£ 9.99

C000221064

STAR TREK®
DUTY, HONOR,
REDEMPTION

STAR TREK®
DUTY, HONOR, REDEMPTION

Novelization by Vonda N. McIntyre

Star Trek II: The Wrath of Khan
Screenplay by Jack B. Sowards
Based on a story by Harve Bennett and Jack B. Sowards

Star Trek III: The Search for Spock
Written by Harve Bennett

Star Trek IV: The Voyage Home
Screenplay by Steve Meerson & Peter Krikes
and Harve Bennett & Nicholas Meyer
Story by Leonard Nimoy & Harve Bennett

Based on *Star Trek* created by Gene Roddenberry

POCKET BOOKS
New York   London   Toronto   Sydney

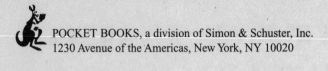

POCKET BOOKS, a division of Simon & Schuster, Inc.
1230 Avenue of the Americas, New York, NY 10020

This book is a work of fiction. Names, characters, places and incidents are products of the authors' imagination or are used fictitiously. Any resemblance to actual events or locales or persons, living or dead, is entirely coincidental.

Introduction copyright © 2004 by Paramount Pictures. All Rights Reserved.
Star Trek® II: The Wrath of Khan copyright © 1982 by Paramount Pictures.
All Rights Reserved.
Star Trek ® III: The Search for Spock copyright © 1984 by Paramount Pictures.
All Rights Reserved.
Star Trek ® IV: The Voyage Home copyright © 1986 by Paramount Pictures.
All Rights Reserved.

STAR TREK is a Registered Trademark of Paramount Pictures.

This book is published by Pocket Books, a division of Simon & Schuster, Inc., under exclusive license from Paramount Pictures.

All rights reserved, including the right to reproduce this book or portions thereof in any form whatsoever. For information address Pocket Books, 1230 Avenue of the Americas, New York, NY 10020

ISBN: 0-7434-9660-4

First Pocket Books trade paperback edition October 2004

10 9 8 7 6 5 4 3 2 1

POCKET and colophon are registered trademarks of Simon & Schuster, Inc.

Manufactured in the United States of America

These titles were previously published individually by Pocket Books.

For information regarding special discounts for bulk purchases, please contact Simon & Schuster Special Sales at 1-800-456-6798 or business@simonandschuster.com.

For Jane and Ole,
with love & snarks

INTRODUCTION

Harve Bennett: The Man Behind the Movies

In a way, collecting these three stories into a single volume seems like a no-brainer. We now think of *Star Trek II: The Wrath of Khan, Star Trek III: The Search for Spock,* and *Star Trek IV: The Voyage Home* as a trilogy. But *Star Trek II* had been conceived as an ending—with the demise of a certain Vulcan—rather than as a first act. It was Harve Bennett, the film's producer and cowriter, who broadened the tale of Spock's death into one of resurrection and reunion. Given that Bennett had never seen *Star Trek* before producing these amazing stories, it was a remarkable feat.

"I was an ignoramus about *Star Trek,*" Bennett admits. "My own show, *The Mod Squad,* had been programmed against it while they were in their first run. And I watched *my* show." So when Bennett was asked to create a follow-up to Paramount's blockbuster, *Star Trek: The Motion Picture,* he had to start from scratch.

"I spent three months watching *Star Trek* episodes," Bennett says. "It was a journey into the dark, but I sure got to be a *Star Trek* appreciator. I finally zeroed in on two episodes, 'City on the Edge of Forever' and 'Space Seed,' as potential source material."

Recalling that many years earlier he had met "Space Seed" guest star Ricardo Montalban, Bennett called the actor to ask how he'd feel about co-starring in a *Star Trek* feature. "Ricardo said, 'Yes. That would be fine,'" Bennett recalls. "And that was the genesis of *Star Trek II.*"

With two key elements in place: "a splendid guest star, and the framework for a classic storyline of 'man against super man,' with Khan as a worthy adversary for Kirk," Bennett and cowriter Jack Sowards began formulating a story. After Art Director Mike Minor showed them a science article about terraforming—making dead planets life bearing, Bennett says, "We took that idea to the next level: life from death. It became the basis for the Genesis Planet and for bringing Kirk's son and a woman he had loved back into his life."

Director Nicolas Meyer soon joined the team. They had one pressing problem to overcome—actor Leonard Nimoy had expressed a reluctance to return in the role of Spock. "We had to lure Leonard back in," Bennett chuckles. "I said, 'What if we pulled a *Psycho?'*" In that film, a major star, Janet Leigh, is killed in an early scene, throwing the audience off-kilter. "So we went to see Leonard," Bennett says, "and told him, 'We're going to give you a great death scene.' Leonard said, 'Oh, that's wonderful!' and signed on."

Unfortunately, it took only days for that "wonderful" idea to leak out, and for thousands of letters protesting the rumor of Spock's impending death to pour in. So Bennett had another inspiration: the Kobayashi Maru test, meant to convince viewers that the character only *appears* to be killed in that early scene. The diversion worked—until, of course, his heartbreaking death at end of the film.

Qualms about Spock's death, however, eventually developed among the filmmakers as well. "The cast and crew started lobbying," Bennett sighs. "By now Leonard really liked being back with this gang. So I suggested, 'Let us lay a little seed here.'" The producer, after all, had experience with bringing back the dead—"I had resurrected the Bionic Woman," he grins. "So I suggested that Spock perform a mind meld and say something. Leonard said, 'I got it. Just shoot it and watch.' When the camera rolled, he put his hand on McCoy's head and said, 'Remember.' It was perfect," the producer recalls. "It was all we needed."

Two days after *Star Trek II: The Wrath of Khan* opened to record box office sales, Bennett got a phone call from Paramount. "It was nine o'clock in the morning," he says. "I heard, 'Okay. Let's get started on number three right now.'"

In Hollywood, this was an unprecedented mandate. "I wrote the last scene of *Star Trek III* that same day," Bennett says. "And it was exactly the way we later shot it. 'Jim. Your name is Jim.' So I knew exactly how the picture would end, with a restored Spock, and that a lot of consequences had to be dealt with. But when? In this movie? Or the next? That's when I started thinking of this as a *three*-act play."

Bennett worried that the Genesis device could be a potential weapon hanging over *Star Trek*'s future. "An analogy with the atomic bomb suddenly came clear to me," he says. "I realized that it had to backfire, and the only way it would was if it had been fraudulently created in the first place. So I decided that David Marcus had done something irregular that had made the formula faulty."

This gave Bennett three things to work with: a pressing timeline for the crew's rescue attempt, the end of the Genesis threat, and a way to dispose of the Marcus family. "The pieces just fell into place," Bennett says. "I wrote it in six weeks."

Bennett again looked back to the original television episodes for a villain. "I thought, 'What could be more frightening than a berserk Klingon?'" And he gave the story a very dark tone; after all, he says, "We were discrediting Kirk's son." The darkness also provided a classic backdrop for resurrecting the dead, and supported Bennett's confidence that, "After the darkness would be the sunlight of Spock's being alive again."

With Leonard Nimoy signed on as director, the team planned a surprise for their audience: the destruction of the *Enterprise*. Bennett explains, "Spock had died to save the crew. Now the *Enterprise* would be sacrificed to save Spock."

Four days after the successful opening of *Star Trek III*, the go-ahead call came from Paramount. Leonard Nimoy again signed on as director. "It was Leonard," Bennett confirms, "who said, 'The crew has to come back and face the music, but there must be something threatening them other than the court-martial. What if something was obliterated in *our* time that proves to be necessary for life in *their* time?'"

"That," Bennett says, "was the click."

Harve Bennett is a producer. In addition to writing, his job is to watch the budget, and this time, he admits, he took it a bit too seriously. "I said, 'What if it's a snail darter?'" Bennett laughs, noting that at the time the tiny, endangered fish was in the news. "If we said snail darters turned out to be the panacea for life, then we could . . .' And Leonard looked at me like I was nuts and said, 'What is that, about an inch long, a snail darter?'" "Yeah, we wouldn't have to do any special effects!" After a moment of cold silence, Bennett realized he was fighting a losing battle. "I said, 'Never mind, we'll get something big.' And Leonard replied, 'What about whales?' I told him, 'We can't do another orca movie with the same black and white fella they have at Sea World.' And that's when Leonard said the magical words: 'What about a humpback?'"

Soon the filmmakers knew that they would write a lighter story, it would include whales, and they would "beam" the whales up in order to solve a problem. They also decided they would use a female in a heroic role. "With those things in place, we called Nick Meyer and said, 'Can you do a rewrite?'" Bennett laughs. "Nick said, 'Sure. I've got two weeks.' He decided that I should write the first part of the movie, which is in the twenty-third century, that he should write the twentieth century sequence on Earth, and that I would do the last section, from when they slingshot back around the sun. And that's exactly what we did."

"I've always looked at the movies as a three-act play," Harve Bennett says.

And so do we. *The Search For Spock* resolves a second act crisis. *The Voyage Home* delivers a final redemption and resolution. The level of sacrifice goes up and up, until the *Enterprise* crew saves Earth herself.

And that's worth a read.

—Terry J. Erdmann

The Wrath of Khan

Better to reign in hell than serve in heav'n

Prologue

CAPTAIN'S LOG: STARDATE 8130.5

STARSHIP ENTERPRISE *ON TRAINING MISSION TO* GAMMA HYDRA. SECTOR *14, COORDINATES* 22/87/4. APPROACHING NEUTRAL ZONE, *ALL SYSTEMS FUNCTIONING.*

Mister Spock, in his old place at the science officer's station, gazed around at the familiar bridge of the Enterprise. The trainees, one per station and each under the direction of an experienced crew member, were so far comporting themselves well.

It was a good group, and the most able of them was the young officer in the captain's seat. Spock expected considerable accomplishments from Saavik. She was young for her rank, and she enhanced her natural aptitude with an apparently inexhaustible capacity for hard work.

Spock listened with approval to the cool narration of the captain's log. Saavik, in command of the *Enterprise,* completed the report and filed it. If she was nervous—and he knew she must be—she concealed her feelings well. Her first command was a test, but, even more, every moment of her life was a test. Few people could understand that better than Mister Spock, for they were similar in many ways. Like Spock, Saavik was half Vulcan. But while Spock's other parent was a human being, Saavik's had been Romulan.

Mister Sulu and Ensign Croy had the helm.

"Sector fourteen to sector fifteen," the ensign said. "Transition: mark." He was a moment behind-time, but the information was not critical to their progress.

"Thank you, Helm Officer," Saavik said. "Set us a course along the perimeter of the Neutral Zone, if you please."

"Aye, Captain."

Sulu watched without comment, letting Croy do his own work and make his own mistakes. The data streamed past on Spock's console.

Spock had not failed to notice Saavik's progress in the use of conventional social pleasantries. Trivial as they may have seemed, learning to use them was one of the most difficult tasks Spock had ever tried to master. Even now, he too frequently neglected them, they were so illogical, but they were important to humans. They made dealing with humans easier.

Spock doubted that Saavik would ever use the phrases with warmth, any more than he would, but she had modified her original icy disinterest, which had come dangerously close to contempt.

Saavik gazed calmly at the viewscreen. She was aesthetically elegant in the spare, understated, esoterically powerful manner of a Japanese brush-painting.

"Captain," Uhura said suddenly, "I'm receiving a signal on the distress channel. It's very faint . . ."

Saavik touched controls. "Communications now has priority on computer access for signal enhancement."

Uhura's trainee worked quickly for several seconds.

"It's definitely an emergency call, Captain."

"Patch it through to the speakers."

Communications complied.

"Mayday, mayday. *Kobayashi Maru,* twelve parsecs out of Altair VI . . ." The voice broke up into static. The trainee frowned and stabbed at the controls on the communications console.

Spock listened carefully. Even computer-enhanced, the message was only intermittently comprehensible.

". . . gravitic mine, lost all power. Environmental controls . . ."

"Gravitic mine!" Saavik said.

". . . hull breached, many casualties." The signal-to-noise ratio decreased until the message slid over into incomprehensibility.

"This is *U.S.S. Enterprise,*" Uhura's trainee said. "Your message is breaking up. Give your coordinates. Repeat: Give your coordinates. Do you copy?"

"Copy, *Enterprise.* Sector ten . . ."

"The Neutral Zone," Saavik said.

Mister Sulu immediately turned his attention from the speakers to his console.

"Mayday, *Enterprise,* we're losing our air, can you help? Sector ten—" The forced calm of the voice began to shatter.

"We copy, *Kobayashi Maru*—" The communications trainee and Uhura both glanced at Saavik, waiting for instructions.

"Tactical data, *Kobayashi Maru.* Helm, what does a long-range sensor scan show?"

Sulu glanced at Croy, who was understandably confused by the screen display. It had deteriorated into the sort of mess that only someone with long experience could make any sense of at all. Sulu replied to the question himself.

"Very little, Captain. High concentrations of interstellar dust and gases. Ionization causing sensor interference. A blip that might be a ship . . . or might not."

The viewscreen shivered. The image reformed into the surrealistic bulk of a huge transport ship. The picture dissected itself into a set of schematics, one deck at a time.

"*Kobayashi Maru,* third-class neutronic fuel carrier, crew of eighty-one, three hundred passengers."

"Damn," Saavik said softly. "Helm?"

Sulu glanced at the trainee, who was still bent over the computer, in the midst of a set of calculations. Croy shook his head quickly.

"Course plotted, Captain," Mister Sulu said, entering his own calculations into the display.

Spock noted with approval Saavik's understanding of the support level she could expect from each of her subordinates.

Sulu continued. "Into the Neutral Zone." His voice contained a subtle warning.

"I am aware of that," she said.

Sulu nodded. "Entering Neutral Zone: mark."

"Full shields, Mister Sulu. Sensors on close-range, high-resolution."

Spock raised one eyebrow. Gravitic mines were seldom deployed singly, that was true, but restricting the sensors to such a limited range was a command decision that easily could backfire. On the other hand, long-range scanners were close to useless in a cloud of ionized interstellar gas. He concentrated on the sensor screens.

"Warning," the computer announced, blanking out the distress call. "We have entered the Neutral Zone. Warning. Entry by Starfleet vessels prohibited. Warning—"

"Communications Officer, I believe that the mayday should have priority on the speakers," Saavik said.

"Yes, Captain." Uhura's trainee changed the settings.

"Warning. Treaty of Stardate—" The computer's voice stopped abruptly. The static returned, pierced erratically by an emergency beacon's faint and ghostly hoot.

"Security duty room," Saavik said. "Security officers to main transporter."

"Aye, Captain," Security Commander Arrunja replied.

"You may have to board the disabled vessel, Mister Arrunja," Saavik said. "They're losing atmosphere and life-support systems."

"The field suits are checked out, Captain."

The intern accompanying McCoy on the bridge hurried to open a hailing frequency.

"Bridge to sickbay," she said. "Doctor Chapel, we need a medical team in main transporter, stat. Rescue mission to disabled ship. Field suits and probably extra oxygen."

McCoy looked pleased by his intern's quick action.

"One minute to visual contact. Two minutes to intercept."

"Viewscreen full forward."

The schematics of the ore carrier dissolved, reforming into a starfield dense and brilliant enough to obscure the pallid gleam of any ship. Ionization created interference patterns across the image.

"Stand by, transporter room. Mister Arrunja, we have very little information on the disabled vessel. Prepare to assist survivors. But . . ." Saavik paused to emphasize her final order ". . . no one is to board *Kobayashi Maru* unarmed."

"Aye, Captain."

"Coordinate with the helm to open the shields at energize."

"Aye aye."

Spock detected a faint reflection at the outer limits of the sensor sphere. The quiet cry of the distress beacon ceased abruptly, leaving only the whisper of interstellar energy fields.

"Captain, total signal degradation from *Kobayashi Maru*."

"Sensors indicate three Klingon cruisers," Spock said without expression. "Bearing eighty-seven degrees, minus twelve degrees. Closing fast."

He could sense the instant increase in tension among the young crew members.

Saavik snapped around with one quick frowning glance, but recovered her composure immediately. "All hands, battle stations." The Klaxon alarm began to howl. "Visual: spherical coordinates: plus eighty-seven degrees, minus twelve degrees. Extend sensor range. Mister Croy, is there a disabled ship, or is there not?"

The viewscreen centered on the ominous, probing shapes of three Klingon cruisers.

"I can't tell, Captain. The Klingon ships are deliberately fouling our sensors."

"Communications?"

"Nothing from the Klingons, Captain, and our transmission frequencies are being jammed."

"Klingons on attack course, point seven-five c," Spock said.

Saavik barely hesitated. "Warp six," she said.

"You can't just abandon *Kobayashi Maru!*" Doctor McCoy exclaimed.

"Four additional Klingon cruisers at zero, zero," Spock said. Dead ahead. Warp six on this course would run the *Enterprise* straight into a barrage of photon torpedoes.

"Cancel warp six, Mister Croy. Evasive action, zero and minus ninety. Warp at zero radial acceleration. Visual at zero, zero. Doctor McCoy," Saavik said without looking back at him, "*Enterprise* cannot outmaneuver seven Klingon cruisers. It will, however, outrun them. If we lure them far enough at their top speed, we can double back even faster—"

"And rescue the survivors before the Klingons can catch up to us again," McCoy said. "Hmm."

"It is the choice between a small chance for the disabled ship, and no chance at all," Saavik said. "If there is in fact a disabled ship. I am not quite prepared to decide that there is not."

The viewscreen confirmed four more Klingon ships dead ahead, and then the *Enterprise* swung away so hard the acceleration affected the bridge even through the synthetic gravity.

"Mister Sulu, Mister Croy, lock on photon torpedoes. Fire . . ." She paused, and Spock wondered whether her early experience—fight or be killed—could, under stress, win out over regulations and the Federation's stated object of keeping the peace. "Fire only if we are fired upon."

"Aye, Captain." Sulu glanced at the young ensign beside him. Croy clenched his hands around the firing controls. "Easy," Sulu said quietly. The ensign started, then forcibly relaxed his hands.

Another blip on the sensor screens: "Enemy cruisers, dead ahead." A third group of ships arrowed toward them, opposing their new course.

Saavik said something softly in a language with which Spock was not ultimately familiar, but by her tone it was a curse.

The Klingons fired on the *Enterprise.*

"Fire at will!" Saavik said.

The viewscreen flared to painful brightness before the radiation sensors reacted to the enemy attack and dimmed the screen to half-intensity. The energy impact was so severe even the shields could not absorb it. Spock held himself steady against the wrenching blow, but it flung Sulu from his post. He crashed into the deck and lay still. McCoy and the intern vaulted down the stairs to the lower bridge and knelt beside him.

"Mister Sulu!" McCoy said. His tricorder gave no reaction. "Spock, he's dead."

Spock did not respond.

"Engineering!" Saavik said.

"Main energizer hit, Captain," Chief Engineer Scott replied.

Saavik slammed her hand down on her controls, transferring command to the helm. She took Sulu's place. Croy fought for data enough to aim the torpedoes.

Saavik did the calculations in her head, keyed them into the console, transferred a copy to Croy's station, and spoke to Scott in the engine room.

"Engage auxiliary power, Mister Scott. Prepare to return fire . . . *now*." She fired. One of the Klingon cruisers fired on the *Enterprise* just as Saavik's torpedo hit. The cruiser imploded, collapsing in upon itself, then exploded in eerie, complete silence. But its deathblow struck the *Enterprise* full force. The screen blazed again, then darkened, with the radiation of the furious attack.

"We're losing auxiliary power, Captain, and our shields along wi' it," Scott cried. "The ship canna take another—"

The scream of irradiated electronics cut off Scott's warning. The enemy ships in pursuit caught up to the Starfleet vessel. At close range, they fired. The *Enterprise* shuddered, flinging Uhura against the railing and to the deck. McCoy left Sulu's inert body and knelt beside the communications officer.

"Uhura—Uhura . . . Oh, my God," McCoy whispered.

Saavik fired at the Klingons, but nothing happened.

"Mister Scott, all power to the weapons systems; it's our only chance."

"Mister Scott . . . is a casualty. . . ." his assistant replied. Her voice was drowned out by a flood of damage reports and pleas for medical help. "Environmental controls destroyed. Life support, nonfunctional. Gravity generators failing."

McCoy cursed at the intraship communications. "Doctor Chapel, I've got to have a team on the bridge! Doctor Chapel! Chris!"

But he got no reply at all from sickbay.

Saavik touched the photon torpedo arming control one last time, delicately, deliberately, yet with the realization that nothing would happen.

"There is no power in the weapons systems, Captain," Spock said. He felt the gravity sliding away. "There is, in fact, no power at all; we are merely bleeding the storage cells."

The enemy ships enclosed them, hovering at the vertices of an impenetrable polyhedron. Spock saw the final attack in the last fitful glow of the viewscreen.

Firing their phasers simultaneously, the cruisers enveloped the *Enterprise* in a sphere of pure energy. Spock imagined he felt the radiation flaming through the ship. He grabbed for a handhold.

His console exploded in his face.

As he fell, he heard the wailing hiss of escaping air, a sound that had been the last experience of all too many spacefarers.

Saavik, clutching at the helm officer's console, fighting the ship's quakes, turned just in time to see Mister Spock fall. For an instant she wished only to be ten years old again, so she could scream with fury and the need for revenge. Doctor McCoy struggled toward Spock, but never made it; the convulsions of the ship flung him down. He screamed, and collapsed with a groan.

Saavik stood up. Her ship, her first command, lay dead in space, her crew was destroyed by her incompetence. She opened the hailing frequencies, not even knowing if any communications were left at all.

"Prepare the escape pods," she said. "All hands, abandon ship." She armed the log buoy and fired it out into space. It would testify to her failure, yet to her honor in accepting the responsibility.

"All hands," she said again. "Abandon ship."

One

Sitting in front of the viewscreen, Admiral James T. Kirk shook his head. He laughed softly, but more at memories than at what he had observed.

"All right," he said. "Open it up."

The wall in front of the video console parted and opened, revealing the destroyed bridge of the *Enterprise.* Kirk got up and walked into it. Acrid smoke burned his eyes, but the heavy-duty ventilation system had already begun to clear the air. He stepped carefully through shattered bits of equipment, over Doctor McCoy's body, and stopped in front of Lieutenant Saavik. She met his gaze without flinching.

"May I request the benefit of your experience, Admiral?"

"Well, Lieutenant, my experience is that the Klingons never take prisoners."

Saavik's expression hardened. Kirk turned all the way around, surveying the wreckage.

This could have happened to me, he thought. *It almost did, all too often and not in simulation, either.*

"Okay, folks," he said. "The fun's over." He glanced at the upper level of the bridge. "Captain Spock?"

Spock got smoothly to his feet. A scattering of breakaway glass shivered to the floor and crunched beneath his boots.

"Trainees to debriefing," he said.

The young crew members, still stunned by the realism of the test, got up and moved toward the exit. The more experienced bridge crew rose from being dead or injured, laughing and joking.

Uhura got up and brushed bits of scorched insulation from her uniform. Sulu turned over and sat up slowly.

"Was that rougher than usual, or am I just getting old?" he said. He climbed to his feet.

Doctor McCoy lounged on the deck, lying on his side with his head propped on his hand.

Kirk stood over him. "Physician, heal thyself."

McCoy gave him a hurt look. "Is that all you've got to say?"

"I'm a Starfleet officer, not a drama critic," Kirk replied.

"Hmph."

"It's too bad you're not a cook," Mister Sulu said to the admiral.

"A cook? Why a cook?"

"You could make fried ham," Sulu said, deadpan.

Jim Kirk started to laugh.

"Fried ham?" Doctor McCoy exclaimed. "I'll have you know I was the best Prince Charming in second grade!"

"And as a side dish," Sulu said in the tones of an obsequious waiter, "perhaps a little sautéed scenery? When it's cooked it's much easier to chew." In an uncanny imitation of Doctor McCoy, he cried, "Mister Sulu! Mister Sulu! Oh, gods, Spock, he's dead!"

McCoy glanced at the ceiling in supplication, but then he could not stand it any longer. He began to laugh, too. From the upper bridge, Spock watched them, his arms folded.

McCoy wiped tears from his eyes. "Mister Sulu, you exaggerate."

"Poetic license," Sulu said.

"Speaking of poetic license, or dramatic realism, or whatever," McCoy said, serious for a moment, "you hit the floor pretty hard. Are you all right?"

"I am, yes, but did they reprogram that simulation? I don't remember its knocking us around quite so badly before killing us."

"We added a few frills," Kirk said. "For effect." He turned toward Saavik, who had watched their interplay as dispassionately as Spock. "Well, Lieutenant, are you going down with the sinking ship?"

He had the feeling she had to draw herself from deep thought before she replied. She did not answer his question but, then, his question had after all been purely rhetorical.

"The simulation is extremely effective," Saavik said.

"It's meant to be." Kirk noticed, though, that she appeared as self-possessed and collected now as when she had entered the simulator, unlike most of the other trainees, who came out sweating and unkempt.

"But I question its realism."

"You think it's an effective simulation, *and* you think it's unrealistic?" Kirk asked.

"Yes, sir." Her imperturbability was not as complete as she pretended; Kirk could see the anger building up. "In your experience, how often have the Klingons sent ten cruisers after a single Starfleet vessel?"

"Lieutenant," Kirk said with an edge in his voice, "are you implying that the training simulation is unfair?"

She took a deep breath and did not flinch from his gaze. "Yes, I should have been more direct. I do not think the simulation is a fair test of command capabilities."

"Why?"

"The circumstances allow no possibility of success."

Jim Kirk smiled. "Lieutenant Saavik, do you think no one who worked on the simulation, and no one who ever took it before, ever noticed that the odds couldn't be beaten?"

She started to reply, stopped, and frowned. "No, Admiral," she said slowly. "I admit I had not considered that possibility."

"You were given a no-win situation. That's something any commander may have to face at any time."

She looked away. "I had not considered that, either." She made the admission only with difficulty.

"By now you know pretty well how you deal with life, Lieutenant. But how you deal with death is important, too, wouldn't you agree?"

"I—" She cut herself off as if she would not trust herself to answer.

"Think about it, Lieutenant," Kirk said. "Just think about it. Carry on." He turned to leave. At the top of the stairs, he came face-to-face with Doctor McCoy. "What's the matter with *you?*"

"You don't think you could manage to push just a little bit harder, do you?" McCoy said softly.

Kirk scowled. "They've got to learn, Doctor. We can't keep the reins forever. Galloping around the cosmos is a game for the young."

He crunched through the debris on the floor and disappeared down the corridor.

Sounding miffed, Uhura said, "What was *that* supposed to mean?"

McCoy shrugged, and shook his head. He and Commander Uhura left together.

Saavik sat alone in the ruins of her first command. She knew she must go to debriefing immediately . . . but she had many things to consider.

Jim Kirk trudged toward the debriefing room. He felt tired, and depressed: and oppressed, by the shining self-confidence of the young people he had been observing. Or perhaps it was by the circumstances of fate that made him the instrument for shaking and scarring that self-confidence. But McCoy was right: he *had* been too hard on Lieutenant Saavik.

He turned the corner and came face-to-face with Spock, who was leaning against the wall with his arms folded.

"Didn't you die?" Kirk asked.

He thought for an instant that Spock was going to smile. But Spock recovered himself in time.

"Do you want to know your cadets' efficiency rating—or are you just loitering?"

"Vulcans are not renowned for their ability to loiter," Spock said.

"Or for their ability to admit terrible character flaws, such as that they're curious."

"Indeed, Admiral? If it will raise your opinion of my character, I suppose I must admit to some curiosity."

"I haven't even got to the debriefing room yet, and you want an opinion." He started down the corridor again, and Spock strode along beside him.

"I seem to recall a Starfleet admiral who referred to this particular set of debriefings as 'a damned waste of time,'" Spock said. "He had a very strong belief that actions were more important than words."

"Did he?" Kirk said. "I don't believe I know him. Sounds like a hothead to me."

"Yes," Spock said slowly. "Yes, at times he was known as a hothead."

Kirk winced at Spock's use of the past tense. "Spock, those trainees of yours destroyed the simulator and you along with it."

"Complete havoc is the usual result when *Kobayashi Maru* comes upon the scene." He paused, glanced at Kirk, and continued. "You yourself took the test three times."

"No!" Kirk said with mock horror. "Did I?"

"Indeed. And with a resolution that was, to put it politely, unique."

"It was unique when I did it," Kirk said. "But I think a number of people have tried it since."

"Without success, you should add. It was a solution that would not have occurred to a Vulcan."

Jim Kirk suddenly felt sick of talking over old times. He changed the subject abruptly. "Speaking of Vulcans, your protégée's first-rate. A little emotional, maybe—"

"You must consider her heritage, Jim—and, more important, her background. She is quite naturally somewhat more volatile than—than I, for instance."

Kirk could not help laughing. "I'm sorry, Spock. The lieutenant is remarkably self-possessed for someone of her age and experience. I was trying to make a joke. It was pretty feeble, I'll admit it, but that seems to be about all I'm up to these days." He sighed. "You know, her tactic might even have worked if we hadn't added the extra Klingon attack group." He stopped at the debriefing room. "Well."

Spock reached out as Kirk started to go in. He stopped before his hand touched Jim Kirk's shoulder, but the gesture was enough. Kirk glanced back.

"Something oppresses you," Spock said.

Kirk felt moved by Spock's concern.

"Something . . ." he said. He wanted to talk to Spock, to someone. But he did not know how to begin. And he had the debriefing to conduct. No, this was not the time. He turned away and went into the debriefing room.

All those kids.

They waited for Admiral Kirk in silence, anxious yet eager. Lieutenant Saavik arrived a moment after Kirk sat down; Spock, his usual emotionless self once more, came in quietly and sat at the very back of the room. Jim Kirk was tempted to declare the discussion over before it had begun, but regulations required a debriefing; he had to fill out a report afterward—

That's all I ever pay attention to anymore, he thought. Regulations and paperwork.

He opened the meeting. He had been through it all a hundred times. The usual protocol was to discuss with each student, in reverse order of seniority, what they would have done had they been in command of the ship. Today was no different, and Kirk had heard all the answers before. One would have stuck to regulations and remained outside the Neutral Zone. Another would have sent in a shuttle for reconnaissance.

Kirk stifled a yawn.

"Lieutenant Saavik," he said finally, "have you anything to add? Second thoughts?"

"No, sir."

"Nothing at all?"

"Were I confronted with the same events, I would react in the same manner. The details might be different. I see no point to increasing your boredom with trivia."

Kirk felt embarrassed to have shown his disinterest so clearly. He reacted rather harshly. "You'd do the same thing, despite knowing it would mean the destruction of your ship and crew?"

"I would know that it *might* mean the destruction of my ship and crew, Admiral. If I could not prove that *Kobayashi Maru* were an illusion, I would answer its distress call."

"Lieutenant, are you familiar with Rickoverian paradoxes?"

"No, sir, I am not."

"Let me tell you the prototype. You are on a ship—a sailing ship, an ocean-going vessel. It sinks. You find yourself in a life raft with one other person. The life raft is damaged. It might support one person, but not two. How would you go about persuading the other person to let you have the raft?"

"I would not," she said.

"No? Why?"

"For one thing, sir, I am an excellent swimmer."

One of the other students giggled. The sound broke off sharply when a classmate elbowed him in the ribs.

"The water," Kirk said with some asperity, "is crowded with extremely carnivorous sharks."

"Sharks, Admiral?"

"Terran," Spock said from the back of the room. "Order Selachii."

"Right," Kirk said. "And they are very, very hungry."

"My answer is the same."

"Oh, really? You're a highly educated Starfleet officer. Suppose the other person was completely illiterate, had no family, spent most of the time getting thrown in jail, and never held any job a low-level robot couldn't do. Then what?"

"I would neither request nor attempt to order or persuade any civilian to sacrifice their life for mine."

"But a lot of resources are invested in your training. Don't you think you owe it to society to preserve yourself so you can carry out your responsibilities?"

Her high-arched eyebrows drew together. "Is this what you believe, Admiral?"

"I'm not being rated, Lieutenant. You are. I've asked you a serious question, and you've replied with what could be considered appalling false modesty."

Saavik stood up angrily. "You ask me if I should not preserve myself so I can carry out my responsibilities. Then *I* ask *you,* what are my responsibilities? By the criteria you have named, my responsibilities are to preserve myself so I can carry out my responsibilities! This is a circular and self-justifying argument. It is immoral in the extreme! A just society—and if I am not mistaken, the Federation considers itself to be just—employs a military for one reason alone: to protect its civilians. If we decide to judge that some civilians are 'worth' protecting, and some are not, if we decide we are too important to be risked, then we destroy our own purpose. We cease to be the servants of our society. We become its tyrants!"

She was leaning forward with her fingers clenched around the back of a chair in the next row.

"You feel strongly about this, don't you, Lieutenant?"

She straightened up, and her fair skin colored to a nearly Vulcan hue.

"That is my opinion on the subject, sir."

Kirk smiled for the first time during the meeting: this was the first time he had felt thoroughly pleased in far too long.

"And you make an elegant defense of your opinion, too, Lieutenant. I don't believe I've ever heard that problem quite so effectively turned turtle."

She frowned again, weighing the ambiguous statement. Then, clearly, she decided to take it as a compliment. "Thank you, sir." She sat down again.

Kirk settled back in his chair and addressed the whole class. "This is the last of the simulation exams. If the office is as efficient as usual, your grades won't be posted till tomorrow. But I think it's only fair to let you know . . . none of you has any reason to worry. Dismissed."

After a moment of silence the whole bunch of them leaped to their feet and, in an outburst of talk and laughter, they all rushed out the door.

"My God," Jim Kirk said under his breath. "They're like a tide."

All, that is, except Saavik. Aloof and alone, she stood up and strode away.

Spock watched his class go.

"You're right, Spock," Kirk said. "She is more volatile than a Vulcan."

"She has reason to be. Under the circumstances, she showed admirable restraint."

The one thing Spock did not expect of Lieutenant Saavik was self-control as complete as his own. He believed that only a vanishingly small difference existed between humans and Romulans when it came to the ability to indulge in emotional outbursts. But Spock had had the benefit of growing up among Vulcans. He had learned self-control early. Saavik had spent the first ten years of her life fighting to survive in the most brutal underclass of a Romulan colony world.

"Don't tell me you're angry that I needled her so hard," Kirk said.

Spock merely arched one eyebrow.

"No, of course you're not angry," Kirk said. "What a silly question."

"Are you familiar with Lieutenant Saavik's background, Admiral?" He wondered how Kirk had come to pose her the particular problem that he had. He could hardly have made a more significant choice, whether it was deliberate or random. The colony world Saavik had lived on was declared a failure; the Romulan military (which was indistinguishable from the Romulan government) made the decision to abandon it. They carried out the evacuation as well. They rescued everyone.

Everyone, that is, except the elderly, the crippled, the disturbed . . . and a small band of half-caste children whose very existence they denied.

The official Romulan position was that Vulcans and Romulans could not interbreed without technological intervention. Therefore, the abandoned children could not exist. That was a political judgment which, like so many political judgments, had nothing to do with reality.

The reality was that the evolution of Romulans and Vulcans had diverged only a few thousand years before the present. The genetic differences were utterly trivial. But a few thousand years of cultural divergence formed a chasm that appeared unbridgeable.

"She's half Vulcan and half Romulan," Kirk said. "Is there more I should know?"

"No, that is sufficient. My question was an idle one, nothing more." Kirk had shaken her, but she had recovered well. Spock saw no point in telling Kirk things which Saavik herself seldom discussed, even with Spock. If she chose to put her past aside completely, he must respect her decision. She had declined her right to an antigen-scan, which would have identified her Vulcan parent. This was a highly honorable action, but it meant that she had no family, that in fact she did not even know which of her parents was Vulcan and which Romulan.

No Vulcan family had offered to claim her.

Under the circumstances, Spock could only admire the competent and self-controlled person Saavik had created out of the half-starved and violent barbarian child she had been. And he certainly could not blame her for rejecting her parents as completely as they had abandoned her. He wondered if she understood why she drove herself so hard, for she was trying to prove herself to people who would never know her accomplishments, and never care. Perhaps some day she would prove herself to herself and be free of the last shackles binding her to her past.

"Hmm, yes," Kirk said, pulling Spock back from his reflections. "I do recall that Vulcans are renowned for their ability to be idle."

Spock decided to change the subject himself. He picked up the package he had retrieved before coming into the debriefing room. Feeling somewhat awkward, he offered it to Kirk.

"What's this?" Jim asked.

"It is," Spock said, "a birthday present."

Jim took the gift and turned it over in his hands. "How in the world did you know it was my birthday?"

"The date is not difficult to ascertain."

"I mean, why—? No, never mind, another silly question. Thank you, Spock."

"Perhaps you should open it before you thank me; it may not strike your fancy."

"I'm sure it will—but you know what they say: It's the thought that counts." He slid his fingers beneath the outside edge of the elegantly folded paper.

"I have indeed heard the saying, and I have always wanted to ask," Spock said, with honest curiosity, "if it is the thought that counts, why do humans bother with the gift?"

Jim laughed. "There's no good answer to that. I guess it's just an example of the distance between our ideals and reality."

The parcel was wrapped in paper only, with no adhesive or ties. After purchasing the gift, Spock had passed a small booth at which an elderly woman created simple, striking packages with nothing but folded paper. Fascinated by the geometry and topology of what she was doing, Spock watched for some time, and then had her wrap Jim's birthday present.

At a touch, the wrapping fanned away untorn.

Jim saw what was inside and sat down heavily.

"Perhaps . . . it is the thought that counts," Spock said.

"No, Spock, good Lord, it's beautiful." He touched the leather binding with one finger; he picked the book up in both hands and opened it gently, slowly, being careful of its spine.

"I only recently became aware of your fondness for antiques," Spock said. It was a liking he had begun to believe he understood, in an odd way, once he paid attention to it. The book, for example, combined the flaws and perfections of something handmade; it was curiously satisfying.

"Thank you, Spock. I like it very much." He let a few pages flip past and read the novel's first line. " 'It was the best of times, it was the worst of times . . .' Hmm, are you trying to tell me something?"

"Not from the text," Spock said, "and with the book itself, only happy birthday. Does that not qualify as 'the best of times'?"

Jim looked uncomfortable, and he avoided Spock's gaze. Spock wondered how a gift that had at first brought pleasure could so quickly turn into a matter of awkwardness. Once again he had the feeling that Jim Kirk was deeply unhappy about something.

"Jim—?"

"Thank you, Spock, very much," Kirk said, cutting Spock off and ignoring the question in his voice. "I mean it. Look, I know you have to get back to the *Enterprise.* I'll see you tomorrow."

And with that, he was gone.

Spock picked up the bit of textured wrapping paper and refolded it into its original shape, around empty air.

He wondered if he would ever begin to understand human beings.

Two

DUTY LOG: STARDATE 8130.4: MOST SECRET

LOG ENTRY BY COMMANDER PAVEL CHEKOV, DUTY OFFICER. U.S.S. RELIANT *ON ORBITAL APPROACH TO ALPHA CETI VI, CONTINUING OUR SEARCH FOR A PLANET TO SERVE AS A TEST SITE FOR THE GENESIS EXPERIMENT. THIS WILL BE THE SIXTEENTH WORLD WE HAVE VISITED; SO FAR, OUR ATTEMPTS TO FULFILL ALL THE REQUIREMENTS FOR THE TEST SITE HAVE MET WITH FAILURE.*

Reliant—better known to its crew, not necessarily fondly, as "this old bucket"—plowed through space toward Alpha Ceti and its twenty small, uninhabited, undistinguished, unexplored planets. Pavel Chekov, on duty on the elderly ship's bridge, finished his log report and ordered the computer to seal it.

"Log complete, Captain," he said.

"Thank you, Mister Chekov." Clark Terrell leaned back in the captain's seat. "Is the probe data for Alpha Ceti on-line?"

"Aye, sir." Chekov keyed the data to the viewscreen so that Captain Terrell could display it if he chose. For now, the screen showed Alpha Ceti VI. The planet spun slowly before them, its surface smudged blurrily in shades of sickly yellow. Nitrogen and sulfur oxides dominated its atmosphere, and the sand that covered it had been ground and blasted from its crust by eons of corrosive, high-velocity winds.

Alpha Ceti VI was a place where one would not expect to find life. If the crew of *Reliant* was lucky, this time their expectations would be met.

And about time, too, Chekov thought. *We need a little luck.*

At the beginning of this voyage, Chekov had expected it to be boring, but short and easy. How difficult could it be to find a planet with no life? Now, several months later, he felt as if he were trapped in a journey that was boring, unending, and impossible. Lifeless planets abounded, but lifeless worlds of the right size, orbiting the proper sort of star, within the star's biosphere, in a star system otherwise uninhabited: such planets were not so easy to discover. They had inspected fifteen promisingly barren worlds, but each in its turn had somehow violated the experimental conditions' strict parameters.

Chekov was bored. The whole crew was bored.

At first the ship had traveled to worlds at least superficially documented by previous research teams, but *Reliant* now had begun to go farther afield, to places seldom if ever visited by crewed Federation craft. The computer search Chekov had done on the Alpha Ceti system turned up no official records except the ancient survey of an automated probe. He had been mildly surprised to find so little data, then mildly surprised again to have thought he had ever heard of the system. Alpha Ceti VI had come up on the list of Genesis candidates for exactly the same reason no one had bothered to visit it after the probe report of sixty years before: it was monumentally uninteresting.

Terrell displayed the probe data as a corner overlay on the viewscreen, and added a companion block of the information they had collected on the way in.

"I see what you mean about the discrepancies, Pavel," he said. He considered the screen and stroked the short black hair of his curly beard.

The probe data showed twenty planets: fourteen small, rocky inner ones, three gas giants, three outer eccentrics. But what *Reliant* saw on approach was nineteen planets, only thirteen of them inner ones.

"I've been working on that, Captain," Chekov said, "and there are two possibilities. Alpha Ceti was surveyed by one of the earliest probes: their data wasn't always completely reliable, and some of the archival preservation has been pretty sloppy. It's also possible that the system's gone through some alteration since the probe's visit."

"Doesn't sound too likely."

"Well, no, sir." Sixty years was an infinitesimal distance in the past, astronomically speaking; the chances of any noticeable change occurring since then were very small. "Probe error is a fairly common occurrence, Captain."

Terrell glanced back and grinned. "You mean maybe we think we're headed for a ball of rock, and we'll find a garden spot instead?"

"Bozhemoi!" Chekov said. "My God, I hope not. No, sir, our new scans confirm the originals on the planet itself. Rock, sand, corrosive atmosphere."

"Three cheers for the corrosive atmosphere," Mister Beach said, and everybody on the bridge laughed.

"I agree one hundred percent, Mister Beach," Terrell said. "Take us in."

Several hours later, on orbital approach, Chekov watched the viewscreen intently, willing the ugly little planet to be the one they were looking for. He had had enough of this trip. There was too little work and too much time with nothing to do. It encouraged paranoia and depression, which he had been feeling with distressing intensity on this leg of their voyage. On occasion, he even wondered if his being assigned here was due to something worse than bad luck. Could it be punishment for some inadvertent mistake, or the unspoken dislike of some superior officer—?

He kept telling himself the idea was foolish and, worse, one that could become self-fulfilling if he let it take him over and sour him.

Besides, if he was being punished it only made sense to assume others in the crew were, too. Yet a crew of troublemakers produced disaffection and disillusion: the ship was free of such problems. Or anyway it had been until they pulled this intolerable assignment.

Besides, Captain Terrell had an excellent reputation: he was not the sort of officer generally condemned to command a bunch of dead-enders. He was soft-spoken and easygoing; if the days stretching into weeks stretching into months of fruitless search troubled him, he did not show the stress. He was no James Kirk, but . . .

Maybe that's what's wrong, Chekov thought. I've been thinking about the old days on the *Enterprise* too much lately and comparing them to what I'm doing now. And what I'm doing now simply does not compare.

But, then—what would?

"Standard orbit, Mister Beach," Captain Terrell said.

"Standard orbit, sir," the helm officer replied.

"What do we have on the surface scan?"

"No change, Captain."

Chekov got a signal on his screen that he wished he could pretend he had not noticed.

"Except . . ."

"Oh, no," somebody groaned.

Every crew member on the bridge turned to stare at Chekov with one degree or another of disbelief, irritation, or animosity. On the other side of the upper bridge, the communications officer muttered a horrible curse.

Chekov glanced down at Terrell. The captain hunched his shoulders, then forced himself to relax. "Don't tell me you've got something," he said. He rose and came up the stairs to look at Chekov's data.

It is *getting to him,* Chekov thought. Even him.

"It's only a minor energy flux," Chekov said, trying to blunt the impact of his finding. "It doesn't necessarily mean there's biological activity down there."

"I've heard that line before," Terrell said. "What are the chances that the scanner's out of adjustment?"

"I just checked it out, sir," Chekov said. "Twice." He immediately wished he had not added the last.

"Maybe it's pre-biotic," Beach said.

Terrell chuckled. "Come on, Stoney. That's something we've been through before, too. Of all the things Marcus won't go for, tampering with pre-biotics is probably top of the list."

"Maybe it's *pre*-pre-biotic," Beach said wryly.

This time nobody laughed.

"All right, get Doctor Marcus on the horn. At least we can suggest transplantation. Again."

Chekov shook his head. "You know what she'll say."

On the Regulus I Laboratory Space Station, Doctor Carol Marcus listened, frowning, as Captain Terrell relayed the information *Reliant* had collected so far.

"You know my feelings about disturbing a pre-biotic system," she said. "I won't be a party to it. The long range—"

"Doctor Marcus, the long range you're talking about is millions of years!"

"Captain, *we* were pre-biotic millions of years ago. Where would we be if somebody had come along when Earth was a volcanic hell-pit, and said, 'Well, *this* will never amount to anything, let's mess around with it'?"

"Probably we wouldn't care," Terrell said.

Carol Marcus grinned. "You have it exactly. Please don't waste your time trying to change my mind about this, it simply isn't a matter for debate."

She watched his reaction; he was less than happy with her answer.

"Captain, the project won't be ready for the next stage of the test for at least three months. There's no pressure on you to find a place for it instantaneously—" She stopped; the unflappable Clark Terrell looked like he was about to start tearing out his very curly, handsomely graying black hair. "Wrong thing to say, huh?"

"Doctor, we've spent a long time looking for a place that would fit your requirements. I'd match my crew against any in Starfleet. They're good people. But if I put them through three more months of this, I'll have a mutiny on my hands. They can take boredom—but what they've got is paralysis!"

"I see," Marcus said.

"Look, suppose what our readings show is the end of an evolutionary line rather than the beginning? What if some microbes here are about to go extinct? Just barely hanging on. Would you approve transplantation then?"

"I can't do that," she said. She chewed absently on her thumbnail but stopped abruptly. *You're a little old to still be chewing your nails, Carol,* she thought. *You ought at least to have cut it out when you turned forty.*

Maybe when I hit fifty, she replied to herself.

"Don't you leave *any* room for compromise?" Terrell asked angrily.

"Wait, Captain," she said. "I'm sorry, I didn't mean that the way it sounded. It isn't that I wouldn't give you a go-ahead. It's that finding a species endangered by its own environment is a fairly common occurrence. There are established channels for deciding whether to transplant, and established places to take the species to."

"A microbial zoo, eh?"

"Not just microbes, but that's the idea."

"What kind of time-frame are we talking about?" Terrell asked cautiously.

"Do you mean how long will you have to wait before the endangered species subcommittee gives an approval?"

"That's what I said."

"They're used to acting quickly—if they don't it's often too late. They need documentation, though. Why don't you go down and have a look?"

"We're on our way!"

"I don't want to give you false hopes," Marcus said quickly. "If you find so much as a pre-biotic spherule, a pseudo-membranous configuration, even a viroid aggregate, the show's off. On the other hand if you have discovered an evolutionary line in need of preservation, not only will you have found a Genesis site, you'll probably get a commendation."

"I'll settle for the Genesis site," Terrell said.

His image faded.

Carol Marcus sighed. She wished she were on board *Reliant* to keep an eye on what they were doing. But her work on Genesis was at too delicate a point; she had to stay with it. Clark Terrell had given her no reason to distrust him. But he was obviously less than thrilled about having been assigned to do fetch-and-carry work for her laboratory. He was philosophically indifferent to her requirements for the Genesis site, while she was ethically committed to them. She could imagine how *Reliant*'s crew referred to her and the other scientists in the lab: a bunch of ivory-tower eggheads, test-tube jugglers, fantasy-world dreamers.

She sighed again.

"Mother, why do you let them pull that stuff on you?"

"Hello, David," she said. "I didn't hear you come in."

Her son joined her by the communications console.

"They're lazy," he said.

"They're bored. And if they've found something that really does need to be transplanted . . ."

"Come on, Mother, it's the military mentality. 'Never put off tomorrow what you can put off today.' If life is beginning to evolve there—"

"I know, I know," Carol said. "I'm the one who wrote the specs—remember?"

"Hey, Mother, take it easy. It's going to work."

"That's the trouble, I think. It *is* going to work, and I'm a little frightened of what will happen when it does."

"What will happen is, you'll be remembered along with Newton, Einstein, Surak—"

"More likely Darwin, and I'll probably get as much posthumous flak, too."

"Listen, they might not even wait till you're dead to start with the flak."

"Thanks a lot!" Carol said with mock outrage. "I don't know what I can hope for from other people, I can't even get any respect from my own offspring."

"That's me, an ingrate all the way." He gave her a quick hug. "Want to team up for bridge after dinner?"

"Maybe. . . ." She was still preoccupied by her conversation with Terrell.

"Yeah," David said. "Every time we have to deal with Starfleet, I get nervous too."

"There's so much risk. . . ." Carol said softly.

"Every discovery worth making has had the potential to be perverted into a dreadful weapon."

"My goodness, that sounds familiar," Carol said.

David grinned. "It ought to, it's what you've been telling me for twenty years." Serious again, he said, "We just have to make damned certain that the military doesn't take Genesis away from you. There're some who'll try, that's for sure. That overgrown boy scout you used to hang out with—"

"Listen, kiddo," Carol said, "Jim Kirk was a lot of things . . . but he was *never* a boy scout." Her son was the last person she wanted to talk about Jim Kirk with. She gestured toward the file David was carrying. "Last night's batch?"

"Yeah, fresh out of the machine." He opened the file of X-ray micrographs, and they set to work.

Jim Kirk pulled the reading light closer, shifted uncomfortably on his living room couch, held the book Spock had given him closer to his eyes, held it at arm's length. No matter what he did, his eyes refused to focus on the small print.

I'm just tired, he thought.

It was true, he was tired. But that was not the reason he could not read his book.

He closed it carefully, set it on the table beside him, and lay back on the couch. He could see the pictures on the far wall of the room quite clearly, even down to the finest lines on the erotic Kvern black-and-white that was one of his proudest possessions. He had owned the small drawing for a long time; it used to hang in his cabin back on the *Enterprise.*

A few of his antiques were alien artifacts, collected offworld, but in truth he preferred work from his own culture, particularly England's Victorian era. He wondered if Spock knew that, or if the Dickens first edition was a lucky guess.

Spock, making a lucky guess? He would be horrified. Jim grinned.

Only in the last ten years or so had the beauty of antiques overcome his reluctance to gather too many possessions, to be weighed down by *things.* It was a long time since he had been able to pick up and leave with one small suitcase and no glance back. Sometimes he wished he could return to those days, but it was impossible. He was an admiral. He had too many other responsibilities.

The doorbell chimed.

Jim started and sat up. It was rather late for visitors.

"Come," he said. The apartment's sensors responded to his voice. Leonard McCoy came in, with a smile and an armful of packages.

"Why, Doctor," Jim said, surprised. "What errant transporter beamed you to my doorstep?"

McCoy struck a pose. "'*Quidquid id est, timeo Danaos et dona ferentis,*'" he said.

"How's that again?"

"Well, that's the original. What people usually say these days is 'Beware Romulans bearing gifts.' Not quite the same, but it seemed appropriate, considering—" he rummaged around in one of the packages and drew out a bottle full of electric-blue liquid, "—this. Happy birthday." He handed Jim the chunky, asymmetric bottle.

"Romulan ale—? Bones, this stuff is so illegal—"

"I only use it for medicinal purposes. Don't be a prig."

Jim squinted at the label. "Twenty-two . . . eighty-three?"

"It takes the stuff a while to ferment. Give it here."

Jim handed it back, opened the glass-paneled doors of the cherrywood Victorian secretary where he kept his dishes, and took out a couple of beer mugs. McCoy poured them both full.

"Is it my imagination, or is it smoking?"

McCoy laughed. "Considering the brew, quite possibly both." He clinked his glass against Jim's. "Cheers." He took a deep swallow.

Jim sipped cautiously. It was a long time since he had drunk Romulan ale, but not so long that he had forgotten what a kick it packed.

Its electric hue was appropriate; he felt the jolt of the first taste, as if the active ingredient skipped the digestive system completely and headed straight for the brain.

"Wow," he said. He drank again, more deeply, savoring both the taste and the effect.

"Now open this one." McCoy handed him a package which, rather than being stuffed into a brown paper bag, was gift-wrapped.

Jim took the package, turned it over in his hand, and shook it.

"I'm almost afraid to. What is it?" He took another swallow of the ale, a real swallow this time, and fumbled at the shiny silver tissue. Strange: he had not had any trouble opening Spock's present this afternoon. A tremendously funny idea struck him. "Is it a tribble?" He started to laugh. "Or maybe some contraband Klingon—"

"It's another antique for your collection," McCoy said. "Your health!" He lifted his glass and drank again.

"Come on, Bones, what is it?" He got one end of the package free.

"Nope, you gotta open it."

Though his hands were beginning to feel like he was wearing gloves, Jim could feel a hard, spidery shape. He gave up trying to get the wrapping off in one piece and tore it away. "I know what it is, it's—" He squinted at the gold and glass construction, glanced at McCoy, and looked down at his present again. "Well, it's . . . charming."

"They're four hundred years old. You don't find many with the lenses still intact."

"Uh, Bones . . . what are they?"

"Spectacles."

Jim drank more ale. Maybe if he caught up with McCoy he would be able to figure out what he was talking about.

"For your eyes," McCoy said. "They're almost as good as Retinax Five—"

"But I'm *allergic* to Retinax," Jim said petulantly. After the buildup the doctor gave about restoring the flexibility of his eyes with the drug, Jim had been rather put out when he turned out to be unable to tolerate it.

"Exactly!" McCoy refilled both their glasses. "*Happy birthday!*"

Jim discovered that the spectacles unfolded. A curve of gold wire connected two little half-rounds of glass; hinged hooks attached to each side.

"No, look, here, like this." McCoy slid one hook behind each of Jim's ears. The wire curve rested on his nose, holding the bits of glass beneath his eyes. "They're spectacles. Oh, and I was only kidding about the lenses being antique. They're designed for your eyes."

Jim remembered a picture in an old book he had. He lowered the spectacles on the bridge of his nose.

"That's it," McCoy said. "Look at me, over the top. Now look down, through the lenses. You ought to be able to read comfortably with those."

Jim got them in the right position, did as McCoy said, and blinked with surprise. He picked up Spock's book, opened it, and found the tiny print in perfect focus.

"That's amazing! Bones, I don't know what to say. . . ."

"Say thank you."

"Thank you," Jim said obediently.

"Now have another drink." McCoy drained the bottle into their mugs.

They sat and drank. The Romulan ale continued to perform up to its usual standard. Jim felt a bit as he had the first time he ever experienced zero gee—queasy and confused. He could not think of anything to say, though the silence felt heavy and awkward. Several times McCoy seemed on the verge of speaking, and several times he stopped. Jim had the feeling that whatever the doctor was working up to, he would prefer not to hear. He scowled into his glass. Now he was getting paranoid. Knowing it was the result of the drink did nothing to relieve his distress.

"Damn it, Jim," McCoy said suddenly. "What the hell's the matter? Everybody has birthdays. Why are we treating yours like a funeral?"

"Is *that* why you came over here?" Jim snapped. "I really don't want a lecture."

"Then what *do* you want? What are you doing, sitting here all alone on your birthday? And don't give me that crap about 'games for the young' again, either! That's a crock, and you know it. This has nothing to do with age. It has to do with you jockeying a computer console instead of flying your ship through the galaxy!"

"Spare me your notions of poetry, please. I've got a job to do—"

"Bull. You never should have given up the *Enterprise* after Voyager."

Jim took another drink of Romulan ale, wishing the first fine glow had lasted longer. Now he remembered why he never developed a taste for this stuff. The high at the beginning was almost good enough to compensate for the depression at the end. Almost, but not quite.

He chuckled sadly. "Yeah, I'd've made a great pirate, Bones."

"That's bull, too. If you'd made a few waves, they wouldn't have had any choice but to reassign you."

"There's hardly a flag officer in Starfleet who wouldn't rather be flying than pushing bytes from one data bank to another."

"We're not talking about every flag officer in Starfleet. We're talking about James T. Kirk—"

"—who has a certain amount of notoriety. It wouldn't be fair to trade on that—"

"Jim, ethics are one thing, but you're crucifying yourself on yours!"

"There are rules, and regulations—"

"Which you are hiding behind."

"Oh yeah? And what am I hiding from?"

"From yourself—Admiral."

Jim held back an angry reply. After a long pause, he said, "I have a feeling you're going to give me more advice whether I want it or not."

"Jim, I don't know if I think this is more important because I'm your doctor, or because I'm your friend. Get your ship back. Get it back before you really do get old. Before you turn into part of your own collection."

Jim swirled the dregs of his drink around in his glass, then looked up and met McCoy's gaze.

The wind nearly knocked Chekov over as soon as he lost the protection of the transporter beam. Alpha Ceti VI was one of the nastiest, most inhospitable places he had ever been. Alpha Ceti VI was worse even than Siberia in the winter.

Driven by the storm, the sand screamed against his pressure suit. Captain Terrell materialized beside him, looked around, and opened a channel to *Reliant*.

"Terrell to *Reliant*."

"*Reliant*. Beach here, Captain." The transmission wavered. "Pretty poor reception, sir."

"It will do, Stoney. We're down. No evidence of life—or anything else."

"I copy, sir."

"Look, I don't want to listen to this static all afternoon. I'll call you, say, every half hour."

". . . Aye, sir."

Kyle broke in. "Remember about staying in the open, Captain."

"Don't fuss, Mister Kyle. Terrell out." He shut down the transmission and turned on his tricorder.

Chekov stretched out his arm; his hand almost disappeared in the heavy blowing sand. Even if whatever they were seeking were macroscopic, rather than microbial, they would never find it visually. He, too, began scanning for the signal that had brought them to the surface of this wretched world.

"You getting anything, Pavel?"

Chekov could barely make out the captain's words, not because the transmission was faulty but because the wind and the sand were so loud they drowned out his voice.

"No, sir, nothing yet."

"You're sure these are the right coordinates?"

"Remember that garden spot you mentioned, Captain? Well, this is it." Chekov took a few steps forward. Sand ground and squealed in the joints of his suit. They could not afford to stay on the surface very long, for these conditions would degrade even an almost indestructible material. Chekov knew what would happen if his suit were torn or punctured. The oxides of sulfur that formed so much of the atmosphere would contaminate his air and dissolve in the moisture in his lungs. Chekov intended to die in some far more pleasant way than by breathing sulfuric and sulfurous acids: some far more pleasant way, and some far more distant time in the future.

"I can't see a damned thing," Terrell said. He started off toward the slight rise the tricorder indicated. Chekov trudged after him. The wind tried to push him faster than he could comfortably walk in the treacherous sand.

Sweat ran down the sides of his face; his nose itched. No one yet had invented a pressure suit in which one could both use one's hands and scratch one's nose.

"I'm getting nothing, Captain," Chekov said. Nothing but one case of creeps. "Let's go."

He got no reply. He looked up. At the top of the hillock, Captain Terrell stood staring before him, his form vague and blurry in the sand. He gestured quickly. Chekov struggled up the sand dune, trying to run, sliding on the slick, sharp grains. He reached Terrell's side and stopped, astonished.

The sand dune formed a windbreak for the small hollow before them, a sort of storm's eye of clearer air. Chekov could see perhaps a hundred meters.

In that hundred meters lay a half-buried group of ruined buildings.

Suddenly he shivered.

"Whatever it is," Clark Terrell said, "it isn't pre-biotic." He stepped over the knife-sharp crest of the dune and slid down its concave leeward side.

After a moment, reluctantly, Chekov followed. The unpleasant feeling of apprehension that had teased and disturbed him ever since they started for Alpha Ceti gripped him tighter, growing toward dread.

Terrell passed the first structure. Chekov discarded any hope that they might have come upon some weird formation of violent wind and alien geology. What they had found was the wreckage of a spaceship.

Chekov would have been willing to bet that it was a human-made spaceship, too. Its lines were familiar. Alien craft always appeared . . . alien.

"These look like cargo carriers," Terrell said.

Chekov leaned over to put his faceplate against a porthole, trying to see inside the ruined ship.

A child popped up, laughed silently, and disappeared.

"Bozhemoi!" Chekov cried, starting violently. He fell backward into the sand.

"Chekov! What the hell—?" Terrell stumbled toward him.

"Face! I saw—face of child!"

He pointed, but the porthole was empty.

Terrell helped him to his feet. "Come on. This place is getting to you."

"But I *saw* it," Chekov said.

"Look, there's the airlock. Let's check it out."

"Captain, I have bad feeling—I think we should go back to *Reliant* and look for different test site and pretend we never came here. Lenin himself said, 'Better part of valor is discretion.' "

"Come along," Terrell said. His tone forbade argument. "And anyway, it was Shakespeare."

"No, Captain, Lenin. Perhaps other fellow—" Chekov stopped and reminded himself of the way Standard was constructed. "Perhaps the other fellow stole it."

Terrell laughed, but even that did not make Chekov feel any easier.

Though sand half covered most of the cargo modules, testifying to some considerable time since the crash, the airlock operated smoothly. In this environment, that was possible only if the mechanism had been maintained.

Chekov hung back. "Captain, I don't think we should go in there. Mister Kyle's warning—" The electrical disturbances in the atmosphere that had disrupted communications and made scanning so difficult gave problems to the transporter as well; Kyle had said that even a covering of tree branches, or a roof (knowing what they expected to find, Chekov and Terrell had both laughed at the caution), could change beaming up from "just barely possible" to "out of the question."

"Mister Kyle has one flaw," Terrell said, "and that is that he invariably errs far on the side of caution. Are you coming?"

"I'll go in, Captain," Chekov said reluctantly. "But you stay outside, *pazhalsta,* and keep in contact with ship."

"Pavel, this is ridiculous. Calm down. I can tell you're upset—"

On *Reliant,* Chekov occasionally got teased for losing his Standard, in which he was ordinarily fluent, when he was angry or very tired.

Or—though his shipmates had no way of knowing this—when he was terrified.

"Look," Terrell said. "I'll go in. If you want to, you can stay here on guard."

Chekov knew that he could not let Terrell enter the cargo ship alone. Unwillingly, he followed the captain into the airlock.

The inner doors slid open. Chekov had to wait a moment, but after his eyes adjusted to the dimness he saw beds and tables, a book, an empty coffee cup: people lived here. They must have survived the crash on the cargo ship. But where were they?

"We've got a breathable atmosphere," Terrell said. He unfastened his helmet. Chekov glanced at his tricorder. Terrell was right: the proportions of oxygen, nitrogen, and carbon dioxide were all normal, and there was barely a trace of the noxious chemicals that made up the outside air. Even so, Chekov opened his helmet seal half expecting the burning pungency of acid vapors.

But the place smelled like every dormitory Chekov had ever been in: of sweat and dirty socks.

Outside, the wind scattered sand against the walls. Terrell went farther into the reconverted cargo hold. His footsteps echoed. There were no sounds of habitation; yet the place did not *feel* deserted.

It felt evil.

"What the hell is all this? Did they crash? And where are they?"

Terrell stopped in the entrance to the next chamber, a kitchen.

On the stove, a faint cloud of steam rose from a pot of stew.

Chekov stared at it.

"Captain . . ."

Terrell was gone. Chekov hurried after him, entering a laboratory, where Terrell poked around among the equipment. He stopped near a large glass tank full of sand. Chekov went toward him, hoping to persuade him to return to the ship, or at least call in a well-armed security team.

"Christ!"

Terrell leapt away from the tank.

Chekov ripped his phaser from the suit's outer clip and crouched, waiting, ready, but there was nothing to fire at.

"Captain—what—?"

"There's something in that damned tank!" He approached it cautiously, his hand on his own phaser.

The sand roiled like water. A long shape cut a stroke across the surface, and Chekov flinched back.

"It's all right," Terrell said. "It's just some kind of animal or—"

The quiet gurgle of a child, talking to itself, playing with sounds, cut him off as effectively as a shout or a scream.

"I told you!" Chekov cried. "I told you I saw—"

"Shh." Terrell started toward the sound, motioning Chekov to follow.

Chekov obeyed, trying to calm himself. So what if there was a child? This was not a world where Chekov would wish to father and try to raise a baby, but obviously at least one couple among the survivors of the cargo ship crash had felt differently. Chekov's fear was reasonless, close to cowardice—

He stepped through a crumpled and deformed passageway and peered into the next chamber.

The crash had twisted the room around, leaving it tumbled on its side, one wall now the floor, the floor and the ceiling now walls. The change made the proportions odd and disconcerting; worse, the floor was not quite flat, the walls not quite straight.

All alone, in the middle of the room, sitting on the floor—the wall—the baby reached out to them and gurgled and giggled with joy. Terrell climbed down from the sideways entrance and approached the child tentatively.

"Well, kid, hi, didn't your folks even leave a baby-sitter?"

Chekov looked around the room. The wall that the ceiling had turned into displayed a collection of sharp, shining swords; Chekov recognized only the wavy-bladed *kris*. He recognized few of the titles of the books on a shelf nearby: *King Lear?* That sounded like imperialist propaganda to him. *Bible?* Twentieth-century mythology, if he recalled correctly.

And then he saw, hanging from the floor-wall, the ship's insignia, and the reason for his terror came at him in a crushing blow.

Botany Bay.

"*Bozhemoi,*" Chekov whispered, "*Botany Bay,* no, it can't be. . . ."

Terrell chucked the baby gently under the chin with his forefinger. "What'd you say, Pavel?"

Chekov lunged forward, grabbed Terrell by the shoulder, and dragged him toward the passageway.

"Wait a minute! What's the matter with you?"

"We've got to get out of here! Now! Captain, please trust me, hurry!"

He forcibly pushed the bigger man up and through the hatch and climbed after him. Angry now, Terrell tried to turn back.

"But the child—"

"I can't explain now!" Chekov cried. "No time! Hurry!" He pushed the captain down the battered companionway, which was too narrow to allow Terrell to put up much struggle. Chekov fumbled with his helmet, got it fastened, and turned on the suit's communicator.

"Chekov to *Reliant,* come in *Reliant.* Mayday, mayday—"

Static answered his pleas.

By the time they reached the laboratory, Terrell had caught his urgency or decided to humor him now and bust him back to ensign later—Chekov did not care which. Terrell put on his helmet and fastened it as they reached the kitchen and ran into the connecting hall. The dormitory was still deserted. Chekov began to hope they might get outside and contact the ship in time. They plunged into the airlock. Chekov continued to call *Reliant,* hoping to get through, determined to reach it the instant he and Terrell left the building.

The door opened. Chekov bolted forward.

He stopped.

They were surrounded by suited figures, each one armed, and every weapon pointed straight at them.

"Beam us up!" Chekov cried into his transmitter.

As he grabbed at his phaser, one of the suited figures lunged forward, disarmed him, and knocked him back into the airlock.

High above, in *Reliant,* Mister Kyle tried again to raise Terrell and Chekov. They had only been out of touch for a little while, true, but the conditions were so terrible on the surface of Alpha Ceti VI that he would have preferred continuous contact.

"Try again," Beach said unnecessarily.

"*Reliant* to Captain Terrell, Kyle here. Do you copy, Captain Terrell? Come in, Captain, please respond. . . ."

He got no reply.

Beach let out his breath in an irritated snort.

"Let's give them a little more time."

Kyle knew as well as Beach did how much Clark Terrell hated to be second-guessed; nevertheless, he was about to protest when a sudden squawk came through his headphone and echoed on the speakers. He flinched.

"What was that?" Beach said. "Did you hear it?"

"I heard it." He channeled the transmission through the computer, enhancing and filtering it. "Stoney, I want to put more power to the sensors."

"You already overrode the alarm—much more and you'll blow out the circuits completely."

"I think they're in trouble."

The transmission returned from enhancement.

"Eeeeebeeeessss . . ." squealed out of the speaker. Kyle slapped his console and forced the signal through the program again.

"Beeeeeeussss . . ."

And again.

Though flattened and distorted, it was Chekov's voice.

"Beam us . . ."

Kyle looked up at Beach.

"Beam us . . ."

"Okay—more power," Beach said. "Get a lock on them!"

"Beam us . . ."

"Beam us . . ."

"Beam us . . ."

Three

When Captain Terrell tried to explain that he and Chekov had been looking for survivors, that they were, in effect, a rescue party, one of the survivors expressed gratitude by backhanding him with the full weight of body and arm and massive suit glove. Terrell sagged.

Chekov did not try to protest their capture. He knew the attempt would be futile.

He and Terrell still wore their suits, though their helmets and phasers had been taken. Escape seemed impossible. Besides the four people holding them, twelve or fifteen others stood in silence around them.

As if they were waiting.

Chekov felt more frightened of what—whom—they were waiting for than of all of them together. Without actually looking at his phaser, Chekov set himself to get to it. He forced himself to relax; he pretended to give up. When in response one of his captors just slightly relaxed the hold, Chekov lunged forward.

He was not fast enough. His hands were jammed up under his shoulder blades, twisting his arms painfully. He cried out. Terrell's captors jerked him upright, too, though he was still half-stunned.

Chekov had no other chance to resist. The pressure on his arms did not ease: it intensified. Through a haze of pain, he sought desperately through old memories to recall everything he could about *Botany Bay*. So much had happened in so short a time that while he remembered the incident itself with terrible clarity, some of the details had blurred. It was a long time ago, too, fifteen years . . .

The airlock hummed into a cycle. The guards forced Chekov to attention, pulled Terrell upright, and turned them both to face the doorway. The bruise on Terrell's face was deep red against his black skin. Sweat ran down Chekov's sides.

A tall figure, silhouetted by the light, paused, stepped out of the chamber, and slowly, deliberately, removed its helmet.

Chekov's breath sighed out in a soft, desperate moan.

"Khan. . . ."

The man had changed: he appeared far more than fifteen years older. His long hair was now white, streaked with iron gray. But the aura of power and self-assurance was undiminished; the changes meant nothing. Chekov recognized him instantly.

Khan Noonien Singh glanced toward him; only then did Chekov realize he had spoken the name aloud. Khan's dark, direct gaze made the blood drain from Chekov's face.

Khan approached and looked them over. The unrelenting inspection shocked Terrell fully back to consciousness, but Khan dismissed him with a shrug.

"I don't know you," he said. He turned toward Chekov, who shrank away.

"But *you,*" he said softly, gently, "I remember you, Mister Chekov. I never hoped to see *you* again."

Chekov closed his eyes to shut out the sight of Khan's terrifying expression, which was very near a smile.

"Chekov, who is this man?" Terrell tried vainly to reassert some authority.

"He was . . . experiment, Captain. And criminal." Though he feared angering Khan, he could think of no other way, and no satisfactory way at all, to describe him. "He's from . . . twentieth century." He was an experiment, a noble dream gone wrong. Genetic engineering had enhanced his vast intelligence; nature had conveyed upon him great presence and charisma. What had caused his overwhelming need for power, Pavel Chekov did not know.

Khan Singh's only reaction to Chekov's statement was a slow smile.

"What's the meaning of this treatment?" Terrell said angrily. "I demand—"

"You, sir, are in a position to demand nothing." Khan's voice was very mild. He could be charming—Chekov recalled that all too well. "I, on the other hand, am in a position to grant nothing." He gestured to the people, to the surroundings. "You see here all that remains of the crew of my ship, *Botany Bay*, indeed all that remains of the ship itself, marooned here fifteen years ago by Captain James T. Kirk."

The words were simply explanatory, but the tone was chilling.

"I can grant nothing, for we have nothing," Khan said.

Terrell appealed to Khan's ragtag group of men and women.

"Listen to me, you people—"

"Save your strength, Captain," Khan said. "They have been sworn to me, and I to them, since two hundred years before you were born. We owe each other our lives." He glanced kindly at Chekov. "My dear Mister Chekov, do you mean you never told him the tale?" He returned his attention to Terrell. "Do you mean James Kirk never amused you by telling the story of how he 'rescued' my ship and its company from the cryogenic prison of deep space? He never made sport of us in public? Captain, I'm touched."

His words were filled with quiet, deadly venom.

"I don't even know Admiral Kirk!"

"*Admiral* Kirk? Ah, so he gained a reward for his brave deeds and his acts of chivalry—for exiling seventy people to a barren heap of sand!"

"You lie!" Chekov shouted. "I saw the world we left you on! It was beautiful; it was like a garden—flowers, fruit trees, streams . . . and its moon!" Chekov remembered the moon most clearly, an enormous silver globe hanging over the land, ten times the size of the moon on Earth, for Captain Kirk had left Khan and his followers on one of a pair of worlds, a twin system in which planet and satellite were of a size. But one was living, the other lifeless.

"Yes," Khan said, in a rough whisper. "Alpha Ceti V was that, for a while."

Chekov gasped. "*Alpha Ceti V!*" The name came back, and all the pieces fell into place: no official records, for fear Khan Singh would free himself again; the discrepancies between the probe records and the data *Reliant* collected. Now, too late, Chekov understood why he had lived the last few days under an increasing pall of dread.

"My child," Khan said, his tone hurt, "did you forget? Did you forget where you left me? You did, I see . . . ah, you ordinaries with your pitiful memories."

If the twin worlds had still existed, Chekov would have seen them on approach and remembered, and warned Terrell away.

"Why did you leave Alpha Ceti V for its twin?" Chekov asked. "What happened to it?"

"*This* is Alpha Ceti V!" Khan cried.

Chekov stared at him, confused.

Khan lowered his voice again, but his deep black eyes retained their dangerous glitter.

"Alpha Ceti VI, our beautiful moon—you did not survey that, did you, Mister Chekov? You never bothered to note its tectonic instability. It exploded, Mister Chekov. It exploded! It laid waste to our planet. *I* enabled us to survive, I, with nothing to work with but the trivial contents of these cargo holds."

"Captain Kirk was your host—" Chekov said.

"And he never appreciated the honor fate offered him. I was a prince on Earth; I stood before millions and led them. He could not bear the thought that I might return to power. He could only conquer me by playing at being a god. His Zeus to my Prometheus: he put me here, in adamantine chains, to guard a barren rock!"

"You tried to steal his ship—"

Ignoring his words, Khan bent down and looked straight into Pavel Chekov's eyes. "Are you his eagle, Mister Chekov? Did you come to tear out my entrails?"

"—and you tried to murder him!"

Khan turned away, and gazed at Clark Terrell. "What of you, Captain? Perhaps you are my Chiron. Did you come to take my place in purgatory?"

"I . . . I don't know what you mean," Terrell said.

"No, you do not! You know nothing of sacrifice. Not you, not James T. Kirk—" he snarled the name, "—no one but the courageous Lieutenant McGivers, who defied your precious admiral, who gave up everything to join me in exile."

Khan's voice broke, and he fell silent. He turned away.

"A plague upon you all."

He swung around on them again. His eyes were bright with tears, but his self-control had returned. The horrifying gentleness of his voice warned of anger under so much pressure it must, inevitably, erupt.

"You did not come seeking me," he said. "You believed this was Alpha Ceti VI. Why would you choose to visit a barren world? Why are you here?"

Chekov said nothing.

"Foolish child." As carefully as a father caressing a baby, Khan touched his cheek. His fingers stroked down to Pavel's chin. Then he grabbed his jaw and brutally forced up his head.

Just as suddenly he spun away, grabbed Terrell by the throat, and jerked him off his feet.

"Why?"

Terrell shook his head. Khan gripped harder.

Choking, Terrell clawed at Khan's gloved hand. Khan watched, a smile on his face, while the captain slowly and painfully lost consciousness.

"It does not please him to answer me," Khan said. His lips curled in a cruelly simple smile. "Well, no matter." He opened his fist, and Terrell's limp body collapsed on the floor.

Chekov twisted, trying to free himself. The two men holding him nearly broke his arms. Chekov gasped. Terrell curled around himself, coughing. But at least he was alive.

"You'll tell me willingly soon enough," Khan said. He made a quick motion with his head. His people dragged Chekov and Terrell into the laboratory and dumped them next to the sand tank.

Khan strode past them, picked up a small strainer, and dipped it into the tank. He lifted it and sand showered out, sliding down through the mesh and flung up by the struggling of the creatures he had snared.

"Did you, perhaps, come exploring? Then let me introduce you to the only remaining species native to Alpha Ceti V." He thrust the strainer in front of Chekov. "Ceti eels," Khan said. The last of the sand spilled away. The two long, thin eels writhed together, lashing their tails and snapping their narrow pointed jaws. They were the sickly yellow of the sand. They had no eyes. "When our world became desert, only a desert creature could survive." Khan took Chekov's helmet from one of his people, an intense blond young man.

"Thank you, Joachim." He tilted the strainer so one of the eels flopped into the helmet.

Joachim spilled the second eel into Terrell's helmet.

"They killed, they slowly and horribly killed, twenty of my people," Khan said. "One of them . . . was my wife."

"Oh, no. . . ." Chekov whispered. He remembered Lieutenant McGivers. She had been tall and beautiful and classically elegant, but, more important, kind and sweet and wise. He had only ever had one conversation with her, and that by chance—he was an ensign, assigned to the night watch, when she was on the *Enterprise,* and ensigns and officers did not mix much. But once, she had talked with him. For days afterward, he had wished he were older, more experienced, of a more equivalent rank. . . . He had wished many things.

When she left the *Enterprise* to go with Khan, Ensign Pavel Chekov had locked himself in his cabin and cried. How could she go with Khan? He had never understood. He did not understand now.

"You let her die," he said.

Khan's venomous glance transfixed him.

"You may blame her death on your Admiral Kirk," he said. "Do you want to know *how* she died?" He swirled Chekov's helmet in circles. Pavel could hear the eel sliding around inside. "The young eel enters its victim's body, seeks out the brain, and entwines itself around the cerebral cortex. As a side effect, the prey becomes extremely susceptible to suggestion." He came toward Chekov. "The eel grows, my dear Pavel Chekov, within the captive's brain. First it causes madness. Then the host becomes paralyzed—unable to move, unable to feel anything but the twisting of the creature within the skull. I learned the progression well. I watched it happen . . . to my wife."

He lingered over the description, articulating every word with care and precision, as if he were torturing himself, embracing the agony as a fitting punishment.

"Khan!" Pavel cried. "Captain Kirk was only doing his duty! Listen to me, please—"

"Indeed I will, Pavel Chekov, in a few moments you will speak to me as I wish."

Pavel felt himself being pushed forward in a travesty of a bow.

He fought, but the guards forced him down. Khan let him look into his helmet, where the eel squirmed furiously.

"Now you must meet my pet, Mister Chekov. You will find that it is not . . . quite . . . domesticated. . . ."

Khan slammed the helmet over Pavel's head and locked it into its fastenings.

The eel tumbled against Pavel's face, lashing his cheek with its tail. In a panic, he clawed at his faceplate. Khan stood before him, watching, smiling. Pavel grabbed the helmet latches, but Khan's people pulled his hands away and held him still.

The eel, sensing the heat of a living body, ceased its frantic thrashing and began to crawl, probing purposefully with its sharp little snout. Pavel shook his head violently. The eel curled its body through his hair, anchoring itself, and continued its relentless search.

It curved down behind his ear, slid beneath the lobe, and glided up again.

It touched his eardrum.

He heard the rush of blood, and its flowing warmth caressed his cheek.

Then he felt the pain.

He screamed.

On board *Reliant,* Mister Kyle tried again and again to reach Terrell and Chekov. His voice was tight and strained.

"*Reliant* to Terrell, *Reliant* to Terrell, come in, Captain. Captain Terrell, please respond."

"For gods' sake, Kyle, stop it," Beach said.

Kyle swung around on him. "Stoney, I can't *find* them," he said. "There's no signal at all!" Several minutes had passed since the cry from Pavel Chekov. The sensor dials trembled in overload.

"I know. Muster a landing party. Full arms. Alert the transporter room. I'm beaming down right now." He headed for the turbo-lift.

"Terrell to *Reliant,* Terrell to *Reliant,* come in, *Reliant.*"

Beach rushed back to the console.

"*Reliant,* Beach here. For gods' sake, Clark, are you all right?"

The pause seemed slightly longer than the signal lag required, but Beach dismissed it as his own concern and relief.

"Everything's fine, Commander, I'll explain when I see you. We're bringing several guests aboard. Prepare to beam up on my next signal."

"Guests? Clark, what—?"

"Terrell out."

Beach looked at Kyle, who was frowning.

" 'Guests'?" Kyle said.

"Maybe we *are* transplanting something."

"*Enterprise* Shuttle Seven, you're cleared for liftoff."

"Roger, Seattle, we copy." Commander Hikaru Sulu powered up the gravity fields, and the square little shuttlecraft rose smoothly from the vast expanse of the landing field.

He glanced around to make sure his passengers were all safely strapped in:

Admiral Kirk, Doctor McCoy, Commander Uhura. Almost like the old days. Kirk was reading a book—was that a pair of spectacles he was wearing? It was, indeed—McCoy was making notes in a medical file, and Uhura was bent over a pocket computer, intent on the program she was writing.

Last night's rain had left today crystal clear and gleaming. The shuttle gave a three-hundred-sixty-degree view of land so beautiful that Hikaru wanted to grab everyone in the shuttle and shake them till they looked: two ranges of mountains, the Cascades to the east and the Olympics to the west, gray and purple and glittering white; the long wide path of Puget Sound, leading north, studded with islands and sliced by the keen-edged wake of a hydrofoil. He rotated the shuttle one hundred eighty degrees to starboard, slowly, facing in turn the solitary volcanic peaks of Mount Baker, Mount Rainier, Mount St. Helens, steaming and smoking again after a two-hundred-year sleep, Mount Hood, and far to the south, rising through towering thunderheads, Mount Shasta.

The shuttle continued its ascent. Distance blurred the evidence of civilization, even of life, stripping the underlying geology bare, until the lithic history of lava flows, glacial advance, and orogeny lay clear before him. A lightning bolt flashed along Mount Shasta's flank, arcing through the clouds.

And then the earth curved away beneath him, disappearing into the sun far to one side and into the great shadow of the terminator on the other.

Uhura reached out and brushed her fingertips against his arm. He glanced around. The computer lay abandoned beside her.

"Thank you," she said very softly. "That was beautiful."

Hikaru smiled, glad to have someone to share it with.

"My pleasure."

She went back to her computer. He homed in on the Starfleet Spacedock beacon and engaged the autopilot. It would be a while before he had anything else to do. He stretched out in one of the passenger seats, where he could relax but still keep an eye on the control display.

The admiral closed his book and pushed his glasses to the top of his head.

"You look a bit the worse for wear, Mister Sulu—is that from yesterday?"

Hikaru touched the bruise above his cheekbone and grinned ruefully. "Yes, sir. I didn't realize I'd got it till too late to do anything about it."

"There's one thing you can say about Mister Spock's protégés: They're *always* thorough."

Hikaru laughed. "No matter what they're doing. That was quite a show, wasn't it?"

"It was, indeed. I didn't get much chance to speak to you yesterday. It's good to see you."

"Thank you, sir. The feeling's mutual."

"And by the way, congratulations, Commander."

Hikaru glanced down at the shiny new braid on his uniform. He was not quite used to it yet.

"Thank you, Admiral. You had a lot to do with it. I appreciate the encouragement you've given me all these years."

Kirk shrugged. "You earned it, Commander. And I wasn't the only commander you've had who put in a good word. Spock positively gushed. For Spock, anyway. And you got one of the two or three best recommendations I've ever seen from Hunter."

"I appreciate your letting me know that, Admiral. Both their opinions mean a lot to me."

Kirk glanced around the shuttle. "Almost like old times, isn't it? Do you still keep in touch with your friend Commander Flynn?"

"Yes, sir—I saw her off this morning, in fact. She made captain, early last spring."

"Of course she did, I'd forgotten. When the memory begins to go—" He stopped, then grinned, making it into a joke. But he had sounded terribly serious. "They gave her one of the new ships, didn't they?"

"Yes, sir, *Magellan.* It left today." It will be a long time before I see her again, Hikaru thought, with regret.

A long time. The new *Galaxy*-class ships were smaller than the *Enterprise,* but much faster. They were most efficient around warp twelve. Only three as yet existed: *Andromeda, M-31,* and *Magellanic Clouds.* Their purpose was very-long-range exploration; commanding such a mission was the career Mandala Flynn, who had been born and raised in space, had aimed for all her life.

Jim Kirk chuckled. Hikaru gave him a questioning glance.

"Do you remember what she said to me, at the officers' reception the day she came on board the *Enterprise?*"

"Uh—I'm not sure, sir." Actually he remembered it vividly, but if Admiral Kirk by chance was thinking of something else, Hikaru felt it would be more politic not to remind him of the other.

"I asked her what her plans were, and she looked me straight in the eye and said, 'Captain, I want your job.' "

Hikaru could not repress a smile. Besides remembering that, he also remembered the shocked silence that had followed. Mandala had not meant it as a threat, of course, nor had Kirk taken it as one. Not exactly. But it had not been quite the best foot for a field-promoted officer, a mustang—someone who had worked up from the ranks—to start out on.

"She got it, too," Kirk said softly, gazing out the window and seeing, perhaps, not the earth below or the angular chaos of the space station far ahead, but new worlds and past adventures.

"Sir? Do you mean you put in for a *Galaxy* ship?" Hikaru felt rather shocked, partly because if Kirk had applied, he must have been turned down, but even more that he had made the request in the first place.

"What? Oh, no. No, of course not. I didn't mean that the way it sounded. She earned her promotion, just as you did yours. I don't begrudge it to either of you." He grinned. "But if I were ten years younger, she might have had a fight on her hands for one of the *Galaxies.*"

"I can't quite imagine you anywhere but on the bridge of the *Enterprise,* Captain Kirk—uh, sorry—*Admiral.*"

"I think I consider that a compliment."

The autopilot emitted a soft beep as it engaged the Spacedock's guide bea-

con. Kirk nodded to Sulu, who returned to the controls, deactivated the autopilot, and engaged the navigational computer and communications system.

"Shuttle Seven to *Enterprise*. Admiral Kirk's party on final approach."

"Shuttle Seven, welcome to *Enterprise*. Prepare for docking."

"Thank you, *Enterprise,* we copy."

When Sulu had completed the preparations, Kirk caught his gaze again.

"By the way, Sulu, I must thank you for coming along."

"I was delighted to get your request, Admiral. A chance to go back on board
the *Enterprise,* to indulge in a bit of nostalgia—how could I pass it up?"

"Yes. . . ." Kirk said thoughtfully. "Nevertheless, I remember how much
there was to do, and how little time there seemed to be to do it in, just before I
got the *Enterprise.*"

"I've looked forward to it for a long time."

"I'm grateful to have you at the helm." He grinned: for a moment the
somber cloud of responsibility thinned, letting out a flash of Captain James
Kirk of the *Starship Enterprise.* He leaned over and said, with mock confiden-
tiality, "Mister Sulu, I don't believe those kids can steer."

Lieutenant Saavik watched *Enterprise* Shuttle Seven as it settled into its transport moorings; its pilot—Commander Sulu, she assumed—was excellent. The
great doors of the starship's landing bay slid closed, and air sighed in to pressur-
ize the compartment.

The other trainees waited nervously for Admiral Kirk. Saavik remained outwardly impassive, though she felt uncomfortable about having to face Kirk after
yesterday's disaster. He had merely added to her humiliation by rating her well
in the series of simulation exams. She believed he should have significantly
downgraded her overall score because of her performance on the final test. She
felt confused, and Saavik disliked confusion intensely.

Captain Spock knew far more about humans in general than Saavik thought
she could ever hope to learn, and more about Admiral Kirk in particular. Perhaps
he could explain Kirk's motives. Since coming on board, though, Saavik had
been too busy to ask him.

"Docking procedures completed," the computer said.

"Prepare for inspection," Spock said. "Open airlock."

All the trainees came to rigid attention as the doors slid open. The computer,
surrogate bo'sun, piped the admiral onto the ship. Kirk paused, saluted the
Federation logo before him, and exchanged salutes with Spock.

"Permission to come aboard, Captain?"

"Permission granted, Admiral, and welcome."

Kirk stepped on board the *Enterprise.*

"I believe you know my trainees," Spock said. "Certainly they have come to
know you."

Kirk looked straight at Saavik. "Yes," he said, "we've been through death
and life together."

Saavik maintained her composure, but only the techniques of biocontrol
that Spock had taught her saved her from a furious blush. She could not make
out Kirk's tone at all. He might be attempting humor.

For the first ten years of her life, Saavik had never laughed; for the first ten years of her life, she had never seen anyone laugh unless they had caused another person pain.

Humor was not Saavik's forte.

Kirk held her gaze a moment, then, when she did not respond, turned away.

"Hello, Mister Scott," he said to the chief engineer. "You old spacedog, Scotty, are you well?"

"Aye, Admiral. I had a wee bout, but Doctor McCoy pulled me through."

" 'A wee bout'? A wee bout of what?"

Saavik paid particular attention to the interchange between the humans. Spock said their words were not necessarily significant. Observe their actions toward one another, their expressions. Assign at least as much importance to the tone of voice as to what is said.

The first thing that occurred after the admiral's question was a pause. Inability to answer the question? Saavik dismissed that immediately. Surprise or confusion? Those were possibilities. Reluctance, perhaps?

Mister Scott glanced at Doctor McCoy—quickly, as if he hoped no one would notice. So: reluctance it was. McCoy returned his look, adding a slight shrug and a small smile.

"Er, shore leave, Admiral," Mister Scott said.

"Ah," Kirk said.

His tone indicated comprehension, though in fact his question had been not answered but avoided. Saavik dissected the encounter in her mind and put it back together as best she could. Mister Scott and Doctor McCoy knew of some event in Mister Scott's life that the admiral wished to know, but which Mister Scott would be embarrassed to reveal. Doctor McCoy agreed, by his silence, to conspire in the concealment; the admiral, by his tone of understanding, had appeared to accede to their plan, yet put them both on notice that he intended to find out exactly what had happened, but at some more convenient, perhaps more private, time.

Saavik felt some satisfaction with the intellectual exercise of her analysis; it remained to be seen if it was accurate.

Admiral Kirk strode along before the line, giving each trainee a stern yet not unfriendly glance. Spock and Scott accompanied him.

"And who is this?" Kirk said, stopping in front of the child.

Peter drew himself up so straight and serious that Saavik wanted to smile. He was blond and very fair; under the admiral's inspection his face turned bright pink. He was a sweet child, so enthusiastic he practically glowed, so proud to be in space at fourteen that he lived within a radiating sphere of joy that could not help but affect those around him.

Even Saavik.

Now, undergoing his very first admiral's inspection, Peter replied to Kirk breathlessly, "Cadet First Class Peter Preston, engineer's mate, *sir!*" He saluted stiffly, fast, and with great eagerness.

Kirk smiled, came to attention, and saluted in the same style.

If he laughs at Peter, Saavik thought, *I shall certainly rip out his liver.*

The civilized part of her, taking over again after the infinitesimal lapse, replied: You most certainly shall not; besides—do you even know where the liver is in a human?

"Is this your first training voyage, Mister Preston?"

"Yes, sir!"

"I see. In that case, I think we should start the inspection with the engine room."

"Aye, sir!"

"I dinna doubt ye'll find all in order," Mister Scott said.

"We shall see you on the bridge, Admiral," the captain said.

"Very good, Mister Spock."

Engineer Scott started toward the turbolift with Kirk; the engine room company followed. Peter flashed Saavik a quick, delighted grin, and hurried after them.

The rest of the ship's personnel dispersed quickly to attend their posts. Spock and Saavik left for the bridge.

"Have you any observations to make, Lieutenant Saavik?" Spock asked.

"The admiral is . . . not quite what I expected, Captain."

"And what did you expect?"

Saavik paused in thought. What *had* she expected? Spock held James Kirk in high regard, and she had based her preconceptions almost entirely on this fact. I expected him to be like Spock, she thought. But he resembles him not at all.

"He's very . . . human. . . ."

"You must remember that, as a member of Starfleet, you are unlikely ever to escape the presence of humans, or their influence. Tolerance is essential; in addition, it is logical."

"You are my mentor, Captain. Your instruction has been invaluable to me—indeed, it is indispensable." They stepped into the main turbo-lift.

"Bridge," Spock said. "Saavik, no one exists who has experiences and heritage similar enough to yours to advise you competently. Even I can only tell you that, as a Vulcan and a Romulan in a world of humans, you are forever a stranger. You will have to deal with strangers who may, at times, seem incomprehensible to you."

"Captain," Saavik said carefully, "I confess that I had not expected the admiral to be quite so representative of his culture. However, I intended no prejudice against Admiral Kirk, nor intolerance of human beings."

The doors to the turbolift opened onto the bridge, ending the conversation.

Peter Preston stood at attention next to the control console that was his responsibility. It was the second backup system for auxiliary power, and its maintenance records showed that except for testing, it had not even been directly on-line for two years. Nevertheless, Peter had checked out every circuit and every memory nexus and every byte of its data base a dozen times over. Sometimes, late at night when the ship was docked without even a skeleton crew on duty, Peter came down and ran his console through its diagnostic programs. He loved being here all alone in the enormous engine room with the echoes of tremendous energy fluxes scintillating around him.

Peter stood last in line for inspection. He could hardly bear the wait. He knew his console was in perfect shape. But what if Admiral Kirk found something wrong? What if—

The admiral stopped in front of him, looked him up and down, and drew one finger along the edge of the console. Looking for dust? There definitely was not any dust.

"I believe you'll find everything shipshape, Admiral," Peter said, and immediately wished he had kept his mouth shut.

"Oh, do you?" Kirk said sternly. "Mister Preston, do you have any idea, any idea at all, how often I've had to listen to Mister Scott tell me that one more warp factor will blow the ship to bits?"

"Uh, no sir," Peter said, quite startled.

"Mister Preston, do you know how they refer to the *Enterprise* in the officers' mess?"

"Uh, no sir," Peter said again, and then thought, *Brilliant line, kid. Why don't you use it one more time and make a* really *good impression?*

"Why, they call it 'the flying deathtrap.' And they aren't referring to the food."

"Sir, that's not true! This is the best ship in the whole Starfleet!"

The admiral started to smile, and Mister Scott chuckled. Peter felt the blood rising to his face. *Oh, no,* he thought, *I fell for it; Dannan warned me, and I still fell for it.* Dannan, his oldest sister, was already a commander; she was twelve years older than he, and he had absorbed her stories, practically through his skin, since before he could remember. If she saw him now, he knew she would tease him about looking like a ripe tomato, he blushed so hard. That is, if she would even speak to him once she found out he'd acted like such a dope.

"And begging the admiral's pardon, *sir,*" Peter said, "but the only person who couldn't see the truth about this ship would have to be as blind as a Tiberian bat! *Sir.*"

Kirk looked at him for a moment. Then he reached into his pocket and pulled out a small spidery little construction of glass and gold wire. He unfolded it, balanced it on his nose, hooked some of the wires around his ears, peered closely through the lenses at the console and over the tops of the lenses at the rest of the engine room, and finally turned to Peter again.

"By God, you're right, Mister Preston. It *is* a good ship."

Doctor McCoy laughed, and so did Mister Scott. For a horrible moment, Peter was afraid one of the three men was going to reach out and pat him on the head, but they spared him that. As they walked away he could not help but hear their conversation.

"Scotty, your cadet's a tiger."

"My sister's youngest, Admiral."

Oh, no, Peter thought, *why did he have to tell the admiral he's my uncle?* Peter himself had told no one in the training group, and he had hoped that neither had Uncle Montgomery. Peter valued his uncle's advice and love and even his occasional crotchetiness, but things would have been easier, clearer somehow, if he were training under someone unrelated to him.

"Crazy to get to space," Mister Scott said. "Always has been."

"Every youngster's fancy," Admiral Kirk said. "I seem to remember it myself."

They stopped at the far end of the engine room; the admiral listened as Mister Scott pointed out improvements added since Kirk's last visit.

Peter ducked out of line, sprinted to the tool bay, rummaged around in his bin for a moment, and hurried to his place again.

At the console next to him, Grenni glanced at him sidelong and muttered, "What the hell you doin', Pres? We're not dismissed yet."

"You'll see," Peter whispered.

Kirk and Scott and McCoy strolled back along the length of the engine room. When they reached Peter, the cadet saluted hard.

Kirk stopped. "Yes, Mister Preston?"

Peter offered him a complicated instrument.

"I believe the admiral asked after this?"

Kirk inspected it.

"What is it, Mister Preston?"

"Why, sir, it's a left-handed spanner, of course."

Mister Scott looked completely and utterly shocked. The admiral's mouth twitched. Doctor McCoy choked down a smile, then gave up and started to laugh. After a moment, Kirk followed suit. Mister Scott managed nothing better than a stiff, grim smile. Peter watched them with his very best total-innocent look.

"Mister Scott," Kirk said, but he was laughing too hard to continue. Finally he stopped and wiped his eyes. "Mister Scott, I think we'd better get these kids on their training cruise before they take over completely. Are your engines up to a little trip?"

"Just give the word, Admiral."

"Mister Scott, the word is given."

"Aye, sir."

Kirk handed the "left-handed spanner" back to Peter and started away. A few steps later, he glanced over his shoulder and winked.

As soon as the turbolift doors slid closed, Jim Kirk collapsed into laughter again. "Do you believe it, Bones?" He was laughing so hard he had to pause between every phrase. "God, what a terrific kid. A left-handed spanner!" Jim wiped the tears from his eyes. "I deserved that one, didn't I? I forgot how much I hated being teased when I was his age."

"Yes, once in a while we old goats need to be reminded how things were back in the mists of prehistory."

Kirk's amusement subsided abruptly. He *still* disliked being teased, and McCoy was well aware of the fact. Jim frowned, not knowing how to take McCoy's comment. "Bridge," he said to the turbolift voice sensor.

"What about the rest of your inspection . . . Admiral?" McCoy said. He let the tone of his voice creep over into not completely benign mockery. Needling Jim Kirk was one of the few ways to get him to take a good hard look at himself.

Getting him drunk certainly had not worked.

"I'll finish it later, Doctor," Jim said mildly. "After we're under way."

"Jim, do you really think that a three-week training cruise once a year is going to make up for forty-nine other weeks of pushing paper? Do you think it's going to keep you from driving yourself crazy?"

"I thought we got this conversation over with last night," Jim said. "You want to know something? It's getting extremely tedious."

"Yeah, concern from one's friends is a bore, isn't it?"

"Sometimes it is," Jim said. "You're a lot better surgeon than you are a psychotherapist."

The turbolift doors opened, and McCoy repressed a curse. A few more minutes and he might have made some kind of breakthrough with Jim.

Or got myself punched in the mouth, he thought. *Some breakthrough.*

Admiral Kirk stepped out onto the bridge of the *Enterprise,* and Doctor McCoy followed him.

McCoy had to admit it was pleasant to be back. He nodded to Uhura, and she smiled at him. Mister Sulu had the helm, though just now it appeared that Lieutenant Saavik, first officer and science officer for the training cruise, would be piloting the *Enterprise* for practice. The main difference, of course, was that now Mister Spock was the captain. He did not relinquish his place to Kirk; to do so would be improper. Heaven forbid that Spock might do anything improper.

"Admiral on the bridge!" Mister Sulu said.

"As you were," Kirk said before anyone could stand up or salute.

"Starfleet Operations to *Enterprise.* You are cleared for departure."

"Lieutenant Saavik," Spock said, "clear all moorings."

"Aye, sir."

She set to work. Kirk and McCoy descended to the lower bridge.

"Greetings, Admiral." Spock nodded to McCoy as well. "Doctor McCoy. I trust the inspection went well."

"Yes, Captain, I'm very impressed," Kirk said.

"Moorings clear, Captain," Saavik said.

"Thank you, Lieutenant." Spock paused a moment and then his eyes got that hooded look that McCoy had learned in self-defense to recognize.

"Lieutenant Saavik," Spock said, "how many times have you piloted a starship out of Spacedock?"

"One hundred ninety-three, sir," Saavik said promptly. And then added: "In simulation."

Kirk absolutely froze.

"In real-world circumstances," Saavik said, "never."

McCoy got the distinct impression that Jim Kirk simultaneously thought of two possible courses of action. The first was to pitch Spock out of the captain's seat and order Mister Sulu to take the helm. The second was to do nothing. He chose the latter. But it was close to a photo finish.

You damned leprechaun! McCoy directed the delighted thought at Spock. *Vulcan discipline, indeed!*

Deliberately avoiding a look at Kirk, pretending ignorance of the admiral's discomfort, Spock glanced at McCoy with a very slight smile. For the Vulcan, that was almost as extreme a reaction as Jim's fit of laughter in the turbolift was for Kirk.

"Take us out, Lieutenant Saavik," Spock said.

"Aye, sir. Reverse thrust, Mister Sulu, if you please."

"Reverse thrust, Lieutenant."

"It is always rewarding to watch one's students examine the limits of their training," Spock said. "Wouldn't you agree, Admiral?"

"Oh, definitely, Captain. To be sure. First time for everything, after all."

The viewscreen showed the Spacedock receding majestically; then it spun slowly from their sight as Saavik rotated the *Enterprise* away.

"Ahead one-quarter impulse power, if you please, Commander Sulu," Saavik said.

Jim opened his month to speak, took a deep breath and closed his mouth abruptly, and grabbed his hands together behind his back. McCoy leaned toward him.

"Hey, Jim," he whispered, "want a tranquilizer?"

Kirk glared at him and shook his head.

The ship accelerated.

"One-quarter impulse power," Mister Sulu said; then, a moment later, "Free and clear."

Kirk quietly released the breath he had been holding.

"Course, Captain?" Saavik asked.

Spock turned to Kirk and raised one eyebrow.

"At your discretion, Captain," Kirk said.

Spock got that expression again, and McCoy's suspicion that the Vulcan was as concerned about Kirk as he was intensified.

"Out there, Lieutenant Saavik."

Kirk started.

"Sir?" Saavik glanced back.

"Out there" was something Jim Kirk had said the last time the *Enterprise* was under his command.

"I believe the technical term is 'thataway,' " Spock said.

"Aye, sir," Saavik said, obviously not understanding.

But McCoy could see that Jim understood.

Four

As soon as the inspection ended, Peter dropped the "left-handed spanner" into its bin and sprinted to his locker. He was late for his math lesson. He scooped up his little computer, banged the locker door closed, turned around, and ran smack into his Uncle Montgomery.

"Uh—" Peter came to attention and saluted. "I'm due in tutorial, sir, with your permission—"

"Permission denied, Cadet. I'll have a few words wi' ye first."

"But, sir, I'll be late!"

"Then ye'll be late! What did ye mean wi' that display of impertinence?"

Oh, boy, Peter thought. *Now I'm in for it.*

"Sir?" he said innocently, stalling for time.

"Dinna 'sir' me, ye young scoundrel! Were ye trying to embarrass me in front of the admiral? In front of James Kirk himself?"

"You didn't have to tell him who I was!" Peter said. "Nobody knew, till now!"

"Aye, is that so? Ye are embarrassed to be my nephew?"

"You know I'm not! It just seems like everybody will think I only got here because of it."

Montgomery Scott folded his arms across his chest. "Ye have so little faith in ye'sel'?"

"I just want to pull my share," Peter said, and saw that *that* was not the right thing to say, either.

"I see," Uncle Montgomery said. " 'Tis not ye'sel' ye doesna trust, 'tis me. Ye think I'd do ye the disservice of letting ye off easy? If ye think ye havna been working hard enough, we'll see if we canna gi' ye a bit o' a change."

I'm definitely going to be late to math, Peter thought. *Lieutenant Saavik will cancel the lesson, and on top of everything else it's going to take me three days to get uncle over his snit. Well, smart kid, was it worth it?*

He remembered the look on the admiral's face when he gave him the "left-handed spanner" and decided that it was.

But not, unfortunately, as far as Uncle Montgomery was concerned.

"You know I don't think that, Uncle," Peter said, trying to placate him.

"Ah, *now* it's 'Uncle'! And stop changing the subject! Ye havna explained thy behavior!"

"He was testing me, Uncle, to see how dumb I am. If that happened, Dannan said—"

"Dannan!" Uncle Montgomery cried. "That sister o' thine has only just missed being thrown in the brig more times than thy computer can count! I'd not take thy sister as a model, mister, if ye know what's good for ye!"

"Wait a minute!" Peter cried. "Dannan is . . . she's—"

It was true she had been disciplined a lot; it was even true that she had nearly been thrown out of Starfleet. But even Uncle Montgomery had told him a million times that once in a while you had to work on your own initiative, and that was what Dannan did. It didn't matter anyway. Dannan was Peter's sister, and he adored her.

"You can't talk about her that way!"

"I'll talk about her any way I please, young mister, and ye shall listen with a civil tongue in thy head."

"Can I go now?" Peter asked sullenly. "I'm already five minutes late, and Lieutenant Saavik won't wait around."

"That's another thing. Ye spend far too much time hanging around after her. D'ye think she's naught to do but endure the attentions of a puppydog?"

"What's *that* supposed to mean?" Peter asked angrily.

"Dinna play the fool wi' thine old uncle, boy. I can see a schoolboy crush—and so can everyone else. My only advice for ye," he said condescendingly, "is dinna wear thy heart on thy sleeve."

"You don't know what you're talking about!"

"Nay? Well, then, be off wi' ye, Mister Know-It-All, if ye are too wise to listen to the advice o' thine elders."

Peter fled from the locker room.

Saavik arrived at tutorial rather late, for the inspection and undocking disarrayed the usual schedule. She was surprised to find that Peter was not there yet, either. Perhaps he had arrived and, not finding Saavik, assumed that the training cruise would change the routine. But she thought he would wait more than two or three minutes. Perhaps Mister Scott had lectured his trainees after the engine room inspection.

That could take considerable extra time, Saavik thought. *I will wait.*

When Spock first requested that Saavik tutor Peter Preston in advanced theoretical mathematics, she had prepared herself to decline. Peter, fourteen, was nearly the same age as Saavik had been when the Vulcan research team landed on her birth-world.

Saavik had feared she would compare the charming and well-brought-up young Peter to the creature she had been on Hellguard. She had feared she would resent the advantages childhood had presented to him and withheld from her. She feared her own anger and how she might react if she released it even for a moment.

When she tried to explain all this to the captain, he listened, considerately and with all evidence of understanding. Then he apologized for his own lack of clarity: he had not made a request; he had given an order which he expected Saavik to carry out as a part of her training. Unquestioning obedience was illogical, but trust was essential. If, in all the years that Saavik had known Spock, she had not found him worthy of trust, then she was of course free to refuse the order. Many avenues of training and advancement would still lie open to her. None, however, would permit her to remain under Spock's command.

Spock had been a member of the Vulcan exploratory expedition to Hellguard. He alone forced the other Vulcans to accept their responsibility to the world's abandoned inhabitants, though they had many logical reasons (and unspoken excuses far more involved) for denying any responsibility. Saavik owed her existence as a civilized being, and possibly her life—for people died young and brutally on Hellguard—to Spock's intervention.

She obeyed his order.

Saavik heard Peter running down the hall. He burst in, out of breath and distracted.

"I'm really sorry I'm late," he said. "I came as fast as I could—I didn't think you'd wait."

"I was late, too," she admitted. "I thought perhaps you were delayed by the inspection, as I was." Saavik had to be honest with herself, though: one of the reasons she waited was that she thoroughly enjoyed the time she spent teaching the young cadet. Peter was intelligent and quick, and while their ages were sufficiently different that Peter was still a child and Saavik an adult, they were in fact only six years apart.

"Well . . . sort of."

"Are you prepared to discuss today's lesson?"

"I guess so," he said. "I think I followed projecting the n-dimensional hyperplanes into n-1 dimensional spaces, but I got a little tangled up when they started to intersect."

Saavik interfaced Peter's small computer with the larger monitor.

"Let me look," she said, "and I will try to see where you began . . . getting a little tangled up."

As she glanced through Peter's work, Saavik reflected upon her own extraordinarily erroneous assumption about the way she would react to Peter. Far from resenting the boy, she found great comfort in knowing that her own childhood was anomalous, rather than being the way of a deliberately cruel universe. Cruelty existed, indeed: but natural law did not demand it.

She learned at least as much from Peter as he did from her: lessons about the joy of life and the possibilities for happiness, lessons she could never feel comfortable discussing with Spock, and in fact had avoided even mentioning to him.

But the captain was far more subtle and complex than his Vulcan exterior permitted him to reveal. Perhaps he had not, as she had believed, given her this task to test her control of the anger she so feared. Perhaps she was learning from Peter precisely what Spock had intended.

"Here, Peter," she said. "This is the difficulty." She pointed out the error in one of his equations.

"Huh?"

He looked blankly at the monitor, his mind a thousand light-years from anything.

"Your tangle," she said. "It's right here."

"Oh. Yeah. Okay." He looked at it and blinked, and said nothing.

"Peter, what's wrong?"

"Uh, nothing."

Saavik remained silent for a moment; Peter fidgeted.

"Peter," Saavik said, "you know that I sometimes have difficulty understanding the way human beings react. I need help to learn. If everything is all right, determining why I thought something might be wrong will pose me a serious problem."

"Sometimes there's stuff people don't want to talk about."

"I know—I don't wish to invade your privacy. But if, in truth, you are not troubled, I must revise many criteria in my analyses of behavior."

He took a deep breath. "Yeah, something happened."

"You need not tell me what," Saavik said.

"Can I, if I want?"

"Of course, if you wish."

He hesitated, as if sorting out his thoughts. "Well," he said, "I had this fight with Commander Scott."

"A fight!" Saavik said with considerable distress.

"Not like punching or anything. But that isn't it; he gets snarked off about little stuff all the time."

"Peter, I think it would be better if you did not speak so of your commanding officer."

"Yeah, you're right, only he's been doing it my whole life—his whole life, I guess. I know because he's my uncle."

"Oh," Saavik said.

"I never told anybody on the ship, only now he's started telling people. He told the *admiral*—can you believe it? That's one of the things I got mad about." He stopped and took a deep breath and shook his head. "But . . ."

Saavik waited in silence.

Peter looked up at her, started to blush, and looked away. "He said . . . he said you had better things to do with your time than put up with me hanging around, he said I'm a pest, and he said . . . he said I . . . Never mind. That part's too dumb. He said you probably think I'm a pain."

Saavik frowned. "The first statement is untrue, and the second is ridiculous."

"You mean you don't mind having to give me math lessons?"

"On the contrary, I enjoy it very much."

"You don't think I'm a pest?"

"Indeed, I do not."

"I'm really glad," Peter said. "He thinks I've been . . . well . . . acting really dumb. He was laughing at me."

"You deserve better than to be laughed at."

He felt humiliated, Saavik could see that. She knew a great deal about humiliation. She would not wish to teach it to another being. She wished she knew a way to ease his pain, but she felt as confused as he did.

"Peter," she said, "I can't resolve your disagreement with your uncle. I can only tell you that when I was a child, I wished for something I could not name. Later I found the name: it was 'friend.' I have found people to admire, and people to respect. But I never found a friend. Until now."

He looked up at her. "You mean—me?"

"Yes."

Inexplicably, he burst into tears.

Pavel Chekov screamed.

Nothing happened. . . .

His mind and his memory were sharp and clear. He was hyperaware of everything on the bridge of *Reliant:* Joachim beside him at the helm, Terrell sitting blank and trapped at first officer's position, and Khan.

Khan lounged in the captain's seat. The screen framed a full-aft view: Alpha Ceti V dwindled, from a globe to a disk to a speck, then vanished from their sight. *Reliant* shifted into warp and even Alpha Ceti, the star itself, shrank to a point and lost itself in the starfield.

"Steady on course," Joachim said. "All systems normal."

"It was kind of you to bring me a ship so like the *Enterprise,* Mister Chekov," Khan said.

Fifteen years before, Khan had flipped through the technical data on the *Enterprise;* apparently he had memorized each page with one quick look. As far as Chekov could tell, Khan remembered the information perfectly to this day. With the knowledge, and with Terrell under his control, Khan had little trouble taking over *Reliant.* Most of the crew had worked on unaware that anything was wrong, until Khan's people came upon them, one by one, took them prisoner, and beamed them to the surface of Alpha Ceti V.

The engine room company remained, working in concert with each other, and with eels.

Out of three hundred people, Khan had found only ten troublesome enough to bother killing.

"Mister Chekov, I have a few questions to ask of you."

Don't answer him, don't answer him.

"Yes."

The questions began.

He answered. He screamed inside his mind; he felt the creature writhing inside his skull; he answered.

Khan questioned Terrell only briefly, but it seemed to give him great pleasure to extract information from Chekov. By the time he finished, he knew each tiny detail of what precious little anyone on *Reliant* had been told about the classified Project Genesis. He knew where they had been, he knew where they were going, and he knew they reported to Doctor Carol Marcus.

"Very good, Mister Chekov. I'm very pleased with you. But tell me one more thing. Might my old friend Admiral Kirk be involved in your project?"

"No."

"Is he aware of it?"

"I do not know."

With an edge in his voice, Khan asked, "Could he find out about it?"

Kirk was a member of the Fleet General Staff; he had access to any classified information he cared to look up. Chekov tried desperately to keep that knowledge from Khan. His mind was working so fast and well that he *knew,* without any doubt, what Khan planned. He knew it and he feared it.

"Answer me, Mister Chekov."

"Yes."

Khan chuckled softly, the sound like a caress.

"Joachim, my friend, alter our course. We shall pay a visit to Regulus I."

"My lord—!" Joachim faced his leader, protest in his voice.

"This does not suit your fancy?"

"I am with you. We all are. But we're free! This is what we've waited for for two hundred years! We have a ship; we can go where we will—"

"I made a promise fifteen years ago, Joachim. You were witness to my oath, then, and when I repeated it. Until I keep my word to myself, and to my wife, I am not free."

"Khan, my lord, she never desired revenge."

"You overstep your bounds, Joachim," Khan said dangerously.

The younger man caught his breath, but plunged on. "You escaped the prison James Kirk made for you! You've proved he couldn't hold you, Khan, you've won!"

"He tasks me, Joachim. He tasks me, and I'll have him."

The two men stared at each other; Joachim wavered, and turned his head away.

"In fifteen years, this is all I have asked for myself, Joachim," Khan said. "I can have no new life, no new beginning, until I achieve it. I know that you love me, my friend. But if you feel I have no right to any quest, say so. I will free you from the oath you swore to me."

"I'll never break that oath, my lord."

Khan nodded. "Regulus I, Joachim," he said gently.

"Yes, Khan."

"That's it," Carol Marcus said to the main computer. "Genesis eight-two-eight-point-SBR. Final editing. Save it."

"Ok," the computer said.

Carol sighed with disbelief. Finally finished!

"Fatal error," the computer said calmly. "Memory cells full."

"What do you mean, memory full?" She had checked memory space just the day before.

The damned machine began to recite to her the bonehead explanation of peripheral memory. "The memory is full when the size of the file in RAM exceeds—"

"Oh, stop," Carol said.

"Ok."

"Damn! David, I thought you were going to install the Monster's new memory cells!"

All their computers stored information by arranging infinitesimal magnetic bubbles within a matrix held in a bath of liquid hydrogen near absolute zero. The storage was very efficient and very fast and the volume extremely large; yet from the beginning, Genesis had been plagued by insufficient storage. The programs and the data files were so enormous that every new shipment of memory filled up almost as quickly as it got installed. The situation was particularly critical with the Monster, their main computer. It was an order of magnitude faster than any other machine on the station, so of course everyone wanted to use it.

David hurried to her side. "I did," he said. "I had to build a whole new bath for them, but I did it. Are they filled up *already?*"

"That's what it says."

He frowned and glanced around the lab.

"Anybody have anything in storage here they've just been dying to get rid of?"

Jedda, who was a Deltan and prone to quick reactions, strode over with an expression of alarm. "If you delete my quantum data I'll be *most* distressed."

"I don't *want* to delete anything," Carol said, "but I just spent *six weeks* debugging this subroutine, and I've got to have it."

At a lab table nearby, Del March glanced at Vance Madison. Vance grimaced, and Carol caught him at it.

"All right you guys," Carol said. "Del, have you been using my bubble bath again?"

Del approached, hanging his head; Vance followed, walking with his easy slouch. They're like a couple of kids, Carol thought. *Like* kids? They *are* kids. They were only a few years older than David.

"Geez, Carol," Del said, "it's just a little something—"

"Del, there's got to be ninety-three computers on Spacelab. Why do you have to put your games on the main machine?"

"They work a lot better," Vance said in his soft beautiful voice.

"You can't play Boojum Hunt on anything less, Carol," Del said. "Hey, you ought to look at what we did to it. It's got a black hole with en accretion disk that will jump right out and grab you, and the graphics are fantastic. If I do say so myself. If we had a three-d display . . ."

"Why do I put up with this?" Carol groaned. The answer to that was obvious: Vance Madison and Del March were the two sharpest quark chemists in the field, and when they worked together their talents did not simply add, but multiplied. Every time they published a paper they got another load of invitations to scientific conferences. Genesis was lucky to have them, and Carol knew it.

The two young scientists played together as well as they worked; unfortunately, what they liked to play was computer games. Del had tried to get her to play one once; she was not merely uninterested, she was totally disinterested.

"What's the file name?" she asked. She felt too tired for patience. She turned back to the console. "Prepare to kill a file," she said to the computer.

"Ok," it replied.

"Don't kill it, Carol," Del said. "Come on, give us a break."

She almost killed it anyway; Del's flakiness got to her worst when she was exhausted.

"We'll keep it out of your hair from now on, Carol," Vance said. "I promise."

Vance never said anything he did not mean. Carol relented.

"Oh—all right. What's the file name?"

"BH," Del said.

"Got one in there called BS, too?" David asked.

Del grinned sheepishly. Carol accessed one of the smaller lab computers.

"Uh, Carol," Del said, "I don't think it'll fit in that one."

"How big *is* it?"

"Well . . . about fifty megs."

"Christ on a crutch!" David said. "The program that swallowed Saturn."

"We added a lot since you played it last," Del said defensively.

"Me? I never play computer games!"

Vance chuckled. David colored. Carol hunted around for enough peripheral storage space and transferred the program.

"All right, twins," she said. She liked to tease them by calling them "twins": Vance was two meters tall, slender, black, intense, and calm, while Del was almost thirty centimeters shorter, compact, fair, manic, and quick-tempered.

"Thanks, Carol," Vance said. He smiled.

Jedda folded his arms. "I trust this means my data is safe for another day."

"Safe and sound."

The deepspace communicator signaled, and he went to answer it.

Carol stored the Genesis subroutine again.

"Ok," the computer said, and a moment later, "Command?"

Carol breathed a sigh of relief, "Load Genesis, complete."

A moment's pause.

"Ok."

"And run it."

"Ok."

"Now," Carol said, "we wait."

"Carol," Jedda said at the communicator, "it's *Reliant*."

She got up quickly. Everyone followed her to the communicator. Jedda put the call up on the screen.

"*Reliant* to Spacelab, come in Spacelab."

"Spacelab here, Commander Chekov. Go ahead."

"Doctor Marcus, good. We're en route to Regulus. Our ETA is three days from now."

"Three days? Why so soon? What did you find on Alpha Ceti VI?"

Chekov stared into the screen. What's wrong? Carol wondered. There shouldn't be any time lag on the hyper channel.

"Has something happened? Pavel, do you read me? Has something happened?"

"No, nothing, Doctor. All went well. Alpha Ceti VI checked out."

"Break out the beer!" Del said.

"But what about—"

Chekov cut her off. "We have new orders, Doctor. Upon our arrival at Spacelab, we will take all Project Genesis materials into military custody."

"Bullshit!" David said.

"Shh, David," Carol said automatically. "Commander Chekov, this is extremely irregular. Who gave this order?"

"Starfleet Command, Doctor Marcus. Direct from the General Staff."

"This is a civilian project! This is *my* project—"

"I have my orders."

"What gold-stripe lamebrain gave the order?" David shouted.

Chekov glanced away from the screen, then turned back.

"Admiral James T. Kirk."

Carol felt the blood drain from her face.

David pushed past her toward the screen.

"I knew you'd try to pull this!" he shouted. "Anything anybody does, you just can't wait to get your hands on it and kill people with it!" He reached to cut off the communication.

Carol grabbed his hand. *Keep hold of yourself,* she thought, and took a deep breath.

"Commander Chekov, the order is improper. I'll permit no military personnel access to my work."

Chekov paused again, glanced away again.

What's going on out there? Carol thought.

"I'm sorry you feel that way, Doctor Marcus," Chekov said. "The orders are confirmed. Please be prepared to hand over Genesis upon our arrival in three days. *Reliant* out."

He reached forward; the transmission faded.

On Spacelab, everyone started talking at once.

"Will everybody please *shut up!*" Carol said. "I can't even think!"

The babble slowly subsided.

"It's got to be a mistake," Carol said.

"A mistake! Mother, for gods' sake! It's perfect! They came sucking up to us with a ship. 'At our disposal!' Ha!"

"Waiting to dispose of us looks more like it," Jedda said.

"David—"

"And what better way to keep an eye on what we're doing? All they had to do was wait till practically everybody is on leave, they can swoop in here and there's only us to oppose them!"

"But—"

"They think we're a bunch of pawns!"

"David, stop it! You're always accusing the military of raving paranoia. What do you think *you're* working up to? Starfleet's kept the peace for a hundred years. . . ."

Silence fell. David could not deny what she had said. At the same time, Carol could not explain what had happened.

"Mistake or not," Vance said, "if they get Genesis, they aren't likely to give it back."

"You're right," Carol said. She thought for a moment. "All right, everybody. Get your gear together. Start with lab notes and work down from there. Jedda, is Zinaida asleep?" Carol knew that Zinaida, Genesis's mathematician, had been working on the dispersal equations until early that morning.

"She was when I left our room," he said. Like Jedda, Zinaida was a Deltan. Deltans tended to work and travel in groups, or at the very least in pairs, for a Deltan alone was terribly isolated. They required emotional and physical closeness of such intensity that no other sentient being could long survive intimacy with one of them.

"Okay, you'd better wake her. Vance, Del, Misters Computer Wizards: I want you to start transferring everything in the computers to portable storage, because any program, any data we can't move we're going to kill—that goes for BH or BS or whatever it is, too. So get to work."

"But where are we going?" Del asked.

"That's for us to know and *Reliant* to find out. But we've only got three days. Let's not waste time."

The doors of the turbolift began to close.

"Hold, please!"

"Hold!" Jim Kirk said to the sensors. The doors opened obediently, sighing. Lieutenant Saavik dashed inside.

"Thank you, sir."

"My pleasure, Lieutenant."

She gazed at him intently; Kirk began to feel uneasy.

"Admiral," she said suddenly, "may I speak?"

"Lieutenant," Kirk said, "self-expression does not seem to be one of your problems."

"I beg your pardon, sir?"

"Never mind. What was it you wanted to say?"

"I wish to ask you about the high efficiency rating."

"You earned it."

"I did not think so."

"Because of the results of *Kobayashi Maru?*"

"I failed to resolve the situation," Saavik said.

"You couldn't. There isn't any resolution. It's a test of character."

She considered that for a moment.

"Was the test a part of your training, Admiral?"

"It certainly was," Jim Kirk said with a smile.

"May I ask how *you* dealt with it?"

"You may ask, Lieutenant." Kirk laughed.

She froze.

"That was a little joke, Lieutenant," Kirk said.

"Admiral," she said carefully, "the jokes human beings make differ considerably from those with which I am familiar."

"What jokes exactly do you mean?"

"The jokes of Romulans," she said.

Do you want to know? Jim Kirk asked himself. You don't want to know.

"Your concept, Admiral," Saavik said, "the human concept, appears more complex and more difficult."

Out of the blue, he thought, *My God, she's beautiful.*

Watch it, he thought; and then, sarcastically, *You're an admiral.*

"Well, Lieutenant, we learn by doing."

She did not react to that, either. He decided to change the subject.

"Lieutenant, do you want my advice?"

"Yes," she said in an odd tone of voice.

"You're allowed to take the test more than once. If you're dissatisfied with your performance, you should take it again."

The lift slowed and stopped. The doors slid open and Doctor McCoy, who had been waiting impatiently, stepped inside.

All this newfangled rebuilding, he thought, and look what comes of it: everything's even slower.

"Who's been holding up the damned elevator?— Oh!" he said when he saw Kirk and Saavik. "Hi."

"Thank you, Admiral," Saavik said as she stepped off the lift. "I appreciate your advice. Good day, Doctor."

The doors closed.

Jim said nothing but stared abstractedly at the ceiling.

Doing his very best dirty old man imitation, McCoy waggled his eyebrows.

"Did she change her hair?"

"What?"

"I said—"

"I heard you, Bones. Grow up, why don't you?"

Well, McCoy thought, *that's a change. Maybe not a change for the better, but at least a change.*

"Wonderful stuff, that Romulan ale," McCoy said with a touch of sarcasm.

Kirk returned from his abstraction. "It's a great memory restorative," he said.

"Oh—?"

"It made me remember why I never drink it."

"That's gratitude for you—"

"Admiral Kirk," Uhura said over the intercom. "Urgent message for Admiral Kirk."

Jim turned on the intercom. "Kirk here."

"Sir, Regulus I Spacelab is on the hyperspace channel. Urgent. Doctor Carol Marcus."

Jim started.

Carol Marcus? McCoy thought. *Carol Marcus?*

"Uh . . . Uhura, I'll take it in my quarters," Jim said.

"Yes, sir."

He turned the intercom off again and glared at McCoy, as if having any witnesses to his reaction irritated him.

"Well, well, well," McCoy said. "It never rains but it—"

"Some doctor you are," Jim said angrily. "You of all people should appreciate the danger of opening old wounds."

The lift doors opened, and Kirk stormed out.

"Sorry," McCoy said after the doors had closed once more. *Well, Old Family Doctor,* he thought, *needling him isn't working; you'd better change your tack if you want to bring him out of his funk.*

On the other hand, McCoy said to himself, depending on what that call is about, you may not have to.

Jim Kirk strode down the corridor of the *Enterprise,* trying to maintain his composure. Carol Marcus, after all these years? It would have to be something damned serious for her to call him. And what, in heaven's name, was going on with McCoy? Every word the doctor had said in the past three days was like a porcupine, layered over with little painful probes veiled and unveiled.

He hurried into his room and turned on the viewscreen.

"Doctor Marcus, Admiral," Uhura said.

The image snowed and fluttered across the viewscreen. For an instant, he could make out Carol's face; then it fragmented again.

"Uhura, can't you augment the signal?"

"I'm trying, sir, it's coming in badly scrambled."

". . . Jim . . . read me? Can you . . ."

What did come through clearly was Carol Marcus's distress and anger.

"Your message is breaking up, Carol. What's the matter? What's wrong?"

". . . can't read you. . . ."

"Carol, what's wrong?" He kept repeating that, hoping enough would get through for her to make out his question.

". . . trying . . . take Genesis away from us. . . ."

"What?" he asked, startled. "Taking Genesis? Who? Who's taking Genesis?"

". . . can't hear you. . . . Did you order . . . ?"

"What order? Carol, *who's taking Genesis?"*

The transmission cleared for a mere few seconds. "Jim, rescind the order." It began to break up again. ". . . no authority . . . I won't let . . ."

"Carol!"

"Jim, please help. I don't believe—"

The picture scrambled again and did not clear. Jim slammed his hand against the edge of the screen.

"Uhura, what's happening? Damn it!"

"I'm sorry, sir. There's nothing coming through. It's jammed at the source."

"Jammed!"

"That's what the pattern indicates, Admiral."

"Damn," Jim said again. "Commander, alert Starfleet HQ. I want to talk to Starfleet Command."

"Aye, sir."

Jim Kirk strode onto the bridge.

"Mister Sulu," he said, "stop impulse engines."

Sulu complied. "Stop engines."

The bridge crew waited, surprised, expectant, confused.

"We have an emergency," Kirk said stiffly. "By order of Starfleet Command, I am assuming temporary command of the *Enterprise.* Duty Officer, so note in the ship's log. Mister Sulu, plot a new course: Regulus I Spacelab." He paused as if waiting for an objection or an argument. No one spoke. He opened an intercom channel to the engine room. "Mister Scott."

"Aye, sir?"

"We'll be going to warp speed immediately."

"Aye, sir."

"Course plotted for Spacelab, Admiral," Mister Sulu said.

"Engage warp engines."

"Prepare for warp speed," Saavik said. Her voice was tense and suspicious; only the regard in which Captain Spock held this human kept her from rebelling. She shifted the ship to warp mode.

"Ready, sir," said Mister Sulu.

"Warp five, Mister Sulu."

The ship gathered itself around them and sprang.

Kirk stepped back into the turbolift and disappeared.

In his cabin, Spock lay on a polished slab of Vulcan granite, his meditation stone. He was preparing himself to sink from light trance to a deeper one when he felt the *Enterprise* accelerate to warp speed. He immediately brought himself back toward consciousness. A moment later, he heard someone at his door.

"Come," he said quietly. He sat up.

Jim Kirk entered, hitched one hip on the corner of the stone, and stared at the floor.

"Spock, we've got a problem."

Spock arched his eyebrow.

"Something's happened at Regulus I. We've been ordered to investigate."

"A difficulty at the Spacelab?"

"It looks like it." He raised his head "Spock, I told Starfleet all we have is a boatload of children. But we're the only ship free in the octant. If something *is* wrong . . . Spock, your cadets—how good *are* they? What happens when the pressure is real?"

"They are living beings, Admiral; all living beings have their own gifts." He paused. "The ship, of course, is yours."

"Spock . . . I already diverted the *Enterprise.* Haste seemed essential at the time. . . ."

"The time to which you are referring, I assume, is two minutes and thirteen seconds ago, when the ship entered warp speed?"

Kirk grinned sheepishly. "I should have come here first, I know—"

"Admiral, I repeat: The ship is yours. I am a teacher. This is no longer a training cruise, but a mission. It is only logical for the senior officer to assume command."

"But it may be nothing. The transmission was pretty garbled. If you—as captain—can just take me to Regulus—"

"You are proceeding on a false assumption. I am a Vulcan. I have no ego to bruise."

Jim Kirk glanced at him quizzically. "And now you're going to tell me that logic alone dictates your actions."

"Is it necessary to remind you of something you know well?" He paused. "Logic does reveal, however, that you erred in accepting promotion. You are what you were: a starship commander. Anything else is a waste."

Kirk grinned. "I wouldn't presume to debate you."

"That is wise." Spock stood up. "In any case, were the circumstances otherwise, logic would still dictate that the needs of the many outweigh the needs of the few."

"Or the one?"

"Admiral—" Spock said. He stopped, then began again. "Jim, you are my superior officer. But you are also my friend. I have been, and remain, yours. I am offering you the truth as I perceive it, for myself and for you."

"Spock—" Kirk said quietly. He reached out.

Spock drew back within himself.

Kirk respected the change. He let his hand fall.

"Will you come to the bridge? I didn't do much explaining, and I think your students wonder if I've mutinied."

"Yes, Admiral. But perhaps we'd best talk with Mister Scott first, so he may explain the situation to his cadets as well."

That day at lunchtime, Saavik went to the mess and got in line. All around her, her classmates speculated about the change in plan, the *Enterprise*'s new course, the admiral's unusual move in taking over the ship. Saavik, too, wondered what all these abrupt changes meant. She leaned toward the view that it was another, more sophisticated, training simulation.

A few minutes after the admiral's order, Captain Spock had returned to the bridge accompanying Admiral Kirk. He assured the crew that Kirk's action had his consent. Yet Saavik still felt uncomfortable about the whole procedure.

She hesitated over her choice of lunch. She would have preferred steak tartare, but the captain considered eating meat—raw meat in particular—an uncivilized practice at best; consequently Saavik ordinarily chose something else when she was to take a meal in his company. She had tried for a long time to conform to the Vulcan ideal, vegetarianism, but had succeeded only in making herself thoroughly sick.

She compromised, choosing an egg dish which came out of the galley in a profoundly bland state, but which could be made nearly palatable by the addition of a large amount of sesame oil and pippali, a fiery spice. Peter Preston had taken a taste of it once, and Saavik had not warned him to use it sparingly. She had had no idea of the effect it would have on a human being. Once he stopped coughing and drinking water and could talk again, he described it as "a sort of combination of distilled chili and nuclear fission."

She wondered where Peter was. They occasionally ate together; but though now was his lunch break, he was not in the cafeteria.

Saavik stopped beside Captain Spock's table. He was eating a salad.

"May I join you, sir?"

"Certainly, Lieutenant."

She sat down and tried to think of a proper way to voice her concern about the admiral's having taken command of the *Enterprise.*

"Lieutenant," Spock said, "how are Mister Preston's lessons proceeding?"

"Why—very well, sir. He's an excellent student and has a true aptitude for the subject."

"I thought perhaps he might be finding the work too difficult."

"I've seen no evidence of that, Captain."

"Yet Mister Scott has asked me to suspend Mister Preston's tutorial."

"Why?" Saavik asked, startled.

"His explanation was that the engines require work, and that Preston's help is needed."

"The engines," Saavik said, "just scored one hundred fifteen percent on the postoverhaul testing."

"Precisely," Spock said. "I have considered other explanations. An attempt by Mister Scott to shield Preston from overwork seemed a possibility."

Saavik shook her head. "First, Captain, I believe Peter feels comfortable enough around me that he would let me know if he felt snowed under—"

" 'Snowed under'?"

"Severely overworked. I beg your pardon. I did not intend to be imprecise."

"I meant no criticism, Lieutenant—your progress in dealing with human beings can only be improved by learning their idioms."

Saavik compared Scott's odd request to her earlier conversation with Peter. "I believe I know why Mister Scott canceled Cadet Preston's tutorial."

She explained what had happened.

Spock considered. "The action seems somewhat extreme. Mister Scott surely realizes that proper training is worth all manner of inconvenience—for student and teacher. Did Mister Preston say anything else?"

"He preferred not to repeat part of it. He said it was . . . 'too dumb.' He seemed embarrassed."

"Indeed." Spock ate a few bites of his salad; Saavik tasted her lunch. She added more pippali.

"Saavik," Spock said, "has the cadet shown any signs of serious attachment to you?"

"What do you mean, sir?"

"Does he express affection toward you?"

"I suppose one might say that, Captain. He appeared quite relieved when I told him that I do not consider him a 'pest.' And I must confess . . ." she said, somewhat reluctantly, "I am . . . rather fond of him. He's a sweet-natured and conscientious child."

"But he is," Spock said carefully, "a child."

"Of course." Saavik wondered what Spock was leading up to.

"Perhaps Mister Scott is afraid his nephew is falling in love with you."

"That's ridiculous!" Saavik said. "Even were it not highly improper, it would be impossible."

"It *would* be improper. But not impossible, or even unlikely. It is, rather, a flaw of human nature. If Cadet Preston develops what humans call a 'crush' on you—"

"Sir?" Now she felt confused.

"A crush, for humans, is something like falling in love; however, it occurs only in very young members of the species and is looked upon with great amusement by older members."

The reasons for Peter's behavior suddenly became much clearer. If this was what he was too embarrassed to tell her about, no wonder. She was well aware how much he disliked being laughed at.

Spock continued. "You must deal with it as best you can, as gently as you can. Human beings are very vulnerable in these matters, and very easily hurt. And, as you quite correctly pointed out, it would be improper—"

Saavik felt both shocked and uncomfortable. "Mister Spock," she said, returning to the title she had used for him for many years, "Peter is a *child*. And even if falling in love is a flaw of human nature, it is not one of Vulcan nature."

"But you are not a Vulcan," Spock said.

Saavik dropped her fork clattering onto her plate and stood up so fast that her chair rattled across the floor.

"Sit down," Spock said gently.

Unwillingly, she obeyed.

"Saavik, do not misunderstand me. Your behavior as regards Cadet Preston is completely proper—I entertain no doubts of that. I am not concerned with him for the moment, but with you."

"I've tried to learn Vulcan ways," she said. "If you will tell me where I've failed—"

"Nor are we speaking of failure."

"I—I don't understand."

"I chose the Vulcan path when I was very young. For many years, I considered it the best, indeed the only, possible choice for any reasoning being. But . . ." He stopped for a moment, then appeared to change the subject. "I spoke to you of tolerance and understanding—"

Saavik nodded.

"I have come to realize that what is proper for one being may not be correct for another. In fact, it may be destructive. The choice is more difficult for someone with two cultures—"

"I have only one!"

"—who must choose between them, or choose to follow another's lead, or choose a path that is unique. You are unique, Saavik."

"Mister Spock, what does this have to do with Peter Preston?"

"It has nothing at all to do with Mister Preston."

"Then what are you trying to say to me?"

"What I am trying to say—and I am perhaps not the most competent person to say it, but there is no other—is that some of the decisions you make about your life may differ from what I might decide, or even from what I might advise. You should be prepared for this possibility, so that you do not reject it when it appears. Do you understand?"

She was about to tell him that she did not, but she felt sufficiently disturbed and uneasy—as, to her surprise, Mister Spock also appeared to feel—that she wanted to end the conversation.

"I'd like to think about what you've said, Captain." Saavik put herself, and Spock, back into their relationship of commander and subordinate.

"Very good, Lieutenant," he said, acquiescing to the change.

She stood up. "I must get back to the bridge, sir."

"Dismissed, Lieutenant."

She started to go, then turned back. "Sir—what about Cadet Preston's tutorial?"

Spock folded his hands and considered the question. "It must resume, of course. However, Mister Scott has made a statement about the condition of the engine room which would be indelicate to challenge. I will wait a day or two, then suggest that the lessons continue. Do you find that agreeable?"

"Yes, sir. Thank you."

Saavik returned to her post. She had a great deal to think about.

Five

Peter Preston stood stiffly at attention. His shoulders ached. He had been there close to an hour, waiting for Commander Scott to inspect—for the third time today—the calibration of Peter's control console.

This is getting old real fast, Peter thought.

His uncle had not cracked a smile or spoken to him in anything but a completely impersonal tone for two days. He was showing considerable displeasure in work that before the training cruise—and before their disagreement—he had unstintingly approved. Just now he was unsatisfied with Peter's maintenance of the console.

Finally the engineer strode over and stopped in front of him.

"Ye ha' stood here a considerable while, Cadet, are ye so sure this is fixed that ye can afford to waste time lounging?"

"The console was ready at eleven hundred hours as you ordered, sir."

"So, ye think *this time* ye ha' it working properly, do ye?"

"Aye, sir."

"We'll see abou' that."

Commander Scott ran it through a diagnostic or two.

"Nay," he said, "now ye ha' a field imbalance, ye've overcompensated. Calibrate it again, Cadet."

In a hesitation of a fraction of a second, Peter thought, *Dannan said there are times when you have to stick up for yourself, but there are times when you have to prove you can take whatever they can dish out.*

"Aye, sir," Peter said. "Sorry, sir."

"As well ye' might be. *Will* ye try to do it right?"

"Aye, sir."

This is definitely one of those times when you have to prove you can take it, Peter thought.

And I can *take it, too.*

He set to work on the console again.

He was still at it when the trainees came back from lunch. Grenni sat down at his station.

"Hey, Pres," he said out of the side of his mouth, "the Old Man's really got it in for you today, doesn't he?"

"Why're you talking like you're in an old prison movie?" Peter said. "He's not going to put you on bread and water just for talking to me."

"You never know."

Peter snorted.

"I told you you shouldn't have pulled that dumb stunt with the admiral," Grenni said.

"Yeah, and I guess you'll keep on telling me, huh?" Peter said. Grenni had all the self-righteousness of twenty-twenty hindsight. That was getting as old as Uncle Montgomery's bad humor.

"Geez, Pres, you're working so hard it makes me tired just to watch you," Grenni said.

"Don't worry," Peter told him. "You won't have to endure the torture much longer. Commander Scott's tantrums never last more than three days. Or hadn't you noticed?"

"No," Grenni said, "I hadn't noticed. But then I haven't had the opportunity to observe him like some people—not being his nephew and all."

Damn, Peter thought. Grenni heard, and that means even if nobody else did, they all know now. *Damn.*

"*Enterprise* to Regulus I Spacelab, come in, Spacelab. Doctor Marcus, please respond."

Uhura's transmissions met with no reply.

She glanced up at Spock.

"It's no use. There's just nothing there."

"But the transmissions are no longer jammed?"

"No, there's no jamming—no nothing."

Spock turned to Kirk, back in his old familiar place on the bridge.

"There are two possibilities, Admiral," Spock said. "That they are unwilling to respond, or that they are unable to respond."

"How long—?"

"We will reach Spacelab in twelve hours and forty-three minutes at our present speed."

Kirk folded his arms and hunched down in the captain's chair. " 'Give up Genesis,' she said. What in God's name does that mean? Give it up to whom?"

"It might help my analysis if I knew what Genesis was," Spock said.

Kirk wrestled with conflicting duties, conflicting necessities.

"You're right," he said finally. "Something's happened—something serious. It would be dangerous not to tell you." He stood up. "Uhura, please ask Doctor McCoy to join us in my quarters. Lieutenant Saavik, you have the conn."

The three officers gathered in Jim Kirk's cabin. Spock and McCoy waited while Kirk proved himself to the highest security safeguards.

"Computer," he said. "Security procedure: access to Project Genesis summary."

"Identify for retinal scan," the computer replied.

"Admiral James T. Kirk, Starfleet General Staff. Security Class One."

An instant's pulse of bright light recorded his eyes' patterns; then the screen blinked in filtered colors as the computer ran its comparison programs.

"Security clearance Class One: granted."

"Summary, please," Kirk said.

The computer flashed messages to itself across its screen for several more seconds, until finally an approval overlay masked the safeguards and encodings.

The summary tape began. Carol Marcus, in her lab, faced the camera.

Kirk recognized her son at the next table. David resembled his mother strongly: slender, with high cheekbones, very fair. His curly hair was more gold, while Carol's was ash blond, but they had the same eyes.

Jim had met David Marcus once, years ago, by chance. He recalled the encounter with no particular pleasure. Though David Marcus did not seem to have anything personal against Jim Kirk—for which Jim was grateful if only for the sake of his memories of Carol—the young scientist clearly had little use for military personnel.

Carol faced the camera like an adversary and began to speak.

"I'm Doctor Carol Marcus, director of the Project Genesis team at Regulus I Spacelab. Genesis is a procedure by which the molecular structure of matter is broken down, not into subatomic parts as in nuclear fission, or even into elementary particles, but into subelementary particle-waves. These can then, by manipulation of the various nuclear forces, be restructured into anything else of similar mass."

"Fascinating," Spock said.

"Wait," said Kirk.

"Stage one of the experiment has been completed here in the lab. We will attempt stage two underground. Stage three involves the process on a planetary scale, as projected by the following computer simulation."

The tape switched to the sharp-edged ultrarealistic scenes of computer graphics.

"We intend to introduce the Genesis device via torpedo into an astronomical body of Earth's mass or smaller."

A gray barren cratered world appeared on the screen.

"The planet will be scrupulously researched to preclude the disruption of any life forms or pre-biotics."

Jim, who had already seen the tape, watched the reactions of Spock and

McCoy. Relaxed and intent, Spock took in the information. McCoy sat on the edge of his chair, leaning forward, scowling as the images progressed before him.

"When the torpedo impacts the chosen target," Carol said, "the Genesis effect begins."

On the screen, the planet quivered; then, just perceptibly, it expanded. For an instant, it glowed as intensely as a star.

"The Genesis wave dissociates matter into a homogeneous mass of real and virtual sub-elementary particles."

The forces of gravity and rotation warred, until it became clear that no structure remained to the planet at all.

"The sub-elementaries reaggregate instantaneously."

An entire world had become a translucent cloud. The mass spread into a disk and almost as quickly coalesced again, reenacting planetary evolution at a billion times the speed.

"Precisely *what* they reform into depends on the complexity of the quantum resonances of the original Genesis wave, and on the available mass. If sufficient matter is present, the programming permits an entire star system to be formed. The simulation, however, deals only with the reorganization of a planetary body."

The sphere solidified, transformed into a new world of continents, islands, oceans. Clouds misted the globe in pinwheel weather patterns.

"In other words," Carol said, "the results are completely under our control. In this simulation, a barren rock becomes a world with water, atmosphere, and a functioning ecosystem capable of sustaining most known forms of carbon-based life."

Wherever the clouds thinned, they revealed a tinge of green.

"It represents only a fraction of the potential that Genesis offers, if these experiments are pursued to their conclusion."

An eerily earthly world revolved silently before them on the screen.

"When we consider the problems of population and food supply, the value of the process becomes clear. In addition, it removes the technical difficulties and the ethical problems of interfering with a natural evolutionary system in order to serve the needs of the inhabitants of a separate evolutionary system."

Carol Marcus returned to the screen.

"This concludes the demonstration tape. I and my colleagues, Jedda Adzhin-Dall, Vance Madison, Delwin March, Zinaida Chitirih-Ra-Payjh, and David Marcus, thank you for your attention."

The tape ended.

"It literally *is* genesis," Spock said.

"The power," Kirk said, "of creation."

"Have they proceeded with their experiments?"

"Carol made the tape a year ago. The team got the Federation grant they were applying for, so I assume they've reached phase two by now."

"Dear Lord . . ." McCoy said. He looked up, stricken. "Are we—can we control this? Suppose it hadn't been a lifeless satellite? Suppose that thing were used on an inhabited world?"

"It would," Spock said, "destroy all life in favor of its new matrix."

"Its 'new matrix'? Spock, have you any idea what you're saying?"

"I was not attempting to evaluate its ethical implications, Doctor."

"The ethical implications of complete destruction!"

Spock regarded him quizzically. "You forget, Doctor McCoy, that sentient beings have had, and used, weapons of complete destruction for thousands of years. Historically it has always been easier to destroy than to create."

"Not anymore!" McCoy cried. "Now you can do both at once! One of our myths said Earth was created in six days, now, watch out! Here comes Genesis! We'll do it for you in six minutes!"

"Any form of power, in the wrong hands—"

"Whose are the right hands, my cold-blooded friend? Are you in favor of these experiments?"

"Gentlemen—" Kirk said.

"Really, Doctor McCoy, you cannot ban knowledge because you distrust its implications. Civilization can be considered an attempt to control new knowledge for the common good. The intent of this experiment is creation, not destruction. Logic—"

"Don't give me logic! My God! A force that destroys, yet leaves what was destroyed still usable? Spock, that's the most attractive weapon imaginable. We're talking about Armageddon! Complete, universal, *candy-coated* Armageddon!"

"Knock it off!" Kirk said. "Both of you. Genesis is already here, Spock, you don't need to argue for its existence."

McCoy started to speak but Kirk swung around and silenced him with a look.

"Bones, you don't need to argue how dangerous it might be if it falls into the wrong hands. We know that. And it may already have happened. I need you both—and not at each other's throats."

Spock and McCoy looked at each other.

"Truce, Doctor?" Spock said.

Grudgingly, McCoy replied, "Truce." Then he added, "Besides, that was a simulation. The whole idea's preposterous—it probably won't even work in real life."

"On the contrary, the probability of success appears extremely high."

"And how would you know, Spock? You haven't known about it any longer than I have."

"That is true. But Marcus is an excellent scientist, and her research team carries impressive credentials."

"Do you know them, Spock?" Kirk asked.

"Adzhin-Dall is a quantum physicist and Chitirih-Ra-Payjh is a mathematician. Neither is well known because their work is not translatable from the original Deltan. But the work itself contains fascinating implications. As for Madison and March, I encountered them some two years ago, at a symposium they attended immediately after attaining their doctoral degrees." He spoke rather dryly because their presentation had been, to say the least, unique.

A decade before, Jaine and Nervek had done the theoretical work in "kindergarten physics"—so-called because it dealt with sub-elementary particles.

Madison and March experimentally validated the theory. Their first breakthrough was the dissolution of elementary particles into sub-elementary particles.

Quarks have fractional charge of one-third or two-thirds, and attributes such as charm and strangeness. The sub-elementary particles had fractional charge as well: four-ninths and one-ninth, the squares of the charges of the quark. According to Madison, they could be sorted further by "five unmistakable marks," which the team had proposed designating taste, tardiness, humor, cleanliness, and ambition.

All this had begun to sound peculiarly familiar to Spock. He searched his memory for resonances. Just as he finally came upon the proper reference, March took over to offer terminology for the particles themselves.

When March recited several stanzas of a poem by a Terran nonsense writer, half the audience responded with delighted laughter and the other half with offended silence.

Spock maintained his reserve, but in truth he had been very tempted to smile.

"We'd like to propose that the sub-elementary particles be designated 'snarks' and 'boojums,'" March had said. "When we picked the names, we didn't realize quite how appropriate they were. But after we worked on the math for a while we discovered that the two entities are actually images of one another, one real, one virtual." He displayed on the auditorium screen a set of formulae, a transformation that proved the mathematical equivalence of the two separate particle-waves.

"Now," March said with a completely straight face, "and with apologies to Lewis Carroll:

"In the midst of the word we were trying to say,
In the midst of our laughter and glee,
We will softly and silently vanish away—
For the Snark was a Boojum, you see."

He and Madison left the podium.

After the presentation, Spock had heard one normally dignified elder scientist say, laughing, "If they get bored with science they can go straight into stand-up comedy," to which her colleague, who was not quite so amused, replied, "Well, maybe. But the jokes are pretty esoteric, don't you think?"

Spock had made a point of attending their question-and-answer session later that day, and during the week-long seminar became fairly well acquainted with them. He had more in common with Madison, whose intellect was firmly based in rationality, than with the high-strung March, whose brilliance balanced on a fine edge of intensity. But Spock had found their company stimulating; he would be pleased to encounter the two young humans again, on Spacelab.

"Spock?" Kirk said.

Spock returned from his reminiscences. "Yes, Admiral?"

"I said, were they your students?"

"Indeed not, Admiral. They are pioneers in the field of sub-elementary particle physics. I am honored to have been a student of theirs."

* * *

Del March glared at the computer terminal. No way was he going to be able to transfer Boojum Hunt. Every portable byte of memory was already packed full of essential Genesis data, and the team still would have to let some go when they blanked the built-in memory cells.

He had a hard copy of the program, of course, a printout, but it would take a couple of hours for the optical-scan to read it back in, and it always made mistakes. Boojum was a real pain to debug. Well, no help for it.

He was glad they would not lose the program entirely. Boojum was the best piece of software he and Vance had ever written. It was an adventure game; yet it paralleled their real-world work of the last few years. Vance referred to it as "the extended metaphor" but agreed that "Boojum Hunt" was a lot more commercial.

Then Del got an idea. When the storm troopers arrived tomorrow, they would be looking for *something*. It would be a shame to disappoint them.

Vance came over and put his hand on Del's shoulder.

"Might's well get it over with, don't you think?"

Del grinned. "No, Vance, listen—don't you think it's about time Mad Rabbit got going again?"

Vance gave him a quizzical look, then began to laugh. He had a great laugh. Del did not have to explain his plan; Vance understood it completely.

Carol returned to the lab. Most of the really sensitive data had already been moved. Only the mechanism of Genesis itself remained. They had another whole day to finish collecting personal gear and to be sure they had erased all clues to their whereabouts.

"I could use a good joke about now," Carol said. She sounded both tired and irritable.

Among other things, she's probably sick of hassling with Dave about Starfleet, Del thought. He really had it in for them—now he had good reason, but it was hardly his newest theme.

"Vance and I just decided to leave something for the troops," Del said. "The latest Mad Rabbit."

"What in heaven's name is a mad rabbit?"

"Do you believe it, Vance, she never heard of us." Del feigned insult. "Carol, we were famous."

"What do you mean, 'were'? You're pretty famous now."

"We were famous in Port Orchard, Del," Vance said mildly. "That isn't exactly big time."

"Port Orchard?" Carol said.

"See?"

"What's Mad Rabbit!"

"I'm Mad," Vance said, "and he's Rabbit."

"As in March Hare. We started a minor revival of Lewis Carroll all by ourselves."

Carol flung up her hands in resignation. "Del, I guess you'll let me in on the secret when you get good and ready, right?"

Del started to explain. "We used to have a company, when we were kids. It still exists; we just haven't done anything with it since—before grad school, I guess, huh, Vance?"

"Reality is a lot more interesting," Vance said. He pulled a chair around and got Carol to sit down.

Del grinned. "If you call quark chemistry reality."

Vance took heed of Carol's impatience, and, as usual, brought Del back on track. "We used to write computer-game software," he said. "Our company was called Mad Rabbit Productions. It did pretty well. In Port Orchard, we were 'local kids make good' for a while." He started to rub the tension-taut muscles of Carol's neck and shoulders.

"I had no idea," Carol said. She flinched as Vance found a particularly sore spot, then began to relax.

"The thing is," Del said, "where the game sold best was to starbases."

"The more isolated the better," Vance added. "They don't have much else to do."

"Not unlike Spacelab," Del said.

But it was true. Spacelab was quite possibly the Federation's least exciting entertainment spot. There wasn't much to do but work. After concentrating on the same subject eighteen hours a day seven days a week for close to a year, Del had been getting perilously close to burnout. He had begun having bizarre and wistful dreams about going out to low dives, getting stoned to the brainstem on endorphin-rock and beer, and picking a fight with the first person to look at him sidewise.

He thought he had outgrown that kind of thing a couple of years before.

When he told Vance about one of his nightmares, his friend and partner suggested they revive their old business. It was perfectly possible, on Spacelab, to get drunk or stoned or both, and Vance was not anxious to have to start dragging Del out of brawls again.

"We wrote Boojum just to play it," Del said. "But why not leave it for *Reliant*—"

Carol giggled. "What a great idea. It seems a shame for them to come all this way for nothing."

They all laughed.

The last couple of days had actually been rather exciting. Everyone had managed to convince each other that the Starfleet orders were some ridiculous, awful mistake, and that as soon as they could get through to somebody in the Federation Assembly, or in the Federation Science Network, everything would be straightened out. Some overzealous petty-tyrant Starfleet officer would get called on the carpet, maybe even cashiered out of the service, and that would be that. All they needed to do was keep Genesis and the data out of the hands of *Reliant*'s captain until he got bored with looking for it and went away, or until they could recruit civilian scientific support and aid.

Looked at that way, it became a big game of hide-and-seek. It was a change in routine, with a tiny potential for danger, just scary enough to be fun.

"I'll put it in the Monster," Del said.

"Oh, I see," Carol said smiling. "This whole thing is a ploy for you guys to get room to play in the main machine."

"You got it," Vance said.

They all laughed again. They had been working forty-eight hours straight. Del felt punchy with exhaustion and marvelously silly.

Carol patted Vance's hand and stood up. "Thank you," she said. "That feels a lot better."

"You're welcome," he said. "You looked like you needed it."

Zinaida entered the lab.

Over the past year, Del had got used to working with her, but he never had managed to get over a sharp thrill of attraction and desire whenever he saw her. Deltans affected humans that way. The stimulus was general rather than individual. Del understood it intellectually. Getting the message through to his body was another thing.

No Deltan would ever permit her- or himself to become physically involved with a human being. The idea was ethically inconceivable, for no human could tolerate the intensity of the intimacy.

Dreaming never hurt anyone, though, and sometimes Del dreamed about Zinaida Chitirih-Ra-Payjh; in his dreams he could pretend that he was different, that he could provide whatever she asked and survive whatever she offered.

The Deltans, Zinaida and Jedda both, were unfailingly cordial to the humans on the station; they comported themselves with an aloofness and propriety more characteristic of Vulcans than of the uninhibited sensualists Deltans were said to be. They seldom touched each other in public, and never anyone else. They kept a protective wall of detachment between themselves and their vulnerable co-workers, most of whom were acutely curious to know what it was they did in private, but who knew better than to ask.

Zinaida greeted them and turned on the subspace communicator. Ever since the call from *Reliant,* one or another of the scientists tried to contact the Federation every hour or so. Except for Carol's half-completed transmission to James Kirk, no one had met with any success.

This time it was just the same. Zinaida shrugged, turned off the communicator, and joined her teammates by the computer.

"Genesis is about ready," she said to Carol. "David and Jedda thought you would want to be there."

Her eyebrows were as delicate and expressive as bird wings, and her lashes were long and thick. Her eyes were large, a clear aquamarine blue flecked with bright silver, the most beautiful eyes Del had ever seen.

"Thanks, Zinaida," Carol said. "We'll get it out of here—then I guess all we can do is wait." She left the lab.

Del knew she still hoped *Reliant* might be called off: if it was, they would not have to purge the computer memories. Once that was done, getting everything back on-line would be a major undertaking. The last thing they planned to do before fleeing was to let the liquid hydrogen tanks—the bubble baths—purge themselves into space. The equipment only worked when it was supercooled; at room temperature, it deteriorated rapidly. Rebuilding would take a lot of time.

Jan, the steward, came in a moment after Carol left.

"Yoshi wants to know what anybody wants him to bring in the way of food."

Yoshi, the cook, had put off his leave till the rest of the station personnel returned from holiday. He was convinced the scientists would kill themselves with food poisoning or malnutrition if they were left completely to their own devices.

"He really shouldn't have to worry about it," Del said.

Jan shrugged cheerfully. "Well, you know Yoshi."

"How about sashimi?"

"Yech," said Vance.

"I think he had in mind croissants and fruit and coffee."

"Jan, why did he put you to the trouble of asking, if he'd already decided?"

"I don't know. I guess so you have the illusion of being in charge of your own fate. Do you know when we're going? Or how long we'll be?"

"No to both questions. We may be gone for a while. Maybe you ought to tell him we suggested pemmican."

"Hell, no," Jan said. "If I do, he'll figure out a way to make some, and it sounds even worse than sashimi."

After Jan left, Del poured himself a cup of coffee, wandered down to his office, and checked to be sure he had got all his lab notes. The top of his desk was clear for the first time since he came to Spacelab. The office felt bare and deserted, as if he were moving out permanently. The framed piece of calligraphy on the wall was the only thing left: he saw no need to put it away, and it seemed silly to take it. He read it over for the first time in quite a while:

Come, listen, my men, while I tell you again
The five unmistakable marks
By which you may know, wheresoever you go,
The warranted genuine Snarks.

Let us take them in order. The first is the taste,
Which is meagre and hollow, but crisp:
Like a coat that is rather too tight in the waist,
With a flavor of Will-o-the-Wisp.

Its habit of getting up late you'll agree
That it carries too far, when I say
That it frequently breakfasts at five-o'clock tea,
And dines on the following day.

The third is its slowness in taking a jest.
Should you happen to venture on one,
It will sigh like a thing that is deeply distressed:
And it always looks grave at a pun.

The fourth is its fondness for bathing-machines,
Which it constantly carries about,
And believes that they add to the beauty of scenes—
A sentiment open to doubt.

The fifth is ambition. It next will be right
To describe each particular batch:

Distinguishing those that have feathers, and bite,
From those that have whiskers, and scratch.

For although common Snarks do no manner of harm,
Yet I feel it my duty to say
Some are Boojums—

—Lewis Carroll
"The Hunting of the Snark"

Del sat on the corner of his desk and sipped his coffee. Exhaustion was beginning to catch up with him, dissolving the fine thrill of defiance into doubt.

Vance came in and straddled a chair, folding his arms across its back. Del waited, but his partner did not say anything. He reached for Del's cup. Del handed it to him and Vance drank some of the coffee. He had always had a lot more endurance than Del, but even he was beginning to look tired.

"I can't figure out what to take."

"I don't know, either," Del said. "A toothbrush and a lot of books?"

Vance smiled, but without much conviction. He drank some more of Del's coffee, grimaced, and handed back the cup. "How many times has that stuff boiled?"

"Sorry. I forgot to turn down the heat."

Vance suddenly frowned and looked around the room. "Little brother . . ." he said.

Del started. Vance had not called him that since high school.

"Little brother, this is all bullshit, you know."

"I *don't* know. What are you talking about?"

"If the military decides to take Genesis, they will, and there's not a damned thing we'll be able to do about it."

"There's got to be! You're beginning to sound like Dave."

"For all our Lewis Carroll recitations, for all our doing our amateur comedian number at seminars—hell, even for all the fun we've had—we've been hiding out from the implications of our work. This has been inevitable since the minute we figured out how to break up quarks en masse without a cyclotron."

"What are you saying we ought to do? Just turn everything over to *Reliant* when it gets here?"

"No! Gods, Del, no."

"Sorry," Del said sincerely. He knew Vance better than that. "That was a stupid thing to say. I'm sorry."

"I mean the exact opposite. Only . . . I don't really know what I mean by meaning the exact opposite. Except, we can't let them have it. No matter what."

All of a sudden the lights started flashing on and off, on and off, and a siren howled. Vance jumped to his feet.

"What the hell—!"

"That's the emergency alarm!" Del said.

They sprinted out of Del's office.

Something must have happened when they tried to move Genesis, Del thought.

Vance, with his longer stride, was ten meters ahead of him by the time they reached the main lab. He ran into the room—

Two strangers stepped out of hiding and held phasers on him. He stopped and raised his hands but kept on walking forward, drawing their attention farther into the lab and away from the corridor. Del ducked into a doorway and pressed himself against the shadows, taking the chance his friend had given him.

"What the hell is going on?" he heard Vance say. "Who are you people?"

"We've come for Genesis."

Damn, Del thought. *We spent the last two days running around in a fit of paranoia about the military, and not one of us thought to wonder if they were telling the truth about arriving in three days.*

He opened the door behind him, slipped into the dark room, and locked the door. He felt his way to the communications console and keyed it on.

"Hi, Del," David said cheerfully. "Can you wait a minute? We're just about to move."

"No!" Del whispered urgently. "Dave, keep your voice down. They're here! They've got Vance and Zinaida."

"What?"

"They lied to us! They're here already. Get Genesis out, fast."

He heard a strange noise in the corridor, searched his mind for what the sound could be, and identified it: a tricorder.

"Dave, dammit, they're tracking me! Get Genesis out, and get out yourselves before they find you, too!"

"But—"

"Don't argue! Look, they're not gonna hurt us. What can they do? Maybe dump us in a brig someplace. Somebody's got to be loose to tell the Federation what's going on. To get us out if they try to keep us incommunicado. *Go!*"

"Okay."

Del slammed off the intercom and accessed the main computer. He *had* to wipe the memories before he got caught. The tricorder hummed louder.

The computer came on-line.

"Ok," it said.

"Liquid hydrogen tanks, purge protocol," Del said softly.

The door rattled.

"We know you're in there! Come out at once!"

"That's a safeguarded routine," the computer said.

"I know," Del said.

"Ok. Which tanks do you wish to purge?"

Somebody banged on the locked door, but it held. Del answered the computer's questions as quickly and as softly as he could speak. As a safety precaution, the liquid hydrogen tanks would not accept the purge command without several codes and a number of overrides. Del assured the program that he wanted everything purged except for one memory bath.

The banging and thumping grew louder. He was almost done.

"All right!" he yelled. "All right, I'm coming." They didn't hear him, or they didn't believe him, or they didn't care.

"What?" the computer said.

"I wasn't talking to you that time."

"Ok. Codes acceptable. Safeguards overridden. Purge routine ready. Please say your identity password."

"March Hare," Del said.

"Ok. Purge initiated."

A moment later, the computer's memory began to fail, and the system crashed.

A laser-blaster exploded the door inward. The concussion nearly knocked Del to the floor. He grabbed at the console and turned it off. The screen's glow faded as the invaders rushed him.

He raised his hands in surrender.

The tanks were venting into space. In about one minute, nothing at all would be left in any of the station's computers. Except Mad Rabbit Productions' Boojum Hunt.

Four strangers came through the ruined door, three with phasers, one with a blaster.

"Come with us." The one with the blaster gestured toward the exit.

Del raised his hands a little higher. "All right, all right," he said to her. "I told you I was coming."

They herded him into the main lab. About twenty people guarded Vance, Zinaida, Jan, and Yoshi. The strangers, rough and wild, sure did not look like Starfleet personnel.

Vance gave Del a questioning glance. Del nodded very slightly: mission accomplished.

A white-haired, cruel-faced man stood up and approached them. Nearly as tall as Vance, he was arrogant and elegant despite his ragged clothing.

"I've come for Genesis," he said. "Where is it?"

"The scientists shipped out of here a couple hours ago," Vance said. "They didn't tell us where they went or what they took. We're just technicians."

The leader of the group turned to one of his people.

Del recognized Pavel Chekov, and cursed under his breath. Captain Terrell stood a bit farther back in the group. Neither appeared to be a prisoner—in fact, they both carried phasers.

"Is this true, Mister Chekov?"

"No, Khan." Pale and blank-looking, Chekov spoke without expression.

"Who is he?" Khan gestured toward Vance.

"Doctor Vance Madison."

Khan took a step toward him. Two of his people grabbed Vance's arms. Del saw what was coming and fought to go to Vance's aid. One of the people behind him put a choke-hold on him.

Khan struck Vance a violent backhand blow to the face, flinging him against his captors. Dazed, Vance shook his head. He straightened up. A thin trickle of blood ran down his chin.

"Do not lie to me again, Doctor Madison."

Khan went back to questioning Chekov.

"Who are these others?"

Chekov said he did not know Yoshi or Jan, bat he identified Zinaida and Del. Del tried to figure out what was going on. What were Chekov and Terrell doing with this bunch of pirates?

"You can save yourselves a great deal of unpleasantness by cooperating," Khan said.

No one spoke.

"My lord—"

"Yes, Joachim?"

"There's nothing in the computer but this."

Khan joined Joachim and gazed down at the computer screen. At first he smiled. That scared Del, because it indicated that Khan had either seen Carol's grant application, or otherwise knew a good deal about Genesis. The opening Boojum graphics closely resembled a Genesis simulation.

Del looked across at Vance, worried about him.

"You okay?"

The woman behind Del tightened her hold on his throat, so he shut up. But Vance nodded. The dazed look, at least, had disappeared.

Khan suddenly shouted, incoherent with rage. "A game!" he screamed. "What do you mean, a game!"

Yoshi was the nearest to him of the station personnel. Khan swung around and grabbed him.

"A game! *Where is Genesis?*" He picked Yoshi up and shook him violently.

"I don't know!"

"He's telling the truth! Leave him alone!" Vance struggled but could not get free.

Khan set Yoshi down gently.

"This one knows nothing of Genesis?" he asked kindly.

"That's right. Whatever you're after, Jan and Yoshi have nothing to do with it. Leave them alone."

Khan drew a knife from his belt. Before anyone understood what he planned, he grabbed Yoshi by the hair, jerked his head back, and cut his throat. Yoshi did not even cry out. Blood spurted across the room. Warm droplets spattered Del's cheek.

"My God!"

Someone—one of Khan's own people—screamed. Khan reached for Jan. Del wrenched himself out of his captors' hands and lunged. The knife flashed again. Jan's scream stopped suddenly and arterial blood sprayed out. Del grabbed Khan, who turned smoothly and expertly and sank his blade to its hilt in Del's side.

"Del!" Vance cried.

Del felt the warmth of the blade, but no pain: he thought it had slid along his skin just beneath his ribs.

He grappled with Khan, straining to reach his throat, but he was outnumbered. Within a few seconds, they had powered him to the floor. That was the worst show he'd put up since the last time Vance dragged him drunk and stoned and bruised out of a bar and made him promise to quit mixing recreational drugs. He had kept the promise, too.

Weird to remember that now.

He pushed himself to his hands and knees. Someone kicked him.

Del cried out in shock and surprise at the pain. He fell, then rolled over onto his back. The ceiling lights glared in his eyes. Everyone was staring at him,

Khan with a faint smile. Del put his hand to his side, which should have ached, but which hurt with a high, throbbing pain.

His hand came away soaked with blood. That was the first time he realized Khan had stabbed him.

They dragged him to his feet. His knees felt weak and he was dizzy.

Four people barely succeeded in holding Vance down.

Khan stood just near enough to tempt Del to kick at him, just far enough away to make any attempt futile and stupid. Del pressed his hand hard against the knife wound. It was very deep. Blood flowed steadily against the pressure.

Yoshi was dead, but Jan moved weakly, bleeding in pulsebeats. Someone moved to help him.

"Leave him!" Khan snarled. "Let him die; he is worthless to me." He gestured at Del. "Hold his arms."

They already held him tightly but they forced his hands behind his back. The wound bled more freely.

Khan turned away and strolled to a nearby workbench. "Your laboratory is excellently equipped," he said matter-of-factly, while everyone else in the room, even his own people, stared horrified at Jan, slowly bleeding to death.

"My gods," Vance whispered in fury. "You're insane!" He strained around. "Chekov! Terrell! You can't just stand there and let him die!"

"Be quiet, Doctor Madison," Khan said easily. "My people and I do what we must; as for young Pavel here, and his captain—I own them. I intend to own you." He idly picked up a large tripod.

"My Lord Khan, yes!" Joachim said. "Control them completely! There are eels on *Reliant,* I'll return to the ship and get them—"

"That will not be necessary, Joachim," Khan said. "Thank you for your suggestion."

"Sir—"

"Tie them up." He fiddled with the tripod.

Khan's people dragged them to a smaller room down the corridor. There, they bound Zinaida and Vance to chairs. Del watched as if from a long distance. He could feel himself slipping down into shock. The whole side of his shirt and his left hip and thigh were soaked with blood. He could not believe what was happening. His reality had suddenly turned far more fantastic than any game he had ever invented.

Del focused on the thought: At least Carol got Genesis away. She *must* have.

Khan's followers flung a rope over the ceiling strut, then dragged Del beneath it and tied his hands. The rope jerked him upright and he cried out. When his feet barely touched the floor, they tied the other end of the rope to a built-in lab table.

"Khan, my lord," Joachim pleaded, "this effort is unnecessary. It would only take a moment—"

"No. Our dear friend the admiral must know what I plan for him when he is in my grasp."

"But, my lord—"

Khan stopped in front of Del.

"Leave us, Joachim."

He had taken the tripod apart; now he held one of its legs, a steel rod half a meter long and a centimeter through.

"Leave us!" He touched Del's face with his long, fine hand. Del tried to turn away, and Khan chuckled.

His people left.

Jan and Yoshi were dead.

Khan smiled.

Vance struggled furiously against the ropes, cursing. Zinaida sat quietly with her eyes closed.

Del met Khan's gaze. His expression was kind, almost pitying.

"Tell me about Genesis, Doctor March."

Del tried to take a breath. The knife wound radiated pain.

"No. . . ." he said.

Khan hardly moved. The steel rod flicked out and struck Del's side.

It hurt so much Del could not even cry out. He gasped.

"Don't!" Vance yelled. "For gods' sake, stop it!"

Khan did not even bother to ask another question. Slowly, methodically, with the precision of obsession, he beat Del unconscious.

Joachim waited.

Khan opened the door. He gripped Joachim by the shoulder.

"We are close to the prize, Joachim. Doctor March will speak to me when he regains consciousness," he said. "Let it be soon, my friend."

Joachim watched him stride away.

He did not want to enter the lab. He had heard what was happening. He did not want to see it. But he obeyed.

Dark streaks soaked through March's shirt where the steel rod, striking, had broken his skin. He had lost a great deal of blood, and the stab wound still bled slowly.

Vance Madison raised his head.

"If there's anything human left in you," he whispered, "untie me. Let me help him." His voice was hoarse.

"I have no wish to die as your hostage." Joachim searched for March's pulse and found it only with difficulty. He was deep in shock. Left alone, he would soon die.

Joachim found an injector in *Reliant*'s portable medical kit. He chose the strongest stimulant it offered, pressed the instrument to the side of March's throat, and introduced the drug directly into the carotid artery.

Del March shuddered and opened his eyes.

Joachim had never seen such an expression before, so much pain and fear and bewilderment. He ran water onto a cloth and reached toward him. The young man flinched back.

"I'm sorry," Joachim said. "I'll try not to hurt you." He gently wiped the sweat from March's face. He need not speak to him at all. But he said, again, "I'm sorry."

Joachim had no excuse to delay Khan any longer. Nevertheless, he stopped before Madison and Chitirih-Ra-Payjh. Madison looked at him with the awful intensity of a gentle man driven to hatred.

"Do you want some water?"

"It's blood I want," Madison said. "Your leader's. Or yours."

Joachim ignored the empty threat. He glanced at Chitirih-Ra-Payjh, who had not moved or spoken or opened her eyes.

"Did Khan question her?"

Madison shook his head.

"Tell him what he wants to know," Joachim said urgently. "He'll break one of you, eventually, and the pain will be for nothing."

"You hate this!" Madison said. "You can't stand what he's doing! Help us stop him!"

"I cannot."

"How can you obey somebody like that? He's crazy, he's flat out of his mind!"

Joachim came close to striking Madison, who had no idea what he was saying. For fifteen years Khan had dedicated himself to the survival of his followers, when he himself had nothing left to live for. Nothing but revenge. Bitterness and hatred had overwhelmed him. Joachim held desperately to the conviction that when his vengeance was behind him, Khan could find himself again, that somehow, someday, Joachim would regain the man to whom he had sworn his loyalty and his life.

"I gave my word," Joachim said.

"When there's no one left," Madison said, "it's you he'll turn on. You must know that."

"I will not oppose him!" Joachim bolted from the room.

Del cringed, expecting Khan to return immediately. But the door slid shut and remained so.

Zinaida opened her eyes and stood up. She flung the ropes aside. Her wrists were raw. She untied Vance.

"Del—" Vance lifted him so the strain on his arms eased. Blood rushed back into Del's hands, stinging hot. The world sparkled. Vance tried not to hurt him but any touch was like another blow. The stimulant made the pain more intense, and prevented his passing out again.

Zinaida loosed the far end of the rope. Vance let him down as gently as he could.

"Oh, gods, Vance, what the hell is happening?"

"I don't know, little brother." He gave Del some water.

They heard a noise from the hallway outside. Del froze.

"I can't take any more—" He looked up at Vance, terrified. "If he starts on me again . . . I'm scared, Vance."

"It's all right," Vance said desperately, "it's all right. I won't let him . . ." He stopped. They both knew it was a futile promise.

Zinaida knelt beside them. She touched Del's forehead. Her hands were wondrously cool and soothing. She had never touched him before.

She bent down and gently kissed his lips. Vance grabbed her shoulder and pulled her away.

"What are you doing?"

"Vance, even a Deltan cannot kill with one kiss," she said softly. "But I can give him . . . Vance, I can give him the strength to die. If he chooses."

The strength to die. . . .

Del felt his best friend shudder.

"I—" Vance's voice caught.

"Del, can you hear me?" Zinaida said.

He nodded.

"I'll do whatever you wish."

"Please . . ." he whispered.

She kissed him once more, then placed her fingertips along his temples. His pain increased, but the fear gradually disintegrated.

Zinaida took her hands away. Del felt very weak, very calm. The stimulant had stopped working. Zinaida turned aside, trembling.

They heard Khan outside, his words indistinguishable but his voice unmistakable. Del took a deep breath.

"Damn, Vance," he whispered, "I would have liked to see your dragons."

"Me too, little brother. Me too." He eased Del to the floor.

The only times Vance had ever been hurt in a fight—the only times he ever got in fights—was getting his partner out of trouble. Del tried to reach out for him, to stop his doing anything stupid, to tell him it was too late.

Just try to stall him, brother, Del thought. *For yourself. . . .*

But he could not move.

Vance pressed himself against the wall beside the door. Seeing what he planned, Zinaida did the same on the other side.

The door opened.

Vance got both hands around Khan's throat before Joachim shot him with a phaser set on stun. Zinaida clawed at his eyes, scoring his cheek, before the phaser beam enveloped her, too, and she fell.

Khan's people lifted Del from the floor. Their hands were like burning coals. Khan gazed straight into his eyes. Del started to understand Joachim's dedication.

"Doctor March. . . ." Khan said.

Del *wanted* to tell him about Genesis. He wanted the hurt to stop, and he wanted Khan to speak a kind word to him—

Del gathered together all the pain, and concentrated on it, and gave way to it.

He could see only shadows.

When Doctor March collapsed, Joachim sprang to his side with *Reliant*'s medical kit, numb with shock, and dread of Khan, at his own failure.

Joachim could not forget what Vance Madison had said. As he tried desperately to revive March, he could feel his leader's vengeful gaze.

"He's dead," Joachim said. And then he lied to Khan for the first time in his life. "I'm sorry, my lord."

Khan said nothing to him. He turned his back.

Madison started to revive from the phaser blast. Khan dragged him to his feet.

"I do not have time to be gentle with you, Doctor Madison," Khan said, "as I was with your friend. I have other, more important quarry to hunt down." He drew his knife. "It takes perhaps ten minutes for a human being to bleed to death. If you say one word or make one gesture of compliance in that time, I will save your life."

Haunted by grief, Madison stared through him. Joachim knew that he would never speak.

Khan ordered his people to tie Madison's ankles and suspend him from the ceiling strut. They obeyed.

Khan would make a small, quick cut, just over the jugular vein; the bleeding would be slower than if he slashed the artery, and Madison would remain conscious longer. But he would die all the same.

Joachim could not bear to watch Khan destroy another human being. He fled.

In the main lab, he contacted *Reliant* and beamed on board. He ran to the captain's cabin, which Khan had taken over as his own. A sand tank stood on the desk. Joachim dug frantically through it with the strainer until he caught two eels. He dumped them into a box, raced back to the starship's transporter room, and returned to Spacelab. He ran, gasping for breath, to the small lab Khan had made a prison.

Joachim was too late to save Madison. He stopped, staring horrified at the pool of blood.

Khan stood before Zinaida Chitirih-Ra-Payjh. She met his gaze without flinching; he seemed offended that she did not fear him.

"My lord!" Joachim said when he could speak again. His voice shook. "Khan, they're all too weak to stand against your force—"

"So it seems. . . ." Khan said softly.

"There's no need for you to . . . to . . ." Joachim stopped. He thrust the box into Khan's hands. "She cannot keep Genesis from you now, my lord." He held his breath, for he could not know how Khan would react.

Khan opened the box, looked inside, and smiled. He set it down and put his arms around Joachim.

"You know my needs better than I myself," Khan said. "I'm grateful to you, Joachim; I could not love you more if you were my son."

He *will* be himself again, Joachim thought, close to tears. As soon as this is over. . . .

Khan broke the embrace gently and turned toward Zinaida Chitirih-Ra-Payjh.

Deltans seek out intensity of experience. Zinaida, like most, had concentrated on the limits of pleasure. Some few Deltans preferred pain; Zinaida had always thought them quite mad. But here, now, she knew she had no other choice than to experience whatever came and learn what she could from it. Jedda and Carol and David needed time to get away. She must give it to them. Besides, Carol was convinced rescue was coming. Perhaps, if Zinaida were strong enough, she might even survive until then. She did not want to die. She thought out toward the empathic link between herself and Jedda, and touched it with reassurance. She knew that if she let him know what had happened, he would try to help her rather than escape.

Khan's hand darted into the box his aide had brought him. He drew it out again. He was holding, pinched between thumb and forefinger, a long, slender, snakelike creature. It probed the air blindly with its sharp snout.

"Mister Chekov would tell you," Khan said, "that the pain is brief."

Zinaida drew back in terror, realizing what they had done to Chekov and Terrell.

This, she could not withstand.

Khan's people pushed her forward and turned her head to the side. The eel slithered across her smooth scalp and over her ear, still probing, searching.

"Jedda—" she whispered. She thought to him all that had happened, so he would know there was no hope, so he would flee, and then she broke the link between herself and her lover forever.

The eel punctured her eardrum. Zinaida screamed in pure horror and despair.

She gave herself to the shadows.

Carol and David and Jedda crept up the emergency stairs toward the main lab. Genesis was safe for the moment, but they were afraid for the others. No matter how reassuring Del had sounded over the intercom, Carol was sure she had, a few minutes later, heard the echo of a cry of pain and fear. David had heard something too. But Jedda kept insisting that everything was all right.

"Dammit!" Carol said again. "*Something's* happening up there and we can't just run away and leave our friends. Not even to save Genesis!"

"Del said—"

"David, Del lives in a fantasy world half the time!" She wished Del were half as steady as Vance; she would be a lot less worried about them both. If Del tried unnecessary heroics, if the Starfleet people overreacted, he could get himself and everybody else up there in more trouble than they could handle.

Carol reached the main level and opened the door at the top of the stairs just a crack.

Zinaida's terrified cry echoed through the hallway. Carol froze.

Jedda's knees buckled and he fell.

"Jedda! What is it?"

Carol knelt beside him. Jedda flung his arms across his face, trying to keep her from touching him. He rolled away from her, pushed himself to hands and knees, and slowly, painfully, got to his feet.

"We must flee," he said dully. "Zinaida is dead, Vance and Del are dead. We can't help them."

"But you said—"

"She was trying to protect us! But she's gone! If we don't run, they'll find us, and take Genesis, and kill us!"

They ran.

Six

That evening, Captain Spock and Doctor McCoy dined with Admiral Kirk in his quarters. Their argument about Genesis continued on and off, but not at such a high level of reciprocal abuse that Kirk became sufficiently irritated to tell them again to shut up.

The intercom broke into the conversation.

"Admiral," Saavik said, "sensors indicate a vessel approaching us, closing fast."

"What do you make of it, Lieutenant?"

"It's one of ours, Admiral. *Reliant.*"

"Why is *Reliant* here?" Spock said.

Kirk wondered the same thing. Starfleet had said only the *Enterprise* was free and near enough to Spacelab to investigate Carol's call.

He hurried out of his cabin. Spock and McCoy followed.

"Isn't Pavel Chekov on *Reliant?*"

They entered the turbolift. It rose.

"I believe that is true, Admiral," Spock said.

The lift doors opened. Kirk stepped out onto the bridge and turned immediately to Uhura.

"*Reliant* isn't responding, sir," she said.

"Even the emergency channels . . . ?"

"No, sir," she said, and tried again. "*Enterprise* to *Reliant,* come in, *Reliant.*"

"Visual, Lieutenant Saavik."

"It's just within range, Admiral."

Saavik turned the forward magnification up full. *Reliant* showed as a bare speck on the screen, but it was growing larger quickly.

"Attempt visual communication," Spock said.

"Aye, sir." Uhura brought the low-power visible light comm-laser online and aimed it toward *Reliant*'s receptors.

"Maybe their comm systems have failed. . . ." Kirk said doubtfully.

"It would explain a great many things," said Spock.

Joachim, still numbed by what had happened back at the Spacelab, blankly watched the *Enterprise* grow on *Reliant*'s viewscreen.

Behind him, Khan chuckled softly.

With Terrell and Chekov gone, Khan was surrounded only by his own loyal people. Soon his revenge would be complete. Then—would he finally be free? Joachim feared the answer.

"Reduce acceleration to one-half impulse power," Khan said; and then, with a crooning, persuasive, ironic tone, "Let's be friends. . . ."

"One-half impulse," the helm officer said.

The laser receptors registered a signal.

"They're requesting visual communications, Khan," Joachim said.

"Let them eat static."

"And they're still running with shields down."

"Of course they are. Didn't I just say we're friends? Kirk, old friend, do you know the Klingon proverb, 'Revenge is a dish best served cold?' "

Joachim risked a glance at his leader. Khan was leaning forward with his hands clenched together into fists and his hair wild around his head; his eyes were deep with exhaustion and rage.

"It is very cold in space," Khan whispered.

* * *

On the viewscreen of the *Enterprise, Reliant*'s image grew slowly.

"*Reliant*'s delta-vee just decreased to one-half impulse power, Admiral," Mister Sulu said.

"Any evidence of damage?"

"None, sir."

"Sir," Saavik said, "if I may quote general order twelve: 'On the approach of any vessel, when communications have not been established—' "

"The admiral is aware of the regulations."

Saavik forced herself not to react. "Yes, sir," she said stiffly.

"This is damned peculiar," Kirk said, almost to himself. "Yellow alert."

"Energize defense fields," Saavik said.

The Klaxon sounded; the lights dimmed. It took only a moment for the backup crew to arrive and staff their battle stations.

"Transmission from *Reliant,* sir. . . . A moment . . . on the short-range band. They say their chambers coil is shorting out their main communications."

"Spock?"

Spock bent down to scan *Reliant*.

"They still haven't raised their shields," Joachim said. Everything that was happening seemed to exist at a very great distance. Only his memories stayed close to him, terrifyingly immediate, flashing into his vision every time he blinked or even let his attention drift: the expression in March's eyes, the blood flowing down Madison's face, the suicide of Chitirih-Ra-Payjh. And he could not forget what Madison had said to him.

"Be careful, Joachim," Khan said. "Not all at once. The engine room, lock on the engine room. Be prepared to fire."

Joachim obeyed. Two hundred years ago, he had given his word; so he obeyed.

Spock studied the scan results. They were precisely the same as the first set: no evidence of damage.

"Their coil emissions are normal, Admiral." And then he saw the signal of a new change that was not normal. "Their shields are going up—"

"*Reliant*'s phasers are locking!" Sulu said at the same moment.

"Raise shields!" Kirk said. "Energize phasers, stand by to—"

Reliant fired.

Peter stood ready at his console, wishing, wishing desperately, that he had something he could really do. The ship was on battle alert, with the Klaxon alarm sounding around him and all the engine room crew—the veterans—hurrying to their places or already completely involved in their work. The trainees could only wait at their backup positions and watch. And a lowly cadet could only grit his teeth and try to pretend he was here for a reason.

Till now, Peter had suspected that the whole trip was an elaborate charade, nothing more than a simulation with real equipment. But maybe he had been wrong. Surely, if this were another test, the veterans would stand back and let the trainees handle everything. Peter's heart beat faster. He wondered how Saavik would analyze it, logically. It would be fun to talk to her about it as soon as it was over, whether or not it was for real! He had not even seen her since Commander Scott postponed his math lessons.

Uncle Montgomery had told Captain Spock that Peter could not be spared because there was too much work in the engine room; but to Peter he said that the lessons would resume only when Peter "stopped neglecting his work." Peter recognized the disparity as an attempt to teach him a lesson without damaging his record, which he appreciated—yet still resented, because he did not think that this was a lesson he needed to learn.

He'll quit in another day or so, Peter thought. Maybe even as soon as we're finished with this. *Whatever* it is.

From out of nowhere, a shock wave slammed him to the deck. A moment later, the noise of the explosion struck. As Peter scrambled up, metal shrieked and a great wind whipped past him. The breach in the hull sucked air from the engine room. An eerie silence clamped down and Peter feared his eardrums had burst. The emergency doors slid abruptly closed, and fresh air poured into the partially depressurized area. Sound returned: he could hear screams, and shrieks of pain, beyond the ringing in his ears.

He grabbed the edges of his console to steady himself. The general alarms moaned at a low pitch.

"Oh, my God!" Grenni cried. His console was alight with warnings. "Pres, we gotta get out of here—"

Peter looked up. Right above them, a heat-transfer pipe hissed thick yellow-green smoke through a crack in the triple-layered unbreakable matrix of the tube. Peter watched with horror. Coolant leak was supposed to be *impossible.*

The radiation signal flashed stroboscopically while the noxious-gas warning hooted. The poisonous coolant gas flooded the trainees' area. Peter's eyes burned. Grenni grabbed his arm and tried to pull him away as the rest of the group fled.

"You're online!" Peter cried.

"Shit!" Grenni yelled. He broke and ran.

Peter fumbled for his respirator. He could barely see by the time he got it on. His chest felt crushed.

The primary control panel was damaged, and Lieutenant Kasatsuki lay unconscious on the deck. She was responsible for the auxiliary power main controls that Grenni and Peter were supposed to back up. Now, Grenni's console blinked and beeped for attention. If no one did anything, auxiliary power would fail completely.

The gas closed in around Peter as he overrode the hardware hierarchy and brought his own machine on-line. Despite the respirator, his eyes still teared and burned.

The screams of pain and fear crashed over him like waves. Commander Scott shouted orders amid the chaos. Peter heard it all, but it was a light-year away; he felt almost as if he had merged with the *Enterprise*—his actions came so smoothly and he knew so easily and so certainly what he had to do.

Back on the bridge, Jim Kirk had his hands full.

"Mister Sulu—the shields!"

"Trying, sir!"

The intercom broke through the disorder.

"Medical alert, engine room!"

McCoy was already halfway to the turbolift. He plunged into it and disappeared.

"I can't get any power, sir," Sulu said.

Kirk slammed his hand down on an intercom button. "Scotty!"

A cacophony spilled from the intercom as every channel on the ship tried to break through.

"Uhura, turn off that damned noise!"

She hit the main cutoff.

Silence.

"Mister Scott on discrete," she said.

"Scotty, let's have it."

His voice sounded strange: throat mike, Jim thought. He's wearing a respirator! What the hell happened down there?

"We're just hanging on, sir. The main energizers are out."

"Auxiliary power," Kirk said. "Damage report."

The forward viewscreen switched over to a schematic display of the *Enterprise,* with a shockingly large red high-damage area spreading outward from the engine room. Kirk and Spock surveyed the report.

"Their attack indicates detailed knowledge of our vulnerabilities," Spock said.

"But who *are* those guys? *Reliant* is under—who?"

"Clark Terrell," Spock said. "A highly regarded commander, one likely neither to go berserk nor to become the victim of a mutiny."

"Then who's attacking us? And *why?*"

"One thing is certain," Spock said. "We cannot escape on auxiliary power."

"Visual!" Kirk snapped. The screen flashed into a forward view from the bridge. *Reliant,* very close, faced them head-on. "Mister Sulu, divert everything to the phasers."

"Too late—" Spock said.

In the viewscreen, *Reliant's* photon torpedoes streaked toward them with an awful inevitability.

The blast of energy sizzled through the ship, searing and melting computer chips, blowing out screens, crashing whole systems. A fire broke out on the upper deck. The acrid odor of singed plastic and vaporized metals clouded the air.

"Scotty!" Kirk yelled. "What have we got left?"

"Only the batteries, sir. I can have auxiliary power in a few minutes—"

"We haven't *got* a few minutes. Can you give me phasers?"

"No' but a few shots, sir."

"Not enough," Spock said, "against their shields."

"Who the hell *are* they?" Kirk said again.

"Admiral," Uhura said, "Commander, *Reliant* is signaling. . . ." She hesitated. "He wishes to discuss . . . terms of our surrender."

Kirk looked at Spock, who met his gaze impassively; he glanced at Saavik, expecting—he did not know what to expect from Saavik. Her self-control was as impenetrable as Spock's.

"On-screen," Kirk said.

"Admiral . . ." Uhura said.

"Do it—while we still have time."

The viewscreen changed slowly, pixel by pixel, filling in a new image that gradually took the form of a face.

"Khan!" Jim Kirk exclaimed.

"You remember, Admiral, after all these years. I cannot help but be touched. I feared you might have forgotten me. Of course *I* remember *you*."

"What's the meaning of this?" Kirk said angrily. "Where's *Reliant*'s crew?"

"Have I not made my meaning plain?" Khan said dangerously. "I mean to avenge myself, Admiral. Upon you. I've deprived your ship of its power, and soon I intend to deprive you of your life."

"*Reliant*'s maneuvering, sir," Sulu said very quietly. "Coming around for another shot."

"But I wanted you to know, as you die, who has beaten you: Khan Noonian Singh, the prince you tried to exile."

"Khan, listen to me!" Kirk said. "If it's me you want, I'll beam aboard your ship. All I ask is that you spare my crew. You can do what you want to me!"

Khan lounged back, smiling pleasantly. He stretched his hands toward Kirk, palms up, as if weighing James Kirk, at his disposal, in one, against the *Enterprise* and Jim Kirk's certain but more remote death, in the other.

"That is a most intriguing offer. It is—" his voice became low and dangerous, "—typical of your sterling character. I shall consider it."

He paused for perhaps as much as a second.

"I accept your terms—"

Kirk stood up. Spock took one step toward him but halted when Kirk made an abrupt chopping gesture, back and down, with his hand.

"—with only a single addition. You will also turn over to me all data and material regarding Project Genesis."

Jim Kirk forced himself not to react. "Genesis?" he said. "What's that?"

"Don't play with me, Kirk. My hand is on the phaser control."

"I'll have to put a search on it, Khan—give me some time. The computer damage—"

"I give you sixty seconds, Admiral."

Kirk turned to Spock.

"You cannot give him Genesis, Admiral," the Vulcan said.

Kirk spoke softly and out of range of the highly directional transmitter mike. "At least we know he hasn't got it. Just keep nodding as though I'm giving orders. Lieutenant Saavik, punch up the data charts on *Reliant*'s command console. Hurry."

"*Reliant*'s command—?"

"Hurry up!" Jim whispered angrily.

"The prefix code?" Spock asked.

"It's all we've got."

"Admiral," Khan said, "you try my patience."

"We're finding it, Khan! You know how much damage you inflicted on my ship. You've got to give us time!"

"Time, James Kirk? You showed me that time is not a luxury, but a torture. You have forty-five seconds."

Mister Sulu turned toward Kirk. "*Reliant*'s completed its maneuver, sir— we're lined up in their sights, and they're coming back."

Saavik found the information Kirk sought, but could see no way it could be of use. "I don't understand—"

"You've got to learn *why* things work on a starship, not just how." Kirk turned back to Khan, trying to put real conviction in his dissembling. "It's coming through right now, Khan—"

"The prefix code is one-six-three-zero-nine," Spock said.

He set quickly to work. Saavik watched the prefix code thread its way through the schematics and dissolve *Reliant*'s defenses. She understood suddenly what Kirk intended to do: transfer control of *Reliant* to the *Enterprise* and lower its shields.

"You have thirty seconds," Khan said, lingering over each word.

"His intelligence is extraordinary," Spock said. "If he has changed the code . . ."

"Spock, wait for my signal," Kirk said urgently. "Too soon, and he'll figure it out; he'll raise the shields again. . . ."

Spock nodded, and Kirk turned back to the viewscreen.

"Khan, how do I know you'll keep your word?"

"Keep my word, Admiral? I gave you no word to keep. You have no alternative."

"I see your point . . ." Kirk said. "Mister Spock, is the data ready?"

"Yes, Admiral."

"Khan, stand by to receive our transmission." He glanced down at Sulu. "Mister Sulu—?"

"Phasers locked. . . ." Sulu said quietly.

"Your time is up, Admiral," Kahn said.

"Here it comes—we're transmitting right now. Mister Spock?"

Spock stabbed the code through to *Reliant* and followed it instantly with the command to lower shields.

Saavik's monitor changed. "Shields down, Admiral!"

"Fire!" James Kirk shouted as Khan, on the viewscreen, cried, "What—? Joachim, raise them—*Where's the override?*"

Mister Sulu bled off all the power the crippled ship could bear and slammed it through to the phasers.

A thin bright hue of light sprang into existence, connecting *Enterprise* and *Reliant* with a lethal filament. *Reliant*'s hull glowed scarlet just at its bridge.

On the viewscreen, Khan cried out in rage and pain as his ship shuddered around him. His transmission faded and the *Enterprise*'s viewscreen lost him.

"You did it, Admiral!" Sulu said.

"I didn't do a damn thing—I got caught with my britches down. Damn, damn, I must be going senile." He glanced up at Saavik and shook his head. "Lieutenant Saavik, you just keep on quoting regulations. Spock, come with me—we have to find out how bad the damage is."

He strode to the turbolift; Spock followed. The doors closed—

Joachim bore Khan's hoarse rage as quietly, and with as much pain, as he would have borne the lash.

"Fire! Fire! Joachim, you fool! Why don't you fire!"

"I cannot, Khan. They damaged the photon controls and the warp drive. We must withdraw."

"No!"

"My lord, we must, we have no choice. We must repair the ship. *Enterprise* cannot escape." He wanted to close his eyes, he wanted to sleep, but he was afraid of his memories and terrified of his dreams. He felt sick unto death of killing and revenge.

—the lift dropped, and the doors opened at the level of the engine room. Kirk took one step forward and stopped, aghast.

"Scotty! My God!"

The engineer stood trembling, spattered with blood, holding Peter Preston in his arms. The boy lay limp, his eyes closed, blood flowing steadily from his nose and mouth.

"I canna reach Doctor McCoy, I canna get through; I must get the boy to sickbay—" Tears tracked the soot on his face. He staggered into the lift. Kirk and Spock caught him. Kirk steadied him while Spock took the child gently from his arms.

"Sickbay!" Kirk yelled.

The turbolift accelerated.

Spock stepped onto the bridge. His shirt was bloody—red blood, darkening to brown: not his own.

Saavik did not show the relief she felt. In silence, Spock joined her at the science officer's station. As Saavik continued to coordinate the work of the repair crews, Spock slid a roster into the input drive. The information quickly sorted itself across the screen: ENGINE ROOM CREW: SLIGHTLY INJURED. SERIOUSLY INJURED. CRITICAL.

PETER PRESTON.

Saavik caught her breath. Spock glanced at her—she felt his gaze but could not meet it.

Saavik's hands began to tremble. She stared at them, thinking, this is shameful. You shame yourself and your teacher: must you bring even more humiliation to Vulcans?

Her vision blurred. She squeezed her eyes closed.

"Lieutenant Saavik," Spock said.

"Yes, Captain," she whispered.

"Take this list to Doctor McCoy."

She swallowed hard and tried to make her eyes focus on the sheet Spock handed her.

The engine room casualty list—? Doctor McCoy had no use whatever for it: indeed it had just come from him.

"Captain—?"

"Please do not argue, Lieutenant," Spock said. His cold tone revealed nothing. "The assignment should take you no more than fifteen minutes; the bridge can spare you no longer."

She stood up and took the copy from his hand. Her fingers clenched on it, crumpling the paper. She looked into Spock's eyes.

"The bridge can spare you no longer, Lieutenant," he said again. "Go *quickly*. I am sorry."

She fled.

McCoy worked desperately over Preston. He had to keep intensifying the anesthetic field, for the boy struggled toward consciousness.

The life-sign sensors would not stabilize. No matter what McCoy did, the boy's physical condition deteriorated. Lacerations, a couple of broken bones, some internal injuries with considerable loss of blood, a hairline fracture of the skull: nothing very serious. But Preston had been directly beneath the coolant-gas leak. Everything depended on how much he had breathed and how long he had been within the cloud before the ventilators cleared it.

McCoy cursed. The damned technicians claimed nothing else but this wretched, corrosive, teratogenic, gamma-emitting *poison* had a high enough specific heat to protect the engines against meltdown. Well, they also claimed its protection was fail-safe.

"Doctor Chapel!" he yelled. "Where's the damned analysis?"

Scott watched him from outside the operating room; the engineer slumped against the glass.

Chris Chapel came in, and McCoy knew the results from her expression.

She handed him the analysis of Preston's blood and tissue chemistry. "I'm sorry, Leonard," she said.

He shook his head grimly. Several of the life-sign indicators were already close to zero, and the boy had begun to bleed internally, massively, far worse than before: the sutures were not holding. And would not. The cell structure had already started to deteriorate.

"I knew it already, Chris. I only hoped . . ."

He withdrew from the operating field and changed the anesthetic mode from general to local. Preston began to come to, but he would not feel any pain.

When McCoy looked up again, Jim Kirk stood next to Scott, gripping his shoulder.

McCoy shook his head.

Scott burst into the operating theater. Kirk followed.

"Doctor McCoy, can ye no'—" His voice broke.

"It's coolant poisoning, Scotty," McCoy said. "I'm sorry. It would be possible to keep him alive for another half hour, at most—I *can't* do that to him."

Scott started to protest, then stopped. He knew as well as any doctor, perhaps better, the effects of the poison. He went to Preston's side and touched the boy's forehead gently.

Preston slowly opened his eyes.

"Peter," Scott said, "lad, I dinna mean—" He stopped. Tears spilled down his cheeks.

Kirk leaned over the boy.

"Mister Preston," he said.

"Is . . . is the word given?" Peter stared upward, intent on a scene that existed in his sight alone.

"The word is given," Kirk said. "Warp speed."

"Aye . . ." Peter whispered.

Saavik stopped at the door to sickbay. She was too late.

Mister Scott came out of the operating room, flanked and half-supported by Admiral Kirk and Doctor McCoy. He was crying. Behind them, Peter's body lay on the operating table.

Doctor Chapel drew a sheet over Peter's face.

Saavik hurled the crumpled list to the floor, turned, and bolted down the corridor. She flung herself into the first room she came to and fumbled to lock the door behind her.

In the darkened empty conference chamber, she tried to calm her breathing; she fought to control the impossible surge of grief and rage that took her.

It isn't fair! she cried in her mind. *It isn't fair! He was only a child!*

She clenched her hands around the top of a chair. As if she were still on Hellguard, she flung back her head and screamed.

For an instant the madness owned her. She wrenched the chair from the deck, twisting and shearing the bolts, and flung it across the room. It crashed against the bulkhead, dented the metal, and rebounded halfway to her.

When Saavik knew anything again, she was crouched in a corner, huddled and trembling. She raised her head.

Darkness raised no barriers to her; she saw the damage she had done.

She was so weak she could control herself once more. Slowly she rose; slowly, without looking back, she left the conference room.

Mister Scott was unable to speak for some minutes. Finally he looked up at Jim Kirk.

"Why?"

Jim looked sadly at Cadet Preston's body. "Khan wants to kill me for passing sentence on him fifteen years ago . . . and he doesn't care who stands between him and vengeance."

"Scotty," McCoy said, "I'm sorry."

"He stayed at his post," Scott said. "When my other trainees broke, he stayed."

"If he hadn't, we'd be space by now," Kirk said.

"Bridge to Admiral Kirk," Spock said over the intercom.

Kirk hurried to open the channel. "Kirk here."

"The engine room reports auxiliary power restored. We can proceed on impulse engines."

Kirk rubbed his temples, drawing himself away from Mister Scott's despair, back to the ship and the whole crew's peril. "Best speed to Regulus I, Mister Spock." He sat on his heels beside Scott. "Scotty, I'm sorry, I've got to know— can you get the main engines back online?"

"I . . . I dinna think so, sir. . . ."

"Scotty—"

". . . but ye'll have my best . . ." He stood up, moving apathetically, speaking by rote. "I know ye tried, Doctor. . . ." He left sick bay like a sleepwalker.

"Damn," McCoy muttered.

"Are you all right?"

McCoy shrugged; weariness lay over him. "I've lost patients before, Jim; God help me, I've even lost kids before. Damn! Jim, Khan lured you here, that's the only way any of this makes sense! He *must* have used your name to threaten Genesis—but how did he find out about it?"

"I don't know—and I'm a lot more worried about keeping him from laying his hands on it. You said it yourself: With a big enough bang, he could rearrange the universe."

"There may still be time. You gave as good as you got."

"I got *beat*. We're only alive because I knew something about these ships that he didn't." Jim sighed. "And because one fourteen-year-old kid . . ." He stopped.

"Shit," he said, and left sick bay.

Seven

The *Enterprise* limped to Regulus I, its crews working nonstop to repair the damage done by Khan. By the time they reached Spacelab, Jim Kirk was able to stop worrying about the immediate fate of his starship; but he became more and more concerned about what he would find at their destination. The space station maintained complete radio silence.

Mister Sulu slid the *Enterprise* into orbit around Regulus I.

"Orbit stabilized, sir."

"Thanks, Mister Sulu. Commander Uhura, would you try again?"

"Aye, sir. *Enterprise* to Regulus I Spacelab, come in, Spacelab. Come in, please. . . ." She received the same reply she had received to every one of the many transmissions she had made in the hours since Doctor Marcus's original call: nothing. "*Enterprise* to Spacelab, come in, Spacelab. This is the *U.S.S. Enterprise*. Please respond. . . ." She turned to Kirk. "There's no response at all, sir."

"Sensors, Captain?"

"The sensors are inoperative, Admiral," Spock said. "There is no way to tell what is inside the station."

"And no way of knowing if *Reliant* is still nearby, either," Kirk said.

"That is correct, Admiral."

"Blind . . . as a Tiberian bat," Kirk said softly. "What about Regulus I?"

"Class D planetoid, quite unremarkable: no appreciable tectonic activity. It is essentially a very large rock."

"*Reliant* could be hiding behind that rock."

"A distinct possibility, Admiral."

Kirk opened a channel to the engine room. "Scotty, do we have enough power for the transporters?"

"Just barely, sir." The engineer's voice sounded tired and lifeless.

"Thanks, Scotty."

Jim Kirk took his spectacles out of his belt pouch, looked at them, unfolded them, turned them over, then folded them again and put them away.

"I'm going down to Spacelab."

"Jim," Doctor McCoy said, "Khan could be down there!"

"He's *been* there, Bones, and he hasn't found what he wants. Can you spare someone? There may be people hurt."

"I can spare *me*," the doctor said.

"I beg your pardon, Admiral," Saavik said, "but general order fifteen specifically prohibits the entry of a flag officer into a hazardous area without armed escort."

"There is no such regulation," Kirk said. That was easier than arguing with her.

She began to speak, stopped, then frowned, trying to decide how to respond to such a bald-faced representation of a lie as the truth.

On the other hand, Kirk thought, *she had a point.*

"But if you want to check out a phaser, Lieutenant Saavik, you're welcome to join the party. Mister Spock, the ship is yours."

"Aye, sir."

"You and Mister Scott keep me up-to-date on the damage reports." He got up and started for the turbolift.

"Jim—" Spock said.

Jim Kirk glanced at his old friend.

"—be careful."

Jim nodded, with a grin, and left.

Doctor McCoy materialized inside the station's main laboratory with his phaser drawn, the safety off.

Some position for a doctor to be in, he thought—ready to shoot off somebody's head. Jim materialized beside him, at an angle, and Saavik behind them both, so they formed a small protective circle.

"Hello!" Jim yelled. "Anybody here?"

The station replied with the echoes of abandonment and silence.

Saavik went to the main computer and turned it on. She spoke to it, but it did not answer her, a sure sign of a badly crashed system.

"Very little remains in any of the computers, Admiral," she said after working with it for a few moments. "The online memories have been wiped almost clean." She loaded the single remaining file, started it running, and watched it for several minutes.

McCoy pulled out his tricorder and scanned the immediate area. He thought he saw a blip—but, no, it faded before he could get a reading on it.

"Sir. . . ." Saavik said.

"Yes, Lieutenant?" Kirk replied.

"This is extremely odd. Only a single program remains. It is very large. It is . . . unique in my experience."

She stood back so Kirk and McCoy could look at the screen display.

"I can make nothing of it."

They frowned at the sizzling, sparking, colorful graphics.

"Another Genesis simulation?" McCoy said doubtfully.

"No. . . ." Kirk said. "My God, Bones, it's a game—if that's all Khan found when he got here . . ." He shook his head. "Phasers on stun. Move out. And *be careful.*"

McCoy moved cautiously down the hall. The lights were very dim, the shadows heavy. Spacelab was enormous: besides the project scientists Spock regarded so highly, the satellite supported and housed several hundred technicians and support personnel. Most of them were on leave now, but there still should be eight or ten people here. So where—?

He caught his breath: a scratching noise, a faint beep from his tricorder. He turned slowly.

A white lab rat, free in the hallway, blinked at him from a dim corner, scrabbled around, and fled, its claws slipping on the tiles.

"I'm with you, friend," McCoy muttered.

Feeling a little easier, he continued. He glanced into the rooms he passed, finding nothing but offices, a small lounge, sophisticated but familiar equipment for a number of fields of study.

If they had to search the entire station, room by room, it would take days. McCoy decided to return to the main lab to see if Jim or Saavik had found anyone.

He opened one last door. Beyond, it was dark.

The hair on the back of his neck prickled. He took a step inside. No strange sound, no strange sight—why did he feel so uneasy?

The smell: sharp, salty, metallic. He smelled blood.

He turned, and a cold hand gently slapped against his face.

"Lights!" he cried, jumping back. His foot slipped, and he fell.

The sensors responded to his voice. Lying on the floor, he looked up.

"My God in heaven . . . !"

Staring at the hanging bodies, McCoy got slowly to his feet. He fumbled for his communicator.

"Jim. . . ."

Five people—a Deltan and four human beings—hung upside down from a ceiling strut. Each one's throat had been slashed. McCoy approached the nearest body, that of a tall black man. His own blood obscured his face. The man next to him had been tortured.

As he waited for Kirk to answer, McCoy gradually got hold of himself. The casual ferocity of the killing gave him a deep, sick sensation.

Jim's voice on the communicator made him start.

"Yeah, Bones?"

"I . . . found them."

"I'll be right down."

"No—! Jim, Doctor Marcus isn't here. *She isn't here.* But the rest . . . they're dead, Jim. Please stay where you are. I'll get a medical team to beam down." He was already trying to think if there was anyone on the ship he could count on besides Chris Chapel to help deal with this horror.

"Kirk out."

McCoy cursed softly.

He took tricorder readings on all the bodies and recorded their position and surroundings. Three of the people had bled to death, one had died of shock, and the Deltan . . . he could detect no cause for the Deltan's death.

What chance is there, McCoy thought, that their murderer will ever come to trial? Not very damned much.

"Oh, my God. . . ." Jim said from the doorway. He stared up, horrified.

"I *told* you not to come down here," McCoy said angrily. "There was no need for you to see what happened." He saw Saavik behind Kirk, her face Vulcan calm. "Or for her to either, dammit!"

Kirk glanced over his shoulder. "Lieutenant, I ordered—"

"I am your escort, Admiral," she said coldly. "Your safety is my responsibility, not the reverse."

"Stay outside, then," McCoy said gently. "Child, it isn't necessary for you to be exposed to this—"

"I am neither a child nor in need of protection."

"Lieutenant Saavik—" Kirk said sharply.

Saavik cut him off. "*Sir.* In order to protect me from sights such as this you would have had to start when I *was* still a child. I will *not* leave you unguarded when a creature who takes such great pleasure in killing—and who would take his most extreme pleasure in your death—is free and in hiding somewhere near. Nor will I stand by idle!"

She paused a moment, looking somewhat abashed by her outburst. She continued in a tone more restrained, but with words no less definite.

"Admiral Kirk, if you in truth prefer an escort who behaves differently, you must order me back to the ship."

Saavik waited, but Kirk said nothing.

She walked carefully across the blood-thick, sticky floor, hesitated a bare moment, and lifted Vance Madison. His body lay limp in her arms, and the rope around his ankles slackened.

"Please cut him down."

Kirk complied.

They lowered the five bodies and found sheets in which to shroud them. Three were Project Genesis scientists, and two were service personnel.

"They even killed the galley chief," Kirk said. His voice sounded stunned.

"The bodies are almost cold," McCoy said. "But rigor hasn't set in yet. Jim, they haven't been dead for very long."

Jim looked around the blood-spattered room.

"Carol . . ." he said.

The search party returned to the main lab.

Saavik heard a noise. She gazed around the lab, finding nothing. But the small sound came again. She drew out her tricorder and scanned with it.

It wailed plaintively. McCoy and Kirk heard it.

"Lieutenant—?" Kirk asked.

"I don't know, sir."

She followed the signal to a large storage locker. As Kirk and McCoy joined her, she reached out and opened the door.

Two more bodies fell out and sprawled at their feet.

Kirk started violently. "My God!"

McCoy knelt down and inspected them with his medical sensor. One was a dark-haired youthful human, the other an older, bearded man, a captain. Both wore the insignia of the *Reliant*.

"They're alive, Jim."

Behind them, the Spacelab's communications screen glowed on. "*Enterprise* to Admiral Kirk, come in, please," Uhura said.

"Why, it's Chekov," Kirk said.

"*Enterprise* to Admiral Kirk," Uhura said again. "Please respond."

"This is Clark Terrell, Jim," McCoy said. "I've served with him." In fact he had known him, rather well, for years.

Chekov moaned.

McCoy frowned at the readings on his sensor. Apparently, Saavik thought, they looked as odd to him as they did to her, despite his enormously greater experience.

Kirk turned Chekov over and supported his shoulders. "Pavel, do you hear me? Pavel, wake up."

"Admiral Kirk!" Uhura said. "Please respond."

"Saavik, tell her we're all right."

"Please acknowledge our signal, Admiral." Uhura's tone became more urgent.

"Some kind of brain disturbance," McCoy said as Saavik hurried across the lab and opened a channel to the *Enterprise*. "It's drug-induced, as far as I can tell."

"Saavik here, Commander Uhura. We're all right. Please stand by. Saavik out."

"Thank you, Lieutenant," Uhura said with relief. "*Enterprise* standing by."

Saavik left the channel open and returned to McCoy and Kirk. *Reliant*'s Captain Terrell was beginning to regain consciousness, and Chekov was almost awake. He opened his eyes and stared blankly at Kirk.

"Pavel, can you hear me?" Kirk said. "What happened?"

"Admiral Kirk. . . ." Chekov whispered. He took a deep breath that turned into a sob. "Oh, God, sir—" His voice failed him, and he cried.

Kirk held him. "It's all right now, Pavel. You're all right. Go on, don't worry; you're with friends now."

Terrell moaned and tried to get up. McCoy hurried to him.

"It's Len McCoy, Captain." McCoy shook him gently by the shoulders. "Clark, do you remember me?"

Terrell's expression was that of a man faced with such horror that he had lost himself in it. "McCoy. . . ." he said slowly. "Len McCoy . . . yes. Oh . . . yes. . . ."

Chekov pulled away from Kirk and struggled to sit up. "Admiral—it was Khan! We found him on Alpha Ceti V. . . ."

"Easy, Pavel. Just tell me what happened."

"Alpha Ceti VI was gone. My fault. . . ."

McCoy and Kirk glanced at each other, both frowning slightly; Saavik, too, wondered how it could be the young commander's fault that a whole world had disappeared. He was clearly still badly confused.

"Khan captured us. He—he can control people, Captain! His creatures—

he—" Chekov began trembling. He clamped his hands over his ears. *"My head—!"*

McCoy came to his side and checked him over with the medical sensor. "It's all right; you're safe now."

Chekov's words came all in an incomprehensible rush. "He made us say things—lies—and made us do . . . other things, but we beat him; he thought he controlled us, but he didn't; the captain beat him—he was strong. . . ." He was shaking so hard he could no longer speak. He drew his knees to his chest and put his head down, hiding his face to cry.

Kirk glanced over at Terrell, who maintained the composure of oblivion.

"Captain, where's Doctor Marcus? What happened to Genesis?"

"Khan couldn't find them," Terrell said with dreadful calm. "He found some of the scientists."

"We know that," Kirk said sharply.

"Everything else was gone. He tortured them. They wouldn't talk; so he killed them. The station was too big for him to search it all before he took *Reliant* and went to kill you too."

"He came damned close to doing that," Kirk said.

"He left us here," Chekov said. He raised his head. His face was wet with tears. "We were . . . no longer any use."

"Does he control all of *Reliant*'s crew?" Saavik asked, wondering if humans were that susceptible to mind control.

"He stranded most of them on Alpha Ceti V."

"He's mad, sir. He lives for nothing but revenge," Chekov said. "He blames you for the death of his wife . . . Lieutenant McGivers."

"I know what he blames me for," Kirk said. He sat with his eyes focused on nothing for some moments. "Carol's gone, but all the escape pods are still in their bays. Where's the transporter room in this thing?" He glanced at Saavik.

"Even the Spacelab specifications were erased from the computer, sir," she said. "However, the *Enterprise* should have a copy in its library files."

They contacted the ship, reassuring Commander Uhura and Mister Spock that they were all right, and had a set of plans for the station transmitted down. Even the decorative printed maps of Spacelab, which ordinarily would have been displayed in its reception area, had been torn down and destroyed.

In the transporter room, Kirk inspected the console settings.

"Mister Chekov, did he get down here?"

"I don't think so, sir. He said searching such a big place was foolish. He thought he would make the captives talk."

"*Somebody* left the transporter on," Kirk said. "Turned it on, used it, and left it on—and no one still alive remained to turn it off."

Saavik figured out the destination of the settings. "This makes no sense, Admiral. The coordinates are within Regulus I. The planetoid is both lifeless and airless."

"If Carol finished stage two, if it was underground," Kirk said thoughtfully, "—she said it was underground. . . ."

"Stage two?" *He must be referring to the mysterious Project Genesis,* Saavik thought.

Kirk suddenly pulled out his communicator. "Kirk to *Enterprise*."

"*Enterprise,* Spock here."

"Damage report, Mister Spock?"

"Admiral, Lieutenant Saavik would recommend that we go by the book. In that case, hours could stretch into days."

Saavik tried to understand what the captain meant by that. It sounded vaguely insulting, unlikely behavior from Captain Spock.

"I read you, Captain," Kirk said after a pause. "Let's have the bad news."

"The situation is grave. Main power cannot be restored for six *days* at least. Auxiliary power has failed, but Mister Scott hopes to restore it in two *days*. By the book, Admiral."

"Spock," Kirk said, "I've got to try something. If you don't hear from us within—" he paused a moment, "—one hour, restore what power you can and get the *Enterprise* the hell away from here. Alert Starfleet as soon as you're out of jamming range. By the book, Spock."

Uhura broke in. "We can't leave you behind, sir!"

"That's an *order,* Spock. Uhura, if you don't hear from us, there won't *be* anybody behind. Kirk out." He snapped his communicator closed and put it away. "Gentlemen," he said to Terrell and Chekov, "maybe you'd better stay here. You've been through a lot—"

"We'd prefer to share the risk," Terrell said quickly.

"Very well. Let's go."

"Go?" McCoy exclaimed. "Go *where?*"

"Wherever they went," Kirk replied, and nodded at the transporter.

Saavik realized what he planned. She went to the transporter and set it for delayed energize, being careful not to alter the coordinates. Kirk stepped up onto the transporter platform. Terrell and Chekov followed, but McCoy stayed safely on the floor and folded his arms belligerently.

"What if they went nowhere?"

Kirk grinned. "Then it's your big chance to get away from it all, Bones."

Doctor McCoy muttered something and stomped up onto the platform.

"Ready," Saavik said. She pressed the auto-delay and hurried up beside the others.

Spacelab dissolved; around them, darkness appeared.

Jim Kirk held his breath, waiting for his guess to be wrong, waiting for solid rock to resolidify around him forever as soon as the transporter beam ended. Fear tickled the back of his mind. The instant he finished transporting, lights blazed on around him.

"Well," Jim said as the rest of his party solidified, "if anybody's here, now they know we're here, too."

He was in a small cavern: several tunnels led from it. The caverns were definitely dug out, not naturally formed. The chamber was haphazardly piled with stacks of notebooks, technical equipment, peripheral storage cells. It had all obviously been transferred from Spacelab in terrible haste.

"Admiral—" Saavik said. She gestured toward the next chamber. Jim could see within it a massive curve of metal.

He followed Saavik into the second cave. It, too, held piles of equipment, but a great torpedo shape dominated everything.

"Genesis, I presume?" Doctor McCoy said.

Without answering, Kirk moved farther into the cavern complex.

Suddenly someone lunged at him from behind a stack of crates, plowing into him and knocking him to the ground. A knife glittered. Jim felt it press against his throat, just below the corner of his jaw, at the pulsepoint where the carotid artery is most vulnerable. When he tried to fight, the knife pressed harder. He could feel the sharpness of its edge. If Saavik or McCoy tried to draw a phaser, he would be bleeding to death before they could finish firing.

"You son of a bitch, you killed them—"

Jim Kirk recognized David Marcus.

"I'm Jim Kirk!" Jim yelled. "David, don't you remember me?"

"We were still there, you dumb bastard, I heard Zinaida scream—"

"David, we *found* them, they were already dead!"

"David—"

Carol's voice.

"Go back, Mother!"

"Jim—"

Kirk strained around until he could see her. The knife dimpled his skin and a drop of blood welled out. He felt its heat.

"Hold still, you slimy—"

"Carol," Jim said, "for Gods' sake, you can't believe we had anything to do with—"

"Shut up!" David cried. "Go back, Mother, unless you *want* to watch me kill him the way he killed—"

Carol Marcus took a deep breath, "I don't want to watch you kill anyone . . . least of all your father."

David looked up at her, stunned.

Feeling stunned himself, Jim slid from beneath the knife and disarmed the boy. Surely Carol had said that just to give him such a chance—

Out of the corner of his eye, he saw Clark Terrell step forward and take the phaser from the Deltan—Jedda Adzhin-Dall, it must be—who had been covering Saavik and McCoy.

"I'll hold on to this," Terrell said.

Jim stood up and turned to Carol.

"Carol—"

He went toward her, and she met him. She smiled, reached out, and gently stroked a fingertip across the hair at his temple.

"You've gone a little gray—" She stopped.

He put his arms around her. They held each other for a long while, but finally he drew back to look her in the eyes, to search her face with his gaze.

"Carol, is it true?"

She nodded.

"Why didn't you tell me?"

"It isn't true!" David shouted. "My father was—"

"You're making this a lot harder, David," Carol said.

"I'm afraid I must make it harder still, Doctor Marcus," Clark Terrell said.

Jim spun around.

Reliant's captain held his captured phaser trained directly on Jim Kirk and Carol Marcus.

"Clark, in heaven's name—" McCoy said.

"Please, don't move." He glanced toward Chekov, who nodded. He came toward McCoy, who made as if to resist. "Even you, Len," Terrell said. McCoy let his hands fall. Chekov disarmed everyone, then joined Terrell in covering them.

"Pavel—" Jim said.

"I'm sorry, sir."

Terrell opened his communicator.

"Have you heard, your excellency?"

"I have indeed, Captain. You have done very well."

Khan.

"I knew it!" David whispered, low and angry. Jim turned, but not in time to stop him. David launched himself at Terrell. Saavik instantly reacted, catching David and flinging him out of the way with all the force of muscles adapted to higher gravity. They collapsed in a heap as Jedda, too, sprang forward after David.

Terrell fired.

Jedda fell into the beam.

He vanished without a sound.

"Jedda!" Carol cried.

"Oh, God. . . ." David said softly.

"Don't move, any of you!" Terrell's hand clenched hard around the phaser. "I don't *want* to hurt you. . . ."

"Captain Terrell, I am waiting."

Chekov started violently at Khan's softly dangerous voice. He was deathly pale and sweating. He began to tremble. The phaser shook in his hand. Jim Kirk weighed his chances of taking it, but they were no better than David's had been.

"Everything's as you ordered, my lord," Terrell said. "You have the coordinates of Genesis."

"I have one other small duty for you, Captain," Khan said. "Kill James Kirk."

On the ground beside David, Saavik shifted slightly, gathering herself.

No, Jim thought, *no, your instincts were right with David. Don't pull the same stupid stunt he did and get yourself killed for nothing, Lieutenant.*

"Khan—" Terrell said. He wiped his forehead on his sleeve and pressed his free hand against the side of his face. "I can't—" Wincing, he gasped in pain.

"Kill him!"

Terrell flung down his communicator. It clattered across stone. Terrell groaned as if he had been struck himself. He gripped the phaser with both hands, shaking so hard he could not aim.

Pavel Chekov raised his phaser slowly, staring at it with utter absorption. His whole body trembled. He aimed the weapon . . .

. . . at Clark Terrell. He tried to fire.

He failed.

Terrell screamed in agony. He forced his phaser around until he had turned it on himself.

"Clark, my God," McCoy whispered. He reached out toward him.

Terrell raised his head. Jim felt the intensity of his plea to McCoy in his horrified gaze.

The only thing the doctor could do for Clark Terrell now was . . . nothing. McCoy groaned and turned away, his face in his hands.

"Kill him, Terrell!" Khan said again. The damaged communicator distorted his voice, but still it was all too recognizable. "Fire, now!"

Terrell obeyed.

He disappeared.

Chekov shrieked. His phaser fell from his shaking hands, and he clutched at his temples as his knees buckled. He quivered and convulsed on the hard rock floor.

McCoy hurried to his side, pulled an injector from his medical pack, dialed it, and stabbed it into Chekov's arm. Chekov struggled a moment more, then went limp.

"Terrell!" Khan said. "Chekov!"

"Oh, my God, Jim—" McCoy said in horror.

Jim hurried to him.

Blood gushed down the side of Chekov's face. Through unconsciousness, he moaned.

Something—a creature, some *thing*—probed blindly from inside his ear. It crawled out of him: a snake, a worm, smeared with blood down its long, slimy length. Jim fought against nausea. He scooped up a phaser.

"Terrell!" Khan's voice was low and hoarse.

Jim clenched his teeth and shuddered, but he forced himself to wait until the creature flopped on the stone, leaving Chekov free.

He fired, and the creature disintegrated.

"Chekov!"

Jim snatched the communicator from the floor.

"Khan, you miserable bloodsucker—they're free of you! You'll have to do your own dirty work now. Do you hear me? *Do you?*"

After a moment, a terrible sound came from the communicator.

Khan laughed.

"Kirk, James Kirk, my old friend, so you are still—*still!*—alive."

"And still your 'old friend'? Well, listen, 'old friend,' you've murdered a lot of innocent people." Kirk looked at Pavel Chekov lying at his feet, close to death. "I intend to make you pay."

Khan laughed again. "I think not. If I was powerful before, I will be invincible soon."

"He's going to take Genesis!" David rushed toward the next cavern.

Saavik and Kirk both sprinted after him. As they rounded the corner, a transporter beam enveloped the Genesis torpedo. Jim raised his phaser. If he could at least damage it before it dematerialized—

David Marcus was directly in his line of fire.

"David, get down!" Jim yelled.

Saavik caught up to David. He struggled with her.

"Let go—I've got to stop him!"

"Only half of you would get there!"

"Get down!"

Saavik dragged David out of Kirk's way.

Jim fired. The phaser beam passed through the empty space where the torpedo had been, and sizzled against the stone.

Jim Kirk wanted to scream. He barely restrained himself from smashing his fist against the cave wall in pure frustration. He only had one chance left.

He found Terrell's communicator.

"Khan, you have Genesis, but you don't have me! You'll never get me, Khan! You're too frightened to come down here to kill me!"

"I've done far worse than kill you, Admiral. I've hurt you. I wish to let you savor the hurt for a little time."

"So much for all your oaths and promises, so much for your vow—to your wife!"

"You should not speak of my wife, James Kirk. She never wanted me to take my revenge. So now I will grant her wish. I will not kill you."

"You're a coward, Khan!"

"I will leave you, as you left me. But no one will ever find you. You are buried alive, marooned in the middle of a dead planet. Forever."

"Khan—"

"As for your ship, it is powerless. In a moment, I shall blow it out of the heavens."

"Khan!"

"Good-bye, 'Admiral.' "

On board *Reliant,* Khan shut off communications to Regulus I and stretched back in his chair. Not quite what he had foreseen, but a most satisfying climax, nonetheless.

Joachim came onto the bridge.

"Well, Joachim?"

"The Genesis torpedo is safely stowed, my lord. The warp drive is still inoperative, but all other systems will be restored within the hour."

"Excellent."

"Sir?"

"What?"

"May I plot a course away from Regulus I?"

"Not yet. Kirk is finished, but I promised him that I would deal with his ship."

"Khan, my lord—"

Khan frowned at his old friend and aide. Joachim had been with him from the beginning, but he had been acting most strangely since they escaped from Alpha Ceti V.

"You are with me, or you are against me. Which do you choose?"

Joachim looked down. "I am with you, my lord." He turned away. "*I* have not changed."

Carol Marcus sat on the floor of the cavern staring at the empty spot where Genesis had been. She pressed the heels of her hands against her eyes. She could not believe that Jedda, too, was gone. Vance, and Del, and Zinaida, and Yoshi and Jan, all dead. All she had left was David.

She could not help being grateful that it was David who survived. Yet at times she had felt like mother to everyone on the station. She had always been the sort of person people told their troubles to.

She grieved for Vance particularly, missing his gentleness, his steadiness. She covered her face.

Despite the pressure of her hands, tears squeezed from beneath her eyelids. She dashed the drops away angrily, forcing back her grief by willpower alone. She could not collapse into the despair she felt: there had to be *some* way to stop what was happening.

She glanced across the cavern toward Jim. She had sworn to herself never to tell him about David, or tell David about him, but telling them the truth had been the only way to keep them both alive. She needed to talk to Jim—to David, too—but since Genesis disappeared they had all three been revolving around each other like satellites, pulled together by her revelation and pushed apart by time and old pain and lack of trust.

"Saavik to *Enterprise*," the young Vulcan—Vulcan? Carol wondered; maybe not Vulcan—lieutenant said into her communicator for about the twentieth time in as many minutes. "Come in, please."

Carol knew how efficient the other ship was at jamming communications. She doubted Saavik would be able to get through.

She heard a soft moan and glanced across to where Doctor McCoy worked over Chekov, who he had feared might die.

"Jim—" McCoy said.

Jim went to his side.

"Pavel's alive," McCoy said. "It'll be rocky for a while, but I think he's going to be all right."

"Pavel?" Jim said gently.

Chekov tried to get up.

"It's okay, Pavel," McCoy said. "You're going to be fine. Just try to rest now."

"Admiral," Lieutenant Saavik said, "I am sorry, I cannot get through to the *Enterprise*. *Reliant* is still jamming all channels."

"I'm sure you did your best, Lieutenant," Jim said.

"It wouldn't make any difference," McCoy said. "If Spock obeyed orders, the *Enterprise* is long since gone. If Spock couldn't obey, the ship's finished."

"So are we, it looks like," David said.

Carol stood up. "Jim," she said, "I don't understand. Why did this happen? Who's responsible for it? Who is Khan?"

"It's a long story, Carol."

"We've got *plenty* of time," David said angrily.

"You and your daddy," Doctor McCoy said, "can catch each other up on things."

"Maybe he is my biological father," David said. "But he sure as hell is not my 'daddy.' Jedda's dead because of him—"

"Because of you, boy!" McCoy snapped. "Because you tried to rush a phaser set on kill. And it isn't one dead, it's two, in case you've lost count."

"It's more than that, Doctor," Carol said. "In case *you've* lost count. Most of them were our friends. Jim, I think you owe us at least the courtesy of an explanation."

He looked up, and she could see that he felt as hurt and confused as she did. "I'll trade you," he said.

Carol closed her eyes, took a deep breath, and let it out very slowly.

"Yes," she said. "You're right. Jim, Doctor McCoy . . . we may be down here for a while—"

"We may be down here forever," McCoy said sourly.

"—so can we *please* call a truce?" Carol asked.

"I just watched an old friend commit suicide!" McCoy said. "I stood by and I let him do it!" He turned away. "You'll have to forgive—" anger and grief cut through the sarcasm; his voice broke, "—my bad humor. . . ."

"Believe me, Doctor, please, I know how you feel."

"Yes," he said slowly. "Of course. I'm sorry."

When he had composed himself, he returned to the group. They sat in a small circle, and Jim tried to explain.

Carol wished he could give her some reason to hope, but when Jim finished, the implications of Genesis in the hands of Khan Singh left her only despair.

"Is there anything to eat down here?" Jim said suddenly. "I don't know about the rest of you, but I'm starved."

"How can you think of food at a time like this?" McCoy said.

"What I think is that our first order of business is survival."

"There's plenty of food in the Genesis cave," Carol said absently. She shook her head in surprise at herself—she should have led them all there long ago, instead of staying in these cold and ugly chambers. Everything that had happened had affected her far more than she was willing to admit: the clarity of her thought, and her ability to trust . . . She got up. "There's enough to last a lifetime, if it comes to that."

"We thought *this* was Genesis!" McCoy said.

Carol looked around her, at the dark rough caves piled messily with equipment and records and personal gear. The series of caves had taken the Starfleet Corps of Engineers ten months in spacesuits to tunnel out: the second stage of Genesis had taken a single day. Carol laughed, but stopped abruptly when she heard her own hysteria.

"This? No, this isn't Genesis. David—will you show Doctor McCoy and Lieutenant Saavik our idea of food?"

"Mother—there's a lunatic out there with Genesis, and you want me to give a *guided tour?*"

"Yes."

"But we've got to— We can't just do nothing!"

"Yes we can," Jim said. He casually removed a bit of equipment from his belt pouch and unfolded it. It was not until he fitted its lenses in front of his eyes that Carol recognized a pair of reading glasses—one of her professors in graduate school had worn the same things: apparently, as far as Carol had ever been able to tell, to enhance his reputation as an eccentric. Jim Kirk wearing glasses?

He looked at his chronometer, took the glasses off again, and put them away.

"Is there really some food down here?" he said.

David scowled.

"David, please," Carol said.

He glared at Kirk. "Keep the underlings busy, huh?" He shrugged. "What the hell." He gestured abruptly to Saavik and McCoy. "Come on."

Saavik hesitated. "Admiral—?"

"As your teacher Mister Spock is fond of saying: No event is devoid of possibilities."

McCoy followed David out of the cavern. Saavik stood gazing at the floor in thought, then abruptly turned and left with them.

Pavel Chekov lay sleeping or unconscious on a pile of blankets.

Jim and Carol were alone.

Carol sat on her heels beside him.

"David's right, isn't he? It's just to keep us busy."

He raised his head. "Why didn't you tell me?"

Carol Marcus had had twenty years to think about how to answer that question, and she had never decided what the answer should be.

"Jim . . . why didn't you ask?"

He frowned. "What?"

"You've known for a long time that I have a son. You know his age, or you could have found out without any trouble. And," she added with an attempt at humor, "I don't believe they take you into the Starfleet Academy unless you can count." The humor fell flat. She did not feel very much like laughing now, anyway. The possibility that Jim Kirk might ask her about David had always existed in her mind; it was one of those possibilities that in the strange and inexplicable way of the human psyche Carol had both dreaded and, on a level she was aware of but never would have admitted to anyone but herself, wished for.

But it had never happened.

"Carol . . . I don't know if you can believe this. I guess there's no reason why you should. But it never even occurred to me that David might be ours. I didn't even know you'd had a child till I got back with the *Enterprise.* And after that I had, I don't know, some trouble putting any kind of life back together. It was like coming to an alien world that was just similar enough to the one I remembered that every time I ran into something that had changed, I was surprised, and disoriented. . . ."

Carol took his hand, cradled his palm, and stroked the backs of his fingers.

"Stop it, Jim. I'm sorry, dammit, I don't know if I'd even have told you the truth if you *had* asked. I swore I'd never tell either of you."

"I don't understand *why.*"

"How can you say that? Isn't it obvious? We weren't together, and there was no way we were ever going to be! I never had any illusions about it, and to give you your due you never tried to give me any. You have your world, and I have mine. I wanted David in my world." She let go of Jim's hand. She had always admired his hands: they were square and strong. "If he'd decided to go chasing through the universe on his own, I'd have accepted it. But I couldn't have stood having you come along when he was fourteen and say, 'Well, now that you've got him to the age of reason, it's time for him to come along with his father.' His father—someone he'd never known except as a stranger staying overnight? Jim, that was the only possibility, and that's *too late* to start being a father! Besides, fourteen-year-olds have no business on a starship, anyway."

He stood up, walked away from her, and pressed his hands and forehead against the wall as if he were trying to soak up the coolness and calmness of the very stone.

"You don't need to tell me that," he said. His shoulders were slumped, and she thought he was about to cry. She wanted to hold him; yet she did not want to see him cry.

"David's a lot like you, you know," she said, trying to lighten her own mood as much as Jim's. "There wasn't much I could do about that. He's stubborn, and unpredictable— Of course, he's *smarter*—that goes without saying. . . ." She stopped; this attempt at humor was falling even flatter than the other.

"Dammit," she said, "does it matter? We're never going to get out of here."

Jim did not respond. He knelt down beside Pavel and felt his pulse. He avoided Carol's gaze.

"Tell me what you're feeling," she said gently.

He sounded remote and sad; Carol tried to feel angry at him, but could not.

"There's a man who hasn't seen me for fifteen years who thinks he's killed me," Jim said. "You show me a son who'd be glad to finish the job. Our son. My life that could have been, but wasn't. Carol, I feel old, and worn out, and confused."

She went to him and stretched out her hand. "Let me show you something. Something that will make you feel young, as young as a new world."

He glanced at Chekov. Carol was not a medical doctor, but she knew enough about human physiology to be able to see that the young commander was sleeping peacefully.

"He'll be all right," she said. "Come on. Come with me."

He took her hand.

She led him toward Genesis.

Unwillingly Jim followed Carol deeper into the caverns. The overhead light-plates ended, and they proceeded into darkness. Carol slid her free hand along the cave wall to guide them. Jim soon realized that it was not as completely dark as it should have been, underground and without artificial illumination. He could see Carol. The reflected light glinted off her hair.

The light grew brighter. With the sensitivity of someone who spent most of his time in artificial light and beneath alien stars, who valued what little he saw of sunlight, Jim knew, without question, that the glow ahead of him was that of a star very like the Sun.

He glanced at Carol. She smiled, but gave no word of explanation.

Without meaning to, Jim began to walk faster. As the light intensified, as its quality grew clearer and purer, he found himself running.

He plunged from the mouth of the cave and stopped. Carol joined him on the edge of a promontory.

Jim Kirk gasped.

His eyes were still dark-adapted: the light dazzled him. The warm breeze ruffled his hair, and he smelled fresh earth, flowers, a forest. A rivulet tumbled down the cliff just next to him, casting a rainbow mist across his face.

A forest stretched into the distance, filling the shell of the lifeless planetoid that had been Regulus I. It was the most beautiful place he had ever seen, a storybook forest from children's tales. The gnarled trees showed immense age and mystery. The grass in the meadow at the foot of the cliff was as smooth and soft as green velvet, sprinkled with wildflowers of delicate blue and violent orange. Where the shadow of the forest began, Jim half expected to glimpse a flash of white, a unicorn fleeing his gaze.

He looked at Carol, who leaned against the cliff next to the tunnel entrance, her arms folded. She smiled.

"You did this in a day?" Jim said.

"The matrix forms in a day. The lifeforms take a little longer. Not much, though." She grinned. "Now do you believe I can cook?"

He gazed out, fascinated at her world. "How far does it go?"

"All the way around," she said. "The rotation of the planet gives us some radial acceleration to act in place of gravity, to probably forty-five degrees above and below the equator. I expect things get a little strange out at the poles." She pointed past the sun. "A stress field keeps the star in place. It's an extreme variable; twelve hours out of twenty-four, it dims down to give some night. Makes a very pretty moon."

"Is it all . . . this beautiful?"

"I don't know, Jim. I haven't exactly had a chance to explore it, and it's a prototype, after all. Things always happen that you don't expect. Besides, the whole team worked on the design." Her tone grew very sad. "Vance drew the map; his section had a note at the far border, way up north, that said 'Here be dragons.' Nobody ever knew if he was kidding or not. Or—maybe Del did." Carol's voice caught; Jim almost could not hear her. "Vance said, once, that it wasn't worth making something up that was so pretty and safe if it was insipid."

She started to cry. Jim took her in his arms and just held her.

Eight

In the storage bay of *Reliant,* Khan completed his inspection of the massive Genesis torpedo. He had tapped its instruction program; though the mechanism itself was complex, both the underlying theoretical basis and the device's operation were absurdly simple.

He patted the sleek flank of the great machine. When he tired of ruling over worlds that existed, he would create new worlds to his own design.

Joachim came into the storage bay and stopped some distance from him.

"Impulse power is restored, my lord," he said.

"Thank you, Joachim. Now we are more than a match for the poor *Enterprise.*"

"Yes, my lord." His tone revealed nothing: no enthusiasm, no glory, not even any fear. Simply nothing.

Khan frowned.

"Joachim, have you slept?"

Joachim flinched, as if Khan had struck him.

"I cannot sleep, my lord."

"What do you mean?"

Joachim suddenly shivered, and turned away.

"I *cannot* sleep, my lord."

Khan watched his aide for a moment, shrugged, and strode out of the storage bay. Joachim followed more slowly.

On the bridge, Khan ordered the ship out of orbit. He had calculated carefully to put Regulus I between *Reliant* and the relative position the *Enterprise* must keep until it regained power. Foolish of Mister Spock to transmit the ship's vulnerability to any who could hear.

Regulus I's terminator slid past beneath them, and they probed into the actinic light of Regulus.

"Short-range sensors."

Joachim obeyed. Khan brought the display to the forward viewscreen and frowned. There was Spacelab, broached and empty. *Enterprise* should have been drifting dead nearby in a matching orbit.

It was nowhere to be found.

"Long-range sensors."

And still nothing. Khan stood up, his fists clenched.

"Where are they?"

In the Genesis cave, Saavik accompanied Doctor McCoy back into the rock caverns. Pavel Chekov had to be moved to where he could be made more comfortable. David Marcus came along to help. They improvised a litter and carried Chekov out of the caverns.

They made the climb down the cliff with some difficulty, but arrived safely in the meadow below. Doctor McCoy made a bed for his patient, who slept so soundly he barely seemed to breathe.

David Marcus lay down in the grass.

"I knew it would work," he said. "If only . . ." He flung his arm across his eyes.

Saavik watched him curiously, if somewhat surreptitiously. David Marcus, it seemed, dealt with grief a good deal better than she did. In addition, despite his original denial, David had assimilated being introduced to his father with considerable grace.

Saavik doubted she would be able to say the same of herself. It would be an unimaginably dreadful event if anyone ever identified the Vulcan family to which one of her parents had belonged. If that ever happened, if they were somehow forced to acknowledge her, the only way either she or they could survive a meeting with honor and mind intact would be for her to kneel before them and beg their forgiveness for her very existence.

And if she ever encountered the Romulan who had caused her to be born . . . Saavik knew well the depths of violence of which she was capable. If she ever met that creature, she would give herself to the madness willingly.

David kept going over and over what had happened on Spacelab. Somehow he should have been able to *do* something; he should have known, despite

Del's reassurance, that his friends were in a lot more trouble than they could handle.

He was afraid he was about to go crazy.

He decided to pick some fruit from the cornucopia tree in the center of the meadow. He was not the least bit hungry, but at least that would give him something to do.

When he stood up, he felt Saavik's gaze. He turned around and looked at her; she was staring so hard, or so lost in thought, that she hardly realized he had noticed what she was doing.

"What are *you* looking at?" he said belligerently.

She started and blinked. "The admiral's son," she said with matter-of-fact directness.

"Don't you believe it!"

"I do believe it," she said.

Unfortunately so do I, David thought. If his mother had only been trying to keep Jim Kirk alive, she would hardly have kept up the deception after the fight. It was far too easy to prove parentage beyond any doubt with a simple antigen-scan. If McCoy couldn't do it with the equipment in his medical pouch, then David could probably jury-rig an analyzer himself from the stuff they'd brought down from Spacelab. It was just because the proof was so easy that he did not see any point to doing the test. It would merely assure him of what he would rather not have known.

He shrugged it off. What difference did it make who his biological father was? Neither the man he had thought it was, who had died before he was born, nor the man his mother said it was, had ever had any part in his life. David could see no reason why that should change.

"What are *you* looking at?" Lieutenant Saavik said.

David, in his turn, had been staring without realizing it. He had always been fascinated by Vulcans. In fact, the one time he had met Jim Kirk, when he was a kid, he had been much more interested in talking to Kirk's friend Mister Spock. David assumed it was the same Mister Spock whom Saavik had earlier been trying to contact. If David had to be civil to a member of Starfleet, he would a whole lot rather it be a science officer than a starship captain.

Funny he had not noticed before how beautiful Saavik was. Beautiful and exotic. She did not seem as cold as most Vulcans, either.

"I—" He stopped. He felt confused. "I don't know," he said finally.

Saavik turned away.

Damn, David thought, *I insulted her or hurt her feelings or something.* He tried to reopen the conversation.

"I bet I know who I'm looking at," he said. "Mister Spock's daughter, right?"

She spun toward him, her fists clenched at her sides. He flinched back. He thought she was going to belt him. But she straightened up and gradually relaxed her hands.

"If I thought you knew what you were saying," Saavik told him, "I would kill you."

"What?" he said. "Hell—trust a member of Starfleet to react like that. Try to give somebody a compliment, and look what you get."

"A compliment!"

"Sure. Hey, look, there aren't that many Vulcans in Starfleet; I figured you were following in your father's footsteps or something."

"Hardly," she said, her voice and her expression chill. "You could not offer a worse insult to Captain Spock than to imply he is, or even could be, my father."

"Why?" he said.

"I do not care to discuss it."

"Why not? What's so awful about you?"

"One of my parents was Romulan!" She spoke angrily.

"Yeah? Hey, that's really interesting. I thought you were a Vulcan."

"No."

"You look like a Vulcan to me."

"I neither look like a Vulcan nor behave like a Vulcan, as far as *other* Vulcans are concerned. I do not even have a proper Vulcan name."

"I still don't see why Mister Spock would be insulted because I thought you were his daughter."

"Do you know anything about Vulcan sexual physiology?"

"Sure. What difference does that make? They still have to reproduce, even if they only try it every seven years." David grinned. "Sounds pretty boring to me."

"Many Romulans find Vulcans sexually attractive. Under normal conditions, a Vulcan would not respond. But the Romulans practice both piracy and abduction, and they have chemical means of forcing prisoners to obey."

She paused. David could tell this was difficult for her, but he was fascinated.

"To lose the control of one's own mind and body—this is the ultimate humiliation," Saavik said. "Most Vulcans prefer death to capture by Romulans and seldom survive if they are driven to act in a way so alien to their natures. The chance that my Vulcan parent even lives is vanishingly small."

"Oh," David said.

"Romulans make a game of their cruelty. A few take the game so far as to father or conceive a child from their coercion, then compel the Vulcan woman to live long enough to bear it, or the Vulcan man to live long enough to witness its birth. That completes the humiliation and confers great social status on the Romulan."

"Hey, look, I'm sorry," David said. "I honestly didn't mean to hurt your feelings or insult Mister Spock."

"You cannot hurt me, Doctor Marcus," Saavik said. "But as I am not entirely a Vulcan, it would be possible for me to hurt you. I would advise you to take care."

She stood up and strode away.

Saavik paced through the meadow, wondering what had possessed her to tell David Marcus so much about her background. She had never volunteered the information to anyone else before, and she seldom spoke about it even to Mister Spock, who of course knew everything. The obvious explanation, that she had wanted to be certain Marcus would never speak in a completely offensive manner to Spock, failed to satisfy her. But she could think of no other.

She climbed down the bank to the edge of the stream, picked up a smooth rounded pebble, and turned it over and over in her hand. She marveled at the complexity of the Genesis wave. In a natural environment a water-worn pebble would take years to form.

She skipped the stone across the surface of the stream. It spun across the current and landed on the other side.

This was without doubt the most beautiful place Saavik had ever seen. It was all the more affecting because its beauty was neither perfect nor safe. She had heard, far in the distance, the howl of a wild animal, and she had seen the sleek shape of a winged hunter skim the surface of the forest. It was too far away for even Saavik to discern whether it was reptile or bird or mammal, or some type of animal unique to this new place.

The only thing wrong with it was that she was here against her will.

She took out her communicator and tried once again to reach the *Enterprise.* But either the signals were still being jammed or no one could answer. And Doctor McCoy was right, too: Mister Spock should by now have taken the ship and departed for a starbase. If he could.

She climbed the bank to return to the meadow.

Doctor Marcus, junior, lay on a hillock at the edge of the forest, staring meditatively at the sky and chewing on a blade of grass. The admiral, Doctor McCoy, and Doctor Marcus, senior, sat nearby under a fruit tree, picnicking on fruits and sweet flowers.

Saavik hesitated to invade their privacy, then recognized that if Doctor Marcus and Admiral Kirk wished to be alone, Doctor McCoy and David would have gone elsewhere. She started across the field toward them. She had several ideas she wanted to propose to the admiral. Anything would be better than standing idly by, in paradise or not, while the world they had come from dissolved into hell.

Admiral Kirk seemed so very calm and relaxed. As she neared the group, Saavik unfavorably compared her own reaction to the *Kobayashi Maru* simulation to Kirk's composure in the face of real death or permanent exile.

Saavik wondered again how Lieutenant James Kirk had reacted to the simulation that had shaken her own assurance. Captain Spock had said Kirk's solution was unique, and that she must ask the admiral herself if she wished to know what it was.

"That's what I call a meal," Kirk said.

"This is like the Garden of Eden," Doctor McCoy said with wonder.

"Only here, every apple comes from the tree of knowledge," Doctor Marcus said; then added, "with all the risk that implies."

She leaned forward and put a bright red flower behind Admiral Kirk's ear. He tried to stop her, but not very hard, and finally submitted.

Jim Kirk felt a bit silly with a flower stuck behind his ear. But he left it where it was, picked a handful of bright purple blossoms from a thick patch nearby, and began to braid them together into a coronet. Noticing Saavik's approach—and her pensive expression—he motioned for her to join them.

"What's on your mind, Lieutenant?"

"The *Kobayashi Maru,* sir," she said.

"What's that?" David asked.

Doctor McCoy explained. "It's a training simulation. A no-win scenario that tests the philosophy of a commander facing death."

"Are you asking me if we're playing out the same story now, Lieutenant?" Jim picked another handful of flowers.

"What did you do on the test, Admiral?" Saavik asked. "I would very much like to know."

Doctor McCoy chuckled. "Why, Lieutenant, you're lookin' at the only Starfleet cadet ever to beat that simulation."

"I almost got myself tossed out of the Academy, too," Jim said. He thought about the time, took out his glasses, and looked at his chronometer again. Not quite yet.

"How did you beat it?"

"I reprogrammed the simulation so I could save the ship."

"What?"

Jim felt rather amused to have startled Saavik so thoroughly.

"I changed the conditions of the test." He smiled. He was not a wizard computer programmer himself; fortunately one of his Academy classmates not only was, but could never resist a challenge. It was Jim, though, who had staged the commando raid—or cat burglary, since no one figured out what he had done till quite a while later—on the supposedly secure storage facility where the simulation programs were kept, in order to substitute his version for Starfleet's.

"The instructor couldn't decide whether to die laughing or blow her stack. I think she finally flipped a coin. I received a commendation for original thinking." With a smile, he shrugged. "I don't like to lose."

"Then you evaded the purpose of the simulation: you never faced death."

"Well, I took the test twice before I decided to do something about it, so I suppose you could say I faced death. I just never had to accept it."

"Until now."

"Saavik, we each face death every day we're alive."

Now it *was* time. He picked up his communicator and opened it.

"Kirk to *Enterprise*. Come in, Mister Spock."

"*Enterprise* to Kirk, Spock here."

Saavik started violently and leaped to her feet.

"It's two hours, Spock. Are you about ready?"

"On schedule, Admiral. I will compute your coordinates and beam you aboard. Spock out."

Everyone was staring at him in shock. Kirk shrugged contritely.

"I told you," he said. "I don't like to lose."

He joined the flower garland into a circle and placed it gently on Carol's hair.

"Energize," Spock said to Transporter Chief Janice Rand. She focused the beam on the party in the middle of Regulus I, increased the power to compensate for several kilometers of solid rock, and energized.

Spock had deduced Kirk's assumptions and intentions. The science officer was curious to know the results of the second stage of Genesis. He suspected that parts of what had been created within the planetoid would be most interesting, considering the odd sense of humor of the team of Madison and March.

He hoped to be able to see it himself and, seeing it, honor the memory of their lives and their work.

The admiral materialized on the transporter platform, and behind him Doctor McCoy and Doctor Marcus, senior, then Lieutenant Saavik and Doctor Marcus, junior, supporting Pavel Chekov between them.

Spock raised one eyebrow. The admiral wore a flower over his ear, while Doctor Carol Marcus wore a floral wreath.

The planetoid must be most interesting, indeed.

Saavik finished saying something interrupted by the beaming process. "—the damage report. The *Enterprise* was immobilized."

"Come, now, Lieutenant," the admiral said kindly. "You're the one who keeps telling me to go by the book."

Kirk suddenly noticed what Spock was looking at, began to blush, and removed the flower. He gallantly offered it to Lieutenant Saavik—who had no idea what to do with it, as no one had ever given her a flower before—and stepped down from the platform.

"Hello, Mister Spock," Kirk said. "You remember Doctor Marcus—" he presented Carol Marcus, "—and I believe you met David before he also became Doctor Marcus."

David Marcus nodded to Spock and helped Saavik carry Chekov down.

"Certainly," Spock said. "Welcome to the *Enterprise.* I was most impressed by your presentation."

"Thank you, Mister Spock," Carol Marcus said. "I wish it were turning out better."

Even Spock could see the effects of strain and exhaustion in her face; the deaths on Spacelab must of course have affected her far more than they did him, not only because she was human and he Vulcan, but because she had been far better acquainted with the people who had died. Words of condolence were such a trivial response to a loss of this magnitude that Spock refused to attempt any.

Doctor McCoy went immediately to the intercom and ordered a medical team and stretcher from sickbay.

"By the book—?" Saavik said.

"Regulation forty-six-A: 'During battle . . .' "

" '. . . no uncoded messages on an open channel,' " Saavik said; and then, to Spock, "It seems very near a lie. . . ."

"It was a code, Lieutenant," he said. "Unfortunately the code required some exaggeration of the truth."

She did not answer; he knew she was troubled by the difference between a lie and a figurative interpretation of reality. He knew precisely how she felt. It had taken him a long time to understand that in some cases no objective difference existed, and that any explanation lay completely within circumstances.

"We only needed hours, Saavik, not days," Kirk said. "But now we have minutes instead of hours. We'd better make use of them."

"Yes, sir," she said, unconvinced.

The medical team arrived, and Saavik eased Commander Chekov to the stretcher. She looked at the flower in her hand for a moment, then placed it carefully beside him.

"Jim, I'm taking Chekov to sickbay," McCoy said.

"Take good care of him, Bones."

"What can we do?" Carol Marcus asked.

"Carol, it's going to be chaos on the bridge in a few minutes," Kirk said apologetically. "I've got to get up there."

"Doctors Marcus," McCoy said, "I can put you both to work. Come with me."

Kirk, Spock, and Saavik hurried toward the bridge. Kirk stopped at the first turbolift, but Spock kept going.

"The lifts are inoperative below C-deck," Spock said, and opened the door to the emergency stairs. He climbed them three at a time.

"What *is* working around here?"

"Very little, Admiral. Main power is partially restored. . . ."

"Is that *all?*"

"We could do no more in two hours. Mister Scott's crew is trying to complete repairs."

They reached C-deck. Spock and Saavik entered the lift. Kirk was breathing hard. He paused a moment in the corridor, wiped his face on his sleeve, and got into the cage.

"Damned desk job," he said softly. "Bridge."

The lift accelerated upward.

James Kirk stepped out onto the bridge of his ship. It still showed the effects of the earlier skirmish, but he could see immediately that most functions had been restored.

Mister Sulu, at his old place at the helm, glanced over his shoulder when the lift doors opened.

"Admiral on the bridge!" he said immediately.

"Battle stations," Kirk said.

The Klaxon sounded; the lights dimmed down to deep red.

"Tactical, Mister Sulu, if you please."

"Aye, sir."

The viewscreen flipped over into a polar view of Regulus I, showing the orbits of Spacelab, *Reliant,* and the *Enterprise.* The two starships were in opposition, one on either side of the planetoid. *Reliant*'s delta-vee coordinates changed as they watched, revealing that Khan's ship had begun a search.

"Our scanners are undependable at best," Spock said. "Spacelab's scanners, however, are fully operational; they are transmitting the position of *Reliant.*"

"Very good, Mister Spock."

Reliant suddenly accelerated at full impulse power.

"Uh-oh," Kirk said.

It would slingshot itself around Regulus I; unless the *Enterprise* accelerated, too, and continued to chase and flee the other ship, around and around the planetoid, his ship would soon be a target again. And with the engines in the shape they were in, they could not stay hidden for long.

"*Reliant* can both outrun and outgun us," Spock said calmly. "There is, however, the Mutara Nebula. . . ."

Kirk took out his glasses and put them on to study the displays. He opened a channel to the engine room.

"Mister Scott—the Mutara Nebula. Can you get us inside?"

"Sir, the overload warnings are lit up like a Christmas tree; the main energizer bypasses willna take much strain. Dinna gi' us too many bumps."

"No promises, Mister Scott. Give me all you've got."

"Admiral," Saavik said, "within the nebula, the gas clouds will interfere with our tacticals. Visuals will not function. In addition, ionization will disrupt our shields."

Kirk glanced over the rim of his spectacles at Saavik, then at Spock. Spock raised one eyebrow.

"Precisely, Lieutenant: the odds will then be even," the Vulcan said.

The crew had taken their battle stations, pushing the bridge into controlled pandemonium. The dimmed lights cast strange shadows; computer screens glowed in eerie colors. Kirk watched the tactical display. *Reliant* was moving so fast it would round the planet's horizon in a few minutes and have the *Enterprise* in line-of-sight. Kirk wanted to be out of phaser and torpedo range yet remain a tempting target.

"Admiral," Saavik asked, "what happens if *Reliant* fails to follow us into the nebula?"

Kirk laughed, though with very little humor. "That's the least of our worries. Khan will follow us."

"Remind me, Lieutenant," Spock said, "to discuss with you the human ego."

"Mister Scott," Kirk said into the intercom, "are you ready?"

"As ready as I can be, Admiral."

"Mister Sulu."

"Course plotted, sir: Mutara Nebula."

"Accelerate at full impulse power—" he hesitated until only a few degrees of arc remained before *Reliant*'s orbit would carry it within sight of the *Enterprise*, "—now!"

On the viewscreen, the coordinates defining his ship's linear acceleration increased instantaneously by orders of magnitude. The *Enterprise* sped out of orbit.

A moment later, *Reliant* rounded the limb of Regulus, and its course and speed altered radically.

"They've spotted us," Mister Sulu said.

Doctor McCoy had nearly finished the workup on Pavel Chekov when the battle stations alarm sounded. He experienced an all too familiar tightening in his stomach. For a long time, he had believed his reaction was as simple as fear, but eventually, the better he knew himself, he realized that it was at least as much the loathing he felt for having to patch up—sometimes to lose— young people who should never have been injured in the first place. Usually they were not as young as Peter Preston . . . but they were seldom very much older.

At least—to McCoy's astonishment and relief—Pavel Chekov had a good chance of recovering. The horrible creature had insinuated its long and narrow length into his skull, to be sure; but although it had penetrated the dura mater, the arachnoid membrane, and the pia mater, all the way to the cerebrum itself, it had not, at the time of its departure, actually destroyed any brain tissue. Instead it had nestled itself in the sulci between the brain's convolutions. No doubt it would have done more damage had it remained much longer, but as it was Chekov should convalesce as if from a severe concussion. McCoy found no evidence of infection. Pavel Chekov was a very fortunate man.

The ship shuddered around him.

"What was that?" David Marcus had been pacing back and forth through sick bay, nervous as a cat, haunted. Just now there was very little to do. If they were lucky, things would continue that way.

"Impulse engines," McCoy said.

"What does that mean?"

"Well, son, I expect it means the chase is on."

"I'm going up there."

"To the bridge? No, you're not. You'd just be in the way. Best stay here, David."

"Dammit—there must be something I can do."

"There isn't," McCoy said. "Nor anything I can do. All we can do is wait for them to start shooting at each other, and wish we could keep them from doing it. That's the trouble with this job."

Khan chuckled at the pitiful attempt of the *Enterprise* to evade him. *Reliant,* accelerating under full impulse power, streaked out of orbit after James Kirk's crippled ship.

"So," he said to Joachim. "They are not so wounded as they wished us to believe. The hunt will be better than I thought, my friend."

Joachim displayed a long-range scan of their course, showing the *Enterprise* and the great opaque cloud of the nebula ahead.

"My lord, we will lose our advantage if we follow them into the dust. I beg you—"

Khan cut him off. Joachim was beginning to sound like a traitor. Khan decided to give him one last chance.

"Rake the *Enterprise,*" he ordered.

The phaser rippled outward, a long finger of dense light. It streaked along the side of the *Enterprise*'s starboard engine nacelle. The starship heeled over and began to tumble, spiraling on its headlong course.

The *Enterprise* lurched; its artificial gravity flexed, trembled, and finally steadied. McCoy closed his eyes a moment, till he regained his balance.

Action commenced, he thought bitterly.

Chekov gave an inarticulate cry and sat up abruptly, his eyes wild.

"Take it easy," McCoy said.

"I must help Captain—"

"*No.* Listen to me, Pavel. You've been through a hell of a lot. You haven't any strength, and you haven't any equilibrium."

"But—"

"You can lie down willingly, or you can lie down sedated. Which will it be?"

Pavel tried again to get up. He nearly passed out. McCoy caught him and eased him back on the bed. The young Russian turned deathly pale.

"*Now* will you stay put?"

Chekov nodded slightly without opening his eyes.

The ship shuddered again. Coming out of the instrument room where she had been helping Chris Chapel, Carol Marcus staggered, then recovered her balance. The flower garland slipped from her hair. She caught it, stared at it as if she had never seen it before, and carefully laid it aside.

"Doctor McCoy, I can't just sit here. I keep thinking about— Please, give me something to do."

"Like I was tellin' David," McCoy said grimly, "there isn't much *to* do. . . ." He realized how desperate she was to stay occupied. "But you can help me get the surgery ready. I'm expecting customers."

Marcus paled, but she did not back off.

If what she and the kid have been through in the last couple of days didn't break them, I guess nothing will, McCoy thought.

Marcus glanced around sickbay.

"Where *is* David?" she said.

"I don't know—he was here a minute ago."

"Ion concentration increasing," Mister Spock said. "Approximately two minutes to sensor overload and shield shutdown."

The ship plowed on. Encountering great quantities of ionized dust and gases, the shields began to re-radiate energy in the visual spectrum. The viewscreen picked it up, sparkling and shimmering. The crisp rustle of static rose over the low hum of conversation and information on the bridge. A tang of ozone filled the air.

Reliant fired again. The *Enterprise* shuddered. If the shields were not quite steady, at least they held.

"*Reliant* is closing fast," Saavik said.

Directly ahead, the nebula's core raged.

"They just don't want us going in there," Kirk said, nodding toward the viewscreen.

"One minute," Spock said.

The turbolift doors slipped open and David Marcus came onto the bridge.

"Admiral, *Reliant* is decelerating."

"Uhura, patch me in."

"Aye, sir."

Khan felt the power of the impulse engines slacken, then whisper into reverse thrust. The gap between *Reliant* and the *Enterprise* immediately widened.

"Joachim, why are we decelerating?"

"My lord, we daren't follow them into the nebula. Our shields will fail—"

"Khan, this is James Kirk."

Khan leaped to his feet with a scream of surprise and anger. James Kirk— still alive!

"We tried it your way, Khan. Are you game for a rematch?"

Khan struggled to gain control over his rage.

James Kirk began to laugh. "Superior intellect!" he said with contempt. "You're a fool, Khan. A brutal, murderous, ridiculous fool."

"Full impulse power!" Khan's voice was a growl.

Joachim stood up and faced him. "My lord, no! You have everything! You have Genesis!" He looked Khan in the eye and this time he did not flinch. Khan strode toward the helm, but Joachim blocked his way.

"My lord—" he said, pleading.

"Full power!" Khan cried.

He struck his friend with the violent strength of fury. The blow lifted Joachim completely off the deck and flung him over the control console. He fell hard against the forward bulkhead, lay still for a moment, then dragged himself to his feet.

"Full power, damn you!" Khan grabbed the controls and slammed full power to the engines.

Spock watched the tactical display. *Reliant* stopped decelerating and plunged forward at full impulse power.

"Khan does have at least one admirable quality," the Vulcan said.

"Oh?" said Kirk. "And what's that?"

"He is extremely consistent." Spock glanced at the ionization readings. The ship had technically been within the nebula for some time. Now it approached a thick band of dust where pressure waves from the original exploding star met and interfered. The energy flux and mass concentration must disrupt the *Enterprise*'s operation.

"They're following us," said Mister Sulu.

"Sensor overload . . . mark." Almost immediately, the image on the viewscreen broke up and shattered.

Sulu piloted the ship blind through the cloud of gas and dust and energy.

Joachim returned to his place at the helm, bewildered into silence. In all the years that he had served his lord, all the times of witnessing the violence to which Khan was prone, Joachim had never himself been subjected to that wrath. Khan had never assaulted him. Until now.

Joachim had been in fights aplenty; he had even, in his younger days, lost a few. None had ever affected him like the single blow from Khan. His hands shook on the controls, partly from humiliation and partly from rage. He had sworn to follow Khan even to death. There was no room for compromise: he had put no conditions on his vow. No conditions for madness, no conditions for betrayal.

Freedom was in Khan's grasp, yet he was throwing it away. Joachim indeed felt betrayed.

The *Enterprise* vanished into a thick projection of dust, a tendril of exploded matter from the pulsar at the nova's center.

"Follow it!" Khan said.

Joachim held his tongue and obeyed.

The viewscreen's image dissolved into random colors, punctuated by the periodic flash of the pulsar's electromagnetic field.

"Tactical!" Khan cried.

"Inoperative," Joachim said, without expression.

"Raise the shields!"

"Inoperative." Joachim saw that the ship's hull could not long withstand the stress of the high concentration of dust, not at the speed it was going. "Reducing speed," he said coldly.

He could feel Khan's gaze burning into him, but this time Khan made no protest.

The *Enterprise* broke through the worst of the dust; visuals and tacticals returned, but the shields were out completely. Sulu changed course, creeping through the nebula's diffuse mass just outside the irregular boundary which would both hide the *Enterprise,* and blind it.

The *Enterprise* hovered outside the cloud, and waited.

"Here it comes," Saavik said.

Reliant plowed slowly through the dust. It would be blind for another few moments.

"Phaser lock just blew, Admiral," Mister Sulu said.

"Do your best, Mister Sulu. Fire when ready."

Sulu believed he could hit the opposing ship, even at this range. Precisely, carefully, he aimed. A moment's pause:

Fire—

The magnetic bearings of a stabilizing gyro exploded, and the *Enterprise* lurched. The phaser beam went wide.

Sulu muttered a curse and plunged the *Enterprise* back into the nebula as *Reliant* spotted them and fired. The photon torpedo just missed, but it expended its energy in the cloud, and a mass of charged particles and radiation slammed into them. He struggled to steady the ship.

"Hold your course," Kirk said. "Look sharp. . . ."

"At *what?*" Lieutenant Saavik murmured. She drew more power to the sensors, tightened the angle, and ran the input through enhancement.

For an instant, the viewscreen cleared. Sulu started involuntarily—*Reliant* loomed on the screen: collision course!

"Evasive starboard!" Kirk yelled.

Too late.

Reliant's phaser blast hit the unshielded *Enterprise* dead-on. The power-surge baffles on the primary helm console failed completely. It carried a jolt of electricity straight through the controls. Half the instruments blew out. Sulu felt the voltage arc across his hands. It flung him back, arching his spine and shaking him like a great ferocious animal, and slammed him to the deck.

Every muscle in Sulu's body cramped into knots. He lurched over onto his face and tried to rise. He could not breathe. The pain from his seared hands shot through him, cold and hot and overwhelming.

He lost consciousness.

When Mister Sulu fell, Saavik leaped to the helm, seeking out which operations still functioned and which had crashed.

"Phaser bank one!" Kirk said. "Fire!"

Saavik's hands were an extension of the controls, her body was part of the ship itself.

She fired.

The *Enterprises* phaser beam sizzled across *Reliant*'s main hull, full force. The blast reverberated across the bridge. Power failed for a moment, and with it artificial gravity and all illumination. Khan gripped the armrests of the captain's chair, holding himself steady, but through the darkness and the shrieks of tortured metal he heard his people cry out and fall.

Joachim pitched forward over the helm controls.

"Joachim!"

The gravity flowed back, returning slowly to normal, and the lights glowed to a bare dimness.

As *Reliant* plunged ahead, unpiloted and blind, Khan sprang to his old friend's side. He lifted him as gently as he could. Joachim cried out in pain. Khan lowered him to the deck, supporting his shoulders. The jagged ends of broken bones ground together, and Joachim's face was bloody and lacerated. He reached out, his fingers spread and searching.

He could not see.

Khan permitted the touch. He laid his hand over Joachim's.

"My lord. . . ." Joachim whispered. "You proved . . . yourself . . . superior. . . ."

Khan could feel the life ebbing from his friend. For a moment, he experienced despair. His sight blurred: he tried to force away the tears but they spilled unchecked down his face. This was what his hatred had bought—

James Kirk would repay the price.

"I shall avenge you," Khan said to Joachim, his voice a growl.

"I wished . . . no . . . revenge. . . ."

Khan laid his friend down carefully. He stood up, his fists clenched at his side.

"I shall avenge you."

After taking the *Enterprise*'s phaser burst, *Reliant* shot away dead straight, without a maneuver. David Marcus thought the *Enterprise* had won. Yet there was no elation from the bridge crew, only concentration on the scattery viewscreen, murmured interchanges of essential information, and tension over all, like a sound pitched just above the range of hearing.

Kirk spoke into the intercom. "Get a medic up here! Stat!"

David pulled himself out of his observer's detachment and hurried to the side of the injured helm officer.

Sulu was not breathing. His hands were badly burned, and his skin was clammy. David felt his throat for a pulse and got absolutely nothing.

David Marcus was not a medical doctor. He knew some first aid, which he had never had to use. He took a deep breath. The air was heavy with the smell of burned plastic and vaporized metal.

He tilted Sulu's head back, opened his mouth, breathed four breaths into him, pressed the heels of his hands over the helm officer's sternum, and compressed his chest rapidly fifteen times in a row. A breath, fifteen compressions. Sulu did not react, but David kept going. A breath, fifteen compressions.

"What's the damage, Scotty?" he heard Kirk say.

For David, everything was peripheral except the life in his hands. The first rule of manual cardiopulmonary resuscitation was and always had been: Don't stop. No matter what, don't stop.

A breath, fifteen compressions.

"Admiral," the engineer said, "I canna put the mains back online! The energizer's burst; if I try to gi' it to ye, 'twill go critical!"

"Scotty, we've got to have main power! Get in there and fix it!"

A breath, fifteen compressions. David's shoulders and arms were beginning to ache.

"It isna possible, sir!" Mister Scott cried. "The radiation level is far too high; i' ha' already burned out the electronics o' the repair robot, and if ye went in in a suit 'twould freeze for the same reason! A person unprotected wouldna last a minute!"

A breath, fifteen compressions. The ache in David's shoulders crept slowly into pain. Sweat rolled down his forehead and stung in his eyes. He could not stop to wipe it away.

"How long, Scotty?"

"I canna say, sir. Decontamination is begun, but 'twill be a while—"

A breath, fifteen compressions. David was breathing heavily himself now. He had not realized what lousy condition he was in. He had worked long hours on Spacelab, but it was essentially a sedentary job; the only exercise he had ever got was playing zero-gee handball with Zinaida, whom he had sometimes accused of using him as a moving wall to bounce the ball off of.

Come on, Sulu, he thought, *give me a little help, man, please.*

A breath, fifteen compressions.

The turbolift doors slid open, and a medical team hurried onto the bridge.

"Hurry—up—you—guys—" David said.

A medic vaulted down the stairs and knelt beside him.

"Any reaction?"

David shook his head. His sweat-damp hair plastered itself against his forehead.

"Keep going," the medic said. She drew a pressure-injector out of her bag, dialed it, and fitted a long, heavy needle to it. "I'm going to try epinephrine straight to the heart. When I tell you, get out of my way but keep breathing for him. Okay?"

David could hardly see because of the sweat sparkling in his eyes. He nodded. The medic ripped Sulu's shirt open, baring his chest. The fabric parted beneath David's hands.

"Okay. Now!"

He moved quickly, sliding aside but continuing to breathe for the helm officer. What was the count for artificial respiration? Fifteen per minute? He held Sulu's head just beneath his jaw but still could feel no pulse.

The medic plunged the needle down.

The reaction was almost instantaneous. Sulu shuddered, and his clammy skin flushed. David felt a pulse, thready and fast. Sulu gasped. David did not know what to do, whether to stop or keep going.

The medic took his shoulder. "It's okay," she said. "You can stop now."

David stopped. He could barely raise his head. He was dripping with sweat and panting. But Sulu was breathing on his own.

"Good work," the medic said.

"How is he?" Kirk said without taking his gaze off the viewscreen.

"Can't tell yet," the medic said. "He's alive, thanks to his friend here."

She flung out a stretcher. It rippled, straightened, solidified.

David staggered to his feet and tried to help her get Sulu onto it. He was not a great deal of use in lifting because his arms were so tired they had gone numb. But once Sulu was on the stretcher, David at least could guide it. While the medic started working on Sulu's burns, David pushed the stretcher to the turbo-lift and down to sickbay.

Pavel Chekov felt and heard the battle begin; he watched the flow of casualties start and increase. He considered himself responsible for everything that had happened. He tried to sit up, but Doctor McCoy had strapped him down—it was a safety precaution, not a restraint, and as the ship rocked and shuddered around him he freed his arms and fumbled for the fastenings. Sickbay spun around him; he had to close his eyes again to get his balance.

For a moment, he lay back. What possible use could he be on the bridge, half-crippled and sick?

Then they brought Mister Sulu in. Doctor Chapel read his life signs grimly, looked at his hands, and cursed under her breath.

Chekov ripped off the restraining straps and forced himself to stand. In the confusion, no one noticed him get up, or if they did they did not try and make him lie down again.

His hearing was still one-sided. At the entrance to sickbay he lost his balance and kept from falling only by grabbing the doorjamb.

Someone took him by the shoulder.

"You'd better lie down again," David Marcus said. Chekov remembered him vaguely and dimly from the painful haze of Regulus I.

"I can't," Chekov said. "I must get to the bridge—Mister Sulu—"

"Hey, look—"

"*Pazhalsta,*" Chekov said, "help me, *bozhemoi,* the ship has nothing but children on its crew!"

David hesitated. Chekov wondered if he would have to try to fight him to get out of sickbay.

David slung Chekov's arm across his shoulder and helped him toward the lift.

Chekov could never have made it to the bridge without Marcus's help. Even half-supported, he felt like he was struggling through a whirlpool.

As the lift doors opened Chekov drew away from David Marcus: Admiral Kirk would send him back if he could not even make it to the bridge on his own feet. David seemed to understand, and let him go without argument.

Chekov walked carefully across the upper level, took a deep breath, and managed to navigate the stairs without falling. At Kirk's elbow he stopped.

"Sir, could you use another hand?"

Kirk glanced at him, startled. Then he smiled.

"Take your place at weapons console, Mister Chekov."

"Thank you, sir."

At the science officer's station, Mister Spock tried to make something of the distorted readings his sensors were receiving.

"Spock, can you find him?"

"The energy readings are sporadic and indeterminate, but they could indicate extreme radial acceleration under full impulse power. Port side, aft."

"He won't stop now," Kirk said. "He's followed me this far; he'll be back. But where the hell *from?*"

Spock considered.

"Admiral," he said. "Khan's intelligence cannot make up for his lack of experience. All the maneuvering *Reliant* has done, bold though it may be, has occurred in a single plane. He takes advantage neither of the full abilities of his ship nor of the possibilities inherent in three degrees of freedom."

Kirk glanced back at him and grinned. "A masterful analysis, Mister Spock. Lieutenant Saavik, all stop."

Saavik decelerated to zero relative motion.

"All stop, sir."

"Full thrust ninety degrees from our previous course: straight down."

"Aye, sir."

"Mister Chekov, stand by photon torpedoes."

"Aye, sir."

The *Enterprise* plunged downward into the shadows of the nebula.

Khan sought any sign of Kirk in the mangled image on his viewscreen. All around him lay the wreckage of the bridge and the bodies of his people. A few moaned, still alive, but he no longer cared. This was a battle to the death. He would be glad to die if he took James Kirk with him.

He scanned the space surrounding *Reliant,* but found nothing. Nothing at all—only the impenetrable energy fields of the nebula.

"Where is Kirk?" he cried. "Where in the land of Hades is he?'

Nothing, no one, replied.

The *Enterprise* hovered within the Mutara Nebula's great dust-cloud. The ship was blind and deaf. Jim Kirk forced himself to sit quiet and relaxed as if nothing worried him. It was the biggest act of his life. The ship was badly hurt; every score of *Reliant*'s weapons had touched him as painfully as any physical blow. And in truth, he had no idea what Khan would try next. He could only estimate, and guess, and hope.

At the helm, Saavik glanced at him with a questioning expression.

"Hold steady, lieutenant," he said.

She nodded once and turned back to her position. Chekov never moved. He hunched over the weapons console. He had looked terrible when he came in, pale and sick and dizzy. But the truth was Kirk needed him; the ship needed him. With Sulu gone—Kirk glanced around the bridge and saw that David had returned. He gestured to him. The young man came down the stairs and stopped beside the captain's seat.

"How's Sulu?"

"They don't know yet," David said. "His hands are a mess—he'll be in therapy for a while. If he lives. They wouldn't say. He might have brain damage."

"You got to him fast," Jim said. "He'd be dead if you hadn't. You gave him the one chance he had. Whatever happens—David, I'm proud of you."

To Jim's surprise and shock, David reacted with a curse.

"What the hell right have you got to be proud of me?" he said angrily.

He stormed back to the upper level of the bridge and stood scowling with his arms folded across his chest. He ignored Jim Kirk's gaze.

Jim turned back to the viewscreen, angry and hurt.

"Stand by photon torpedoes," he snapped at Chekov.

"Photon torpedoes ready, sir."

The interchange with David had broken Jim's concentration. He felt irritated and foolish to have tried to make peace and friends with the boy and to have been so thoroughly rebuffed. It served him right for thinking about personal matters when the ship was in danger. He forced himself back to the problem at hand.

"Lieutenant Saavik."

"Aye, sir."

He had been tempted to say, "Dive! dive! dive!" earlier, but refrained; now he kept himself from ordering the young Vulcan officer to let the ship surface. This was not, after all, a submarine, and they were not hunting an enemy U-boat.

Too many old novels, Jim, he thought.

If he failed, his crew would have not a comforting sea to receive them, but unforgiving vacuum filled with nothing but radiation.

"Accelerate. Full impulse power at course zero and plus ninety. Just until the sensors clear." That would get them out of the worst of the dust. "Then all stop."

"Aye, sir," she said, and executed the command.

The artificial gravity was holding, but at a level tentative enough that Kirk could feel the acceleration: straight up. The viewscreen was still dead, but as they rose out of the gas cloud it slowly cleared.

The roiling mass of dust and gases draped away from Jim Kirk's ship like the sea around the flanks of a huge ocean mammal. They rose: and *Reliant* lay full ahead.

Bull's-eye! Jim Kirk thought.

"Mister Chekov—!"

"Torpedoes ready, sir!"

"Fire!"

Chekov fired.

The torpedoes streaked away.

In the pure silence of hard vacuum, the torpedoes touched the enemy ship and exploded. *Reliant*'s starboard engine nacelle collapsed, spun, tumbled, and gracefully, quietly, exploded.

Reliant responded not at all. The ship drifted steady on its course.

"Cease fire," Kirk said. "Look sharp."

The bridge crew reacted with silence, watching, waiting. Too soon to be certain. . . .

"Match course, Lieutenant," Kirk said to Saavik.

She obeyed: the *Enterprise* followed *Reliant*, maneuvering slightly till their relative speeds were zero, and *Reliant* appeared dead in space.

"Our power levels are extremely low, sir," Lieutenant Saavik said.

Kirk switched the intercom to the engine room. "Mister Scott, how long before you can get the mains back online?"

"At least ten minutes, sir, I canna send anyone in till after decontamination."

Kirk glowered and snapped the channel off. "Commander Uhura, send to Commander, *Reliant:* Prepare to be boarded."

"Aye, sir."

Her long, fine hands moved on her instruments.

"Commander, *Reliant,* this is *U.S.S. Enterprise.* Surrender and stand by for boarding. I repeat: Stand by for boarding."

Lying on the deck of the bridge of *Reliant,* Khan heard the triumph of the *Enterprise* communications officer. He groaned and forced himself to sit up. He would not accept defeat. Blood ran down the side of his face, and his right arm was shattered. He could see the bone protruding from his forearm. He felt the pain and accepted it, then put it aside. Shock intoxicated him and put a fine edge on his anger.

He crawled to his feet. His crushed arm flopped against his side. He picked up his useless right hand and thrust it beneath his belt, holding it steady and out of his way.

"No, Kirk," he whispered. He smiled. "Our game is not over yet. I am not quite prepared to concede."

"*Reliant,* stand by and prepare for boarding." The viewscreen was dead, but Khan did not need it to know that the *Enterprise* was approaching him, secure and arrogant in the certainty of its conquest.

Khan staggered from the bridge, toward the storage bay. . . .

Laughing.

Back on the *Enterprise,* Mister Spock kept a close eye on his instruments and waited for a reply from *Reliant.* Perhaps Khan had been killed in the final barrage. Perhaps.

Spock did not believe it. The engines, both impulse and warp, were destroyed, and the bridge had been damaged, but he saw no evidence of a break in the hull in that area.

"*Enterprise* to *Reliant,*" Commander Uhura said again. "You are to surrender your vessel and prepare for boarding by order of Admiral James T. Kirk, Starfleet General Command."

Nothing.

"I'm sorry, sir," Uhura said. "No response."

Kirk stood up. "We'll beam aboard. Alert the transporter room."

Spock's attention was drawn to an odd energy pattern on one of his sensors. He focused and traced it: *Reliant.*

"Admiral, *Reliant* is emitting the wave form of an energy source I have never before encountered."

David Marcus, from his place near the turbolift, frowned and hurried to the science officer's station. He leaned over to look at Spock's sensor.

"My God in heaven," he said.

Spock raised one eyebrow.

"It's the Genesis wave!" Marcus said.

"What?"

Marcus turned toward Admiral Kirk. His face paled.

"Khan has Genesis!" David Marcus said. "He's armed it! It's building up to detonation!"

"How long—?"

"If he kept our programming . . . four minutes."

"Shit," Kirk said. He leaped up the stairs and slammed his hand against the turbo-lift controls. "We can beam aboard and stop it! Mister Spock—"

"You can't stop it!" David cried. "Once it's started there's no turning back!"

Kirk rushed back to his place and stabbed the intercom buttons.

"Scotty!"

Kirk received no answer but static. He spoke anyway.

"Scotty, I need warp speed in three minutes or we've had it!"

The intercom crackled. No reply.

Spock watched all that occurred. He knew what Mister Scott would say if he could even be reached: Decontamination would take at least another six minutes, and no human being would last long enough in the radiation flux even to begin the jury-rigging necessary to bring main engines online. He knew, from studying the Marcuses' data, the incredible velocity of the Genesis wave, and he knew the speed his ship could go under damaged impulse engines. It was no match.

"Scotty!"

Spock made a decision.

"Saavik!" Kirk said. "Get us out of here, full impulse power!"

"Aye, sir." She was prepared: at the order, the *Enterprise* spun one hundred eighty degrees in place and crawled away from *Reliant.*

Spock permitted himself a moment of pride. Saavik would make a fine officer: she would fulfill the potential he had detected in the filthy, barbarous, half-breed Hellguard child. He wished he would be able to guide her a little further.

But this way, she would be freer to find her own path.

When the doors to the turbolift opened, responding to Jim Kirk's abandoned order, Spock stepped inside.

Khan Noonian Singh felt hot blood flowing from his temple, from his arm, inside his body. He coughed blood and spat it out. His cold hand caressed the Genesis torpedo. It was armed and ready.

He staggered and fell to his knees.

"No," he said. "No, I will not die here. . . ."

He stumbled into the turbolift. It pressed upward beneath him. When it reached the bridge, he had to crawl to leave it. He collapsed finally at the top of the stairs, but he could see the viewscreen.

The *Enterprise* crept away at a painfully slow speed. Khan began to laugh. The pain caught up to him, and he coughed. He was bleeding into his lungs, into his belly. He did not have much time. But it would be enough.

"You cannot escape me, James Kirk," he murmured. "Hades has taken me, but from his heart I stab thee. . . ."

He watched the *Enterprise,* turned tail and fleeing, terrified. He laughed.

Agony took him, and he cried.

"For hate's sake . . . I spit my last breath at thee. . . ."

Joachim's body lay only an arm's length from him. His wife's body, dust, lay half a light-year distant. Soon neither space nor time would have any meaning, and he would join his love and his friend.

He crawled to Joachim, reached out, and touched his rigid hand.
Darkness enclosed his spirit.

Spock entered the engine room. Scarlet warning lights flashed through it, bloodying the forms of its crew. Doctor McCoy knelt in the middle of the main chamber, trying to save the life of an injured crew member.

The rest of the crew struggled to put more power to the impulse engines, knowing—they *must* know—that their efforts were useless. When the Genesis wave began, it would spread until it reached hard vacuum, engulfing and degrading every atom of matter within the Mutara Nebula, gas or solid, living or dead.

Without speaking or acknowledging his presence, Spock strode past Doctor McCoy to the main reactor room. He touched the override control.

"Are you out of your Vulcan mind?"

McCoy grabbed his shoulder and dragged him around by sheer force of will, for certainly the doctor's strength could not match Spock's.

Without replying, Spock looked at the doctor. He felt detached from everything: from the ship, from their peril, from the universe itself.

"No human can tolerate the radiation in there!" McCoy cried.

"But Doctor," Spock said, feeling a certain terribly un-Vulcan affection for the man who opposed him, "you yourself are fond of pointing out that I am not human."

"You can't go in there, Spock!"

Spock smiled at Doctor McCoy. He was so completely and comfortingly predictable. Spock could go through their conversation in his mind and know everything the doctor would say, everything he himself would reply. The result was the same.

"I regret there is no time for logical argument, Doctor," he said. "I have enjoyed our conversations in the past."

With that peculiarly human atavistic instinct for danger, McCoy drew back, knowing what he planned. But Spock was too quick for him. His fingers found the nerve in the junction of McCoy's neck and shoulder. He exerted pressure. McCoy's eyes rolled back, and he collapsed. Spock caught him and lowered him gently to the deck.

"You have been a worthy opponent and friend," he said.

He finished the coding for the manual override of the reactor room and stepped into the screaming radiation flux.

At first it was quite pleasant, like sunlight. Spock moved toward the reactor. The radiation increased, and his body interpreted it as heat.

He reached toward the damping rods. An aura of radiation haloed his hands; the rays spread forward, outward, even back, penetrating his body. He could see his own blood vessels, his bones. It was most fascinating.

As he worked, he recalled the events in his life that had given him intellectual, and even—he could admit it now, and who was to despise him?—emotional pleasure. Fragments of music—Respighi, Q'orn, Chalmers—and particular insights in physics and mathematics. Bits of friendship, and even love, which he never could acknowledge.

He drew the rods from their clamps; the radiation caressed him like a betraying lover.

He accepted the regrets of his life, the expectations he had never been able to fulfill: neither Vulcan nor human, he was unable to satisfy either part of his heritage. Perhaps his uniqueness compensated in some small way. He had tried to convey that possibility to Saavik, who must face and overcome the same trials.

Radiation sang in his ears, almost blocking the cries of Mister Scott and Doctor McCoy, on the other side of the radiation-proof glass, shrieking at him to come out, come out.

"Captain, please—!" Scott screamed.

The only real captain of the *Enterprise* was and ever had been James Kirk. Spock had kept the ship in trust; but now it was time to return it to its true master.

Spock could feel the very cells of his body succumbing to the radiation. He wiped the perspiration from his face and left a smear of dark blood on his sleeve. Mottled hematomata spread across his hands.

Pain crept from his nerve ends to his backbone, toward his mind, and he could no longer hold it distant.

He flexed his fingers around the manual control that would bring the main engines back into use. He strained against it, and the wheel began to turn. His tortured bones and flesh opposed the control under which he held himself. He could feel his skin disintegrating against the smooth metal, which grew slick with his blood.

"Dear God, Spock, get out of there, man!" McCoy pounded on the glass.

Spock smiled to himself. It was far too late.

The main engines groaned, and protested, and burst back into use.

The bridge main viewscreen showed *Reliant* receding, but slowly, so slowly.

"Time!" Jim Kirk said again. It could be no more than a minute since last he had asked: they had a few seconds left and no more.

"Three minutes, thirty seconds," Saavik said.

"Distance from *Reliant*."

"Four hundred kilometers," Chekov said.

Jim glanced at David. Meeting his gaze, his son shook his head.

"Main engines online!" Chekov shouted.

"Bless you, Scotty," Kirk said. "Saavik—*go!*"

She pushed the ship into warp speed without any proper preparation.

Reliant dwindled to a speck in the viewscreen.

The speck became light.

The Genesis wave hurtled toward them through the nebular dust, dissolving everything in its path. Jim watched, his hands clenched. Saavik forced one more warp factor out of the straining ship, and it plunged from the nebula into deep space.

The huge collapsed cloud began to spiral around the nexus that had been *Reliant*. It quickly coalesced, shrinking behind them. Kirk watched, awed.

"Reduce speed," he said softly.

Saavik complied. The new planet stabilized in their sight.

The turbolift doors opened, and Carol Marcus came onto the bridge. She did not speak.

Jim heard her, turned, reached toward her.

"Carol, my God, look at it . . ." It was so beautiful it made him want to cry. Carol took his hand.

Kirk opened a channel to the engine room.

"Well done, Scotty," he said.

He glanced over his shoulder at the science officer's station.

"Spock—"

He stopped, looked around the bridge, and frowned.

"Where's Spock?"

In front of him, Saavik shuddered. Her shoulders slumped. She did not face him.

"He left," she whispered. "He went . . . to the engine room." She covered her face with her hands.

Kirk stared at her, horrified.

"Jim!" McCoy's voice was harsh and intense over the intercom. "I'm in the engine room. *Get down here, Jim—hurry!*"

For the first time since he began his pursuit of Khan Singh, James Kirk felt cold fear.

"Saavik, take the conn!"

He sprinted for the lift.

Nine

Jim Kirk pounded down the corridors of his ship. They had never seemed so long, so cold.

He caught himself against the entryway of the engine room. It was a shambles: every emergency light flashing, sirens wailing, injured crew members moaning as the medical team tended to them.

He finally managed to catch his breath.

"Spock—?"

Scott and McCoy, near the impenetrable glass panels of the reactor room, turned toward him with horror in their faces. He understood instantly what had happened, what Spock had done. Jim forced his way past them to the hatch control. Scott dragged him away.

"Ye canna do it, sir, the radiation level—"

"He'll die!"

McCoy grabbed his shoulders. "He's dead, Jim. He's already dead."

"Oh, God. . . ."

Jim pressed against the heavy glass window, shielding away reflections and light with his arms and hands.

On his hands and knees, trying to stand up, Mister Spock hunched beside the door.

"Spock!"

Spock barely raised his head, hearing Jim's voice through the thick panel. He reached for the intercom, his hand bloody and shaking.

"Spock. . . ." Jim said softly.

"The ship . . . ?" His face was horribly burned, and the pain in his voice made Jim want to scream with grief.

"Out of danger, out of the Genesis wave. Thanks to you, Spock."

Spock fought for breath.

"Spock, damn, oh, damn—"

"Don't grieve. The good of the many . . ."

". . . outweighs the good of the few," Kirk whispered. But found he no longer believed it; or even if he did, he did not care. Not this time.

"Or the one." Spock dragged himself to his feet, and pressed his bleeding hand against the glass.

Jim matched it with his own, as if somehow he could touch Spock's mind through the glass, take some of his pain upon himself, give his friend some of his own strength. But he could not even touch him.

"Don't . . . grieve. . . ." Spock said again. "It had to be done. I alone could do it. Therefore it was logical. . . ."

Damn your logic, Spock, Jim thought. Tears spilled down his face. He could barely see.

"I never faced *Kobayashi Maru,*" Spock said. His voice was failing; he had to stop and draw in a long shuddering breath before he could continue. "I wondered what my response would be. Not . . . I fear . . . an original solution. . . ."

"Spock!"

Saavik's voice broke in over the intercom.

"Captain, the Genesis world is forming. Mister Spock, it's so beautiful—"

Infuriated, Kirk slammed the channel closed, cutting off Saavik's voice. But Spock nodded, his eyes closed, and perhaps, just a little, he smiled.

"Jim," he said, "I have been, and will be, your friend. I am grateful for that. Live long, and prosper. . . ."

His long fingers clenched into seared claws; the agony of the assault of radiation overcame him. He fell.

"Spock!" Jim cried. He pounded the glass with his fists. "Oh, God, no . . . !"

McCoy tried to make him leave. Jim snarled and thrust him violently away. He hunched against the window, his mind crying denial and disbelief.

Much later that night, Lieutenant Saavik moved silently through the dim corridors of the *Enterprise.* She saw no one: only a few crew members remained on duty, forced to grapple with their exhaustion.

When she reached the stasis room, she paused, reluctant to enter. She drew a deep breath and went into the darkness.

Far too many of the stasis boxes radiated the faint blue glow that showed they were in operation. Protected by the stasis fields, the body of Peter Preston and the bodies of the other people who had died on this mission waited to be returned to their families.

But Captain Spock's will stated that he was not to be taken to Vulcan; his wishes would be respected.

His sealed coffin stood in the middle of the chamber. Saavik laid one hand against its sleek side. Her grief was so intense that she could react with neither rage nor tears.

In the morning, James Kirk had decreed, Spock's body would be consigned to space and to a fast-decaying orbit around the Genesis world, where it would burn in the atmosphere to ashes, to nothing.

Saavik sat cross-legged in the corner, rested her hands on her knees, and closed her eyes. She could not have explained to anyone why she was here, for her reason was irrational.

On Hellguard, if someone died at night and was not watched, their body would be gone by morning, stripped by scavengers and torn to bits by animals. Seldom was anyone buried. Saavik had never cared enough about anyone on Hellguard to remain with them through the night.

Captain Spock and Peter Preston did not need a guard, not here on the *Enterprise*. But this gesture was the only one she could make to them, the only two people she had ever cared about in the universe.

She stayed.

She hoped Spock had heard her before he died. She had wanted him to know that Genesis worked, partly because he had respected the people who built it, so many of whom had died to protect it, but primarily because its formation meant his sacrifice had been meaningful. The creation was the result of destruction, and the *Enterprise* and all its crew would have been caught up in that instant's cataclysm had Spock failed to act as he did. Saavik had wanted Spock to know the destruction had ended, and the creation had begun.

She knew Admiral Kirk misunderstood what she had done, and why. But Saavik's essential inner core had dictated her actions then, as it did now. Admiral Kirk's opinion was of no significance.

Tears slid down Saavik's face.

Yet she remained free of the madness. Rage was absent from her sorrow. She hoped, someday, that she might understand why. Someday.

The hours passed, and Saavik let her thoughts wander. She remembered hiding, shivering and hungry, hoping to steal a piece of bread or a discarded shred of warming-fabric, outside the Vulcan exploration party's Hellguard camp. Saavik had spied on the Vulcans as they argued till dawn, with unvarying courtesy and considerable venom, about the Romulans' castoffs, particularly the half-breed children.

That was the first time Saavik had had any idea who and what she was. Only Spock had given her the potential for something more.

When, during the final battle with Khan, Saavik realized Spock had left the bridge, she *knew* what he planned and what the result would be. She had been a moment away from trying to stop him.

Only the control he had taught her had kept her at her post, because it was her duty. She had regretted her action—her failure to act—ever since. In death Spock affected all those around him, just as he had in life. Someone should have taken his place whose passing no one would lament.

She might have been able to stop him: though his experience was enormously greater, Saavik was younger than he, and faster.

If she *had* been able to stop him, would she have had the courage to take his place? She wanted to believe she would have; for had she not, everyone on the ship would be dead, dissolved into sub-elementary particles and reformed into the substance of the Genesis world.

Saavik had no belief in soul or afterlife. She had read various philosophies; she accepted none. A person died; scavengers destroyed the body. That was all.

Yet as the hours passed and her concentration deepened, her feeling that somehow, somewhere, Spock's consciousness retained some of its integrity grew stronger.

"Spock," she said aloud, "can you see what has happened? Are you there? Are you anywhere? A world has formed; the Genesis wave is still resonating within the nebula, forming a new sun to give the world light and sustain its life. Soon the wave will die away, and the universe will have another star system. But it will be one among millions, one among billions, and you taught me to value uniqueness. Your uniqueness is gone."

Suddenly she opened her eyes. She thought, for a moment, she had heard something, some reply—

Saavik shook her head. The strange hours before morning could give one any mad thought.

Mister Sulu woke slowly, coming to consciousness in the dim night illumination of sickbay. He had a raging headache, he felt as if someone were sitting on his chest, and his hands hurt. He tried to get up.

A moment later, Doctor Chapel was at his side. She made him lie down again.

"What happened?" His voice came out a hoarse croak. He tried to clear his throat. "Why—"

"The oxygen dries your throat," Doctor Chapel said. "It will go away." She held a glass so he could take a sip of water.

"We've been pretty worried about you," she said. "You're all right, though; everything's going to be all right."

He tried to touch the sore spot in the middle of his chest, but the palms of his hands were covered with pseudoskin, and he could not feel anything. He realized what the soreness must be. He frowned.

"Did I have to be resuscitated?" he asked.

Chapel nodded. "David Marcus saved your life."

"I don't remember. . . ."

"You shouldn't expect to. You were nearly electrocuted. A little memory loss is normal. Your brain scan is fine."

"What about Khan?"

"Dead." She stood up. "Go back to sleep, Hikaru." He reached out: his hands were too stiff to stop her, but she paused.

"Chris," he said, "something more is wrong. What is it? Please."

"Mister Spock," she said very softly.

"Spock—! What—?"

"He's dead."

"Oh, gods. . . ."

Chris Chapel started to cry. She hurried away.

Sulu stayed where he was, stunned with disbelief.

Jim Kirk sat alone in the dark of his cabin. He had not moved in hours; his mind kept turning in circles, smaller and smaller, tighter and tighter.

Someone knocked on his door.

He did not answer.

A pause. The knock again, a little louder.

"What do you *want?*" he cried. "Leave me alone!"

The door opened, and Carol stood silhouetted in the light from the corridor outside. She came in and closed the door.

"No, Jim," she said. "I won't leave you alone. Not this time." She knelt before him and took his hands in hers.

He slumped down; his forehead rested on their clasped hands.

"Carol, I just don't . . . I keep thinking, there must be something I could have done, that I should have done—" He shuddered and caught his breath, fighting the tears.

"I know," Carol said. "Oh, Jim, I know." She put her arms around him. As Jim had held her when she grieved for her friends, she held him.

When he slipped into an exhausted, troubled sleep, she eased him down on the couch, took off his boots, and covered him with a blanket from his bed. She kissed him lightly. Then, since there was nothing else she could do for him, she did leave him alone.

When morning came, Saavik rose smoothly from her place in the corner of the stasis room. She had found a measure of serenity in her vigil, a counterweight to her grief. She bid a final farewell to her teacher, and to her student, and left the stasis room. She had many duties to take care of, duties to the ship, and to Mister Spock.

The ship's company assembled, in full dress, at 0800 hours. Saavik took her place at the torpedo guidance console and programmed in the course she had selected.

Accompanied by Carol Marcus and David Marcus and Doctor McCoy, Admiral Kirk came in last.

The ship's veterans, the people who had known Mister Spock best, stood together in a small group: Mister Sulu, Commander Uhura, Doctor Chapel, Mister Chekov, Mister Scott. They all watched the admiral, who looked tired and drawn. He stood before the crew of the *Enterprise,* staring at the deck, not speaking.

He took a deep breath, squared his shoulders, and faced them.

"We have assembled here," he said, "in accordance with Starfleet traditions, to pay final respects to one of our own. To honor our dead . . ." He paused a long time. ". . . and to grieve for a beloved comrade who gave his life in place of ours. He did not think his sacrifice a vain or empty one, and we cannot question his choice, in these proceedings.

"He died in the shadow of a new world, a world he had hoped to see. He lived just long enough to know it had come into being."

Beside Admiral Kirk, Doctor McCoy tried to keep from breaking down, but failed. He stared straight ahead, with tears spilling down his cheeks.

"Of my friend," Admiral Kirk said, "I can only say that of all the souls I have encountered his was—" he looked from face to face around the company of old friends, new ones, strangers; he saw Doctor McCoy crying, "—the most human."

Admiral Kirk's voice faltered. He paused a moment, tried to continue, but could not go on. "Lieutenant Saavik," he said softly.

Saavik armed the torpedo guidance control with the course she had so carefully worked out, and moved forward.

"We embrace the memory of our brother, our teacher." Her words were inadequate, and she knew it. "With love, we commit his body to the depths of space."

Commander Sulu moved from the line. "Honors: *hut.*"

The ship's company saluted. Mister Scott began to play his strange musical instrument. It filled the chamber with a plaintive wail, a dirge that was all too appropriate.

The pallbearers lifted Spock's black coffin into the launching chamber. It hummed closed, and the aiming lock snapped into place.

Saavik nodded an order to the torpedo officer. He fired the missile.

With a great roar of igniting propellant, the chamber reverberated. The bagpipes stopped. Silence, eerie and complete, settled over the room. The company watched the dark torpedo streak away against the silver-blue shimmer of the new world, until the coffin shrank and vanished.

Sulu waited; then said, "Return: *hut.*"

Saavik and the rest returned to attention.

"Lieutenant," the admiral said.

"Yes, sir."

"The watch is yours," he said quietly. "Set a course for Alpha Ceti V to pick up *Reliant*'s survivors."

"Aye, sir."

"I'll be in my quarters. But unless it's an emergency . . ."

"Understood, sir."

"Dismiss the company."

He started out of the room. He saw Carol, but he could not say to her what he wanted to—not here, not now; he saw David, watching him intently. The young man took a step toward him.

Jim Kirk turned on his heel and left.

Saavik dismissed the company. She gazed one last time at the new planet.

"Lieutenant—"

She turned. David Marcus had hung back from the others, waiting for her.

"Yes, Doctor Marcus?"

"Can we stop the formality? My name's David. Can I call you Saavik?"

"If you wish."

"I wanted to tell you that I'm sorry about Mister Spock."

"I, too," she said.

"When we talked the other day—I could tell how much you cared about him. I'm sorry it sounded like I was insulting him. I didn't mean it that way. To him or to you."

"I know," she said. "I was very harsh to you, and I regret it. Starfleet has brought you only grief and tragedy. . . ."

David, too, glanced at the new planet, which his friends on Spacelab had helped to design.

"Yeah," he said softly. "I'll miss those folks, a *lot*. It was such a damned waste. . . ."

"They sacrificed themselves for your life, as Spock gave himself for us. When I took the *Kobayashi Maru* test—" She paused to see if David remembered the conversation, back on Regulus I. He nodded. "—Admiral Kirk told me that the way one faces death is at least as important as how one faces life."

David looked thoughtful, and glanced the way James Kirk had gone, but of course his father had long since departed.

"Do you believe, now, that he is your father?" Saavik asked.

He started. "No. Maybe. I don't know."

Saavik smiled. "We perhaps have something in common, David. Do you remember what *you* said to *him?*"

"When?"

"When you tried to kill him. You called him, if my memory serves me properly, a 'dumb bastard.' "

"I guess I did. So?"

"He is not—to my knowledge—a bastard. But I am. And if Admiral Kirk *is* your father, then I believe the terminology, in its traditional sense, fits you as well."

He stared at her for a moment, then laughed. "I'm beginning to think the 'dumb' part fits me even better."

He reached out quickly and touched her hand.

"I really want to talk to you some more," he said suddenly. "But there's something I have to do first."

"I must return to the bridge," Saavik said. "It is my watch."

"Later on—can I buy you a cup of coffee?"

"That would be difficult: one cannot buy anything on board the *Enterprise.*"

"Sorry. That was kind of a joke."

"Oh," Saavik said, not understanding.

"I just meant, can we get together in a while? When you're free?"

"I would like that," Saavik said, rather surprised at her own reply and remembering what Mister Spock had said about making her own choices.

"Great. See you soon."

He hurried down the corridor, and Saavik returned to the bridge.

The admiral closed the door of his cabin behind him and leaned against it, desperately grateful that the ceremony was over. He wondered what Spock would have thought of it all: the ritual, the speeches. . . . He would have said it was illogical, no doubt.

Jim Kirk unfastened his dress jacket, pulled it off, and pitched it angrily across the room. He dragged a bottle of brandy off the shelf and poured himself a shot. He glared at the amber liquor for a while, then shoved it away.

Too many ghosts hovered around him, and he did not want to draw them any closer by lowering his defenses with alcohol. He flung himself down on the couch. The blanket Carol had tucked around him the night before lay crumpled on the floor.

He smelled the pleasant, musty odor of old paper. He tried to ignore it, failed, and reached for the book Spock had given him. It was heavy and solid in his hands, the leather binding a little scuffed, the cut edges of the pages softly rough in his hands. Jim let it fall open. The print blurred.

He dug into his pockets for his glasses. When he finally found them, one of the lenses was shattered. Jim stared at the cracked, spidery pattern.

"Damn!" he said. "Damn—" He laid the book very carefully on the table; he laid the glasses, half-folded, on top of it.

He covered his eyes.

The door chimed. At first he did not move; then he sat up, rubbed his face with both hands, and cleared his throat.

"Yes," he said. "Come."

The door opened. David Marcus came in, and the door slid closed behind him. Jim stood up, but then he had nowhere to go.

"Look, I don't mean to intrude—" David said.

"Uh, no, that's all right, it's just that I ought to be on the bridge."

David let him pass, but before Jim got to the door his son said, "Are you running away from me?"

Jim stopped and faced David again.

"Yes," he said. "I guess I am." He gestured for him to sit. David sat on the couch, and Jim sat in the chair angled toward it. They looked at each other uncomfortably for a while.

"Would you like a drink?" Jim asked.

David glanced at the abandoned snifter of brandy on the table; Jim realized how odd it must look.

"No," David said. "But thanks, anyway."

Jim tried to think of something to say to the stranger in his sitting room.

"I'm not exactly what you expected, am I?" David said.

"I didn't *expect* anything," Jim told him ruefully.

David's grin was crooked, a little embarrassed. "That makes two of us." His grin faded. "Are you okay?"

"What do you mean?"

"Lieutenant Saavik was right . . . You've never faced death."

"Not like this," Jim admitted reluctantly. "I never faced it—I cheated it; I played a trick and felt proud of myself for it and got rewarded for my ingenuity." He rubbed his eyes with one hand. "I know *nothing*," he said.

"You told Saavik that how we face death is at least as important as how we face life."

Jim frowned. "How do you know that?"

"She told me."

"It was just words."

"Maybe you ought to listen to them."

"I'm trying, David."

"So am I. The people who died on Spacelab were friends of mine."

"I know," Jim said. "David, I'm truly sorry."

The uncomfortable silence crept over them again. David stood up.

"I want to apologize," he said. "I misjudged you. And yesterday, when you tried to thank me—" He shrugged, embarrassed. "I'm sorry."

"No," Jim said. "You were perfectly correct. Being proud of someone is like taking some of the credit for what they do or how they act. I have no right to take any of the credit for you."

He, too, stood up, as David appeared to be leaving.

"Then maybe I shouldn't—" David stopped. Then he said, very fast, "What I really came here to say is that *I'm* proud—proud to be your son."

Jim was too startled to reply. David shrugged and strode toward the door.

"David—"

The young man swung abruptly back. "What?" he said with a harsh note in his voice.

Jim grabbed him and hugged him hard. After a moment, David returned the embrace.

Epilogue

On the bridge of the *Enterprise,* Lieutenant Saavik checked their course and prepared for warp speed. The viewscreen showed the Genesis world slowly shrinking behind them. Doctor McCoy and Doctor Marcus, senior, watched it and spoke together in low tones. Saavik worked at concentrating hard enough not to notice what they were saying. They were discussing the admiral, and it was quite clearly intended to be a private conversation.

The bridge doors opened. Saavik, in the captain's chair, glanced around. She stood up.

"Admiral on the bridge!"

"At ease," Jim Kirk said quickly. David Marcus followed him out of the turbolift.

Doctor McCoy and Carol Marcus glanced at each other. McCoy raised one eyebrow, and Carol gave him a quick smile.

"Hello, Bones," Kirk said. "Hi, Carol. . . ." He took her hand and squeezed it gently.

"On course to Alpha Ceti, Admiral," Saavik said. "All is well."

"Good." He sat down. "Lieutenant, I believe you're acquainted with my . . . my son."

"Yes, sir." She caught David's gaze. He blushed a little; to Saavik's surprise, she did too.

"Would you show him around, please?"

"Certainly, sir." She ushered David to the upper level of the bridge. When they reached the science officer's station, she said to him, softly, straight-faced, "I see that you did, after all, turn out to be a bastard."

James Kirk heard her and stared at her, shocked.

"That is a . . . 'little joke,' " she said.

"A private one," David added. "And the operative word is 'dumb.' "

Saavik smiled; David laughed.

Jim Kirk smiled, too, if a bit quizzically.

McCoy leaned on the back of the captain's chair, gazing at the viewscreen.

"Will you look at that," he said. "It's incredible. Think they'll name it after you, Doctor Marcus?"

"Not if I can help it," she said. "*We'll* name it. For our friends."

Jim thought about the book Spock had given him. He was remembering a line at the end: "It is a far, far better thing that I do, than I have ever done; it is a far, far better rest that I go to, than I have ever known." He could not quite imagine Spock's questing spirit finally at rest.

Carol put her hand on his. "Jim—?"

"I was just thinking of something. . . . Something Spock tried to tell me on my birthday."

"Jim, are you okay?" McCoy asked. "How do you feel?"

"I feel . . ." He thought for a moment. The grief would be with him a long time, but there were a lot of good memories, too. "I feel young, Doctor, believe it or not. Reborn. As young as Carol's new world."

He glanced back at Lieutenant Saavik and at David.

"Set our course for the second star to the right, Lieutenant. 'The second star to the right, and straight on till morning.' "

He was ready to explain that that, too, was a little joke, but she surprised him.

"Aye, sir." Saavik sounded not the least bit perplexed. She changed the viewscreen; it sparkled into an image of the dense starfield ahead. "Warp factor three, Helm Officer."

"Warp three, aye."

The *Enterprise* leaped toward the distant stars.

The Search for Spock

The needs of the one

One

Spock was dead.

The company of the *Enterprise* gathered together on the recreation deck to remember their friend.

Doctor Leonard McCoy, ship's surgeon, moved half a pace into the circle. As he raised his glass in a final toast, he glanced at each of his compatriots in turn.

Admiral James Kirk and Doctor Carol Marcus stood on either side of Carol's grown son, David Marcus. David was Jim's son, as well, unknown until now, but now acknowledged.

Commander Uhura, Chief Engineer Montgomery Scott, Commander Pavel Chekov, and Hikaru Sulu, recently promoted to commander, had clustered together along one arc of the circle. Every member of the ship's company showed the strain of the harrowing past few days, except Lieutenant Saavik. Her Vulcan training required her to be imperturbable, and so she appeared. If her Romulan upbringing gave her the capacity to feel grief or loss or anger at the death of Spock, her teacher, McCoy could see no shadow of the emotions.

McCoy had known the rest of the ship's company, the trainees, only a short time, not even long enough to learn their names. He knew for sure only that they were terribly young.

"To Spock," McCoy said. "He gave his life for ours."

"To Spock," they replied in unison, except for Jim, who brought his attention back to the ship from some other time, some other place, a thousand light-years distant.

A moment after the others had spoken, he said, "To Spock."

Everyone else drank. McCoy put his glass to his lips. The pungent odor of Kentucky bourbon rose around his face. He grimaced. The liquor was raw and new, straight out of the ship's synthesizer. He had nothing better. The *Enterprise*'s mission had been an emergency, an unexpected voyage into tragedy, and Leonard McCoy had come most poorly prepared.

He lowered the drink without tasting it.

"To Peter," Montgomery Scott said. His young nephew, Cadet Peter Preston, had also died in the battle that took Spock's life. Scott made as if to say more, could not get out the words, and instead drained his glass in one gulp. Again, McCoy could not bring himself to choke down any liquor.

When all the glasses had been refilled, David Marcus stepped forward.

"To our friends on Spacelab," he said.

McCoy pretended to drink. He felt as if the alcohol fumes alone were making him drunk.

When no one else came forward to propose a toast, the quiet circle dissolved into small groups. Almost everyone had begun to feel the effects of the liquor, but the drinking was a futile effort to numb their grief.

Whose stupid idea was it to have a wake, anyway? McCoy wondered. Who thought this would help? And then he remembered, Oh, right, it was me and Scott.

He orbited the serving table. It gleamed with an array of bottles. He picked one up, paying little attention to what it was, and filled another glass. McCoy and Scott had spent all day preparing for the wake. The synthesizer had tried to keep up with their programming, but it was badly overloaded. Ethyl alcohol was a simple enough chemical, but the congeners any decent liquor required were foreign to the ship's data banks. Everything smelled the same: strong and rough.

Montgomery Scott beetled toward McCoy, stopped, and gazed blankly at the table full of half-emptied bottles. McCoy picked one at random and handed it to the ship's chief engineer.

"That's scotch," he said. "Or anyway, close enough."

Scott's eyes were glazed with exhaustion and grief.

"I recall a time, when the lad was nobbut a bairn, that he . . ." Scott stopped, unable to continue the story. "I recall a time when Mister Spock . . ." He stopped again and drank straight from the bottle, choking on the first gulp, but swallowing and swallowing again. Obsession and compulsion drove him. He and McCoy had planned the wake and insisted on holding it, though it was foreign to the traditions of most of the people on board and quite alien to the traditions of one of its subjects.

"This isna helping, Doctor," Scotty said. "I canna bear it any longer."

McCoy climbed onto a chair. Looking down, he hesitated. The deck lay ridiculously far away and at a strange angle, as if the artificial gravity had gone on the blink. McCoy steadied himself and stepped up on the table, placing his feet carefully between bottles bright with amber. Then he remembered an alien liquor called "amber" by Earth people. He had not ordered it from the synthesizer because it required the inclusion of an alien insect to bring out its fullest flavor, like the worm in tequila. McCoy felt vaguely sick.

His foot brushed one of the bottles—quite gently, he thought—and the bottle crashed onto its side. It spun around and its contents gurgled out, spilling across the table, splashing on the floor. McCoy ignored it.

"This is a wake, not a funeral!" he said, then stopped, confused. Somehow that sounded wrong. He started again. "We're here to celebrate the lives of our friends—not to mourn their deaths!" Everyone was looking at him. That bothered him until he thought, Why did you get up on the table, if you didn't want everyone to look at you?

"Grief," McCoy said slowly, "is not logical."

"Bones," Jim Kirk said from below and slightly behind him, "come down from there."

Even in his odd mental state, McCoy could hear the edge in Kirk's voice. Twenty years of friendship, and Kirk was still perfectly capable of pulling rank. McCoy turned and staggered. Jim grabbed his forearm and tightened his grip more than necessary.

"Whatever possessed you to say such a thing?" Kirk said angrily. Even the anger was insufficient to hide the pain.

"Don't know what you mean," McCoy said. Permitting Admiral Kirk to help him, he stepped down from the table with careful dignity.

David Marcus had inherited his mother's tolerance for alcohol. He had drunk several shots of some concoction as powerful and as tasteless as Everclear. Despite a certain remoteness to his perceptions, he felt desperately sober. His hands remained rock-steady, and his step was sure.

McCoy and Scott had insisted, cajoled, ordered, and bullied until nearly the whole ship's company congregated in the recreation hall for this ridiculous wake. Alone or in pairs, people stood scattered throughout the enormous chamber. Across the room, Doctor McCoy and Admiral Kirk exchanged words. Kirk looked both angry and concerned. McCoy adopted a belligerent air.

They're both completely pickled, David thought. *Fixed like microscope slides. James T. Kirk, hero of the galaxy, is drunk. My illegitimate father is drunk.*

David had not yet quite come to terms with the recent revelation of his parentage.

"Doctor Marcus—"

David started. He had been so deep in thought that he had not noticed Commander Sulu's approach.

"It'd probably be easier if everybody just called me David," he said.

"David, then," Sulu said. "I understand that I owe you some thanks."

David looked at him blankly.

"For saving my life?" Sulu said, with a bit of a smile.

David blushed. He automatically glanced at Sulu's hands, which had been badly seared by the electrical shock from which David had revived him. The artificial skin covering the burns glistened slightly.

Sulu turned his hands palm-up. "This comes off in a couple of days—there won't even be any scars."

"I almost killed you," David said.

"What?"

"It's true I did resuscitation on you. It's also true that I did it wrong. I'd never done it before. I'm not a medical doctor, I'm only a biochemist."

"Nevertheless, I'm alive because of what you did. Whether you erred or not, you kept me from death or brain damage."

"I still screwed up." *Like I may have screwed up everything I've done for the last two years,* David thought

"It might not matter to you," Sulu said. "But it makes some difference to me." He turned away.

David blushed again, realizing how churlish and self-centered he had sounded. "Commander . . . uh . . ." He had no idea how to apologize.

Sulu stopped and faced David again.

"David," he said, carefully and kindly, "I want to give you some advice. When we get back to Earth, you and your mother are going to be the center of some very concentrated attention. Some of it will be critical, some of it will be flattering. At first you'll think the abuse is the hardest thing to take. But after a while, you'll see that handling compliments gracefully is an order of magnitude more difficult." He paused.

David looked at the floor, then raised his head and met Sulu's gaze.

"But I need to learn to do it?" David asked.

"Yes," Sulu said. "You do."

"I'm sorry," David said. "I really am glad you're okay. I didn't mean to sound indifferent. After they took you to sickbay I realized I'd done the procedure wrong. I didn't know if you'd make it."

"Doctor Chapel assures me that I'll make it."

David noticed that Sulu avoided mentioning McCoy, but thought better of saying so. He had stuck his foot in his mouth far enough for one day.

"I'm glad I could do something," David said.

Sulu nodded and walked away. David had not noticed if Sulu drank during the toasts, but the commander appeared to be completely sober.

He might be the only sober person on the ship right now, David thought.

But then David saw Lieutenant Saavik, all alone, watching the party without expression. He watched her, in turn, for several minutes. Back on Regulus I, she had told him that Spock was the most important influence in her life. He had rescued her from the short, brutal life that a halfbreed child on an abandoned Romulan colony world could look forward to. Spock had overseen her education. He had nominated her to a place in the Starfleet Academy. He was, David supposed, the nearest thing she had to a family. That was a delicate subject. She seldom discussed how the cross that produced her must have come about.

David walked up quietly behind her.

"Hello, David," she said, without turning, as he opened his mouth to speak.

"Hi," he said, trying to pretend she had not startled him with her preternatural senses. "Can I get you a drink?"

"No. I never drink alcohol."

"Why not?"

"It has an unfortunate effect on me."

"But that's the whole point. It would help you loosen up. It would help you forget."

"Forget what?"

"Grief. Sadness. Mister Spock's death."

"I am a Vulcan. I experience neither grief nor sadness."

"You're not all Vulcan."

She ignored the comment. "In order to forget Mister Spock's death, David, I would have to forget Mister Spock. That, I cannot do. I do not wish to. Memories of him are all around me. At times it is as if he—" She stopped. "I will not forget him," she said.

"I didn't mean you should try. I just meant that a drink might make you feel better."

"As I explained, its effects on me are not salutary."

"What happens?"

"You do not want to know."

"Sure I do. I'm a scientist, remember? Always on the lookout for something to investigate."

She looked him in the eye and said, straight-faced, "It causes me to regress. It permits the Romulan elements of my character to predominate."

David grinned. "Oh, yeah? Sounds interesting to me."

"You would not like it."

"Never know until you try."

"Have you ever met a Romulan?"

"Nope."

"You are," she said drily, "quite fortunate."

Carol Marcus felt very much alone at Mister Spock's wake. She sat on the arm of a couch, concealed by the subdued light and shadows of a corner of the room. She felt grateful for the translucent wall that alcohol put between her and the other people, between her and her own emotions. She knew that the purpose of a wake was to release emotions, but she held her grief in tight check. If she loosed it, she was afraid she would go mad.

The pitiful gathering insulted the memory of her friends more than exalting it. Perhaps Mister Scott and Doctor McCoy believed it adequate for Captain Spock and Mister Scott's young nephew. But the mourning of a few veteran Starfleet members and a surreptitiously drunken class of cadets, barely more than children, gave Carol no comfort for the loss of her friends on the Spacelab team. She kept expecting to hear Del March's cheerful profanity, or Zinaida Chitirih-Ra-Payjh's soft and musical laugh. She expected Jedda Adzhin-Dall to stride past, cloaked in the glow of a Deltan's unavoidable sexual attraction. And she expected at every moment to hear Vance Madison's low, beautiful voice, or to glance across the room and meet his gaze, or to reach out and touch his gentle hand.

None of those things would ever happen again. Her collaborators, her friends, were dead, murdered in vengeance for someone else's error.

Jim Kirk managed to get McCoy down from the table and away from the center of attention before the doctor had made too much of a fuss, and, Kirk hoped, without making a fool of either of them.

"I think you've drunk too much, Bones," he said.

"Me?" McCoy said. "I haven't had *nearly* enough."

Kirk tried to restrain his anger at McCoy's juvenile behavior. "Why don't you get some sleep? You'll feel better in the morning."

"I'll feel awful in the morning, Jim-boy. And the morning after that, and—"

"You'll feel worse if you have to deal with a hangover *and* the results of a big mouth."

McCoy frowned at him blearily, obviously not understanding. Kirk felt a twinge of unease. McCoy generally made sense, even when he had had a few too many. In fact, his usual reaction to tipsiness was to become more direct and pithier. Kirk glanced around, seeking Chris Chapel. He hoped that between them they might get McCoy either sobered up or asleep. Chapel was nowhere to be seen. He could hardly blame her for avoiding the wake. He wished he were somewhere else himself. He had come only because McCoy insisted. Jim supposed Chris had decided that the hard time McCoy and Scotty would give her for absenting herself would be less unpleasant than attending. Jim suspected she was right.

"Come on, Bones," he said. Back in sick bay, the doctor might be persuaded to prescribe himself a hangover remedy and go to bed.

"Not going anywhere," McCoy said. He shrugged his arm from Kirk's grasp. "Going over there." He walked slowly and carefully to an armchair and settled into it as if he planned to remain till dawn. Getting him to his cabin now would create a major scene. On the other hand, McCoy no longer looked in the mood to make proclamations. Jim sighed and left him where he was.

Jim wandered over to Carol. She was alone, surrounded by shadows. They had barely had time to talk since meeting again. Jim was not altogether sure she wanted to talk to him. He did want to talk to her, though, about her life since they last had seen each other, twenty years ago. But mostly he wanted to talk to her about David. Jim was getting used to the idea of having a grown son. He was beginning to like the idea of coming to know the young man.

"Hi, Carol," he said.

"Jim."

Her voice was calm and controlled. He remembered that she had always been able to drink everybody under the table and never even show it.

"I was thinking about Spacelab," she said. "And the people I left behind. Especially—"

"You did fantastic work there, you and David."

"It wasn't just us, it was the whole team. I never worked with such an incredible group before. We got intoxicated on each other's ideas. I could guide it, but Vance was the catalyst. He was extraordinary—"

"Spock spoke highly of them all," Jim said. It surprised him, to be able to say his friend's name so easily.

"Vance was the only one who could keep his partner from going off the deep end. He had a sort of inner stillness and calm that—"

"They were the ones who designed computer games on the side? A couple of the cadets were talking about them."

". . . that affected us all."

"David and our Lieutenant Saavik seem to be hitting it off pretty well," Jim said. David and Saavik stood together on the other side of the recreation hall, talking quietly.

"I suppose so," Carol said without expression.

"She has a lot of promise—Spock had great confidence in her."

"Yes."

"I'm sorry I had to meet David—and you and I had to meet again—in such unhappy circumstances," he said

The look in her eyes was cold and bitter and full of pain.

"That's one way to put it," she said

"Carol—"

"I'm going to bed," she said abruptly. She stood up and strode out of the recreation room.

Jim followed her. "I'll walk you to your cabin," he said. He took her silence for acquiescence.

With some curiosity, Saavik watched Admiral Kirk and Doctor Marcus leave together. Of course she knew that they had been intimate many years before. She wondered if they intended to resume their relationship. She had observed the customs of younger humans, students, while she was in the Academy, however, and she now noted the absence of any indication of strong attraction between Marcus and Kirk. Perhaps older humans observed different customs, or perhaps these individuals were simply shy. Mister Spock had told her that she must learn to understand human beings. As a project for her continuing education in their comprehension, she resolved to study the admiral and the doctor closely and see what transpired.

After Doctor Marcus and the admiral left the recreation hall, Saavik returned her attention to the gathering as a whole. She wondered if there was something in particular she was supposed to do. Keeping her own customs after the deaths of Mister Spock and Peter Preston, she had watched over their bodies the night before Mister Spock's funeral. Only yesterday morning she stood with the rest of the ship's company and sent his coffin accelerating toward the Genesis planet. She wished she could have sent young Peter's body into space, too. He had loved the stars, and Saavik believed it would have pleased him to become star-stuff. But his body was the responsibility of Chief Engineer Scott, who had decreed he must be taken back to Earth and buried in the family plot.

Everyone assumed Captain Spock's casket would burn up in the outer atmosphere of the Genesis world. So Admiral Kirk had intended. But Saavik had disobeyed his order. Instead, she programmed a course that intersected the last fading resonance of the Genesis effect. When the coffin encountered the edge of the wave, matter had exploded into energy. Within the wave, the energy that had been Spock's body coalesced into sub-quarkian particles, thence, in almost immeasurable fractions of a second, to normal atomic matter. He was now a part of that distant world. He was gone. She would never see him again.

She wondered how long she would be affected by the persistent, illogical certainty that he remained nearby.

"David," she said suddenly, "what is the purpose of this gathering?"

David hesitated, wondering if he understood it well enough to explain it to anyone else. "It's a tradition," he said. "It's like Doctor McCoy said a while ago, it's to celebrate the lives of people who have died."

"Would it not make more sense to celebrate while a person is still living?"

"How would you know when to have the celebration?"

"You would have it whenever you liked. Then no death would be necessary. The person being celebrated could attend the party, and no one would have to feel sad."

David wondered if she was pulling his leg. He decided that was an unworthy suspicion. Besides, he could see her point.

"The thing is," he said, "the funeral yesterday, and the wake today . . . they aren't really for the people who died."

"I do not understand."

"They're for the people who are left behind. People—humans, I mean—need to express their feelings. Otherwise we bottle them up inside and they make us sick."

This sounded like the purest hocus-pocus to Saavik, who had spent half her life learning to control her emotions.

"You mean," she said, "this procedure is meant to make people feel better?"

"That's right."

"Then why does everyone look so unhappy?"

David could not help it. He laughed.

The door to Carol's cabin sensed her and slid open. She stopped. Jim stopped. Carol said nothing. Jim tried to decide on exactly the right words.

"Carol—"

"Good night Jim."

"But—"

"Leave me alone!" she said. The evenness of her voice dissolved in anger.

"I thought . . ."

"What? That you could come along after twenty years and pick up again right where you left off?"

"I was thinking more in terms of 'we.' "

"Oh, that's cute—there never was any 'we'!"

"There's David."

"Do you think you're so great in bed that no woman would ever want another man after you? Do you think I've spent all these years just waiting for you to come back?"

"No, of course not. But—" He stopped. That she might be involved with someone else simply had not occurred to him, and he was embarrassed to admit it. "Of course I didn't mean that," he said. "But we were good together, once, and we're both alone—"

"Alone!" Her eyes suddenly filled with tears.

"Carol, I don't understand."

"Vance Madison and I were lovers!"

"I didn't realize," he said lamely.

"You would have, if you'd listened. I've been trying to talk about him. I just wanted to talk about him to somebody. Even to you. I want people to remember what he was like. He deserves to be remembered. I dream about him—I dream about the way he died—"

Jim took a step backward, retreating from the fury and accusation in her voice. His old enemy, Khan Noonien Singh, had murdered all the members of the Genesis team except Carol and David. The people he captured refused to give him the information he demanded, so he killed them. He opened a vein in Madison's throat and let him slowly bleed to death.

Carol flung herself into her cabin. The door slid shut behind her, cutting Jim Kirk off, all alone, in the passageway outside.

David finally stopped laughing. He wiped his eyes. Saavik hoped he would explain to her what he found so funny.

She watched him intently. He looked up. Their gazes met.

He glanced quickly away, then back again.

David's eyes were a clear, intense blue.

She reached toward him, realized what she was doing, and froze. David touched her before she could draw away.

"What is it?" he said. He wrapped his fingers around her hand in an easy grip.

He could not hold her hand without her acquiescence, for she could crush his bones with a single clenching of his fist. This she had no intention of doing.

"For many years," Saavik said, "I have tried to be Vulcan."

"I know."

David was one of the few people with whom she had ever discussed her background. Though she had learned to control her strongest emotions most of the time, she never pretended to herself that they were nonexistent.

"But I am not all Vulcan, and I will never be," she said, "any more than Mister Spock. He said to me . . ." She paused, uncertain how David would react. "He said I was unique, and that I must find my own path."

"Good advice for anybody," David said.

Saavik drew her hand from David's grasp and picked up his drink. She barely tasted it. The raw, imaged alcohol slid fiery across her tongue, and the potent fumes seemed to go straight to her brain. She put down the glass. David watched her curiously.

"David," she said hesitantly, "I am under the impression that you have positive feelings toward me. Is that true?"

"It's very true," he said.

"Will you help me find my path?"

"If I can."

"Will you come to my cabin with me?"

"Yes," he said. "I will."

"Now?"

In reply, he put his hand in hers again, and they walked together from the recreation hall.

Jim Kirk strode down the corridor, upset, angry, embarrassed.

He nearly ran into his son and Lieutenant Saavik.

"Oh—Hi, kids." He collected himself quickly. Long years of experience had made him an expert at hiding distress from subordinates.

"Uh . . . hi," David said. Saavik said nothing; she simply gazed at him with her cool imperturbability.

"Got to be too much for you in there?" Kirk said, nodding toward the rec hall behind them. "I never should have let McCoy and Scott have their way about it."

They looked at him without replying. After a long hesitation, Saavik finally spoke.

"Indeed," she said, "it is not a ceremony Captain Spock would have approved. It is neither logical nor rational."

Kirk flinched at the echoes of Spock's voice in Saavik's words. He had known Spock longer than she had, but she had spent more time working with the Vulcan in the past few years, when Kirk was tied to a desk by an unbreakable chain of paperwork.

"Perhaps you're right," he said. "But funerals and wakes aren't for the person who is dead, they're for the people left behind."

"It is interesting," Saavik said, "that David said precisely the same thing. I fail, however, to grasp this explanation."

"It isn't easily explained," Kirk said. "And I can understand why you wouldn't think of Spock in relation to a gathering where everybody was doing their best to get drunk. I was going to go to the observation deck, instead. Have either of you been up there? David, surely you haven't had a chance to see it. Would you like to come along?"

"I am familiar with the observation deck," Saavik said.

"I'd sure like to see it," David said, "any other time. But Lieutenant Saavik wanted to check some readings on the bridge."

Kirk glanced from David, to Saavik, and back. Saavik started to say something, but stopped. A blush colored David's transparently fair complexion. Kirk realized that he had put his foot in his mouth for the second time in ten minutes. He, too, began to blush.

"I see," he said. "Important work. Carry on, then." He turned and strode quickly away.

Saavik watched him until he had passed out of sight around a corner.

"Nothing needs to be checked on the bridge, David," she said.

"I had to say something," David said. "I didn't want to discuss our personal affairs with him. It isn't any of his business."

"But why did he not remind you that the computer would announce any change in the ship's status?"

"I don't know," David said, though he knew perfectly well.

"He has not commanded a starship in a long time," she said. "Perhaps he forgot."

"That must be it."

They continued down the corridor to Saavik's cabin. Inside, David blinked, waiting for his eyes to accustom themselves to the low light. The room held no decorations, only the severe furnishings standard issue in Starfleet, but the warm and very dry air carried a hot, resiny scent, like the sunbaked pitch of pine trees at high noon in summer.

Saavik stopped with her back to David.

"Saavik," David said, "I just want you to know—maybe we don't need to worry, but where I was raised it's good manners to tell you—I passed all my exams in biocontrol."

"I, too," she said softly. "I always regarded learning to regulate the reproductive ability merely as an interesting exercise. Until now . . ." Her voice trailed off.

David realized that she was trembling. He put his hands gently on her shoulders.

"I have traveled far, and I have seen much," Saavik said. "I have studied. . . . But study and action are very different."

"I know," David said. "It's all right, it will be all right."

Saavik reached up, and her hair fell free around her shoulders. It was thick and soft and dark, and it smelled of evergreens.

Jim Kirk did go to the observation deck. He opened the portals and spent a long time staring at the stars. After a while, the romantic in his soul overcame the admiral in his mind. The pain and grief surrounding Spock's death eased, the embarrassing encounter with David and Saavik began to seem humorous, and even his misunderstanding of Carol's wishes became less lacerating in his memory. The whole galaxy lay around him.

He fancied he could still see the star of the Genesis world, far behind, a hot white star red-shifted toward yellow as the *Enterprise* raced away, an unimposing young star made fuzzy by the planetary nebula that surrounded it, by the remnants of the Mutara Nebula. The matter in the nebula had been blasted apart by the Genesis wave, blasted beyond atoms, beyond subatomic particles, beyond quarks, down to the sub-elementary particles that Vance Madison and his partner Del March had whimsically named "snarks" and "boojums."

Khan had set off the Genesis wave in an attempt to destroy Jim Kirk, an attempt that had very nearly succeeded. Thus he set in motion—what? Even Carol could not say. The resonances in the wave were designed to work upon a very different environment. No one could know what had come into existence on the Genesis world without going back and exploring it. Jim Kirk had many reasons for wanting to see that done and, what was more, for wanting to do it himself.

First he had to return to Earth. To accomplish that, he needed a crew that in the morning would be able to think of something other than their hangovers. Realizing that he had been up here all alone for nearly an hour, he decided it was about time to go back to the recreation deck and shut things down.

He closed the portals against the stars.

David dozed in the intoxicating warmth of Saavik's body. Vulcans—and, David supposed, Romulans, too—had a body temperature several degrees above that of human beings.

"Lying next to you is like lying in the shade on a hot summer's day," Saavik said.

David chuckled sleepily. "You must be psychic."

"Only slightly," she said. "Vulcans and Romulans both have the ability in some measure. My talent for it is quite limited. But why do you say so now?"

"I was just thinking that lying next to you is like being in the sun on the first warm day of spring."

She turned suddenly toward him and hugged him close. Her hair fell across his shoulders. He put his arms around her and held her. She had been raised first among Romulans who rejected her, then in the Vulcan tradition which denied any need for closeness or passion. He wondered if anyone had ever held her before.

She drew back and lay beside him, barely touching him, as if ashamed of her instant's impulse. David was not so ready to ignore the intimacy.

He traced the smooth, strong line of Saavik's collarbone with the tip of one finger. He had never been with anyone like her in his life. He caressed the hollow of her throat and cupped his hand around the point of her left shoulder. He had felt the scar on her smooth skin earlier, but just then the time had been wrong for questions. Now, though, he touched the scar in the dark and found it to be a complex, regular pattern.

"How'd you get that?" he asked.

She said nothing for so long that David wondered if his bad habit of asking questions off the top of his head had got him into trouble again.

"Sorry," he said. "Idle curiosity—it's none of my business."

"It is a Romulan family mark," Saavik said.

"A family mark!" She had told him that she did not know the identity of either of her parents, that she did not even know which parent was Vulcan and which Romulan. "Does that mean you could find your family?"

"David," she said, and he thought he could detect a hint of dry humor in her voice, "why would I want to find my Romulan family?"

Since the likelihood was that a Romulan had borne or sired her in order to demonstrate complete power over a Vulcan prisoner, David could see her point.

"I never heard of family marks," he said.

"That is not surprising. Information about them may only be passed on orally. It is a capital crime in the Romulan empire to make permanent records of them."

"Why don't you have the mark removed? Doesn't it remind you of— unpleasant times?"

"I do not wish to forget those times," Saavik said, "any more than I wish to forget Mister Spock. All those memories are important to me. Besides, it may have its use, someday."

"How?"

"Should I have the misfortune to encounter my Romulan parent, it is absolute proof of our relationship."

"But if you don't want to know your Romulan parent . . ."

"The family mark permits me to demand certain rights," Saavik said. "It would be considered very bad manners to refuse a family member's challenge to a death-duel."

"A duel!"

"Yes. How else avenge myself? How else avenge my Vulcan parent, who surely died with my birth?"

David lay back on the narrow bunk, stunned by Saavik's matter-of-fact discussion of deep, implacable hatred.

"I never thought Vulcans as demanding an eye for an eye and a tooth for a tooth."

"But I am not—as Vulcans never cease to remind me—a proper Vulcan."

"Wouldn't it be easier, wouldn't it be safer, to—I don't know, sue the Romulans for reparations?"

"Spoken like a truly civilized human," Saavik said. "But if I am only half a Vulcan, I am in no part human. Mister Spock was right—I must follow my own path."

David moved his hand from her shoulder. The intensity of her feelings surprised him, though it should not, not any more, not after tonight.

"Don't worry, David," Saavik said, in response to his unease. "I am hardly going to defect to the Romulan Empire in order to find a creature I have no real wish to meet. The chance of my ever meeting my Romulan parent is vanishingly small."

"I guess," David said. The Federation had, at best, fragile diplomatic relations with the Romulans. It was a connection like a fuse, continually threatening to burst into flame and ignite a more serious conflagration.

Saavik guided his hand back to her shoulder.

"It feels good when you touch it," she said. "The coolness of your hand is soothing."

"Were you born with it? Or is it a tattoo?"

"Neither. It is a brand."

"A brand!"

"They apply it soon after one is out of the womb."

"Gods, what a thing to do to a little baby. Good thing you can't remember it."

"What makes you think I cannot remember it?"

Horrified, David said, "You mean you *can?*"

"Of course. The white glow is the first beautiful thing I ever encountered, and its touch was the first pain. Do you not remember your own birth?"

"No, not at all. I don't have any reliable memories before I was two or three. Most people don't."

"But most people do, David," Saavik said. "At least, in my experience. Perhaps you mean most humans do not?"

"Yeah," David said. "Sorry. Bad habit."

"No offense taken. I am always glad to learn something new about a fellow intelligent species. The last few hours have been very rewarding. I have learned a great deal."

David did not know quite how to take that, so he replied with an inarticulate "Hmm?"

"Yes," Saavik said. "I feel that my experiments have been most instructive."

"Is that all I am to you?" David said. "An experiment?" He suddenly felt very hurt and disappointed, and he realized that his attraction toward Saavik was a great deal more than physical, something much deeper and much stronger.

"That is one of the things you are to me," she said in an even tone. "And not the least. But not the most, either. You have helped me learn that I have capabilities I believed I did not possess."

"Like—the capacity to love?"

"I . . . I am unprepared to make that claim. I do not even comprehend the concept."

David laughed softly. "Neither does anybody else."

"Indeed? My research is unfinished—I thought I simply had not encountered a satisfactory definition."

"It isn't something you can quantify."

"Someone should conduct experiments."

"Experiments!" David said, slightly shocked.

"Certainly. Perhaps we might collaborate on a paper."

"Saavik—"

"I have heard a speculation. I am curious to know whether it is true, or merely apocryphal."

"All right," David said, beyond surprise. "What speculation is that?"

Saavik turned toward him, propped herself up on one elbow, and let her hair spill over his shoulder and across his chest.

"It is," she said, "that Romulans are insatiable. Would you care to test this hypothesis?"

David laughed. He reached up and touched her face in the dark. He traced the lines of her lips, and found that she was smiling. She had just discovered another capability that few people would suspect her of possessing. She had a terrific sense of humor.

"Why don't we do that?" David said.

Jim Kirk strode into the recreation hall.

The wake had deteriorated even further. Cadets stood alone or in small groups, sinking into silent depression. Scott clutched a drink and talked continuously and intensely to a single captive trainee. McCoy lay sprawled in his chair. As a catharsis, this gathering was a wretched failure. It succeeded only in intensifying everyone's feelings of pain and loss and guilt. Kirk stopped by a small group of cadets.

"I think it's about time to pack it in for the night," he said. "You're all dismissed."

"Yessir," one of the cadets said. Her relieved smile, quick, and quickly hidden, was the first smile Kirk had seen all day.

The cadets, just waiting for an excuse to escape the sepulchral atmosphere, all accepted his order without objection or argument. The trainees still sober enough to be ambulatory helped their friends who had overindulged. Within a few minutes, the only cadet left was the one listening to Mister Scott's tirade. Kirk joined them. The cadet looked pale and drawn.

"Scotty—" Kirk said, when Scott paused for breath.

"Aye, Captain, life doesna make sense sometimes, I was just sayin' to Grenni here, 'tis the good ones go before their time—"

"Mister Scott—"

"—there's no denyin' it. The boy had guts. He had potential—"

"Commander Scott!"

"Aye, sir? What's wrong, Admiral? Why are ye soundin' so perturbed?"

Kirk sighed. "Perturbed, Mister Scott? Whatever makes you think I'm perturbed? You're dismissed, Cadet."

"Yes, sir. Thank you, sir." The cadet's voice shook. He fled.

"Mister Scott, we'll reach Regulus tomorrow, and I need a coherent crew. Go to bed."

"But my poor bairn—I wished to have all o' us sing a song for him. Do ye know 'Danny Boy,' Captain?"

"That's an order, Mister Scott."

"Aye, sir." Scott commenced to sing. " 'O Danny boy, the pipes, the pipes are calling—' "

"Mister Scott!"

Scott stopped singing and gazed at him blearily, blinking and confused, as Kirk's tone finally got through to him.

" 'Sing "Danny Boy" ' is not an order. 'Go to bed' is an order."

"Oh. Begging your pardon, sir. Aye, sir."

Scott glanced around him, as if searching for something. Suddenly he looked very tired and old. He trudged away.

McCoy was the last member of the wake remaining. Jim sat on his heels beside McCoy's chair. The doctor snored softly.

"Bones," Jim said, shaking him softly. "Bones, wake up."

McCoy flinched, muttered something incomprehensible, and lapsed back into snoring.

"Come on, old friend." Jim dragged McCoy's arm across his shoulder and hoisted him to his feet. McCoy sagged against him and muttered a few more words. Jim froze.

"What?"

McCoy straightened up, swaying, and looked Kirk directly in the eye.

"Using a metabolic poison as a recreational drug is totally illogical."

McCoy collapsed.

Two

Doctor Christine Chapel watched herself function efficiently. She felt very much like two different people, one performing as she should, the other separated from the world by shock. She felt numb and clumsy. That she could function at all astonished her. Yet she did what needed to be done, caring for the crew members, mostly young cadets, who had been injured during Khan's attacks; dispensing hangover remedies to those who had neglected to take a preventive after Mister Spock's wake; and looking in occasionally on Leonard McCoy. She was extremely concerned about him.

She paused in the doorway of the cubicle in which she and Admiral Kirk had put him the night before. She left the lights on very low. She suspected that when Leonard woke, his headache would be a credit to its species.

He moaned and muttered something. Chris moved farther into the small room, squinting to see better in the dim light. Leonard tossed on the bunk, his face shining with sweat. His tunic was soaked. Chris felt his forehead. His temperature was elevated, not yet dangerously so, but certainly enough to make him uncomfortable.

"Leonard," she said softly.

He sat bolt upright, staring straight ahead. Slowly he turned to look at her. He moved in a way she had never seen him move before, but in a way that was eerily familiar.

"Vulcans," he said, in a voice much lower than his own, "do not love."

Chris took an involuntary step backward.

"How dare you say that to me?" she said, in a quiet, angry voice. The pain pierced through the numbness to her enclosed, repressed grief and spread like fire through her. She turned, hiding her face in her hands. She could not break down now. The ship had to have a doctor, and McCoy was in no shape to take over.

The obsession she had had with Spock for so long still embarrassed her, though it had burned out years before. She had forced herself beyond it by sheer determination and by the power of the knowledge that what she desired from him, he simply could not give. His inability to respond to her had nothing to do with Christine Chapel. He had never had the choice between "interested" and "uninterested." All his training and experience required him to be disinterested, and so he had behaved.

Once Chris accepted that, she began to appreciate his unique integrity. It took a long time for her to get over her youthful fantasies, but once she did, her fondness for Spock strengthened. Losing a friend, she had discovered in the past few days, was much worse than losing a remotely potential and unrequiting lover. Accepting Spock's death, she thought, would be an even longer and more difficult task than persuading herself not that he never would love her, but that he never could.

She took her hands from her face and straightened up, under control again. This was a bad time to cry. Leonard McCoy's sense of humor was quirky, but not cruel. For him to say what he had said to her meant either that something was seriously wrong or—the simplest, if least flattering, possibility—that he was still intoxicated.

Saavik woke suddenly and sat up, startled. Mister Spock was speaking to her. His deep voice still echoed in her cabin. Saavik was not prepared to answer him. She was dazzled by strange dreams and fantasies.

"But I am not a Vulcan," she said. "You said to me—"

She stopped. He was not here—he had never been here. Spock was gone.

Spock's voice had sounded so real . . . but what she thought was reality was a cruel dream, and what for a moment had seemed impossible fantasy was real.

David lay sleeping beside her, cool and fair. She touched his shoulder lightly. He stirred gently but did not wake. Saavik wondered if she could be going mad with grief, or with guilt. She did not feel mad.

But Spock's voice had seemed so real . . .

Delicately, Farrendahl nibbled at the fur-covered web of skin at the base of the first and second fingers of her right paw. A bad habit, she knew it, one she had picked up from a human shipmate who bit his nails. A human's nails were such flimsy things that it hardly mattered whether they were damaged or properly sharp, but Farrendahl would never sink so low as to bite her claws. They were far too useful.

At times like these, though, she needed a nervous habit to fall back on. Her primate-type crewmates either objected to or thought amusing the more obvious forms of grooming. Never mind that she found them soothing.

Farrendahl did not like to be laughed at. Primates, humanoids as they preferred to call themselves in Standard, could be astonishingly repellent when they laughed.

Farrendahl sat on her haunches in the navigator's hammock, chewing on her paw and blinking at the unfamiliar stars. Having passed out of Federation space and into the gray area between set borders some hours before, the ship now fell under the protection of no one. It had become potential prey to all. This, Farrendahl disliked intensely.

A signal came through her console. She blinked at it, too, then in response to the new order changed the course of the ship for the third time in a single circadian. The resulting course, if left unchanged, would bring the ship face to face with the Klingons. This, Farrendahl disliked even more.

No wonder their mysterious passenger was unwilling to name a destination. No wonder the ship's grapevine sprouted rumors of an enormous payment to the captain. Great wonder, though, if the captain passed on part of his largesse in the crew's bonuses without a confrontation.

"I dislike the scent of this," Farrendahl said. She growled softly in irritation. "It smelled bad when we began, and its odor has become progressively more putrid."

Her compatriot bared his teeth in that offensive primate way, and an intermittent choking noise came from his throat. In short, he laughed.

"Since when do cats learn anything useful from their sense of smell?" he said.

Compatriot—! A high-class word to apply to any member of this ship's crew of ill-mannered, poorly reared mercenaries.

"Since when," Farrendahl said to Tran, "have I been a cat?" Instead of baring her teeth, which another member of her own species would have recognized as a threat, she placed her paw on the scarred control panel. She stretched out her fingers so her paw became a hand, then slowly extended her claws. The sharp tips scratched the panel with a gradual, hair-raising shriek.

"A cat?" Tran exclaimed. "Did I call you a cat? Who in their right mind would call you a cat?"

"I saw a cat once," Farrendahl said matter-of-factly. "It was digging through a garbage heap in a back alley on Amenhotep IX. I disliked it. Please explain the similarities between it and me."

"Don't push it, Farrendahl."

"But I desire to be enlightened."

"All right. Both of you were in the back alley, weren't you?"

Farrendahl leapt, knocking Tran to the deck. The artificial gravity, set for economy's sake at an annoyingly low intensity, turned her attack and Tran's fall into a most unsatisfactory series of slow bounces. But they ended up as Farrendahl planned, with the human on the floor and her claws and teeth at his throat. This was a main reason she never bit her claws.

"And was there not an ugly monkey-looking creature in that same back alley, only insensible from noxious recreational drugs?"

"Probably there was," Tran said, laughing again.

Farrendahl bristled her whiskers out, acknowledging Tran's good-humored surrender. She was about to release him when the captain walked in on them. He stopped, folded his arms across his chest, and glared at the crew members.

"If you two haven't any work, I can find some," he said. "We don't have time for your continual horsing around."

Farrendahl growled softly and rose, extending her hand to Tran to help him rise. He leaped to his feet like a gymnast in the low gravity.

"A cat, a monkey, now a horse," Farrendahl said in a low voice. "Perhaps our mysterious mission is to transport a menagerie."

Tran chuckled and returned to his place at the control console.

"I heard that," the captain said. "Ten demerits."

"You're in a charming mood today, Captain," Farrendahl said. She ignored the threat of demerits. She had already earned so many that ten more scarcely counted. Demerits were a source of great hilarity among the crew, ever since the time they precipitated a minor mutiny. One planetfall, on a more or less civilized world and after a long, boring journey, the captain forbade Farrendahl, Tran, and several others to leave the ship. Too many demerits, he said. Farrendahl said nothing. She simply ignored him, and she and the others went out anyway.

He could have left while they were rousting around. He could have locked them off the ship and hired another crew. But he stayed where he was, leaving the ship open to them when they returned. Apparently he preferred his tried and semi-competent, if insolent, people to a new bunch that he would have to have trained.

He continued to assign demerits, but that was the only time he ever referred to them, and he never again tried to use them for anything.

The captain ignored Farrendahl's smart remark and paused at the control console. Farrendahl despised him on every possible level. He possessed power and the title of captain not because he deserved them or had earned them but simply because he owned the ship. He knew little about running it and less about the computers that formed its guts.

"Perhaps you are concerned that we will discover what you are being paid for this trip," Farrendahl said, putting him on notice that they all did know and that they all expected their cut.

He glared at her as she slipped smoothly into the navigator's hammock. He kept his silence. He was a bully, but he was also a coward, and he avoided any serious confrontation with Farrendahl.

"When do we find out where we are really going?"

"When you need to know," he said.

"Waste of fuel," Farrendahl said just loudly enough for him to hear. It amused her that he would worry the comment around in his mind, trying to find a way to conserve the fuel wasted by their roundabout route. If he had ever learned to pilot his ship himself, he would not have to depend on Farrendahl. She supposed she should be grateful for his lack of application.

The contempt in which she held him was diluted by her awareness of her own failings and limitations. She had been disappointed when, after the "mutiny," the captain capitulated to his impertinent crew. But she might have found another berth—whatever else she was, she was an able navigator, and now and then a shipmaster turned up who was willing to waive small matters like papers and background. She could have found another place, but she did not. Inertia kept her in the same, riskless position. Beneath her contempt for the captain lurked a certain contempt for herself. Perhaps they deserved each other.

The captain remained by the console, his attitude that of one studying the readings, his eyes with the blank stare of someone who had no idea what he was looking at.

"We're on course," Farrendahl said, "as long as you don't have any more changes in mind. Unless you do, I am going to sleep."

Lacking any reply, she slid from the hammock and padded away toward her cabin.

David stepped out of the turbolift, onto the bridge. Saavik, already on duty, glanced over her shoulder at him. A look passed between them that they innocently assumed no one else noticed or understood. Saavik returned her attention to her work as if it were easy for her. David wrestled himself back to this morning and away from last night.

It must be nice, David thought, *to have the ability to control your feelings so completely.* Being able to focus one's attention on a single subject gave remarkable results.

"Good morning, David," James Kirk said.

"Uh, hi." David could not bring himself to call Kirk "father." More than twenty years lay between them, years during which they could have known each other. David wondered what he would be like if he had known James Kirk as his father when it might have made a difference. He had found some reason to respect the Starfleet officer. Affection would take longer.

Kirk responded to David's unease. "How would you feel about calling me 'Jim'?"

"Okay, I guess."

Kirk paused for a moment, then turned away again. David realized he had hurt the admiral's feelings with his lukewarm response.

"This is going to take some getting used to," he said.

"Yes," Kirk said. "For me, too. We need to talk about it. In private."

David took the hint and kept the personal matters to himself, saving them for someplace other than the bridge of the *Enterprise*.

"There it is," Kirk said.

In the viewscreen, Regulus I hung dark and mysterious before them. The barren worldlet had always given David an eerie feeling. It had never evolved life. It had never had a chance of evolving life. It had no water and no air and too little gravity to hold either one. But Genesis had changed all that. The planetoid's interior had been turned into an entire, new, inside-out world, one with an ecosystem designed from scratch by Carol Marcus's team. It was like a Jules Verne novel brought to reality, and David was proud of his part in creating it. The memory of the short time he had spent beneath the surface of the world remained as a warm glow of pride and power. He wanted to go back inside and explore. No experiment ever turned out precisely as one planned. David wanted to discover the unexpected results. They were always the most interesting.

Spacelab drifted in its orbit, a shadowed silver flash against the limb of the planetoid. The Starfleet science ship *Grissom* lay in a matching orbit, waiting for the *Enterprise*. The ship and the laboratory satellite gradually entered the shadow of their primary, vanishing into the featureless darkness. David shivered. He had lived and worked on the research station for two years. He had called it home. Now it felt alien and threatening. If hauntings were possible, it must be haunted. On Spacelab, no one was left alive. The bodies of the people Khan had murdered lay waiting to be returned to Earth and to their graves.

As the transporter beam faded from the newly materialized form of Captain J.T. Esteban, James Kirk waited to greet him. Esteban stepped down. They shook hands.

"Welcome aboard, J.T.," Kirk said. "It's been a while."

"It has that," Esteban said. "An eventful while, too. You folks have things in quite a tizzy, back home."

Kirk led Esteban to the nearest turbolift. "I don't believe I follow you," he said.

"Will Doctor Marcus be available, Jim?" J.T. said. "I need to talk to the both of you."

They stepped into the lift. "Officer's lounge," Jim said, and felt the faint acceleration as the lift whisked them toward their destination. "I'll have Doctor Marcus paged." Kirk contacted Uhura. "Uhura, Kirk here. Would you ask Doctor Marcus to meet Captain Esteban and me in the officer's lounge?"

"Certainly, Admiral."

"Thanks. Kirk out." He turned off the intercom. He could sense the tension in the captain of the *Grissom*. "What's going on, J.T.?"

"I just think it would save time to talk to you both at once." Esteban was deliberately misunderstanding the question, and Jim did not push it. They tried to make small talk, but it was strained.

"The galaxy ships are already paying off," Esteban said. "Have you heard?"

"We've been out of touch," Jim said drily.

"Of course. But a subspace transmission just came through—it made all the news services. *Magellan* is in Andromeda. It just completed the first close-range observation of a supernova."

"That's very impressive," Jim said. And for all his offhandedness, he *was* impressed. Andromeda! Another galaxy, millions and millions of light-years away. A different ship, with a different crew and a different commander, had reached it first. He made a mental note to tell Mister Sulu the news of *Magellan,* for Sulu and the galaxy ship's captain, Mandala Flynn, had been the closest of friends for a long time.

They reached the officer's lounge and went inside. Carol had not yet arrived.

"Jim?"

"Eh?" Kirk realized J.T. had spoken to him, but had no idea what he had said. "I'm sorry, what did you say?"

"I said *Magellan* is a bit of a technological trick. It's too small to do anything but quick and dirty scouting missions. And if they encounter hostiles, what can they do but turn tail and run?"

"No doubt you're right," Jim said. He tried to imagine something that might cause Mandala Flynn to turn tail and run. He failed.

"No, it's *Excelsior* that's the wave of the future," J.T. said.

The door to the lounge slid open to admit Carol Marcus, accompanied by David. Carol nodded to Jim coolly; if she was not still angry at him, at best she was not yet willing to forget about last night's conversation.

"Carol," Jim said, "this is J.T. Esteban, commanding the *Grissom*. J.T., Doctor Carol Marcus, and her son . . ." Jim paused, thinking he really should say, "Our son," but deciding not to because it would take so long to explain. "Her son, Doctor David Marcus."

"Two for the price of one," David said.

Jim chuckled and Carol smiled. Missing the joke, J.T. rubbed his jaw and frowned.

"This is sensitive information," he said. "I only expected Doctor Marcus, senior."

David's smile vanished. "I can take a hint," he said. He headed toward the door, the irritation in his voice mirrored in his stiff-shouldered walk.

"David—" Jim said, but David kept walking.

"David, wait," Carol said.

David hesitated, then glanced back.

"David is a full member of the Genesis team, Captain Esteban," Carol said. "He and I are the only surviving principal investigators. Anything you have to say about Genesis, you must say to him as well as to me."

"The first thing I have to say is I wish you'd called it something else," Esteban said.

"I don't understand what you mean."

"It's too late now, but it wasn't the wisest move you could have made, in terms of PR. Never mind that, for the moment. Doctor Marcus—" He addressed David this time. "I apologize for my bad manners. Please come sit down with the rest of us. We have a great deal to talk over."

They sat around one of the small tables next to the star portals, and Esteban described the circumstances they would return to on Earth.

"The news of the Genesis effect created . . . shall we say, a sensation," J.T. said uncomfortably.

In all the years Jim had known J.T. Esteban, he had never seen him lose his composure. Anything and everything, no matter how strange, no matter the stress, he had always taken easily, even phlegmatically, in his stride. Jim had read the reports of some of his missions. Esteban had come up against extraordinarily challenging events, and he had prevailed. To see him so agitated about Genesis disturbed Jim more than anything the younger Starfleet officer could tell him.

"Of course it did," David said. "That's sort of the point, isn't it? We've made possible the elimination of poverty. We've made the reasons for war completely untenable—"

"You've created a device that could destroy the galaxy. That's what our adversaries perceive, not universal peace and plenty. They have demanded multilateral parity—"

"You mean they want Genesis, too," Carol said.

"Precisely."

"Why don't you give it to them?" David said.

"David!" Jim said, shocked. "We didn't just go through—the last few days—so we could turn Genesis over to an enemy power. Your friends didn't die resisting Khan so you could hand over the discovery to the next person who demanded it."

"That was different," David said. "Khan wanted it for revenge. Revenge against you."

Jim scowled, but did not reply to the jab.

"I'm not talking about giving it to every crazy who comes along," David said. "I'm talking about making Genesis openly available for transforming lifeless worlds."

"That is absolutely outside the realm of possibility," J.T. said.

"But that's what we made it for!"

"My dear boy," J.T. said.

Jim winced, seeing David bristle.

"My dear boy," J.T. said, "we can't give it to anyone else. That would be too dangerous."

"The Federation is the only organization with the wisdom to decide on its use?" Carol said dryly.

"I'm glad you understand Starfleet's—the Federation's—position, Doctor Marcus," J.T. said, missing the irony the same way he always missed jokes.

"Oh, I understand it, all right," Carol said. "That doesn't mean that I accept it."

"I knew it!" David shouted. "You just can't keep your hands off any discovery, can you? You have to grab it and hoard it and twist it until you can figure out a way to use it for destruction!"

"David, relax," Jim said.

"We would hardly have to do much figuring, now, would we?" Esteban said. "The evidence for the destructive power of Genesis is its first deployment. It completely recreated the substance of the Mutara Nebula, a volume of space some hundred astronomical units in radius. It destroyed *Reliant* and all the people on board. It nearly destroyed the *Enterprise,* and it did cause the death of—"

"Indirectly," Jim Kirk snapped. "We were involved in hostilities—"

"Because of Genesis!"

"Not entirely," Jim said. David was right: Khan had intended to use Genesis to wreak revenge upon James Kirk. But he had stumbled upon the project by chance, then turned it to his purposes. He had succeeded better than he could have known.

"You're hardly being fair, Captain," Carol said. "The Genesis device was obviously never meant—in any form—to go off inside a ship. That particular device was never intended to go off within a nebula."

"But that's precisely my point, Doctor! After all that's happened, how can you argue that the device cannot be an instrument of terrorism?"

"But if everybody has it there isn't any need for terrorism!" David said.

Carol was touched by David's naivete, Jim was surprised by it, and J.T. thought he was being deliberately, perhaps even maliciously, dense.

"Your discovery may eliminate poverty. But it'll hardly change the natures of sentient beings. It won't eliminate greed or lust for power or simple error, and it most certainly won't eliminate ideology. The drive to convert people's minds and hearts has caused more grief, more suffering, more loss of life than any desire for property, riches, or even the necessities of survival."

"Very eloquent, Captain," David said sarcastically. "I take it you mean our ideology requires us to pervert Genesis into a weapon before anybody else gets a chance to?"

"It's hardly productive to ascribe malicious motives to everybody who disagrees with you, David," Jim said sharply.

"What has to be done with Genesis isn't up to me to say," J.T. said. "Or to any of us."

"You're entitled to your opinion," Carol said.

David jumped to his feet. "I always said the military'd try to take Genesis away from us! I suppose if I try to call the Federation Science Network in on this, you'll throw me in the brig!"

"Sit down and shut up, David," Jim said. "If anybody gets thrown in the brig on this ship, it'll be by me. And you're making it mighty tempting to send you to bed without your supper."

David glared at him with a sudden flare of resentment that surprised Jim completely.

"Try it and see how far you get!" David glared at Kirk, then at Esteban. "I don't see any point in continuing this discussion." He stalked away.

"Come back here, David," Jim said.

"Do you think you can make me? You and who else?" He strode from the lounge.

Jim started to rise.

Carol put one hand on his arm.

"Let him go, Jim. He'll be all right when he cools down." She smiled. "That's another way he's like you."

"I was never that hot-headed!"

Carol looked at him askance. Jim reluctantly sat down again.

He realized that J.T. was watching them with both curiosity and confusion. He deserved at least some explanation.

"David is my son, as well as Carol's," he said.

"Oh," J.T. said. "Er . . . I didn't realize you had any children."

Neither did I, Jim thought, but what he said out loud was, "Just the one."

"How did we get off on this track, anyway?" J.T. said. "What I asked you here to tell you is that *Grissom* has been ordered to the Mutara sector to make a complete survey of the Genesis world. We can hardly discuss it, with our allies or with our adversaries, unless we know more about the effect and its consequences. Doctor Marcus, I've been directed to transfer you to my ship."

"What?" Carol said.

"Obviously, we need you to supervise the observations—"

"Forget it," Carol said.

"I beg your pardon?"

"What the hell do you think I am? 'Transfer' me? Like a crate of supplies? Do you think I'm a robot?"

"I'm sorry, Doctor. I don't follow you at all."

"Six people died on Spacelab. I·was responsible for them—and they were my friends! I owe them. At the very least I owe them the courtesy of telling their families what happened!"

"Their families know of the tragedy . . ."

"What did you do—send telegrams? My gods!"

"I feel sure things were handled with more . . . more delicacy than you suspect."

"I don't care," Carol said. "I'm not going back to Genesis, not now. I won't discuss it any further."

"But—"

"The subject is closed."

She stood abruptly and strode from the lounge, leaving Jim and J.T. together in awkward silence.

"Well," J.T. said finally, "I didn't handle either one of them very well, did I? Maybe if I ask her again a little later—?"

"I wouldn't advise it," Jim said.

Valkris knelt on the floor of her cabin, meditating. The low gravity of the mercenary's ship made the discipline very difficult. Remaining in one position for a great length of time required no strength of will, where gravity put little stress on the body.

Meditation was one of the few ways she had of passing the time during the miserable boredom of space travel when one was merely a passenger, a lone passenger at that. She had been more accustomed to flying her own ship, before her family fell upon hard times.

This mission would rebuild her family's fortune and its honor. She resisted unseemly pride: it was merely her duty to repair the damage done to all their reputations by the actions of her older brother. Kiosan had never forgiven their family for choosing Valkris, rather than him, to lead them.

In his despair and envy he set out to prove how spectacularly correct the family had been to overlook him. He reneged on all the vows he had made when he came of age. He put aside his veil and showed his face to the world. He addicted himself to pleasure, and he showed no desire to change. Valkris offered him the opportunity to return to the family three times, and even a fourth, though the fourth offer strained her sense of aesthetics. Not only did he refuse— he dared her to break her own word and join him.

Valkris had disowned her brother with a regret so intense that to this moment she felt the pain. But Kiosan's actions had sent their family's reputation and merit into an inexorable slide that could not be reversed unless he repented or she released him. So Valkris had set him free. To all her other blood kin, he was dead. But he was still very much alive to Valkris, and when she thought of him, as she often did, she wished him well in his freedom and envied him more than a little.

She had made vows, too. Every member of each of the great families took the vows upon coming of age. Despite the example of her older brother, Valkris was unable to break them. Every action she had taken since accepting her position had been intended to benefit the family. She had never fled a duel. She had never even lost a duel, though she bore scars from wounds that would have proven her honor even had she yielded to the opponent who inflicted them. Because of her reputation for ferocious tenacity, she had not been challenged in some years. Valkris did not fight for an afternoon's entertainment. She had buried more opponents than she had permitted to be helped from the field.

It was good that the family would recover from Kiosan's foolishness. It was better that it was Valkris who designed the recovery, and who would carry it out.

She extended both her hands and clenched her fingers into fists, feeling the tension and the strength in her long, strong muscles. She rose smoothly to her feet and made a hand signal before the sensor of the intercom.

"Yes?" the captain of the mercenary vessel said after a moment.

"The gravity in my cabin is very weak. I require it to be increased."

"There's a matter of the extra fuel to run the grav generators."

"You will not lose by acceding to my requests, Captain," Valkris said. She was tired enough of his pettiness to consider making him a challenge. She resisted the unworthy impulse. She could gain no honor by vanquishing such a creature. He had no style.

"Very well," the captain said disagreeably.

A short time later the gravity in Valkris' cabin began to increase. She knelt again and composed herself for meditation. When the force increased well beyond that of her homeworld, she simply smiled and set herself to find the discipline she had been seeking.

Saavik did her work automatically. She had practiced on the bridge of the *Enterprise* so often that the responses came without her conscious thought. Any change, any anomaly, would call itself to her attention instantly. For the moment everything was normal—as normal as it could be for a half-crippled ship—so Saavik could think of other things.

She thought about David, she thought about Mister Spock, and she thought about the strangeness of her life. Mister Spock had helped her transform herself from a starving, abandoned, illiterate child-thief into a polished, controlled, and well-educated Starfleet officer. Under most circumstances she was the very model of Vulcan propriety. That had been her goal, until her last conversation with Spock. "You must find your own path," he had said. The wisdom of his words impressed her. He had told her she might find herself considering possibilities that she knew he would not approve. She should not, he said, dismiss them on that criterion alone. Instead, she should remain open to them.

The path she had chosen last night led into the unexplored regions of her Romulan heritage. Spock would most certainly not have encouraged such a journey. For that reason Saavik found even more cause to admire his insight into her character and his own.

Saavik thought about her life, she thought about Mister Spock, and she thought about—her thoughts kept coming back to—David.

"Lieutenant Saavik."

"Yes, Admiral." Saavik turned to face Admiral Kirk, who had just stepped onto the bridge with an unfamiliar officer: Captain Esteban of the *Grissom,* by his uniform and insignia.

"J.T.," Kirk said, "this is Lieutenant Saavik. Lieutenant, Captain Esteban is on a survey trip to Genesis. He needs someone along who has a scientific background, and who witnessed the creation of the world. Doctor Marcus has declined to go. Would you care to volunteer?"

"Aye, Admiral," she said. She thought of David. The words tasted bitter. She turned back to her console.

Chapel paused at McCoy's bedside and felt his forehead again. His fever had receded, and she had heard him move restlessly as if he were about to wake up.

"Chris?"

"Yes, Leonard." She tried to keep the ragged wariness from her voice, but the pain still showed. Whatever his excuse for saying a very Vulcan thing to her in a creditable imitation of Spock's voice, it had still hurt her badly.

"What's going on? What happened?"

"What do you mean, Leonard? Since you spoke to me last? Since last night? Since we left Spacedock? What's the *matter* with you?"

"I . . . I don't know. Everything seems so strange."

She felt concerned enough about him to turn on the medical sensors above his bed. She had held off doing so earlier because she knew what he would say if he awoke to find them quietly talking to themselves over his head.

"What're you doing? I'm not sick. I don't need those damned blinkenlightzen interrupting my sleep."

Chris managed to laugh. "That's more like it," she said. She watched the sensors through a couple of cycles. Nothing seemed amiss. Leonard's temperature had dropped to normal. His body chemistry showed no evidence of the metabolic breakdown products of alcohol. But if he had not been drunk last night . . . what had affected him? She turned off the sensors.

"What time is it?" he asked.

"Eight hundred hours."

"Good lord."

Without comment, Chris let him sit up. If he was well enough to help, all the better.

"Leonard," she said.

"Hm?"

"Why did you say that to me?"

"What?"

"A little while ago you woke up, and you said, 'Vulcans do not love.' "

"My gods, Chris," he said, shocked. "Did I? I'm *sorry.* All night I've been having those horrible dreams where you can't tell if they're real or not. I can't even remember anything about them except how frightening and how real they were. I guess I must have been dreaming . . . about Spock."

"I see," she said.

"I never would have said such a thing if I'd known what I was saying. Will you accept my apology?"

"Yes," she said. Wanting to forget about it as soon as possible, she changed the subject. "Are you well enough to go on duty? Someone has to accompany Carol Marcus to Spacelab. I think it should be one of us."

"Good gods—Jim isn't going to let anybody go down there—!"

He jumped out of bed. Chris caught him when he staggered and nearly fell.

"I'm all right—just stood up too fast."

"Uh-huh." She helped him sit on the edge of the bed. "You're in no condition to leave the ship—especially since I don't know what's wrong with you."

"But—"

"Don't be an ass, Leonard. You can stay here and rest under your own authority, or you can stay under Admiral Kirk's orders. Your choice."

"I forbid you—" He stopped. "Sorry. Chris, I've already been down there— I've seen . . . what happened to Carol Marcus's friends. Letting her see it would be cruel."

"I saw the records you made—surely you didn't think I'd take Carol into *that*—" The violence of the murders flashed unbidden into her mind. "*Grissom's* medical officer has already taken a team into the space station," Chris said. "The . . . casualties . . . are in stasis. The sites are in order." The technical words made the descriptions easier to say.

"Chris, if you're sure—"

"What I said before still holds. You're staying here, under any circumstances."

McCoy stopped trying to hide his exhaustion. He sagged back on his bunk.

"I'm just overtired," he said. "Don't trouble Jim with this."

"That's up to you."

"I'll stay in sickbay."

Chris nodded, relieved at his acquiescence.

The codes and the documentation for Genesis had to be retrieved from Regulus I; the bodies of Khan's victims had to be formally identified and transferred to the *Enterprise.* Carol walked toward the transporter room, dreading the task that faced her. David, beside her, suddenly touched her elbow and drew her to a halt.

"What's the matter, David?"

"There's no reason for you to go down there. I can . . . take care of everything."

"I hardly need to be protected by my own son," Carol said. "This is my responsibility."

"Mother—"

"David, we both lost friends in this disaster," Carol said. One of the ways she could hold off her grief was by reminding herself continually that she was not alone.

"—I know that Vance was more than just a friend to you."

"I know you know it. Did you think we thought we were secret lovers?" She herself had thought it must be obvious to everyone, because she had felt as if she were walking around in a perpetual glow, a bit like the way David and Saavik looked this morning. Right after she and Vance had become lovers, David said offhand to her that he did not understand why the two of them spent so much time together. "Del's a lot more interesting," David had said. "Vance is okay, but he's kind of, well, boring, I think." And Carol, amused that David had not caught on, replied, "Then you don't know Vance very well." Vance was quieter than his partner, more reserved, and steadier. Del possessed a fragile ego and a quick temper, and Carol, for all that she acknowledged his brilliance, thought he was a little crazy. Vance, though . . . Vance was the sanest person she had ever known. Del might be interesting to be around—as in the old Chinese curse, "May you live in interesting times." Being with Vance was simply and purely fun.

David had seemed to catch on, eventually, though now was the first time they had directly discussed it. Far from being jealous, as certain psychological theories would have made him, he had subsequently become much better friends with Vance, which had pleased Carol tremendously.

"I just thought," David said, "if you didn't have to see him . . ."

Carol took his hand and held it between hers. "David, losing Vance is the most painful thing I've ever experienced. I still don't believe he's gone. Because of our work, I *have* to go down to Spacelab. But even if I didn't, I'd have to go anyway. Do you understand?"

"I don't think so," he said.

"If I don't . . . If I don't see him, I'll never be able to believe he's dead. I have to accept it."

David hugged her suddenly.

"I'm so sorry," he whispered. "I'm so damned sorry. When you and he were together, you looked happier than I ever saw you before. It just isn't fair—!" His voice broke, and he did not try to say more.

Carol hugged him, then drew back and scrubbed her sleeve across her eyes.

"We'd better go," she said.

Three

Carol Marcus and Christine Chapel materialized within the stasis room of Spacelab. The blue glow of the stasis fields leaked eerily from the edges of five of the chambers. Carol hesitated a moment, then opened the first one. She looked down at the shrouded figure, then drew the cloth from the pale face of a very young man, who had died with an expression of terror.

"This is Jan." She said his full name and his I.D. number for the identification record that Chris was making. "He was our steward. He hadn't been on

Spacelab for long. A freighter stopped by a few months ago, and when it left he stayed behind. He said he was working his way across the galaxy. He wanted to see everything there is to see. 'I know that's impossible,' he told me, 'but it's too good a line to pass up.' He wrote poetry, but he would never let anyone read it." She covered his pale face again, closed his chamber, and opened the second one, which protected an older man with flecks of gray in his black hair. After identifying him for the record, Carol said, "Yoshi, our cook, shouldn't have been here at all. He was due for leave, with the rest of Spacelab's staff. But when he found out a few of us were staying, he said he would, too, because otherwise we would all forget to eat and make ourselves sick with malnutrition. I think, though, that he stayed because he was as fascinated by Genesis as the rest of us. He didn't want to miss the second phase of the experiment."

Carol glanced at Chris. "Is the machine getting this? I want you to get it all."

Chris nodded. Carol was well aware that nothing was needed beyond a formal identification, but Chris recognized the private eulogies to be a facet of Carol's grief. "Yes," she said. "I'm getting it."

The third chamber held a fair, handsome young man who looked completely at peace.

"Delwin March," Carol said. "He and Vance Madison were partners. They practically invented a whole field of physics. They called it 'kindergarten physics' because it dealt with sub-elementary particles. They used to go to conferences and drive their older colleagues to distraction by refusing to take anything seriously. As far as we know yet, the two particles they discovered are the basis of the whole universe—and they named them 'snarks' and 'boojums,' out of a Lewis Carroll poem. I didn't get along very well with Del March. There was a streak of fury and pain in him that frightened me. I didn't understand it. I couldn't do anything about it and I couldn't do anything to help him. The only person who could reach him when he began to sink into that anger was his partner, and all Vance could do was keep him from hurting himself too badly." She brushed a lock of light brown hair from March's forehead and covered his face with his shroud.

The fourth chamber held the body of a Deltan woman. Her face was stately and elegant and extraordinarily beautiful. "Zinaida Chitirih-Ra-Payjh was one of the finest mathematicians in the Federation. We couldn't have gotten past stage one of Genesis without her." Carol smiled sadly. "All the boys, Jan and David and Del—poor Del, particularly—and some of the young women on the station—fell desperately in love with her, of course. Almost every human here fell in love with her or her partner or with both of them." She glanced at the recorder. "Jedda Adzhin-Dall isn't here. He died by phaser, down inside Regulus I." She sighed. "Deltans have a powerful effect on humans. Zinaida and Jedda handled it beautifully. They were polite and cool and amused. They knew, I think, that nothing will douse a crush quicker than amusement. Everybody wondered what they did in their cabin together. I doubt anybody ever got up the nerve to ask. I think they laughed—not cruelly, but just because human beings must have seemed so silly and immature to them." She put the palm of her hand along the side of Zinaida's face. "Dear Zinaida . . ." Carol glanced at Chris. "Leonard said he could not find a cause of death," she said matter-of-factly.

Chris hesitated, disturbed by Carol's eerie calm. But refusing to answer would be close to lying.

"Deltans can will themselves to die," she said. "If they find themselves in intolerable conditions. I think she wouldn't have felt any pain."

"She wouldn't have been frightened of pain," Carol said. "She would have seen it as a challenge—maybe even as an opportunity to experience something she hadn't chosen to encounter before." She replaced the shroud carefully. She opened the last chamber.

"This is Vance Madison." Her hands shaking, she uncovered his face. It was strong, intelligent, determined. The light glinted like jewels in his very curly black hair. "I used to tease Del and him by calling them 'twins,' because they were so completely different. Fair and dark, white and black, short and tall, quick-tempered and serene . . . crazy and sane." Her calm voice suddenly broke. "Oh, damn, Chris, now I have to believe he's dead . . ."

Chris Chapel turned off the recorder, went to Carol, and put her arms around her while she cried. "I know," Chris said. "I understand."

After Carol and Chris beamed down to Spacelab, Saavik and David stepped up on the transporter platform to beam into Regulus I's new ecosystem.

"Energize," Saavik said.

"Lieutenant," the cadet said hesitantly, "I can't find a clear place to beam you to."

"What?" David said. "It's full of open spaces in there."

Saavik joined the cadet at the console and inspected the readings.

"It is true, David. The surface in range of the beam is covered with some amorphous material. Even the tunnels are filled." The readings were completely different from what she had expected. She scanned further until she found a relatively empty spot. "Beam me here, cadet," she said. "I will report what I find."

"Saavik, wait a minute—" David said.

She returned to the platform. "I will either return immediately or send for you. Energize."

The cadet obeyed.

Saavik experienced the brief disorientation of dematerialization. She arrived on Regulus I, beneath the planetoid's surface and within one of the tunnels dug as a staging area for the second phase of the Genesis project. She held her communicator open and her phaser ready, should the changes threaten her.

She found herself in a very small clearing left by the random arrangement of a tangled mass of undergrowth. Vines completely filled the tunnel in which Doctor Marcus and her team had hidden the Genesis records.

"Saavik to *Enterprise*. I have reached the surface. David, the flora has grown into the tunnels and filled them. Is this what you intended?"

"No. Not at all—but like I told you, things always happen that you don't expect. I'm coming down."

"Wait a moment. I will clear a place for you." First she tried to push aside the beautiful flowering tendrils, but they sprang back into place. In trying to move them, she crushed some of the stems and blossoms. The damaged foliage released a pungent and entrancing scent.

Saavik set her phaser to very-short-range disintegrate. She had checked the phaser out precisely because David had told her that the Genesis experiment was so complex that its outcome could not be predicted in every detail. She had not, however, expected to be attacked by the vegetation.

The scarlet-edged green leaves withered and vanished before the beam of her phaser. The sweet, spicy fragrance intensified. She opened her communicator.

"Saavik to *Enterprise*. Cadet, can you lock onto the cleared area?"

"Aye, Lieutenant."

David materialized beside her. He looked around and whistled in surprise.

"I take that to mean you did not expect anything like this," Saavik said.

"It's even more viable than we thought! My gods, look at the growth, even under artificial light!"

Saavik forbore to puncture his enthusiasm by pointing out that the ball of glowing plasma deeper inside the planetoid gave light no more "natural" than did the overhead fixtures illuminating the tunnels. The mass of reacting gases was held to the proper density by magnetic fields and kept in place by stress fields. It and the surrounding shell of the planetoid existed in an essentially unstable relationship.

"I would call this 'overgrowth,' David. And we still must reach the Genesis records: We do not have much time."

"Hey, I designed these vines—at least give me a chance to admire my own handiwork for a minute, will you?"

"Admire the ones behind us. I must destroy some of the ones in our path. Please do not take it personally." Before she fired her phaser she added, "They are very beautiful. And the scent is aesthetically pleasing."

"Thanks."

Through the intertwining foliage, Saavik could just see the great pile of portable memory banks that held the Genesis research. As she cut a path in that direction, David plucked a spray of leaves from a vine, crushed them, and inhaled the scent.

"They'll grow berries in a couple of months. Ought to make great wine."

Saavik reached the cache of Genesis records. She focused her phaser to a tight beam, powered it down to its minimum level, and used it like a scalpel to remove the undergrowth from the boxes. As she finished, David approached. He put his arms around her from behind and rubbed the leaves together between his hands. The refreshing perfume rose up around her face.

"Wouldn't you like to try some wine that tasted like these smell?"

Saavik holstered her phaser and took David's hands between her own. She stroked the backs of his hands with her fingers and grasped his wrists, feeling the cool throb of his pulse.

"The scent requires nothing more," she said. "It is complete in itself. It is perfect, very much like its designer."

He let the leaves fall to the ground and hugged her more tightly, burying his face in her hair. She wanted nothing more than to respond to his caress.

Her communicator beeped.

"I'd never design a bird that made a silly noise like that," David whispered in Saavik's ear. "Must have been my mother, she was never very good at music. Let's ignore it."

"It would merely make more silly noises," she said. "And when it stopped, a whole flock of its comrades would come looking for it, accompanied by a whole flock of cadets playing at being security officers." She kissed him quickly and pulled out her communicator. Chuckling, David brushed the last remnants of his vines from the storage boxes.

"Saavik here."

"How long will you be, Lieutenant?" Admiral Kirk said. "Captain Esteban wants to leave for the Mutara sector as soon as possible."

"A few more minutes, Admiral," Saavik said. "We have located the Genesis records and are preparing to beam them up."

"Very well. Shake a leg. Kirk out."

With a curious frown, Saavik closed the communicator. " 'Shake a leg'?" she said to David. "How would that be of benefit? Is it an exercise?"

"It's an idiom, it means hurry up. Why did he tell you Esteban's plans?"

"Because he has ordered—" She stopped, and then, to be fair, she said, "Or, rather, he strongly invited me to volunteer to accompany *Grissom* to Genesis. Such invitations are not wisely declined."

"What? Damn! So he's trying to cut me and Mother out of the follow-up! Saavik, do you know what this means?"

"It means he is under the impression that you do not care to go—he said you had declined."

"The hell I did!"

"But he said—Oh. Perhaps he meant Doctor Marcus, senior."

"He didn't even ask *me!* Son of a bitch!"

"Surely if you tell him you wish to go—"

"He'll probably think of some way to stop me. He'll try, anyway. Especially now that you're going."

David made Saavik acutely uncomfortable when he referred to the admiral in such an angry, abusive tone.

"Why do you speak of him like this, David? I was under the impression that you and he had found reason to accept each other."

"So was I. For a while. But maybe I was wrong. Maybe we're too different." He blew his breath out in exasperation, then suddenly grinned. "I have an idea. Let's let him wait. Let's blast a trail to the interior and see what's going on there."

Saavik put her hand on her phaser and very nearly drew it. She was so tempted by his invitation that the strength of her desire shocked her.

"I would like that very much," she said.

"Great. Let's go."

"What I would like is very far from what I must do."

"Oh, come on—a few minutes won't hurt."

"It would take hours to clear a trail through the tunnels."

He snatched playfully at her phaser. She avoided him easily, and not at all playfully.

"Spoilsport," he said. "I thought you were different, but you're just like everybody else in Starfleet."

"I am like no one else at all, in Starfleet or outside it," she said.

"Indoctrinated in the military mind."

"You are provoking me, David."

As she pulled out her communicator, David grabbed again for her phaser, this time with more determination. Reacting automatically, she grasped his hand in a move Commander Sulu had taught her in a self-defense class. The phaser went flying.

"Let go! Geez, what are you doing?"

"The technical term is 'kotegaeshi,' " Saavik said.

"I don't give a shit what it's called—will you let go!"

He dug the nails of his free hand into her fingers to try to make her release him. She put enough twist on his wrist to hurt if he resisted.

"Okay, okay!" he said.

Before she could put the communicator away and retrieve her phaser, the *Enterprise* signaled again.

"*Enterprise* to Saavik," Admiral Kirk said. There was a definite edge to his voice. "Will you get a move on, Lieutenant?"

"Immediately, Admiral," she said. "The Genesis records are cleared of foliage. The transporter beam may now lock onto them."

"Preparing to beam up," the cadet in the transporter room said through the communicator.

"Think you can cut me out of my own project, do you, you filthy warmonger?" David shouted before Saavik could close the channel.

"David? What are you talking about?" Kirk's tone was hurt and surprised.

"I'll tell you what I'm talking about—"

Saavik snapped the communicator closed and slapped it back in place on her belt.

"What is wrong with you?" Saavik had begun to get used to David's impulsive actions. Until now he had never seemed maliciously irresponsible.

The transporter beam glowed; the boxes of Genesis records sparkled and disappeared.

Saavik dragged David around till she could reach her phaser. It had fallen into a tangle of vines. She had to rip it loose from the tendrils that had curled around it. The pungent scent rose up to enclose her.

She felt dizzy. She shoved the phaser against her belt and fumbled for the communicator.

"Saavik to *Enterprise*. Beam us up."

"One moment, please, Lieutenant. We have to clear the platforms."

"Quickly!" She slipped to her knees. The stone floor of the tunnel felt very hard and cold. Tiny tendrils of David's beautiful vines dug into the solid rock. Saavik struggled to her feet. Her grip on David's hand loosened and he came toward her, reaching again for her phaser.

The transporter beam enveloped and dematerialized them.

Jim Kirk stormed into the transporter room just as Lieutenant Saavik and David appeared on the platform among the piles of boxes that the cadet had shoved untidily aside.

David and Saavik were holding hands.

Charming, I'm sure, Kirk thought, *but hardly the place or time—and damned foolish to do while being transported. Lucky neither had lost an arm.*

"I take it you have something to say to me, young man," Kirk said to David.

The young scientist pulled his hand free of Saavik's and strode forward to meet his father.

"You bet I do."

Behind them, Saavik took one step forward and felt her knees begin to buckle. Before she could fall, she sat down quickly on the edge of the platform. David and the admiral argued, David resentfully, the admiral indignantly, neither listening to the other. Saavik stopped listening to both of them.

"Saavik, are you okay?" The cadet crouched beside her, concerned.

"Yes . . . of course." She had to draw on all her Vulcan training to find enough strength to rise. She had not had much sleep in the past several days, but she should be able to function effectively for much longer without rest. She had done so before, in practice. She felt ashamed and embarrassed.

"Admiral," she said. Neither he nor David heard her. "Admiral Kirk!" she said more loudly, breaking into the argument.

Kirk swung around to face her. "What *is* it, Lieutenant?"

"May I be dismissed? I must prepare to transfer to the *Grissom.*"

"All right, yes. Dismissed."

Saavik sat in her cabin, grateful for its dry warmth and the dim, scarlet-tinged light. Her preparations remained incomplete, but she needed a moment to collect herself and to think about her own and David's inexplicable behavior.

Absently she drew her phaser and plucked away the delicate pink tendrils. Many climbing plants have the ability to coil themselves around whatever solid object they contact. This species moved quickly, but she had seen others that were faster. Its ability to probe into solid rock was exceptional—if she had seen what she thought she saw. She wished for time to explore Regulus I. She was, she thought, nearly as anxious as David to know the full results of the Genesis programs.

Saavik lifted a crushed vine-leaf to her nose to experience again the dazzling scent. The fragrance twined around her like the tendrils around her phaser.

Dizziness hit her. Saavik jerked the leaf away. She gazed at it, frowning. She put it aside, went to the synthesizer panel, and requested the ship's computer to send her a sampling envelope. When it appeared, she swept together all the bits of David's vine. Repressing the wish to inhale their redolent essence, she sealed them within the clear plastic.

Jim Kirk folded his arms across his chest. "David, I don't understand what you're so angry about. Carol said she didn't want to go back to the Mutara sector—naturally I assumed you didn't want to go, either."

"You should have asked me," David said stubbornly. He felt tremendously relieved that his mother was not willing to return yet, and terrified and angry that he might be forbidden to do so. "I'll tell you why you expect me to do exactly what she does—it's because everybody you know has jumped when you said 'frog' for so long that you don't think anybody has a mind of their own!"

Jim chuckled. "You don't know the people I know, if you think that. Look, I've apologized—I don't see that there's much else I can do, if you're determined to sulk."

"You can send me out on *Grissom*."

Jim hesitated. "Are you sure that's wise?"

"Why isn't it wise?"

"I just thought . . ."

David glared at him belligerently. Jim took a moment to sort through his own feelings.

"I'll be honest with you, David. I was hoping you'd stay on board the *Enterprise*. I've wanted a chance to talk to you. I can't make up for all the years that I didn't know you—"

"No," David said coldly. "You can't."

Taken aback by David's reaction, Jim said, "Whether you like it or not, I am your father."

"You can't spend twenty years ignoring my existence—"

"David, I didn't—"

"—and just waltz in and expect me to shower you with filial piety!"

"All I want is for us to try to be friends."

"It's too late! It's too damned late for you to come along and try to make friends with me!"

They were getting nowhere; they were succeeding only in antagonizing each other. Jim decided to try to defuse the argument until they both could cool down.

"I hope you're wrong, David," he said. "But I think I understand why you're angry and disappointed. I hope someday you can forgive me, or even accept me. In the meantime let's try at least to be civil to each other. For your mother's sake."

"For my mother's sake! Since when did you give a damn about my mother?"

"You aren't going to let up, are you?" Jim was both angry and hurt. Every concession he had tried to make, David had thrown back in his face. "Get your things together—*Grissom* warps out of orbit in an hour."

He stalked out of the room.

David knocked softly on the door of his mother's cabin. He waited, then knocked again. The door finally slid open. Darkness faced him.

"Mother?"

"Yes, David." Her voice was very quiet.

"Your things that were down inside the cave—I brought them back up with me."

"Thank you." She turned on a light.

"They told me you didn't want to go back to the Mutara sector."

"No," she said. "Not now. I can't, not now."

"I volunteered to. I think it's important that one of us be in the reconnaissance party."

She looked at him in silence.

"I understand why you want to go back to Earth," David said. "I should, too, probably."

"I'd hoped . . ." she said softly.

"Mother, this is essential. *Somebody's* got to keep an eye on Starfleet. To be sure they tell the truth about what happened out there. We can't just let them have free rein, not after everything that's happened."

"I know," she said. "You're right that one of us should go. Probably both of us should."

"No!" he said quickly, then forced his voice back under control when she reacted to his intensity. "It isn't going to be anything but a fast survey. Somebody's got to keep them honest, but it won't take both of us. Mother, I'm leaving you to do the hard job all alone—"

"I have to do it alone," she said. "It's only that I've been afraid . . ."

"Of what?"

"There's a reason I never told you Jim Kirk is your father, David. There are a lot of reasons, but the main one was selfish."

"I don't understand."

"I was afraid that if you found out that your father was a starship captain, you'd be off on the next ship, flying around the galaxy, and I'd never see you again." She sighed. "I told Jim I want you in my world, not in his. But I should have let you make the decision."

"What decision?" He laughed. "Mother, can you really see me on the crew of this ship?" He jerked to attention. "Yessir. Aye-aye sir. I'll be glad to swab the poop deck, sir." Slowly and deliberately, he crossed his eyes.

Carol could not help but laugh. "I don't think starships have poop decks, David."

"They'd probably invent one just for me to swab. I'd never make it in the military."

"Only . . ."

"What?"

"You've met your father, and you're about to go off on a starship."

"Yeah, but note carefully that it isn't *his* starship. Honest, Mom, I'm not going to up and join Starfleet." He hugged her. "I won't even be gone very long. Promise."

"I know."

"They're leaving soon. I better go."

"Good-bye, David. Be careful."

"I almost forgot—" He reached under his shirt and drew out a folded piece of drafting fabric. "Our Starfleet friends sealed the Genesis records, but I insisted on checking them over before they locked them away. I didn't know if they'd let either of us in there again. Who knows who they'll turn everything over to, back on Earth. So . . ." The shiny, silvery material slipped out of its folds and lay soft and unwrinkled in his hands. Dark blue lines and stippling marked it. "I stole this for you when nobody was looking." He handed her the map of the second phase of Genesis.

After drawing the map of the ecosystem for Regulus I, Vance Madison had made a copy for each member of the team. They had all contributed to the plan, and they had all been looking forward to comparing the map with the eventual outcome. The vines in the staging area hinted at greatly divergent results. David wondered if he—if anyone—would ever get the chance to explore Regulus I's interior.

Carol took the map from him and smoothed it out across her lap.

"David . . . thank you." She touched the outer reaches of the map, near the north pole. Inside the shell of the world, centrifugal acceleration created an artificial gravity. But as one curved around toward the poles, the force would become more acutely angled to the surface. The radius of spin would shorten. Thus one would seem to be climbing up an increasingly steeper hill, against a steadily decreasing force.

The team had left the odd environment of the poles almost uncolonized by their creations, for they had primarily been interested in inventing life forms that would be useful on a new world. Carol was rather pleased with her silk heather, and Yoshi had suggested the cornucopia tree, which produced several different kinds of fruit at each season. Vance had invented a small carnivore that he fancifully named the white rabbit, and Del responded by designing the March hare. Its main distinction, he claimed, was complete lunacy. The way he described it, it sounded like a cross between a howler monkey and a gecko. Carol smiled, thinking that it was characteristic of the two young men to design a "rabbit" that was not a rabbit, and a "hare" that was not a hare. When they presented their creations at the weekly design meeting, Carol had laughed and threatened to make up something they could call the mad hatter.

None of those creations lived out toward the poles. At the very top of the map, in spidery script, Vance had written "Here be dragons."

"I wonder if there really are dragons," Carol said softly.

Saavik arrived in the transporter room, ready to beam on board *Grissom,* but found herself all alone. As she was punctual, she felt it safe to assume the others had not left without her.

Waiting in the empty, dim transporter room, she sought something to occupy her mind. Someone spoke her name.

"Captain—?" She turned around, looking for the speaker.

No one else had yet entered the room. The deep shadows offered no hiding places.

"Who is there?" she said.

It occurred to her that someone might be trying to play a joke on her, though no one had ever done so before. No one had ever even told jokes to her. Until a few days ago she had considered them completely frivolous, and thus beneath notice. Jokes could be based in cruelty, she knew, but it was usually a sort of benign cruelty.

Cruel it would be, and not the least bit benign, to play a joke on Saavik by calling out her name, in Mister Spock's voice.

"Saavikam—"

She clapped her hands over her ears. The voice spoke in Vulcan, using a Vulcan form of address.

"*Saavikam,* why did you leave me on Genesis?"

The voice was audible only to her.

It was not a joke.

"Mister Spock," she whispered, "why are you not at peace? I watched over you, and I sent your body into the new world. I thought that would please you . . ."

She heard voices in the corridor. Bringing herself back to some semblance of composure, she pulled her hands from her face and straightened her tunic.

Admiral Kirk and Captain Esteban entered.

"Hello, Lieutenant," the Admiral said. "I see you're on time. Think how much we could get done, J.T., if we were as organized and imperturbable as Lieutenant Saavik."

Nothing Kirk had said to Saavik required a reply, so she remained silent. She felt neither organized nor imperturbable.

This time she did feel as if she were going mad.

Saavik had experienced mind-meld several times during her life, most often with Spock. The touch of his mind was the first civilized experience she had ever had. The touch of a mind was unique. It was impossible to mistake the mind of a person one had touched for that of any other sentient being, strange or familiar. Yet the voice Saavik had felt, the consciousness that had just cried out to her, had felt like Mister Spock's. Which it could not have been.

"You're very quiet, Lieutenant. Are you having second thoughts about this mission? You did volunteer, you know—you can change your mind."

"No!" she said more forcefully than she had intended.

He gave her a quizzical look, not precisely a remonstration, but not approval either.

"No, sir," she said in a more collected tone. "I believe it is extremely important for me to go on this mission."

"Very well. Where the devil is David?"

"He'd better hurry along if he's coming," Esteban said. "I can't wait all day."

"*Is* David coming, Admiral?" Saavik asked.

"He better be," Kirk said. "He read me the riot act about not asking him in the first place."

At that moment David strode in, a small pack slung over his shoulder.

"We were just about to give up on you," Kirk said.

"I was saying good-bye to my mother," David said. "Any objections?"

"None at all," Kirk said mildly.

Kirk shook hands with Captain Esteban.

"Good to see you again, J.T. Let's not leave it so long before we cross paths again."

"We'll be back in a month or six weeks, Jim."

"We'll plan to get together then." Kirk turned to Saavik and, to her surprise, extended his hand to her. She shook it gingerly.

"Good luck, Lieutenant. Take care of my son."

"Aye, sir," she said, and wondered how many layers a human being, accustomed to the ambiguities and "little jokes" of Standard, would find in his order.

"David."

Kirk reached out to his son. When David warily grasped his hand, Kirk drew the young man toward him and into a bear hug.

"Take care of yourself, son," he said.

David extricated himself rather less gracefully than he might. David's mercurial character, Saavik thought, was not ready to forgive what had passed between him and the admiral.

"Don't worry," David said. "There's nothing dangerous in the Mutara sector anymore. Nothing dangerous at all."

Kirk watched the young people—Esteban, David, and Saavik—vanish from the transporter platform. Off into the unknown. He did wish he were going with them.

Instead, he called the bridge and asked Commander Sulu to warp out of orbit and head back toward Earth. Then Kirk himself headed for sickbay.

McCoy was up and working. His façade was excellent, but Kirk could tell it was only a façade. To Kirk, McCoy appeared pale and fragile and distracted, despite the gentle joke he made with an injured young cadet, despite the steadiness of his hands and the certainty of his voice.

"Good morning, Bones," Kirk said. "Talk to you in your office?"

"Hi, Jim. Sure. One minute."

McCoy joined him in the office as soon as he had finished with his patient. "What's up? Need a good hangover remedy?"

"I might ask you the same question."

McCoy gave up his jocular pose. "But I wasn't—" He stopped. "Never mind. It doesn't matter. I owe you an apology anyway. Scotty wanted to have a wake for his nephew, and I thought, Why not include Spock? All I can say is it seemed like a good idea at the time."

"It's over and done," Jim said. "If I'd thought about it I probably would have put my foot down before the whole thing got up any momentum. My only excuse is I had other things on my mind. But I'm worried about you. Last night, you were acting . . . odd."

"Odd?" McCoy chuckled. "I'm not surprised. The synthesizers aren't quite up to decent liquor."

Kirk frowned, detecting a false note in McCoy's dismissal of last night's events.

"I don't mean drunk. You didn't act drunk."

"I didn't?" McCoy exclaimed, all too heartily. "I must be out of practice."

"Don't you remember what you said?"

"About what?"

"You stood up on a table and said 'Grief is not logical' in a pretty damned good imitation of Spock's voice. That isn't your usual sort of . . . humor."

"That isn't humor of any sort," McCoy said. "I must have been farther gone than I thought."

"Tell me what's wrong," Jim said. "Bones, let me help."

"Sure—you can help by accepting my apology and forgetting what it is I'm apologizing for."

When McCoy wanted to avoid interrogation, he could sidestep with the best of them. Jim had not quite reached the point of trying to get an answer out of his old friend by pulling rank. Besides, when had it ever done him any good, with McCoy, to assert his authority as a starship captain?

"Apology accepted. Forgetting—that's going to take a little longer. If you want to talk, you know where to find me."

Kirk returned to the bridge, still disturbed about McCoy, and feeling that his visit to sickbay had been very nearly futile.

On board *Grissom*, Saavik thanked the duty officer for giving her a cabin assignment. The young Vulcan did not bother to stop by her room. She had nothing with her to drop off, and a more pressing matter to attend to than observing the decor of *Grissom*'s cabins.

She felt the faint shift in the ship's gravity fields that indicated they had warped out of orbit. *Grissom,* a small, fast ship, could travel between Regulus and the Mutara sector much more quickly than the crippled *Enterprise.*

Saavik entered the main laboratory and stopped short.

Before her stood a being like a column of rippled crystal. Saavik had never met a Glaeziver before. They were very rare. They intended and planned to be extinct within a hundred Standard years. Their planet had been destroyed in the nova of its star. They possessed such strong ties to their world that they never found another on which they felt anything but alien. And so they disbanded, scattering throughout the Federation and perhaps even beyond.

It occurred to Saavik that if Genesis could be programmed to copy their lost world closely enough, they might change their collective decision to die. If they possessed a world to return to, they might choose to live.

"Hello," Saavik said formally. "How may I address you?"

The utter motionlessness of the being gave Saavik the impression of enormous potential energy preparing to translate itself into motion. When the Glaeziver stirred, it did so with a controlled power that belied the delicacy of its form. The many transparent strands making up its substance brushed together with a chiming like jewels in the wind. ,

"You're well-mannered for an opaque being," the Glaeziver said. Its voice was like a cymbalon. "If you can pronounce my name, you may use it." It spoke a beautiful word like a song, which Saavik reproduced as best she could.

"Not bad," the Glaeziver said. "You may call me that, if you like. I prefer it to Fred."

" 'Fred'?" Saavik said.

"One of my co-workers fancies that my name sounds like a phrase of Chopin's. How may I address you?"

"My name is Saavik."

"How do you do, Saavik. What can I do for you?"

"I wish to analyze a sample from the interior of Regulus I. May I use your equipment?"

"Can you talk and work at the same time?"

"Certainly."

"In that case, I'll make you a deal. We will analyze your sample on my equipment while you tell me what has been going on out here—inside Regulus I, and in the Mutara."

"That appears a fair trade to me," Saavik said.

"Great. What kind of analysis do you want—macroscopic, molecular, atomic, sub-atomic?"

"Molecular, please."

"You got it."

Glaezivers had a reputation for being very formal and standoffish. Saavik found it quite interesting that the being had held to formality during their introductions, but spoke very casually otherwise. It was very easy to think of it as "Fred."

Saavik's cabin was standard for a Federation ship, designed and intended for a human being. The lighting imitated the spectrum of Earth's star, and the temperature conformed to the temperate regions of their home planet. Saavik glanced around the room, approving of its lack of extraneous decoration and its communications terminal, disapproving of the heavily padded furniture. She preferred hard chairs and a sleeping mat.

She reprogrammed the environmental controls. The light dimmed and reddened, and the temperature began gradually to rise. Saavik sat down for the first time since arriving on *Grissom*. Preparing for the survey of Genesis and analyzing the sample from Regulus I had given her plenty of work, for which she was grateful. It took her mind off the fears she had had for her own sanity.

But since leaving the *Enterprise*, she no longer sensed Spock's presence. If she still believed in ghosts—as she had when she was little, for things happened on Hellguard that an uneducated and unsophisticated child could explain no other way—she would have believed Spock's shade to be haunting the *Enterprise*. But she did not believe in ghosts anymore. She believed that for a short while she had been at least a little bit insane.

And now? To test herself, to test the silence, Saavik took the risk of opening her mental shields. She closed her eyes and reached out, seeking any resonance, real or imagined, of Spock.

After some minutes she opened her eyes again. She had found nothing.

The echo of her teacher had vanished. He was gone, and Saavik grieved for him. But at least she was not mad.

She picked up the printout of the Regulus I sample and reread the analysis.

Someone knocked on her door.

"Come."

David entered, smiling. "Hi. Guess what. I'm right next door. Great, huh?"

"That depends. Have you come to your senses?"

"What? Are you talking about what happened down in the Genesis cave?" He shrugged it off. "Yeah, sure, sorry—I don't know what got into me. I guess I was overexcited."

"That is your explanation?"

"What's the matter? I'm sorry I tried to take your phaser—that was dumb. If it's any comfort, you twisted the hell out of my wrist. I can still feel it. And, look, there's a bruise here on my hand where you put your thumb."

"You should not have resisted," Saavik said. "You injured yourself with your own violence."

"And you got your revenge."

"Why do you assume I want revenge? Or that I would take pleasure in hurting you? That is beside the point. You know that I do not use recreational drugs. Even if I did, I was on duty when we beamed down to the Genesis caves. How could you not warn me?"

"Saavik, what are you talking about?"

Saavik was prepared for a laugh and a claim of "a little joke." She was not prepared for deliberate obtuseness. She handed him the printout.

He scanned it.

"Interesting organic makeup. What is it?"

"You should know. You designed it."

"I never did. I never saw this set of molecules before in my life."

"David, that is an analysis of the Genesis vines—the vines you created."

"It's nothing like. Well, superficially, maybe. But this whole subset of molecules—"

"I ran the samples twice," Saavik said. "I am hardly infallible, but this summary *is* accurate."

"But it shouldn't look like this. I don't even know what half the stuff is."

"This," Saavik said, pointing to a heterocyclic compound, "is an extremely potent psychoactive alkaloid."

"What!" David looked at it more closely. "My gods, it could be, couldn't it?"

"It is. It is also the reason we behaved as we did—why we nearly abandoned our tasks to go exploring, like two irresponsible children—"

" 'We'?" David said, rubbing his wrist. "You could have fooled me, if you were about to do anything out of line."

"I came very close to it," Saavik said. "The active ingredient in those vines is a narcotic."

"I designed it so you could brew tea out of the leaves if you wanted. I put a lot of caffeine in it, that's all."

Saavik could see the resemblance between the molecule in question and caffeine, but it had gone through considerable mutation to become what it was.

"I think you would not want to brew tea out of this plant," Saavik said. "Or make wine of its fruit."

"You never know," David said.

Saavik raised one eyebrow.

"Just kidding," David said.

Four

Phase three of Genesis spun like a mobile drifting in the breeze. David watched the newly-formed star system on the *Grissom*'s viewscreen. Despite his calculated calm, he was astonished that the new world was his creation. So far it looked like the programs had worked perfectly. The lack of a sun for the world to orbit had enabled the star-forming subroutine. The great dust-cloud of the Mutara Nebula had provided plenty of mass to form a small, hot star.

David leaned against the bridge rail. He felt out of place and in the way, despite the ship's being there at least partly because of him. Behind him, at the main sensor station, Saavik seemed to David very much in place, cool and controlled.

She had forgiven him for the incident in the Genesis caves back on Regulus I. David truly had not designed a plant containing a chemical of the potency they found. They had talked about what might have gone wrong. The changes in the experiment's outcome were of a far greater magnitude than David had expected. He was still trying to convince himself that everything really had evolved nearly the way the Genesis team intended, only a little more so. He was not ready to admit any serious doubts to himself, much less discuss them with anyone. Even Saavik.

Saavik completed the current log entry.

". . . We are approaching destination planet at point zero three five. So noted in ship's log."

She removed the data cube from the recorder and delivered the log to Captain Esteban to certify and seal.

"Very well, Lieutenant." To the helm officer, he said, "Execute standard orbital approach."

"Standard orbit, aye."

"Communications. Send a coded message for Starfleet Commander, priority one . . ."

He paused for a moment. David decided, with a smile, that the captain was thinking over his message to be sure it would not include a single informal word.

" 'Federation science vessel *Grissom* arriving Genesis planet, Mutara sector, to begin research. As ordered, full security procedures are in effect. J.T. Esteban, commanding.' "

"Aye sir, coding now."

David found the security on *Grissom* restrictive and a little scary. Genesis had always been, in theory, a secret project. Acceding to the security requirements had been the only way they could get the research funded. The whole team had taken a rather lackadaisical attitude toward the rules, mostly by thinking about them as infrequently as possible. They had all been certain that the first implementation of the project would make secrecy impossible.

That's one thing we were right about, David thought. But now the authorities wanted to try to clamp the lid back down.

On *Grissom,* dealing with Starfleet directly instead of one step removed,

David had the distinct impression that they wished he knew nothing about the project and that they would have denied him clearance if they could have done so without looking ridiculous.

Captain Esteban turned toward him. "Doctor Marcus," he said, "it's your planet."

Astonished, and pleased despite himself, David grinned. "Thank you, Captain. Begin scanning, please." He joined Saavik at the science station as she activated the macroscopic scanner. It glowed into life, forming a schematic of the world before them. The schematic showed a stable sphere, with core, mantle, crust and oceans, absolutely indistinguishable from a naturally evolved world.

Well, what did you expect? David asked himself. *That it would be flat?*

Suddenly he laughed, and all his doubts and fears evaporated in the sheer pleasure of inspecting his handiwork.

"This is where the fun begins, Saavik!" he said.

She replied, *sotto voce,* "Like your father . . . so human." Then, turning on the recorder, she took the irony and humor out of her voice. "All units functional, recorders are on. . . . Scanning sector one. The foliage is in a fully developed state of growth. Temperature, twenty-two point two degrees Celsius."

"Sector two . . . indicating desert terrain," David said. "Minimal vegetation, temperature thirty-nine point four."

At several team presentation meetings the discussion had centered on whether to include desert or any other severe climates at all. Vance said he was not interested in working on anything "so beautiful it's sappy," Del (as usual) agreed with Vance. Zinaida persisted, as Deltans often did, in quoting the Vulcan philosophy, "infinite diversity in infinite combinations." David wondered how Vulcans liked being quoted by the Federation's most renowned sensualists. He himself had pushed for trying to make Genesis a shirt-sleeve environment from pole to pole. That would have been quite a challenge. He was, however, outvoted.

"Sector three," Saavik said. "Sub-tropical vegetation."

David glanced across the bank of sensors. They must be scanning a region where several different ecotypes blended into one another.

"Temperature—" Saavik said. She stopped and checked her readings again. "Temperature decreasing rapidly."

My gods, look at that, David thought. *Infinite diversity indeed.*

"It's snow," he said. "Snow in the same sector. Fantastic!" He could not get a topographical map off the sensor he was using, but he assumed they must be looking at a snowcapped mountain upthrust in the midst of subtropical forest edged by desert.

"Fascinating," Saavik said.

"All the varieties of land and weather known to Earth within a few hours' walk!" David knew he was exaggerating, just a bit, but for a time the team had engaged in a sort of informal competition to see who could design the most complicated conditions within the smallest area. Nobody had quite come up with a workable way to juxtapose arctic and equatorial climates, but everyone had developed a different method of coming close. Some of the schemes were positively Byzantine. The trouble was, Carol eventually declared the competition out of hand and said she would not include any of the results in the Genesis device.

Maybe she changed her mind, David thought.

"You must be very proud of what you and your mother have created," Saavik said.

David gazed at the sensors and felt some of his doubts and fears beginning to creep back.

"It's a little early to celebrate," he said.

One of the sensors erupted into frantic beeping. Saavik started, then covered her surprise by bending intently over the monitor.

"Same sector," she said evenly. "Metallic mass."

"Underground, right?" David said. "Probably an ore deposit."

"Negative," Saavik said. "It is on the surface, a manufactured object."

Manufactured! David thought. *Debris from Khan's ship? The Genesis torpedo? But that was impossible—anything in range of the Genesis wave had disintegrated into a plasma of sub-elementary particles. Then he realized—*

"There's only one thing it could be!" he said.

He glanced at Saavik. Surely the same answer must have occurred to her. She gazed intently at the sensors.

"Short-range scan," David said.

Esteban joined them at the console and glanced over the readings.

"Approximately two meters long," Saavik said. "Cylindrical in form . . ."

"A photon tube—!"

Saavik continued to avoid David's look.

She's upset, David thought, *and she's embarrassed about being upset. I don't blame her—If I thought I'd buried a friend, and then his coffin turned up . . .*

"Could it be Spock's?" Esteban asked.

David had noticed that the captain did not much like being surprised.

"It has to be," David said. There were several ways it could have reached the surface of the Genesis world without burning up in the atmosphere like a shooting star. "The gravitational fields were still in flux. It must have soft-landed."

"In code to Starfleet," Esteban said. " 'Captain Spock's tube located intact on Genesis surface. Will relay more data on subsequent orbits.' "

"Yes, sir," said the communications officer. "Coding your message."

Saavik continued to stare at the changing sensors. David neither questioned nor challenged her. Instead, he reached out and put his hand over hers. Still she said nothing, but she did not draw away from him, either.

As the ship passed over the surface of the new world, crossing the terminator into darkness, the sensor's beeps grew fainter and fainter. The ship moved out of line-of-sight of the torpedo tube and the signals cut off abruptly.

J.T. Esteban thoughtfully stroked his thumb under his jaw and considered what to do. Spock's coffin was supposed to have been launched in a standard burial orbit, one that should have resulted in complete ablation. There should be nothing at all left of it. That it had landed intact created all sorts of problems, from the possibility of contamination to the responsibility for retrieving the casket and either re-launching it (J.T. would send it into the star, so there could be no mistake), or holding a formal interment on the surface of Genesis. Technically, Spock's most recent C.O. should make the decision. But with any luck, someone at Starfleet HQ would give the word. Jim Kirk could do without going through the wringer again over the death of a friend.

Under any other circumstances, J.T. might have taken it upon himself to decide what would be done, but not this time—not when it involved something as important as Genesis.

PERSONAL LOG OF JAMES T. KIRK

WITH MOST OF OUR BATTLE DAMAGE REPAIRED, WE ARE ALMOST HOME. YET I FEEL—UNEASY. AND I WONDER WHY. PERHAPS IT IS THE ERRATIC BEHAVIOR OF SHIP'S SURGEON LEONARD MCCOY, OR THE EMPTINESS OF THE VESSEL. MOST OF OUR TRAINEE CREW HAVE BEEN REASSIGNED. LIEUTENANT SAAVIK AND MY SON DAVID ARE EXPLORING A NEW WORLD. THE ENTERPRISE FEELS LIKE A HOUSE WITH ALL THE CHILDREN GONE. . . . NO, MORE EMPTY EVEN THAN THAT. THE NEWS OF SPOCK'S TUBE HAS SHAKEN ME. IT SEEMS THAT I HAVE LEFT THE NOBLEST PART OF MYSELF BACK THERE, ON THAT NEWBORN PLANET.

Jim Kirk stalked the bridge of the *Enterprise*. Sorting out his thoughts in his personal log had failed to diminish his unease.

He paused next to the science station, where Spock always sat. He put his hands on the back of the chair.

The transmission from Esteban, on Genesis, troubled him. He felt unreasonably angered and betrayed at the news that Spock's coffin had soft-landed. Kirk had ordered a trajectory that should have burned the tube to ashes in the upper atmosphere of Genesis. Whether Spock's body returned to its constituent atoms quickly, in fire, or slowly, in the earth of a new world, surely did not matter to the Vulcan any longer. But Kirk, who wished the flames for himself when he died, had made a decision and given an order, and some unforeseen and unknown conspiracy of the universe had served to defy him.

Starfleet had sent the medical rescue ship *Firenze* out to meet the *Enterprise* and to transport all but a few of its trainee crew, injured and healthy alike, back to Earth, so at least he no longer had a boatload of children to worry about.

The *Enterprise,* though patched and limping, was out of immediate danger. It could easily have made it to Alpha Ceti V to rescue *Reliant*'s crew, whom Khan marooned when he hijacked their ship. But before the light of *Firenze*'s engines had fairly red-shifted out of the visible spectrum, Starfleet recalled the *Enterprise* to Earth and sent another ship to Alpha Ceti V. "The *Enterprise* is fully capable of carrying out this mission," Kirk had said, and HQ replied, with a fine disregard for irony, "But, Admiral, your ship is dangerously shorthanded." By then Kirk did not know whether to laugh, cry, or blow his stack. He decided, instead, to make the best of it.

David's decision to return with *Grissom* to the Genesis world disappointed Kirk. Carol was barely speaking to him. One relationship that had started well and one that he had thought to resume were dissolving into nothingness.

And finally, there was Leonard McCoy. Kirk *was* worried about him. Kirk could have understood grief; he could even have understood a refusal to admit to grief. He could not comprehend McCoy's disjointed conversation, his brief episodes of intense activity, and his speaking Spock's words in Spock's voice.

For a while Kirk had felt good about having his ship back, but the price of regaining it was far too high.

Get hold of yourself! he thought. He turned away from Spock's station.

"Status, Mister Sulu?"

"On course, Admiral," Sulu said. "Estimating Spacedock in two point one hours."

"Very well." Kirk returned to his own place on the bridge. "Mister Chekov, I need a pre-approach scan. Take the science station, please."

Chekov hesitated. Kirk understood his reasons, but the ship could not function without the science station. Someone had to take Spock's place. The sooner Kirk and Chekov and everybody else got used to that, the better.

"Yes, sir," Chekov said. He stood, left the helm, and moved to the science station.

"Uhura," Kirk said, "any response from Starfleet on our Project Genesis inquiries?"

"No, sir," Uhura said. "No response."

"Odd . . ." Kirk murmured. He was accustomed to having his questions answered without delay. Esteban had been infuriatingly obscure about the public reaction to the Genesis effect. He had piqued Kirk's curiosity. Apparently, though, Kirk was just going to have to wait until he got back to headquarters to find out what was going on.

He opened an intercom channel to the engine room.

"Scotty, progress report?"

"We're almost done, sir," Scott replied. "Ye'll be fully automated by the time we dock."

"Your timing is excellent, Mister Scott," he said. "You've fixed the barn door after the horse has come home." Scott's jury-rigged automation would help relieve the ship's shorthandedness . . . for about the last hour of the return trip. "How much refit time till we can take the ship out again?"

"Eight weeks, sir—"

Kirk started to protest, but before he could get a word out, Scott spoke again.

"—But ye dinna have eight weeks, so I'll do i' for ye in two."

Kirk had the feeling the Scot had been waiting for a very long time to spring that line on him. In the same spirit, he said, "Mister Scott—have you always multiplied your repair estimates by a factor of four?"

"Certainly, sir. How else would ye expect me to keep my reputation as a miracle worker?"

"Your reputation is secure, Scotty." He turned off the intercom. "Commander Sulu, take the conn. I'll be in my quarters."

"Aye, sir," Sulu said.

Kirk climbed the stairs to the upper level of the bridge. Before he got within range of the turbo-lift's sensors, one of the few trainees who had remained on board half-rose.

"Sir—I was wondering—?"

The cadet was an electronics specialist who had kept the navigational computer going during and after the battle, when Spock was no longer able to do so. Ignoring the breach of protocol, Kirk dredged in his memory and came up with the youth's name.

"Yes—Foster, is it?"

"Aye, sir," Foster said. The pleasure and embarrassment at being recognized brought a red blush to his dark face. "I wondered, when we get home—what should we expect? Does anybody back on Earth know what happened out there?"

"Will they give us a hero's welcome?" Kirk smiled gently, for some of the youngsters, Foster among them, had behaved extraordinarily well for being half-trained and inexperienced. "Lord knows, son, they ought to. This time we paid for the party with our dearest blood."

He took the last step into the turbolift's sensor field. The doors opened, and he disappeared between them.

When the doors closed, cutting him off from the bridge, he let the mantle of command fall away from his shoulders. He slumped against the wall. The respite would be short, but at least during the ride to his quarters he could be free of responsibilities.

The lift slowed and stopped, and the doors slid open. Almost as a reflex, Kirk straightened up.

McCoy stood in the doorway. He looked as if he had not slept in days, and as if, when he tried to sleep, he had lain down in his clothes. The beard repressor he used had worn off at least twenty-four hours ago. He needed a shave.

He entered the elevator, turned to stand side by side with Kirk, and gazed nonchalantly at the ceiling. The lift hummed into motion again.

"Bones," Kirk said, a greeting with a hint of a query in it.

"Jim," McCoy said stiffly, ignoring the implied question.

Kirk waited, hoping McCoy would offer some explanation for his appearance, hoping he would show some sign of snapping out of his strange behavior.

McCoy continued to stare at the ceiling.

"Are you planning," Kirk said with irritation, "to shave today?"

"*Quo vadis,* Admiral?" McCoy said.

"What is *that* supposed to mean?" Kirk searched McCoy's face, hoping to find—what? A flash of his friend's intelligence and good sense pushing him beyond the guilt he felt for Spock's death? There was nothing McCoy could have done, nothing any of them could do. If Spock had not behaved as he had, the Vulcan would not have been the only one to die. They all would be dead. But McCoy regarded any death as a personal failure.

"What is our destination?" McCoy asked. He articulated each word precisely, without contractions. No trace of his southern accent showed, though usually it was strongest when he was under stress.

"We'll be orbiting Earth in two hours," Kirk said.

"Then we are headed in the wrong direction." He spoke as if to the air, without turning toward Kirk, without taking his gaze from the ceiling.

"Bones, don't do this! This is me, Jim. Your friend."

When McCoy spoke, his voice took on a peculiar, low timbre. "And I have been, and always shall be, yours."

Kirk suddenly shivered. The chill of fear infuriated him. He wanted to grab McCoy and shake him back to his senses.

"Damn it, Bones! Don't quote Spock to me! I have enough pain of my own. I don't need your—your self-indulgence."

McCoy slowly turned toward him. His eyes were glazed. "You left me," he said in a completely matter-of-fact tone. "You left me on Genesis. Why did you do that?"

"What the hell are you saying?"

McCoy blinked slowly, then suddenly reacted to what he himself had just said.

"I don't know . . . I just . . ." He stopped. "Why did we leave Spock?"

"Bones! You must deal with the truth. He's gone." Kirk gripped McCoy's upper arms. His intensity increased. "Spock is *gone*. We both have to live with that."

McCoy stared at him a moment, then lifted his hands and grasped Kirk's forearms in a gesture of understanding and gratitude. They stayed like that only a split second before McCoy pulled away.

The turbolift stopped; the doors opened. McCoy took one hurried step out, then swung back to face Kirk.

"I can't get him out of my head, Jim! I'd give the whole state of Georgia if someone could tell me why."

The doors slid closed again, shutting Kirk off, alone, angry, and confused.

Valkris rose to her feet, taking only detached notice of the smoothness with which she moved. The high gravity, the hours in one position, had no effect on her. She had never meditated in such an intense gravity field before. She wished she had discovered its beneficial properties much sooner.

The cabin held all her material possessions, which were honorably few in number. Valkris' wealth resided in the holdings of her bloodline, in her responsibilities, and in the duties she had carried out for her family. It resided particularly in the duty she had carried out toward her brother.

"Kiosan, dear brother, may you drink and carouse and gamble for all time," she said softly, without a trace of irony or anger.

She picked up her headcloth, put it on, and drew the sheer fabric across her face. She could see perfectly, and felt comforted to know that the material was opaque from the other side, opaque to the barbarians with whom she must treat.

Then she left her cabin for the first time since the voyage had begun.

Valkris strode through the corridors of the ship, as repelled now by the shabby, dirty vessel as she had been when first she boarded. The trip were better made on a sturdy, high-powered ship of Valkris' family's own production, but, alas, that was not to be. Not in this region of space.

A shadow moved.

Valkris stopped short, reaching for the dueling knife that hung almost, but not quite, concealed at her side.

The shadow stepped forward, resolving itself into the feline form of the ship's navigator. Farrendahl glided toward her, stalking four-legged, calmly inspecting her.

"Milady passenger," Farrendahl said softly, a purr in her voice. "To what event do we owe the honor of your company?"

"Milady navigator," Valkris said. "Does a simple constitutional qualify as an event?"

"I wonder," said Farrendahl.

The single most exciting thing Valkris had ever seen was a performance of a hunt by a troupe of Farrendahl's people. One of the reasons Valkris had chosen this ship above another was her research into the crew. She had hoped to speak with Farrendahl and to learn more about her civilization and her people, who had been in space thousands of years longer than any other known species. Farrendahl's kind did not claim planets, they did not colonize, they did not take territory. They only explored, and hunted, and made their homes beyond the frontiers of space. Perhaps, to them, the exploration and the hunt were the same.

These were the first words the two had exchanged. When Valkris had come on board, she realized she could not take time to socialize. She had much to think over, much to work out. She preferred action to meditation, but her meditation had brought her to certain conclusions, and now she rather wished she had chosen not to hire this particular ship.

"Perhaps milady passenger would care to divulge our destination? I am the navigator; I must know it eventually."

"I think not," Valkris said. "As we are nearly there."

"But there's no star system within a parsec!"

"Nevertheless," Valkris said.

Farrendahl bristled out her whiskers and growled softly, a thoughtful sound. "A rendezvous, then," she said.

"I did not say so."

"You did not have to."

Farrendahl's presumption amused and delighted Valkris. It also made her very sad.

But then she thought, *If one were worthy . . . if one were sufficiently perceptive . . .*

The handle of the dueling knife still lay cool in Valkris' hand, but now she had no thought of drawing the blade.

The sheath of the knife was encrusted with flakes of minerals, so finely cut they appeared as gemstones. The sheath ended in a heavy mass of fringe that was also thickly hung with cunningly milled discs of mica in all the colors of the spectrum. Each frequency of color meant something different, some honor or remembrance. Many—her dueling records—were transparent and colorless, the representation of emptiness, nothingness, death. She chose to carry only one that was black; her disinclination to carry a disc for each member of her family was the only fault her bloodline could hold against her.

She unfastened the length of fringe and drew it from beneath her robe.

"Milady navigator," she said to Farrendahl, "I wish to give you a gift." She slid the sparkling strands across her palm. The sharp discs touched together with a sound as silver as water. "This might benefit you, one day. It has no intrinsic value. It is . . . symbolic." She offered it to Farrendahl. "Be careful," she said. "The edges are quite sharp."

The navigator accepted the decoration gingerly. "Milady passenger . . . why do you honor me?"

"You might," Valkris said, "call it a whim."

"But I might not." Farrendahl stroked the strands so gently that she did not need to fear the razor edges. Her delicate, clawed fingers singled out the black shard of mica. "Who is this?" she said.

Valkris felt pleased beyond reason and dignity. Few in this region of space would understand, as the navigator did, what she had been given, much less the significance of its details. If anything she had underestimated Farrendahl, not overestimated her.

"It is my brother, Kiosan," she said. "He, or any member of my bloodline, would recognize what you hold, and honor it."

Farrendahl looked up at her, seeking the explanations that Valkris could not speak aloud.

"Milady passenger," Farrendahl said, "your hand is bleeding."

"Yes," Valkris said. "It does not matter."

She strode down the passageway without looking back.

Farrendahl watched the mysterious passenger glide away. The ceremonial fringe, with its adornment of electronically readable glass-chip records, hung heavy in her hands.

Farrendahl did not understand why the passenger would wish to warn her, a stranger. She did not understand why she had offered the warning in a symbolic and obscure way rather than directly. But she did understand what the warning was. At least she thought she did. And if she was right, she had to make a decision instantly.

Farrendahl attached the fringe to her belt, for she carried no knife to which to fasten it. Then she sprang into a run, four-legged, and loped down the corridor.

She slid to a stop at Tran's cabin and raked her claws across the surface of the door, scratching the paint and the metal underneath. Like the passenger's bleeding hand, that did not matter any more.

"What is it?" Sleep slurred Tran's voice. Like most primates, he woke slowly. But for a primate he was all right.

"Let me in," Farrendahl said.

The door opened, and she paced into the darkness. In a moment she could see. Tran sat in a tangle of blankets, blinking the sleep from his eyes.

"What's the matter?"

"Get up. Hurry. We're leaving."

"Leaving—?"

"Do you trust me?"

"In what context?" he said, sounding more awake.

Farrendahl growled and turned on the computer terminal on the wall of Tran's cabin.

"I have no patience for discussions of anthropoidal philosophy," she said. She reproduced a security-breaching program she had developed long ago, tunnelled into the ship's computer, and disabled certain alarms. "I am leaving this ship. I am leaving now. I have good reason. You may come, or you may stay. It is of no moment to me which you choose."

Tran threw off the blankets and reached for his pants. "Then why are you bothering to tell me?"

Farrendahl did not bother to reply. She hid her tracks in the computer with a flimsy cover that would break down under any scrutiny, but she doubted anyone would have the chance even to begin an investigation.

"I guess if I've been promoted from pithecanthropoid to anthropoid—" Tran fastened his belt and reached for his shirt.

"No time for all that foolishness!" Farrendahl said. She grabbed his wrist and dragged him out of his cabin. He snatched up his shirt and his boots and carried them with him. Farrendahl raced down the corridor, pulling Tran behind her.

Valkris swept into the control room.

"We're nearly there," the captain said when he noticed her.

"We are there," she said. "Kill all velocity."

The captain frowned, then nodded to the crew member at the control console, giving assent to his passenger's order.

"Where the hell's Farrendahl?" he said.

The ship vibrated faintly as it decelerated to counteract the forward momentum. And—was that a slight sideways shudder, as of a small craft exiting its mother ship? Valkris could not be certain.

"We have no more need of a navigator, Captain," she said evenly.

"Delta-vee zero."

"Scan the area," the captain ordered.

Valkris smiled to herself as the scanning began. It continued for some minutes. Valkris retired to shadows in the back of the chamber, rather enjoying the curious and very nervous glances of the disreputable rogues around her.

"Nothing, Captain," the crew member said.

"Steady . . . steady, boys. Keep scanning." The captain gave Valkris a poisonous glance. "I thought you people were reliable. Where the hell is he?"

"He has been here for some time. I can feel his presence."

"Don't give me your Klingon mumbo-jumbo! There ain't another vessel in this whole damned sector!"

Valkris noticed the reaction among the crew to what their captain had said, and by it she understood that none but he, on this nominally Federation ship, had known till now who or what she was.

"Put me on the hailing frequency," Valkris said, ignoring his impertinence. Nothing could affect her or offend her now.

"Sure," the captain said, sourly and sarcastically, "whatever games you want to play." He opened the channel for her, and nodded that it was ready.

Valkris grasped the end of her headcloth, using her uninjured right hand, and drew it slowly aside.

The crew reacted uneasily to her appearance, their recent suspicions confirmed, new fears engendered. Renegades they might be, but they were renegades within the Federation, still a part of it. Valkris' people were their antagonists, unknown and dangerous.

Approaching the transmitter, Valkris moved from shadows into light.

"Commander Kruge, this is Valkris. I have obtained the Federation data, and I am ready to transmit."

"Well done, Valkris. Stand by."

Everyone in the control room, even the captain, started at the rough, powerful voice that crashed out of the speaker. The voice spoke a few words which only Valkris recognized, for they were in a Klingon language. Now knowing precisely what Kruge planned, she turned toward the viewport, watched, and waited.

"Oh, my gods," one of the crew members whispered.

Like a ghost, like a creature of mist and fog, the Klingon fighter glowed into existence before the renegade merchant ship, very close, threatening. The Klingon craft had the same effect as its master's powerful voice.

"What the hell . . . ?" the merchant captain said.

Valkris herself had never seen the cloaking device in action before. It impressed and fascinated her. She watched carefully until the ship had taken complete and solid shape.

"Transmit data," Commander Kruge said.

Valkris withdrew the data record from an inner pocket of her robe and inserted it into the transmission enclosure. The monitor blurred with the high-speed transmission. Valkris could not resolve the images, but she knew every frame of what she was sending.

"Transmission completed, Commander. You will find it essential to your mission."

Valkris's hot blood streamed down her slashed wrist and palm and between her fingers, soaking the inner folds of her robe, growing cold. She was beginning to feel the effects of loss of blood.

In the language of Kruge and Valkris, which possessed an almost limitless number of forms and variations, every utterance had many layers, many meanings. When Kruge spoke again, he switched to the most formal variation. Valkris understood it, as did all well-born members of their society, but she had never spoken it, or had it spoken to her, outside the classroom. She felt honored, and she knew for certain that Kruge would keep the vows he had made to her.

"Then you have seen the transmission," Kruge said, implying regret and inevitability.

"I have, my lord," Valkris replied, granting permission in the second stratum and offering forgiveness as the third.

"That is unfortunate," Kruge said, accepting what she gave him and affirming that it was neither frivolously given nor lightly accepted.

"I understand," Valkris said. She made all three strata the same, for she wanted him to know that she understood what she was doing and why, that she understood what he was doing and why, and that she understood that he would make certain the promises made to her would be kept.

"Thrusters," Kruge said, in the form of their language used by commanders to subordinates.

In the viewport, the Klingon fighter changed. The wings of its aft armament section swung from neutral into attack. The vessel rotated, arcing around until its bulbous command chamber thrust toward the merchant ship.

The merchant captain turned on Valkris in a fury.

"What's going on? When do we get paid off?"

"Soon, Captain," Valkris said. "Quite soon." She spoke again, in formal tongue, to Kruge. "Success, Commander. And my love." She did love him, indeed, as the instrument of her bloodline's redemption.

She felt curiously lightheaded and happy. Happiness had deserted her for far too long. She was glad to experience it this one last time.

"You will be remembered with honor," Kruge said. Then he switched dialects again. Valkris knew he was speaking so she would be sure to hear his command: "Fire!"

The Klingon fighter swept toward them like a hunting falcon. Valkris did not see the beams of energy, for their destructive force reached the merchant ship at the same instant as the coherent light that formed them. The ship quaked. People shouted, then screamed. Valkris smelled the acrid smoke of burning insulation and flash-burned computer circuits. She heard the terrible hiss of escaping air.

I have shown my face to the world long enough, she thought. It is time to return to the customs of my family.

Her left hand was dark with blood. It marred the whiteness of the veil as she covered her face for the last time.

"For gods' sake!" the merchant captain cried. "Make him help us! We'll keep your damn secrets, just don't let him space us!"

Valkris closed her eyes.

The bulkhead imploded upon her.

The merchant ship exploded into slag. A shock wave of pure energy battered its scout ship, which Farrendahl had gentled out into space and concealed against the side of the larger craft. At the instant of the explosion, Farrendahl hit the acceleration hard, cut it just as abruptly, and fired all the steering rockets at once. The maneuver blasted the scout out of its hiding place along the merchant's flank and put so much roll, pitch, and yaw on the scout that it would look like merely another bit of exploded debris.

Tran shouted an inarticulate curse.

The scout was far too small to carry gravity, so the spin had its full effects on the occupants. Farrendahl struggled to keep her bearings and her consciousness. When she could stand the erratic tumbling no more, she gradually engaged the steering rockets and brought the scout to a steadier course. She dared not do it quickly lest the attacker notice that this bit of the ship moved under its own power.

"So 'we may have to just turn around and go back inside,' huh?" Tran said, still stunned and dizzy. That had been the only explanation Farrendahl would give him, till now, and now the explanation was obvious.

She used the aft scanners. Through the expanding, thinning cloud of debris,

Farrendahl saw the Klingon ship send one last blast of energy against the destroyed merchant, then turn away from its kill and head toward Federation territory.

"Where did it come from?" Tran said.

"Out of the ether," Farrendahl said.

The scout ship carried too little fuel to reach the nearest inhabited star system. She plotted a low-fuel course toward the nearest shipping lane, where they stood an excellent chance of being picked up. It would take them a while to get there. Just as well: before they were rescued, they would need to fabricate a believable and innocuous explanation for their plight.

Commander Kruge watched the ramshackle merchant ship go violently and silently to pieces under his fire. He stroked the spiny crest of his mascot, Warrigul, who sat by his side whining and hissing with excitement.

The demise of an opponent offered more satisfaction if the death came slowly, but the merchant was too easy a catch to be treated as an opponent. Besides, Kruge deigned to give Valkris a clean finish.

He nodded to his gunner, who reacted to the unusual order without question or hesitation. He fired the beams and blew the merchant ship beyond atoms.

The few remaining bits of debris tumbled away. Kruge felt completely satisfied. His only regret was never meeting Valkris face to face. He had heard much of her, both before her bloodline came to grief and after. Her information would win for him a great triumph; her death would return her family to its previous place in their society's hierarchy. Kruge doubted that the family had another member to choose who would be the match of the formidable Valkris. He wondered if he himself could match her. He was good, but she was renowned as a duelist. Now he would never have the chance to test himself against her.

Kruge rose and surveyed the work pit. His command chair stood at a level that put him well above the heads of the crew members. None looked at him. Each bent intently over the task at hand, fearing a charge of laziness and the resulting discipline. Kruge could find some breach of regulations under almost any circumstances, but having just asserted his dominance over the merchant ship, he felt no need to assert his complete authority over his crew.

He removed the data plaque from the recorder and slipped it under his belt.

Warrigul rubbed its head against Kruge's knee. Its spines scraped against the heavy fabric of the commander's trousers. Kruge reached down and scratched behind his pet's ears. Warrigul leaned harder against him. It was the only creature on board about whose loyalty the commander had no doubt whatsoever. Everyone else might be a spy, a challenger, a traitor.

Kruge glanced at his assistant. As usual, Maltz reacted badly to ambush. The officer was deplorably sensitive to violence. Kruge kept him on because he was an excellent administrator and follower-of-orders, because Maltz seldom thought for himself, and because while he might betray Kruge—anyone might become a betrayer—he would never challenge his commander. It was inconceivable that any of their superiors would consider Maltz a suitable replacement for Kruge. Maltz not only supported Kruge's position, he insured it. Therefore Kruge pretended never to notice behavior that some less devious commander might not have tolerated.

"I'll be in my quarters," Kruge said. "Execute a course to the Federation boundary."

"Yes, my lord!" Maltz said, and hurried to do his bidding.

Kruge started away. Warrigul trotted after him, growling. One of the crew members in the work pit flinched. He glanced away from his work long enough to be certain Warrigul was not growling at him, then looked quickly down at his console again. Kruge stopped. His boots were on a level just above that of the crew member's head. The crew member reluctantly raised his head when he realized Kruge was not going to move.

Kruge gestured casually at Warrigul.

"You may have the honor of feeding my pet," he said.

Struggling to keep the fear from his expression, the underling nodded vigorously. Kruge was so amused that he decided not even to discipline him for failing to answer properly.

The commander strode toward his quarters, where he kept a secure dataviewer. He was exceedingly anxious to watch what Valkris had obtained for him.

Five

Federation science ship *Grissom* sailed out of the darkness and into sunrise, crossing the terminator of the brand-new world. David was excited and pleased by what he had seen so far. For a first try, Genesis was a smashing success. Saavik, as usual in public, showed no emotion. He wished they could go off somewhere and talk so he could find out what she really thought.

"New orbit commencing," she said. "Coming up on sector three."

She was upset by their discovering Captain Spock's coffin down on the surface, David knew it, but she hid the fact well. David decided to try to persuade Captain Esteban to send some people down to bury the tube.

"Short-range scan," he said.

Saavik studied the sensors. "As before, metallic mass. Verifying triminium photon tube. No new data."

"Check for trace radiation. Infrared enhancement." David had observed Captain Esteban's tendency toward overcautiousness. He would surely want to have proof that the tube was safe before he permitted anyone to approach it.

"Residual radiation only," Saavik said. "The level is minimal."

The sensor output changed abruptly. David started violently and hurried to Saavik's side. Studying the monitor intensely, she adjusted the controls. But the new sound meant more than simple interference. Instead of fading, it sharpened and strengthened.

"I don't believe it," David said.

Captain Esteban, who had been hovering around them for the whole two hours of the first orbit, leaned over his shoulder to see the screen.

"What is it?"

"If our equipment is functioning properly," Saavik said, "the indications are . . . an animal life form."

Esteban folded his arms. "You said there wouldn't be any," he said to David.

"There *shouldn't* be any. We only enabled the plant forms in the Genesis matrix."

Captain Esteban seemed unwilling to accept what David had tried to tell him several times: that Genesis was an *experiment*. Besides being a prototype, the torpedo had detonated in an environment completely different from the one it had been designed to affect. And who knew what Khan Noonien Singh might have done while he possessed the device? However obsessed he was, he had to have been a brilliant man. He could surely have discovered how to turn on the programs the team had disabled for the first use of Genesis.

That must be what happened, David thought, if this reading isn't just a sensor gremlin. If Khan was going to use Genesis to create a world for his people to live on, he would have wanted the complete ecosphere, animals included. He would have known he couldn't import any species from Earth—that's for damned sure!

But David had to wonder why it had taken a full orbit to find the first animal life form.

He pushed away his worries. Animal life was decidedly not a symptom of the things David had most feared might go wrong.

Good grief, now you're sounding like Esteban, David said to himself. *You're demanding a complete analysis to ten decimal places before you have enough information for a first approximation. Go ahead and form a hypothesis if you want, but don't turn it into a natural law before you've collected any data.*

Then he thought, *Holy Heisenberg, what if Vance's dragons really are down there? That would please Mother.*

Saavik had been working while David daydreamed and Esteban hovered.

"Cross-referenced and verified," she said. "An unidentified animate life form."

Saavik had been trying to analyze her own reaction to the discovery of Spock's coffin. At the time of Spock's funeral, sending his body to intersect the Genesis wave, to disintegrate into its sub-elementary particles and be incorporated into the very fabric of the new world, had seemed to Saavik an elegant solution, one Spock would have approved. Disobeying Admiral Kirk's orders so flagrantly had troubled her slightly, but her loyalty to Spock was of a higher order entirely. In truth, she believed she was the only person who could understand him and appreciate his life.

Now, having disobeyed Admiral Kirk's instructions, having chosen an orbit of her own design, she must take the responsibility for what had happened. But—what *had* happened? She was dealing with forces that no one yet completely understood. Again and again David had stressed the potential for unexpected events. Perhaps the potential reached as far as inexplicable occurrences . . .

For something—or *someone*—was down there on that planet.

Saavik glanced at David and saw that he was as perplexed as she, yet both delighted and excited. She wished they could go off in private and discuss what they had found.

Esteban rubbed his jaw.

"Do you wish to advise Starfleet, sir?" the communications officer said.

"Wait a minute," Esteban said. "We don't know what we're talking about here."

"Why don't we beam it up?" David said, just to watch Esteban react.

"Oh, no, you don't!" Esteban said sharply. "Regulations specifically state, 'Nothing shall be beamed aboard until danger of contamination has been eliminated.' Can you guarantee that?"

David reflected that it was no fun to pull someone's leg if he never eventually realized his leg was being pulled.

"Not from here, no," the young scientist said.

"Captain," Saavik said, "the logical alternative is obvious. Beaming down to the surface is permitted—"

" 'If the captain determines that the mission is vital and reasonably free of danger.' I know the book, Lieutenant Saavik."

"Captain, please," David said. He was getting sick and tired of having Starfleet regulations quoted at him in regard to his own project. "We'll take the risk. We've got to find out what's down there!"

"Or who," Saavik said, very softly.

David glanced at her, startled.

Esteban nodded thoughtfully to David. "All right," he said. "Get your gear. I'll put you down next time around."

"Thank you, *sir*," David said.

Starfleet Cadet R. Grenni awoke in the trainees' dorm. He felt groggy, and his head ached. He had slept too much. He had nothing else to do. Whenever he slept, he had nightmares—but even the nightmares were better than the things he remembered.

He wished he were back on the *Enterprise*. At least there he would have work to do. He had volunteered to stay, but he had been transferred to *Firenze* along with most of his other classmates. Only a few essential cadets had been left on board the *Enterprise*. Obviously, Commander Scott had not considered Grenni essential.

When *Firenze* reached Earth, Starfleet gave all the trainees several weeks' leave. If they had deliberately planned to torture Grenni, they could not have chosen a better way.

His message light was glowing. He stumbled to the reception panel. Hands trembling, heart beating violently, he accepted the communication. They had caught up to him, they had realized their mistake. This must be his summons to a court-martial—

A small packet fell into the slot. Reluctantly, he opened the door. The envelope bore the seal of Starfleet in gold and blue. He picked it up and fumbled at the flap until it came loose.

"By order of Admiral James T. Kirk," he read, "you are presented with the gold star of valor, jeweled . . ."

The gold star was for conspicuous bravery. The jewel signified an engagement in which lives had been lost. Humans received a ruby. It stood for blood. Grenni's hands started to shake. He blinked rapidly, forcing away tears. He barely made it through the rest of the message. It commanded him and the rest of his class to appear at Starfleet headquarters a few days from now, for the formal presentation of the medal.

The delicate gold star, with ruby, fell out of the envelope and into his hand.

On the bridge of the *Enterprise,* Jim Kirk leaned back in the captain's seat. Before him, Spacedock grew slowly larger. The ship was nearly home. Kirk felt almost as he had in the old days. He could almost forget the *Enterprise* was running on automatic because it had even less than a skeleton crew. He could almost forget that the ship was patched and scarred and battle-worn. He could almost forget the empty chair behind him.

Almost.

"Stand by, automatic approach system," he said. "Advise approach control."

"Approach control, this is *U.S.S. Enterprise,*" Uhura said. "Ready for docking maneuver."

The controller came back with a crisp, clear voice. "*Enterprise* is cleared to dock."

"Lock on."

Sulu transferred control to Spacedock. "Systems locked."

"Spacedock," Kirk said, "you have control."

"Affirmative, *Enterprise.* Enjoy the ride, and welcome home."

"*Enterprise* confirms. With thanks."

The ship approached the dock in a huge curve, arcing around its flank and spiraling in to approach threshold number fifteen. The great enclosed docking bay allowed people to work outside the ship, yet it protected them from the free radiation of space. The *Enterprise* sailed closer and closer to Spacedock, heading straight at the closed radiation-shield doors.

Kirk never liked having to give up direct control of his ship.

Finally, at what seemed to him the last second, the massive doors parted silently. The *Enterprise* coasted in and moved slowly and silently into the bay. It passed ships under construction and ships under repair, ships in storage, and decommissioned ships only waiting to be dismantled.

The enormous bay stretched off into darkness, with only a single pool of light in its entire length. The *Enterprise* came abreast of the lights, where NX 2000, *U.S.S. Excelsior,* floated among its acolytes as they readied it for its first voyage. It was a beautiful ship, sleek and new, its burnished hull untouched by radiation or micrometeorites or battle.

"Would you look at that?" Uhura said.

"My friends," Kirk said, "the great experiment: *Excelsior,* ready for trial runs."

Kirk glanced at Sulu, approving of his restraint. *Excelsior* was Sulu's next assignment, his first command. In many respects, Sulu was Kirk's protégé. The admiral was proud of the young commander. Kirk searched his heart for envy and found none. *Excelsior* belonged to Sulu. Kirk's ship was the *Enterprise,* and he wanted none other.

"It has transwarp drive," Sulu said matter-of-factly.

"Aye," Scott said, "and if my grandmother had wheels, she'd be a wagon."

"Mister Scott," Kirk said with mild reproof.

"I'm sorry, sir, but as far as I'm concerned, there's nothin' needed for space travel that *this* old girl doesn't already have."

"Come come, Scotty," Kirk said. "Young minds. Fresh ideas." His voice grew dry. "Be tolerant."

Sulu smiled to himself, refusing to be baited by the conversation. Behind his calm façade he glowed with pride. *Excelsior* was *his* ship, the ship he had worked so hard and waited so long to command. He knew its lines by heart. He had had considerable say in its design. He was so proud of the ship that even Mister Scott's criticisms could not get very far under his skin.

He had been around and around about *Excelsior* with Scott. Scott thought *Excelsior* was a kludge, full of extraneous bells and whistles. Sulu was beginning to think that Scott was turning into a sort of high-tech Luddite, wanting to go just so far and no farther, afraid of any more advances.

The engineer would change his mind if he ever got a chance to work inside those engines. Sulu gazed at his ship, and the sight of it gave him nearly enough pleasure to overcome the tragedies of the past few days, nearly enough pleasure to overcome his natural reserve and make him laugh aloud.

After the *Enterprise* passed *Excelsior,* Sulu noticed movement behind the row of small ports along the upper level of Docking Bay 15, the ports that opened out from the cafeteria. Sulu looked more closely.

Everyone sitting up there, drinking coffee, shooting the breeze, relaxing, saw the *Enterprise*'s approach. As the great ship limped its slow, stately way to its berth, all along the line the people rose in silent acclamation.

Jim Kirk, too, grew aware of the homage. He fought with powerful and conflicting emotions. When the controller demanded his attention, he felt glad of the distraction.

"*Enterprise,* stand by for final docking procedure."

"Standing by. Mister Sulu, activate moorings. Stand by umbilical and gravitational support systems."

"Aye, sir. Moorings activated. All systems standing by."

"Admiral!" Chekov exclaimed. "This is not possible!"

"What is it, Mister Chekov?"

"Energy reading from C deck . . . from inside Mister Spock's quarters."

"Mister Chekov, I ordered Spock's quarters sealed!" Kirk said angrily.

"Yes, sir, I sealed room myself. Nevertheless, I am reading life form there."

"Mister Chekov," Kirk said, his voice angry and quiet, "this entire crew seems on the edge of obsessive behavior concerning Mister Spock." Chekov opened his mouth to protest. Kirk cut him off with a sharp gesture. "I'll have a look. Mister Sulu, continue docking procedure."

Kirk strode from the bridge. As the doors closed behind him, Chekov shrugged fatalistically. He saw what he saw. In an assertion of Vulcan logic that had seemed completely illogical to Chekov, Spock had always refused to lock his cabin, or even to go through the security procedures with the computer that would permit it to be locked if he chose. Vulcans never used locks. It was a matter of principle with Spock. Because of the damage to the electronic systems of the *Enterprise,* Chekov had not been able to initiate the procedures himself when Kirk ordered the cabin closed off. Instead, Chekov secured the door mechanically, that is, with an alarm, with sensors, and with a lead seal and stamp from the ship's archives. Consequently, someone *could* have broken in.

And unless the sensors had gone completely wonky (which was also possible), apparently someone had.

Kirk strode toward Spock's room, his temper frayed and just short of breaking. If one of the cadets had entered Spock's room, if this was some tasteless and thoughtless practical joke—then Kirk would soon be giving someone a lesson in the uses of black humor.

An alarm was ringing softly. Kirk broke into a run, then slowed abruptly so as to come upon the intruder unaware.

At Spock's door he stopped short. A violent force had ripped away the seal and wrenched open the door, as if an intruder of enormous strength had been too distressed, too desperate, to try any method but direct force.

Kirk touched the alarm, and it faded to silence. He squinted, but saw nothing through the darkness. He stepped cautiously forward, waiting for his eyes to become acclimated to the low light.

"Jim . . . help me . . ."

Kirk gasped. The voice was Spock's.

"Take me up . . . up the steps . . . of Mount Seleya . . . through the hall of ancient thought . . ."

Kirk clenched his fists. His hands were shaking with anger and shock. He peered more deeply into the shadows and saw—

The indistinct form plunged toward him out of the darkness, knocking him aside. Kirk grabbed it and wrestled with it. Its strength was enormous. Somehow he got a judo hold on his opponent and wrenched him down and into submission. They both fell to the floor and into the lights from the corridor.

McCoy struggled against him.

"Bones! What the hell are you doing? Have you lost your mind?"

McCoy stared at him blankly. "Help me, Jim. Take me home." His voice rasped, totally drained of strength.

"That's where we are, Bones," Kirk said gently. "We are home."

"Then . . . perhaps there is still time. . . . Climb the steps, Jim. . . . Climb the steps of Mount Seleya. . . ."

"Mount Seleya? Bones, Mount Seleya is on Vulcan! We're home! We're on Earth!"

McCoy's empty stare continued. Kirk loosed his hold on the doctor's arm.

"Remember!" McCoy said.

In Spock's unmistakable voice.

"Remember!"

Kirk knelt on the cold deck, frozen with shock.

"Admiral," Uhura said through the intercom, "docking is completed. Starfleet Commander Morrow is on his way for inspection."

McCoy shuddered, tried to rise, and fainted. Kirk caught him before he hit the floor.

"Uhura! Get the medics down here! Get them now!"

He held McCoy, feeling the doctor's pulse race frantically, thready and weak.

"Bones, it's all right," he said. "It will be all right."

But he wondered, *Will it? What in heaven's name is happening to us all?*

The skeleton crew of the *Enterprise* assembled in the docking chamber in preparation for Starfleet Commander Morrow's review.

"Tetch-hut!"

The boatswain's pipe wailed eerily, the doors slid open, and 'fleet Commander Morrow stepped on board, his aide close behind.

"Welcome aboard, Admiral."

Morrow grasped Kirk's shoulders. "Welcome home, Jim," he said. He tightened his hands. "Well done."

He embraced Kirk. The sincere affection between them was of long standing. Morrow had been Kirk's first commanding officer. He had sponsored him for his captaincy, and again for his promotion to the general staff.

"Thank you, sir," Kirk said, as Morrow stepped back. To break the tension he said wryly, "I take it this is not a *formal* inspection?"

A ripple of half-repressed laughter spread through the small group.

"No. At ease, everyone." Morrow glanced around. "Where's Doctor McCoy?"

Kirk hesitated. "Indisposed, sir."

"Ah," Morrow said, "too bad." Taking the hint, he dropped the subject. "Well. You have all done remarkable service under the most . . . difficult . . . of conditions. You'll be receiving Starfleet's highest commendations. And more important—extended shore leave."

The youngsters, particularly, reacted with pleased surprise and anticipation.

"That is—shore leave for everyone but you, Mister Scott. We need your wisdom on the new *Excelsior.* Report there tomorrow as Captain of Engineering."

"Tomorrow isna possible, Admiral," Scott said, "And forbye, with all appreciation, sir, I'd prefer to oversee the refitting of the *Enterprise.* If it's all the same to ye, I'll come back here."

"I don't think that's wise, Mister Scott."

"But, sir, no one knows this ship like I do. The refit will take a practiced hand. There's much to do—" He glanced at Kirk. "It could be *months.*"

"That's one of the problems, Mister Scott."

"Well, I *might* be able to do i' for ye a little quicker—"

"You simply don't know what you're asking."

"Then perhaps the admiral would be so kind as to enlighten me."

"I *can* cut you new orders to stay and oversee the *Enterprise*—" he said.

"I'd thank ye for that."

"—but the orders would have to be for you to oversee the ship's dismantling."

Jim Kirk felt the blood drain from his face. He could hear exclamations of shock from the crew around him.

"I'm sorry, Mister Scott," Morrow said. "There isn't going to be a refit."

"But ye canna do that!"

"Admiral, I don't understand," Kirk said. "The *Enterprise*—"

"Is twenty years old. Its day is over, Jim." His sorrow was sincere, but he made no pretense that the order was anything but final. "The ship is obsolete. We kept it on as a training vessel, mainly because you insisted. But after this last trip . . . well, it's clear just by looking at the ship that it's seen its last encounter."

"Ye've no e'en done an inspection!" Scott cried. "Ye canna just look at a ship and condemn it to the scrap heap! All ye need do is gi' me the materiel I requisitioned—"

"Your requisitions have been through a thorough analysis. We gave the ship every point we could—I made sure of that. But it simply isn't cost-effective to bring it back to optimum."

" 'Cost-effective'!" Scott muttered angrily. " 'Optimum'! What d'ye—"

"Scotty," Kirk said gently.

Scott opened his mouth, saw the look on Kirk's face, closed his mouth, and resentfully subsided.

"Scotty, go on over to *Excelsior* for the time being—"

"Nay!" Scott said. "Do ye no' understand? It isna possible!"

"Indeed?" The frost in Morrow's single word lowered the temperature ten degrees. He was not used to having his orders questioned, much less directly refused.

"My nephew Peter is still on board the *Enterprise*," Scott said. "His body is. I must take him home, to my sister. To his grave."

The admiral relented. "I see. Of course, you must go to Earth. But Mister Scott, the preliminary test of the engines is urgent. You're the best man for the job. In a day or so—"

"I canna promise. I *willna*. Some things there be that are more important than starships, and one of them is family, one of them is ties of blood."

He hurried from the docking bay.

Kirk turned to Morrow.

"Admiral, I requested—I'd hoped to take the *Enterprise* back to Genesis."

"Genesis!" Morrow exclaimed. "Whatever for?"

"Why—a natural desire to help finish the work we began. Doctor Marcus is certainly going to want to return—"

"It's out of the question. No one else is going to Genesis."

"May I ask why?"

Morrow sighed. "Jim . . . in your absence, Genesis has become a galactic controversy. Until the Federation Council makes policy, you are all under orders not to discuss Genesis. Consider it a quarantined planet . . . and a forbidden subject."

Morrow's expression forbade argument in general, and argument before the assembled ship's crew in particular.

"Dismissed," Kirk said.

Sulu broke off from the rest of the crew of the *Enterprise* before they reached the transporter room. He had no reason to return to Earth immediately, and no desire whatever for shore leave. All he wanted was to get back to *Excelsior.* He had gone on the *Enterprise* training cruise as a favor, out of courtesy to James Kirk. He should have been back on board his own ship days ago.

"Commander Sulu," Morrow said.

Sulu turned back. "Yes, sir?"

"Where are you going?"

"To *Excelsior,* sir. I'm several days late as it is."

"Would you come with us, instead, for the time being?"

Sulu hesitated, but Morrow had given him, however subtly, a direct order if he had ever heard one.

"If you please," Morrow said.

"Yes, sir." Sulu followed, trying to ward off a deep feeling of apprehension.

Morrow did not speak to him again until they had beamed back to Starfleet headquarters on Earth. The Starfleet Commander bid good-bye to Kirk and the others. Sulu waited for an explanation. When everyone else had gone, Morrow motioned to Sulu to accompany him. They went into his office, and he closed the door.

"Please sit down, Commander," he said.

Sulu complied.

"I appreciate your patience," Morrow said. "I have a delicate situation here that I hope you can help me out with."

Sulu resisted the obvious invitation to offer to do anything he could.

"How much do you know about Genesis?" Morrow asked.

"I know who developed it, I know what it does. I've seen it work." He knew a few of its technical details, for though he had not seen Carol Marcus' fabled proposal tape, he hardly needed to. The ship's grapevine had described it quite thoroughly.

"Do you know what its effect back here has been?"

"No, sir."

"The uproar has been . . . well . . . considerable. There's going to be a Federation inquiry, and a summit meeting. I'm afraid I'm going to have to ask everyone who was on board the *Enterprise* during this recent . . . incident . . . to keep themselves available to offer testimony. This will pose no difficulties for the others. But in your case . . ."

Sulu saw where this was all heading. He rose in protest.

"Please sit down, Commander," Morrow said.

"May I assume that the Admiral has already rewritten my orders?" Sulu said stiffly. He remained standing.

"Yes. I'm sorry."

"Permanently?"

"I sincerely hope not, Commander. In a few months, when this has all blown over . . ."

Sulu held back his protest. He knew that it would do no good, and furthermore that he could only humiliate himself by making it.

"So many factors are involved," Morrow said. "The ramifications of the Genesis incident complicate matters beyond any of our expectations. But above that, our investment in *Excelsior* precludes our keeping it in its berth indefinitely. The shakedown cruise must occur as scheduled. Captain Styles will take over for you while you're otherwise occupied."

"I see," Sulu said. Anger made his words tight and hard, but he did not raise his voice. He also did not say, What about afterwards? Do you really expect me to believe that afterwards, after Styles has had a chance to command that ship, that he'll turn *Excelsior* over to me without a protest?

All this was equally obvious to Morrow, who at least had the good grace to look embarrassed. "Commander, after all the turmoil has died down, I promise you Starfleet will make this up to you. Even if things don't turn out quite as we expect, you'll find your cooperation well rewarded."

No ship existed, no ship was even planned, that came close to *Excelsior.* Sulu feared that once he lost it, he lost it forever. Being told that something could make up for that was so outrageous, so absurd, that Sulu nearly burst out laughing.

"I will find that reward quite fascinating to contemplate," Sulu said bitterly. "If the Admiral will pardon me, I have—absolutely nothing to do."

Morrow frowned at him, not knowing how to interpret what Sulu said.

Without waiting to be dismissed, Sulu turned and strode from the lavishly appointed office.

Dannan Stuart awakened at sunrise, in her mother's house. The young starfleet pilot could smell the new-cut hay from the field beyond the horse pasture. The bird that had been singing all night, confused by the huge full moon, twittered into silence. Dannan flung off the bedclothes and wrapped herself in her silken. It clasped itself around her.

The floor creaked beneath her bare feet. She leaned on the sill of the small window and looked out across the valley. The wall of the house was half a meter thick, for Dannan's mother's house was five hundred years old and more. Its massive walls insulated the interior against the occasional summer heat of northern Scotland, and against the continual damp cold of winter. Today would be a perfect day, cool and sharp, the sun bright. A better day for saying hello than saying good-bye.

The valley glowed with dawn. Dew lay thick on every surface. Dannan could see a darker path through the silvered grass, where her little brother's old pony had made its way to the creek to drink. Dannan remembered coming home from school on vacation and looking out on mornings just like this, to see young Peter riding Star bareback and bridleless at a gallop across the field. She remembered all the times she had been mean and impatient, when the prospect of taking care of a pesky child had been too much to bear. Often she had been too busy to pay him much heed. She had been so eager to go off drinking and carousing with her friends that she had pushed Peter aside. All he had ever wanted, since he was old enough to understand what Dannan planned for her life, all he had ever wanted from her was to hear her tell her stories.

Poor kid, she thought, *poor brother. We did have some fun, in the last few years, but I regret all the times I closed you out and went my own way. I hope you found it in your heart to forgive me.*

She whistled from the window. A few minutes later Star trotted slowly over the crest of the hill. He was old and stiff, and he had been retired since Peter went away to school. The bay pony's black muzzle was speckled with white.

Dannan climbed down the steep, twisty stairs to the main floor of the house, grabbed a carrot and a piece of bread from the kitchen, and ran through the back yard to the pasture fence. The dew was cold on her feet, but the water beaded up on the silken. The motion of her running spun the droplets sparkling into the sunlight.

Star whickered at her and reached his head over the fence for the treats she brought. He nipped up the bread with his soft, mobile lips and crunched the carrot in two bites. Dannan rubbed his cheek, then traced the unusual five-pointed marking of white on his forehead.

When Peter came home and whistled, Star whinnied like a colt and galloped to him, age and arthritis forgotten.

"Poor old boy," Dannan said. "You're lucky, you never have to understand he isn't coming back. Maybe you'll even forget him."

She gave the pony one last pat and trudged back across the wet grass. The house peered at her from beneath eyebrows of thick willow thatch, where the edge of the roof had been trimmed in graceful curves to leave the upstairs windows open to the light.

In the kitchen she made a pot of coffee and put the morning's bread in to bake, though she did not feel very hungry. She had not, since hearing the news of Peter's death on board the *Enterprise.*

The kitchen led into her mother's studio. Dannan could smell the heavy odor of wet clay and the sharper electric tang of ozone from the kiln. Dannan rubbed her fingers around the fluid shape of the mug from which she drank her coffee. Her mother sent her sculptures and commissions into the city to be fired in her co-operative's radioactive kiln. The radiation interacted with the glazes she used, producing an unusual depth and patina. But the things she threw for use around the house, she fired in the traditional way in her studio.

She had spent all day, and most of the night, in the studio. Dannan had left her alone. It was her mother's way, in bad times, to close herself off with her work. Dannan would have liked to talk about what had happened and about Peter, but she knew her mother would not be able to do that for some while yet.

Dannan heard a brief, shivery sound from the street outside, a sound she knew well but seldom heard in her mother's house. Dannan preferred traveling here by more ordinary means, by train or ground car. The time gave her a chance to make the transition from high tech to countryside. Beaming in, besides being too expensive to use very often for personal business, was terribly abrupt.

But the sound of a transporter beam was unmistakable. The loud knock at the front door confirmed her assumption.

She hurried into the hallway and opened the door just as her uncle, Montgomery Scott of Starfleet, raised his hand to rap insistently again.

"Hush, Uncle," she said. "Mother's asleep—don't you know what time it is?"

"Nay," Uncle Montgomery said. "I dinna think to look."

"It's just past dawn." Even thirty years on a starship should not have taken his ability to glance at the height of the sun and realize it was early; but, then, even thirty years on a starship had not changed his indifference to the subtler niceties of social interaction.

Montgomery stood on the doorstep just off the deserted cobbled street. One of the things Dannan loved about this house was that its front door led directly into the village and its back into the countryside. She had grown up here, she was used to it, but friends she had brought home from school for a visit, when she was in the Academy, never failed to find it surprising.

"Well?" said Uncle Montgomery. "Are ye going to let me in or are ye going to stand in the street all day in thy skivvies?"

"Don't insult my clothing," Dannan said. "It's sensitive to discourtesy."

"I knew I should ha' beamed straight in," he muttered.

Dannan stood aside to let him pass. Even Uncle Montgomery had better manners than to beam directly into a private home, whether it belonged to his sister or not.

He tramped to the kitchen and looked at the coffeepot with distaste.

"Is there no tea?"

"You know where it is as well as I do," Dannan said. She sat down and hooked her bare feet over a rung of the chair.

"I'm in no mood for thine impertinence, young lady," he said.

"We're not on Starfleet ground now," she said. She resisted pointing out that even when they were on Starfleet ground, she was only one grade in rank beneath him and thus rated being treated as a colleague rather than as a subordinate. "We're both guests in Mother's house, and I think we should call a truce."

He shrugged and sat down without getting himself any tea. He fidgeted in silence for some minutes.

"When is the funeral?" he finally asked.

"Ten o'clock," Dannan said.

He lapsed again into silence. Dannan could not think of any subject to bring up that would not cause one or the other or both of them pain. They had never got along very well. He had opposed her joining Starfleet, saying she was too spoiled and undisciplined ever to succeed. When she did succeed, he never acknowledged it. He never said a word to indicate that he had been wrong. Dannan assumed he was still waiting for her to fail.

The message system chimed softly and the reception light turned on. Grateful for the diversion, Dannan rose to check it.

The message was addressed to her. This surprised her. No one but Hunter, her commanding officer, knew where she had gone. She turned it on.

Dannan immediately recognized the image that formed before her. Peter had described Lieutenant Saavik in his letters more than once. She was just as beautiful as he had said. She had great presence; she gave the impression of strength, intelligence, and depth. Dannan began to understand why Peter had spent so much time talking about her when he wrote.

"Please forgive me for intruding upon your privacy," the young Vulcan said. "My name is Saavik. I cannot convey my message in person, as I am unable to accompany the *Enterprise* to Earth. I knew your brother, Peter Preston. He spoke of you often, with admiration and with love. He was my student in mathematics. He was quick and diligent and he found great satisfaction in the beauty of the subject." The image of Saavik hesitated. "Though I was the teacher, he taught me many things. The most important lesson was that of friendship, which I had never experienced before I met your brother. I may discover other friends, but I will cherish the memory of Peter always. I would not have been able to speak of these feelings had I never met him; that is one of the things he taught me. He was a sweet child, a wholly admirable person, and he saved many lives with his sacrifice. This is perhaps as little comfort to you as it is to me, but it is true." Saavik paused, collecting herself, Dannan thought, fighting to keep her emotions hidden, as her culture demanded. "I hope that someday we may meet, and speak of him to each other. Farewell."

The image on the tape faded out. Dannan removed the message disk and slid it inside her silken, which obediently formed a pocket for it.

Dannan returned to the kitchen.

"What was that?"

"Just a message," Dannan said, trying to keep her voice steady. "Uncle, what happened?" When she asked the question, her voice did break.

"I canna tell ye," he said. " ' 'Tis all top secret."

"But everybody already knows about Genesis," Dannan said. "Trust Starfleet to put something everybody already knows under seal! But I don't care about that. I just want to know what happened to Peter!"

"I'll not have you maligning Starfleet—"

"What was he doing on the *Enterprise*, anyway? Why was he under your command?"

"Because ye wouldna take him under yours!"

"I'm his sister! It wasn't proper for either one of us to train him!"

"Proper! Who says it isna proper? I'll not be accused of favoritism by an impudent—"

"Favoritism!" She laughed angrily. "I'll bet you demanded three times as much from Peter as you did from anyone else! Favoritism! Others might accuse you of that, but your family knows better!"

" 'Tis for the family that I arranged to teach him! I didna want him to be ill-taught—"

"Is that why you won't tell me what happened? Did you push him beyond his abilities? Did you put him where he shouldn't have been?"

"None o' the bairns should ha' been where they were," he said so sadly that

Dannan felt a twinge of pity through her grief. "They were all pushed beyond their abilities."

"By Admiral James Kirk," Dannan said bitterly, softly. "Admiral Kirk, who—"

"I willna tolerate slander!"

"I'm not saying anything everybody else hasn't been saying for days," Dannan said. "The last two times he got his hands on the *Enterprise,* the captains died. First Decker, now Spock. If I had command of a ship I wouldn't let him within a light-year of it!"

"Ye dinna know anything about the situations! And ye'll never get wi'in a light-year of command if any friend o' the admiral hears ye speaking like that!"

"Or if you have anything to say about it?"

" 'Twillna take a report from me for thy superiors to see ye are too hot-headed for command."

What happened to the truce? Dannan thought. *Did I start this? I didn't intend to, if I did.*

"All I wanted to know was what really happened to my brother," she said.

Uncle Montgomery stood up, stalked out into the yard, and would not speak to her again.

Later that morning, Dannan endured the memorial for Peter. She barely listened to it. Today was the first time in years that she had been in a church. She sat next to her mother, holding her hand.

The pastor described Peter as an obedient and dutiful little boy—a boring creature, not very similar to what he had been as a child, and nothing at all like the sharp and independent young man he had been well on his way to becoming. Dannan wanted to jump up and push the clergyman aside and read everyone her last letter from Peter, written just before he died, received after she knew he had been killed. She smiled, thinking of the practical joke he had played on Admiral Kirk. That took nerve, it did, to face down a general officer.

The last line in his letter was, "Lieutenant Saavik says we are friends. I'm glad. I think you would like her. Love, Peter."

She thought he was right. She hoped she had a chance to meet Saavik someday, face to face.

The eulogy ended. Everyone rose and filed out to the churchyard. The raw pit of Peter's grave gaped open in the hard, cold autumn ground. A few dead leaves scattered past, rustling against Dannan's boots. They came from the oak grove that encircled the top of the low hill behind the church. The grove was sacred, or haunted, or cursed, depending on whom one asked about it. Dannan remembered winter nights long ago in front of the fireplace, and summer nights around a campfire, telling deliriously scary stories about the creatures and spirits who lived among and within the trees.

In the oak grove, a dark shape moved. Dannan started.

It was nothing. Just the wind, shaking a young tree (but there were no young trees in the grove, only ancient ones that did not quiver in the wind), or a dust-devil (but weather like today's never produced dust-devils). Who would hide up in the grove? Who would come to a funeral and fear to attend it? Who would prefer the solitary strangeness of the grove to the company of friends?

At the side of the grave, Dannan's mother bent down, picked up a handful of the cold, stony earth, and scattered it gently onto the coffin of her youngest child. Dannan followed, but she clenched her hand around the dirt until the sharp stones cut into her hand. She flung it violently into the grave. The rocks clattered hollowly on the polished wood. The other mourners looked up, startled by her lack of propriety.

She did not give a good God's damn for propriety. She wanted to bring her brother back, or she wanted to take revenge on the renegade who had killed him, or she wanted to punch out her uncle's lights. These were all things she could not do.

Tears flowing freely, Uncle Montgomery scooped up a handful of dirt and dropped it into Peter's grave.

"Ashes to ashes, dust to dust . . ."

"To fully understand the events on which I report," James T. Kirk said, "it is necessary to review the theoretical data on the Genesis device."

Kruge leaned back in the command chair, contentedly rubbing Warrigul's ears as he contemplated his prize. The image of Admiral James Kirk dissolved into the simulated demonstration of the Genesis device.

The translator changed the words from the standard language of the Federation of Planets into Kruge's dialect of the high tongue of the Klingon Empire.

"Genesis is a procedure by which the molecular structure of matter is broken down, not into subatomic parts as in nuclear fission, or even into elementary particles, but into sub-elementary particle-waves."

The torpedo arced through space and landed on the surface of a barren world. The rocky surface exploded into inferno. The planet quivered, then, just perceptibly, it expanded. For an instant it glowed as intensely as a star. The fire died, leaving the dead stone transformed into water and air and fertile soil.

Kruge casually transferred his attention to his officers, Maltz and Torg. A few minutes before, alone in his cabin, he had watched the recording that Valkris sacrificed her life to acquire. Now, playing it again for his two subordinates, he was more interested in observing their reaction to the presentation.

"The results are completely under our control. In this simulation, a barren rock becomes a world with water, atmosphere, and a functioning ecosystem capable of sustaining most known forms of carbon-based life."

Torg watched intently, all his attention on the screen. The young officer was in a state of high excitement, indifferent to any potential danger. Maltz gazed at the screen with wonder and admiration.

The human narrating the tape thanked her listeners. Kruge smiled to himself at that, wondering what she would say to *this* audience. He made the tape pause.

"So!" he said. He looked at Torg. "Speak!"

"Great power!" Torg said eagerly. "To control, to dominate, to destroy." He scowled. "*If* it works."

Kruge made no response. He scratched Warrigul beneath the scaly jaw. The creature pressed up against his leg, whining, sensing the tension and excitement.

Kruge turned his ominous gaze on Maltz.

"Speak!"

"Impressive," Maltz said thoughtfully. "They can make planets. Possibilities are endless. Colonies, resources—"

"Yes," Kruge said gently. He noticed with satisfaction Maltz's chagrin at his tone, and his surprise. "New cities, homes in the country, your mate at your side, children playing at your feet . . ." As Kruge's voice grew more and more sarcastic, Maltz's expression changed from one of satisfaction to one of apprehension. ". . . And overhead, fluttering in the breeze—the flag of the Federation of Planets!" He fairly growled the last few words, and Warrigul snarled in support. "Oh, charming!" Kruge said. He sneered at Maltz. "Station!"

"Yes, my lord," Maltz said quickly, knowing better than to try to defend himself when he had so completely lost his ground. He hurried to his post and made himself very inconspicuous.

Kruge regarded Torg. "It works. Oh, yes, it works." He touched the controls of the player to let the tape continue.

"It was this premature detonation of the Genesis device that resulted in the creation of the Genesis planet." On the screen, a *Constellation*-class Federation starship fled the expanding wave that turned the dust and gases of a nebula into a mass of energy and sub-elementary particles, thence into a blue new world.

Kruge turned off the machine, removed the information insert, and slipped it beneath his belt.

"Tell this to *no one*," he said to Torg. He glanced significantly across the control room at Maltz.

"Understood, my lord."

"We are going to this planet," Kruge said. "Even as our emissaries negotiate for peace with the Federation, we will *act* for the preservation of our people. We will seize the secret of this weapon—the secret of ultimate power!"

Torg nodded, nearly overwhelmed by the magnitude of what he had seen. "Success," he whispered. "Success, my lord."

"Station!"

"Yes, my lord!"

Torg returned to his position. At Kruge's side, Warrigul whined and slavered, reacting to the emotions of its master. Kruge dropped to one knee to soothe the creature.

"My lord," said the helm officer, speaking carefully in the tongue of subordinates. "We are approaching Federation territory."

"Steady on course," Kruge snapped, easing his impatient first stratum with a second stratum of approval. "Engage cloaking device."

"Cloaking device—engaged."

From within the ship, it was a most odd and satisfying sensation. The ship and all its contents and all its occupants became slightly transparent. Voices grew hollow, like echoes.

Warrigul howled in protest. Lower subordinates shuddered at the keening cry, knowing that the cloaking device put the creature's temper on a thin edge. It had a similar effect on people. Once in a while it would, without warning, drive someone mad. But this time everyone survived the transition sane. Kruge smiled and stroked his beast, satisfied in the knowledge that outside the cloaking field, his ship was completely invisible.

Six

Saavik stepped onto the transporter platform beside David.

"Transporter room," Captain Esteban said through the intercom. *"Stand by to energize."*

"Transporter room standing by."

"Energize."

The beam caught Saavik up and dissolved her. A moment later it reassembled her, atom by atom, on the surface of the world David had helped to create.

From her point of view, the world solidified around her. She had no real sensation of being torn asunder and put back together. Throughout the entire process she could feel sensations from her body, feel the weight of the backpack on her shoulders, hear and see and think.

The Genesis world lay wreathed in silver haze. Great primordial fern-trees reached into the air then drooped down again with the weight of their own leaves. The fronds had captured miniature pools of glittering rainwater.

David appeared beside her and looked around with wonder.

"It really is something, isn't it?" he said.

"It is indeed," Saavik said. She took her tricorder from her belt and turned it on. David did likewise. The bio readings were what she had expected, similar to the long-range scans. The animate life signals matched nothing she had ever seen before, but they definitely existed.

David set off through the forest as Saavik switched the emphasis on her tricorder and scanned again. She raised one eyebrow in astonishment.

"This is most odd, David," she said.

He glanced impatiently back.

She frowned and took out her communicator. "Saavik to *Grissom.*"

"Grissom here."

"Request computer study of soil samples for geological aging."

"I'll handle that later," David said.

Saavik wondered why his voice was so sharp and tense. She, too, was anxious to proceed, but not to the point of recklessness.

"My readings indicate great instability."

"We're not here to investigate geological aging, we're here to find life forms!" He scanned around with his tricorder. The signals changed and strengthened. "Come on!" He hurried off between the trees.

Saavik felt an intense uneasiness, but she followed David.

"Grissom to landing party." Even through the communicator, Saavik could

hear the worry in Captain Esteban's voice. *"We show you approaching indications of radioactivity. Do you concur?"*

"Affirmative, Captain. But our readings are well below the danger level."

"Very well. Exercise caution, Lieutenant. This landing is 'captain's discretion.' I'm the one who's out on a limb here."

Saavik stood in the midst of a profoundly unknown world and replied, straight-faced, "I will try to remember that, Captain."

She strode after David, who had hurried several hundred meters ahead of her. He paused to take readings, and she caught up to him. Her tricorder showed strange and fluctuating life-signs. She flipped the setting quickly from bio to geo and got the same disturbing readings of instability. At the very least this area would be prone to severe earthquakes.

Reluctantly Saavik changed the sensor again.

The metallic mass she had detected from on board *Grissom* lay very near. She glanced in the direction of the reading. Before her the trees thinned out into a blaze of sun. The air was very warm and very humid. Saavik could not see beyond the sun's dazzle in the steamy haze.

She walked toward the source of the readings. Before her, just out of sight, lay a casket that held the body of her teacher. She did not need to see it to be certain he was dead. Because now, she was certain. Her speculations in response to the life-sign readings had been fantasies, dreams, wishes. She felt nothing of the neural touch that had disturbed her so deeply back on the *Enterprise.* If Spock were nearby, if by some incredible action of the Genesis wave, or some unsuspected ability of the Vulcan-human cross, he had returned, Saavik would perceive him. Of that she felt quite sure.

David pushed his way through the thick fronds of the fern-trees and into the glade beyond. The sunlight burst upon him and he stood still, blinking.

Saavik moved more slowly out of the green shade, giving her eyes the few seconds they needed to adapt.

"It *is* Spock's tube!" David said. He squinted at it, trying to screen out the light.

"David . . ." She pointed to the base of the tube.

A mass of pale, moist worms writhed and wriggled in the shadow of the casket. A few fell from the cluster into the sunlight and frantically burrowed into the dark loam.

His eyes now accustomed to the brightness, David saw what she was pointing at. He took one step toward the slimy creatures and stopped. A muscle along the side of his jaw tightened, and he swallowed hard.

"Well," he said bitterly. "There's our life-form reading. It must have been microbes, caught on the surface of the tube. We shot them here from the *Enterprise.*" His voice was tinged with irony and disappointment. "They were fruitful, and multiplied." He looked around the otherwise peaceful glade. "Probably contaminated the whole planet."

Saavik could think of several other explanations for the presence of the worms, but as the casket appeared still to be sealed, she hoped David's explanation was correct.

"But how could they have changed so quickly . . . ? Did you program accelerated evolution into Genesis?" Perhaps the creatures were far more complicated than they appeared at first glance. She focused her tricorder on them, but could not reproduce the reading that had brought her here.

David approached the torpedo tube. His tricorder bleated and clicked, registering the increased radiation flux and confirming the torpedo tube as the source. Nevertheless, the level was well below the danger point.

David grimaced, then forged ahead, kicking his way through the worms. Saavik followed until she realized what he intended to do. She stopped, unwilling to see again the terrible burns on Spock's sculpted face, preferring not to consider the effects of climate.

She started despite herself when David slowly raised the lid of the bier. He stared down into the casket.

"Saavik . . ."

Pushing a path through the worms with her boots, Saavik joined him.

". . . He's gone," David said. He reached into the empty coffin and drew out the black shroud. "What is it?" he asked.

She took the silvery, silky piece of heavy black fabric from his hands.

"It is Spock's burial robe," she said, her voice even, but her thoughts in disarray.

Saavik heard a low, threatening rumble. The ground shook gently beneath her feet. Merely a temblor, not a true quake, but a precursor to and a promise of events more violent.

As the quivering of the earth faded away, a frightened cry echoed through the forest. A mammal? A predatory bird? A creature unique to this world? David spun toward the sound, that lonely shriek of pain, then, when the echoes had faded and the cry came no more, he looked back at Saavik.

She felt sure he was thinking, as was she: No highly evolved microbe screamed that scream.

Dannan fidgeted on the sofa in the living room. It was early evening, and beginning to grow dark outside. The day seemed to have stretched on forever.

Uncle Montgomery sat on the other side of the room, in silence and in shadows.

Dannan's mother had vanished back into her studio. Everyone in the family knew better than to disturb her when the door was closed. That was one of the things Peter's father had never been able to get through his head; it was the final bit of selfishness Dannan's mother could not tolerate. Dannan returned from school once to find, rather to her relief, that the elder Preston had packed up his things and departed, muttering about eccentric artists and heading for—he said—a Federation colony, on the first available ship. Dannan had smiled to hear that, for if he thought an artist who did not like to be interrupted when she was working was eccentric, wait until he met the people who shipped out to colonies. He had not been a bad person, just a self-involved one who should perhaps never have tried to join a family. Dannan wondered if anyone knew where he was, to let him know about Peter.

Dannan rose, crossed the living room, and took in one stride the three steps up to the foyer. She slipped into her boots and went out the front door, into the village. She made her way down the steep cobbled street to the river's edge, thence through the town and back to the churchyard, the cemetery, and the old oak grove.

The evening was extraordinary. In the west, the sun lined the horizon from below in a thick ochre gold. The color shaded upward into a soft, intense, and glowing mauve. Dannan could not describe the sky in terms of clear spectral colors, only in mixes and delicate hues. What color did one name the region where the sky shaded from predominantly gold to predominantly violet? She could not answer. In the east, the enormous blood-red harvest moon began to glide above the horizon. The just-set sun and the just-risen full moon combined to create a lavender twilight.

Tonight was the autumn equinox. Dannan spent most of her life on starships, where every day was the same length and one counted one's time by the artificial measurement of star dates. When she came home, to a place where seasons still mattered and time was more subjective, she experienced the days and nights and dawns and evenings, the colors and sounds and scents, as a brand-new discovery.

Twilight remained when she reached the graveyard, though the livid gold horizon had faded and the sky had changed from lavender to deep blue. Stars glinted here and there, bright and steady in the cold, still air. They were never as clear as they were in space. She was glad Peter had at least had a chance to see them from above the atmosphere.

Dannan sat on her heels by Peter's grave. Beneath the flowers that lay thick and fragrant upon it, the raw earth smelled of rocks and ripped turf. She could make out his name, and the summation of the short years of his life, carved into gray granite. He lay among ten previous generations of his family, the first of his generation to die. Because of the family's tradition of taking the name of one's parent of the same gender, her brother was the only Preston among many Scotts, more Stuarts, a scatter of MacLaughlins, and one Ishimoto, a great-uncle Dannan remembered with great fondness.

She wished she had some memento of space to leave on Peter's grave, some alien bloom to put down to remind everyone that he had dreamed of and sought after and loved the stars.

As the moon rose higher, Dannan saw a hard glint among the flowers littering Peter's grave. She reached between the soft petals and picked up the bit of gold. It was a medal, the star of valor, with ruby. She wondered for an instant if it was Peter's, if her mother or her uncle had put it here, but in the same instant she recognized it as the wrong form for a posthumous medal. It was not engraved with name or place, so it had not yet been formally presented. It had to belong to one of Peter's classmates.

A sound broke the silence that lay easily over the graveyard.

At first Dannan identified the noise as a dog, a lost puppy. She stood up and waited to hear it again.

It came from the oak grove.

Dannan strode toward the trees. Fallen leaves crunched beneath her boots. All the scary childhood stories about ghosts and changelings passed through her mind, though she knew the sound came from someone who was merely flesh and blood.

Besides, she thought, *I'm a Starfleet officer, remember? With citations for bravery of my own.*

Big deal.

She heard the sound again: a sob.

"Come on out," she said.

The usual silence of the grove was one of calm. This was the breathless quiet of concealment and apprehension.

"Come on," Dannan said. "It's cold out here."

The young man scuffed out of the trees, the red coat of his uniform black in the moonlight. He stopped before her, hanging his head.

"Who are you?"

"One of Peter's shipmates."

He was several years older than Peter, he must have been a third or fourth year student, while Peter was only first.

"Is this your medal?"

"Yes."

"Why?"

He still did not look up.

"I thought Peter deserved it more than I did."

"Because he's dead and you're alive?" Dannan was about to tell him how brutally often the difference came down to nothing but chance.

"No!" he said before she could continue. "No!" He hung his head lower, if that were possible. His voice was muffled and reluctant. "Because he stayed . . . and I ran."

Dannan stepped toward him with a flare of shock and surprise and anger. She wanted, quite simply, to kill him. She was perfectly capable of doing it with her bare hands.

But then the boy did raise his head, as if baring his throat to accept her revenge. He made no move to defend himself. The utter defeat was all that saved him.

She understood why he had lurked in the grove during the funeral, and why he had not shown himself. She did not understand why he was still here.

"Get out of here," she said. "Why don't you just go home?"

His shoulders slumped. "I can't," he said. "I'm AWOL, for one thing . . . and I used up all my money getting here. I don't know how to get back."

"That shows great foresight," Dannan said. "Is that what they teach you at the Academy these days?" She sighed. "You'd better come with me."

Dannan took Grenni back to her mother's house, wondering what the devil to do with him.

Uncle Montgomery had not moved from his place in the corner when Dannan returned, and the door to the pottery studio still was closed.

"I believe you know this gentleman," Dannan said sarcastically to her uncle as Grenni followed her into the living room. "He came . . . for Peter's funeral."

Uncle Montgomery greeted Grenni with every indication of pleasure and gratitude for his presence.

" 'Tis good o' ye to come pay thy respects to our bairn—"

"Stop it!" Grenni cried. "Why do you keep being so nice to me? You know where my station was—you must know Pres is dead because of me!"

Scott stared at him.

"You know he was the only one in our section who held his post! I was cadet commander, I should have ordered him out of danger!"

"He'd no' ha' gone," Scott said.

"Then neither should I."

"Perhaps not," Scott said. "Then we would have two funerals to attend today, instead o' one." He rose and approached the boy, took him by the shoulders, and looked him in the eye. "Dinna get me wrong, boy. Ye did a cowardly thing. Now ye must decide if ye are fit for the career ye've chosen. If this is thy character—"

"It isn't!" Grenni said. "I don't know what happened—I don't understand why it happened. I never did anything like that before in my life!"

Montgomery Scott nodded. "Ye hadna been properly prepared for what we faced. 'Tis at least as much my fault."

"Are you saying—you forgive me?"

"Aye."

Grenni looked at Dannan. "Do you forgive me too, Commander?"

"Not bloody likely," Dannan said.

Her uncle and the cadet both looked at her, shocked.

"Dannan—" her uncle said, raising his voice in protest.

"But I'm sorry!" Grenni cried. "I didn't mean it! If I could make it up—"

"Make it up? Make up for the death of my brother?" Her voice was cold with contempt. "I don't think so."

"I know there's nothing I can do, that's what makes it so awful—"

"Ye dinna want to be vengeful, Dannan," her uncle said.

"No," she said, surprised to find that vengeance was not what she wanted. "You're right, Uncle. But so are you, Cadet. There's nothing you can do. . . ."

Uncle Montgomery stood up angrily. "Ye always were a cold-hearted little—"

". . . and that's what makes it so hard," Dannan said.

Her uncle put his arm over the boy's shoulders. "Come along, Cadet. 'Tis time to go home." He sent one quick glare at Dannan. "Tell thy mother farewell, I canna wait any longer for her to come out."

He and Grenni left the house. A moment later Dannan heard the electric sparkle of a transporter beam. The window next to the front door glowed briefly, and then turned dark again.

Jim Kirk stared out the window of his apartment at the night and at the bridges on the bay, lines of light leading out of and into an infinity of fog. Reflections overlaid the distant city. Jim turned to them and raised his glass.

"To absent friends," he said.

Uhura, Chekov, and Sulu raised their glasses in response. They all drank.

"Admiral, is it certain?" Hikaru said. "What's going to happen to the *Enterprise*—?"

"Yes," he said. "It's to be decommissioned."

"Will we get another ship?" Pavel said.

We? Jim thought. *Is there a "we" anymore? The ship to be dismantled, the crew dispersed, McCoy in shock and doped to the gills, and . . . Spock dead.*

"I can't get an answer," he said. "Starfleet is up to its brass in galactic conference. No one has time for those who only stand . . . and wait."

"How is Doctor McCoy, sir?" Uhura said.

"That's the 'good' news," Jim said dryly. "He's home in bed, full of tranquilizers. He promised me he'd *stay* there. They say it's exhaustion." He sighed.
"We'll see."

His doorbell chimed.

"Ah," Jim said. "It must be Mister Scott, fresh from the world of transwarp
drive. Come!"

The door responded to his voice and whirred open.

Expecting Scott, Jim started at the sight of a much taller figure standing
cloaked and hooded in a Vulcan robe, half hidden by the shadows in his foyer.
Jim felt panic brush against him, bringing the fear of madness. He thought for
an instant that, like Leonard McCoy, he was beginning to perceive the ghost of
Spock in every patch of darkness, in dreams and wakefulness alike.

The figure reached up and drew back its hood.

"Sarek!" Jim exclaimed.

Ambassador Sarek strode into the light. He looked as he did the first time
Jim had met him, well over a decade before. He had not aged in that time. He
would by now, Jim reflected, be nearly one hundred twenty years old. He
looked like a vigorous man of middle age, which, of course, was precisely
what he was. But a Vulcan of middle age, not a human being. He had many
years left to look forward to, just as Spock, his son, should have had over a
century.

"Ambassador," Jim said, feeling flustered, "I—I had no idea you were on
Earth . . ." His words trailed off. Sarek said nothing. "You know my officers, I
believe," Kirk said.

Sarek showed no inclination to acknowledge the others. He moved to the
window and stared out, his back to the room.

"I will speak with you alone, Kirk," he said.

Kirk turned toward his friends. They regarded him with questioning expressions, each clearly uneasy about leaving him alone in Sarek's intimidating presence.

"Uhura, Pavel, Hikaru—perhaps we'd better get together again another
evening." Kirk put into his tone a confidence of which he was far from certain.
With a gesture he silenced Pavel's hotheaded objection before it started; he
shook Hikaru's hand, appreciating his equanimity, and he returned Uhura's
embrace as he showed his three compatriots to the door.

"We're here," she said, "when you need us."

"I know," he said. "And I'm grateful."

He let them out, watched the door close behind them, and turned back to
Sarek with considerable apprehension.

Sarek remained at the window, silhouetted black against black. Kirk
approached him. He stopped a pace behind him, and the silence stretched on.

"How . . . is Amanda, sir?" Kirk asked.

"She is a human being, Kirk. Consequently, she is in mourning for our son.
She is on Vulcan."

"Sarek, I'm bound here to testify, or I would have come to Vulcan, to
express my deepest sympathies. To her, *and* to you—"

Sarek cut off Kirk's explanation and his sympathy with a peremptory gesture. "Spare me your platitudes, Kirk. I have been to your government. I have seen the Genesis information, and your own report."

"Then you know how bravely your son met his death."

" 'Met his death'?" Sarek faced Kirk, and the cold expressionlessness of his eyes was more powerful than any grief or fury. "How could you, who claim to be his friend, assume that? Why did you not bring him back to Vulcan?"

"Because he asked me not to!" Kirk said, rising to the provocation.

"He *asked* you not to? I find that unlikely in the extreme."

Sarek stopped just short of calling Kirk a liar, which did not serve to improve the admiral's temper.

"His will states quite clearly that he did not wish to be returned to Vulcan, should he die in the service of Starfleet. You can view it—I'll even give you his serial number."

"I am aware of his serial number," Sarek said with contempt. "I am also aware that Starfleet regulations specifically require that any Vulcan's body be returned to the homeworld. Surely this would override the dictates of a will."

"The trivial personal wishes of an individual?" Kirk did not give Sarek a chance to reply to his barb. "I'll tell you why I followed Spock's request rather than the rules of Starfleet," he said bitterly. "It's because in all the years I knew Spock, never once did you or any Vulcan treat him with the respect and the regard that he deserved. You never even treated him with the simple courtesy one sentient being owes another. He spent his life living up to Vulcan ideals— and he came a whole hell of a lot closer to succeeding than a lot of Vulcans I've met. But he made one choice of his own—Starfleet instead of the Vulcan Academy—and you cut him off!"

He stopped to catch his breath.

"My son and I resolved our disagreement on that subject many years ago, Kirk," Sarek said mildly.

Kirk ignored the overture. "For nearly twenty years I watched him endure the slights and the subtle bigotry of Vulcans! When he died, I was damned if I would take him back to Vulcan and give him over to you so you could put him in the ground and wash your hands of him! He deserved a hero's burial and that's what I gave him—the fires of space!" He stopped, his anger burned to ashes, yet he thought, *And I can think of a few dogs I would have liked to put at his feet.*

Sarek behaved as if Kirk's outburst had never occurred, as if he believed that by refusing to acknowledge it, he caused it not to exist.

"Why did you leave him behind? Spock trusted you. You denied him his *future.*"

Jim felt entirely off balance and defensive. He had no idea what Sarek was talking about. If Kirk had hoped to accomplish anything by exposing to Sarek the anger he had built up over the years, he had failed, miserably, spectacularly, completely.

"I—I saw no future!"

"You missed the point, then and now. Only his body was in death, Kirk. And *you* were the last one to be with him."

"Yes, I was . . ." *My gods,* Jim thought, *is Sarek trying to tell me that if I had behaved differently—Spock might still be alive?*

"Then you must have known that you should have come with him back to Vulcan."

"But—why?"

"Because he asked you to! He entrusted you with . . . with his very essence, with everything that was not of his body. He asked you to bring him to us, and to bring that which he gave you, his *katra,* his living spirit."

Sarek spoke with intensity and urgency that served merely to disguise, not to hide, his deep pain and his loss. Jim had received the response he intended to provoke. He wished he had been gentler.

"Sir," he said quietly, "your son meant more to me than you can know. I'd have given my life if it would have saved his. You must believe me when I tell you he made no request of me." If there was a chance for him to live, Kirk cried out in his mind, why *didn't* Spock ask me for help?

"He would not have spoken of it openly."

"Then, how—"

Sarek cut him off. "Kirk, I must have your thoughts."

Jim frowned.

"May I join your mind, Kirk?"

Jim hesitated, for the Vulcan mind-meld was not the most pleasant of experiences. The human perception was trivial, Vulcans claimed, compared to the discomfort Vulcans underwent in order to mingle their refined psyches with the disorganized thought processes of human beings. It was clear, however, that Sarek needed information that Jim did not possess in his own conscious mind. Acceding to the mind-meld was the one thing Jim could do, perhaps the only thing, that might give Sarek some peace.

"Of course," he said.

Sarek approached him and placed his hands on Jim's face, the long forefingers probing at his temples. His gaze never met Kirk's. He seemed to be looking straight through him. Kirk closed his eyes, but Sarek's image remained.

The sensation was as if Sarek's slender, powerful hands reached straight into his brain.

Kirk traveled back through time. The recent message from *Grissom* brought a strong resonance of hope from Sarek: My son's body may yet exist—perhaps there is still time! Time to save him for the Hall of Ancient Thought. . . .

And James Kirk understood that even if Sarek found what he sought, Spock was lost to the world he had lived in. Only a few individuals, trained for years in Vulcan philosophic discipline, could communicate with the presences that existed in the Hall of Ancient Thought. If Sarek found what he was looking for, he would give Spock a chance at immortality . . . but not another chance at life.

Sarek's powerful mind forced Jim farther back in time. Jim's memories of Spock's death, which had barely begun to ease, returned with the cruel clarity of dream.

"He spoke of your friendship."

Jim could not tell if Sarek uttered words or communicated through the mental link. Likewise he could not be sure if he himself replied aloud, or in silence.

"Yes . . ."

"He asked you not to grieve . . ."

"Yes . . ."

"The needs of the many outweigh . . ."

". . . the needs of the few—"

"Or the one."

The image of Sarek faded from Jim's mind. Spock appeared, horribly burned and dying.

"Spock . . ." Jim said.

"I have been . . . and always shall be . . . your friend," Spock said. "Live long . . . and prosper."

"No!" Jim shouted, as if by force of will he could twist the dictates of the universe and mortality to his wishes.

The illusion drained away like a spent wave, leaving Jim soaked and shaken. He experienced one last, hopeless thought from Sarek: What I thought destroyed, my son's body, is found; but his soul is irrevocably lost.

He broke the contact between them.

Jim's knees buckled. Sarek caught and supported him. Jim pressed the heels of his hands against his closed eyes, trying to drive back the sharpened memories.

"Forgive me," Sarek said. "It is not here. I assumed he had melded his mind with yours. It is the Vulcan way, when the body's end is near."

"But he couldn't touch me! We were separated!"

"Yes," Sarek said. "I see, and I understand." He turned away, weariness— even age—apparent in the set of his shoulders. "Everything that he was, everything that he knew, is lost. I must return to Vulcan, empty-handed. I will join Amanda. We will mourn our son. We will mourn for the loss of his life, we will mourn for the loss of his soul." Without a word of farewell, he started toward the door.

"Wait!" Kirk cried. "Please . . . wait." Like a man trying to scale a crumbling cliff he clutched at fragile branches, and they pulled loose from the rock. "Sarek, surely he would have found a way! If there was so much at stake, Spock *would have found a way!*"

Sarek strode toward the door and Kirk feared he would sweep out of the room without a backward glance, hinting at possibilities, abandoning them.

Sarek slowed, hesitated, turned. "What are you saying, Kirk?"

"What if he melded his mind with someone else?"

Seven

The flight recorder from the *Enterprise* lay under seal and under guard. Even Admiral James T. Kirk had to do some fast talking and some throwing around of his authority to see it, much less to bring in an outside observer. Though Sarek knew all there was for any diplomat to know about Genesis and about the last voyage of the *Enterprise,* whoever had cleared him for those reports had not thought to include the flight recorder. This caused what seemed to Kirk like an endless delay. However esteemed Sarek might be within the Federation, he was not a member of Starfleet. Then, when the ambassador finally received special clearance to view the data, Kirk was absolutely refused permission to transmit the recording anywhere outside the records storage center. He and Sarek had to go to it.

Kirk arrived at the center chafing under the limitations of surface travel. He found it incredibly frustrating to be forced actually to traverse the distance from one point to another, rather than to have a convenient transporter beam at his beck and call.

Finally all the distance had been covered, all the permissions had been granted, all the forms had been signed and sealed and retina-printed, and he and Sarek entered a viewing cubicle that would display data from the *Enterprise*'s flight recorder.

Ordinarily the recorder would lie essentially suppressed, quiescently tracking only the routine mechanical functions of the ship. An alert increased its powers of observation and set it to making a permanent record of the ship's crucial areas. The engine room monitor had watched Khan's attack and Spock's last moments of life.

Jim Kirk had already relived Spock's death once today, in an all too realistic fashion. He wondered, as he keyed into the player the star date he wished to observe, why he had fought so hard to be permitted to see it again. He could leave Sarek alone with it and let the Vulcan make of it what he would. But in the end Kirk could not abandon his responsibilities to Spock or—if his suspicions proved true—to McCoy.

"Engine room, flight recorder, visual," the computer voice announced. "Star date 8128 point seven eight." It froze at the decimal he had chosen. "Point seven eight . . . point seven eight . . ."

On the screen, Spock lay dying against the glass of the radiation enclosure, frozen in time.

"Back!" Kirk snapped. "Point seven seven."

The random access search skipped to the last words between James Kirk and Spock.

"Back! Point six seven."

"Flight recorder, visual. Star date 8128 point six seven, point six seven—" The tape had reached the point before Kirk left the bridge, before Spock entered the radiation chamber, a time when the *Enterprise* was still in imminent danger of being caught up in Khan Singh's detonation of the Genesis device. Spock was poised in freeze-frame at the radiation chamber control console.

"Go."

Spock's image flowed into life. McCoy entered the picture, intercepting Spock before he reached the chamber. They argued in eerie silence. Spock guided McCoy's attention toward Mister Scott, who lay half-conscious on the floor. As soon as McCoy turned his back, Spock felled him with a nerve pinch.

And then . . . Spock knelt down and pressed his hand to Doctor McCoy's temple. Spock's lips formed the silent word:

"Remember."

"Hold," Kirk said. The image froze. "Augment and repeat." The scene scrolled smoothly back. The central image expanded. "Audio," Kirk said.

Spock guided McCoy's attention toward Mister Scott, who lay half-conscious on the floor. As soon as McCoy turned his back, Spock felled him with a nerve pinch.

Spock knelt down and pressed his hand to Doctor McCoy's temple.

"Remember!" Spock said.

"Freeze!" Kirk said. He struggled against hope and excitement to retain his composure. "Bones . . ." Kirk said softly. All the doctor's tortured behavior, his confusion—

"One alive, one not," Sarek said. "Yet both in pain."

"One going mad from pain," Kirk said. "Why—why did Spock leave the wrong instructions?"

"Do you recall the precise words, Kirk?" Sarek cocked his eyebrow at Kirk and saw that he did not. He repeated a phrase from Spock's will as he had plucked it from Kirk's mind. " 'Failing a subsequent revision of this document, my remains are not to be returned to Vulcan—' " He paused. "Spock did not . . . did not believe that his unusual heritage would permit the transfer of his *katra*. He did leave the possibility open."

"But he never made a revision. He left only—"

"—The good Doctor McCoy," Sarek said. "Who, if the process had worked properly, would have known what to do. Perhaps Spock was correct. Perhaps he was unable to transfer . . ."

"He transferred *something*! And it's driving McCoy insane!"

"Had Doctor McCoy ever experienced the mind-meld before?"

"A couple of times, in emergencies."

"How did he react?"

"He didn't like it. To put it mildly."

Sarek raised his eyebrow again but forbore to remark upon the comment. "Did he become physically ill, afterwards?"

"I don't know. He wouldn't necessarily have said so if he did."

"He is undergoing an allergic reaction."

"What?"

"It is unusual, but not unprecedented. McCoy's mind is rejecting what Spock gave to him."

Kirk fought an impulse to laugh. He lost.

"You find this amusing?" Sarek said stiffly.

"No—yes, I'm sorry, Sarek, I can't help it. McCoy would find it hilarious, if he were in any shape to appreciate it. Come to think of it, Spock would, too."

"I find that highly unlikely," Sarek said. "Since the result is that McCoy was unable to assimilate the new information even so far as to rescind the provision of Spock's will that may now destroy both of them." He shook his head. "It would have been better if Spock had been near another Vulcan when he died. He did not prepare well, Kirk. He left too many factors open to chance—"

"This is hardly the time to criticize Spock!" Kirk said angrily. "Or to deplore Murphy's Law, for that matter."

"What is 'Murphy's Law'?"

" 'Whatever can go wrong, will go wrong.' "

"How apropos."

"What do we do to make things right?"

"It may already be too late."

"Sarek—!"

Sarek gazed at the frozen screen in silence.

"The fact that Doctor McCoy retains even a semblance of sanity gives me some cause for hope. You are fortunate that you failed in your plan to burn my son like a barbarian chieftain. Had it succeeded, McCoy would surely be lost to us by now. The mind and the body are not a duality, they are parts of a whole. If one is destroyed, the other must disintegrate. If they are separated . . . the greater the distance, the greater the strain, until it becomes intolerable."

"The strain on McCoy, you mean."

"Precisely."

"What must I do?"

"You must recover Spock's body from the Genesis world," Sarek said. "You must bring it, and Doctor McCoy, to Mount Seleya, on Vulcan. Only there is the passage possible. Only there can both find peace."

"What you ask," Kirk said, "is difficult."

"You will find a way, Kirk. If you honor them both, you must."

Kirk glanced again at the frozen image of his two closest friends.

"I will," he said. "I swear it."

Even before Jim Kirk and Sarek had left the records storage center, the questions the ambassador had left unanswered began to trouble Jim.

"Sarek," he said, "if I succeed in what you ask . . . will Spock know? I mean—will he be aware of himself? Will he retain his individuality?"

"He will not be as you knew him," Sarek said.

"I understand that!" Kirk said. The lessons of the mind-meld remained fresh in his consciousness. "That wasn't my question."

"Your question is one that cannot be answered in a few simple words, Kirk. There is no time—"

"I'll take the time!"

Sarek regarded him coolly. "Will you take ten years of your life? First you must learn to speak Vulcan, and then you must dedicate yourself to study. In ten years you might approach the simplest questions of this philosophy . . . and the question you have asked is far from the simplest."

"Ambassador, with all due respect—that explanation is getting pretty stale! 'I cannot answer your question because humans are too immature to understand. Humans are too uncivilized—' "

"I said nothing against humans. Do you forget that Spock's mother is human? She has studied the discipline of ancient thought these many years. She has earned a place among the adepts and the teachers. Granted, she is extraordinary. But even you might reach a moderate level of comprehension—"

"I get the picture," Kirk said, irritated. "It still comes down to, 'None of your business.' Is that what I'm supposed to say to Harry Morrow, when I ask him to bend regulations into the fourth dimension?"

"You must say what you think best," Sarek said, without irony.

Hikaru Sulu leaned forward in his leather armchair.

"Admiral, I—"

"No!" Kirk said sharply. "Don't answer me now. I want you to think it over first."

The image of James Kirk faded abruptly from the 'phone screen.

On the surface, what Kirk had asked Sulu to do was not very difficult. A volunteer mission, a few days out, a few days back. But if worse came to worst, the consequences could be grave. Kirk had not softpedaled the most severe of the possibilities.

Kirk's intensity troubled Hikaru. It was Kirk who had first commented on the crew's obsession with the death of Spock, and now he himself seemed obsessed and driven. What he hoped to accomplish was not entirely clear to Hikaru—who had the definite impression that Kirk was not clear on the details, either.

But it was certain that Kirk felt responsible for Spock's death, and that he could not accept it. Hikaru believed Kirk had taken on this mission to expiate the guilt he felt, and he understood Kirk well enough to know that he would never be free of the guilt, or of his grief, until he completed what he had sworn to do.

Cold rain skittered against the window. Hikaru sat in the dark for an hour, thrashing questions around in his mind.

He admitted to himself that he feared for James Kirk's sanity.

The house was very quiet. He shared it with four other people, but tonight he was the only one home. He was, in fact, the lone member of the household on Earth. Only rarely was everyone home at the same time, but even more rarely was everyone else gone.

I shouldn't be home, either, he thought. *Dammit!*

He got up and went out the back door into the garden. Without his noticing, the rain had stopped and the sky had cleared. The full moon was risen halfway to its zenith. The wet lawn felt cold against his bare feet and the air was ozone-washed. In the near distance, the sea rushed against the shore and away.

His mind chased itself around in circles. He needed to think about something else for a while, or better yet to think of nothing at all. He began to move in a *bo* routine, *bō-no-ikkyo*, though his *bo*, his wooden staff, was back in the house along with his *gi*, and the black belt and *hakama* he had only recently earned when he passed his *shodan* test.

Tsuki, deflect, *tsuki*, *yokomen*, *yokomen*—

Over the years he had studied a number of martial arts. He was an excellent fencer, and he had progressed to the first of the several degrees of brown belts in judo. But his interest in judo had always had more to do with the fact that he was learning it from Mandala Flynn (he believed she had the same feeling about fencing, which he had taught her). Aikido was different. It was a martial art dedicated to non-violence, to demonstrating to one's opponent the futility of violence. He had been training for some years now. The thrill of being promoted to *shodan,* of putting on for the first tune the black belt and the *hakama,* the long wide pleated black trousers, was just as intense as what he had felt when he received the orders giving him command of *Excelsior.*

Yokomen, kakushibo, sweep, reverse, thrust, *dogiri*—

Usually he could lose himself in the motions, but tonight the question he had been asked and the decision he had still to make remained uppermost in his mind, spoiling the flow and the peace of the routine.

James Kirk planned to return to Genesis, whether he got help and the *Enterprise* from Starfleet, or merely a blind eye turned when he departed.

If he was denied permission, or expressly forbidden to go . . .

Sulu thought of his magnificent new ship, up in Spacedock, waiting for him, nearly ready to fly. That was where he should be, not down here Earthbound, waiting for debriefings, waiting to testify, waiting to find out from Starfleet whether he had kept his nose clean enough to rate being given back his command.

They had no right to take it from me in the first place, he thought. But they did, and they made very clear the conditions under which I might hope to regain it.

Yokomen, tsuki, yokomen, sweep and turn—

He lost the rhythm and the pattern. He stopped. He blotted the sweat from his forehead, from the sides of his face.

He weighed *Excelsior* against what James Kirk had asked of him. He weighed his ambitions against his allegiance; he weighed the future and the past.

He made a decision, without regret and without reservation.

He swirled back into the routine, moving lightly over the springy wet grass while the last fall roses perfumed the air. The pattern of his motions was smooth and pure, the way he hoped and tried to form his life.

Saavik ran through the steamy, humid glade, pushing aside rain-laden fronds that doused her with cascades of sun-warmed water. She followed the sound of the cry, pierced to her center by its despair. The tricorder in her hand beeped and clicked with life-sign readings, but she hardly glanced at it. Its data were superfluous.

She burst from the forest. It ended so abruptly that she stopped. David hurried up behind her, breathing hard.

"Not so fast," he said between gasps. "We don't know what that scream was." He bent over to catch his breath. "It might be a predator—it might be one of Vance's dragons."

Saavik wondered who had designed this section of the landscape. Enormous cactuslike trees stretched bulbous fingers to the sky. On the rocky surface, gray, leathery succulents spread their thick leaves like wounded wings, soaking up the sun.

The ground quivered gently beneath Saavik's feet. It was like a caress—but the illusion shattered when the pain-filled cry came again. Whatever made that sound experienced no pleasure from the trembling land.

Saavik strode forward, the gravel of the desert crunching beneath her boots and sliding beneath her heels. The rounded, waterworn stones made the surface treacherous and slippery and difficult to negotiate.

"Was this a 'little joke'?" she said to David.

"What?"

"Waterworn stones, in a desert that has never seen water? False history, false geology."

"We wanted to make it seem real," David said. "Layered. Not as if everything were brand-new."

"In that, you certainly succeeded." The cacti might each have been a thousand years old. The succulents might have been left over from an earlier age, living fossils of the beginnings of evolution.

She continued deeper into the forest of cacti. The dryness was a relief after the oppressive humidity of the glade, but what glimpses she could get between the gnarled and looming trunks hinted at another abrupt change of climate.

A hundred meters farther on, the ground was covered with snow.

The rumble of a temblor surrounded her. She tensed—and the cry came yet again. She had been expecting it—

We hear the cry whenever the ground quakes, she thought. As if there were some direct connection. . . . But she amended her hasty deduction. She did not have enough data to draw a significant conclusion, and besides, the creature, the being, might simply be frightened by the earthquakes.

"Grissom *to ground party. What's going on down there?"*

Saavik stopped and flipped open her communicator.

"Saavik here, Captain. We have strong life sign readings, bearing zero-one-five. We are proceeding to investigate."

"All right, Saavik, I concur. . . . But be advised that we are *tracking a severe and unnatural age curve for the planet. The harmonic motion of the core is increasing in amplitude at a rate that is making me* very *nervous."*

Saavik covered the microphone of the communicator. David was staring in the direction of the snow, apparently ignoring her conversation with Captain Esteban.

"Do you have an explanation?"

"Later," he said with an intensity that belied his outward indifference to Esteban's information. He gestured impatiently. "Let's *go!*" Without waiting, he started toward the snow-covered bluffs beyond the desert, moving away from her in more important ways than simple distance.

Saavik uncovered the communicator pickup. "*Grissom,* your message acknowledged. Will advise. Saavik out."

She snapped shut the communicator and followed David across the desert. He had already passed beyond the limits of the twisted cactus trees. A breeze ruffled his curly golden hair. With every step he took the wind grew stronger. By the time Saavik reached the edge of the forest, the wind had begun to swirl flakes of dry snow against David's feet. He was only about fifty meters ahead of her. She stepped out of the shelter of the cacti, into the whine of the wind. The temperature dropped precipitously, perhaps thirty degrees in as many paces. The wind howled past them.

David reached the first patch of solid snow, stopped, and gazed down at something. Saavik joined him. A trail of small, blurry footprints led from the edge of the snow and up the white-blanketed slope. The wind had obscured their outlines. A sudden flurry of snow threatened to bury them entirely.

The sky held no clouds. The snow was not falling; it was, rather, being carried by the wind from some other source. The icy, stinging flakes cut the visibility to almost nothing.

Saavik sat on her heels and looked closely at the vanishing footprints. She shook her head and rose to her feet.

"Those are not, I think, the tracks of *Sauriform Madisonii,*" she said. Neither, though, were they the tracks she had hoped to find.

In the Starfleet officers' lounge, Jim Kirk feigned calm as he waited for Harry Morrow's reply. Morrow stared silently out into the night, his reflection black on black against the wide expanse of the window that stretched seamlessly from one side of the lounge to the other. The Starfleet commander's expression remained unreadable. Kirk forced himself not to clench his fists.

"No," Morrow said finally. "Absolutely not, Jim. It's out of the question."

All the repressed tension fueled Kirk's words. "Harry—Harry, I'm off the record now. I'm not speaking as a member of your staff. I'm talking about thirty years of service. I have to do this, Harry. It has to do with my honor—my life. Everything I put any value on."

He cut off his plea when a steward stopped at his elbow with a tray, removed empty glasses, replaced them with full ones. Jim held himself silent. After an interminable time, the steward left.

"Harry—"

"Jim," Morrow said carefully, "you are my best officer, and if I *had* a best friend, you'd be that, too. But I am Commander, Starfleet, so I don't break rules."

"Don't quote rules, Harry! We're talking about loyalty! And sacrifice! One man who died for us, another at risk of deep—permanent—emotional damage—"

"Now, wait a minute!" Morrow said. "This business about Spock and McCoy and mind-melds and—honestly, I have never understood Vulcan mysticism. Nor do I understand what you hope to accomplish—I'm sorry! I don't want you to make a fool of yourself. Understand?"

"Harry, you don't have to *believe.* I'm not even sure *I* believe. But if there's even a chance that Spock has an . . . an eternal soul—then that is *my* responsibility."

"Yours!"

"As surely as if it were my own." He leaned forward. "Harry, give me back the *Enterprise!* With Scotty's help—"

"No, Jim! The *Enterprise* would never stand the pounding."

Kirk realized that Morrow had not understood a word he had said all evening. Harry did not believe him and did not trust him. Worse, he would not permit him to draw on a thirty years' friendship to help him complete a task that bound him as strongly as any Starfleet mission he had ever undertaken.

"You've changed, Harry," he said with anger and contempt. "You used to be willing to take some risks."

"I used to have different responsibilities than I have now," Harry said sadly. "Jim, I'm not completely unsympathetic to your request, believe me. I'll contact Esteban. If anything comes of . . . what *Grissom* has found on Genesis, I will of course order them to bring it back."

"How long—?"

"At least six weeks."

"Impossible. Harry, Leonard McCoy is being driven mad! He wasn't properly prepared for what happened to him, he wasn't trained—in six weeks the damage could be fatal!"

"You're not dictating any terms here! *Grissom*'s mission is vital—we have to have the data on Genesis before we can make a decision about it! And you want me to order them to turn around and come straight back so you can—save a dead man's soul? Can't you see how that would sound? No. I'm sorry."

"I repeat: give me back my ship."

"I'm sorry, Jim. I can't let you have the *Enterprise*."

"Then I'll find a ship—I'll hire a ship!"

"Out of the question!" Morrow said again. "You can hire one—but you won't get it anywhere near Genesis. The whole Mutara sector is under quarantine. No one goes there until the science team gets back, and probably not even then. Council's orders."

"Then let me speak to the Council!" Jim's voice rose, so absorbed was he in the urgency of his quest. "Harry, please! I can make them understand!"

He realized that every person in the lounge was either staring at him or making a noticeable effort to avoid doing so. He drew back, forcing his temper back under control.

"No, *you* understand," Morrow said. "You simply have no conception of the political realities of this situation. Tensions are strung so tight you could play them like a piano! The Council has its hands full trying to deal with delegations from both the Romulan and the Klingon Empires. My gods, Jim, can you imagine the repercussions if you go in there and announce your personal views on friendship and metaphysics?" He shook his head slowly, stroked the condensation in stripes down the side of his glass with his forefinger, and clenched his fist. "Jim—! Your life and your career stand for rationality, not intellectual chaos. Keep up this emotional behavior, and you'll lose everything. You'll destroy yourself!"

As one friend accused him of abandoning lifelong rationality because of a duty to another friend who had continually perceived him as totally illogical, Jim Kirk felt an almost hysterical urge to laugh.

"Do you hear me, Jim?"

Jim stared at him for a long time, searching for some way to respond to having been so irrevocably refused. He sagged back in his chair.

"Yes, I hear you," he said. He truly was not sure if he had heard everything Harry Morrow had said to him, but it did not matter. He sighed. "I . . . just had to try."

"Of course," Morrow said. "I understand."

Jim said nothing, certainly not, *No, you don't, you don't at all.*

"Now take my suggestion, Jim," Morrow said kindly. "Enjoy your leave—and let all this tension blow away."

"You're right," Kirk said with reluctance. He picked up his glass and raised it to Morrow. "Thanks for the drink."

"Any time."

Jim set it back down without tasting it, rose, and walked from the lounge, eyes front. He was very much aware of Morrow, watching him with concern, very much aware of all the other senior Starfleet officers, deliberately avoiding him.

This was the world in which he had lived for thirty years, the world in which he always before felt comfortable and welcome. The palpable chill said: The pressure finally got to him, Jim Kirk finally cracked.

The rumors would fly across Starfleet at transwarp speed, grow, and take on a life of their own.

He left the lounge, stepping out into the terminal of the spaceport. Restrained conversation and low lights gave way to brilliant illumination and the hubbub of crowds. He felt more out of place here than he ever had on any alien world. He wondered if there was any place left for him at all.

He looked around, feeling conspicuous in his Starfleet uniform. Finally he found Sulu and Chekov. They were a hundred meters across the terminal, wearing civilian clothes and sitting together on a circular bench, people-watching. Chekov wore a jumpsuit of relatively severe tailoring, while Sulu wore jeans and sandals and an embroidered white Filipino festival shirt. Sulu saw Kirk first and nudged Chekov. They waited for him with elaborate casualness. Kirk glanced around carefully, looking for other Starfleet personnel. He wished he had asked the two younger officers to wait for him somewhere more private. The way things stood, the less they were seen with him the better. He needed their help, but with any luck he might be able to get them out of all this relatively unscathed.

He saw no one else he recognized, so he joined Sulu and Chekov.

"The word, sir?" Sulu said.

"His word is no," Kirk said, gesturing with a jerk of his head back toward the senior officers' lounge. "But my word . . . is given."

"Count on our help, sir."

"I'll need it, Hikaru." He had nearly slipped, nearly said, "Thank you, Commander." But he remembered hearing about Sulu asking to be removed from the captain's list, and he even turned down the *Excelsior.* Kirk knew it was loyalty to him that has cost Sulu his own command. While it was Sulu's choice Kirk felt responsible.

"Shall I alert Doctor McCoy, sir?" Chekov asked.

"Yes. He has . . . a long journey ahead."

Leonard McCoy strode down the crowded street. His body felt like someone else's. He could smell the pungent scent of eight different volatile recreational drugs. He was familiar with them all, of course: he was, after all, a doctor. But he should not be able to sort them out so efficiently from the surrounding smells of the dirty street, the fog, the rain, incense and warm oil from one establishment, raw meat from another. He could hear more clearly than usual. He listened to five simultaneous conversations, one in Standard, two in more traditional Earth languages, and two—no, that was a single conversation being carried out in two different dialects of the same offworld tongue.

He arrived at the meeting place. He paused before its brightly lit come-hither sign. He could feel the colors of the neon script illuminating his face with another dozen different languages, evenly divided between Earth and other worlds. He rubbed the scratchy stubble on his jaw. There was something else he was supposed to be doing, something Jim had told him to do. *Oh. Right.* Jim had told him to shave and put on more beard repressor. *Was this as important?* He remembered what it was he was doing. It definitely was more important than shaving.

But is it the right thing? he wondered. *There's still time to turn back, go to the nearest hospital, confess to being stark raving mad, and make them lock me up before I get violent.*

He reached into his pocket, but it was empty. He had forgotten his tranquilizers. He shrugged. They had not been doing him much good anyway.

He plunged into the tavern.

The noise, the smoke, the appalling scent of sizzling meat assaulted him. He staggered and only managed to keep from falling by grabbing onto the nearest person. She turned, ready to fight, then looked at him more closely and laughed.

"Honey, you look like you're having a tough time of it," she said. She supported him easily. She was half a head taller than he. Her heavy, curly black hair spread around her head and down her back. She wore the black leather pants and jacket favored by independent couriers, with the jacket fastened only at the bottom and nothing beneath it. The skin of her throat and the inner curves of her breasts looked like warm sable. She was black on black on black, except her eyes, which were a piercing pale blue. He stared up at her and fell in love with her instantly. Only that saved him from abandoning his appointment and asking her for the help he needed. He did not want to drag anyone he loved into the trouble he was heading for.

"I'm . . . I'm all right," he said. He drew himself up straighter. He still had some dignity.

She kept a steadying hand on his elbow. "Sure?"

"Yes," he said. "Yes, thank you."

"Okay." She let him go.

Somehow he kept his feet and continued farther into the bar. A tiny plane whizzed past his face. Startled, he stepped back and nearly fell. A second plane whined past, its propellers blurred, minuscule guns blazing with a sharp snapping sound like a fire of pitch-pine.

The planes were holograms. Nearby, two youths lay in game couches, their eyes closed and their hands on antiqued controls. Behind their eyelids they were experiencing the dogfight of the two early twentieth century biplanes. McCoy watched the three-dimensional images zoom high over the heads of the bar patrons. Each aircraft was the size of his hand, and exquisitely detailed. Suddenly they dove straight toward him. The Spad 7 vanished into his shirt front, the Albatros D-III close behind. He hardly had time to flinch. He looked over his shoulder to watch them soar into the heights again, unscathed by their passage through his strange and alien body. The fleeing Spad suddenly executed an elegant loop-the-loop, came up behind the Albatros, and quite abruptly shot it out of the sky. The Albatros screamed into a dive, emitted holographic flame and clouds of holographic smoke—and disappeared a handsbreadth from the floor. The Spad zoomed victoriously toward the ceiling and faded away.

"Gotcha!" cried one of the youths.

"Okay, okay—want to make it three out of five?"

"That is a wager."

They were dressed alike—McCoy wondered if that was some new style he had been too out of touch to notice—and they looked so alike that it was impossible to tell if they were two of one gender, two of the other, or one of each. He supposed they knew. That was, after all, the thing that mattered.

McCoy pushed on ahead. The illumination was very dim, but he could see quite clearly, in an odd and glowing way that he had never experienced before. Nevertheless he could not find the person he was looking for. Instead he found a small unoccupied booth in the corner of the room and settled down to wait.

Beneath the din of the tavern he heard footsteps quickly approaching. He glanced up.

"Long time, Doc," Kendra said.

"Yeah," he said. "Yeah . . ." He would have liked to talk over old times with her. "Anyone . . . been looking for me?"

"I have," she said. "But what's the use?" She smiled. "Well. What'll it be?"

"Altair water." He drew himself up grandly. " 'Specially carbonated from underground fissures.' "

Kendra snorted at his recitation of the advertisement.

"Not your usual poison."

"To expect one to order poison in a bar is not logical," he said, and then he realized—though it surprised him to hear a tavern employee admitting it—that of course she meant alcohol, which was indeed a poison despite its wide use as a recreational drug.

Then he wondered what in heaven's name he was talking about. He simply did not want a drink, that was all. He had not had a drink since—since before Spock died, as it happened. *This is it,* he thought. *Sheer lunacy. I'm talking to myself. I always talk to myself, though, it helps me think. Have since I was only a tad. Doesn't mean a thing. As Freud said, Sometimes a cigar is only a cigar.* He noticed Kendra watching him curiously. "Excuse me," he said. "I'm on medication."

"Got it." She went away to get his water. As her footsteps receded among the hubbub, another set approached.

The alien slid into the booth beside him. "Hello! Welcome to your planet."

"I think that's my line, stranger," McCoy said.

"Oh, forgive. I here am new. But you are known, being McCoy from *Enterprise.*"

"You have me at a disadvantage, sir. You are—?"

"I name not important. You seek I. Message received. Available ship stands by."

"Good. How soon and how much?"

"How soon is now. How much . . . is where."

"Where . . . ?"

"Is yes. Where?"

"Somewhere in the Mutara Sector."

"Oh. Mutara restricted. Take permits many . . . money—more."

"There aren't going to be any damn permits!" McCoy shouted. "How can you get a permit to do a damn illegal thing?" He glanced around hurriedly to see if anyone had noticed his outburst, then continued in a softer, more conspiratorial tone. "Look, price you name, money I got."

"You name place, I name money. Otherwise, bargain no."

"All right, dammit! It's Genesis. The name of the place we're going to is Genesis."

"Genesis!" The being recoiled.

"Genesis, yes! How can you be deaf," he muttered, "with ears like that?" *I used to say the same thing to Spock,* McCoy thought.

"Genesis allowed is not. Is planet forbidden."

"Now listen to me, my backwards friend!" He lurched forward and grabbed the alien's collar. "Genesis may be 'planet forbidden,' but I'm damn well—"

A hand closed around his arm. McCoy tried to pull away, but the grip tightened painfully. He looked up. The civilian, an ordinary man, so ordinary he should have looked out of place here, but did not, smiled at him pleasantly. When he leaned forward he loomed, and McCoy realized how big he was.

"Sir, I'm sorry, but your voice is carrying," he said. "I don't think you want to be discussing this subject in public."

"I'll discuss what I like, and who the hell are you?"

The alien tried to pluck McCoy's hands from his collar. McCoy considered going for his throat, but instead clenched his hands harder around the fabric. The civilian tightened his grip again.

"Could I offer you a ride home, Doctor McCoy?"

What shreds of control McCoy had regained disintegrated.

"Where's the logic in offering me a ride home, you idiot! If I wanted a ride home, would I be trying to charter a space flight?" He scowled, beginning to perceive the civilian as an obstacle to his quest. "How the hell do you know who I am?"

The plain young man lowered his voice. "Federation security, sir."

McCoy realized just how serious an obstacle the young man was. He lurched away, loosing his grasp on the alien and trying to break the security man's grip. He crashed into Kendra, bringing his Altair water, which tumbled off her tray and splashed over the alien's face and shoulders. The alien leaped to his feet, brushing at the drops and stains. Kendra, surprised by the fray, fell backwards against the next table, sending icy drinks into customers' laps.

"You—you horrible doctor!" the alien cried, still brushing at the water.

"Come in here and punch people, will you?" yelled a customer as bits of crushed ice slid down the front of his sheer trousers. "Whyn't you go across the street where you belong?" He punched the alien, who rolled with the blow, let himself fall over a chair that tripped up the ice-drenched patron, chose the better part of valor, and left his commission behind him.

McCoy bowed to the wisdom of his former and all too brief colleague and headed for the door. Unfortunately the Federation man still had hold of his arm. He brought McCoy up short. McCoy swung around, panicked, and grabbed the man at the vulnerable point between neck and shoulder. He squeezed with all his strength and turned to flee without even waiting to see what happened.

Nothing had happened at all.

The Federation man, his grip unbroken, dragged McCoy to a halt. He looked into the doctor's eyes. "You're going to get a nice, long rest, Doctor," he said gently. "Please come along."

McCoy had a choice: walk or be carried.

He walked.

Eight

Saavik followed the blurry, half-obscured tracks across the snow. The wind blew ice crystals against her face, whipping them across her cheeks and freezing them to her eyelashes. She squinted to try to see into the blizzard. Movement caught her eye, and she headed toward it. The snow made ghosts all around her. She would have believed she was seeing phantoms if David's tricorder had not continued to bleat rhythmically.

She trudged through the snow, cold and unhappy, trying to ignore both sensations. But she discovered that once she had released her self-discipline, even for only a few days, she could not easily regain the complete Vulcan control she had worked so hard to learn.

With the discovery of the creatures around Spock's coffin, her hopes had crashed; a few moments later, when she saw that the coffin was intact, unsealed, and empty, her hopes had risen just as abruptly. This emotionalism was dangerous; in addition, it was illogical, for even when she dropped her mental shields completely, she could find no sense of Spock anywhere.

She knew she had erred. Whatever happened, whatever she and David found, she must re-establish dominance over her feelings and aspire to eradicating them.

Now she understood why Vulcans denied themselves any indulgence in passion. It was to protect themselves from pain.

Saavik shivered and pressed forward against the howling wind and the snow.

The ground rose beneath her. She was climbing the flank of a glacier. In only a few kilometers' distance it had changed from a thin blanket of snow to a sheet of ice many meters thick.

The frequency of the tricorder's output increased until it was nearly a continuous shriek, even louder than the wind. Saavik stopped and motioned for David to turn the thing off.

Beneath the ragged whine of the wind, the skittering of snow across the ground, the creaking of the ice beneath her feet, Saavik heard a weak and frightened whimper. She walked toward it. Her boots crunched through the frozen crust. The snow reached halfway to her knees. The uneven footprints before her trailed atop the surface. She wondered if she was following some small and vicious predator that a member of the Genesis team had made up as "a little joke," a little joke that now perhaps was injured and desperate. Saavik was growing impatient with the collective humor of the group. Her phaser made a comforting weight in her hand.

A great mass of stone, one moment concealed by the snow, the next a wall of tumbled gray blocks before her, thrust abruptly from the surface of the glacier. The ice had crumpled and cracked all around it, piling up in great heaps to either side.

Saavik saw the child.

He crouched in the meager shelter of a rock overhang, naked, shuddering uncontrollably with the cold. He saw her and tried to scrabble deeper into the cleft, clumsy on his injured leg.

David saw the boy and gasped.

"Your comrades appear to have added a humanoid species to the Genesis matrix," Saavik said. She crushed out the spark of fury that rose in her against such presumption. She could not afford to lose her temper, not here, not now.

"We didn't," David said. "I'm sure nobody did. We discussed it, because we realized it was possible. But nobody did it. Nobody even argued for it—it was obvious to all of us that it would be completely unethical to include an artificial intelligence in the first experiment. Besides, nobody could have put such a complex program into the matrix without everybody else noticing."

"David, the evidence is before your eyes." She bolstered her phaser, opened the side pocket of her coat, and drew out Spock's burial robe. She stepped toward the child, carrying the heavy cloth in one hand, her other hand empty and outstretched.

"No," David said. "The evidence is behind us, in Spock's empty coffin."

She looked at him sharply, unwilling to let herself begin to hope again.

The little boy huddled against cold stone, too tired to flee any farther. The wind whipped his scraggly black hair around his face and shoulders. The cold had given his skin a peculiar pallid tint. Saavik sat on her heels beside him and touched his shoulder gently. He flinched violently and stared at her, wide-eyed. She brushed her fingertips across his cheek. He continued to watch her, motionless, as she pushed back his hair, revealing his ears.

He was a Vulcan.

Saavik stared at him with wonder. She did not know what this could mean. Now was no time for analysis. The cold and the wind were too powerful. Whoever or whatever the boy was, she had to get him off the glacier.

She hoped she had shown him she meant him no harm. Moving slowly and carefully, she brought the black cloth forward, opened it slowly so he could see what she was doing, and wrapped it around his shoulders. He touched it with wonder, then hugged it tight.

"I am Saavik," Saavik said in Vulcan. "Can you speak?"

He cocked his head at her, but did not reply. She felt no resonances from him, no mental emanations, no hint of Spock's powerful intelligence. He was, rather, an innocent, a blank.

"It was the Genesis wave," David said. "It must have been. His cells could have been regenerated. Reformed . . ."

Still moving carefully so as not to alarm the child, Saavik drew out her communicator. David's theory was the most outrageous she could imagine . . . and the simplest.

"Saavik to *Grissom*. Captain Esteban, come in please."

"Esteban here, Saavik. Go ahead."

"We have found the source of the life signs. It is a Vulcan child, the equivalent of eight or ten Earth years of age."

There was a very long pause before Esteban replied.

"A child! That's . . . extraordinary. How did he get there?"

"It is Doctor Marcus' opinion that this is—that the Genesis effect has in some way regenerated—Captain Spock."

Back on board the *Grissom*, J.T. Esteban clamped his jaw tight shut to keep it from dropping. He glanced over at his science officer, who stopped staring at the speaker from which Saavik's announcement had come and met Esteban's gaze with an expression of complete, bewildered, speechless perplexity.

"Ah, Saavik," Esteban said, slowly, carefully, trying to figure out how to reply without saying that he thought she and David Marcus had gone stark staring bonkers. *"That's . . . ah . . . extraordinary. What would you, ah, like to do next?"*

"Request permission to beam aboard immediately."

He wanted to stall them for a bit. It was possible that some glitch in the Genesis programs bad produced powerful hallucinogens, or even that one of its denizens could take on the form of someone the observer would most desire to see. He could not take the chance of beaming such a thing on board. Of course there was always the possibility that what Saavik was describing was exactly what was happening. . . .

"Saavik . . . do Doctor Marcus' instruments show any chance of, er, radioactive contamination?"

After a short pause, Saavik replied, "None that he can detect, sir."

"Well. All the same, I'm going to advise Starfleet and get instructions."

"I am sure Starfleet would approve, sir," Saavik said.

"Nevertheless . . . let's do it by the book. Stand by on this channel." He nodded to his communications officer. "Go."

"Starfleet command, this is *U.S.S. Grissom* on subspace coded channel ninety-eight point eight. Come in, please."

The comm officer flinched as a high whine came through the earpiece.

"Sir," the comm officer said to Esteban, "something's jamming our transmission. An energy surge."

"What's the location?"

"Astern, sir. Aft quarter."

"On-screen."

The viewscreen flickered from a forward view to the aft pickup. The starfield lay empty behind them, empty except for an odd interference pattern in one corner. Esteban frowned, wondering if the maintenance of the pickup had been let go.

The interference pattern suddenly coalesced and solidified.

Out of nothing, a ship appeared.

Down on the surface of Genesis, Saavik and David waited impatiently for a response from Esteban. To Saavik's embarrassment, she was beginning to shiver from the cold. The child had stopped watching them. He hunched shivering in the black cloth, his eyelids drooping.

"Don't sleep," Saavik said, shaking him gently. He did not respond.

"Just like good old J.T. to leave us here freezing our butts off while he puts in a call to Starfleet," David said. "Let's get off this glacier, anyway."

Saavik nodded. Between them, they got the child to his feet. His injured leg collapsed beneath him. They would have to carry him, then call *Grissom* back when they got to a more hospitable spot.

As she was about to put her communicator away, it shrieked and squealed. *"Oh, my God!"* It was Esteban's voice. *"Red alert! Raise the shields!"*

"Captain," Saavik said, "what is it?"

"We're under attack! Stand by for evasive—stand by for—"

The cracked voice dissolved in a rattle of static.

"Captain! Captain Esteban, come in please!"

Deep space replied to her with silence.

On the bridge of the Klingon fighter, Commander Kruge watched the Federation science ship open out like a flower with a center of flame. The wreckage exploded and expanded beyond the limits of his own ship's port. Kruge's anger was only a little less explosive.

He swung around toward his gunner.

"I told you," he said dangerously, in the lowest of the low dialects, "engine section only!"

"A fortunate mistake," the gunner said. His crest flared up in excitement until he realized how Kruge had spoken to him. "Sir . . . ?"

"I wanted prisoners," Kruge said, layering all the strata of his words with contempt. At his side, Warrigul growled.

The gunner's crest flattened against his skull. Kruge gestured to Maltz.

"Offer him a chance to regain his honor," Kruge said.

Maltz stopped before the gunner's station and drew his ceremonial blade.

The gunner cringed. "Sir, please, no—it was an error!"

Maltz willed the gunner to get hold of himself and bow to the inevitable with grace. Maltz offered him his own honor blade. Every member of the crew watched, mesmerized.

Instead of accepting it and doing the proper thing, the gunner lurched backward from his station.

"Sir, no!" he cried. He stumbled toward Kruge, his hands outstretched in supplication. "Mercy, sir—"

Kruge drew his phaser and fired. The gunner disintegrated in a flare of energy.

"Animal," Kruge muttered. Warrigul snorted in agreement and rubbed up against his leg.

Maltz sheathed his blade, glad that its edge had not been sullied with the blood of a coward.

"Sir," Torg said, "may I suggest—"

Kruge whirled around to confront him. The commander still gripped the handle of his phaser, his frustration undiminished.

"Say the wrong thing, Torg, and I will kill you, too!"

"I only mean to say, my lord, that if it is prisoners you want, we interrupted a transmission from the planet's surface. I have traced it." He gestured to the screen. "These life signs may be the very scientists you seek."

Kruge strode to his side, glared at the screen, and analyzed the readings. One was clearly human, the other two less distinctive. Vulcan, perhaps, or Romulan. Human was to be expected; humans were the troublemakers of the galaxy, as far as Kruge was concerned. It annoyed him thoroughly that the Romulans might be involved in this. No doubt they had abandoned their commitments to the Klingon Empire and rushed straight to conclude an alliance with the Federation, in return for a share in Genesis.

And he, Kruge, was about to catch them at the treachery.

"Very good," he said to Torg, who stood even straighter with the pleasure of his commander's approval. "Very good."

The Vulcan boy huddled against Saavik's side, unable to understand the events taking place overhead, unable even to understand that events *were* taking place overhead, but upset and frightened by David and Saavik's reaction.

"*Grissom,* this is Saavik, come in please—"

The emergency channel replied with static. Suddenly Saavik snapped the communicator closed. Her transmission would clearly and easily mark their position.

"Saavik, my gods, what happened to them?"

"It would seem that *Grissom* was destroyed by an enemy attack," she said.

Saavik thought with regret of Frederic, the Glaeziver, whose counsel she had grown to value in the short time she had known him. He had understood what Genesis might mean for him and his kind, and now he was gone.

"Destroyed . . . ?" Stunned, David looked up, as if he might see the remains of the ship drifting dead in the new sky.

Saavik put away her communicator. It was useless now. She picked up the Vulcan child and started across the ice. She was very worried about the boy. He was so cold he had ceased even to shiver.

The ground quaked gently beneath her feet. Some distance away, ice shuddered, squealed, and ruptured. The child cried out weakly and began to tremble again. His pain did not ease until the temblor faded.

Saavik reached the place where, half an hour earlier, the snowfield had ended. Now it stretched onward and she could not see its edge. She hitched the child higher against her shoulder and ploughed on.

David caught up to her.

"Saavik—that means we're stranded down here!"

"Logic indicates that is the case," she said. The glacier seemed never-ending. It must be flowing at an incredible rate.

"How can you be logical at a time like this? We have to get the hell off this planet!"

"We must get out of the snow, first," she said. "I think it likely that we would freeze before we would starve, on this world."

"We have to get off Genesis!" David said again.

"That will be difficult," Saavik said. It took considerable effort to make any headway through the deep, soft snow. She trudged on.

"Why don't you just call for help!"

She looked at him. His demand was most curious, the result, no doubt, of panic. He knew her communicator was nothing but a local transceiver. *Grissom* had been the only Federation ship within its range. Whatever destroyed it was the only ship she would reach if she called again.

David's reaction disturbed her greatly. He was more frightened of remaining on the world he had created than he was of transmitting a Mayday that would be picked up by enemies. He was more distressed by having to remain in a paradise he had helped design than he was by the destruction of an entire ship and its crew.

"I have already made one transmission too many," she said.

David's shocked expression revealed his comprehension. He did not ask her to call for help again.

The snow ended as abruptly as it had begun. The edge of the ice moved perceptibly, creeping and grinding its way across the desert floor. Saavik stepped out of cold and into abrupt, welcome heat. She carried the child across a hundred meters of the water-worn stones, to a place where he would be safe for at least a few minutes. The snow on her hair and the ice on her eyelashes melted quickly. Cold drops slid down her face. She lowered the child to the ground, brushed away the dissolving snow with half-numbed hands, and helped him to lie in a warm and sunny spot.

David sank down nearby, drew his knees to his chest, and laid his face against his folded arms.

Saavik sat on her heels beside him.

"David," she said gently.

He said nothing.

"David, it is time for truth between us." She put her hands on his shoulders in what she hoped might be a comforting gesture. But what did she know of comfort? She was neither Vulcan, never needing comfort, never able to give it, nor was she Romulan, able to give full rein to her passions. "This planet is neither what you intended nor what you hoped for, is it?"

David let his hands fall. "Not exactly," he said.

"Is it what you feared?"

"I didn't think this would happen—!"

"But you have not been surprised by anything we have discovered, no matter how bizarre."

"There was one set of equations, I wasn't quite certain about them. . . ."

"You were overruled by the other members of the Genesis team?"

"I . . . I didn't want to make a big thing of them. . . ."

"Surely you pointed them out?"

"Why should I?" he snapped, on the defense. "I'm a mere biochemist, as my young genius physicist colleagues kept trying not to remind me. If Madison and March didn't think their creation was going to dissolve back into protomatter—"

"Protomatter!" Saavik exclaimed. "David, you are saying the entire system is unstable—and dangerously unpredictable! As an ethical scientist—"

"It shouldn't have happened! It hasn't, yet, maybe it won't. Maybe it wasn't a mistake at all—"

"And perhaps the ground tremors are in our minds, and the harmonic vibrations we detected from *Grissom* were instrument malfunction . . ." She shook her head. "Oh, David."

"I just figured, if it worked out for fusion, it would work out for us."

"What are you talking about?"

"The first time anybody started a fusion reaction—the first time on Earth, I mean. It was a bomb, of course—"

"Naturally," Saavik said.

"They didn't know for sure if they'd set off a chain reaction of all the hydrogen in the atmosphere. But they took the chance. They did it anyway."

"Indeed."

"Well, at least there's precedent."

"I am glad to see you are able to maintain your sense of humor," Saavik said.

"Dammit, Saavik, if those equations weren't right, the whole project collapsed—permanently! All I had was a suspicion, and it was a suspicion about a probability function at that! There was only a one in a million chance that the worst would happen even if the worst *could* happen. Besides, if we'd tested Genesis the way we intended to, instead of having it blown up by your admiral's—"

"Your father's—"

"—friend Mister Khan, there wouldn't have been anybody on the planet to be in danger!"

"You did not tell your collaborators," Saavik said. "Even after detonation, you did not tell Carol—"

"If I had, it wouldn't be just us stuck here! Mother would never have gone back to Earth, not if she'd known. She'd have taken the whole responsibility on herself . . . when it was mine to accept."

"Just like your father . . ." Saavik said sadly. "You changed the rules." She knew now that Genesis would never benefit anyone. It would never create new resources, it would never provide a new home for Frederic's people, it would only, ever, cause grief and anguish and disaster.

"If I hadn't, it might have been years—or never!"

All Saavik could think was that if Genesis had been delayed or abandoned, none of the recent events would have happened. *Reliant* would never have visited the world on which Khan Noonien Singh and his people were marooned. Khan would never have obtained a starship. He would never have led his people on his mission of vengeance. The scientists on Spacelab would not have been murdered. The *Enterprise* and its crew of children never would have been attacked. Peter Preston would still be alive. Genesis would not have existed to be used as a weapon, and Mister Spock would not have had to sacrifice his existence to save his ship and his crewmates.

Spock would not have died.

Nor would he have been resurrected. The child possessed the substance of her teacher, but he lacked his mind, his experience, his individuality.

Saavik rose to her feet and stood looking down at David. A dangerous fury began to form.

"And how many have paid the price for your impatience?" Saavik said. "How many have died? How much damage have you caused—and what is yet to come?"

He raised his head. His belligerence dissolved in grief and anguish, but Saavik was still too close to the madness to forgive him. She fled from him, her fists clenched so hard that her nails cut into her palms. When she had run a hundred paces she stopped.

Saavik cried out to the dying world, a long, hoarse shriek of rage and pain.

For a jail cell, it was not half bad.

Leonard McCoy lay on the bunk with his arm flung across his eyes.

The bunk was no wider than his shoulders, the floor was badly worn, gray, spongy linoleum, and he could not turn out the lights, but, still, it was not too bad. For a jail cell.

McCoy felt quite calm and rational and single-minded, despite having been forbidden any tranquilizers. After he had prowled the cell, pacing back and forth and inspecting every crack and corner of it, after he had come to the conclusion that he could not escape (that was the one other thing wrong with it, of course: he could not pass through the open doorway; the force field threw him back into the room at every try, more forcefully and more painfully each time. But, then, it *was* a jail cell), the compulsion to return to the Mutara Sector and Genesis had vanished as suddenly and completely as it had appeared.

He wondered about that. It seemed like a terribly logical reaction to have. . . .

McCoy dozed off.

"You got a visitor, Doc."

McCoy started out of troubled sleep, wondering where he was and how he had gotten there, and then remembering. *Not a dream, after all. Too bad.*

"Make it quick, Admiral," the guard said. "They're moving him to the Federation funny farm."

McCoy peered sideways from beneath his arm and saw the guard and Jim Kirk standing outlined by the force field. Jim shook his head sadly.

"Yes, my poor friend," he said. "I hear he's fruity as a nutcake."

Oh, you do, do you? McCoy thought. *A "funny farm," eh? Is that the kind of respect anybody with a few problems gets in here? Besides, I know my rights— they can't send me anywhere without a hearing.*

However, they had put him in here without a hearing. Genesis had not only frightened the Federation and Starfleet, it had put them into a total panic. McCoy wondered what would happen when Jim called his lawyer for him, as McCoy intended to ask him to do. He wondered if the administration of this prison would even admit to an attorney that he was here.

"Two minutes," the guard said.

McCoy watched the grid of the force field dim and fade. He had to struggle against the sudden compulsion to leap up and try to fight his way out. Since the guard was head and shoulders taller than he, and armed at that, such a course was definitely not logical. As Jim stepped inside the cell, the urge diminished in proportion to the strength of the reappearing energy barrier.

Jim knelt beside the cot.

"Jim—" McCoy said.

"Shh." He raised his hand, shielding it from the surveillance camera. "How many fingers?"

His fingers parted in the Vulcan salute.

"That's not very damned funny," McCoy said.

"Good," said Jim. "Your sense of humor has returned." He reached into his pocket.

"The hell it has!" Two minutes, and Jim wanted to spend it trading one-liners. McCoy wanted a lawyer and he wanted out of here. It was ridiculous to maintain the pretense of being asleep, so he sat up.

Jim drew out a spray injector.

McCoy frowned. "What's that?"

"Lexorin."

"Lexorin! What for?"

"You're suffering from a Vulcan mind-meld, Doctor."

"Spock—?"

"That's right."

"That green-blooded, pointy-eared son of a bitch. It's his revenge for all those arguments he lost—"

"Give me your arm. This will make you well enough to travel." He fumbled around with the automatic hypo, putting himself in considerable danger of shooting himself in the hand. "How do you do this, anyway?"

"Give it here," McCoy said. He took the hypo and pushed up his own sleeve. "This once, Admiral, you're beyond your capabilities."

Outside the prison, Hikaru Sulu ran his hands through his hair to muss it, tucked one side of his ruffled civilian shirt in and left the other free, hyperventilated for a few breaths, and, when he thought he had a properly flustered air about him, flung open the door and rushed into the reception area. The two guards looked up from their card game, startled by the appearance of another visitor so late at night.

"Where's Admiral Kirk?" Sulu said urgently.

One of the guards looked him up and down.

"He's with a prisoner. What's it to you?"

"Get him quickly! Starfleet Commander Morrow wants him—right now!"

The guard snorted with irritation, glanced at his partner and shrugged, laid his cards aside, and fumbled around for his electronic key. He vanished into the cell block. His partner glanced speculatively at the facedown cards, glanced at Sulu with unconcealed disdain, and flipped his partner's poker hand face up. Then, watching Sulu with a faint sneer, he turned the cards back over.

Sulu simply watched as if he saw men cheat their partners every day and thought nothing of it. It was to his advantage if the guard assumed he was a powerless flunky.

The guard stretched and yawned.

"Keeping you busy?" Sulu said to the big man.

"Don't get smart, Tiny."

Sulu frowned. He had to remind himself forcibly that he was supposed to be someone's messenger boy.

"This man is sick! Look at him!" Kirk's muffled voice came from beyond the cell-block door.

The guard heard, too, and rose to his feet. Sulu took a step forward, ready to distract him. The console did the job for him.

The signal buzzed insistently. The guard frowned, glanced at the cell block door, and snatched up the receiver. Sulu relaxed, centered himself, and waited. These few minutes were crucial. A glitch now could destroy the whole plan.

"Sixth floor holding," the guard said. He listened to his earphone. "Yeah, come on up and get him, his visitor's just leaving. . . . What? Some admiral, name of Kirk."

Sulu could hear the squawk of protest from the receiver. He also heard a crash and thud from within the cell block, but the guard was too distracted to notice.

"How the hell am I supposed to know *that?*" the guard snarled. "He's a damned admiral—! All right!" He flung down the earpiece and headed for the door. He heard the commotion beyond.

The door to the cell block opened and Admiral Kirk stepped through, supporting Doctor McCoy.

"What the hell is going on?"

Sulu tapped the guard on the shoulder.

"Dammit, I told you—" The guard swung toward him, punching at Sulu's head as he turned.

Sulu stepped into and around the strike, cutting down with his hands to redirect the force of the blow. As the big man stumbled forward, off-balance, Sulu drew him in, pivoted, and spiraled him up. The guard ran out from under himself, and Sulu completed the spiral into the ground. The wall interposed itself. Sulu's opponent hit it with a thud—a hollow thud, Sulu fancied—and slid slowly and limply to the floor.

The form had not been perfect for *yokomenuchi iriminage,* and throwing one's partner into the wall was rather bad form. But, then, this was the real world.

Besides, Sulu hated to be teased about his height.

Sulu glanced up. Kirk was watching appreciatively.

"The side elevator," Sulu said. "Agents on their way up."

Kirk nodded. He and McCoy hurried out the side door. Sulu paused by the master console. He reached beneath it, sought out the central processor, and applied the confuser he had put together. A moment later it rewarded him with a small fireworks display and the acrid smell of burned semiconductors.

Sulu started after Kirk. He reached the door, paused, and glanced down at the unconscious guard.

"Don't call me 'Tiny,' " he said.

Someone should have told the man that in Sulu's chosen martial art, being short was an advantage.

Sulu caught up to Kirk and McCoy and helped support the doctor.

"I'm all right," the doctor muttered. But he did not try to pull away. He was steadier than the last time Sulu had seen him. Apparently Sarek's lexorin had worked.

Admiral Kirk pulled out his communicator and flipped it open.

"Unit two, this is one. The *Kobayashi Maru* has set sail for the promised land. Acknowledge."

"Message acknowledged," Chekov replied, his voice sounding tinny from the small speaker. *"All units will be informed."*

Kirk closed his communicator. McCoy seemed to gain strength from the interchange and, perhaps, from regaining his freedom. He cocked his eyebrow at Kirk.

"You're taking me to the promised land?"

"What are friends for?" said Kirk.

On board *Excelsior,* Montgomery Scott waited for the turbo-lift. He kept his hand thrust deep in his pocket. The sharp corners of a small and nondescript chunk of semiconductor, elegant only at the microscopic level, bit into his palm.

The lift arrived, the doors slid open, and Captain Styles stepped out. Scott started. He had not expected to see anyone, particularly not Captain Styles. He managed to greet the officer civilly; technically, after all, Styles was his superior officer.

Superior officer, indeed, Scott thought angrily. *Taking this ship from our own Mister Sulu with nae a second thought nor a protest. 'Tis nae thing superior in that.*

"Ah, Mister Scott," Styles said. "Calling it a night?"

"Aye, Captain, yes," Scott said, trying to maintain his frozen smile.

"Turning in myself. Don't know if I'll be able to sleep, though—I'm looking forward to breaking some of the *Enterprise*'s speed records tomorrow."

"Aye, sir," Scott said through clenched teeth. "Good night." Scott got into the lift. As soon as the doors slid closed between him and Styles, he scowled.

His whole time on *Excelsior* had been like a replay of the arguments he had had with Mister Sulu about the ship. Only this time, Scott lost most of the arguments. Scott would never admit it to Sulu, but *Excelsior* was, indeed, a miracle of engineering. He had expected it to be full of complications, but its systems were elegantly integrated, clean, and nearly flawless. Scott, of course, had been looking for the flaws.

"*Level* please," the ship's computer said.

There were a few things on the ship that Scott did not like, such as the faintly insolent baritone voice of the computer. Had he the charge of *Excelsior,* that would change.

"Transporter room," he said.

"*Thank you,*" said the computer.

"Up your shaft!"

The lift jerked into motion.

"Temper, temper," Scott said.

Saavik and David struggled up the steep flank of the mountain, seeking a vantage point from which to watch for other survivors of *Grissom.* David believed it was at least possible that a few others might have had enough warning to escape. He knew Saavik thought the possibility unlikely, but she had not tried to persuade him it was impossible. In fact, she had barely spoken to him since his confession about Genesis. When he suggested they climb to higher ground, she merely shrugged, picked up the Vulcan boy, and started toward the mountain that rose abruptly from the surrounding desert.

"Are you mad at me?" David asked hesitantly.

She kept on climbing. But after another twenty meters she said, "Were I to permit the less civilized part of my character to dictate my reactions, I would be infuriated with you."

"I had to do it!" David said. "It shouldn't have put anyone in danger, and if it worked—"

"Yes," she said. "So you have said."

"I knew if I told you, I'd lose you as my friend," David said, despondent.

Saavik stopped and laid the Vulcan boy down gently in the shade of a tree, out of the penetrating blue-white sunlight. Then she faced David and took his hands in hers.

"You have not lost me as a friend," she said.

"But—you must hate me, after all this!"

"I am angry," she said, not bothering to conceal her feelings behind a philosophical comparison of Vulcans and Romulans, no longer trying to claim that she did not possess those feelings at all. "If I understand them properly, anger and hatred are two very different emotions. And again, if I understand correctly—it is unusual to hate a person that one loves."

"Saavik—" He tightened his grasp on her hands.

"Perhaps I am not capable of love, as humans know it," Saavik said. "But as you cannot explain it, I am free to define it for myself. I choose to define it as the feelings that I have for you."

She looked into his eyes. She felt in his wrists his cool, strong pulse. She drew her hands up his arms, to his shoulders, to the sides of his face. He moved toward her and put his arms around her. She kissed him. David felt as if he were dissolving in a white-hot flame, or tumbling unprotected through a solar flare.

Saavik drew away.

"We must go on," she said. "We cannot stay here."

As she started toward the Vulcan boy, she heard a strange sound. She glanced back the way they had come.

"David," she said with wonder, "look."

Far below, the glacier lapped at the foot of the mountain, surging up in slow-motion waves. As David and Saavik watched, the ice crept forward, piling and folding and crushing itself against immovable stone, squealing and cracking and shrieking. The ice had completely engulfed the desert, inundating it like a silver flood.

Scott materialized in the dark. He hated being transported into darkness.

"Chekov?" he whispered.

"Welcome home, Mister Scott," Chekov said. *"Zdrastvuyte, tovarisch."*

"None o' your heathen gibberish, Chekov," Scott said. "How did ye get on board?"

"We have ways," Chekov said.

"Which ways, in particular?"

"Partner of 'Unit three' was taking advantage of her good nature, was late for job. Will be more difficult for 'Unit one.' "

"All right," Scott said. "Let's get some life in tae this old tub." He squinted across the transporter room of the *Enterprise*. He could barely make out Chekov's hands in the faint glow of the console's controls.

"How was trip?" Chekov said.

"Short," Scott said. "Let's get to work."

Uhura replied to the ten P.M. check.

"Roger. Old City Station at twenty-two hundred hours. All is well."

She made a few adjustments to the controls of the Earth-based transporter to which she had been assigned. This was a peaceful posting; she had been here since four this evening and, officially, she had transported no one in or out. The schedule listed no travelers—officially—for the rest of the night.

She became aware that Lieutenant Heisenberg was watching her closely, with a slight frown of curiosity. He leaned back in his chair, his hands clasped behind his head and his feet up on the console.

"You amaze me, Commander," he said.

"How is that?" she said mildly.

"You're a twenty-year space veteran—yet you ask for the worst duty station in town. I mean, look at it—this is the hind end of space."

"Oh, peace and quiet appeal to me, Lieutenant." Uhura smiled a private smile.

"Maybe it's okay for someone like you, whose career is winding down."

Uhura raised an eyebrow at that remark, but let it pass.

"But me," Heisenberg said, "I need some challenge in my life. Some adventure. Even just a surprise or two."

"You know what they say, Lieutenant. Be careful what you ask for: you may get it."

"I *wish*," he said with feeling.

Uhura glanced at the clock. She had tried to persuade Heisenberg to go home early, on the grounds that there was hardly enough work for one person, let alone two. Unfortunately, he had declined. Apparently he felt slightly guilty about arriving an hour late. She wished he would choose some other day to make it up, but that was life.

The door slid open.

Admiral Kirk, Doctor McCoy, and Commander Sulu entered and headed straight for the transporter platform without a pause. Kirk appeared intent, but intent on something and somewhere else, distracted from this place and time. McCoy looked exhausted, but steady. Sulu caught Uhura's gaze and offered her his unshadowed smile.

"I talked to Sarek," Uhura heard Kirk say softly to McCoy. "I'm worried about him, Bones. The strain on him—"

Heisenberg dropped his feet to the floor and sat up very straight in his chair.

"Gentlemen," Uhura said. "Good evening."

"Good evening, Commander," Admiral Kirk said. "Everything ready?"

"Yes, Admiral." She swept her hand through the air in a gesture of welcome. "Step into my parlor."

Uhura saw Heisenberg's jaw go agape as he recognized the travelers. He was the one factor of uncertainty in this equation. She hoped he would behave sensibly. She began setting controls.

"Commander," he whispered, "these are some of the most famous people in Starfleet. Admiral Kirk! My gods!"

"Good for you, Lieutenant," she said.

"But it's damned irregular—no orders, no encoded ID—"

"All true," she said agreeably.

Heisenberg glanced over her shoulder and frowned at the settings she had entered.

"That's the *Enterprise,*" he said in a low and worried voice.

"And another one for you, Lieutenant. You're doing very well tonight."

"But the *Enterprise* is sealed—we can't beam anybody directly on board!"

"Can't we?"

"No, we can't—It's directly against orders, we can't just let people waltz in here and go on board a sealed ship, no matter who they are!"

Uhura was rather glad he was making the objection, for in the long run it would serve to keep him out of trouble.

"What are we going to do about it?" he exclaimed.

"*I'm* going to do nothing about it. *You're* going to sit in the closet."

"The *closet!*" He backed off from her. "Have you lost all sense of reality?"

"But this isn't reality, Lieutenant," she said sweetly. "This is fantasy." She drew out her concealed pocket phaser and leveled it at him. It was set on stun, of course, but stun was more than sufficient for this exercise. She hoped Heisenberg would not make her use it. Waking up from phaser stun was rather unpleasant. Uhura wished him neither harm nor physical discomfort. His psychic discomfort, though, was another thing entirely. She owed him a little psychic discomfort, after that snarky remark about her career.

"You wanted adventure?" she asked. "How's this? Got your old adrenaline going?"

Heisenberg nodded.

"Good boy," she said. "Now get in the closet."

She touched a key and the door to the storage closet, just behind him, slid open. She gestured with the phaser and he backed into it.

"Wait—"

She closed the door.

"I'm glad you're on our side," McCoy said.

She smiled.

"Let's go," Kirk said. "Uhura, is it on automatic? Come on, get up here."

"No," she said.

It took him a second to realize what she had said. His expression changed from distraction to amazement.

" 'No'?" he said. "What do you mean, 'no'?"

"I realize that the Admiral is . . . somewhat unfamiliar with the word—"

Kirk opened his mouth to speak, but she cut him off.

"—but somebody's got to stay behind and put enough glitches in communications so you don't have every ship in the sector coming after you."

"You can do it from the *Enterprise*—"

"No, I can't. It's too easy to jam. Admiral, there's no time to argue! Prepare to energize!"

"What about—?" He gestured toward the closet.

"Don't worry about Mister Adventure. I'll have him eating out of my hand." If I have to, she thought. "Go with all my hopes, my friends."

Kirk nodded, acquiescing. "Energize."

She activated the beam.

Nine

After the figures of Kirk, Sulu, and McCoy turned to sparks and vanished, Heisenberg started pounding on the inside of the closet door. Uhura ignored him and set to work opening the communications channels that she would need to interfere with as soon as Spacedock realized what was going on.

Uhura was in her element at the console. She infiltrated every important communications channel between headquarters and the fleet. By the time the tangle got straightened out, the *Enterprise* would be halfway to Genesis. If the ship could evade any pursuit sent directly from Spacedock, then Admiral Kirk should be able to carry out his mission. If it could be carried out.

Sulu felt his body form around his consciousness, and then he was standing on the bridge of the *Enterprise* with Kirk and McCoy solidifying beside him. The ship's systems were running at standby level, and the bridge felt very empty with only five people. At the navigation console, Chekov raised his hand in greeting. Scott rose from the command chair to greet Kirk.

"As promised, 'tis all yours, sir," he said. "All systems automated and ready. A chimpanzee and two trainees could run her."

"Thank you, Mister Scott," Kirk said drily. "I'll try not to take that personally." He drew aside, with McCoy, and faced the other three. "My friends," he said. "I can't ask you to go any farther. Doctor McCoy and I have to do this. The rest of you do not."

Taking the *Enterprise* to Genesis would require a good deal more than "a chimpanzee and two trainees," and everyone on the bridge knew it. Sulu strode down the steps and took his place at the helm. Yesterday he had made a decision on where to place his loyalties. He saw no reason to change his mind now.

"Admiral," Chekov said, "we're losing precious time."

"What course, please, Admiral?" Sulu said, entering a course for the Mutara sector.

Kirk glanced from Chekov, to Sulu, to Scott.

"Mister Scott—?"

"I'd be grateful, Admiral, if ye'd give the word."

Kirk hesitated, then nodded sharply. "My word is given. Gentlemen, may the wind be at our backs. Stations, please!"

Kirk took his own place in the command seat.

"Clear all moorings. . . ."

Sulu centered his attention on the impulse engines. They had not, of course, received the overhaul Scott had wished to give them, and they responded hesitantly, irritably, erratically, just as they had on the way in. The warp drive would be equally rocky.

The ship backed hesitantly from its slip and swung toward the entrance of Spacedock.

"Engage auto systems," Kirk said. "One quarter impulse power."

The *Enterprise* reached the berth in which *Excelsior* lay. Sulu gave the new ship a single glance and pushed the longing, and the temptation for regret, out of his mind.

Sulu started hearing consternation over the communications channels, as sensors and alarms and Starfleet personnel on late-night watch began to realize what was happening. The *Enterprise* drifted like a ghost ship past *Excelsior*, toward the huge closed spacedoors. He heard the beginning of a command to secure them, a command that was abruptly and rudely cut off by a screech of static. A moment later a raucous voice spilled over the channel. Sulu recognized the voice of a popular comedian.

He grinned. Everything Uhura did, she did with flair and humor. Crossing Starfleet channels with those of a system-wide entertainment network might well produce an interesting hybrid.

Quite, as Spock would have said, fascinating.

"One minute to spacedoors," Sulu said.

McCoy fidgeted on the upper bridge level.

"You just gonna *walk* through them?"

"Calm yourself, Bones," Kirk said.

"Sir," Chekov said, "Starfleet Commander Morrow, on emergency channel. He orders you to surrender vessel."

"No reply, Mister Chekov. Maintain your course."

Sulu set the communications monitor to steady scan. At one channel it paused long enough for him to hear, "What the hell do you mean, *yellow alert?* How can you have a *yellow alert* in *Spacedock?*"

The soundtrack of an old movie cut off the reply: "Who *are* those guys?"

The one thing Uhura could not do was prevent people on Spacedock from seeing what was happening. Everyone at the space station knew the *Enterprise* was being decommissioned. By now they would have begun to notice something distinctly odd.

"Thirty seconds to spacedoors," Sulu said.

"Sir, *Excelsior* is powering up with orders to pursue," Chekov said.

Sulu switched the viewscreen to an aft scan. They all watched *Excelsior* come alive, preparing for the chase.

"My gods," McCoy said. "It's gaining on us just sitting there."

Sulu switched back to a forward scan. The spacedoors filled the viewscreen completely.

"Steady, steady," Kirk said. "All right, Mister Scott?"

"Sir—?" Scott answered distractedly, for his concentration was fixed on smoothing out his infiltration routine.

"The *doors,* Mister Scott."

"Aye, sir, workin' on it."

Sulu had his hands on the controls to apply full reverse thrust when the doors finally cracked open and revealed the bright blackness of space beyond. The doors slid aside for the bow of the *Enterprise.* With a hands-breadth to spare, they were free.

"We have cleared spacedoors," Sulu said.

"Full impulse power!"

Sulu laid it on. The *Enterprise* shuddered and plunged ahead.

Behind them, *Excelsior* burst out into space.

Uhura had left the channels clear enough for the *Enterprise* to know what was going on, but she was also insuring that no ship could be sent after them by radio or subspace communications.

All they had to do was elude *Excelsior.*

"*Excelsior* closing to four thousand meters, sir," Chekov said.

"Mister Scott," Kirk said, "we need everything you've got now."

"Aye, sir. Warp drive standing by."

"Kirk!" Captain Styles' voice burst through the chatter and static. "Kirk, you do this and you'll never sit in a captain's chair again!"

Kirk ignored him; Sulu gritted his teeth. In the background of the channel he could hear *Excelsior* preparing to apply a tractor beam.

"Warp speed, Mister Sulu," Kirk said.

"Warp speed."

The ship collected itself and lurched into warp.

Excelsior's communications switched to subspace.

"No way, Kirk," Styles said. "We'll meet you coming back! Prepare for warp speed! Stand by transwarp drive!"

Damned showoff, Sulu thought. Excelsior *could catch the* Enterprise *with warp speed alone; with transwarp it would overshoot its quarry and, indeed, have to come back to meet it.*

As the *Enterprise* struggled toward the Mutara sector, Sulu aimed the visual sensors aft. On the viewscreen, the tiny point of light that was *Excelsior* shone white behind them. Scott watched with a self-satisfied smirk. Sulu glanced at Scott, and wondered.

Excelsior's aura blue-shifted as the new ship accelerated toward them.

The blue-shift died, and the ship's light reddened as the *Enterprise* accelerated away from it. Sulu's sensors revealed *Excelsior* to be intact, but without power. He felt more than a little ambivalent about what was happening.

"*Excelsior* is adrift in space," he said.

When Captain Styles' call for a tow came through from *Excelsior,* Uhura intercepted and damped it, feeling considerable satisfaction.

Take over Hikaru's ship, will you? she thought. *You can just sit there and stew for a while.*

"Commander, let me out of here!"

She ignored Heisenberg's shouts and his pounding on the door, until she was afraid he was making so much noise that someone else would come along and hear him.

"Heisenberg!" she shouted. "Shut up!"

"Let me out! What the hell is going on?"

"If you don't be quiet I'll use this phaser on you!" She continued working. Some of the safeguards had come into play against her. Each new disruption was increasingly difficult to accomplish. Tracers had already been sent out. She had only a few minutes left before she must flee, if she were to complete one final self-appointed task before the authorities caught up with her. She did not doubt that by this time tomorrow she would be in jail.

"Commander," Heisenberg said, not shouting this time. "What's going on? Maybe I can help."

She stopped replying; she had enough already to occupy her attention.

"Commander Uhura, please, if you'd just told me—"

He sounded sincere, but she did not know him well enough to know how good an act he could put on. Besides, she needed no help. If he was looking for excitement, he would surely find it if she let him out of the closet—he would find it for a few minutes, and perhaps spend the rest of his life regretting it, or trying to make up for it. The best thing she could do for him was leave him where he was. That way, it would be clear to Starfleet that he had nothing to do with helping James Kirk steal the *Enterprise.* Heisenberg might find himself embarrassed to be locked up by an officer whose career was winding down . . . but it would be less embarrassing than a court-martial.

She had done what she could here. She set the transporter controls on automatic. Starfleet would be able to trace her by the coordinates on the console, but by then she hoped it would not matter.

"Heisenberg!" she said.

"What?" he said irritably.

"Somebody will be along to let you out in a few minutes. I'm sorry I had to lock you up, Lieutenant. It was for your own good."

"Yeah, sure."

Uhura stepped up on the transporter and dematerialized.

* * *

Mister Scott paused behind Sulu, at the helm. On the viewscreen, *Excelsior* dwindled and vanished behind them.

"I dinna damage thy ship permanently, lad," Scott said softly.

Sulu glanced up. What to do to *Excelsior* had been left up to Scott, and it was a relief for Sulu to know the change was temporary. He nodded, grateful for the reassurance.

"Mister Scott," Kirk said, "you're as good as your word."

"Aye, sir. The more they overthink the plumbin', the easier it is to stop up the drain."

There are always a few flaws in a new application of technology, Sulu thought.

"Here, Doctor," Scott said to McCoy. He took his hand out of his pocket and handed McCoy a dull gray wafer. "A souvenir, as one surgeon to another."

McCoy accepted it. His hand shook slightly. He clearly had no idea what it was.

"I took it out o' *Excelsior*'s main transwarp computer," Scott said. "I knew Styles surely wouldna be able to resist trying it out."

"Nice of you to tell me in advance," McCoy said.

Kirk hooked his arm over the back of his command chair. "That's what you get for missing staff meetings, Doctor," he said. He surveyed the bridge, taking in everyone. "Gentlemen, your work today was outstanding. I intend to recommend you all for promotion." His voice turned wry as he added, "In whatever fleet we end up serving."

Sulu caught Chekov's glance.

"In fleet of ore-carriers of Antares Prison Mine," Chekov said, only loud enough for Sulu to hear.

Kirk stood and laid his hand on Sulu's shoulder.

"Best speed to Genesis, Mister Sulu," Kirk said.

Uhura had never visited the Vulcan embassy. The stately building stood in a genteel neighborhood in the city, on a hilltop overlooking the sea. The ocean was black and silver in the dark; the moon was one night past full. Uhura materialized on the sidewalk in front of the ambassador's residence, for it was protected against penetration by unauthorized transporter beams. She walked into the pool of light around the gate and pressed the buzzer.

"Yes?" The video screen tucked discreetly into a recess in the stone pillar remained featureless. The tiny camera next to it, pointing directly at her, was surely in use.

"I would like to speak with Ambassador Sarek," she said.

"The ambassador cannot see visitors this evening. You may make an appointment and return during reception hours."

"But it's urgent," Uhura said.

"What is your request?"

"It's private," she said, remembering how reticent Spock had always been about his background and his family.

"Sarek is occupied," the faceless voice said. *"I cannot disturb him unless I know your name and your business."*

"I am Commander Uhura, from the starship *Enterprise*," she said. "You may tell Ambassador Sarek that my business . . . concerns Genesis."

"Wait," said the emotionless voice.

She waited.

She could feel the minutes ticking away, minutes during which her trail would be traced. She knew the process well enough to be able to estimate just how quickly the trace could be done, and when that amount of time had passed she began to listen for the shining satin sound of a transporter beam. Fog rolled in from the sea. She shivered.

She touched the signal button again.

"We respectfully request that you wait." The voice had so little inflection that she wondered if it came from a machine, and a machine poorly programmed for Standard at that.

"I'll be forced to go, soon," she said. "If I can't see Sarek I must leave him a message—but I'd prefer to speak to him in private. It will only take a moment!"

"Please contain your emotions."

She wanted to kick the gatepost, that was how contained her emotions were. But she knew it would do her no good, and probably break her foot as well.

She heard a transporter beam, very near. She pressed herself against the stone gatepost, trying to conceal herself in the shadows. She could not hide from the materializing security team for long. She had considered transporting to some other location and proceeding here on foot, but they would have deduced where she was heading. They probably would have arrived before she did.

She pressed the call-button again.

"We respectfully request that you wait," the flat voice said again.

"I'm about to be taken," she said. "Please tell Sarek—"

The gates swung slowly open. The distance to the residence was about a hundred meters, and the hundred meters was her distance. She plunged inside just as the security team reached her. They chased her across the dark grounds of the Vulcan embassy. She outraced them to the residence, to no avail. The door remained closed. She turned.

One of the security officers strode up the stairs and took her arm.

"Please come with us, Commander. It'll be a lot easier if you don't make any fuss."

"I'll come with you if you'll just give me ten minutes to speak with Ambassador Sarek. It's desperately important!"

The security officer shook her head. "I'm sorry," she said. "That's impossible. It's directly against orders."

She led Uhura down the stairs and halfway back to the gate.

"Do your orders include invading the sovereign territory of an allied power?"

Sarek had crossed the distance between them and the wide steps of the embassy with such long and silent strides that no one had seen him approach. His commanding presence was accentuated by his long black cape, his drawn, intense features, his dark and deepset eyes. To Uhura he looked as if he had neither eaten nor slept since word of Spock's death reached him.

The head of the security team blushed scarlet, knowing she had overstepped her authority. She put the best face on it that she could.

"That was not our intention, sir," she said. "Several people from the last mission of the *Enterprise* have shown . . . evidence of severe mental difficulties. We're trying to get them to treatment. If you'll give me leave to take Commander Uhura to the hospital—"

"I will do no such thing. Commander Uhura has requested political asylum, and I have granted it. I give you leave to remove yourselves from the embassy grounds."

The security officer stood her ground and spoke to Uhura. "Commander, is this what you want? It could mean exile. But we might all be able to get out of this pretty clean. If I give you your ten minutes—off the record—will you come with us?"

Uhura considered it, but she had burned too many bridges today.

"No," she said. "I'm staying here."

The security commander took a deep breath and let it out slowly. "Very well." She turned to Sarek. "My government will contact you immediately with a formal request for extradition."

"That is up to your government. Good evening."

The security commander led the team from the grounds of the embassy, and the gate closed behind them.

"Thank you, sir," Uhura said. She was shivering violently. "I came to tell you—"

"Come inside, Commander," he said. "There is no need to stand in the cold and the damp . . . and in public . . . for our conversation."

Kruge materialized on the surface of the Genesis world, near enough to the high-order life signs to track them, but far enough away that they would remain ignorant of his arrival, and he could come upon them unawares. At his side, Warrigul appeared, shivering with excitement and whining, but whining almost soundlessly. The beast had been trained to recognize potential combat and to behave in a suitable manner. If Kruge ordered Warrigul to attack, the attack would be silent.

The commander inspected the glade as his sergeant and crew member materialized behind him. The place pleased him, with its dark earth smelling of mould, the tall-stalked plants that bore drooping, leathery leaves, the heat and actinic brightness of the brilliant new sun.

Kruge pulled out his tricorder and scanned with it. He located the metallic mass around which so much activity had lately centered. It lay deeper in the glade, perhaps fifty paces. Some minor life signs surrounded it, but the signs lacked the high order that would betray the presence of the prisoners he hoped to take. Still, they had been there, so there he would go too, and pick up their trail.

He set off between the gnarled stalks of the leather plants. Warrigul padded along at his side; the sergeant and the crew member brought up the rear.

The ground began to quiver. Kruge stopped. The quake intensified, till the leather plants all swayed and thumped together with a low and hollow sound. A frond broke away from its stalk, making a heavy liquid crunching noise, and the long thick leaf thudded to the ground like some dying thing at the dead-end of its evolution.

As the earthquake reached its peak, Kruge heard a long and high-pitched hissing shriek, like nothing he had ever heard before. He started toward the noise, striding steadily across the rocking surface. He made note, for future use, of the fact that his two subordinates did not follow him till the quake ceased and he was a good twenty paces ahead of them. Only Warrigul stayed with him.

He nearly stumbled over his pet when it stopped short, took a step backward, and growled.

The thick gray-green vegetation thinned slightly, letting a sharp white column of sunlight pierce the canopy to illuminate the Federation torpedo casing that had engendered so much interest.

All around its base, like the monsters in the story of Ngarakkani, a myth of Kruge's people, writhed a great mass of sleek scaled creatures. The creatures saw him, or smelled him, or felt the vibration of his footsteps, and rose up in a many-headed tangle to hiss and scream.

Kruge heard the sergeant whisper a protective curse. Kruge smiled to himself, gestured to Warrigul to sit and stay, and strode toward the casket. He ignored all but the largest of the creatures, which had squirmed to the top of the torpedo tube and coiled there. It raised its head, weaved toward him and away, hissed, and squealed a challenge. It reached as high as his shoulder.

He stepped into its sudden strike and grasped its throat, then drew it from the slithering group and raised it up to inspect it. It twisted in his hands. Several others coiled around his boots. He ignored them, as he ignored his two companions, though he was aware of everything, most particularly including the impression the scene must be making. Like the hero Ngarakkani, he would wrestle with the demons and defeat them.

The creature whipped its long lashing tail around his neck and began to squeeze. Kruge thought to unwind it from him, but its strength exceeded his. The harsh scales of its belly cut into his throat, squeezing the breath out of him. Darkness slipped slowly down around him.

The creature had tricked him into going on the defensive. He let its body tighten around him; he turned to the attack. He grabbed its throat with both his hands and squeezed. He began to twist.

He heard its bones begin to crunch. As he began to lose consciousness, its strength suddenly dissipated and it sagged away from him.

He cast the limply writhing body to the ground.

His subordinates gazed upon him with awe. He intensified their reaction by ignoring it. He *tsked* to Warrigul, who leapt up and sprang to his side, snarling at the twitching body of the creature.

Kruge pulled out his communicator.

"Torg," he said easily, "I have found nothing of consequence. I am continuing the search."

David sat forlornly on a stone outcropping. His world spread out around his vantage point. It was beautiful. It was strange, and growing stranger. It was destroying itself. The vines back on Regulus I had been a warning that he should have heeded, as he should have heeded the rogue equation in the primary Genesis description. Evolution was running wild. Each species was growing and changing and aiming for its own extinction, without creating any diversity, any new forms, to take over when the old died out. Not that it much mattered. If his estimates were right, the evolutionary process would be only about half done when the more violent geological processes tore the whole planet apart. Soon after that, the subatomic attractions would break down, and the entire mass of what had been the Mutara Nebula, what had been Genesis and its new star system, would degenerate into a homogeneous, gaseous blob, a fiery, structureless plasma: protomatter.

His shadow stretched far down the hillside as the sun set behind him. Night approached, a dark border overwhelming day. It reached the edge of Spock's glade. The group of delicate fern-trees had grown and coarsened, turning from a patch of feathery emerald green to a smudge of bulbous gray, just in the few hours since he had left it.

He and Saavik had found a vantage point, but so far David had detected no sign of other intelligent life. His tricorder showed nothing, but it was of limited range. He had heard nothing over his communicator; if anyone else had fled *Grissom* before it was shot down, they were as reluctant to broadcast their presence to their attackers as was David. Perhaps they were listening to each other's static.

More likely, no one else had survived. But until he was sure, he was keeping his communicator set to the Federation emergency channel.

Night fell quickly on Genesis. The land below the promontory had grown too dark for David to see anyone, friendly or malevolent. Darkness obscured everything, even the field of silver ice now covering the desert, nearly surrounding the glade, and grinding away at the base of the mountain itself. David rose and trudged back up the hill. Gnarled black trees with twisting exposed roots loomed over him, and great broken slabs of stone projected from the ground. Soon he reached the narrow, hidden cave they had stumbled upon.

He stepped inside, expecting the pale steady illumination of the camp light from Saavik's kit. Instead he encountered darkness.

"Saavik—?" he whispered, but before her name had passed his lips she had uncovered the light again. She held her phaser aimed straight at him. She let her hand fall.

"Your footsteps . . . sounded different," she said, in explanation and apology. She put the phaser away again. "This place is most discomforting."

The Vulcan child whimpered. He lay huddled on a bed of tree branches, his face to the stone wall. Saavik had laid her coat over him. She turned to him, touched his shoulder, and said a word or two of comfort. David did not speak the language she was using, but he recognized it when he heard it.

"Why are you talking to him in Vulcan?" he said.

Saavik shrugged. "I know it is not logical. I know he cannot understand, but he would not understand any other language, either, and Vulcan is . . . the first language Spock taught me."

David glanced at the child. "It's hard to think of him as Spock," he said.

"He is only a part of Spock. He is the physical part. The mind exists only in potential. He might perhaps become a reasoning being, with time and teaching. He is not so different from what I was when . . . when he found me—a scavenger, illiterate certainly, almost completely inarticulate . . ."

She shivered. He sat down next to her and put his arm across her shoulders. "You're cold."

"I choose not to perceive cold," she said. She did not respond to his embrace.

The child suddenly cried out. David glanced up apprehensively, for they were beneath tons of stone. The gentle quake that followed the cry left the cave undisturbed, but the child moaned in pain. Saavik slid from beneath David's arm and went to the boy's side to tuck the black cloth and her maroon jacket more closely in around him.

"Sleep," she said softly, in Vulcan.

David pulled out his tricorder and made a quick geological scan. The results gave him no comfort.

"This planet is aging in surges," he said.

"And Spock with it," Saavik said quietly.

David glanced at her, then at the boy, who had flung himself over.

"My gods—" David said.

An hour before, the child had had the appearance of a boy of eight or ten. Now he looked more like a thirteen- or fourteen-year-old.

"The child and the world are joined together," Saavik said. She looked at David steadily, as if wishing—or daring—him to interpret events in a different way.

David had nothing to say that would give her, or himself, any comfort. He nodded.

"The Genesis wave is like a clock ticking . . . or a bomb," he said. "For him and for the planet. And at the rate things are going . . ."

"How long?" Saavik asked. She thought that if they must die, sooner would be less painful than later. But though she accepted the logic of that conclusion, she was not yet ready to stop fighting for every instant of life left to her.

"Days . . . maybe hours," David said. "It's a chaotic system, Saavik. Which variable will pass the energy threshold and cause everything to disintegrate into protomatter . . ." He shook his head. "It's completely unpredictable." He looked away, and then, in such a low tone that Saavik almost did not hear him, he said, "I'm sorry."

She nodded, accepting both his verdict and his grief.

"It will be hardest on Spock," she said. "Soon . . . he will feel the burning of his Vulcan blood."

"I don't understand," David said.

I should not have spoken of pon farr, *she thought. It is not logical to burden David with one more thing about which he can do nothing. No one has ever found a way to free Vulcan men of the loss of emotional and physical control they endure every seventh year of their adult lives.*

She was saved from having to choose between an explanation and a lie by the abrupt querulous bleating of David's tricorder.

He pulled the instrument out and frowned over the life signs.

"Whoever they are," he said, "they're getting closer."

Saavik estimated one chance in a thousand that other refugees from *Grissom* caused the signs, and five to ten chances in a thousand that whoever was tracking them had other than malicious intent. In all the other possibilities, the beings who had destroyed *Grissom* sought Saavik and David in order to inflict the same fate upon them. Still . . . a chance, even if it was the chance to become a prisoner, was better odds than the certain death they faced by remaining on Genesis.

Saavik stood up. "I will go—"

"No!" David said sharply. "I'll do it. Give me your phaser."

Saavik did not want David, untrained as he was, to go out alone on a spy mission. She glanced at the Vulcan boy. She did not want to leave him alone, either, and she particularly did not want to leave David alone with him. She realized it would be marginally less dangerous, for David, if he were to go spying on the unknown entity.

And she could see that his guilt impelled him to undertake the mission. She offered him her phaser.

He touched her hand, took the weapon, and hurried out into the darkness.

A moment later the Vulcan child cried out in agony, just before the ground began to tremble.

Ten

The *Enterprise* sped free through space.

Excelsior lay far behind, still waiting for a tow. The communications channels were just beginning to come clear again. Kirk wondered if Uhura was all right. She was levelheaded. When Security came to the transporter station she should simply have thrown up her hands and surrendered. But accidents could happen, and Kirk could not help but worry. Nevertheless he was grateful to her, for without her help he might have the whole fleet converging on him. The one thing he knew he could not do, even to save McCoy's sanity and Spock's soul, was fire on another Starfleet ship.

"Estimating Genesis 2.9 hours, present speed," Sulu said.

"Can we hold speed, Scotty?" Kirk asked.

"Aye, sir, the *Enterprise* has its second wind now."

"Scan for vessels in pursuit," Kirk said.

"Scanning . . ." The voice was an eerie facsimile of Spock's. "Indications negative at this time."

Kirk turned toward the science station. McCoy, at Spock's old place, looked up and blinked.

"Did I . . . get it right . . . ?" he asked.

"You did great, Bones," Kirk said. "Just great."

"Sir, Starfleet is calling *Grissom* again," Chekov said. "Warning about us."

"Response?"

Chekov glanced worriedly at his console. "Nothing. As before."

"What's *Grissom* up to?" Kirk said. "Will they join us, or fire on us?" he said, half to himself. "Mister Chekov, break radio silence. Send my compliments to Captain Esteban."

"Aye, sir."

Kirk rose and went to McCoy's side.

"How we doing?" he said.

McCoy gave him a thoughtful and slightly sardonic glance, the look of a doctor who recognizes a bedside manner when it is being inflicted upon him.

"How are *we* doing?" he said. "Funny you should put it quite that way, Jim." He paused, as if listening to a second conversation. "*We* are doing fine. But I'd feel safer giving him one of my kidneys than getting what's scrambled up in my brain."

"Admiral," Chekov said, "there is no response from *Grissom* on any channel."

"Keep trying, Mister Chekov. At regular intervals."

Carol Marcus hurried up the steps of the tall Victorian house and knocked on the door. She waited apprehensively, looking back over the small town of Port Orchard. Beyond it, water sparkled slate-gray and silver in the autumn sun. The chilly salt air fluttered against the rhododendrons that grew all around the porch. They were heavily laden with the buds of next year's flowers. She had hoped to see them in bloom, in the spring. But if that had still been possible, she would not have had to come here now, all alone.

The door opened. Carol turned, still dazzled by sunlight on the sea.

"I'm terribly sorry not to arrive when I said I would—I got lost," she said. "I have something to give to Del March's family, but I couldn't find the address, I ended up in a park—" She stopped suddenly. She was practically babbling. "I'm sorry," she said more calmly. "I'm Carol Marcus."

"Come in." Vance's mother took Carol's hand and led her inside. Her voice possessed the same low, quiet timbre as Vance's. Her hand in Carol's felt frail. "I'm Aquila Madison, and this is Terrence Laurier, Vance's father."

Both Vance's parents were tall and slender, as he had been. Carol had expected them to be about her own age, for Vance had been only a few years older than David. But they were both considerably older than she, perhaps as much as twenty years. Aquila's close-cropped curly hair was iron-gray. Terrence wore his longer, tied at the back of his neck, but it, too, had gone salt-and-pepper from its original black.

A leaded glass door opened from the foyer. Terrence and Aquila showed Carol into their living room. It was a high-ceilinged, airy place, carpeted with antique Oriental rugs. Aquila and Terrence sat side by side on a couch in front of the tall windows. Carol sat facing them and wondered what to say to them, how to start.

"Del never did outgrow that joke," Aquila said.

"I thought I'd written the address down wrong," Carol said. "Do you mean he meant people to go to a park?"

"No, my dear," Aquila said, "he meant people to think they'd written the address down wrong."

"I don't understand. Where does his family live?"

"He has none," Terrence said. "None he'll admit to, anyway."

"Then where did he live?"

"He lived here," Aquila said.

"What you have to understand about Del," Terrence said, "is that he made up nearly everything about himself—his name, his home, the relatives that only existed in a computer file, his background before he was twelve—everything."

"But his records," Carol said. "In this day and age—"

"He didn't need too much," Terrence said. "Not here—a false address, a few counterfeit relatives and school records. He had an uncanny rapport with computers, and the voice synthesizer he built stood in for an adult as long as nobody asked to meet it face to face. He was so young no one thought to be suspicious of him."

"As it was, he and Vance had been friends for a year before Terrence and I realized just how odd some of the odd things about him were. Vance knew, but he couldn't persuade Del to trust us."

"How did you find out?"

"I tried to go to his house once," Terrence said. "I went out all fired up with the intention of either jumping down somebody's throat for never getting the kid any decent clothes, or offering to get him some myself."

"When we finally found out where he was living—it was an abandoned house—we persuaded him to move in here. We have plenty of room." Aquila made a quick gesture with one hand, indicating the house, the surroundings.

Carol found herself already under the spell of Terrence and Aquila's home. It had the comfortable and comforting ambiance of a place lived in by people who loved each other, of a place lived in and cared for and cared about by the same people for a long time. Vance had told her that the Madisons, Aquila's family, were some of the first black landholders in the area. Her ancestors had settled here three hundred years ago, long before the Federation, even before the region had been admitted to statehood in the previous political entity.

"Did you adopt him?"

"We wanted to. But he was terrified that if we found his people and asked them to give up legal custody, they'd make him go back. Arguing didn't do any good—"

Carol nodded. She had been in a few arguments with Del March.

"—and besides, he might have been right."

"We didn't press him about it. We were afraid he might run away from us, too, and we were already very fond of him. Though he could be quite trying."

"He did have a reputation for being . . . a little wild," Carol said.

"In college, yes," Aquila said. "Once he was of age and didn't have to fear being shipped back to—whatever he was running from—he didn't have to be careful never to attract any attention. He did get . . . 'a little wild.' We were awfully worried about him for a few years. So was Vance . . ."

"I didn't get to know him as well as I should have," Carol admitted. "We just never got off on the right foot. He and my son David were very close, though." Carol reached into her pack and drew out a roll of parchment. "I think you should have this. It was Del's—he kept it on the wall of his office. And Vance made it."

Aquila unrolled the parchment. In his strong, even calligraphy, Vance had copied seven stanzas of Lewis Carroll's "The Hunting of the Snark." Those were the stanzas from which Madison and March had taken the terminology for the sub-elementary particles they had described and discovered. Carol remembered the end of the poem: "For although common Snarks do no manner of harm,/Yet I feel it my duty to say/Some are Boojums—"

Aquila and Terrence read it over. Aquila smiled, brushed her fingertips across the parchment, and read it a second time. Terrence raised his head. He and Carol looked at each other. They could no longer avoid talking about Vance.

"I loved your son," Carol said. "I don't know if he told you, about us—"

"Of course he did," Aquila said. "We were looking forward to your vacation next spring, we were hoping you would come with him when he visited."

"I would have. He told me so much about you . . . Aquila, Terrence, he was such an extraordinary man. I'm so sorry—" She had to stop. If she said any more, she would start to cry again.

"Carol," Terrence said, "what *happened* out there? We never thought Vance would work on a military project—"

"It wasn't!" Carol said. "Oh, it wasn't! It was supposed to be just the opposite."

She told them about the project, and the least painful version of their son's and their foster son's deaths that she could without lying to them. But it still came down to the Spacelab team's being caught in the middle of someone else's quarrel.

When she finished, her voice shaking, Terrence and Aquila were desperately holding each other's hands. Carol stood up. She did not want to inflict her own grief on them anymore, and she thought they might want to be alone.

"I wish—I wish I could have met you next spring. I'm so sorry . . . I'd better go."

Aquila rose. "That's foolish, Carol. It's a long trip back, and it's nearly dark."

It *was* a long trip back. Port Orchard was a historical reference site, so it was against the rules to beam in. The only way to get here was by ferry or ground car.

"We had already planned for you to stay over," Terrence said.

When she realized they meant it, Carol agreed, not only because of the long trip. She was grateful to them simply for making the offer, grateful to them for not hating her, and glad to be able to spend more time in the company of two people who reminded her so strongly of the person she had loved.

Saavik started awake, unable to believe she had fallen asleep, and, at the same time, unsure what had awakened her. She stood up and looked out over Genesis at night. Here and there across the land faint lights, like the shadows of ghosts, drifted between twisted trees.

It is merely bioluminescence, Saavik thought. *What the humans call fox-fire, and Romulans call devil-dogs. And Vulcans? What do Vulcans call it? No doubt they speak of it in chemical formulae, as no doubt so should I.*

She was standing on the rocky promontory that thrust out below the cave mouth. She had come out here to keep watch, and because she was afraid her exhausted restlessness might wake the Vulcan child. Genesis had permitted itself a short respite between its convulsions, and the boy had drifted off into his first painless sleep.

Saavik's tricorder beeped again, and she realized how long David had been gone. She considered, decided to take the chance of transmitting, and opened her communicator.

"Saavik to David." She waited. "Come in, David."

Only static replied. She closed the communicator quickly, more worried than she cared to admit, for worry was not only an emotion, but a completely unproductive use of energy.

A low, moaning cry came from the cave. Saavik braced herself against the inevitable ground tremor that echoed the child's pain. Rocks clattered down the hillside. Saavik sprinted for the cave entrance, dodging boulders and raising her arms to ward off a rain of gravel. The huge trees rocked and groaned.

She stopped just inside the cave. The boy huddled against the wall as if he could draw in its coolness and take upon himself a stony calm. His muscles strained so taut they quivered, though the earthquake had faded. This paroxysm had nothing to do with the convulsions of the dying world.

"Spock," she said softly.

Startled, he flung himself around to face her.

He had changed again. Before, she could see him only as a Vulcan child. Now she could see in him her teacher, her mentor—Spock. He was younger than when she first encountered him. But he was Spock.

The fever burned in his face and in his eyes. He fought what he could not understand. He struggled to gain some control over his body and his world.

Saavik knew that he would fail.

"So it has come," she said to him in Vulcan. She moved closer to him, speaking quietly. "It is called *pon farr.*"

He could not understand her words, but her tone calmed him.

"Will you trust me, my mentor, my friend?" *I know it is no longer you,* she thought, *but I will help you if I can, because of who you used to be.*

The sound of his labored breathing filled the cave. She knelt beside him. She was not certain that anything she could do would ease his pain. They were not formally pledged, psychically linked.

His body was so fevered she could feel the heat, so fevered it must burn him. She touched his hand and felt him flinch as a thread of connection formed between them. She guided his right hand against hers, then put her left hand to his temple. His unformed intelligence met her trained mind, and she used the techniques he had taught her—it seemed so long ago, in another life—to soothe his fear and confusion. Saavik felt the tangled tautness of his body begin to relax.

Spock reached up and gently touched her cheek. His fingers followed the upward stroke of her eyebrow, then curved down to caress her temple, as Saavik met the gaze of his gold-flecked brown eyes.

* * *

The viewscreen wavered with the *Enterprise*'s change of state from warp speed to sub-light. The new star and its single planet spun where only a few days before the Mutara Nebula filled space with dense dust-clouds. Despite everything, Jim Kirk remained taken by the world's beauty.

"We are secured from warp speed," Sulu said. "Now entering the Mutara sector. Genesis approaching."

"What about *Grissom,* Mister Chekov?" Kirk asked.

"Still no response, sir."

Sulu increased the magnification of the viewscreen and put a bit of the ship's limited extra power to the sensors, but he could find no trace of *Grissom,* either.

"Bones," Kirk said tentatively, "can you give me a quadrant bi-scan?"

He glanced back at McCoy. The doctor hunched unmoving over Spock's station. After a moment he spread his hands in frustration and defeat.

"I think you just exceeded my capability . . ."

"Never mind, Bones." Kirk gestured to Chekov. "Mister Chekov—"

"Yes, Admiral." Chekov joined McCoy and took over.

"Sorry," McCoy said shakily.

"Your time is coming, Doctor. Mister Sulu, proceed at full impulse power."

"Full impulse power," Sulu said.

"There is no sign of ship, Admiral," Chekov said. "Not *Grissom,* not . . . anything."

"Very well, Mister Chekov. Continue scanning."

Kirk rose and joined McCoy.

"You all right?" he asked softly.

"I don't know, Jim," McCoy said. "He's . . . gone, again. I can feel him, it's almost as if I can talk to him. But then he slips away. For longer and longer, and when he . . . comes back . . . my sense of him is weaker."

Kirk frowned. McCoy had not added that he, too, felt weaker, but he did not have to. It was obvious to Kirk that the doctor's strength was slowly draining away.

"Keep hold of him, Bones," he said. "Keep hold of yourself. We're almost there."

Saavik smoothed Spock's tangled hair. The fever had broken, the compulsion had left him. He slept, and he would live. She wondered if she had done him a kindness by saving his life. He was still completely vulnerable to the convulsions of Genesis, which would continue to torture him.

She sighed. She had done what she thought was right.

She was terribly worried about David. He should have returned long ago. She drew out her communicator and opened it, but on second thought put it away. Spock would sleep for some time, so she could safely leave him alone. It would be better for all of them if Saavik sought David without using her communicator and advertising their presence. She rose and started for the cave entrance.

She heard something—footsteps. This cursed world made sounds difficult to identify accurately, a task she would have found ridiculously easy anywhere else. Hoping it was David but believing it was not, she pressed herself against the cave wall.

A great dark shape filled the entrance. The tall and massive humanoid figure carried a sensor that sought out his quarry.

A Klingon—!

While he still stood blinking in the darkness, Saavik launched herself at him. If she could overcome him and escape into the woods with Spock—

Roaring with fury, he spun, knocking her back against the cave wall. His bones were so heavy and his muscles so thick that she could barely get a grasp on him, even on his wrist. He flung his arms around her and began to squeeze, shouting angrily in a dialect of Klingon that she did not understand. She struggled, pressing her hands upward. Klingons had different points of vulnerability than humans, who were different again from Vulcans and Romulans. She broke his grasp for an instant and smashed her fists into the sides of his jaw. He staggered backward, dazed by the transmission of energy from the maxilla into the skull.

Saavik heard laughter.

Two of his comrades had followed him into the cave. They stood beside Spock, who sat watching, half-awake and confused. Both were armed; they held their weapons aimed at Spock. They taunted her—again in a dialect she did not know, but the meaning was clear: Get him, little one, beat him if you can, and we will laugh at him for the rest of the trip. Beat him and lose anyway, because we hold your friend hostage.

She stepped back, spreading her hands in a gesture of surrender.

Enraged by the others' mockery, her opponent rushed at her with a raging curse. He struck her a violent backhand blow that flung her against the cave wall.

The impact knocked her breath from her. She sagged against the stone, her knees collapsing. She pressed herself against the cave wall, barely managing to hold herself upright.

Her opponent snapped a harsh reply to his laughing companions, dragged Saavik's wrists behind her back, twisted her arms, and pushed her forward out of the cave. The other two pulled Spock to his feet and roughly hurried him outside.

Saavik stumbled down the rocky trail to the promontory. Dawn lay scarlet over Genesis, turning the trees a deep and oppressive maroon. Overnight the thick gnarled trunks had sprouted tens of thousands of spindly, barbed branches that flailed at the people passing beneath them. A thorn caught in Saavik's shirt and tore it. Another tangled in her hair. She tried to look back, to see if Spock was all right. With only the shroud to wrap around him, he was terribly vulnerable. But her captor forced her faster down the trail. The branches thrashed and clattered, as if whipped by a violent wind.

But there was no wind.

Even the stones had changed. The sharp thrust of the promontory was rounded, smoothed, and darkened with a patina of age that implied a thousand years of erosion. A Klingon officer stood upon it in an attitude of possession, gazing out over the forest below. A creature stood at his side.

His hunting party flung Saavik and Spock roughly down behind him.

Saavik lay still, clenching her fingers in the dirt and struggling to control her anger. If she surrendered to the madness now, she could only bring death to them all.

The commander turned slowly.

"So!" he said. He spoke in Standard, but his faint accent did nothing to disguise his impatience. "I have come a long way for the power of Genesis. And what do I find?"

He gestured sharply as Saavik pushed herself to her knees.

The rest of his landing party dragged David forward and shoved him down. He sprawled on the stone beside Saavik. She gasped at the dark bruises on his face, the blood on his mouth, the scratches and welts on his arms and hands. He looked ashamed. She wanted to touch him, she wanted to protect him from any more pain, but she knew if she betrayed any concern for him their captors would use it against them.

"What do I find?" the commander said again. "Three children! Ill-bred children, at that. It's only what one might expect of humans, but you, and you—" He glared at Saavik, then at Spock, and then he laughed. "So much for Vulcan restraint," he said.

His creature echoed his laugh with a growling whine.

Saavik rose to her feet, very slowly, her rage so great she trembled.

"My lord," she said. Her voice was so calm, so cold, that it astonished her. "We are survivors of a doomed expedition. This planet will destroy itself in hours. The Genesis experiment is a failure."

"A failure!" The commander laughed with every evidence of sincere good humor. "The most powerful destructive force ever created, and you call it a *failure*—?" He took one step forward. Saavik had to raise her head to look at him. He was head and shoulders taller than she. "What would you consider a success, child?" He chuckled. "You will tell me the secrets of Genesis."

"I have no knowledge of them," Saavik said.

"Then I hope pain is something you enjoy," he said.

Saavik was accustomed to being taken at her word, but she knew she could not hope for that courtesy from the enemy commander. Genesis had taken six primary investigators plus a laboratory full of support personnel eighteen months of solid work and all their lifetimes of experience to create. Even if Saavik had belonged to the team, she would not be able to say, in a few simple words, how to recreate their project.

The Klingon sergeant hurried forward with an open communicator. The commander cut off his words.

"I ordered no interruptions!"

"Sir!" said a voice from the communicator. "Federation starship approaching!"

Saavik and David caught each other's glance, hardly daring to hope.

The commander glared at them, as if they had called the starship to them at this particular moment, simply to frustrate him.

"Bring me up!" he said. And to his landing party, "Guard them well."

He and his creature vanished in a dazzle of light.

Kruge reformed on board his ship and strode to the bridge. Torg saluted him and gestured to the viewport.

"Battle alert!" Kruge said. As the bridge erupted into activity around him, he folded his arms across his chest and observed the *Constellation*-class Federation starship that sailed slowly toward him. He smiled.

It was his, as firmly in his possession as the three child-hostages on the surface of Genesis.

Warrigul pressed up against his leg. Kruge reached down and scratched his creature's head. Warrigul hissed with pleasure.

The *Enterprise*'s search for *Grissom* continued fruitlessly. Kirk wondered if, somehow, it had finished its work and headed back to Earth. Traveling at warp speed, they might easily have missed it. No doubt David was back home already, having coffee with Saavik. Or laughing with his mother about that lunatic James Kirk, rushing off in a stolen ship on a self-imposed mission that no one else could understand. Kirk pressed the heels of his hands against his eyes.

"Sir—" Chekov said.

"What is it, Commander?"

"I'd swear something was there, sir . . ." Chekov peered at his instruments, which had flickered with the sensor-signature of a small vessel, but now stubbornly continued to show absolutely nothing. "But . . . I might have imagined it. . . ."

"What did you see, Chekov?"

"For one instant . . . *Scout*-class vessel."

"Could be *Grissom*," Kirk said thoughtfully. "Patch in the hailing frequency."

Chekov did so, and nodded to Kirk.

"Enterprise to *Grissom,"* Kirk said. "Come in, *Grissom*. Come in, please."

"Nothing on scanner, sir," Chekov said.

"Short-range scan, Mister Chekov. Give it all the focus you've got. Onscreen, Mister Sulu."

Chekov focused the beam, and Sulu switched the viewscreen, which showed nothing but empty space.

On the bridge of his fighter, Commander Kruge listened to the Federation ship's unguarded transmission:

"I say again, Enterprise *to* Grissom. *Admiral Kirk calling Captain Esteban, Lieutenant Saavik, Doctor Marcus. Come in,* Grissom!"

"Report status," Kruge said, keeping his voice offhand, but secretly rejoicing. Kirk! Admiral James T. Kirk, and the *Enterprise!* If he returned home having vanquished the legendary Federation hero, and bearing Genesis as well—!

"We are cloaked," said Torg. "Enemy closing on impulse power, range five thousand."

"Good." Kruge stroked the smooth scales of Warrigul's crest and murmured to his creature, "This is the turn of luck I have been waiting for. . . ."

"Range three thousand," Maltz said.

"Steady. Continue on impulse power."

"Yes, sir!"

Kruge noted Torg's intensity, Maltz's uneasiness.

"Range two thousand."

"Stand by, energy transfer to weapons. At my command!"

"Within range, sir."

Kruge turned slightly. After a moment, his new gunner raised his head and froze, noting Kruge's attention.

"Sight on target, gunner," Kruge said. "Disabling only. Understood?"

"Understood *clearly,* sir!"

"Range one thousand, closing."

"Wait," Kruge said, as the *Enterprise* loomed larger in his viewport. "Wait. . . ."

At the same time, Kirk studied the enhanced image on the viewscreen of the *Enterprise.*

"There," he said. "That distortion. The shimmering area."

"Yes, sir," Sulu said. "It's getting larger as we close in—"

"—And *it's* closing on *us.* Your opinion, Mister Sulu?"

"I think it's an energy form, sir."

"Yes. Enough energy to hide a ship, wouldn't you say?"

"A cloaking device!"

"Red alert, Mister Scott!" Kirk said.

"Aye, sir."

The Klingon vessel must have beamed someone on board. Chekov would have had only a second or two to catch a glimpse of the ship. If his attention had wandered for a moment . . .

"Mister Chekov," Kirk said, "good work."

"Thank you, Admiral."

The lights dimmed. The Klaxon alarms sounded: a bit redundant, Kirk thought, since every living being on the ship was right here on the bridge.

"Mister Scott, all power to the weapons system."

"Aye, sir."

McCoy stood up uneasily. "No shields?"

"If my guess is right, they'll have to de-cloak before they can fire."

"May all your guesses be right," McCoy said.

Kirk tried not to think what the appearance of this disguised ship, in place of *Grissom,* must mean.

"Mister Scott: two photon torpedoes at the ready. Sight on the center of the mass."

"Aye, sir."

The *Enterprise* sailed closer and closer to an indefinable spot in space, more perceptible as *different* if one looked at it from the corner of the eye. The ship was very nearly upon it when—

Sulu saw it first. "Klingon fighter, sir—"

The Klingon craft appeared before them as a spidery sketch, transparent against the stars, quickly solidifying.

"—Arming torpedoes!"

"Fire, Mister Scott!"

The torpedoes streaked toward the Klingon ship. It was as if their impact solidified the ship while simultaneously blasting a section of it away. The fighter tilted up and back with the momentum of the attack. It began to tumble.

"Good shooting, Scotty," Kirk said.

"Aye. Those two hits should stop a horse, let alone a bird."

"Shields up, Mister Chekov," Kirk said.

"Aye, sir." He accessed the automation center and tried to call up the shields. Nothing happened.

"Sir," he said in concern, "shields are unresponsive."

Scott immediately turned to his controls, and Kirk turned to Scott.

"Scotty—?"

With a subvocal curse, Scott bent closer over his console. "The automation system's overloaded. I dinna expect ye to take us into combat, ye know!"

On the smoke-clouded bridge of his wounded ship, Kruge stumbled over a dim shape and fell to his knees. He touched the shape in the darkness—

Warrigul.

His beast, which he had owned since he was a youth and Warrigul only a larva, lay dying. Ignoring the chaos of the damaged bridge, Kruge stroked the spines of Warrigul's crest. His pet responded with a weak, whimpering growl, convulsed once, and relaxed into death.

Kruge rose slowly, his hands clenched at his sides.

Torg's voice barely penetrated the white waves of rage that pounded in his ears.

"Sir—the cloaking device is destroyed!"

"Never mind!" Kruge shouted. There would be no more hiding from this Federation butcher. "Emergency power to the thrusters!"

"Yes, my lord."

The lights on the bridge further dimmed as the thrusters drained the small ship's power, but the tumbling slowed and ceased. The ship stabilized.

"Lateral thrust!"

Torg obeyed, bringing the ship around to face the *Enterprise* again.

"Stand by, weapons!"

Jim Kirk watched the Klingon craft come round to bear on his ship.

"The shields, Scotty!"

"I canna do it!"

"Ready torpedoes—" The order came too late. The enemy ship fired at nearly point-blank range. The *Enterprise* had neither time nor room to maneuver. "Torpedoes coming in!" Kirk cried, bracing himself.

The flare of the explosion sizzled through the sensors. The viewscreen flashed, then darkened. The ship bucked violently. Kirk lost his hold and fell. The illumination failed.

"Emergency power!"

The *Enterprise* responded valiantly, but the bridge lights returned at less than half intensity. McCoy helped Kirk struggle up.

"I'm all right, Bones." He lunged back to his place. "Prepare to return fire! Mister Scott—transfer power to the phaser banks!"

"Oh, god, sir, I dinna think I can—"

"What's *wrong?*"

"They've knocked out the damned automation center!" He smashed his fist against the console. "I ha' no control over anythin'!"

"Mister Sulu!"

Sulu's gesture of complete helplessness, and Chekov's agitated shake of the head, sent Kirk sagging back into his chair.

"So . . ." he said softly. "We're a sitting duck."

He watched the enemy fighter probe slowly closer.

Kruge, in his turn, watched the silent, powerful Federation ship drift before him.

"Emergency power recharge," Torg said, "forty percent . . . fifty percent. My lord, we are able to fire—"

Kruge raised his hand, halting Torg's preparations for another salvo.

"Why hasn't he finished us?" Kruge said. He suspected Kirk wanted to humiliate him first. "He outguns me ten to one, he has four hundred in crew, to my handful. Yet he sits there!"

"Perhaps he wishes to take you prisoner."

Kruge scowled at Torg. "He knows I would die first."

"My lord," Maltz said, from the communications board, "the enemy commander wishes a truce to confer."

"A truce!" Kruge's training and better judgment restrained his wish to fire, provoke a response, and end the battle quickly and cleanly. "Put him on-screen," he said more calmly, then, to Torg, "Study him well."

The transmission from the *Enterprise*, enhanced and interpreted, formed Kirk's three-dimensional image in the area in front of and slightly below Kruge's command post.

"This is Admiral James T. Kirk, of the *U.S.S. Enterprise*."

"Yes," Kruge said, "the Genesis commander himself."

"By violation of the treaty between the Federation and the Klingon Empire, your presence here is an act of war. You have two minutes to surrender your crew and your vessel, or we will destroy you."

Kruge delayed any reply to the arrogant demand. Kirk was neither ignorant nor a fool. He must know that officers of the Klingon Empire did not surrender. And no one with a reputation like his could be a fool. Was he trying to provoke another attack, so he could justify destroying his enemy or increase his valor in the defeat? Or was there something more?

"He's hiding something," Kruge said. "We may have dealt him a more serious blow than I thought."

Torg looked at him intently, trying to trace his superior's thoughts. "How can you tell that, my lord?"

"I trust my instincts," Kruge said easily. He toggled on the transmitter. "Admiral Kirk, this is your opponent speaking. Do not lecture me about treaty violations, Admiral. The Federation, in creating an ultimate weapon, has turned itself into a gang of interstellar criminals. It is not I who will surrender. It is you." He paused to let that sink in, then gambled all or nothing. "On the planet below, I have taken prisoner three members of the team that developed your doomsday weapon. If you do not surrender immediately, I will execute them. One at a time. They are enemies of galactic peace."

Listening to the transmission with disbelief, Kirk pushed himself angrily from his chair. "*Who is this?* How dare you—!"

"Who *I* am is not important, Admiral. That I have *them,* is." He smiled, baring his teeth. "I will let you speak to them."

On the surface of Genesis, far below, the landing party listened via communicator to the battle and to the interchange between Kirk and Kruge. Saavik

listened, too, buoyed by the appearance of the *Enterprise,* disturbed by its failure to instantly disable and capture the Klingon ship. A Klingon fighter was no
match for a vessel of the Constellation class. Saavik could only conclude that
Kirk had come back to Genesis before his ship was fully repaired. She glanced
at Spock, who sat wrapped in his black cloak and in exhaustion that was nearly
as palpable. The reports *Grissom* had sent back must have brought James Kirk
here. She then glanced at James Kirk's son, and saw the hope in David's bruised
face. She hoped, in her turn and for all three of them, that he would not be disappointed.

The Klingon commander snapped an order. The sergeant in charge of the
landing party replied with a quick assent and motioned to his underlings. They
dragged Saavik, David, and Spock to their feet. Spock staggered. His face
showed hopeless pain. The planet's agony, which came to him without warning
and frequently—more and more frequently as the hours passed—tortured him
brutally.

The sergeant thrust his communicator into Saavik's face. His meaning
was clear: she must speak. She tried to decide if it would be better to reassure
Admiral Kirk that his son and his friend were alive, or if she should maintain
her silence and by doing so withhold the Klingons' proof that they had prisoners.

The sergeant said a single word and Saavik felt her arms being wrenched
upward behind her back. She called on all her training. Though the leverage
forced her on tiptoe, she neither winced nor cried out. She stared coldly at the
sergeant.

He clenched the fingers of his free hand into a fist. Saavik did not flinch
from him. He gazed at her steadily, then smiled very slightly and made a silent
motion toward David. The crew member restraining him twisted his arms piti-
lessly. David gasped. The sergeant prodded Saavik in the ribs. He did not need to
be able to speak Standard to indicate that he would hurt either or both of her
friends until she did his bidding. She closed her eyes and took a deep breath. She
could not bear to bring them any more pain.

"Admiral," she said, "this is Saavik."

"Saavik—" Kirk hesitated. *"Is . . . David with you?"*

"Yes. He is. As is . . . someone else. A Vulcan scientist of your acquaintance."

"This Vulcan—is he alive?"

"He is not himself," Saavik said. "But he lives. He is subject to rapid aging,
like this unstable planet."

Before Kirk could answer, the sergeant turned to David and thrust the communicator at him.

"Hello, sir. It's David."

"David—" Kirk said. His relief caught in his voice, then he recovered himself. *"Sorry I'm late,"* he said.

"It's okay. I should have known you'd come. But Saavik's right—this planet
is unstable. It's going to destroy itself in a matter of hours."

"David . . ." Kirk sounded shocked, and genuinely sorrowful for his son's
disappointment. *"What went wrong?"*

"I went wrong," David said.

The silence stretched so long that Saavik wondered if the communication had been severed.

"David," Kirk said, *"I don't understand."*

"I'm sorry, sir, it's too complicated to explain right now. Just don't surrender. Genesis doesn't work! I can't believe they'll kill us for it—"

The sergeant snatched the communicator from David.

"David—!" Kirk shouted. But when David tried to reply, his captor wrenched him back so hard he nearly fainted. Saavik took one instinctive step toward him, but she, too, was restrained, and for the moment she had no way to resist.

The sergeant permitted them to listen to the remainder of Kruge's conversation with Admiral Kirk.

"Your young friend is mistaken, Admiral," Kruge said. His voice tightened with the emotions of anger and desire for revenge. "I meant what I said. And now, to show my intentions are sincere . . . I am going to kill one of my prisoners."

"Wait!" Kirk cried. *"Give me a chance—"*

Saavik did not understand the order Kruge next gave to his sergeant—that is, she did not understand the words themselves, which were of a dialect she did not know. But the intent was terribly clear. The sergeant looked at Spock, at David, at Saavik.

His gaze and Saavik's locked.

The sergeant had been vastly impressed by his captain's offer of final honor to his gunner, and vastly horrified by the gunner's inability to accept the offer and carry out the deed. He recognized in Saavik a prideful being. As Kruge had shown magnanimity to the gunner, the sergeant would show it to this young halfbreed Vulcan. He would give her the chance to maintain her honor at her death.

He drew his dagger. The toothed and recurved edges flashed in the piercing light of the sun. He raised it up; he offered it to her.

Saavik knew what he expected of her. She understood why he was doing it, and she even understood that it was meant as a courtesy.

But she had never taken any oath to follow his rules.

She raised her hands, preparing to grasp the ritual dagger. She could feel the attention of every member of the landing party. They were so fascinated, so impressed by their sergeant's tact and taste, that they had nearly forgotten their other captives. Saavik would take the knife—then lay about her with it, distract them, cry "Run!" to her friends, and hope they had the wit to take the chance she offered them. With any luck at all she might escape, too, in the confusion, but that matter was quite secondary to her responsibility to David and to Spock.

She reached into herself to find the anger that had been building up for so long, the berserk rage that would give her a moment's invincibility. The fantastically recurved blade of the knife twisted in her vision. Her attention focused to a point as coherent and powerful as a laser. She touched the haft of the knife.

"No!" David cried. He flung himself forward, breaking out of the inattentive hold, and plunged between Saavik and the sergeant.

It took Saavik a fatal instant to understand what had happened.

With a snarl of rage, the sergeant plunged the dagger into David's chest.

"David, no—!"

David cried out and collapsed. Saavik went down with him, breaking his fall. She held him, trying to stanch the blood that pulsed between her fingers. She could not withdraw the knife, for it was designed to do far more damage coming out than going in. David grasped weakly at the hilt and Saavik pushed his hands away.

"David, lie still—"

If she could just have a moment to help him, a moment to try to meld her consciousness with his, she could give him some of her strength, some of her ability at controlling the body. She knew she could keep him alive.

"David, stop fighting me—"

He was very weak. He stared upward. She did not think he could see her. Her own vision blurred. He tried to speak. He failed. She struggled to make contact with him, to touch his mind, to save him.

"Help me!" she cried to the landing party. "Don't you understand, you can never replicate Genesis without him!"

If any of them understood her, they did not believe her.

The Klingon commander did not rescind the death sentence he had ordered. Saavik felt David slipping away from her.

"David—"

He reached up. His hand was covered with blood. He touched her cheek.

"I love you," he said. "And I wish . . ."

Saavik had to bend down to hear him, his voice was so weak.

"I wish we could have seen Vance's dragons . . ."

"Oh, David," Saavik whispered, "David, love, there are no dragons."

Three of the landing party dragged her from him.

Saavik's fury erupted without focus or plan. The madness took her. She flung herself backwards, turning. She clamped her hands around the throat of the nearest of her captors. He gagged and choked and clawed at her hands. She perceived the blows and shouts but they had no effect on her. She perceived the limpid hum of a phaser and felt the beam rake over her body. Her fingers tightened. The phaser whined at a higher pitch. Hands clawed at her, trying to break her grip, failing.

The phaser howled yet a third time. The sound penetrated Saavik's blue-white rage, searing her mind from cerebrum to spinal cord.

She collapsed to the rocky ground and lost consciousness.

Eleven

Pale and tense, Jim Kirk pushed himself from the command seat. His fingernails dug into the armrests and he sought desperately for time. The channel from the surface of Genesis spun confused voices around him, but the Klingon commander smiled coolly from the viewscreen, impervious and confident.

"Commander!" Kirk shouted.

"My name," his opponent said, *"is Kruge. I think it is important, Admiral, that you know who will defeat you."*

"At least one of those prisoners is an unarmed civilian! The others are members of a scientific expedition. Scientific, Kruge!"

" 'Unarmed'?" Kruge chuckled. *"Your unarmed civilian and your scientific expedition stand upon the surface of the most powerful weapon in the universe, which they have created!"*

"Kruge, don't do something you'll regret!"

"You do not understand, Admiral Kirk. Since you doubt my sincerity, I must prove it to you. My order will not be rescinded." He glanced aside and snapped a question to someone out of Kirk's view.

Kirk heard the beginning of a reply.

A cry of agony and despair cut off the words.

"David!" Jim shouted. "Saavik!"

He could make out nothing but the sounds of struggle, anger, and confusion. The transmission jumped and buzzed—Kirk recognized the interference of a phaser beam, reacting with the communicator. He was shaking with helplessness. The uncertainty stretched on so long that he thought for an instant of rushing to the transporter room and beaming into . . . into whatever was happening on the surface of Genesis. But even in his desperation he knew that he would be too late.

Commander Kruge watched, harsh satisfaction on his face.

Finally the voice transmission from Genesis cleared to silence.

"I believe I have a message for you, Admiral," Kruge said, and spoke a command to his landing party.

Again there was a delay. Jim could feel the sweat trickling down his sides. A voice came from Genesis, but it was one of impatient command in a dialect of Kruge's people that Kirk had never even heard before.

"Saavik . . . David . . ." Kirk said.

"Admiral . . ."

Even when Saavik was angry—and Kirk had seen her angry, though she might have denied it—her voice was level and cool. But now it trembled, and it was full of grief.

"Admiral, David—" Her voice caught. *"David is dead."*

Kirk plunged forward as if he could strangle Kruge over the distance and the vacuum that separated them by using the sheer force fury gave his will.

"Kruge, you spineless coward! You've killed—my—son!"

At first Kruge did not react, and then he closed his eyes slowly and opened them again, in an expression of triumph and satisfaction.

"I have two more prisoners, Admiral," he said. *"Do you wish to be the cause of their deaths, too? I will arrange that their fate come to them . . . somewhat more slowly."* He let that sink in. *"Surrender your vessel!"*

"All right, damn you!" Kirk cried. He sagged back. "All right." He became aware of McCoy, at his side. "Give me a minute, to inform my crew."

Kruge shrugged, magnanimity in his gesture. But his tone reeked of contempt. *"I offer you two minutes, Admiral Kirk,"* he said, enjoying the irony of turning James Kirk's commands back upon him. *"For you, and your gallant crew."*

His communication faded. Kirk sat staring at the viewscreen as the image scattered and reformed into space, stars, the great blue curve of Genesis below, and the marauding Klingon fighter.

"Jim," McCoy said. He took Kirk by the shoulder and gripped it, shaking him gently, trying to pull him back out of despair. "Jim!"

Kirk recoiled from his help. He stared at him for a moment, hardly seeing him, hardly aware anymore of the reason he had come to this godforsaken spot in space. He knew that if he did surrender, he would sacrifice the lives of all his friends. And he realized, suddenly, that if he gave Kruge the opportunity to tap into the *Enterprise*'s Genesis records, the information would lead inevitably to Carol Marcus. Kruge might be bold, but he was not a fool; he could not threaten Carol directly. But Kirk would be a fool to discount the Empire's network of spies, assassins . . . and kidnappers.

"Mister Sulu . . ." he said. "What is the crew complement of Commander Kruge's ship?"

"It's about—" Sulu had been thinking of a smart and angry kid, a young man on the brink of realizing an enormous potential, his life drained out into the world he had tried to make. Sulu forced his voice to be steady; he forced his attention to the question he had been asked. "A dozen, officers and crew."

"And some are on the planet. . . ." Kirk said. He faced his friends, who had risked so much to accompany him. "I swear to you," he said, "we're not finished yet."

"We never have been, Jim," McCoy said.

"Sulu, you and Bones to the transporter room. Scott, Chekov, with me. We have a job to do." He slapped the comm control. "*Enterprise* to Commander, Klingon fighter. Stand by to board this ship on my signal."

"No tricks, Kirk," Kruge replied. *"You have one minute."*

"No tricks," Kirk said. "I'm . . . looking forward to meeting you. Kirk out."

Kirk gathered with Chekov and Scott at the science officer's station and opened a voice and optical channel direct to the computer.

"Computer, this is Admiral James T. Kirk. Request security access."

He experienced a moment of apprehension that Starfleet might have blocked the deepest levels of the computer. A bright light flashed in his eyes, taking a pattern for a retina scan. No: no one in Starfleet had expected him to commit an act as outrageous and absurd as stealing his own ship. The order to him to sit still and do nothing, though it would cost the life of Leonard McCoy, was deemed to be sufficient protection for the *Enterprise*. They had not bothered to protect the ship in any more subtle way. If they had, no doubt the ship's computer would have begun shouting "Thief, thief!" the moment he stepped on board.

"Identity confirmed," the computer said.

"Computer . . ." Kirk said. He took a deep breath, and continued without pause. "Destruct sequence one. Code one, one-A . . ."

As Kirk recited the complex code, he ignored Scott's stunned glance. The only way he was going to get through this was by keeping it at a distance, by making the decision and carrying it out with no second-guessing.

Kirk finished his part of the process and stood aside.

Chekov stepped forward, his expressive face somber.

"Computer," he said slowly, "this is Commander Pavel Andreievich Chekov, acting science officer."

The computer scanned Chekov's dark eyes and recognized him.

Was it Kirk's imagination, or did the identification take longer for Chekov than it had for Kirk? It must be his apprehension and his nerves and his sense of the clock ticking away that last minute. The computer was merely a machine, a machine with a human voice and some decision-making capabilities, but it was not designed to be self-aware. It could not possess intimations of mortality. It would not delay identifying Chekov to give itself a few more moments of existence, nor would the injuries begun by Kirk's code slow it in any fashion perceptible to a human being. The end would be quick and clean, a matter of microseconds.

"Destruct sequence two, code one, one-A, one-B . . ."

The computer was merely a machine; the ship was merely a machine.

"Mister Scott," Kirk said, his voice absolutely level.

"Admiral—" Scott said in protest.

"Mister Scott—!"

Scott could stop the sequence. Kirk experienced a mad moment when he hoped the engineer would do just that.

Scott looked away, faced the computer's optical scan, and identified himself. "Computer, this is Commander Montgomery Scott, chief engineering officer." The light flashed white, bringing the lines of strain on his face into sharp relief.

"Identification verified."

"Destruct sequence three, code one-B, two-B, three . . ."

"Destruct sequence completed and engaged. Awaiting final code for one-minute countdown."

If the computer were merely a machine, if the ship were merely a machine, how could Jim Kirk perceive grief in its voice? It was just that, he knew: his perception, not objective reality. He and Spock had had many arguments about the difference between the two. They had come to no agreement, no conclusions.

The last word remained James Kirk's.

"Code zero," he said. "Zero, zero destruct zero . . ."

This time there was no delay.

"One minute," the computer said. "Fifty-nine seconds. Fifty-eight seconds. Fifty-seven seconds . . ."

"Let's get the hell out of here," Jim Kirk said angrily.

On the bridge of the fighter, Torg felt his commander's gaze raking him and the heavily armed boarding party. Torg understood the compliment his commander offered him by permitting him to lead the force. Maltz alone would remain behind with Kruge. Admiring his commander's restraint, Torg wondered if he himself, in Kruge's position, would have the strength to let another lead the assault. By forgoing that perquisite, Kruge would gain the more important prize of seeing Kirk brought to him, thoroughly beaten, a prisoner.

Torg felt some slight apprehension about the size of his force relative to the crew of a ship such as the *Enterprise*. He wondered if the two remaining hostages would truly secure the submissive behavior of the enemy. He knew that if the positions were reversed, Kruge would sacrifice two hostages without hesitation.

"They do outnumber us, my lord—" Torg thought to point out that even a few rebels among the crew could make significant trouble.

His crest flaring, Kruge turned to him. "We are Klingons! When you have taken the ship, when you control it, I will transfer my flag to it and we will take Genesis from their own memory banks!"

"Yes, my lord," Torg said. Kruge delivered into his hands the disposition of any rebels. Torg would deliver the ship into the hands of his commander.

"To the transport room," Kruge said. He saluted Torg. "Success!"

The intense thrill of excitement nearly overwhelmed the younger officer. No one had ever spoken to him in such a high phase of the language before.

"Success!" he replied. As he ordered his team into formation and away he heard Kruge contact the Federation admiral again. The conversation followed him via the ship's speakers.

"Kirk, your time runs out. Report!"

"Kirk to Commander Kruge. We are energizing transporter beam . . ."

Torg arranged his party in a wedge, with himself at the apex.

"Transporter, stand by," Kruge said.

"Ready, my lord." Torg grasped the stock of an assault gun, a blaster, the weapon he particularly favored over a phaser.

". . . Now."

The beam spun Torg into a whirlwind that swept him away.

As his body reformed aboard the *Enterprise*, he held his weapon at the ready. But no rebels waited to resist him.

No one waited at all. Over the speakers, a soft and rhythmic voice kept the ship's time. An alien custom, no doubt, as inexplicable and distracting as most alien customs.

"Forty-one seconds. Forty seconds . . ."

Torg descended from the transporter platform. He was prepared for an attack, even more than a surrender. He was not prepared for . . . nothing.

He led his force from the transporter room and toward the bridge. By the time he reached it, the eerie silence beneath the computer voice had drawn his nerves as taut as his grip on his blaster.

The bridge, too, lay empty and quiet.

"Twenty-two seconds. Twenty-one seconds . . ."

Torg drew out his communicator.

"It's a trap," one of the team members said. The fear in his voice infected every one of them.

Torg silenced him with a poisonous glance that promised severe discipline when the time was right. He opened a channel to his commander.

"My lord, the ship appears to be . . . deserted."

"How can this be?" Kruge said. "They are hiding!"

"Perhaps, sir. But the bridge appears to be run by computer. It is the only thing speaking."

"What? Transmit!"

Torg aimed the directional microphone at the computer speaker, which continued its rhythmic chant. "Six seconds. Five seconds . . ."

"Transport! Maltz, quickly, lock onto them—!"

The alarm in Kruge's voice terrified Torg, but he had no time to react.

"Two seconds. One second."

The transport beam trembled at the edge of his perceptions—

"Zero," the computer said, very softly.

—but it reached him too late.

Saavik lay on the cold, rocky hillside. The effects of the stun beams were fading, yet she was barely able to move. The madness had possessed her, and now she must pay its price. Her rage had drained her of strength. David's death had drained her of will. His blood stained her hands.

She forced herself to rise. The young Vulcan watched her, curious and impassive. His form was that of Spock, but the Spock she had known had never been indifferent to exhaustion or to grief. She stood up. David's body was only a few paces away.

The sergeant snapped an order at her. She understood its sense, but chose to ignore it. The crew member she had tried to throttle leaped forward and struck her, knocking her down. Even the sound of his laughter was not enough to anger her now.

She staggered back up. The guard flung her to the ground again. Saavik lay still for a moment, digging her fingers into the cold earth, feeling the faint vibrations of the disintegrating world.

She pushed herself to her feet for a third time. The guard clenched his fist. But before he could attack, the sergeant grabbed his arm. The two glared at each other. The sergeant won the contest. Neither moved as Saavik took the few steps to David's body and knelt beside him. She put her hand to his pallid cheek.

When David was near, she had always been aware of the easy and excitable glow of his mind. Now it had completely dissolved. He was gone. All she could ever do for him was watch his body through the night, as she had watched Peter and as she had watched Spock. On the *Enterprise* the ritual had been only that. But on this world his body was vulnerable to predators, indigenous or alien.

Saavik gazed into the twilight. If the *Enterprise* was in standard orbit, she should be able to locate it as a point of light in the sky. Working out the equations in her head forced her to collect her mind and concentrate her attention. When she was done she felt unreasonably pleased with herself.

Am I becoming irrational? she wondered. *Under these conditions, feeling pleased at anything, much less at the solution of such a simple process, must surely be irrational.*

She looked for the *Enterprise* in the spot she had calculated it should be.

She found the moving point of light.

And then—

The transporter beam ripped James Kirk from his ship and reformed him on the surface of Genesis. One after the other, McCoy, Sulu, Chekov, and Scott appeared around him, safe. They all waited, phasers drawn, prepared for pursuit. They had timed their escape closely. The enemy boarding party could have perceived the last glint of their transporter beam, could have tracked them by the console settings, and could have followed them. But they remained alone.

The air was cold and damp and heavy with twilight. All around, a hundred paces in all directions, iron-gray trees reached into the air, then twisted down, twining around each other like gigantic vines. They formed a wide circle around an area clear of trees but choked with tangled, spiny bushes. He took a step toward the forest, where he and his friends could find concealment, and where he would not be able to see the sky. But the thorns ripped into his clothing and hooked into his hands. The scratches burned as if they had been touched with acid. Jim stopped.

Unwillingly, he looked up.

Stars pricked the limpid royal blue with points of light. This system contained only a single planet and no moon. All its sky's stars should be fixed, never changing their relationship to one another. But one, shining the dull silver of reflected light, moved gracefully across the starfield on its own unique path.

Slowly and delicately it began to glow. Its color changed from silver to gold. Then, with shocking abruptness, it exploded to intense blue-white. The point of motion expanded to a blazing, flaming disk, a sphere, a new sun that blotted out the stars.

Jim felt, or imagined, the radiation on his face, a brief burst of heat and illumination as matter and antimatter met and joined in mutual annihilation.

The *Enterprise* arced brilliantly from its orbit. For an instant it was a comet, but the gravity of the new world caught it and held it and drew it in. It would never again curve boldly close to the incandescent surface of a sun, never again depart the gentle harbor of Earth to sail into the unknown. The gravity of Genesis turned the dying ship from a comet to a falling star. It spun downward, trailing sparks and cinders and glowing debris. It touched the atmosphere, and it flared more brightly.

Just as suddenly as it appeared, it vanished. One moment the *Enterprise* was a glorious blaze, and the next the sky rose black and empty.

It seemed impossible that the stars should remain in their same pattern, for even fixed stars changed after an eternity.

"My gods, Bones . . ." he whispered. "What have I done?"

"What you had to do," McCoy said harshly, his voice only partly his own. "What you've always done: turned death into a fighting chance to live." He faced Jim squarely and grasped his upper arms. "Do you hear me, Jim?"

Jim stared at him, still seeing a flash of the afterimage of the new falling star, still feeling the death of his ship like sunlight searing his face. He took a deep breath. He nodded.

The tricorder Sulu carried had been reacting to the new world since the moment they appeared, but Sulu had barely heard it. Now it forced itself on his attention.

"Sir, the planet's core readings are extremely unstable, and they're changing rapidly—"

Kirk wrenched his attention to the immediate threat. "Any life signs?"

"Close." He scanned with the tricorder. "There."

"Come on!"

Kirk strode through the clearing toward the distorted trees. This time the thorns seemed to part for his passing.

The holographic viewer, which had blazed with light, hung dark and flat; the port looked out on empty space.

Kruge slowly realized how many blank seconds had passed during which he had failed to act, or even to react. The great ship which he had held in thrall had dissolved in his grasp.

Confused and uncertain, Maltz waited by the transporter controls. He had directed the beam to the landing party, touched them, held them—then nothing remained on which to lock.

Kruge was unable to believe what the alien admiral must have done.

"My lord," Maltz said hesitantly, "what are your orders?"

My orders? Kruge thought. *Do I retain the right to give orders? I underestimated him—a human being! He did the one thing I did not anticipate, the one thing I discounted. The one thing I would have done in his position.*

"He destroyed himself," Kruge said aloud.

"Sir, may I—?"

If I had known one of the prisoners was his son—if I had interrogated them before sacrificing one—! Kruge flailed himself with his own humiliation. Killing Kirk's son was stupid! It made Kirk willing to die!

"We still have two prisoners, sir," Maltz said with transparent concern, for he had received no real response from his commander, no acknowledgment of his presence or of their predicament, since the enemy ship exploded and died. "Perhaps their information—"

Kruge turned on him angrily. "They are useless! It was Kirk I needed, and I let him slip away."

"But surely our mission has not failed!" Maltz exclaimed. They had come seeking Genesis; they retained two hostages who had some knowledge of it, perhaps enough to reproduce it. By his cowardly suicide, Kirk had abandoned them to their captors. Surely Kruge would not let one setback destroy him because of pride. . . .

"Our mission is over," Kruge said. "*I* have failed. A human has been bolder and more ruthless than I. . . ." His eyes were empty. "*That* . . . is the real dishonor."

—and then, the point of light that was the *Enterprise* flared into a nova and scattered itself across the sky.

Saavik gasped.

The ship vanished.

She felt the loss of other lives and dreams much more sharply than she felt the certainty of her own impending death. That did not seem to matter much anymore. It would have very little effect on the universe.

Spock cried out violently, foretelling an inevitable quaking of the planet. The night rumbled; the ground shook. In the distance, Genesis echoed Spock's agony. Beyond the forest, a fault sundered the plain, splitting it into halves, then ramming the halves one against the other. One edge rose like an ocean wave, overwhelming and crushing the other, which subsided beneath it. The sheer faces of stone ground against each other with the power to form mountains.

A wash of illumination flooded ground and sky. A brilliant aurora echoed the earthquake lights, and ozone sharpened the air.

The planet was dying, as the *Enterprise* had died, as every person Saavik had ever cared about had died, as she expected, soon, to die.

Her guards turned away to gaze into the looming, sparkling curtains of the aurora. Even above the rumblings of the quake, Saavik could hear the electric sizzle of the auroral discharge. The guards watched and marveled. The undertones of their voices revealed fear.

Instead of fading, the quake intensified. The massive trees rocked. The loud *snap!* of breaking branches reverberated across the hillside. The guards looked around, seeking some place where they might be safe and realizing no such place existed on this world.

The ground heaved. It flung a massive tree completely free, ripping it up by its roots and propelling it onto the bare promontory. The guards plunged out of its reach and stood huddled together, terrified, stranded between the clutching, grasping trees and the abyss.

The resonances of Genesis tortured Spock. Saavik touched David's soft, curly hair one last time. She could do nothing for him, not even guard him till the dawn. This world would never see another sunrise.

She rose and picked her way across the ragged, trembling surface. Behind her the sergeant spoke into his communicator, a note of panic in his voice. Though Saavik could not understand the words, she could well imagine what he was saying.

Only static replied. Perhaps, when the *Enterprise* destroyed itself, it had destroyed the marauder as well. If that was true, then they were marooned down here after all.

Spock lay prone, shuddering, clenching his long fingers in the dirt. Saavik began to speak to him in Vulcan. If she could calm him enough to approach him, she might join with his mind and alleviate some of his pain.

So intent was she that she did not even hear the guard stride up behind her. He shoved her roughly aside. She stumbled on the broken ground.

"No!" she cried as the guard reached down to jerk Spock to his feet. "No, don't touch him!"

She was too late.

He reached down and grabbed Spock's arm. Spock reacted to the touch as if it burned. He leaped to his feet with a cry of pain and anger, lifted the guard bodily, and flung him through the air.

The guard smashed into a contorted tree with a wrenching crunch of broken bone. His body slid limply to the ground and did not move again.

As the sergeant drew his phaser, Saavik struggled to her feet.

"Be easy," she said to Spock in Vulcan, "be easy, I can help you."

Spock covered his face with his hands and cried out to the darkness in a long, wavering ululation. He had aged again, aged years, during the short time the guards had kept them apart. Saavik touched him gently, then enfolded him and held him. He was so intent on his own inner contortions that he did not even react.

The sergeant approached, his phaser held ready. He was frightened to the brink of ridding himself of his murderous prisoner, his commander's wishes and ambitions be damned. Saavik glared at him over her shoulder. He would not reach Spock without going through her first.

A tetanic convulsion wracked Spock's body, arching his spine and forcing from him a shuddering, anguished scream.

In the dark forest on the side of the mountain, Jim Kirk heard a shriek of agony. He redoubled his pace. He plunged up the steep slope. The faint trail wound between trees that would have done credit to Hieronymus Bosch. The scarlet aurora threw moving shadows across his path. Kirk struggled upward between whipping branches that moved far more violently than the plunging of the earth could account for.

Sulu paced him, with Chekov close behind. McCoy followed at a slightly greater distance. Kirk gasped for breath. The heavily ionized air burned in his throat.

He burst out into a clearing. Saavik stood in its center, supporting—someone—and a Klingon sergeant threatened her with a phaser.

"Don't move!" Kirk cried.

The sergeant spun in astonishment, leading with his phaser. Kirk fired his own weapon. The beam flung the sergeant backwards. He hit the ground and did not move again.

Kirk ran past the sergeant without a second glance. He slowed as he approached Saavik, who turned toward him, cradling an unconscious young man in her arms.

"Bones—" Kirk said softly.

McCoy panted up beside him and gently took her burden from her. When his hand brushed Saavik's arm, she gasped and jerked away as if he had given her an electrical shock. She took a step back, staring at him. Kirk touched her elbow, startling her.

"Sir—" she said. Her voice broke, and she staggered. He caught her and drew her close.

"Easy, Saavik," he said. "Take it easy. It's all right."

"I tried," she whispered. "I tried to take care of your son . . ."

The auroras burned in the sky and lit the clearing with a ghastly glow. Jim saw, beneath a twisting tree, the body of his son.

He hugged Saavik one last time. She took a long shuddering breath and straightened up, allowing him to break the embrace.

He left her with McCoy and the others and slowly crossed the clearing. His boots crunched on fallen leaves.

Jim knelt beside David's body.

"My son. . . ." A poem whispered to him from a long-ago time. " 'To thee no star be dark . . . Both heaven and earth . . . friend thee forever . . .' "

Fallen leaves drifted across David's body, shrouding the young man in a tattered cloth that shone scarlet and gold when the auroras flared, a cloth of autumn leaves, from a world that had barely experienced its spring.

Twelve

Jim closed his eyes tight, fighting back the tears. He heard footsteps nearby. He opened his eyes and raised his head. His vision blurred, then cleared. Saavik stood before him.

"What happened?" he said.

"He . . . he gave his life to save us," she said. She stopped, then shook her head and turned away. She said, very softly, "That is all I know."

"Jim!"

Kirk stood quickly, responding to McCoy's concerned shout. He forced himself away from his grief, away from the dead and toward the living.

McCoy hunched over the body of the young person whom Saavik had so fiercely protected. Kirk knelt down beside them, and in the changing light he saw—

He gasped. "Bones—!"

"Bozhemoi!" Chekov exclaimed.

In all the years from the time James Kirk met Spock until the time of Spock's death, the Vulcan had not much changed. He aged more slowly than a human being. No one knew if he would age as slowly as a Vulcan. Kirk had always been aware that he would not live to see Spock old, and he had not known him as a youth. The Vulcan lying unconscious before him *was* a youth . . . but he was also, unmistakably, Spock.

Spock. Alive.

Kirk wanted to laugh, he wanted to cry, he wanted instant certain answers to all the questions tumbling over each other in his mind. *My gods,* he thought, *Spock—alive!*

And then he had to wonder, *What does this mean for McCoy?*

"Bones—?" he said again.

"All his metabolic functions are highly accelerated," McCoy said. He made his diagnosis calmly, despite its implications. "In lay terms—his body is aging. Fast."

"And—his mind?"

McCoy glanced at his tricorder again and shook his head. "The readings of a newborn, or at best an infant of a few months—his mind's a void, almost a *tabula rasa*." He glanced up. "It would seem, Admiral," he said drily, "that I have all his marbles."

"Is there *anything* we can do?"

McCoy shrugged. Kirk glanced at Saavik.

"Only one thing, sir," she said. "We must get him off this planet. He is . . . bound to it in some way. He is aging, as is this world."

The young man moaned. The ground shuddered as violently as he did. Saavik knelt beside him.

"And if he stays here?"

Saavik looked up.

"He will die."

Kirk withdrew as a blaze of lightning flooded the clearing. He had to do something . . . and only one possibility remained.

He opened his communicator.

"Commander Kruge," he said. "This is Admiral James T. Kirk. I am . . . alive and well on the surface of Genesis." He paused. He received no reply except crackling electrical interference. "I know this will come as a pleasant surprise for you," he said, "but, you see, my ship was the victim of . . . an unfortunate accident. I'm sorry about your crew, old boy. But *c'est la vie,* as we say back on Earth."

His answer was another convulsion of the ground, another crash of static, another blinding burst of light from the cloudless sky.

"Well?" Kirk said angrily. "I'm waiting for you—what's your answer?" He forced himself to relax his grip on his communicator, to be patient, to wait and think. "I have what you want," he said desperately. "I have the secret of Genesis! But you'll have to bring us up there to get it. Do you hear me?"

Static drowned out any possibility of an answer. The sky and the earth rumbled, the young Vulcan moaned, the trees groaned and cracked, and in the background the aurora rustled, soft and eerie. A tremendous crash of lightning and thunder obliterated sight and sound. His shoulders slumping, Jim Kirk folded his communicator and stowed it carefully away. He blinked a few times, trying to drive away the afterimages that made his eyes water. He turned back to the remnants of his crew, whom he had led to their doom.

He joined them, but he did not know what to say to them. Spock lay sprawled on the ground, his arm flung across his face. The others were gathered around him, astonished to find him alive. Kirk sat on his heels beside them, not knowing what to say. "Thank you" and "I'm sorry" seemed terribly inadequate.

"Drop all weapons!"

Startled, Kirk spun toward the voice.

The sky was a luminous backdrop, a curtain of wavering auroral light pierced intermittently by stars. Against it stood a huge shadow. It loomed above them on the pinnacle of stone.

Kirk rose carefully, drawing his phaser and dropping it, then spreading his empty hands. Sulu, Chekov, and McCoy followed suit, but Saavik remained kneeling beside Spock.

The looming figure came a few steps toward them. The phaser glinted in his hand. The hair of his crest rose.

"Over there," said Commander Kruge. "All but Kirk." He gestured to a trampled spot on the hillside.

Kirk made a slight gesture of his head. McCoy, Sulu, and Chekov reluctantly obeyed. Saavik remained where she was, next to Spock. Kirk heard the Klingon commander draw in a long, angry breath.

"Go *on,* Lieutenant," Kirk said softly. He feared that she would argue, but finally she stood and joined the others.

Commander Kruge spun open his communicator. "Maltz," he said, "the prisoners are at our first beam coordinates. Stand by."

Kirk took one step toward Kruge, who reacted by raising the phaser.

At least I have his full attention, Kirk thought.

"You should take the Vulcan, too," he said easily.

"No."

"But, why?"

"Because," Kruge said, "you wish it." Keeping his gaze on Kirk, he picked up the phasers and flung them, one by one, over the promontory and down the side of the mountain. Then he spoke into the communicator in his own language. Kirk did not understand the words, but it must have been the order to transport. The energy flux pulsed around Kirk's friends.

"No—!" Saavik cried, but the beam attenuated her voice. She vanished with the others.

Only a few hundred meters away, the whole hillside suddenly split open with a great roar of tortured rock. Scarlet light and intense heat fanned out of the fissure. The glowing magma thrust upward through the breach in the planet's crust. The waterfall that tumbled down the hillside flowed into the crack and over the molten rock, exploding into superheated steam.

Kruge strode closer to Kirk.

"Genesis!" He shouted over the cacophony of the dying planet. "I want it!"

"Beam the Vulcan up," Kirk said. "Then we talk."

"Give me what I want—and I'll consider it."

"You fool!" Kirk cried. "Look around you! This planet is destroying itself!" Kruge smiled.

"Yes," he said. "Exhilarating, isn't it?"

Kirk stared at him, speechless, then recovered himself.

"If we don't help each other, we'll all die here!"

"Perfect!" Kruge said triumphantly. "That's the way it shall be!" He loomed over Kirk, smiling his wolfish smile. *"Give me Genesis!"* he said. Each word struck like a blow.

As if in reply, Genesis heaved and pitched beneath him. The outcropping on which he stood shattered and flung him forward. He lost his balance and fell. His phaser skittered across the stone, sliding down the hillside to the edge of the earth fault.

As Kruge struggled up, Kirk plunged forward and tackled him. Kirk's breath rushed out as if he had run into a solid wall. Kruge roared with anger and caught him in the side with his fist. He fell hard but managed to roll to his feet. Kruge ran toward his phaser. Kirk sprinted toward him and tackled him at the knees. They both went down. Half-stunned, staggering, Kruge rose. But Kirk managed to get up first. He pressed his advantage, hitting with short, sharp jabs that did little real damage but kept his opponent off-balance and flailing. He ducked beneath Kruge's long, powerful arms and hit him again. Kirk's knuckles were raw. Each blow shot pain up his hands.

The livid glow of magma haloed the Klingon commander. He swung and missed. His momentum pitched him around. Kirk sprang at him and hit him one more time with his battered hands.

Kruge fell.

He tumbled over the edge of a bit of broken ground.

Kirk looked over the precipice. Kruge stood on a second cliff, just above the rumbling magma. Steam and smoke roiled around him.

Looking up at Kirk, he laughed.

Infuriated, Kirk sprang down on him. The heat slapped him. He struggled with Kruge. The size and relative youth of the Klingon commander began to overwhelm him. Kruge broke Kirk's hold and slammed him in the chest with both hands. The impact flung Kirk violently back against the cliff's rock wall. Dazed, Kirk slid toward the ground. He barely managed to prevent himself from falling. He was soaked with sweat. He struggled up. Kruge regarded him from the edge of the pit. The scarlet darkness silhouetted the Klingon commander, who waited, hands on hips, for Kirk to regain enough of his strength to be a fitting opponent.

The magma surged from below, scraping against the side of the cliff. Rocks fell, clattering hollowly. Great hexagonal columns of basalt split away from the cliff and collapsed like the trunks of ancient trees. The column on which Kruge stood fractured and began to sink. The magma swallowed its base.

The whole column began to topple. Kruge balanced upon it, the heat rising around him in waves. To Kirk it looked as if the commander were enjoying his peril, testing his nerve.

"Jump, damn you!" Kirk cried.

And still Kruge delayed. The column of stone continued to tilt, to sink.

Kruge leaped. But he had waited an instant beyond the last moment. He fell short. He slammed up against the fragmenting columns, gripping the edge, his feet dangling into the glowing pit.

Kirk sprinted to the edge of the cliff and knelt, peering down at Kruge, who looked up at him with his teeth slightly bared in an expression that was more a mocking smile than a threat.

"Now," Kirk said, "you'll give me what I want—"

Kruge lurched upward, trying to get his arm over the edge of the cliff, trying to gain leverage. Kirk let him flail at the heated stone.

"You're going to get us off this planet!" Kirk said.

Kruge snarled something. Whatever it was, it was not agreement. He slipped precariously down.

"Don't be a fool!" Kirk cried. "Give me your hand—and live!"

The commander lunged toward Kirk. Kirk jerked back. Kruge's fingers grazed his throat, then slipped away. He started to fall, but with a supernatural effort he vaulted upward again and grabbed Kirk's leg.

Kruge abandoned his hold on the cliff and clenched both hands like claws around Kirk's ankle.

Jim Kirk felt himself sliding along the rough surface of the cliff, off-balance, only a handsbreadth from the edge. He struggled back, digging his fingers between the hexagonal patterns where the basalt continued to fragment. His fingernails ripped, and he left streaks of blood on the dark stone as he slipped farther and farther over the edge. The fierce heat of the magma gusted up around him.

He heard Kruge laughing again, laughing with contempt and victory, laughing at the death of Kirk's son, at Kirk's determination to save his friends, at Kirk's defeat, and at Kirk himself.

"Damn you!" Kirk cried in a rage. "I have had—enough—of *you!*" He kicked out angrily, and again, desperately.

Kruge's grip loosened, faltered, and broke.

Kirk scrambled back onto the cliff.

Kruge tumbled down, with nothing to break his fall but the glowing magma.

The basalt columns shuddered and split away from each other, tumbling one after the other into the pit. The cliff was disintegrating beneath Jim's feet. He raced for the higher cliff, leaped, caught its edge, and dragged himself up its face. He lay panting on solid ground, exhausted. He had no choice but to get up and keep going, for the solid ground was no longer solid. Other cracks opened, engulfing twisted, warty trees that exploded into flame and smoke, swallowing the hillside's streams, gushing superheated steam. Jim struggled to his feet. Spock sprawled, unconscious, near a blood-red glowing fissure.

The hot white spark of the Genesis sun burst above the horizon, piercing the darkness and the steam and the smoke. Long shadows sprang into existence. They moved and wavered like wraiths with the convulsions of the ground.

Kirk knelt beside Spock and gently turned him over.

He cursed softly.

This was Spock, Spock as he had known him. In only a few minutes he had traveled from youth to maturity. In a few more minutes he would progress to age, thence to . . . death. He moaned, as the pain of the world to which he was chained penetrated even his exhaustion and deep unconsciousness. The sound lanced through Jim Kirk.

The sun was rising so fast he could feel its progress. The rays grew hotter as their angle changed, and the shadows shortened. The planet's rotation was increasing as the world tore itself apart.

Jim looked up at the sky. Even the stars had faded in the dawn. It was too bright even to search for the reflected light of the single ship that remained in orbit around Genesis—if it had not already fled the unstable star system.

He glanced around, found Kruge's phaser, and scooped it up. Then he slid one arm beneath Spock's limp body, heaved him onto his shoulder, and pushed himself to his feet. He opened his communicator, muffled the pickup by rubbing his thumbnail back and forth across it, did his best to copy Kruge's low, harsh voice, and repeated the last words Kruge had transmitted.

Then he waited. His legs were trembling with fatigue. He raised the communicator to try once more—

And felt the gentle tingle of a transporter beam forming around him. It dematerialized his body, and Spock's, and carried them away.

Saavik materialized aboard a Klingon fighter. The others appeared around her. A single officer of the ship observed their arrival.

Saavik measured the distance to his weapon with her gaze. She glanced sidelong at Captain Sulu. He stood in a completely relaxed attitude of appraisal. He was ready. If two at once—

The officer gestured with his phaser. It was set to fire in a wide fan. It was clear that if anyone moved suspiciously, the officer would stun them all simultaneously and dispose of them at his leisure.

Doctor McCoy suddenly cried out in pain and fell to his knees. Chekov and Scott quickly moved to help him. Saavik and Sulu remained where they were, but they both realized they were at too great a disadvantage. As Sulu turned away to help the others with McCoy, he muttered, "I wonder what O-sensei would have said about phasers?"

Saavik held back from touching McCoy again. When he brushed against her, back on Genesis, it was not the doctor she sensed, but Mister Spock. McCoy carried in him the unique pattern of her teacher, trapped and blind and weakening. The experience left Saavik thoroughly shaken.

Nevertheless, it explained a great deal. And it opened so many possibilities . . . possibilities which would be closed again if they all remained prisoners, and above all if Genesis destroyed itself before those remaining on its surface could be rescued.

Composed once more, Saavik mentally ran through the forms of address in the high tongue of the Klingon Empire. She was unfamiliar with the lower dialects she had heard the other crew members speak, but no matter. It would surely be better to speak to the Klingon officer in a form too high than in one too low. If she could speak to him without offending him, she might have some chance of persuading him to rescue those left behind. She might even be able to persuade him to surrender, for the high tongue was a very persuasive language.

Whatever she did, she had only a little time. The ship lay oriented so its forward port faced Genesis directly. The tectonic activity had become so violent that even from this distance she could see the great rifts in the planet's crust and the glowing fires of its interior. Its orbit around its sun was decaying rapidly; the star's blue-white disk grew larger as Saavik watched. Before the planet destroyed itself, its surface conditions would be lethal.

"Worthy opponent," she said, hoping that her accent was not too atrocious, "we find ourselves in a delicately balanced position."

He glanced at her sharply and frowned. His hand tightened on the grip of his phaser.

"You are one," Saavik said, "and we are five." She neglected to point out that Doctor McCoy was in no state to join in any opposition. "Furthermore, this entire star system will soon degenerate into a plasma of subelementary particles. If we do not rescue our respective shipmates and flee, we will all perish."

"Stop!"

She stopped. The tone of his voice gave her little choice.

"Why do you speak to me in this manner?" he said. He spoke quite acceptable Standard.

"I did not know you spoke our language," she said.

"Of course I speak your barbarian pidgin—do you think me so ignorant of my enemies? But you speak to me in Kumburan, and I am Rumaiy. Could it be that you have not been taught the difference?"

"It could be," Saavik admitted. "I did not intend offense."

"Could it be that you believe the slanderous cant put about, that Kumburanya are in the ascendancy over Rumaiym?"

"I confess to an unforgivable ignorance of the subject," Saavik said, not altogether truthfully. She had been told at the Academy that the language she was studying was the only significant one in the Klingon Empire. That did not

288 Vonda N. McIntyre

seem quite the appropriate response just now. "In the Federation we employ a single language in public, so we may all communicate."

"Reductionists!" he said with contempt. "Obliterators of diversity!" He muttered something unpleasant in a language Saavik did not know, and then he started to say something which she feared would be a lengthy tirade against the social or political group that opposed his own.

"But I am not ignorant about the world below us," Saavik said quickly, taking the risk of incurring his anger by interrupting him. "And it is close to destroying itself. Look at it! You cannot pretend the signs do not exist! We must cooperate to survive!"

"I have my orders."

"Orders from a commander unaware of the dangers on the surface, or beneath it—a commander who may even now be dead? If you value diversity . . . my worthy opponent, this system will soon lose its diversity completely. In a matter of hours it will consist of nothing but a homogeneous mass of highly entropic protomatter."

The officer said nothing, but gazed at Saavik thoughtfully.

The communicator erupted in a muffled burst of static. Saavik cursed silently, for it broke his consideration. She would have to start persuading him all over again—if she got the chance. No doubt this was his commander with new orders, orders that could not be of any benefit to Saavik and her companions.

When she heard the voice she started. She glanced at Captain Sulu and knew her suspicion was correct, because he was forcing himself not to react, not to burst out in surprised and relieved laughter. They both looked surreptitiously up at the command seat.

The officer hesitated before replying to the order. Saavik dug her nails into her palms.

The officer touched controls.

Then they all waited.

The last thing Jim Kirk saw on the surface of Genesis was the body of his son, drifted over with scarlet leaves and outlined by the fires of the world that had meant so much to him.

That world faded like a dream.

A transporter chamber solidified into reality around Jim Kirk. He blew his breath out in a sharp reaction of relief, for if he had been under suspicion he might have found his and Spock's atoms spread all over space by the transporter beam.

Dredging from the depths of his mind the layout of a Klingon fighter, he settled Spock's body more firmly on his shoulder and headed for the control room. He saw no one as he strode through the corridors, and he could not help but think, with some trepidation, that this was precisely the sort of emptiness the boarding party had confronted on the *Enterprise*. He drew the phaser. It fit his hand strangely, having been designed for different joints and different proportions.

Doors opened for him. He stepped into the control room.

Kruge's second in command revealed no surprise when Kirk entered. Like Kirk, he held a phaser. Unlike Kirk, he was alone. Even if he fired now, he would fall to Kirk's phaser, and the prisoners behind him would become his captors.

"Where is Commander Kruge?" he asked. He spoke as if the question were his final duty. Kirk knew, then, that his masquerade had not fooled the officer for a moment.

"Gone," Kirk said. "Dead. Engulfed by Genesis."

Defeated and resigned, the officer spread his hands. Kirk nodded once, sharply.

Saavik vaulted from the work-pit and relieved Maltz of his phaser. Chekov helped McCoy to his feet. The strain in the doctor's face, the strain of having been removed again from proximity to Spock, began to ease.

"How many more?" Kirk said.

"Just him, sir!" Scott said.

Kirk lowered Spock to the deck. "Bones, help Spock! Everyone else find a station."

Saavik put Maltz's phaser in her belt, and waited. Slowly, reluctantly, he drew his dagger and surrendered it to her.

"You!" Kirk said to him. "Help us, or die!"

"I do not deserve to live!"

"Fine—I'll kill you later! Let's get out of here!"

He sprinted to a place on the bridge, leaving Kruge's second confused and defeated. Everyone else had already taken a spot. Kirk trusted that they had all spent their time here trying to figure out which instrument performed which function.

Beyond the viewpoint, the Genesis sun contracted and brightened. It was a few minutes, no more, from nova. The instability of the planet affected its orbit in an accelerating manner. As the path decayed, the world spiraled toward the sun, drawing the ship along with it.

Kirk glanced at the beautiful and unfamiliar alien script, of which he could not read a word.

"Anybody here read Klingon?" he said.

No one answered, though Saavik glanced at him sharply, then looked away as if she were embarrassed.

Just like Spock, Kirk thought. She considers it a personal failing if she can't do absolutely everything.

"Well, take your best shot," Kirk said to his friends.

"If you can bypass into this module—" Chekov said to Scott.

Scott made a sound of disgust. "Fine, but where's the damn antimatter inducer?"

"This?" Chekov replied. "No, this!"

"This," Scott said, "or nothing." He touched alien controls, took a deep breath, and moved another control to its farthest extent.

The ship whined. Everyone flinched as the sound wavered, then relaxed as it steadied and strengthened.

Sulu occupied a station as if it were built for him.

"If I read this right, sir, we have full power."

Kirk did not doubt that the young commander read it right.

"Go, Sulu!"

The ship arced around, accelerated out of orbit, and hurtled at warp speed from the deteriorating system.

There was no conversation, there were no orders, there was simply a consensus between people who had known each other long and well. At what he judged to be a safe distance, Sulu pulled the fighter back from warp speed. If navigating the *Enterprise* was like driving a team of proud and immensely powerful draft horses, handling the Klingon ship was like being perched on the back of a skittish two-year-old colt during its first race. Sulu oriented it so the viewport faced the system they had just fled.

The planet fell toward its sun, which burned with an intense blue-white light. Stellar flares burst from the incandescent surface, reaching out to capture anything within their grasp.

The only thing within their grasp was the Genesis world. With shocking suddenness, the sun engulfed it.

The Genesis world was gone.

"Good-bye, David," Jim Kirk whispered.

The disk of the star expanded, exploding to millions of times its previous volume until it was nothing but a tenuous, vaguely luminescent, spiral cloud of plasma.

"It will form another world," Saavik said.

Kirk glanced at her sharply.

"The protomatter will condense to a plasma of normal matter," she said. "The plasma will cool. It will condense to dust, thence to a star and a family of planets. This time, lacking the Genesis wave, it will be stable. A surface will harden, oceans will form, the sun's radiation will induce chemical reactions. Life will begin. In time . . . it may evolve as David and his friends intended."

"In millions of years," Kirk said.

"No, Admiral," she said. "In billions of years."

"I'm glad you find some comfort in the long view, Lieutenant," Kirk said.

Sulu spoke, breaking the uneasy tension between Kirk and Saavik. "We're clear and free to navigate," he said.

"Best speed to Vulcan, Captain." Kirk fell gratefully back into the role he knew best. "Mister Chekov, take the prisoner below."

"Aye, sir."

"Wait!" Kruge's second in command drew back from him and turned angrily on Kirk. "You said you would kill me."

"I lied," Kirk said, and gestured for Chekov to get him off the bridge.

After a quick and dirty self-taught course on the finer details of navigating a Klingon fighting craft, Sulu laid in a course for Vulcan. Saavik puzzled out the communications system.

"Lieutenant Saavik of Federation science ship *Grissom,* calling Starfleet Communications. Come in, please."

"Communications to Grissom. *We've been trying to reach you folks for days! A freighter just picked up a lifeboat with a couple of survivors from a merchant vessel—they claim Klingons raided their ship!"*

"It is likely their claim is true," Saavik said. "We . . . experienced a similar encounter."

"Are you all right?"

"I regret that we are not. We have a serious and continuing emergency. We have incurred many fatalities. We need your cooperation."

"You have it, Lieutenant. What do you require?"

"A patch into your library's data-base, and a general message to all ships between Mutara sector and Vulcan."

"The patch is made." The Starfleet communications officer paused a moment, then said in a startled voice, *"Lieutenant, what communications protocol are you using? What the devil are you flying?"*

"Please stand by," Saavik said. She instructed the Starfleet data-base and waited for the information she needed before she replied to the question. She assumed her answer would cause consternation at the very least. At worst it would result in so much suspicion that the data link would immediately be broken, and hunters would be sent out for their heads.

A new voice broke into the channel. *"Cut that damned data link! Lieutenant Saavik! This is Starfleet Commander Morrow. What the hell is going on out there? Let me speak with Esteban!"*

"I am sorry, sir," she said. "That is impossible."

He cursed softly. *"I want some explanations! Have you seen the* Enterprise?"

"The *Enterprise* is not within our range, sir," she said. She did not know how to react to her new-found ability to dissemble nearly as well as a human being.

"What is the message you want us to relay?" Morrow said.

" 'Klingon fighter on course to Vulcan—' " Saavik heard exclamations of astonishment. She continued. " 'This ship is not an adversary. It is held by a contingent of Federation personnel. It is running with shields down and weapons disabled. Essential that we reach Vulcan. Delay will result in further casualties. *This ship is not an adversary.*' "

"A Klingon fighter! Lieutenant, I ask again, Where is Grissom? *What in blazes is going on out there?"*

"Saavik out." She shut down the channel.

"Good work, Lieutenant," Kirk said. He had known perfectly well that if he or anyone else from the *Enterprise* contacted Starfleet they would have been ordered to return immediately to Earth, to surrender. They were without doubt already under arrest, albeit in absentia.

Saavik could think of no suitable way to respond to a compliment for dishonesty. Instead, she transferred the Starfleet data to Captain Sulu's station. He gave her a smile of thanks.

She brought up the second information module on her own screen and began to read the dense Vulcan prose.

"Estimating Vulcan at point one niner," Sulu said.

Federation ships dogged their path, but none offered a direct challenge. Saavik left her ship's systems open to surveillance, but continued to let Starfleet believe that she was the only Federation member on board.

"Lieutenant," Kirk said, "transmit a message to Ambassador Sarek. Tell him we bring McCoy, and Spock. Tell him . . . Spock is alive. Ask him to prepare for the *katra* ritual."

"Aye, sir. But . . ." She was still trying to sort out the basic facts of what she had just finished reading. She could hardly presume to comprehend the philosophy. For centuries, the most intellectual citizens of Vulcan had dedicated their lives to its study without claiming to have reached the limits of its meaning.

"But what, Lieutenant?"

"I do not know if that is possible." Her lack of knowledge brought home to her, with redoubled force, her profound isolation from Vulcan society.

"What? What are you saying?"

"The *katra* ritual is meant to deposit Spock's consciousness in the Hall of Ancient Thought. Not back into his body."

"But we have Spock—alive! Why can't they return his *katra?*"

"The circumstances are most unusual. The procedure you suggest is called *fal-tor-pan,* the refusion. The conditions required to perform it have not occurred for millennia. There is considerable disagreement about whether it succeeded then, whether it could succeed at all, and indeed whether it should succeed. The elders may not choose even to attempt it."

"And if they don't? What will happen to Spock?"

Saavik wished she could avoid answering James Kirk as easily as she had avoided the questions of Starfleet Command.

"He will remain," she said finally, unwillingly, "always as he is . . ."

Kirk looked blankly at her, then turned and strode from the bridge.

Spock lay on one of the pallets in the small sick bay. McCoy stood beside him, his hand on the pulse-point at Spock's throat. The weak, thready beat pulsed far too slowly for a Vulcan. McCoy passed his scanner over Spock's body. The fragile, feeble signal gave him no confidence. Spock had stopped aging since they freed him from Genesis, but he had fallen into a deep unconsciousness. As the strength of his body ebbed, so did the strength of his spirit.

"Spock," McCoy said softly, desperately, "I've done everything I know to do. Help me! You stuck me with this, for gods' sake, teach me what to do with it!" He paused, without much hope, and received no answer from within or without. "I never thought I'd ever say this to you," he said, and thought, *You green-blooded* . . . but the old, familiar gibe rang hollow, and he could not bring himself to speak it aloud. "I've missed you. I couldn't . . . I couldn't bear to lose you again." He could feel his own strength failing him. In despair, he hid his face in his hands.

He felt the touch of another hand. Jim Kirk stood beside him, one hand on McCoy's shoulder, the other on Spock's. Their lives had been intertwined for so long. . . .

Jim's face was full of grief, and yet of determination. He gripped McCoy's shoulder hard, as if, like a Vulcan, he could transfer to him some of his strength.

Thirteen

Vulcan.

A desert world, limited in material resources, yet limitless in the intellectual and philosophical achievements of its inhabitants.

Saavik gazed upon it and wished what she had wished since the first time she learned about this planet. She wished she belonged here. She wished she had some right to this world, some claim to a place upon it and within its society. She had none of those things. She suspected she could never earn them, no matter her achievements.

"Home, eh, Lieutenant?"

"I beg your pardon, Admiral?" Saavik said.

Kirk nodded toward the viewport. "Vulcan."

"Vulcan is not my home, sir. I have never been here before."

"Oh," he said, taken aback. "I would have thought you would at least have visited it."

"I have never been invited to Vulcan, sir." She tried to speak as she had been taught, without emotion. She almost succeeded, but Kirk sensed something of her isolation.

"I think we'll find that we're welcome," he said gently.

"The planet Vulcan is in hailing distance, Admiral," Captain Sulu said.

"Thank you, Sulu. Saavik—send a message to Ambassador Sarek. Tell him we're coming in."

She obeyed. A ground station accepted her message. She waited for an answer.

"Rescue party—"

In reaction to the voice, everyone on the bridge swung toward the speaker. Sulu gave a cheer of surprise and delight that mirrored all their feelings. Hearing Uhura's voice, knowing she was well and free, was the first purely joyful thing that had happened to any of them in far too long.

"—this is Commander Uhura. Permission is granted to land on the plain at the foot of Mount Seleya. Ambassador Sarek is ready." She paused. Her voice close to breaking, she said, *"Welcome. Oh, welcome back."*

The fighter shivered as its wings spread into flying configuration. Sulu felt the energy of the ship glide into his hands and arms and suffuse his body with a powerful glow. He had never flown anything like this ship before. He had developed a considerable and more than grudging respect for the engineering abilities of the opponents of the Federation.

He wondered what would happen to the ship. No doubt Starfleet would seize it and send it back to Earth to be dismembered and analyzed. The idea pained him greatly.

He realized that this was quite probably the last time he would ever fly any ship, of any sort.

"Commander Sulu," Kirk said, "you're on manual."

He nodded. "It's been a while, sir." He had not landed a ship of this size without gravity propulsion since his student days. And, of course, he had never landed a craft of this design. "Here we go. Retrothrusters!"

The ship replied, responding like a dream. The dust of the plain at the foot of Mount Seleya billowed up around it as it settled to the ground.

The ramp hissed out and lowered itself to the ground. Spock's friends carried his litter out into the scarlet dusk of Vulcan.

At the foot of the ramp, Kirk stopped short and looked out amazed. The plain led to the temple. To either side of the long steep path, Vulcans stood watching and waiting, curious and silent. Here and there a torch flared against the dim light.

"My gods . . ." Kirk whispered.

"Much is at stake," Saavik said.

Kirk knew little of the Vulcan philosophy of what he was about to ask, and he cared less. All he wanted to hear was an acquiescence to his demand.

The light faded to the state of dimness where everything took on an eerie cast. More torches flared. Kirk heard running footsteps before he could tell where they came from.

Uhura appeared before him. Jim embraced her with his free arm. Uhura's eyes were bright with tears.

"Sarek is waiting," she said. "Above—"

She slipped in between Kirk and Sulu and helped carry the stretcher up the long path to the crest of the hill, where the temple loomed dark and mysterious.

Strange music teased the limits of Kirk's hearing. As he trudged up the slope the music grew only a little louder. It and the flaring of the torches were the only sounds. The enormous crowd of people watched somberly and in utter silence.

Kirk's legs began to ache. He had fought off his exhaustion for so long that he could not even remember when last he had slept. He kept going.

A young child let go her father's hand. She walked with great dignity to Spock's side, and followed for a few paces. She looked down into his face, saluted him, and whispered, "Live long and prosper, Spock." Then she slipped away and vanished into the crowd again.

Sarek waited on the steps of the temple, accompanied by several dignitaries and by six members of the priesthood. The tall, stately women watched with utter impassivity.

Finally Sarek strode forward to meet them. Kirk stopped, no longer sure what he should do.

The music faded so gradually that he was uncertain of the transition between sound and silence.

Sarek gazed at Spock. He reached down and placed his long, graceful hands against the sides of Spock's face. Kirk wanted nothing more than to grab him and shake him and make him explain what would happen now. He glanced sidelong at McCoy, who had reached the raw edge of his strength.

Sarek said nothing. He took one pace backward and nodded to the members of the priesthood. They moved between Kirk and his friends so easily, so gently, and with such assurance that they hardly seemed to be displacing them. The women took Spock in their hands and carried him away. Sarek followed.

Kirk watched, astonished. The Vulcans carried Spock easily, but their hands were not underneath his body.

They were on top of it.

Kirk hurried after them.

He passed between massive stone pillars and stopped at the edge of a circular, slightly dished platform. An altar rose at its far side. T'Lar, the leader of the Vulcan priesthood, waited in stately silence as her subordinates brought Spock to her. They began a low chant that penetrated to the bones.

Sarek paused and faced Kirk.

"This is where you must wait."

Unwillingly, Kirk obeyed. The music began again. Sarek faced the altar as his son's body sank gently to the age-smoothed granite and lay motionless as stone. The music and the chant ceased simultaneously.

"Sarek," T'Lar said. Her voice, barely a whisper, carried to them sharp and clear. "Sarek, child of Skon, child of Solkar. The body of your child breathes still. What is your wish?"

"I ask *fa-tor-pan*," Sarek said. "The refusion."

"What you seek has not been done since ages past. It has succeeded only in legend. Your request is not logical."

"Forgive me, T'Lar," Sarek said. He sounded very tired, and Kirk realized this must be the most difficult thing he had said in a hundred twenty years. "My logic falters . . . where my son is concerned."

T'Lar looked beyond Sarek to Kirk and his friends. She looked Kirk straight in the eye. Her gaze, as sharp as a weapon, touched him, then granted him mercy. She turned her attention to McCoy.

"Who is the keeper of the *katra?*" The question, clearly, lay in ritual; she knew the answer to what she asked.

Sarek nodded at McCoy. McCoy stared straight ahead, fixed by the power of T'Lar's eyes.

"Bones—" Kirk said urgently under his breath.

McCoy finally replied. "I am," he said hesitantly. "McCoy . . . Leonard H." He took a long breath of the rarefied air of Vulcan. "Son of David and Eleanora . . ."

"McCoy, son of David, son of Eleanora . . ."

McCoy shivered.

"Since thou art human, and without knowledge of our philosophy, we cannot expect thee to understand fully what Sarek has requested. The circumstances are extraordinary. Spock's body lives. With thine approval, we will use all our powers to return to his body that which thou dost possess: his essence. But, McCoy . . ."

T'Lar let the silence surround them and press down against them. Kirk could see the faint sheen of sweat on McCoy's forehead.

"You must now be warned," T'Lar said, speaking with complete formality. "The danger to you is as grave as the danger to Spock."

Now Kirk shivered, and tried to tell himself it was only the rapid cooling of a desert at night.

"You must make the choice." T'Lar waited for McCoy's reply. Her dispassionate expression offered neither encouragement nor warning.

McCoy, in his turn, let the silence stretch out.

"I choose the danger," he said. Under his breath, to Kirk, he muttered, "Helluva time to ask."

Kirk repressed a smile and fought down a laugh, knowing it to be a laugh of apprehension. He and McCoy both knew the choice to be between madness and the risk of death.

"Bring him forward!" T'Lar said.

Sarek led McCoy across the long empty platform and stopped before the altar. Kirk knew he could do nothing, yet he hated letting McCoy go alone, to face . . .

A bolt of heat lightning shattered the silence.

McCoy let Sarek draw him forward to the altar. Abruptly he stood all alone.

Spock lay before him, and T'Lar stood above them both. McCoy was aware of music, a rhythmic chant, and the thin sharp sighing of the wind. The powerful voice of the Vulcan leader echoed around him. "All that can be done, shall be done, though it take full turn of the Vulcan sun."

T'Lar stroked her fingers along his temple. Her touch was like fire, and he gasped. An alien consciousness stirred deep within his mind. Terror-stricken, he struggled against it.

The voice he heard was wordless and silent, yet so loud he feared it would strike him deaf. He could not see, and he feared he had been blinded as well.

"Yes! Strive, fight! Employ the power of thine alien emotions! Wrest back thy life!"

Thunder pounded at him, and he screamed.

Built high on the slopes of Mount Seleya, the retreat of the adepts of the discipline of ancient thought had grown and changed over many generations. Its hallways and galleries cut deep into bedrock. It was said that they looped back upon themselves and never reached an end; it was said that one could wander through them for a lifetime and never walk the same path twice.

Amanda Grayson, student and adept of the discipline, citizen of Earth, knew of no one who claimed complete familiarity with the maze. Most of the deepest caverns had long fallen into disuse. Even the most ascetic of Vulcans preferred open spaces, open air, and the heat of the huge red sun.

The retreat overlooked the plain at the foot of Seleya. Amanda stepped out onto her balcony, into darkness. The face of the retreat stretched away to either side, a long stream of carven rock. Its organic curves and graceful arcs flowed easily and imperceptibly into balconies, pathways, entrances, windows.

Amanda put her hands on the smooth surface of the parapet. The stone held the heat of the day, though the air had already grown chilly.

Long stretches of time often passed during which the plain far below remained deserted. In all the years Amanda had studied the discipline, she had never seen more than a few people at a time approach the temple. Citizens who had reached the death of the body were brought to Mount Seleya by close family members, perhaps by comrades with whom they had formed intellectual ties.

The student-adepts then helped the citizen sever the bond between body and mind, between substance and soul. After that, the body could go to dust and ashes, but the presence retired to the Hall of Ancient Thought. Always before, the student-adepts carried out the procedure in private, in an atmosphere of calm.

All that was changed. An enormous, silent, curious crowd had gathered on the plain. Their torches cast an eerie glow over the land, the courtyard, the temple. The light was far too dim for Amanda to see the processional, but she knew every detail of the ceremony. She followed it, in her mind, as if she could affect it with her imagination and carry it to the conclusion she sought. And perhaps she could. She dared not try to reach out to her son with her thoughts, not now, not yet, but her heart was with him.

T'Mei knocked softly on the door, entered, and paused at the balcony's doorway. The young Vulcan was still many years away from adding "adept" to her title of student, which Amanda had done not too long before. Adepts of the discipline never abandoned the appellation, "student." They preferred always to be reminded that the universe still held things they did not know. T'Lar, the most learned of them all, had recently and without comment ceased to use the title "adept." She now called herself merely student.

"Amanda?"

"Yes, child."

"Do you need anything?"

"No, my dear," Amanda said. "I don't need anything, except to have my wishes answered."

"I cannot do that," T'Mei said.

Amanda smiled. "I know it. Come stand by me."

T'Mei joined Amanda on the balcony. She moved so gracefully, with such self-possession, that she made hardly a sound. Her dark gold hair fell free past her waist.

"One of your wishes is to be in the temple," T'Mei said.

"Yes. I never thought I'd live to see the time when my own son was a subject of the discipline. Certainly I never would have wished it! But now I *do* wish I could be there. Spock is balanced between refusion and oblivion—and I can't even help him!" She slapped the parapet with anger and frustration. From the time of her marriage to Sarek she had known that to adopt Vulcan manners completely would be her destruction. Exhibiting her emotions beyond all courtesy would have run counter to her own upbringing, but neither did she try to smother or deny her feelings. At the beginning of her training, this all-too-human characteristic counted against her, but she proved herself worthy nonetheless.

Once in a while she appreciated, and even envied, the equanimity of Vulcans. For Amanda, the days since Spock's death had been an unending succession of powerful emotions: grief when the news first came, and hope of saving his presence, then a desperate anguish when it seemed that even Spock's *katra* had been lost. And now she was faced with the powerful, incredible possibility that her son still might live.

But it hasn't been easy for Sarek, either, Amanda thought. *Equanimity or no, he's felt these past days deeply.*

T'Mei rested her elbows on the parapet and gazed thoughtfully down at the temple.

"It would be most fascinating to attend the refusion," she said. "It is unlikely that this precise constellation of circumstances will recur in our lifetimes."

"Or in this millennium," Amanda said. "But I want to be down there for personal reasons—not historical ones."

"Your position is ironic," T'Mei said. "A student-adept, yet a relative of the subject, when the subject is unique."

"Ironic's hardly the word for it," Amanda said. No student-adept could ever participate in, or even observe, the transfer of a close relative. The *katra* was fragile and easily lost. To free it from the bearer and place it in the Hall of Ancient Thought, the student-adepts formed delicate, temporary psychic ties around it, and dissolved them again on completing the passage. If mental connections already existed between a subject and an adept, as they did when the two belonged to the same family, the resonances created an interference that invariably proved disastrous.

How the interference might affect the refusion, no one even attempted to speculate.

When James Kirk's message arrived, it had a galvanic effect on the inhabitants of the retreat. Many questions had to be answered instantly, questions that for generations had been discussed, analyzed, and debated without any final resolution. Amanda would have had no time to prepare her case, even had she wished to argue against her exclusion from the ritual—which she did not. She knew from the beginning that she could not be a member of the group that assisted her son. She understood the logic of avoiding such a completely unnecessary risk. But her intellectual acceptance of matters did absolutely nothing to diminish her emotional desire, her need, to be in the temple, to try to help.

"It is unfortunate that you must forgo participating in this unique experience," T'Mei said.

"I don't give a hang for the uniqueness of the experience!" Amanda said angrily. She had to switch to Standard to get her point across. Vulcan was far too refined for what she had to say. "Dammit! Right this minute I wish I'd never studied the discipline!"

"Amanda," T'Mei said, perplexed, "I do not understand."

"If I weren't a student-adept, I wouldn't endanger Spock just by being near him! At least I could be down there! At least Sarek and I could be together tonight!"

She turned away from T'Mei and stared down at the bright sparks of the torches. She was furious at her helplessness at the injustice of the universe, too furious even to cry.

T'mei stood beside her in silence, unable to comprehend her hope, her grief, her anger, or her love.

Jim Kirk was exhausted. He had spent the long cold Vulcan night knowing he could do nothing but wait, knowing that it would make sense . . . that it would be logical . . . to rest. But he was too tired to sleep, too keyed up. It seemed that this night he might lose all the people who meant the most to him. He had lost David already, and he had not even been permitted to contact Carol and tell her what had happened. Or, rather, he had not been prevented, but it had been made clear to him that if he left the mountain and the temple before the end of the ritual, he would not be able to return. To the Vulcans, the stricture seemed completely logical. To Kirk, it seemed a cruel choice. In the end, he had stayed. He could not help his friends, but he could not leave them, either, not when they both ran such a tremendous risk.

Jim envied Scotty, sprawled against a stone pillar, gently snoring. Chekov sat with his knees pulled to his chest, his arms folded, his head down. Uhura lay on the stone with her cheek pillowed on her hand, as lithe as a cat, and, Jim thought, as alert, even in sleep. Saavik waited for the dawn, her legs crossed beneath her, her hands palm down and relaxed, her eyes open and unblinking. Sulu knelt motionless on the stone, sitting *seiza* with his eyes half closed.

Kirk strode from one pillar to the next and back again, trying to fight off the bone-deep chill. At night, what little moisture was in the Vulcan air condensed out as frost. Kirk's lungs ached and his throat was dry and raspy.

He made himself sit down; he pretended to rest. The stars in Vulcan's empty sky were marvelously bright and clear. The dawn-wind began to blow, cold and harsh, whipping up dust-devils from the desiccated land.

Within the space of a few breaths the stars faded and vanished, and the sky changed from black to a brilliant royal purple. The dawn-wind died abruptly. The scarlet disk of Epsilon Eridani burst above the horizon, casting impenetrable shadows through the temple and searing the desert as it had at every dawn for countless millennia.

A gong rang.

Kirk leaped to his feet.

T'Lar appeared first. She lay supine in a sedan chair carried by the dignitaries who had waited silently all night long. Kirk took a step toward her, but she neither stirred nor opened her eyes. The power she wielded had drained and exhausted her, leaving her wan and frail. The Vulcans bearing her toward the dawn passed Kirk without acknowledging his presence.

McCoy stepped wearily into the sunlight that pierced the shadows, behind the altar. Though Sarek supported him, the doctor was moving under his own power. The members of the priesthood, tall and serene in their long hooded cloaks, followed behind. The Vulcans remained completely impassive, showing neither exultation nor despair.

For gods' sakes, Jim cried in his mind, *what happened? What happened?*

At the end of the procession, a single figure, robed in stark white, moved past the altar. The hood was so deep, the robe so brilliantly white, that the thick scarlet light of dawn obscured the being's features rather than illuminating them.

Nearby, Saavik drew a quick breath—of recognition? Of distress? Jim Kirk could not tell.

He became aware of his shipmates, if that term had any meaning for them anymore. They clustered close around him, Sulu and Uhura on his right, Chekov and Scott on his left, the engineer stiff and sore and sleepy. Saavik stood a little apart from the rest.

As the procession crossed the platform, Sarek broke off from the group and brought McCoy to join his friends. Sulu moved forward to help support him.

"Leonard—" Jim said.

"It's all right. . . ." McCoy said. Weariness faded his voice to a whisper. "I'm all right, Jim."

Sulu drew McCoy's arm across his shoulders and supported most of his weight. McCoy managed a smile, a grip of his hand on Sulu's upper arm, as he accepted the aid gratefully.

The white-robed figure at the end of the procession walked past without a glance or hesitation. Jim still could not see beneath the hood, but he knew the stride, the carriage. Saavik started toward the figure, but Jim grabbed her arm. He could not stop her if she chose to break free, but she halted at his touch.

"What about . . . Spock?" Jim said to Sarek.

"I am not sure," Sarek said. "Only time will answer." He turned his head toward the robed figure, then back to Jim.

"Kirk. I thank you." Sarek's voice, if not his words, admitted that the night's work might have failed. "What you have done is—"

"What I have done, I had to do," Kirk said harshly. He thought he saw a flicker of sympathy, even of pity, in Sarek's eyes. He did not want pity.

"But at what cost? Your ship." The lines around his eyes deepened. "Your son. . . ."

Jim felt that if he acknowledged what Sarek was trying to say to him, his whole being would shatter with grief.

"If I hadn't tried, the cost would have been my soul."

Sarek nodded, accepting Jim's unwillingness to speak any further or any deeper. He turned and walked silently away. Vulcan's star hung just above the horizon, an enormous scarlet disk, silhouetting first the procession, then a tall and solitary figure. The wind whined mournfully and fluttered the edge of the white robe.

Jim shaded his eyes with his hands, squinting into the dawn for one last glimpse of his old friend.

Live long, he thought. Live long and prosper.

And the figure slowly turned.

One of the members of the procession heard or sensed his motion and reached back, but Sarek stayed her hand. The sun shone incandescently through the fabric of the white hood, from behind, casting the face into deep shadow.

He hesitated, then walked slowly toward Jim Kirk and his friends.

He stopped, reached up, drew the hood back from his face, and let it fall to his shoulders.

The pain had left Spock's face, the pain, and the horrible emptiness. His deep gaze questioned Jim gently and wordlessly. An intent intelligence, impatient with uncertainty, lit his eyes.

He glanced from Jim to each of his other shipmates in turn: Sulu, Uhura, McCoy, Chekov, Scott; and finally Saavik. It seemed to Jim that he reached the brink of recognition with each of them, but could not quite cross the boundary.

Spock returned his gaze to Jim Kirk. The hot wind of Vulcan wailed over the desert with a keening cry.

"I know you . . ." His voice rasped across the words. "Do I not?"

"Yes," Kirk said. "And I, you."

"My father says you have been my friend. You came back for me."

"You would have done the same for me," Kirk said, willing Spock to remember something from *before,* something that had happened before they brought him home.

"Why would you do this?" Spock asked.

"Because—" Kirk fumbled for words that would form even a tenuous connection between past and present. "Because the needs of the one outweighed the needs of the many."

Spock stared down at him, still without real recognition. He turned away again and took a few uncertain steps toward his father, toward the other Vulcans. Kirk reached out, but he knew he had been right when earlier he prevented Saavik from stopping him. They might provide a key, but none could force Spock to remember.

What could I have said? he wondered. *What was the right thing?*

He let his hands fall.

A few paces away, Spock paused. He looked up into the deep sky.

"I have been . . ." he said.

At his strained and tortured voice, Jim moved instinctively toward him.

". . . and always shall be . . . your friend. . . ."

"Yes," Jim whispered. "Yes, Spock."

Spock half turned. "The ship," he said. "Out of danger . . . ?"

"You saved the ship, Spock. You saved us all! Don't you remember?"

Spock said nothing for a moment. He cocked his head, as if listening to some faraway inner voice. He arched his eyebrow and slowly faced Jim Kirk.

"Jim," he said softly. "Your name is Jim."

"Yes!" Jim's voice broke, and he caught his breath.

Spock nodded once, briefly, as if acknowledging to himself that he had found the proper path. He glanced at McCoy, and then at the others.

Suddenly all his old shipmates clustered around him, laughing and crying at the same time. None of them knew for certain an instant of what the future would bring, but each knew that for now, for this moment, everything was all right.

The Voyage Home

Home is the place where, when you have to go there,
They have to take you in

Prologue

The traveler sang.

Amid its complexities and its delicate, immensely long memories, it sang. In the complete cold of deep space, the song began at one extremity, spun in circles of superconducting power and speed, and evolved. It culminated in the traveler's heart, after a time counted not in micromeasures, but on the galactic scale of the formation of planets.

The traveler sent each finished song into the vacuum. In return it received new songs from other beings. Thus it wove a network of communication across the galaxy. Oblivious to the distances, it connected many species of sentient creatures one with the other.

From time to time it discovered a newly evolved intelligence to add to its delicate fabric. On those rare occasions, it rejoiced.

On much rarer occasions, it grieved.

The traveler followed a long curve, spiraling inward from the perimeter of the galaxy to the center, then spiraling outward again. It traveled through eons, embroidering its course with the music of intelligences.

The touch of the songs gave it a joy that held its single vulnerability. It was immune to the radiation of exploding stars. It could protect itself against any damage by mere matter. But if any of its threads of communication parted, grief and agony possessed it.

When the song of one of its entities changed from delight and discovery to distress and confusion, pain and fear, the traveler listened, it decided, and it gathered up the tremendous energy it needed to change its course.

Singing reassurance, the traveler turned toward the other side of the galaxy, toward a small blue planet circling an ordinary yellow sun.

Admiral James T. Kirk paced back and forth in a vaulted stone chamber, ignoring the spectacular, sere view spanning one entire wall. Vulcan's red sun blazed outside, but the retreat of the students—adepts of the discipline of ancient thought—remained cool, shielded by the mountain from which it was carved.

"Relax, Jim," Leonard McCoy said. "You won't get to see T'Lar any faster by running in place. You're making me tired."

"I don't care if I see T'Lar or not," Jim said. "But they've had Spock practically incommunicado for three days. I want to be sure he's all right before we leave."

"Whether he is or not, there isn't much you can do about it now." The doctor managed a wan smile. "Or me, either, I suppose."

"No," Jim said gently. "You did your part. You saved his life." Jim worried about McCoy almost as much as he worried about Spock. The doctor's exhaustion troubled him. Even a quick flash of McCoy's usual wit, a snap of irony, would ease Jim's concern.

"Are we leaving?" McCoy asked. "You've had word from Starfleet?"

"No. But we've got to return to Earth. At least, I do. I have to answer for my actions. For disobeying orders. For losing the *Enterprise.*"

"You won't be alone," McCoy said.

"I don't want anybody to try to be a hero for my sake!" Jim said. "I bear the responsibility—"

"Who's talking about taking responsibility?" McCoy said. "I'm talking about getting off Vulcan. Jim, this damned gravity is squashing me. If I have to live in it much longer, I'll turn into a puddle of protoplasm."

Jim laughed. "That's more like it, Bones."

"Kirk. McCoy."

A young Vulcan stood in the doorway.

Jim stopped laughing. "Yes? Do you have news of Spock?"

"I am T'Mei. I will take you to T'Lar."

She turned, her long dark robe brushing softly against the stone floor. She wore the deep blue of a student of the discipline. Only once, many years ago, had Jim met any other Vulcan as fair as she, with blond hair and blue eyes and a golden-green cast to the skin.

"I'll just wait here and you can tell me all about T'Lar afterward," McCoy said.

T'Mei glanced back. "McCoy, it is you, not Kirk, that I am requested to guide."

"What does she want?"

"I am her student, not her interpreter."

"Come on, Bones," Jim said. "I'm sure T'Lar will satisfy your curiosity."

"I've had about as much curiosity as I can take right now, thanks just the same." But he pushed himself from his chair. Grumbling under his breath, he followed T'Mei down the long corridor. Jim accompanied them.

The Vulcan student ushered them to a chamber, then silently departed. Jim and McCoy entered the presence of the discipline's high adept.

Though T'Lar had divested herself of the ceremonial garments of the rite of *fal-tor-pan,* neither the effect of her personality nor her power depended on the trappings of her rank. Even in a plain green robe, her white hair arranged severely, the elderly Vulcan emanated dignity and authority.

"We have examined Spock," she said without preliminaries. She spoke to McCoy. "The transfer of his *katra,* his spirit, is complete."

"Then he's all right," Jim said. "He's well again, he can—"

When she glanced at him, he fell silent. She returned her attention to McCoy.

"But you, McCoy, were not properly prepared to accept the transfer. I have determined that he retains certain elements of your psyche, and certain elements of his personality and his mind remain in your keeping—"

"What!" McCoy exclaimed.

"I will continue to facilitate the transfer between you, until it is complete." She rose. "Please come with me."

Beside Jim, McCoy stiffened.

"What are you saying?" Jim said. "That Bones has to go through *fal-tor-pan* again? How much do you think he can take?"

"This has nothing to do with you, Kirk," T'Lar said.

"Anything concerning my officers has something to do with me!"

"Why must you humans involve yourselves in matters you cannot affect?" T'Lar said. "I will create a simple mind-meld. In time, the process will permit Spock and McCoy to separate themselves."

"In time?" McCoy said. "How long is 'in time'?"

"We cannot know," T'Lar said. "The refusion of the *katra* with the physical body has not been attempted within historical memory, and even in legend the transfer proceeded from Vulcan to Vulcan."

"What if I prefer not to undergo another mind-meld?"

"You will cripple Spock."

"What about McCoy?" Jim said.

"I think it likely that the force of Spock's psychological energy will once again possess McCoy, as it did when he held Spock's *katra*."

McCoy grimaced. "I don't have much choice, do I?"

"No," T'Lar said. "You do not." She gestured toward a curtained entrance. "The facilitation room. Come."

McCoy hesitated. Jim moved to his side.

"Kirk," T'Lar said, "you must stay behind."

"But—"

"You cannot help. You can only hinder."

"What's to prevent me from following?"

"Your concern for the well-being of Spock and McCoy."

"It's all right, Jim," McCoy said. T'Lar led him into the facilitation room. They disappeared into the darkness beyond the curtain. Nothing but a drape of heavy fabric held him back.

Jim paced the anteroom, fuming.

McCoy followed T'Lar into the facilitation room. Spock waited, his expression dispassionate. He wore a long white Vulcan robe, so different from the uniform in which McCoy was used to seeing him. Otherwise he looked the same, black hair immaculately combed, short bangs cut straight across his forehead. His deep-set brown eyes revealed nothing.

"Spock?"

McCoy had known the Vulcan, who was also half-human, for a long time. But Spock neither spoke to him nor acknowledged his existence. He did not even quirk one upswept eyebrow. His human side seemed more deeply suppressed than it had for many years.

T'Lar beckoned to McCoy. Neither power nor accomplishment had endowed her with patience. Spock lay down on a long slab of granite. Its crystalline matrix sparkled in the dim light. McCoy paused beside an identical slab, glaring at it with antipathy.

"Haven't you people ever heard of featherbeds?" he said.

Neither T'Lar nor Spock responded. McCoy hitched himself onto his slab and lay on the hard stone.

T'Lar placed one hand at McCoy's temple and the other at Spock's. An intense connection entwined all three people. McCoy flinched and closed his eyes.

"Separate yourselves," T'Lar whispered hoarsely, "one from the other. Become whole again . . ."

Jim waited impatiently. He was used to being in control. He was used to acting. He was not used to cooling his heels and having his questions put off.

Intellectually he understood what T'Lar had told him. He, and they, and most of all Spock and McCoy, were involved in a unique occurrence. Only in legend had a dying Vulcan given up his *katra,* his spirit, yet lived to reclaim it. Spock's death and regeneration in the Genesis wave gave the Vulcans a challenge they had not faced within their history.

Both McCoy, who unknowingly accepted Spock's *katra,* and Spock, who must reintegrate his memories and his personality with his physical self, had been in extreme danger.

"Admiral Kirk?"

Jim started, rising to his feet.

"Admiral Cartwright!"

The new Commander of Starfleet entered the anteroom. Cartwright offered his hand. Jim shook it warily.

"What are you doing on Vulcan?" Jim said.

"I came to talk to you, of course. I want to know what happened straight from you, not from reports or gossip or even from Harry Morrow. You left him one hell of a mess to end his tenure."

"And to begin yours."

"It comes with the job. But I've got to know what happened, and you're going to have to tell the story to the Federation Council."

"I know."

"How soon can you leave Vulcan?"

"That I don't know."

"I don't mean this as a polite request. You've already disobeyed enough orders to hold you for the rest of your career."

"I didn't have any choice. I asked for Harry Morrow's help and he refused it. Sarek's request—"

"Sarek should have made his request through regular channels."

"There was no time! Leonard McCoy was going mad, and Spock would have died."

"I didn't come here to argue with you," Cartwright said. "You and your people have caused an enormous amount of trouble. I can't vaporize the charges against you. Much as I might like to deal with this within Starfleet, it's gone too far for that. The Federation Council demands your presence. So far, all anyone is talking about is an inquiry. If you come immediately, an explanation may suffice. If not, you'll face a criminal trial."

"On what charge?" Jim said, shocked.

"The murder of Commander Kruge, among other things."

"Murder! That's preposterous. I tried to get him off Genesis and he tried to pull me into a pit of molten lava! Kruge invaded Federation space, he destroyed a merchant ship, he instigated espionage, he destroyed the *Grissom* and everyone on board! He killed David Marcus—" Jim's voice faltered.

"I know." Cartwright's voice softened. "I know you're grieving. I'm very sorry. But you must return to Earth and tell your side of the story. If you refuse, the assumption will be that you've no answer to the Klingon Empire's claims."

"I can't leave Vulcan. Not yet."

"Why not? When *can* you leave?"

"Because McCoy—and Spock—are still in danger. I can't leave Vulcan until I know they're all right."

"It's hardly abandoning them to leave them in the hands of the Vulcans. They'll be in the care of the finest medical technologists in the Federation. What more do you think you can do?"

"For Spock, I don't know. But McCoy—it isn't medical technology he needs. He needs support. He needs a friend."

"Leonard McCoy has many friends," Cartwright said. "I'm sure he has one who can stay with him who isn't under indictment."

"I'll come to Earth as soon as I can," Jim said.

"Then I have to give you this." Cartwright drew out a folded paper and handed it to Jim.

"What is it?" It was thick, ragged-edged paper, heavy with a Federation seal. The Federation only used paper for the most formal of purposes.

"A copy of the inquiry order."

Jim broke the seal and scanned it. "I'm still not coming."

"You're disobeying a direct order, Admiral Kirk." Cartwright's brown eyes narrowed and his dark face flushed with anger.

"Yes," Jim said, equally angry. "And it's easier the second time."

"I've done all I can for you," said Starfleet Commander Cartwright.

His second's hesitation gave Jim Kirk one last chance to concede. Jim said nothing. Scowling, Cartwright turned and stalked from the anteroom.

Jim cursed under his breath. He shoved the order into his pocket and paced impatiently. In one more minute he was going to rip down that curtain—

The drape rustled. Haunted and drained, McCoy stood in the entryway.

"Bones?"

"It's over . . . for the moment."

"Haven't they completed the process?"

McCoy shrugged.

"Is something wrong?"

"Vulcans jump up and walk away after a mind-meld," the doctor said. "I shouldn't be any different, right?"

Jim smiled. "Right."

McCoy fainted.

McCoy slept. Jim sat at the foot of the bed, rubbing the bridge of his nose. McCoy suffered merely from exhaustion, the Vulcans said. The doctor would recover in time for the next facilitation session. When that might be, or how many more sessions might be required, they could not answer.

Jim rose, silently left McCoy's room, and returned to his own. He sat down at the communications terminal, made a request, and waited with both impatience and dread for a reply. Even the technology of the twenty-third century took a few moments to route a call from Vulcan to Earth.

The "please wait" pattern on the screen of the comm unit flicked out, replaced by the pattern of Carol Marcus's household computer concierge.

"Doctor Marcus cannot reply at this time," the concierge said. "Please leave identification and location so she may return your call."

Jim took a deep breath. "This is Jim Kirk again."

He had been trying to call Carol Marcus since the morning after his arrival on Vulcan. Every time, he had failed to reach her. By now she must know of the death of her son David. It both relieved and distressed Jim that he would not be the one to tell her. But he had to talk to her.

"It's extremely urgent that I speak with Carol," he said. "Please have her call me as soon as possible."

"She will receive your message." The pattern faded.

Jim rubbed his eyes with the heels of his hands. He had barely known the young man, yet David's death affected him as if a piece of his heart had been ripped away and burned to ashes. It would almost have been easier—

Easier! he thought. *No, nothing could make it easier. But if I'd known him, I'd have at least the comfort of memories of Carol's son. My son.*

Carol Marcus sat cross-legged on the observation deck of the courier *Zenith,* staring down at a glittering green planet.

"Doctor Marcus." The ship's computer voice glided easily over the intercom. "Doctor Marcus. Please prepare to beam down."

Carol rose reluctantly.

It would be so easy, she thought, *so easy just to stay on board and keep traveling from world to world and never have to talk to anyone, never risk getting close to anyone again, never have to tell anyone that a person they love has died . . .*

She left the observation platform and headed for the transporter room.

Carol Marcus felt it her duty to speak to the families of her friends and co-workers on the Genesis project. And so she found herself orbiting a world known familiarly as Delta, the homeworld of Zinaida Chitirih-Ra-Payjh and Jedda Adzhin-Dall, two mathematicians, two friends who had died.

The casket bearing Zinaida's body stood on the transporter platform. Jedda had died by phaser, and nothing at all remained of him.

Carol stepped onto the platform. She did not know what she would say to the people waiting below. She had not known what to say to the parents of Vance Madison or the families of the others. She only knew she had to control her own grief so she would not add it to the grief of others.

"Energize," she said.

The beam took her to the surface of Delta. A rosette of light surrounded her. A dazzling stained-glass window cast colors across the reception room's pale slate floor.

Two Deltans waited for her, a woman and a man, Verai Dva-Payjh and Kirim Dreii-Dall. *Partners* was the closest word in Standard to describe the relationship of these two people to Zinaida and Jedda. They had formed a professional and economic and sexual partnership that should have lasted for decades.

They approached her. Like most Deltans, they were supernaturally beautiful. Verai, heavyset and elegant, had mahogany skin, pale eyelashes, and fair eyebrows like the most delicate brush strokes of a Chinese painting. Unlike Deltan women, who grew no hair on their heads, Kirim had fine, rose-colored hair. He wore it long and free, spilling in great waves over his shoulders and down his back nearly to his knees. The red mark of mourning on the forehead of each did nothing to detract from their beauty.

Carol blushed. Human beings could not help their response to Deltans; nevertheless the powerful sexual reaction embarrassed her. Deltans never took advantage of humans, always holding themselves aloof. But Verai and Kirim approached her more closely than Zinaida or Jedda ever had. Verai offered Carol her hand. Carol stepped back in confusion.

"You have not been in contact with Earth," Verai said.

"No. Not since I left."

The stained-glass window cast patterns over them. Verai and Kirim grasped her hands. She had never been touched by a Deltan before. Both grief and comfort flowed into her.

"I'm sorry," she said. Tears sprang to her eyes. "Your partners—"

"We know," Verai said. "And we are grateful that you came to us. We will speak of them, and remember them. But we must speak of someone else as well."

Holding Carol's hands, Verai and Kirim told her of the death of her son.

Shocked speechless with grief and horror, Carol sank to the floor and stared at the window's light. The pattern crept across the floor with the motion of the sun. In the warmth of the hall she started to shiver.

"Come with us, Carol," Verai said. "We will grieve for our partners, and we will grieve for your son."

In a visitors' chamber of the habitation, Lieutenant Saavik of Starfleet also failed to reach Carol Marcus.

Perhaps, thought the young Vulcan, *Doctor Marcus will never speak to me or to anyone else who participated in the Genesis expedition. She must know of David's death by now. It is possible that she has no wish to be reminded of it by those who witnessed it.*

She rose from the terminal, left her room, and stepped onto a balcony that overlooked the plain at the foot of Mt. Seleya. After so many years and so much hope, she finally found herself on Vulcan, beneath its great scarlet sun. She hoped that the Vulcans would permit her, a half-Romulan, to remain long enough to walk in their world's deserts and explore its cities.

She returned to the cool shadows of the habitat. Loud footsteps approached. One of her human shipmates, no doubt; Vulcans moved more quietly.

"Fleet commander!" she said, surprised.

Blinking, the new commander of Starfleet brought his attention back from somewhere else. The tall, black-skinned officer carried a compact travel case. He looked both angry and in a hurry. Yet now he stopped.

"You are Lieutenant Saavik, are you not?"

"Yes, sir."

"Do you know where the transporter is? My ship's about to warp out of orbit."

"Certainly, sir. I will show you."

He followed her deeper into the maze of stone corridors.

"You handled yourself well on Genesis, Lieutenant," he said. "You won't be named in the indictment."

"The indictment, sir? Surely Admiral Kirk and his shipmates aren't to be punished for saving Spock's life!"

"I hope not. Despite everything, I hope not."

"I, too, am alive because of the admiral's actions. Had Admiral Morrow permitted him to depart for the Genesis world without delay, the science vessel *Grissom* and all hands might have been saved as well."

"It isn't your place to second-guess the Commander of Starfleet," Cartwright said. "The Genesis project was a disaster, but your part in it was fully admirable. That won't be forgotten, I promise you."

"I do not look for credit from these events," she said. "Too many people lost their lives. A survivor should not gain benefit." *Especially,* she thought, *a Starfleet officer who survived because of the death of a civilian.*

They reached the transporter room. Cartwright programmed in a set of coordinates and climbed onto the platform.

"Nobody will get much benefit out of Genesis," Cartwright said grimly. "But that isn't your concern. I'll trust you to comport yourself as well during your Vulcan assignment as you did on Genesis. Good-bye, Lieutenant. Energize."

"What Vulcan assignment?"

But the computer responded to his command; the transporter beam swept Cartwright away before he could hear her question, before he could reply.

Perhaps Cartwright simply meant her time on Vulcan until new orders arrived from Starfleet. But he had sounded like he meant something more.

Surely Admiral Kirk would know. Perhaps he would have a moment to explain.

She knocked at the entrance of the admiral's chamber.

"Come."

She pushed aside the curtain.

James Kirk stared disconsolately at the comm terminal's disconnect pattern. It occurred to Saavik that he, too, must have been attempting to contact Carol Marcus. He, too, must have failed.

She hesitated. The question of her assignment seemed trivial now. She saw the indictment order lying crumpled on the desk. At least she did not have to tell him that news.

"Yes, Lieutenant?" He glanced at her. His expression held the pain of loss and uncertainty, the kind of pain that could only be eased with knowledge.

"Sir," she said hesitantly. "May I speak with you?"

"Certainly, Lieutenant." He rose.

"It is about . . . about David."

He flinched. "Tell me."

She wanted to say, "I should have died in his place. I am a member of Starfleet, and he was a civilian, and I should have protected him. I could have protected him, had he not acted when he should have restrained himself."

But for all Saavik's uncertainty about human beings and their often incomprehensible emotions, she knew as surely as she knew anything that she could not help James Kirk accept his son's death by saying he should not have died.

"David died most bravely, sir," Saavik said. "He saved Spock. He saved us all . . . I thought you should know." She also wanted to say, "I loved your son. He taught me that I am capable of love. But that was not something a junior lieutenant could say to a flag officer of Starfleet, nor was it something someone trying to be a Vulcan should ever admit to anyone. She kept her silence."

James Kirk did not reply in words. His hazel eyes glistened. He gripped her shoulders, held tight for a moment, then dropped his hands.

Saavik slipped past the curtain and left him alone. She could do nothing more for his grief.

Commander Hikaru Sulu climbed into the Klingon fighting ship. The sharp, acrid smell of seared plastic and fused electronic circuits permeated the air. He entered the command chamber. He had managed to nurse the bird all the way to Vulcan, but it would never take off again without repairs. Maybe it would never take off again at all. He settled into the command chair, tied a universal translator to the computer, and requested a complete set of damage reports.

Salvaging the fighter is worth a try, he thought. *And if I succeed, I'll have a ship. A ship of my own.*

Amanda Grayson listened to Spock reading out loud from a fragile bound volume of ancient Vulcan poetry. She wanted to touch him, to reassure herself that he was alive.

He paused. "Reading out loud is very slow, Mother. And the words of this piece are archaic."

"Try to hear the beauty in them, my dear," she said. "No one on Vulcan writes poetry anymore. Those lines are a thousand years old."

"If no one writes poetry, why must I read it?"

"Because I didn't read it to you when you were a child. We have another chance, and I won't make the same mistake twice. I want you to be able to enjoy beauty and poetry and laughter."

He cocked his eyebrow, a heartbreakingly familiar gesture. Moment by moment he crept back toward himself. But Amanda wanted to take this second chance to help him release his other half, the half of himself that he had always held in check.

"Beauty and poetry and laughter are not logical," Spock said.

"I agree," she said. "They are not."

He frowned, puzzled. He read another stanza, stopped, and closed the book.

"I am tired, Mother," he said. "I will meditate. I will consider what you have said."

One

The traveler accelerated to a tremendous speed, but the galaxy spanned an enormous distance. The traveler perceived that its journey had lasted for only an instant. But in that instant—the mere time of a half-life of the minor isotope of the eighteenth element, the brief interval in which a small blue planet would revolve around its ordinary yellow sun three hundred times—the troubled music from that blue world ripped apart into incoherence. The songs faded, and finally they died. Now the traveler hurtled toward the silence, its own song a cry. As the stars sped past and it received no response, it gradually transmuted its music into a dirge.

The Romulans might come raiding out of the Neutral Zone at any time.

Captain Alexander stared at *Saratoga*'s viewscreen and into the silent Neutral Zone. Three months on yellow alert was bad for anyone's nerves. She was as jumpy as the rest of her crew, but she could not admit it.

It had been like this ever since the Genesis disaster. Diplomats, Starfleet, the Federation, the shadowy oligarchy of the Klingons, even the mysterious Romulan Empire reacted to Genesis by exciting themselves like electrons in a plasma of mutual suspicion.

Subspace communications brought each day's proceedings of the Genesis inquiry to every ship and starbase. Everyone had an opinion about Admiral James T. Kirk's actions, his motives, his ethics.

When the inquiry returned its findings, the Klingons might disagree with the conclusions. They might go to war. If that happened, Alexander must be prepared, for the Romulans, their allies, to join them. So far, though, the inquiry served the interests of the Klingons much more efficiently than open conflict.

Alexander could not understand why Kirk did not return to Earth to defend himself. It was as if he had surrendered without fighting, as if he did not care whether the inquiry condemned or vindicated him.

"Captain—"

"Yes, Lieutenant."

"I'm receiving—" Suddenly, with a curse, the *Saratoga*'s Deltan science officer snatched the earphone from his ear. Sgeulaiches, the communications officer, yelped in pain and pulled the transmission membrane from its vibratory sensors.

"Mister Ra-Dreii! What happened?"

"A transmission, Captain, of such power that it overcame the volume filters. A rather stimulating experience," he said with irony. He listened to the earphone gingerly.

318 Vonda N. McIntyre

"Source?"

"The Neutral Zone, Captain."

"The Romulans?"

"No. Nor the Klingons, unless they have completely altered their communications signature."

"Visual sensors."

"The energy density hinders localization," Sgeulaiches said.

Watchful excitement tingled along Alexander's spine.

"Volume filters back in service and intensified, Captain," Chitirih-Ra-Dreii said.

"Let's hear it," Alexander said.

The transmission's cacophony filled the bridge.

"The universal translator—" Chitirih-Ra-Dreii said. He abruptly cursed again, using an epithet far up the hierarchy of Deltan curses. Deltans did not even bother with minor curses. "Overloaded, Captain. Useless."

The gibberish bucked and broke over the speakers.

Alexander felt more excited than angry. This might make the months of patrol worthwhile. Every starship captain possessed the ambition to make a first contact: an encounter with something new, something unknown.

"I want to see our guest, Lieutenant Sgeulaiches," Alexander said. "And send out a universal greeting. Let them know we're here."

"Yes, Captain."

Alexander detected no change in the wailing noise, no indication that the transmission's source detected her transmission, no acknowledgment of the Saratoga's presence.

"Found it, Captain! Maximum magnification."

An object caught starlight and flung it out again. All the information the sensors could glean about the object—damned little, Alexander noted—appeared in a stat window in the corner of the viewscreen. Alexander whistled softly. Whatever the object was, it was big.

"Evidence of Romulan ships?"

"None, Captain."

Alexander frowned. "They should have seen that thing. They ought to be pursuing it. They ought to be accusing us of sending intruders into their territory. Where are they?"

The object approached.

"Helm—wait for it." This whole business reminded Alexander a little too strongly of the Kobayashi Maru test.

"Aye, Captain," the helm officer said. The Saratoga's impulse engines countered the ship's momentum.

"Overlay."

An information overlay dimmed the primary image on the viewscreen.

If the object remained on its current course, it would intersect the system of an average yellow star, Sol, the system of Alexander's homeworld, Earth.

"Cancel," she said stiffly. The overlay dissolved. The intruder was much closer now.

The surface of the long, cylindrical construction erupted here and there with antennae. The construction's metallic skin bore a brushed finish. Or . . . a shiny finish had been dulled by eons of space travel, touched by micrometeoroids or stroked by stellar winds perhaps once a year, once a century, till a uniform pattern of microscopic scratches created its velvety skin.

"What do you make of it?"

"It appears to be a probe, Captain," the science officer said. "From an intelligence unknown to us."

"Continue transmitting," Alexander said. "Universal peace and hello in all known languages. And get me Starfleet Command."

"Starfleet, Captain."

"Starfleet Command," Alexander said, "this is the *Starship Saratoga*, patrolling sector five, the Neutral Zone. We are tracking a probe of unknown origin on apparent trajectory to the Solar system. We have attempted first contact on all frequencies. We have received no intelligible response and no acknowledgment."

"Continue tracking, *Saratoga*. We will analyze transmissions and advise."

"Roger, Starfleet," Alexander said. "Relay transmissions."

The science officer relayed a copy of the probe's transmissions back to Starfleet. His sardonic smile as much as said, "Analyze away, and see what *you* make of it."

"*Saratoga* out," Alexander said.

"Range four hundred thousand kilometers and closing."

The ship reverberated with the probe's transmission. The bridge lights faded.

"Mister Ra-Dreii, what's causing that?"

"Captain, their call is being carried on an amplification wave of enormous power."

"Can you isolate the wave?"

"Negative. It's affecting all our systems—"

The dim half-intensity illumination flickered as the probe's cry plunged through the *Saratoga* and overwhelmed it.

"Red alert," Alexander said calmly. "Shields up. Helm, reduce closing speed."

"Captain, our impulse engine controls have been neutralized!"

"Emergency thrusters." This was going the *Kobayashi Maru* test one better. Or one worse.

"No response, Captain."

The probe plunged toward them. The volume of its transmission increased, as if the probe could grip the fabric of matter and space-time itself and force it to vibrate to its will. *Saratoga* quivered.

All power failed.

"Emergency lights!" Alexander shouted over the impossible scream of the probe.

In the feeble scarlet glow, the officers wrestled to win some reaction from deadened controls. The viewscreen wavered into a blurry half-intensity image.

"Damage report!" Alexander snapped.

"Captain, all systems are failing," Chitirih-Ra-Dreii said. "We are functioning on reserve power only."

The enormous bow of the probe plowed toward them. Its body stretched back endlessly.

"*Saratoga* is out of control," Alexander said. "Secure for collision."

The probe's immense length flashed past, just above the upper curve of *Saratoga*'s hull. It left them behind in a sudden silence and dimming scarlet light.

It headed toward Earth.

"They've finished us," Chitirih-Ra-Dreii whispered, his voice hoarse. "And we don't even know why, we don't even know what they want."

"Give me whatever you've got on the emergency channel," Alexander said. "Mister Ra-Dreii, prepare stasis."

The signal strength hovered at such a marginal level that Captain Alexander might drain the last of *Saratoga*'s reserves and never get through to Starfleet. But she had no choice.

"Starfleet Command, this is *Saratoga*," Alexander said. "Can you hear me? Come in, please. Starfleet Command, come in." She paused, hoping for a response but receiving none. "Any Federation ship, Mayday, Mayday. Please relay this message to Starfleet. Earth is in danger. Repeat—"

The air grew heavy with exhaled carbon dioxide. Chitirih-Ra-Dreii and Engineering struggled to restore the life-support systems, but failed. Alexander ordered the rest of her crew into stasis and repeated the message of danger till the signal strength fell to zero.

The Federation did not reply.

Sarek of Vulcan stepped from the transporter center into the cool, damp brightness of Earth. He could have beamed directly to Federation headquarters, but he preferred to make his way on foot. On any world where conditions permitted, he chose to walk in the open air and on the open ground. In this way he could make himself familiar with a new environment. This was something Amanda had taught him. He often wondered why Vulcans did not habitually do the same thing, for it was quite logical.

Sarek had expected never to return to diplomatic service after his retirement. He had never expected to visit Earth again. But now, two journeys in three months disarranged his contemplative existence. He had made his first voyage to accuse James Kirk. He made this voyage to defend him.

The planetary government of Vulcan had come perilously close to forbidding the second voyage. Sarek had to delve deep into his reserves of logic and persuasion to win their agreement. Many members of the government claimed no interest in James Kirk's fate; they offered Sarek the hypothesis that since Kirk had neutralized a series of events that he himself had begun, a balance had been reached. Kirk must face the consequences of his actions alone. If Vulcans acted, the balance would be destroyed.

Perhaps, Sarek thought, *the charge Representative T'Pring made is correct. Perhaps I have spent too much time on Earth. I have certainly, in the eyes of other Vulcans, spent too much time in the company of human beings, or at any rate in the company of one human being. Yet I cannot imagine following any other path for my life, and, at the end of our debate, even the flawlessly logical sword-edged blade of T'Pring's mind finally turned to my persuasion. She argued on my behalf.*

As he walked, he reaccustomed himself to Earth's low gravity and weather conditions. Fog, gathering beneath the catenaries of the Golden Gate Bridge, crept through the streets and flowed around the hills. Sarek drew his cloak around him, marring the fine pattern of condensation that collected on the heavy fabric.

Sarek arrived at Federation headquarters moments before he was scheduled to speak. In the foyer, Commander Christine Chapel hurried to meet him.

"Sarek, thank you for coming."

"I left Vulcan as soon as I was able after your message arrived. Do the findings of the inquiry still go against James Kirk and his shipmates?"

"It isn't going well for him. For any of them." She sounded worried. "He's made a lot of friends in his career. But a lot of enemies as well. There are people—outside the Federation, and in it too—who would like to see him brought down."

"But he saved Spock's life, and the life of Lieutenant Saavik," Sarek said. "Furthermore, he acted on my behalf and at my request. It is preposterous that he should be punished."

"Sir," Chapel said, "you've made enemies too."

"It is illogical," Sarek said. "But it is true."

"Mister Ambassador, has Spock recovered?"

"He is recovering. However, the experience is not without effect. He has undergone changes, but he is Spock."

"I'm glad," she said.

Sarek followed Chapel into the surprising darkness of the council chamber. A harsh glare flashed over the stepped ranks of seats and turned the councilors' varied complexions a uniform scarlet. The floor, the very air, shook with a subsonic rumble. On a holographic screen above the chamber, a violent explosion roiled and rumbled.

A thunderous voice filled the room. "All the members of the boarding party perished horribly in this Federation trap. All but one of Commander Kruge's heroic crew died by a devious hand, and Commander Kruge himself was abandoned, to perish on the surface of an exploding planet!"

The holographic image faded. The only light remaining radiated upward from the witness box, illuminating the flushed and angry heavy-featured face of Kamarag, the Klingon ambassador to the United Federation of Planets. Sarek had encountered Kamarag before. He knew him as an obdurate opponent.

A great starship appeared above Kamarag: the *Enterprise,* bright against a background of black space and multicolored stars. A second explosion filled the chamber with the actinic light of warp engines gone critical. Beside Sarek, Commander Chapel gasped. The nictitating membranes flicked across Sarek's eyes, protecting him from a glare that caused most of the sighted beings in the chamber to blink and murmur. When their vision cleared, they saw what Sarek observed: the destruction of the *Enterprise.* The battered ship struggled against

322 Vonda N. McIntyre

its death, fighting to stay in the sky, but another explosion racked it, and another, and it fell from space into atmosphere. It glowed with the friction of its speed. It burned. It disappeared in ashes and in flames.

Distressed, Chapel turned away.

How very like a human, Sarek thought, *to grieve over a starship.*

"But one fatal error can destroy the most sinister plan," Kamarag said. "The mission recordings remained in the memory of our fighting ship! Officer Maltz transmitted them to me before he, too, died. Did he die, as the Federation claims, a suicide? Or was it convenient to eliminate the last objective witness?"

The image of a small band of humans appeared. The mission recorder focused on the face of James Kirk.

"There!" Kamarag shouted. "Hold the image! *Hold!*"

The image froze: James Kirk gazed at his dying ship.

"Observe!" Kamarag said in a low and dangerous voice. His brow ridges pulsed with anger; his heavy eyebrows lowered over his dark, deep eyes. "The quintessential devil in these matters! James T. Kirk, renegade and terrorist. He is responsible for the murder of the Klingon crew and the theft of their vessel. But his true aims were more sinister. Behold the real plot and intentions!"

One image of James Kirk dissolved into a second. The new image, uniformed, calm, well groomed, gazed out at the audience.

"To fully understand the events on which I report," Kirk said, "it is necessary to review the theoretical data on the Genesis device."

A complex diagram glowed into being.

"Genesis is a procedure by which the molecular structure of matter is broken down, not into subatomic parts as in nuclear fission, or even into elementary particles, but into subelementary particle-waves."

The diagram solidified into a torpedo, and the torpedo arced through space to land on a barren world. The effect of the device spread out from the impact like a tidal wave of fire, racing across and finally covering the rocky surface of the planetoid. When the glow faded, stone and dust had become water and air and fertile soil.

"The results are completely under our control," James Kirk said. "In this simulation, a barren rock becomes a world with water, atmosphere, and a functioning ecosystem capable of sustaining most known forms of carbon-based life."

Sarek knew about the Genesis device. He did not need to watch its simulation. Instead, he observed the councilors. Most had known little if anything about the secret project. They reacted with amazement or shock or silent contemplation, depending on their character and their culture.

"Even as the Federation negotiated a peace treaty with us, Kirk secretly developed the Genesis torpedo. This dreadful weapon, disguised as a civilian project, was conceived by Kirk's paramour and their son. It was test detonated by the admiral himself!"

Kamarag waited for silence among the agitated councilors. Sarek gathered his own energy. The holographic screen contracted upon itself, squeezing its image to nothingness. The chamber's lights rose.

"James Kirk called the result of this awesome energy the 'Genesis Planet.' A gruesome euphemism! It was no more and no less than a secret base from which to launch the annihilation of the Klingon people!" He paused again, letting his outrage affect the council chamber. He drew himself up. "We demand the extradition of Kirk! We demand justice."

"The Empire has a unique point of view on justice, Mister President," Sarek said. He strode into the chamber and descended the stairs. "It is not so many years past that the Empire recognized James Kirk as a hero, and honored him for preventing the annihilation of the Klingon people. One must wonder what political upheaval could have changed their opinion so precipitously."

"It is Kirk who changed!" Kamarag clamped his fingers around the edge of the lectern and leaned toward Sarek, fixing him with an expression of hatred and fury. "From concealing his treachery to exposing it, as Genesis proves!"

"Genesis was perfectly named," Sarek said. "Had it succeeded, it would have meant the creation of life, not death. It was the Klingons who drew first blood while trying to possess its secrets."

"Vulcans are well known," Ambassador Kamarag said coldly, "as the intellectual puppets of the Federation."

"Your vessel did destroy *U.S.S. Grissom*. Commander Kruge did order the death of David Marcus, James Kirk's son. Do you deny these events?"

"We deny nothing," Kamarag said. "We have the right to preserve our species."

"Do you have the right to commit murder?"

The councilors and the spectators reacted to Sarek's charges. Sarek stood in silence, unaffected by the noise rising around him. The president rapped the gavel.

"Order! There will be no further outbursts from the floor."

After quiet returned, Sarek mounted a dais and faced the council president. This put his back to Ambassador Kamarag. It was an action both insult and challenge.

"Mister President," Sarek said, "I have come to speak on behalf of the accused."

"This is a gross example of personal bias! James Kirk retrieved Sarek's son." Kamarag's voice grew heavy with irony. "One can hardly blame Sarek for his bias—or for letting his emotions overwhelm a dispassionate analysis."

Sarek ignored the retaliatory insult. His attention remained on the council president. He refused to be distracted by Kamarag's outbursts or by the whispers and exclamations of the councilors. During his many years away from Vulcan, Sarek had learned that such reactions to an altercation did not necessarily indicate the intention to interfere. However high the technologies of their worlds, however polished their educations, most sentient beings could easily be diverted from important issues by the promise of entertainment. And a fight between Ambassador Kamarag and Sarek of Vulcan would be entertainment indeed.

Sarek greatly preferred the Vulcan way. Perhaps the council president had also studied Vulcan methods, for he remained calm until the uproar subsided.

324 Vonda N. McIntyre

"Mister Ambassador," the president said to Kamarag, "with all respect, the council must deliberate. We will consider your views—"

"You intend to let Kirk go unpunished," Kamarag said, his tone low and dangerous.

"Admiral Kirk has been charged with nine violations of Starfleet regulations—"

"Starfleet regulations!" Kamarag snorted with disgust. "This is outrageous! There are higher laws than Starfleet regulations! Remember this well: there will be no peace as long as Kirk lives."

He swept down from the witness box and strode from the council chamber. In the shocked silence that followed his ultimatum, the heels of his boots thudded loudly on the polished floor. His security guards surrounded him; his staff snatched up their equipment and hurried after him.

Disturbed, finally, by Kamarag's reaction, the president turned his attention to Sarek. "Sarek of Vulcan, with all respect," he said. "We ask you to return Kirk and his officers to answer for their crimes."

The president's request told Sarek much. The inquiry would find that charges were justified. James Kirk and his friends would face court-martial.

Kirk and the others had risked their careers and their lives at Sarek's request. They had willingly gone through an ordeal that most of the beings in this chamber could not even imagine. This was their reward.

"With respect to you, Mister President," Sarek said evenly. "There is only one crime: denying James Kirk and his officers the honor they deserve."

The president hesitated, as if hoping Sarek might relent. Cold and silent, Sarek met his gaze.

An aging sun gave the planet Vulcan its two simple constants: the appalling heat, and the dry red dust. The climate wrung Jim out. The atmosphere's scanty oxygen forced humans to take a maintenance level of tri-ox. Tri-ox made Jim almost as lightheaded as oxygen deprivation. He supposed that at least it caused less neuron loss.

For all their long civilization, Jim thought, Vulcans never bothered to invent air conditioning. I wonder what logic explains that?

Near sunset, Jim crossed the plain at the foot of Mt. Seleya and paused by the Klingon fighting ship. In the long shadow of its swept-wing body the temperature fell a few degrees, but the inside of the ship would be an oven. He and the others worked on the ship at night. During the day they slept in the relative coolness of the mountain habitat, they did what work they could outside the Klingon fighter, and they worried. No one second-guessed either Jim's choice or their own decisions. But everyone worried.

Jim worried most about McCoy. Whatever the facilitation sessions were doing for Spock, they drained McCoy more completely as they progressed.

He heard a scraping noise above him. He went back outside and tried to see the dorsal surface of the ship from the top rung of the ladder.

"Who's there?" he called.

"Just me."

"Bones? Are you all right?" He chinned himself on the edge of the wing and climbed onto the ship. He was hypersensitive to any hint of odd behavior on McCoy's part, but he tried not to show it.

"T'Lar says Spock doesn't need any more facilitation sessions," McCoy said, without turning around. He sat back, regarded his handiwork critically, and made one last stroke with his paintbrush.

Jim looked over McCoy's shoulder. The doctor had struck out the Klingon identification script; above it he had spelled out *"H.M.S. Bounty."*

"We wouldn't want anybody to think this was a Klingon ship, would we?"

Jim chuckled. "You have a fine sense of historical irony, Bones."

"Jim, I think we've been here just about long enough. How about you?"

"Not just about long enough. Too long." He gripped McCoy's shoulder. "And everyone's had long enough to consider the question. We'll vote tonight."

They climbed down again. At the top of the ladder, Jim took a long breath, let it out, and entered the ship. The heat closed in around him. By dawn the temperature would be nearly tolerable. James Kirk was accustomed to living in the perfectly controlled environment of a starship. Back home he lived in San Francisco, a city with an even and moderate climate.

"I'm *never* going to get used to that smell," McCoy said.

The heat intensified the pungent, slightly bitter odor of the materials of an unfamiliar technology.

"It isn't that bad," Jim said. "You never used to be this sensitive to unusual smells."

"Don't tell me how I've changed, Jim," McCoy said. "I don't want to hear that anymore." His good mood vanished. "I've got work to do in sickbay." He disappeared down the corridor.

Jim walked down the long neck of the Klingon fighter to the command chamber. The differences far outnumbered its similarities to the *Enterprise*. He and his officers had all taken a crash course in the obscure dialect of Klingon in which the controls were labeled. Bits of tape with scribbled reminders littered all the consoles. Chekov's mnemonics were in Russian. Sulu's were in three different languages, only one of which used the Roman alphabet.

Jim sat at Uhura's station and glanced over her notes, which were in Standard. He turned on the system.

"Vulcan communications control."

"James Kirk, requesting subspace to Delta. Private channel, please."

"Subspace channels are blocked with heavy interference. Please try again at a later time."

Jim cursed softly. His every attempt to contact Carol Marcus had met with failure. Perhaps she was avoiding him, out of grief or out of fury. Or both. He remembered what she had told him the first time he and David had met: "You have your world, and I have mine. I wanted David in my world."

Her reluctance had been justified. James Kirk's world was wondrous and dangerous. In seeking out the wonder, David encountered the danger. It destroyed him.

Jim envied Carol's knowing the boy. What would his own life have been like, if he had been told about David and invited to participate in his childhood? But he had not. He had never known David as a child; no one would know David in his maturity.

Jim treasured his few memories of the arrogant and intelligent and sensitive young man who had been his son. He grieved for David's death and for lost chances.

At sunset, Jim cleared his throat, straightened his shoulders, and rose. It would be all too easy to withdraw into his grief. But he still had responsibilities, even if the end of his responsibility turned out to be leading friends to the ends of their careers, or worse.

He climbed down the ladder and waited for the officers of the destroyed starship *Enterprise* to gather.

Montgomery Scott was the first to straggle across the plain toward the *Bounty*. The chief engineer appeared exhausted. He had not been himself since the destruction of the *Enterprise*—nor had anyone in the group, but the starship's last mission had hit Scott particularly hard. He lost his beloved nephew, Peter Preston, during Khan Noonien Singh's suicidal attack. Then he lost his ship. Scott was chief engineer of the *Enterprise* before Jim took command and after flag rank took Jim away from starships and from space. Jim could hardly count the times Scott had pulled some mechanical or electronic rabbit out of an invisible hat to keep the *Enterprise* from certain destruction. This time Scott had done more than fail to save the starship. He had concurred in its annihilation.

"Good evenin', Admiral," the engineer said.

"Hello, Scotty. Don't go in yet. We'll vote tonight."

"Aye, sir."

They waited. Pavel Chekov and Commander Uhura crossed the plain together. As they approached, Pavel, the youngest of the group, made another in a series of jokes about serving on ore carriers. The evening wind ruffled his dark hair. As collected and cool as always, Uhura managed to smile at Chekov's joke.

"We vote tonight," Jim said. Serving on an ore carrier was perhaps the best they could hope for. Even Chekov's usually irrepressible sense of humor crumbled.

As for Uhura, Jim could not tell what she felt or what she thought. During their entire three months on Vulcan, she had never revealed any discouragement. More than once, her strength and certainty had kept the group's morale from bottoming out.

Sulu ran toward the ship from the other side of the plain. Sweat plastered his straight black hair to his forehead.

In choosing to help Jim fulfill Sarek's request, the young commander had given up more than anyone else. Had he remained on Earth, he would now have his own command. The starship *Excelsior* had been taken from Sulu and given to another officer because of James Kirk. Sulu had never voiced a word of regret over the choice he had made.

During their exile, Sulu had begun studying a Vulcan martial art. Tonight, as he approached, Jim saw a new bruise forming on Sulu's wrist.

The Vulcans described the art as meditative. Jim had watched one training session, and he considered the art brutal. Concerned about his officer, Jim had suggested two months ago that Sulu might consider getting more rest. Sulu replied in the most civil terms imaginable that Admiral Kirk should mind his own business.

And Sulu had been right. Now he looked as elemental as the blade of a saber, as if he had deliberately tested himself, seeking and finding a point beyond regret or fear. Vulcan's heat and gravity had purified him to essentials, and tempered him to steel.

McCoy climbed down the ladder. The group was complete.

"Have you all decided?" Jim said.

"Is nothing to decide, Admiral," Chekov said. "We return to Earth, with you."

"How do you know I'm planning to return?" Jim said.

At that, even Uhura looked shocked. "Admiral!"

"I bear the responsibility for what's happened," Jim said. "No, don't object. If I return alone, Starfleet may choose to overlook the rest of you. If I don't return, they may concentrate on finding me and leave you in peace. At the embassy back on Earth, Sarek granted Uhura asylum. The Vulcans will never break that promise. If any of the rest of you request it, I'm certain Sarek will arrange your protection."

"And spend the rest of our lives learning logic on Vulcan?" McCoy said. "Not likely."

"Any of you who wish it could take the *Bounty* to one of the colony worlds, out by the boundary, where people don't ask too many questions."

Chekov laughed. "Even on boundary, sir, people would ask questions of human people flying Klingon fighter. Even disguised as it is." He gestured toward the ship's new name.

McCoy snorted. "Come on, Jim, enough of this. You're not about to become a colonist—or a pirate—and we all know it. Let's vote."

"Very well," Jim said. "All those in favor of returning to Earth . . ."

Sulu raised his hand. His motion was like a challenge, not a gesture of defeat. McCoy and Uhura and Chekov followed his lead. Finally, listlessly, Scott joined the others.

"Scotty, are you sure?"

"Aye, sir, I just . . . I just keep thinkin' . . ."

"I know, Scotty. I know."

Jim, too, raised his hand. He gazed at each of the others in turn, then nodded.

"The record will show," he said, "that the commander and officers of the late starship *Enterprise* have voted unanimously to return to Earth to face the consequences of their actions in the rescue of their comrade, Captain Spock." He hesitated. He tried to express his gratitude for their loyalty, but the words would not come. "Thank you all," he said, his voice tight. "Repair stations, please."

At first no one had believed the ship would fly again. At the beginning, Scott vehemently denied any possibility of making the ship spaceworthy. Sulu gracefully argued him into a challenge that interested him enough to put at least a hairline crack in his depression. Throughout the endeavor, Scott alternated between bleak despair at the monumental task and grim determination to conquer all the difficulties.

Every time they solved one problem, another came up. Now Jim understood how the captain of an eighteenth-century sailing ship must have felt, stranded in the New World, thousands of miles from home, attempting to repair a broken mast or a stove-in hull. But Jim could not go into the forest, cut down a tree, and fashion from it a new piece of equipment (Vulcan had no forests, in any event, and the citizens protected the few ancient trees that remained); he could not repair the hull, even temporarily, by stretching a canvas sail over the holes. His job had become one of convincing Vulcan quartermasters and bureaucrats that giving him and his people the equipment they needed made perfectly logical sense.

Jim would have preferred to go into a forest and cut down a tree.

Jim found Scott. The engineer stood beneath the body of the little ship, gazing critically at a patch on the hull.

"Mister Scott, how soon can we get under way?"

"Gi' me one more day, sir," Scott said. "The damage control is easy. Reading Klingon is hard."

Jim nodded, straight-faced, and refrained from reminding Scott of all the times he had declared the project impossible. Scott climbed up the landing ladder and disappeared inside.

McCoy stopped next to Jim and folded his arms across his chest. "They could at least send a ship for us."

Jim had neglected to tell McCoy about his argument with Admiral Cartwright. The doctor did not need any more stress.

"What do you have in mind, Bones?" Jim said, trying to be jocular. "A nice little VIP yacht?"

"They should insist on it. Instead of a court-martial—!"

"I lost the *Enterprise,* Bones!"

"You lost the *Lydia Sutherland,* too. They didn't court-martial you that time."

"But I was a hero that time, Bones. This time . . ." He shrugged. "Starfleet could have waived court-martial. They didn't choose to. Besides, it isn't the trial that matters, it's the verdict."

"The verdict where we're all sentenced to spend the rest of our lives mining borite? It's adding insult to injury for us to have to come home in this Klingon flea trap."

"Don't let Commander Sulu hear you say that. Anyway, I'd just as soon go home under our own steam. And we could learn a thing or two from this flea trap. Its cloaking device cost us a lot."

McCoy glanced up the landing ladder and squared his shoulders. He took a deep breath of the dusty air, as if he could stock up before having to go inside. "I just wish we could use it to cloak the smell." He climbed up the ladder and disappeared into the *Bounty.*

Saavik sat cross-legged in her spare stone chamber. She let her hands rest lightly on her knees, closed her eyes, and settled her thoughts.

Saavik had dreamed of coming to Vulcan since she learned of its existence and of her own heritage. She felt more comfortable here than on any other world to which she had traveled, even Earth, where she had spent some years, and Hellguard, where she had spent her childhood. Like most other Romulan-Vulcan half-breeds, she had been abandoned very young. Her usefulness to her Romulan parent ended with her birth. Hellguard's usefulness to the Romulans ended soon thereafter. Only the arrival of a Vulcan exploratory party saved Saavik from a short, hard life of struggle for subsistence. When they found her, she was a filthy and illiterate little thief. But Spock detected potential in her. When all the other members of the exploration team preferred to pretend the half-breeds never existed, Spock rescued her, arranged for her education, and sponsored her entrance into Starfleet.

Since his return from the Genesis world, Spock had not spoken to her. The revival had changed him. No one but Spock knew what he recalled from his past life, and what he had to relearn. Perhaps he had forgotten her. She was too proud to plead for his attention, and she was trying too hard to be a proper Vulcan to admit that she missed his friendship. Even if he did forget her, and never remembered her again, she would always be grateful to him for giving her the chance to become a civilized being.

In his earlier life, Spock had acknowledged her existence, but Saavik still did not know why. She believed herself to be the product of abduction and coercion, while Spock descended on his father's side from a Vulcan family renowned and respected for centuries. He commanded respect with his very name, both because of his family and because of his own achievements. Saavik did not even possess a proper Vulcan name.

The single similarity between them was that neither was completely Vulcan. Even that similarity held great differences. Mister Spock's mother was a human being. Amanda Grayson descended from a human family whose accomplishments could not be denied, even if its lineage could be traced only ten generations. Her own accomplishments rivaled any Vulcan's. Even if Amanda had possessed no background worth mentioning, Saavik would have respected and admired her. In their brief acquaintance, Amanda had shown her great kindness. She had made it possible for Saavik to stay on Vulcan.

Saavik, on the other hand, did not even know which of her parents had been Vulcan and which Romulan. She had gone to some trouble to avoid finding out, for tracing her Vulcan parent could gain her no acceptance.

She absently touched her shoulder, rubbing the complex scar of the family mark she bore. Someday the information it contained would reveal her Romulan parent, upon whom she had sworn revenge.

Saavik brought herself to a more recent past.

"Computer."

"Ready," replied the discipline's ubiquitous, invisible computer.

"Record deposition."

"Ready."

"I am Saavik, lieutenant of Starfleet. I last served on the starship *Grissom,* an unarmed exploratory vessel, Captain J. T. Esteban, commanding. Captain Esteban proceeded to the Mutara sector, conveying Doctor David Marcus to the Genesis world. Doctor Marcus was a member of the group that designed Genesis.

"*Grissom* warped into orbit around Genesis. David Marcus and I transported to the surface to investigate the effect of the Genesis torpedo. We found an Earth-type planet with a fully evolved biosphere. Tracking the signals of a being more highly evolved than the Genesis data allowed, a being that should not have existed on the new world, we discovered a Vulcan child of the age of about ten Earth-standard years. It was the opinion of Doctor Marcus that the Genesis wave had regenerated the physical form of Captain Spock, who had been buried in space and whose casket and shroud we found empty on the surface of the world.

"Soon thereafter, we lost contact with *Grissom*. Some hours later, a Klingon expedition arrived on Genesis. They made prisoners of Doctor Marcus, the young Vulcan, and me. The Vulcan and the planet both aged rapidly. It became clear that the Vulcan would die if he was not removed from the influence of the degenerating Genesis wave."

Again, she did not reveal her knowledge of the reasons for the degeneration. A flaw in the Genesis program made the whole system dangerously unstable; it eventually caused the new world to decay into protomatter, to destroy itself. David had suspected this might happen, but in his enthusiasm for the project he persuaded himself he was wrong. Saavik saw no reason to tarnish his reputation as a scientist. Doing so could only cause more pain.

"The Klingon expeditionary force refused to believe the truth about Genesis, that the experiment had failed. They demanded the equations, believing Genesis to be a powerful weapon. Knowing that it could be used in such a way, David—Doctor Marcus—bravely refused to reveal the information, despite threats on all our lives.

"At this juncture, Admiral James T. Kirk returned to Genesis at the request of Sarek of Vulcan, to recover the body of Captain Spock. Commander Kruge, of the expeditionary party, demanded the Genesis equations of Admiral Kirk, and threatened him with the deaths of the hostages if he did not comply. To prove his determination, Kruge ordered a death. . . . He ordered my death. Doctor David Marcus, protesting, drew the attack to himself. He was unarmed. He was murdered. The killing was unprovoked."

Saavik's hesitation lasted only the blink of an eye, but during that moment, she reexperienced David's death. He should not have died. Saavik had the training and the responsibility to protect civilians. But he had interfered before she could stop him. She felt the warmth of his blood on her hands as she tried to save him by giving him some of her own strength. The Klingon war party forced her away from him and permitted him to die.

"Admiral Kirk and his companions escaped from the *Enterprise*. The majority of the Klingon warriors sought him on board the starship. It self-destructed, destroying them. On the Genesis world, Admiral Kirk fought Commander Kruge in hand-to-hand combat, defeated him, and tried to persuade him to surrender. Kruge preferred to perish with Genesis.

"I have no doubt," Saavik said, "that at the least Admiral Kirk's actions prevented two deaths: Captain Spock's, and mine. I believe it probable that he prevented Genesis from falling into the hands of an opposing power. Though the ideals of Genesis failed, Admiral Kirk prevented them from being perverted into a most terrible weapon.

"I am Saavik of Starfleet," she said again. "I have been assigned to Vulcan at the request of Doctor Amanda Grayson, but I will return to Earth willingly to testify on behalf of Admiral Kirk and his companions. I swear on my oath as a Starfleet officer that the words I have spoken are true. End recording."

"Recording ended," the computer replied.

"Electronic copy."

The computer obediently created an electronically readable copy of her testimony and delivered it to her chamber. Saavik slipped the memory chip into her pocket and hurried to the landing field.

James Kirk raised a hand in greeting.

"You have decided," Saavik said.

Kirk nodded. "We lift off tomorrow."

"To Earth?" Saavik had always believed the admiral and his friends would choose to face their accusers.

"Yes."

"Admiral, I would like to continue my work on the ship until you leave."

"Thank you, Lieutenant Saavik."

She drew the memory chip from her pocket. "I have made a deposition."

"Thank you, Lieutenant." He accepted the chip.

"If it is insufficient, I will return to Earth to testify."

"Is Vulcan a disappointment, Saavik? Do you want to leave?"

"No, sir!" She collected herself once more. On Vulcan she felt strong and powerful; she felt completely in control of her life for the first time since she could remember. And this reaction struck her as very strange and wonderful, for she had no idea what the future would bring to her.

Saavik wanted to explain all this to Admiral Kirk, but the words were far too emotional.

"No, sir," she said again. "Amanda has made me welcome. She is teaching me many things."

"And Spock?"

"Mister Spock . . . is in the hands of the student-adepts," Saavik said. "I have not spoken with him. I cannot help him here."

"You aren't alone," the admiral said. "No, Saavik. I appreciate your offer. But I think you should stay on Vulcan."

"Thank you, sir."

She climbed the *Bounty*'s landing ladder, taking the rungs two at a time. At the hatch, she glanced back at the admiral.

James Kirk stood alone in the dusk, gazing up at Mt. Seleya, his expression suddenly uncertain.

Two

The traveler called, but it no longer expected any reply. The pain of the loss had begun to fade. The traveler brought other programs into play as it approached the insignificant blue planet. Because it had fallen silent, the traveler could act upon it. The world that had appeared so promising had proved inhospitable, and so must be changed. When the traveler had completed its work, the world would be ready for a rebirth of intelligent life.

The traveler ranged closer to the planet, plowing through the electromagnetic flux of the yellow star's spectrum. Other stray waves of radiation passed across the traveler, but it had been designed to withstand such energy, not to attend to it.

Soon its work would begin. The possibilities of the future began to wipe away the disappointment of loss.

From a balcony carved into the living rock of Mt. Seleya, Spock could see a great distance across the plains of his chosen homeworld. As the huge red sun set and twilight gathered, his attention focused on the landing field at the foot of the mountain. He watched as the small party of human beings who had brought him to Vulcan gathered beneath the battered wings of their Klingon warship. He deduced the purpose of their meeting; when they parted, he deduced their decision.

The Starfleet lieutenant who had also accompanied them to Vulcan joined Admiral Kirk and spoke to him briefly. Spock knew that she had been on the Genesis world, and he knew she had been instrumental in saving his life. But he knew very little else about her. This troubled him, for each time he saw her, he thought he knew everything about her. Then the knowledge faded, as unrecoverable as the memory of a dream. She became a stranger again.

Spock raised the hood of his heavy white robe and let the fabric settle around his face. During the past three months of intensive memory retraining, he should have recovered or relearned all the information he needed to conduct his life and his career. When he looked down the mountainside into the twilight and saw James Kirk, he could bring into his conscious memory an enormous amount of data about the man. He had first met James Kirk on the occasion of Kirk's taking over command of the starship *Enterprise* from Captain Christopher Pike. No Starfleet officer had ever attained the rank of captain at a younger age than James Kirk. His rate of promotion to flag rank had been similarly precocious. That much was in the records. But Spock also knew that at first he had doubted his ability to work with James Kirk, and the captain had a similar reaction to his new science officer. That was true memory, recovered from the *katra* left in McCoy's keeping when Spock died.

Only experience would reveal where Spock's true memory required more augmentation. It was time to complete his final testing.

On the landing field below, Admiral James Kirk looked upward, as if seeking Spock out. Without acknowledging him, Spock turned away and entered the domain of the student-adepts of the Vulcan discipline of ancient thought.

He paused in the entrance of the testing chamber. The computer had frozen all three screens: "MEMORY TESTING INTERRUPTED." Spock entered the chamber, sat before the screens, and composed himself.

"Resume."

Three problems appeared simultaneously. The computer demanded the chemical formula for yominium sulfide crystals; asked, "What significant legal precedent arose from the peace pact between Argus and Rigel IV?"; and presented him with a challenge in three-dimensional chess. He wrote the formula with one hand; replied, "It is not the province of justice to determine whether all sentient beings are created equal, but to ensure that all such beings are given equal opportunity and treatment under the law"; and moved his queen. White queen took the black knight. "Check," he said. The first screen demanded the electron structure of the normal state of gadolinium; the second requested an outline of the principal historical incidents on the planet Earth in the year 1987; the third remained static. He typed "$1s^2 2s^2 2p^6 3s^2 3p^6 3d^{10} 4s^2 4p^6 4d^{10} 4f^7 5s^2 5p^6 5d^1 6s^2$" and recited the watershed events of Earth, 1987, old dating system. He glanced at the chess screen. The computer had not yet answered his challenge. "You are in check," he said. The computer replied by presenting him with an image to identify. The second screen demanded, "Who made the first advances on toroidal space-time distortion, and where?" "The image is a two-dimensional projection of a three-dimensional theoretical representation of a four-dimensional time gate as proposed by the Andorian scientist, Shres; Ralph Seron did the original toroid work at Cambridge, Massachusetts, Earth, in 2069, and you are still in check." The computer's rook took Spock's queen. Spock instantly moved his white pawn and captured the black rook.

"Checkmate."

All questions ceased. All three screens cleared. A legend appeared, in triplicate: "MEMORY TESTING SATISFACTORY."

The central screen dissolved and reformed: "READY FOR FINAL QUESTION?"

"I am ready," Spock said.

The question appeared before him and to either side, filling his vision, central and peripheral.

"HOW DO YOU FEEL?"

Confused, Spock gazed at the central screen. He drew his eyebrows together in thought. The screen flashed the question at him, urging him to reply.

"I do not understand," Spock said.

The screen continued to flash, demanding an answer.

Spock heard the faint rustle of soft fabric against stone. He glanced over his shoulder.

Amanda, student-adept of the Vulcan discipline of ancient thought, Spock's human mother, stood in the doorway.

"I do not understand the final question," Spock said.

"You are half human," Amanda said. She crossed the room, stopped beside him, and put her hand on his shoulder. "The computer knows that."

"The question is irrelevant."

"Spock . . . the retraining of your mind has been in the Vulcan way, so you may not understand feelings. But you are my son. You have them. They will surface."

Spock found this statement difficult to accept, for he could recall no evidence that what she said was true, no occasion when he had reacted as she said he must. Yet he trusted her judgment.

"As you wish," he said, "since you deem feelings of value. But . . . I cannot wait here to find them."

"Where must you go?" Amanda said.

"To Earth. To offer testimony."

"You do this—for friendship?"

"I do this because I was there."

She touched his cheek. "Spock, does the good of the many outweigh the good of the one?"

"I would accept that as an axiom," Spock replied. Her touch revealed her concern, her disquiet, and her love.

"Then you stand here alive because of a mistake," Amanda said. "A mistake made by your flawed, feeling, human friends. They have sacrificed their futures because they believed that the good of the *one*—you—was more important to them."

Spock considered. "Humans make illogical decisions."

She looked at him, sadly, patiently; she shook her head slightly. "They do, indeed."

Spock raised one eyebrow, trying to understand the incomprehensible motives of human beings.

Doctor Leonard McCoy let the door of the *Bounty*'s sickbay close behind him. He sagged into a chair designed for someone of entirely different build. The ship, particularly his cabin, felt completely alien. He had managed to bring some familiarity to sickbay alone. He had begged, borrowed, and scrounged medical equipment and supplies on Vulcan. However short and safe the trip, he would not go into space without medical capabilities. Some of the *Bounty*'s instruments he had been able to adapt to humans and Vulcans; others he had found useless or incomprehensible.

He had had neither opportunity nor desire to make his sleeping quarters feel more homelike. He did not expect to spend much time on this alien ship. But where he would be spending his time in the future, he did not know.

He rubbed his temples, wishing away the persistent headache. Wishing had about as much effect on it as the medications he had tried and given up on.

McCoy was troubled. Despite T'Lar's assurances, McCoy still felt the presence of Spock in his mind. He hoped it was just a shadow, a memory of the memories he had carried during those few interminable days. Though he did not believe that he and Spock were entirely separate, he had said nothing. He did not want to go through any more facilitation sessions. They delved too deeply; they made him face parts of himself he preferred not to acknowledge. They opened him up to the Vulcans as surely as if he were being dissected. And the Vulcans could not understand. After each session they withdrew from him farther and farther, as if he were some experimental animal gone wrong, some freak of nature. Even Spock withdrew, never speaking to him before or after the sessions, though he should have understood McCoy better than any other being in the universe.

McCoy certainly understood Spock. That was one of the things that troubled him. He could understand how appalled and repelled the Vulcans were when they stripped the civilized veneer from McCoy's emotions and left his psychic nerve endings bare. He could even understand their cold curiosity about him. The Vulcans had given him the ability to stand aside from his own being and act as an objective observer. It was not an ability he had ever encouraged in himself. He knew far too many doctors who prided themselves on their objectivity, who could separate themselves completely from a patient in pain. They might be technically competent, even brilliant; technically they might even be far better doctors than McCoy. But he could not work like that, and he had never wanted to. There was more to being a doctor than technical expertise. Now, though, McCoy felt as if he might be forced into such a mold. If he could no longer understand the feelings of his patients, he was worse than useless as a doctor.

McCoy could find only one defense, and that was to accentuate his reactions, both positive and negative, to let them loose instead of putting them under any restraints.

If Spock and the other Vulcans thought he was emotional before, just wait.

After a long night, Jim Kirk climbed down from *H.M.S. Bounty.* He breathed deeply of the cool thin air, trying to escape his persistent light-headedness. The little ship hunched over him, ungainly on the ground, but spaceworthy again.

Vulcan's harsh and elegant dawn surrounded him. The cloudless sky turned scarlet and purple as the sun's edge curved over the horizon. Light reflected from the atmosphere's permanent faint haze of dust.

High above, a shape glided into sunlight from Mt. Seleya's shadows. Jim watched in amazement as the wind-rider soared and circled. Few humans— indeed, few Vulcans—ever saw the rare creature. Too delicate to bear any touch less gentle than air, it lived always in the sky, hunting, mating, giving birth, and dying without ever touching the ground. Even after death it flew, until the winds dissociated its body into molecules, into elements.

It spiraled upward, directly over the *Bounty.* Vulcan's sun, low on the horizon, illuminated the wind-rider from below. Jim realized that at any other sun angle, the translucent creature would be nearly invisible. But with the light reflecting off the undersides of its wings, he could see the tracing of its glassy hollow bones beneath a tissue-thin skin covered with transparent fur. The creature soared spiraling to a peak. It arched over backward and dove straight toward him, its brilliant gold eyes glittering. Jim caught his breath, afraid the ground would smash it or the turbulence of the air rip it apart. Twenty meters overhead it swooped upward again. It sailed away.

Jim did not understand how a beast of such delicacy had survived the fall; but Jim Kirk was not the first person to be mystified by a wind-rider. No one, not even Vulcans, claimed to understand how they withstood the violent wind and sandstorms that sometimes racked the world.

Jim wondered if seeing a wind-rider meant good luck in Vulcan mythology; he wondered if any Vulcan would admit an omen of luck existed. For while Vulcans preserved their ancient myths, modern Vulcans were far too rational to believe in luck.

What Vulcans believed did not matter. Jim felt as if seeing a wind-rider meant good luck in his own mythology. He climbed back into the *Bounty*, heartened.

Sulu and Scott had directed the repair of the worst of the damage the *Enterprise* had done. Admiral James Kirk took his place in the control chamber of the Klingon fighter, doubting he would ever feel comfortable in the commander's seat. It had been designed for a member of a species that averaged rather larger than human beings.

"Systems report," he said. "Communications?"

"Communications systems ready," Uhura replied. "Communications officer—ready as she'll ever be."

"Mister Sulu?"

"Guidance is functional. I've modified the protocols of the onboard computer for a better interface with Federation memory banks."

"Weapons systems?"

"Operational, Admiral," Chekov said. "And cloaking device is now available in all modes of flight."

"I'm impressed, Mister Chekov. A lot of effort for a short voyage."

Chekov grinned. "We are in enemy vessel, sir. I didn't wish to be shot down on way to our own funeral."

"Most prudent," Jim said. "Engine room. Report, Scotty."

"We're ready, sir. I've converted the dilithium sequencer into somethin' less primitive. And, Admiral, I've replaced the Klingon food packs. They gi' me sour stomach."

"Appreciated by all, Mister Scott."

In the silence that followed, Jim became aware that the attention of everyone on the bridge centered, expectantly, upon him.

"Prepare for departure," he said in a matter-of-fact tone.

Sulu began the prelaunch checklist, and in a moment Jim was surrounded by the low, intense chatter of preparation. This was always the moment when the captain of a starship sat at storm's eye, observing everything, responsible for everything, but with no physical tasks. He could only think of where he was taking his people, what he was taking them back to face.

He glanced around the bridge. In the shadows of the passageway that led into the neck of the *Bounty*, Saavik hesitated on the threshold, her uncertainty clear. She was not as unexpressive as a Vulcan.

Jim rose and joined her. "Well, Saavik, I guess this is good-bye."

"I should accompany you back to Earth, Admiral," she said hesitantly. "I have considered—I am prepared . . . I need nothing. I would request a moment to take my leave of Amanda."

"No, Saavik. Starfleet's put you on detached assignment to Vulcan, so you're staying on detached assignment to Vulcan." He spoke quickly to forestall her argument. She would undoubtedly present it with flawless logic, choosing responsibility over her own wishes. "There's no point in another of us being brought up on charges of insubordination, now, is there?"

"But—"

"Your recorded deposition will be sufficient for the inquiry, Lieutenant. You'll follow your orders. Is that understood?"

She raised her head, her dark eyes narrowing in a flash of anger and rebellion, but the moment's lapse into emotion lasted only an instant before her Vulcan training overcame her Romulan upbringing.

"Yes, sir."

The *Bounty* vibrated at a low, throbbing frequency as it prepared for liftoff.

"Hurry, now," Jim said, trying to maintain a hearty cheerfulness. "You have a great deal to learn on Vulcan. Almost as much as Spock. And you'll be a better Starfleet officer for your stay here. Besides, you're the only one who knows everything that happened on Genesis—" His own memories swept in close around him. His cheer failed and his voice caught. He recovered himself, not as quickly as a Vulcan. "You may be able to help Spock regain access to his true memories."

"My knowledge has not as yet been required in Captain Spock's refusal," Saavik said stiffly. "But I will follow my orders."

"Apparently we won't see Spock before we leave," Jim said, keeping his voice neutral. "If the subject should come up, tell him I wished him . . . good-bye and good luck."

"Should I converse with Captain Spock, Admiral, I shall endeavor to give him your message."

Jim watched Saavik go. The hatch slid open at her approach. To Jim's astonishment, Spock appeared in the hatchway. He wore his long, pale robe. Saavik stopped.

"Good day, Captain Spock," Saavik said.

"Live long and prosper, Lieutenant," Spock said, his voice and face expressionless.

He stepped past her, never glancing back. Saavik's control faltered with deep pain. She watched Spock, but when her gaze intersected Jim's, she brought herself up short, turned, and disappeared.

Apparently the Vulcans in charge of Spock's memory training had not thought it desirable to remind him of Saavik and his importance in her childhood. Perhaps time would bring him the recollection.

Spock stopped before him. "Permission to come aboard, sir."

"Permission granted," Jim said. "But we're preparing for liftoff, Spock. We've spent as much time on Vulcan as we can afford. I'm glad to have the chance to say good-bye—"

"I request permission to accompany you to Earth, sir."

"To Earth? What about your retraining? What about the elders?"

"My retraining is as complete as study permits. The elders . . . would prefer that I stay, but I have declined their invitation. Subject to your decision, of course."

"Of course I grant you permission, Spock. Welcome aboard."

"Thank you, Admiral."

338 Vonda N. McIntyre

"Jim, Spock. *Jim.* Remember . . . ?" It startled Jim to have Spock revert to titles. "Your name is Jim," Spock had said to him, after the refusion. Jim wondered if the elders' program had re-formed Spock as a perfect Vulcan, without personality, character, or even the remnants of emotion to hold in check.

"It would be improper to refer to you as Jim while you are in command, Admiral." Spock hesitated and glanced down at himself. "Also, I must apologize for my attire." He frowned slightly. "I . . . I seem to have misplaced my uniform."

"Well, I . . . find that understandable." Spock was not the only member of the group without a uniform. Jim started to smile.

Spock raised one eyebrow, questioning.

"I mean," Jim said, "you've been through a lot."

Spock did not respond.

Jim sighed. "Station, please," he said.

Spock crossed the bridge to the science station and took his position. Jim watched him, suddenly doubtful about the wisdom of taking Spock along. Spock did not yet seem to be quite his old self. But the trip to Earth should be uneventful, and Spock was not under a council directive to appear and explain his actions.

Maybe this trip is just what Spock needs, Jim thought. *Maybe.*

Besides, Spock had made his decision to leave Vulcan many years ago. Jim did not want to involve himself in complicity with the Vulcan elders, supporting an "invitation" that might keep Spock here into the unforeseeable future.

"You sure this is such a bright idea?"

McCoy had appeared silently at Jim's shoulder. He gazed skeptically at Spock.

"What do you mean?" Jim said, irritated to have McCoy voice in such bald terms the same question he had been thinking.

"I mean *him,* back at his post, like nothing happened. I don't know if you've got the whole picture, but he isn't exactly working on all thrusters."

"It'll come back to him," Jim said, still trying to persuade himself.

"Are you sure?"

Dissembling was one thing; lying directly to his old friend was another. Jim glanced across the bridge to where Spock sat, communing with his computer.

"That's what I thought," McCoy said.

"Mister Sulu," Jim said abruptly. "Take us home."

Saavik strode across the landing field. Behind her, the *Bounty* gathered itself for takeoff. Saavik did not alter her pace. Amanda waited at the edge of the landing pad, staring past her at the ship with an unreadable expression. The wind caught a stray lock of her hair and fluttered it against her throat.

Amanda held out her hand. Saavik hesitated, then grasped it and turned to stand with her as the ship lifted off. It rose on a cloud of dust and power, then plunged forward, climbing slowly as it vanished between the peaks and canyons of Mt. Seleya's range.

Saavik glanced at Amanda when *Bounty* had disappeared. Saavik suddenly felt glad that she had stayed, for tears tracked Amanda's cheeks, and her fingers felt very thin and frail in Saavik's strong hand.

Chief Medical Officer Christine Chapel stood in the midst of the chaos of Starfleet Command's major missions room. Huge curved windows presented a 180-degree view of San Francisco Bay, but no one inside could pay any attention to the calmness of the scene outside. Major missions vibrated with tense communication in many languages, many accents. All the news was bad.

An unknown object was approaching Earth with appalling speed and appalling power. It passed Starfleet ships, and the ships ceased to communicate. Nothing even slowed it down.

Chapel had spent the morning coordinating efforts to reach the crippled ships. But she was running out of personnel, she was running out of rescue ships, and communications became progressively more difficult. The probe showed no sign of running out of ways to stop Starfleet vessels on its headlong plunge toward Earth.

The president of the Federation Council entered. The chaos of the missions room hushed for a moment. The president joined Starfleet Commander Admiral Cartwright at the central command console. Chris hoped they knew something about the probe that she did not, but both men looked intent and grim.

Chapel joined Janice Rand at one of the consoles in the missions room.

"Janice?"

Rand looked up, her expression grim. "Every ship in ten days' radius is already on its way back."

She gestured toward her screen, a three-d representation of part of Federation space, centered on Earth. A multitude of ships moved toward that center at high warp speeds. Some had already begun to gather in a protective phalanx. The unknown signal plowed steadily toward the phalanx. It left in its wake a scattering of motionless, dimming sensor points.

"As for the more distant ships . . . at the rate this thing is going, Chris, by the time they return, there may not be anything to return *to*."

"We don't *know* what the probe's intentions are," Chris said. "We can't be certain . . ."

Janice glanced up at her. Chris stopped grasping at spider-silk hopes that dissolved in her hands.

"If I call the ships back," Janice said, "I may be calling them to their destruction."

"We may need them," Chapel said. "For evacuation."

"They can't evacuate anybody if they're destroyed! We don't even know what happened to the *Saratoga* and the others! That . . . that *thing* has completely disrupted communications from the entire sector."

"It's my job to be prepared," Chapel said. "Evacuation may be our only choice."

"But where can they go?" Rand said softly. She returned her attention to her console. "That thing is getting stronger, Chris," Janice Rand said. Her shoulders slumped as she stared at the screen. "I wish Admiral Kirk were here now," she said. "I wish he were here with the *Enterprise*."

Three

The traveler reached the star system of the nondescript blue planet. The voices it sought remained silent. It passed the system's outer worlds, frozen rocky spheres and great gas giants, and it sang its grief to space and all worlds' skies. Its sensors traced the planet's surface, cutting through the electromagnetic radiation that often surrounded such worlds. It found several small spaceborne nodes of power and drained them.

This was a marginally acceptable world. The traveler could give it new voices. First its surface must be sterilized. The traveler would lower the temperature until glaciers covered the land and the seas froze solid. Whatever had destroyed the intelligence that once existed here would itself be destroyed. After a few eons, the traveler would permit the temperature to rise again, leaving a tropical world devoid of life. Then the traveler could reseed.

The traveler centered its attention on a wide expanse of ocean and began feeding power to the focus.

An enormous sea wave burst upward and exploded into steam. The traveler observed and approved the results. It intensified its power discharge, which plunged into the ocean and vaporized tremendous volumes of water. The vapor rose into the atmosphere and collected into a cloud cover that rapidly thickened and spread, obscuring the surface of the world.

On the surface of Earth, it began to rain.

The invincible probe crossed the orbit of Jupiter. The Federation waited in hope and fear.

With terrifying rapidity, clouds gathered over the surface of the earth. Rain scattered, pelted, scoured the land.

The last hopes faded with the proof of the probe's malevolence.

Captain Styles pounded through the corridor and into the turbo-lift. His orders were specific and desperate: "Stop the intruder." Starfleet Commander Cartwright's intensity had penetrated the badly scrambled channel. "Captain, if you fail . . . it's the end of life on Earth."

Styles did not consider failure. The prospect of action excited him. His ship, *Excelsior,* Starfleet's newest and most powerful, had been held in reserve as a last defense against the unknown. Now the waiting had ended.

It's a good thing, he thought, *that Montgomery Scott's little trick with the engine control chips didn't damage* Excelsior *permanently. If we were crippled now. . . . Helping steal the* Enterprise, *even losing the obsolete old bucket, is a trivial charge compared to sabotage. People care what happens to this ship.*

Anyway, Styles cared. He cared what other people thought about it. He cared what people thought about him. He was determined to erase the memory of the humiliation Scott and Kirk had caused him. *Excelsior* would meet the unknown probe and vanquish it. Styles would save his homeworld, and everyone in the Federation would talk about *Excelsior* and its captain instead of bringing up the heyday of the *Enterprise* and James T. Kirk.

"Open channel to Spacedock control."

"Channel open, sir."

"Styles to Spacedock control."

"You're cleared to depart, Captain."

The transmission broke into static as the controller ordered Spacedock doors to open.

"Would you like to clear up that channel a little, Lieutenant?" Styles said to his communications officer.

"I'm trying, sir. This is a direct hookup; it shouldn't have any interference."

"I'm aware of that—" A shriek of gibberish squealed through the speakers. The communications officer flinched. Styles cursed. "Helm, prepare for departure."

The helm officer engaged the controls. "No response, sir!" she said. "*Excelsior* has no power!"

"Engineering!"

"Captain Styles, the impulse engines are drained, and warp potential is failing!"

"Excelsior, *stand by,*" Spacedock control said. The voice buzzed and jumped through the interference. *"Spacedock doors are inoperative! Repeat, malfunction on exit doors."*

"This is *Excelsior,* control. Never mind the damned doors—we've got no power! What's going on?"

A second voice, almost indistinguishable, penetrated the weird interference. *"Space doors not responding. All emergency systems nonfunctional."*

Styles glanced up through the clear dome that covered *Excelsior*'s bridge. A Spacedock observation deck loomed overhead.

On it, all the lights were going out.

"Engage reserve power." Spacedock control was a whisper among screams of incomprehensible interference. *"Starfleet command, this is Spacedock on emergency channel. We have lost all internal power. Repeat, we have lost all power . . ."*

The signal faded to nothingness.

The probe sped past Mars with little opposition and settled into orbit around the earth.

Tokyo: cloud cover ninety-five percent. The spattering rain froze to sleet.

Juneau: cloud cover ninety-seven percent. Icy snow plummeted from the sky.

Leningrad: cloud cover one hundred percent. It was too cold to snow. The city hunkered in the freezing darkness, as if for an early winter of conventional brutality. Its citizens, accustomed to their winters, were well prepared to survive till spring.

But this time, spring might never come.

Sarek of Vulcan stood on the observation platform of Starfleet's major missions room. Through the hours he had watched as Federation personnel searched for some response to the probe, some way to stop or escape it. The hum of voices gradually receded before the increasingly frantic data stream from machines stretched to overload. The people were exhausted, for the information had been pouring in for hours and they had no response to give it.

Sarek stepped down from the platform and crossed the main floor, listening and watching, trying to form some synthesis of the data that might explain what had happened, and why. The probe's incomprehensible cry resonated through the information channels, erratically disrupting communications.

He paused beside Christine Chapel, who was trying to direct rescue and evacuation on a world which ships could not leave. She stood by Janice Rand, staring in despair at the information that told her she would fail. Sarek gazed at the same information without comment or expression.

All over the globe the temperature dropped rapidly, and the curve kept growing steeper, with no indication of any plateau.

Chapel raised her head. "In medicine, no matter how good you are, no matter how much you know and how powerful your equipment is, you always come to times when you're helpless. But . . . not like *this*."

She put her hands on the back of Janice Rand's chair. Sarek observed the trembling of her hands before she clenched her fingers and regained her control.

A few centuries before, a group of Earth scientists had calculated what would happen if a nuclear war blasted dirt and soot and water vapor into the atmosphere. The results would have been devastating: a years-long winter of total cloud cover, a nonexistent growing season, famine, plague, and death for human beings and most other species. That single paper offered understanding of the utter finality of nuclear war; it had helped human people learn to fight to understand each other as hard as they had previously fought to destroy each other. And so Earth and its population survived to join and enrich a civilization that spanned a large portion of an arm of the galaxy.

The calculations that had warned Earth's powers of their folly had been made under the assumption that most of the bombs would explode in the northern hemisphere. In that event, most of the atmospheric debris would circulate through the wind and weather currents north of the equator, leaving the southern hemisphere less affected.

The probe was not so kind. Its disruption affected the earth from poles to equator.

"The rescue ships are getting close, Chris," Janice Rand said. "We have to tell them something soon."

"I know," Chapel replied.

Rand's screen revealed a small fleet of ships, several already within the orbit of Pluto. Perhaps they were already within the grasp of the probe, for no one could show any evidence of limits to its power.

Sarek glanced at Chapel, one eyebrow raised.

"No ship has approached the probe without being neutralized," Chapel said to Sarek. "The approaching rescue ships may suffer the same fate. It seems unlikely that the probe will allow them to carry out any evacuation."

Above, on the observation level, the council president stood with Starfleet Commander Cartwright. He had the whole planet to worry about, not just a few ships whose arrival would make little if any difference to the fate of the earth and its people.

"Try to get through to them," Chapel said to Rand. "Tell them to stand off. Maybe if they wait, the probe will finish, and leave . . ."

Sarek nodded, approving of her logical conclusion. He turned without a word, climbed back to the observation level, and gazed out into the bay. Tall waves roughened the surface of the water, as if reaching to join the thick, dark clouds rolling in from the sea. Already the clouds had obscured the upper curves and peaks of the bridge. A bolt of lightning flashed across the water. Glass shivered and rattled in the rumble of thunder.

Nearby, the council president and Starfleet Commander Cartwright discussed the possibilities, which now were desperately limited. They had no more power than Chapel to overcome the probe. Perhaps it came from an intelligence so great that the Federation was nothing to it but an anthill or a beehive, or from an intelligence so cold that the destruction of sentient beings concerned it not at all. Perhaps it did not even perceive Earth's transmissions as attempts at communication.

Sarek's acute hearing sorted the familiar voices of Cartwright and the president from the constant gibberish of computers offering more and more information that became less and less useful. The two men had to decide what, if anything, to do. Whatever they decided, without sunlight the earth could not long survive.

"Status report, please," the council president said.

His adjutant replied, his voice not quite steady. "The probe is over the South Pacific. No attempts at dissipating the clouds have had any effect. Estimate total cloud cover by next orbit."

"Notify all stations," Cartwright said suddenly. "Starfleet emergency, red alert. Switch power immediately to planetary reserves."

"Yes, sir."

The president joined Sarek by the observation window. "Sarek . . . Is there no answer we can give this probe?"

Sarek shook his head, for he had no resources to offer. "It is difficult to answer if you do not understand the question." He could conceive of only one logical response. The president could not save Earth, but he might save other beings by offering a warning. If he transmitted all the information they possessed, some other world might discover a defense against the probe.

"Mister President, perhaps you should engage the terminal distress signal, while we still have time."

The president gazed out the window. During his silence, the waves increased in amplitude and the rain increased its intensity. Huge drops hit with perceptible force and streaked down the glass as if to score its shining surface. When finally the president spoke again, his words surprised Sarek.

"You shouldn't be here, Sarek," he said. "You came to Earth to aid a friend. Not to die. I wish I could change things. I am sorry."

"I see no reason to indulge in regrets for events I cannot alter," Sarek said. "I would ask only one thing."

"It's yours, if it's in my power to grant it."

"A moment on a communications channel, after the warnings have been transmitted. To call Vulcan."

"Of course."

The data stream echoing through major missions suddenly failed to silence. The threnody of the probe reverberated through the chamber.

Over the bay, snow began to fall.

The *Bounty* sped toward Earth through warp space.

"Estimating planet Earth, one point six hours, present speed," Sulu said.

"Continue on course," Admiral Kirk replied.

"Aye, sir." Sulu checked the systems. Some, especially the power plant, already showed signs of strain. The instrument readings hovered barely within normal ranges. The *Bounty* would convey the group to Earth, but Sulu doubted the ship could give much more. He felt sorry for that. Sulu had many ambitions, and almost all of them centered on Starfleet, space travel, exploration. But he suspected that Starfleet would forbid him to fly another starship for a very long time. Even flying a battered captured enemy ship was better than being grounded.

But the enemy ship could also get him and his companions killed. If the power blew, the cloaking device would go first. The *Bounty* would appear as an intruder. It was essential for Starfleet to be aware of their approach, and so far the Federation had not replied to Uhura's subspace transmissions. Unusual interference permeated this region of space, and she had received in reply nothing but an eerie silence. So no one knew that the survivors of the *Enterprise* were flying to Earth in a Klingon fighter.

Or they know, Sulu thought, *and they've decided to let us sweat for a while.*

"Mister Chekov, any signs of Federation escort?" Kirk said.

And if we do get an escort, Sulu thought, *will it escort us—or put us under arrest?*

"No, sir," Chekov said. "And no Federation vessels on assigned patrols."

"That's odd," Kirk said.

"Admiral, may I speak with you?" Uhura said.

"Certainly, Commander." Kirk rose and joined Uhura at her station. "What have you got, Uhura?"

"I'm getting something awfully strange," Uhura said. "And very active. Overlapping multiphasic transmissions. . . . It's nothing I can translate. It's gibberish."

"Can you separate them?" Kirk said.

"I've been trying, sir. They're unfocused, and they're so strong they bleed out into adjacent frequencies and harmonics. And their positions . . . lead in the direction of Earth."

"Earth!"

"Yes, sir. I'm trying to sort it out."

Like Sulu and everyone else in the command chamber, Spock overheard the conversation between Admiral Kirk and Commander Uhura. Curious, Spock picked up an earphone and listened in as Uhura attempted to extract a comprehensible message from the garble that filled the frequencies.

When Leonard McCoy appeared at the entrance to the control chamber, then strolled in, Spock took care to show no reaction. He had not spoken directly to McCoy since . . . before. He had not even been in his presence without T'Lar as a barrier between them. Speaking to McCoy should be no different from speaking to any other human being, and yet Spock felt a strange reluctance to do so.

"Hi," McCoy said. "Busy?"

"Commander Uhura is busy," Spock said. "I am monitoring."

McCoy looked at him with a strange expression. "Well. Just wanted to say—nice to have your *katra* back in your head, not in mine."

McCoy smiled. Spock could not imagine why.

"I mean," McCoy said, "I may have carried your soul, but I sure couldn't fill your shoes."

"My shoes?" Spock said. "What would you intend to fill my shoes with? And why?" Spock seldom wore shoes. On shipboard, in uniform, he wore boots. On Vulcan he ordinarily wore sandals. "I am wearing sandals," Spock said. This seemed wrong to him. "How would one go about filling a pair of sandals?"

"Forget it," McCoy said abruptly. "How about covering a little philosophical ground?"

Spock tried to reconcile McCoy's words and tone, which he interpreted as flippant, with the tension in his body, the intensity in his gaze.

"Life. Death. Life," McCoy said. "Things of that nature."

"I did not have time on Vulcan for deep study of the philosophical disciplines."

"Spock, it's me!" McCoy exclaimed. "I mean—our experience was unique."

"My experience was unique," Spock said. "Your experience was essentially the same as that of anyone accompanying a Vulcan to that Vulcan's death. It is true that you were untrained and unprepared; this caused T'Lar great difficulty in freeing my *katra*—"

"T'Lar!" McCoy exclaimed. "What about me? I thought I was going crazy! I was arrested, drugged, thrown in jail—"

"—and it caused you some distress," Spock said. "For this I apologize, but I could see no other choice."

"Never *mind* that," McCoy said. "Do you think I'm complaining about helping save your life? But, Spock—you really have gone where no man has ever gone before. And in some small part, I shared that experience. Can't you tell me what it felt like?"

The Vulcan elders had asked him the same question, and he had not replied. He continued to resist the demand that he delve into his memory of the subject. Yet he had no logical reason for his reluctance.

Even if he did force himself to recall the experience, he doubted he could express it to McCoy in words the doctor or any human—except perhaps Amanda Grayson, who had studied Vulcan philosophy—could understand. Spock was not altogether sure he could express it to any sentient being.

"It would be impossible to discuss the subject without a common frame of reference."

"You're joking!" McCoy exclaimed.

"A joke . . ." Spock said, sorting through his memory, "is a story with a humorous climax." He wondered why McCoy had accused him of making a joke. In the first place the comment seemed an utter non sequitur. Spock could

346 Vonda N. McIntyre

not understand how it followed from their previous discussion. In the second place, McCoy must be under some serious misapprehension if he thought Spock would deliberately attempt to make a joke.

"Do you mean to tell me," McCoy said, "that I have to die before you'll deign to discuss your insights on death?"

The chaotic tangle of sound suddenly sorted itself out, distracting Spock from McCoy's unanswerable questions. "Most strange," Spock murmured.

"Spock!" McCoy said.

"Pardon me, Doctor," Spock replied. "I am hearing many calls of distress."

"I heard a call of distress, too, and I answered it," McCoy said angrily. "You—" He cut off his furious protest. "What do you mean? What calls of distress?"

"Captain!" Uhura exclaimed.

Kirk strode to her side. "What did you find?"

"Overlapping distress calls. Maydays from starships, and—"

"Let's hear them!" Kirk said. "Have you got any visuals? Put them onscreen."

Uhura complied. The Maydays flicked onto the holographic viewing area, each overriding the next, each different but very much the same: starships overtaken and drained by a huge spacegoing object that blasted their power supplies and sailed past at high warp, without answering their greetings or their supplications.

The blurry image of the president of the Federation Council formed before them. His message broke and dissolved, but Uhura had captured enough that its meaning could not be mistaken.

"This is . . . president of . . . grave warning: Do not approach planet Earth . . . To all starships, repeat, do not approach!"

Shocked, Admiral Kirk cursed under his breath.

The president's image faded and the strange spacegoing construct replaced him.

"Orbiting probe . . . unknown energy waves . . . transmission is directed at our oceans. Ionized our atmosphere . . . all power sources failing. Starships are powerless." Suddenly the transmission came through with utter clarity. The president leaned forward, intent and intense.

"Total cloud cover has enveloped our world. The result is heavy rain and flooding. The temperature is dropping to a critical level. The planet cannot survive beneath the probe's force. Probe transmissions dominate all standard channels. Communication is becoming impossible. Earth evacuation plans are impossible. Save yourselves. Avoid the planet Earth." He paused, closing his eyes wearily, opening them again to stare blankly from the screen. "Farewell."

Jim Kirk listened to the transmission with disbelief. What *is* that thing? he thought. "Uhura, can you let us hear the probe's transmissions?"

"Yes, sir. On speakers."

A blast of sound overwhelmed them with its eerie strangeness.

"Nothing we have can translate it," Uhura said. "Neither the *Bounty*'s original computer nor our universal translator."

"Spock, what do you make of it?" Jim said.

"Most unusual," Spock said. He gazed at the visual transmission, taking in all the available information, analyzing it, trying to synthesize a hypothesis. "An unknown form of energy, great intelligence, great power. I find it illogical that its intentions are hostile . . ."

"Really?" McCoy said sarcastically. "You think this is its way of saying 'Hi there' to the people of Earth?"

"There are other intelligent life forms on Earth, doctor. Only human arrogance would assume the message was meant for humanity."

McCoy scowled. He glanced sidelong at Jim. "I liked him better before he died."

"Bones!" Jim said in protest, knowing Spock could not help but have heard.

"Face it, Jim!" McCoy said. "Everything he used to have that made him more than a green-blooded computer, they've left out this time." He stalked away and stopped near the visual transmission, staring morosely at the images of destruction.

"Spock," Jim said, "are you suggesting that this transmission is meant for a life form other than human beings?"

"It is at least a possibility, Admiral. The president did say that the transmission was directed at the Earth's oceans."

Jim frowned, considering. "Uhura, can you modify the probe's signals by accounting for density, temperature, and salinity?"

"For underwater propagation? I'll try, sir."

He waited impatiently as Uhura played the communications console like a complex musical instrument, like a synthesizer creating an entire orchestra. The probe's signal mutated as she filtered it, altered its frequency, enhanced some parts of the sound envelope, and suppressed others. Slowly it changed, till it wailed and cried in a different voice, still alien, yet strangely and tantalizingly familiar. Jim searched his memory for the song, but the knowledge remained out of reach.

"This is what it would sound like underwater?"

"Yes, sir."

"Fascinating," Spock said. "If my suspicion is correct, there can be no response to this message." He strode toward the exit hatch of the control chamber.

"You recognize it, Spock?" Jim asked, but Spock offered no response. "Spock! Where are you going?"

"To the onboard computer room. To confirm my suspicions." He vanished through the hatchway without a word of explanation.

Jim headed after him. When he realized McCoy was following, he stopped and turned back. He was as concerned about McCoy's mental state as he was about Spock's. For all their vast knowledge and long history, Vulcans were neither omniscient nor omnipotent. They might not have freed McCoy as completely as they claimed.

And Bones might be right, Jim thought, trying to persuade himself that he was worrying to no purpose. Maybe they did use the opportunity of retraining Spock's mind to create the perfect Vulcan, a being of complete logic and no emotion at all . . .

"Stay here, Bones," he said.

"No way," McCoy said. "Somebody has to keep an eye on him."

"Yes. Me."

"Oh, no," McCoy said. "*You* think he's all right."

Spock gazed at the computer screen, waiting for the results. He felt as if he were taking still another memory test. He wondered if he would pass it. The result would be of intellectual interest.

Admiral Kirk and Doctor McCoy stood close behind, their anxiety disquieting. He wondered why they were acting this way, for he had already told them that his hypothesis, even if true, could have no effect.

The computer replayed the probe's song, then played another, not identical but similar: a melody of rising cries and whistles, clicks and groans. He had heard it before, but only in a fragmented, half-remembered form.

The computer displayed the image of a huge creature, an inhabitant of Earth's seas, and identified it: *Megaptera novaeangliae.*

Spock had passed his own memory test.

"Spock?" Admiral Kirk said, his voice tight.

"As I suspected," Spock said. "The probe's transmissions are the songs sung by whales."

"Whales?"

"In particular, the humpback whale, *Megaptera novaeangliae.*"

"That's crazy!" McCoy exclaimed.

Spock found McCoy's highly emotional state to be most discomforting. He tried to ignore it.

"Who would send a probe hundreds of light-years to talk to a whale?" McCoy said.

"It's possible," Admiral Kirk said thoughtfully. "Whales evolved on Earth far earlier than human beings."

"Ten millions of years earlier," Spock said. "Human beings regarded them, as they regarded everything else on the planet, as resources to be exploited. Humans hunted the whale, even after its intelligence had been noted, even after other resources took the place of what humans took from whales. The culture of whales—"

"No one ever proved whales *have* a culture!" McCoy exclaimed.

"No. Because you destroyed them before you had the wisdom to obtain the knowledge that might form the proof." McCoy started to object again, but Spock spoke over him. "The languages of the smaller species of cetaceans contain tantalizing hints of a high intellectual civilization. Lost, all lost. In any event, the pressure upon the population was too great for the whales to withstand. The humpback species became extinct in the twenty-first century."

He glanced at the screen. The computer displayed the immense form of a humpback whale, bloated and graceless in death. Human beings flensed the carcass. Great thick chunks of the whale's body flopped onto the deck, and the whale's blood stained the sea dark red. Spock observed his colleagues. Kirk and McCoy watched, fascinated and horrified, unable to resist the scene of an intelligent creature's death and dismemberment.

"It is possible," Spock said, "that an alien intelligence sent the probe to determine why they lost contact. With the whales."

"My God . . ." McCoy whispered.

"Spock, couldn't we simulate the humpback's answer to this call?"

"We could replay the sounds, but not the language. We would be responding at best in rote phrases, at worst in gibberish."

"Does the species exist on any other planet?"

"It died out before humans had the ability to transplant it. It was indigenous to Earth. The Earth of the past."

"If the probe wants a humpback, we'll give it a humpback," McCoy said. "We've reintroduced other extinct species by cloning frozen tissue samples—"

"The same difficulty remains, Doctor McCoy," Spock said. "The reason great whales have not been reintroduced to Earth's seas is that no great whales still exist to teach them survival, much less communication. You could clone a whale, of course—but you would create a lonely creature with no language and no memory of its own culture. Imagine a human child, raised in complete isolation. Imagine . . . my own existence, had you refused to undergo *fal-tor-pan*. No. A cloned whale, crying its despair, could bring only further destruction. Besides," he said, considering practicality, "I doubt Earth could survive for the years it would take to grow a cetacean to maturity."

"That leaves us no choice," Kirk said. "We've got to destroy the probe before it destroys Earth."

"The attempt would be futile, Admiral," Spock said in a matter-of-fact tone. "The probe would neutralize us easily, as it has neutralized every other starship that has faced it, each one more powerful than the craft you command. Fleet Commander Cartwright's orders to all Starfleet vessels are to turn away."

"We can't! Orders be damned, I *won't* turn away from my homeworld! Isn't there any alternative?"

Spock considered Admiral Kirk's question as an interesting intellectual exercise.

"There is one, of course," he said. "The obvious one. I could not guarantee its success, but the attempt would be possible."

"The alternative isn't obvious to me," the admiral said.

"We could attempt to find some humpback whales."

"You just said there aren't any except on the Earth of the past," McCoy said.

"Your memory is excellent, Doctor," Spock replied. "That is precisely what I said."

"Then how . . . ?" McCoy glanced from Spock to Kirk and back again. "Now wait just a damned minute!"

Admiral Kirk made an instant decision. Spock recalled that this was James Kirk's characteristic behavior.

"Spock," Kirk said, "start computations for a time warp." He turned toward McCoy. "Come on, Bones. Let's pay Scotty a visit."

McCoy started to protest, but Kirk left the computer room, pulling McCoy along behind him. Spock watched them go, bemused. Kirk had asked him a question and he had answered it, never intending to base any action on his information. Still, it would be an interesting challenge to see if he could successfully solve the mathematical problem Admiral Kirk had posed him.

Turning back to the computer, Spock overrode the report on humpback whales and began to compose the complex equations.

Four

The traveler's joy overcame the distress of losing contact with the beings of this little world. The planet lay enshrouded in an impenetrable cloud. Great thunderstorms wracked it. Where they did not flood the land they seared it with lightning, setting fires that added soot and ash and gases to the roiling clouds. The globe's temperature continued to fall. Soon the rain would turn to snow from poles to equator. The insignificant life that remained would perish from the cold. After the world became sterile, and the clouds rained themselves out, and the particulate matter settled, the carbon dioxide left in the atmosphere would aid in the world's rapid warming. Then the traveler could begin its real work.

Until then, it need only wait.

Doggedly, McCoy followed Jim through the neck of the *Bounty*. The plan disturbed him deeply, but the reasons for his discomfort took time to puzzle out.

"Jim," he said, "are you sure this is the right thing to do?"

"I don't understand what you mean," Jim said.

"Time travel," McCoy said. "Trying to change the future, the past—"

"We aren't trying to change the future or the past, Bones. We're trying to change the present."

"But we're the past of other people's future."

"That's the most sophistic argument I ever heard," Jim said.

McCoy forged on, trying to ignore the edge in Kirk's voice. "What if we change something that makes a difference to history?"

"But that's the whole point, Bones. To make a difference."

"Don't evade my question—you know what I mean!"

Jim strode on in silence.

"In the old days, on the *Enterprise*," McCoy said, "we had the same kind of disaster to face. And sometimes we had to do the hardest thing in the universe. Sometimes we had to do nothing."

Jim's stride hesitated, but he kept going.

"Jim—what would the Guardian say?"

Jim swung around, grabbed McCoy by the front of his shirt, and shoved him against the bulkhead.

"Don't talk to me about the old days on the *Enterprise!*" Jim shouted. "Don't talk to me about the Guardian of Forever! I went back in time to save your life—and I had to stand by and watch someone else I loved die! I had to stand by while Edith died—*and do nothing!*"

"It was the right thing to do."

"You didn't think so at the time. I'm not sure I think so now. Ever since, I've wondered, what if I'd saved her? What if I'd brought her back? Everything would have been . . . so different . . ."

"It wouldn't have worked. You couldn't have brought a twentieth-century person into a twenty-third-century world and expected her to adapt."

"You don't know that!"

"Jim," McCoy said, "she wouldn't have come."

"She loved me!"

"So what? She had a mission in her life, and she wouldn't have given it up to go with you. No matter how much she loved you. And if you'd brought her against her will, even to save her life, she would have seen it as a feeble excuse and she would have seen it as betrayal."

Jim stared at him, shocked by the blunt recital of the truth. "What's the matter with you, Bones?"

"Let go of me," McCoy said.

Jim loosed his rigid grip on McCoy's shirtfront. "You're telling me to stand back and watch what's left of my family die. You're telling me to write off my homeworld—and yours. I won't do it! And I can't believe you want me to! The future hasn't happened yet, Bones! If I start believing that nothing I do can—or should—change it, then what's the point of anything?"

"I don't know, Jim. I just know you shouldn't do this."

"And just how," Jim said, "do you propose to stop me?" He turned away and left McCoy standing in the corridor.

McCoy had no answer to James Kirk's rage, but as his old friend strode away, he still sought to counter the intuitive force of Jim's argument.

Upset and angry, Jim Kirk entered the engine room of the *Bounty.* Everything about McCoy's argument troubled him: the argument itself, the doctor's having proposed it, and the possibility that McCoy might be right. Could Spock's suggestion, if Jim carried it out, cause some traumatic change in the universe? The possibility, even the probability, existed whenever one began interfering with the vectors of space-time. Jim had faced enormous personal danger and worse emotional pain in order to keep from disrupting the past, and thus the future he lived in.

But I'm not going to disrupt the past, he thought. *I'm going to enter it and remove something that's going to be destroyed anyway.*

He intended to change his own present. He could not make himself believe that what he planned was wrong.

Besides, Jim thought, *if the plan posed so much danger—beyond the obvious danger to my people and my ship, which I suppose Spock did not consider germane—Spock never would have suggested it in the first place.*

If Jim did nothing, Earth would die. He put McCoy's objections from his mind, for he feared that if he let them affect him he would fail. If he tried and failed, Earth would die anyway.

"Scotty!"

"Aye, sir?" Scott said, appearing from behind a complex webwork of engine structure.

"Come with me to the cargo bay, would you?"

"Aye, sir."

The engineer accompanied him into the huge, empty chamber. McCoy followed in perturbed silence. Jim found it difficult to estimate the dimensions of the oddly proportioned and dimly lit space.

"Scotty, how long is this bay?"

"Abou' twenty meters, Admiral."

"That ought to be enough. Can you enclose it to hold water?"

Scott pondered. " 'Twould be easy wi' a force field, but there isna sufficient force field capability in the *Bounty*. 'Twould have to be done mechanically. I suppose I can, sir. Are ye plannin' to take a swim?"

"Off the deep end, Mister Scott," McCoy said grimly.

Jim ignored him. "Scotty, we have to find some humpbacks."

"Humpbacked . . . people?"

"Humpback whales. They're fifteen or sixteen meters in length. They'll mass about forty tons."

"They willna have much room to swim."

"It doesn't matter. They won't have to stay in the hold for long. I hope."

"Long or short, sir, I canna be sure abou' the ship. 'Twill handle only so much mass."

"You'll work it out, Scotty. You've got to. Tell me what you'll need, and I'll do my best to get it for you. And remember: *two* of them."

"Two, Admiral?"

"It takes two to tango, Mister Scott."

As he headed for the bay hatch, he heard Scott mutter softly, "The great flood, and Noah's ark. What a way to finally go . . ."

Halfway across the cargo bay, McCoy caught up to him.

"You're really going to try this! Aside from everything else—time travel in this rust bucket?"

"We've done it before." The ship would make a full-power warp-speed dive toward the sun, letting the gravity field accelerate it. If it picked up enough velocity, it would slingshot around the sun and enter a time warp. And if not—

"If you *can't* pick up enough speed," McCoy said, as if reading his thoughts and completing them, "you fry."

"We could land on Earth and freeze instead," Jim said, his tone grim. "Bones, you don't really prefer me to do nothing—?"

"I prefer a dose of common sense and logic! Never mind the ethics of the situation. You are proposing to head backward in time, find humpback whales, bring them forward in time, drop them off—and hope they tell this probe what to go do with itself!"

"That's the general idea."

"That's crazy."

"If you've got a better idea, now's the time."

McCoy held his gaze a moment, then looked away. He did not have a better idea.

Jim entered the *Bounty*'s control chamber. Spock had returned to his station. Incomprehensible equations flickered across his computer screen. Jim took his place and turned on the intercom so his voice would reach Scott.

"Could I have everyone's attention, please." It seemed strange to him, but appropriate, to request their attention rather than expecting it. "Each of you has a difficult decision to make. The information that Mister Spock and Mister Scott have offered leads me to believe that it is possible, though risky, to go backward in time and obtain two humpback whales, the species with which the probe is trying to communicate. If the attempt is successful, it could mean the survival of Earth. But we have no guarantee of success. The *Bounty* could be destroyed. We might all die."

He paused, waiting for a reaction. No one spoke. Finally Sulu gave him a curious glance.

"You mentioned a difficult decision, Admiral."

"I intend to make the attempt, Commander Sulu. But anyone who wishes to remain in our own time is free to take one of the rescue pods and leave the ship before we enter the probe's apparent sphere of influence. An entire flotilla of rescue craft is hovering outside the solar system, unable to risk a close approach to Earth. It's likely they could rendezvous with a rescue pod within a few minutes—a few hours at most. Remaining behind is probably . . . the sensible thing to do."

"You need somebody to fly this beast," Sulu said, and turned back to his console.

"Would anyone care to cast an opposing vote?"

Spock glanced up only long enough to cock one eyebrow.

"I think what you have here is consensus, Admiral," Chekov said, and also returned to his console.

Uhura acted as if Jim had never asked if anyone cared to abandon the group. "Conditions on Earth appear to be getting worse, sir," she said.

"Scott here, Admiral. Wi' the proper materials—the proper twentieth-century materials—I'll be able to build ye a tank."

"Thank you, Mister Scott." Jim glanced at McCoy.

"You know how I feel about this, Jim," McCoy said.

"Then you'd better take a pod and get out fast."

"Who said anything about getting out? I'm not getting into any rescue pod."

"Very well," Jim said. "We will proceed without delay. . . . Thank you all." He turned to the science officer. "Mister Spock, your computations?"

"In progress, Admiral."

"Uhura, get me through to Starfleet Command."

"I'll try, sir."

In all his years on Vulcan, on Earth, and on many worlds in between, Sarek had never observed such weather. Waves of rain and sleet pounded against the windows. A repair crew had tried to shore up the glass, but the seals had sprung again. Water sprayed through the cracks and pooled on the floor. Lightning burst continuously, turning the night's darkness brighter than Earth's yellow day.

Sarek always felt cold on Earth. In the past, he had always found it possible simply to acknowledge the fact and then ignore it. He had been well trained to ignore the trivial matter of physical comfort. But now, as Starfleet Command diverted all its remaining power in an attempt to maintain communications, the temperature within the building fell to match the ambient temperature outside, which itself continued to fall. Sarek felt colder than he had ever felt in his life. He tried to increase the metabolism of his body to compensate, but he could not outdistance the chill.

Shivering, Sarek gazed through the observation window. Torrential rain whipped across the waves of the bay and pounded against the glass. The clouds darkened overhead. Lightning bursts illuminated each individual raindrop to form an instant's still picture of a billion tiny glowing spheres. Simultaneous thunder shook the platform, the building, the world.

Apparently serene amid the chaos, Sarek listened to Cartwright and the council president and Chief Medical Officer Chapel attempting to maintain some coherence among the rescue attempts. Sarek did not offer his aid, because he knew he could do nothing. No one could be evacuated from Earth because of the probe, but the probe ignored the movement of people from coastal regions to higher elevations.

Perhaps it ignores them, Sarek thought, because it knows any such attempts to be futile. People will be saved from drowning only to freeze; people may be saved from freezing only to starve.

He had been offered a place on a transport to the interior of the continent; he had refused.

He found a certain irony in what had happened. In returning to Earth to plead on behalf of the man who had saved Sarek's son's *katra,* and his life, Sarek would lose his own life and soul. For he had accepted that he would die here on Earth. His *katra* would never be transmitted to the Hall of Ancient Thought, because no one would be left alive to accept it.

Snow had already begun falling just a few kilometers inland. The hills to the east, like mountains, bore caps of snow. As Sarek gazed through the window, the rain driven in off the bay ceased to streak the glass and began instead to burst upon it and stick and flow in wet, slushy droplets of sleet.

Communications within Starfleet Command continued to deteriorate. Sarek could barely make out the reflections of the screens' blurry images. Humans scurried back and forth in futile activity. Chief Medical Officer Chapel had been on duty for nearly forty-eight hours. She slumped in a chair with her face in her hands. Fleet Commander Cartwright clenched his hands around the railing of the observation platform, tense with strain.

Sarek had spent the past few hours preparing himself, permitting himself a moment to consider his successes and releasing his regrets. Only one remained: no reserve power could be spared, no communications channel remained clear enough, for him to transmit a message to Vulcan, to Amanda. He had written to her, but he doubted she would ever receive his message. All he wished to tell her must remain forever unsaid.

"Sir!" Janice Rand turned toward Cartwright. Her rain-streaked image wavered in the glass. "I'm picking up a faint transmission—it's Admiral Kirk!"

"On-screen!" Cartwright said.

Sarek turned from the shadow world of the reflections to the real world behind him. The blurry image on the screen was hardly sharper than its reflection, and Kirk's words came through utterly garbled. The picture faded to noth-ingness, to a resonance of the probe.

"Satellite reserve power," Cartwright said. "Now."

The screen flickered, cleared, blurred. Sarek made out Kirk's form, and the control boards of the Klingon fighter ship . . . and the vague silhouette behind him, unmistakably of a Vulcan, unmistakably Spock. Kirk said something, but static muffled his words.

He is coming to Earth, Sarek thought. *All ships have been ordered away. But instead of obeying, he will come. He has been ordered to Earth. But instead of disobeying, he will come.*

James Kirk was incapable of standing by while his homeworld died. But Sarek also knew that there was no logical way to save it. The Klingon ship would face the probe and be destroyed. So, too, Kirk and all his companions would die.

"Analysis," Kirk said. His voice rose and faded in the static and the reso-nance. A strange cry whistled and moaned in the background. For a moment Sarek thought it was the probe, and then he realized it was not. "Probe call . . . Captain Spock's opinion . . . extinct species . . . humpback whale . . . proper response . . ."

His voice and image both failed, but Sarek had already gleaned Spock's explanation of the probe's intent and desire. A bright stroke of pride touched the elder Vulcan's equanimity.

"Stabilize!" Cartwright exclaimed. "Emergency reserve!"

"Do you read me?" Kirk said clearly. His image snapped into focus, then immediately deteriorated. "Starfleet, if you read, we are going to attempt time travel. We are computing our trajectory . . ."

"What in heaven's name—?" the fleet commander said.

The power failed utterly.

"Emergency reserve!" Cartwright said again, his voice hoarse.

"There *is* no emergency reserve," the comm officer said.

The groan of tortured glass and metal cut through the scream of the wind and the pounding of rain and waves. Sarek understood what Kirk proposed to do. Somehow, in the madness of its desperation, the plan possessed an element of rationality.

"Good luck, Kirk," Sarek said. "To you, and to all who go with you."

The shoring struts on the window failed. The glass imploded, spraying cold sharp shards. Cries of fear and freezing needles of sleet and wind formed Sarek's last perception.

Five

The sun blazed across the viewscreen. The *Bounty* plunged toward it. The light grew so intense that the screen blacked it out, creating an artificial eclipse. Tongues of glowing gas, the corona, stretched in a halo around the sun's edge.

"No response from Earth," Uhura said. "The solar wind is too intense. We've lost contact."

"Maybe it's just as well."

The artificial gravity of the *Bounty* wavered. The acceleration of impulse engines on full punished the ship. The solar storms stretched and grasped for the *Bounty* as it sped toward a fiery perihelion just above the surface of the star.

"Ready to engage computer, Admiral," Spock said.

"What's our target in time?" Jim asked.

"The late twentieth century.".

"Surely you can be more specific."

"Not with this equipment. I have had to program some of the variables from memory."

"Just how many variables are you talking about?"

"Availability of fuel components, change in mass of the vessel as it moves through a time continuum at relativistic speeds, and the probable location of humpback whales. In this case, the Pacific basin."

"You've programmed that from memory?"

"I have," Spock said.

Beside him, McCoy looked at the ceiling in supplication. " 'Angels and ministers of grace, defend us.' "

"Hamlet," Spock said. "Act one, scene four."

"Mister Spock," Jim said with some asperity, "none of us has doubts about your memory. Engage computer. Prepare for warp speed."

Sulu collected the *Bounty* for transition. "Ready, sir."

"Shields, Mister Chekov."

"Shields up, Admiral."

"May fortune favor the foolish," Jim said softly.

"Virgil," Spock said. "The *Aeneid.* But the quote—"

"Never mind, Spock!" Jim exclaimed. "Engage computers! Mister Sulu, warp speed!"

The warp engines impelled the ship forward. The light of the sun's corona shimmered. The *Bounty* plunged through successive bands of spectral color as the frequency of the light increased through yellow, to intense blue-white, to a penetrating actinic violet.

"Warp two," Sulu said.

The *Bounty* shuddered within the drag and twist of warp drive, within the magnetic field and the gravity of the sun.

"Warp three . . ."

"Steady as she goes," Jim said.

"Warp five . . . warp seven . . ."

A tentacle of the corona reached out and entwined the *Bounty,* squeezing it mercilessly.

"I don't think she'll hold together, sir!" Scott's voice on the speaker sounded faint and tinny. The ship struggled for its life.

"No choice now, Scotty," Jim said.

"Sir, heat shields at maximum!"

"Warp nine," Sulu said. "Nine point two . . . nine point three . . ."

"Mister Sulu, we need breakaway speed!"

"Hang on, sir . . . nine point seven . . . point eight . . . breakaway thresh-old . . ."

"Steady," Jim said. "Steady . . ."

A mass of data swept over the viewing area. It would be close, all too close, too close to the sun and too close to the speed, with no margin left.

"Now, Mister Sulu!"

The heat of the sun overrode the shields. A tendril of acceleration insinuated itself through the gravity.

The *Bounty* blasted out of its own dimensions of space and plunged into time.

Jim remembered . . .

Glimpses of his past returned to him at random. He saw the *Enterprise* exploding out of space and burning in the atmosphere of Genesis. He saw David Marcus lying dead among the ruins of his dreams. He saw Spock as a youth—on Genesis, Spock had aged. But Jim's memory crept backward and the aging reversed. The Vulcan's living body grew younger. As the images flowed faster and faster, Jim watched all his friends become younger and younger. Spock had changed least, in the time that Jim had known him, for the life of a Vulcan spanned more time than any human's. McCoy lost the lines that years in space had drawn in his face, till he looked as he had when James T. Kirk, lieutenant's stripes fresh on his sleeves, first met him. Jim remembered Mister Scott, who had been doubtful at first of a brash young captain's ability to command the finest ship in Starfleet. He remembered Carol Marcus, as she had been when he returned her to Earth, as she had been when they parted so many years before, as she was when they first met.

Jim's mother smiled and shook her head, bemused by some exploit, and as he watched she too grew younger, though she seemed hardly to change whether the years passed forward or backward.

Jim recalled Uhura the evening he met her, singing an Irish folk song and playing a small harp; he recalled Sulu, a youth just out of the Academy, beating him soundly in a fencing match; he recalled meeting Chekov, an ensign on duty during low watch, when late at night Jim haunted the bridge of his new ship. He saw his nephew, Peter Kirk, change from a young man at peace with himself and his past to a young boy, grief-stricken after the loss of both his parents.

And among those clear images drifted memories fainter and more ghostly. Jim saw his sister-in-law, Aurelan, dying in shock as the parasitic creatures of Deneva took over her mind. He saw his older brother, Sam, already dead of the same awful infestation. And yet he also saw them on their way to Deneva, in happier times, and he saw Sam as a youth, laughing, challenging him to a race across the fields of the Iowa farm; as a boy, climbing to their tree house; and as a child, looking down at him, one of the first memories Jim Kirk could recall. He saw his friend Gary Mitchell, mad with power, dying in a rock slide on an alien planet, and at the same time he saw him as an ambitious lieutenant, and as a wild midshipman their first year at the Academy. Jim heard echoes of their discussions: what they would do, where they would go, and all that they would achieve.

And Jim caught a quick, vague glimpse of his father, George Samuel Kirk, a remote and solitary man, who seemed alone even when he was with his family.

Finally he saw nothing but a long and featureless gray time.

A tremendous noise roused him from his fugue. The ship had survived its plunge through solar winds. Heat penetrated from the *Bounty*'s seared skin and pooled in the control chamber. Sweat trickled down Jim's back. The instruments showed all systems within the limits of normalcy. Everyone else on the bridge—even Spock—gazed dreamily into nothingness. The temperature began to fall as the ship radiated energy back into space.

"Mister Sulu," Jim said. He received no reply. "Mister Sulu!" Sulu glanced around, startled from his own reverie. "Aye, sir?" Jim watched as they all drew themselves back from their reveries to now . . . but when was *now?*

"What is our condition?"

Sulu glanced at his control panel. "Braking thrusters have fired, sir."

"Picture, please."

A blue and white globe rotated lazily, its clouds parting here and there to reveal familiar continents.

"Earth," Jim said softly. "But when?" At least they had outdistanced the probe, for the probe's impenetrable, roiling cloud cover no longer enclosed the planet. "Spock?"

"Judging by the pollution content of the atmosphere, I believe we have arrived at the late twentieth century."

"Well done, Mister Spock."

"Admiral!" Uhura exclaimed. "I'm picking up whale songs on long-range sensors!" She patched the signal into the speakers. The eerie cries and moans and whistles filled the control chamber.

"Home in on the strongest signal," Jim said. "Mister Sulu, descend from orbit."

"Admiral, if I may," Spock said. "We are undoubtedly already visible to the tracking devices of this time."

"Quite right, Spock. Mister Chekov, engage cloaking device."

Chekov complied. The *Bounty* remained visible inside itself, yet it lost a certain substantiality. Jim had a brief impression of riding toward a phantom planet in a phantom ship. Perhaps McCoy should have named the Klingon fighter *Flying Dutchman.*

The *Bounty* swept down out of space, drawing its wings into their sleek and streamlined atmospheric configuration. The ship bit into the air, slowing as it used friction and drag to help its braking.

The leading edges of its wings glowed with heat. Ionized molecules of gas rippled from the heat shields over the bow. The *Bounty* passed into night. The ship rode a fiery wave toward Earth, a brilliant shooting star in the dawn sky.

"We've crossed the terminator into night," Sulu said.

"Homing in on the west coast of North America," Spock said.

"The individual whale song is getting stronger. This is strange, Admiral. The song is coming from San Francisco—"

"From the city?" Jim said. "That doesn't make sense."

"Unless they're stranded in the bay," Sulu said. "Or—held captive?"

"It's the only one I can pick up," Uhura said. "And it's being broadcast. But there's no way to tell if it's live or from a recording."

"Is it possible . . ." Jim said. "Is it possible that they're already extinct in this time?"

"They are not yet extinct," Spock said.

"Then why can't Uhura find more than one?" Jim snapped.

"Because," Spock said evenly, "this is the wrong time of year for humpbacks to sing."

"Then why—"

"I do not know, Admiral. Information on great whales is severely limited in our time. Much has been lost, and much was never learned. May I suggest that we begin by discovering the origin of these signals?"

"Admiral!" Scott's voice overrode the song of the whale on the speakers. "Ye and Mister Spock—I need ye in the engine room."

Jim rose immediately. "Continue approach," he said, and headed out of the control chamber. Spock followed at a more dignified pace.

When Spock entered the engine subroom beside the power chamber, he understood the trouble before Scott spoke. The glow of dilithium crystals should have provided a brilliant illumination. Instead, the transparent power chamber radiated only the dimmest of multicolored light from the planes and angles of the crystalline mass. The dilithium now consisted of a crystal lattice changing into a quasicrystalline form. The crystals were diseased. As Spock watched, the plague spread. It was as if diamonds were decomposing into graphite or coal. For the *Bounty*'s purposes, the dilithium crystal was essential, the dilithium quasicrystal utterly useless.

"They're givin' out," Scott said. "Decrystallizin'. Ye can practically see 'em changin' before ye. After a point, the crystal is so compromised that ye canna pull any energy from it at all."

"How soon before that happens, Mister Scott?" Kirk said. "Give me a round figure."

Scott considered. "Twenty-four hours, give or take, stayin' cloaked. After that, Admiral, we'll be visible, or dead in the water. More likely both. We willna have enou' power to break back out of Earth's gravity. I willna even mention gettin' back home."

Kirk glared at the crystals. Spock wondered if he thought that the force of his anger could make them shift their energy states in an impossible spontaneous transformation.

"I can't believe we've come this far, only to be stopped," Kirk said. "I won't believe we'll be stopped." He chewed thoughtfully on his thumbnail. "Scotty, can't you recrystallize the dilithium?"

"Nay," Scott said. "I mean, aye, Admiral, 'tis theoretically possible, but even in our time we wouldna do it. 'Tis far easier, never mind cheaper, to go and mine new dilithium. The recrystallization equipment, 'twould be too dangerous to leave lyin' abou'."

"There *is* a twentieth-century possibility," Spock said. During his brief study of his mother's species' history and culture, he had been particularly intrigued by the human drive, one might almost say instinct, to leave extremely dangerous equipment "lyin' abou'."

"Explain," Kirk said.

"If memory serves," Spock said, "human beings carried on a dubious flirtation with nuclear fission reactors, both for energy production and for the creation of weapons of war. This in spite of toxic side effects, the release of noxious elements such as plutonium, and the creation of dangerous wastes that still exist on Earth. The fusion era allowed these reactors to be replaced. But at this time, some should remain in operation."

"Assuming that's true, how do we get around the toxic side effects?"

"We could build a device to collect the high-energy photons safely; we could then inject the photons into the dilithium chamber, causing crystalline restructure. Theoretically."

"Where would we find these reactors? Theoretically?"

Spock considered. "The twentieth-century humans placed their land-based reactors variously in remote areas of low population, or on fault lines. Naval vessels also used nuclear power. Given our destination, I believe this latter possibility offers the most promise."

Thinking over what Spock had said, Jim headed back to the control chamber.

At the helm, Sulu looked out across twentieth-century Earth. He kept the *Bounty* hovering above San Francisco. The city avalanched in light down the hillsides that ringed its shore. The lights ended abruptly at the bay, as if the wall of skyscrapers caught them and flung them upward.

"Is still beautiful city," Chekov said. "Or was, and will be."

"Yes," Sulu said. "I've always wished I had more time to get to know it. I was born there."

"I thought you were born on Ganjitsu," Chekov said.

"I was raised on Ganjitsu. And a lot of other places. I never lived here more than a couple of months at a time, but I was born in San Francisco."

"It doesn't look all that different," McCoy said.

Jim returned to the control chamber, and overheard McCoy's comment.

"Let's hope it isn't, Bones," he said.

But it did look different to Jim. He traced out the city, trying to figure out why the scene made him uneasy. Unfamiliar tentacles of light reached across the water: bridges. In his time, the Golden Gate Bridge remained as a historical landmark. But the other bridges no longer existed. The lights must be the headlamps of ground cars, each moving a single person. Jim located the dark rectangle of undeveloped land that cut across the eastern half of the city.

"Mister Sulu," he said, "set us down in Golden Gate Park."

"Aye, sir. Descending."

As the *Bounty* slipped through the darkness, Jim discussed the problems they had to solve with his shipmates.

"We'll have to divide into teams," he said. "Commanders Chekov and Uhura, you draw the uranium problem."

"Yes, sir," Chekov said. Uhura glanced up from the comm board long enough to nod.

"Doctor McCoy, you, Mister Scott, and Commander Sulu will build us a whale tank."

McCoy scowled. "Oh, joy," he said, almost under his breath.

"Captain Spock and I," Jim said, "will attempt to trace the whale song to its source."

"I'll have bearing and distance for you, sir," Uhura said.

"Right. Thanks." Jim gathered them together with his gaze. "Now, look. I want you all to be very careful. This is terra incognita. Many customs will doubtless take us by surprise. And it's a historical fact that these people have not yet met an extraterrestrial."

For a second no one understood what he meant. They lived in a culture that included thousands of different species of sentient beings. To think that they would meet people for whom a nonhuman person would be an oddity startled and shocked them all.

They looked at Mister Spock.

Spock, who often felt himself an alien even among his own people, did not find Admiral Kirk's comment surprising. He considered the problem for a moment.

When he had in the past been compelled to pass for human among primitive humans, his complexion had aroused little comment and no suspicion. His eyebrows had engendered comment, but only of a rather pernicious kind that could easily be ignored. Of the several structural differences between Vulcans and humans, only one had caused him any difficulty: his ears.

He opened his robe, untied the sash of the underrobe, and retied the sash as a headband. The band served to disguise his eyebrows, but, more important, it covered the pointed tips of his ears.

"I believe," he said, "that I may now pass among twentieth-century North Americans as a member of a foreign, but not extraterrestrial, country."

James Kirk gave a sharp nod of approval. "This is an extremely primitive and paranoid culture. Mister Chekov, please issue a phaser and communicator to each team. We'll maintain radio silence except in extreme emergencies." Jim glanced around to see that everyone understood the dangers they faced. Given the fears of the people of the late twentieth century, perhaps it would be better if his people did not look official. "Scotty, Uhura, better get rid of your uniform insignia."

They nodded their understanding and complied.

"Any questions?" Kirk said.

No one spoke.

"All right. Let's do our job and get out of here. Our own world is waiting."

Monday mornings were always worst as far as garbage was concerned. His heavy gloves scraping on the asphalt, Javy scooped up the loose trash and pitched it into the park garbage can. He and Ben were only supposed to empty the cans, but Javy hated seeing Golden Gate Park trashed after every weekend, so sometimes he broke the rules.

Belching diesel fumes into the foggy, salt-tinged air, the truck backed toward him. Javy hoisted the can onto his shoulder and pitched the contents into the garbage crusher. His first few weeks on the job, he had thought of a different metaphor for the machine every day, but there existed only a limited number of variations on grinding teeth or gnashing jaws. His favorite literary image contained a comparison of the garbage-crushing mechanism to a junkyard machine smashing abandoned cars into scrap. Minor garbage and major garbage. He had not quite got it worked out yet. So what else was new? He tried comparing the unfinished metaphor to the persistently intractable novel he was trying to write in the same way he compared the garbage crusher and the car crusher. Minor unfinished business and major unfinished business. Maybe he should try putting the manuscript into the garbage crusher.

You're really straining your symbolism here, Javy, he told himself.

He hoisted the second can and dumped the contents into the crusher.

Sometimes he wondered if he should go back to teaching. But he knew that if he did, he would get less work done on the novel than he did now. He needed a job of physical labor. Now the book went better than before. But he still could not finish it.

Javy jumped on the back of the truck and hung on till the next pickup spot, where a whole row of cans waited. Ben climbed down and joined him.

"And then what happens?" Ben said.

Javy was telling him a scene from the novel. Every book on writing and every creative writing teacher he knew of said that writers who talked about their stories never wrote them. For years Javy believed it and never told anyone anything till after he had written it down. But recently he had met a writer, an actual published writer.

"Everybody's different, Javy," the writer had said. "Don't ever let anybody tell you you've got to work the same way they do. Don't let them make your rules for you. They'll screw you up every time. You're supposed to be in the rule-breaking business." He was drunk, so maybe it was all bull, but just as an experiment, Javy broke that first law of writing and talked about a story. To Ben, as it happened. And then he went home and wrote it. He had not sold it yet, but at least he had finished the damned thing. So far it had three reject slips. Javy was getting attached to his reject slip collection. Sometimes that worried him.

He grabbed a crumpled newspaper off the ground and flung it after the other garbage.

"Come on, Javy, what happens?" Ben said. He dumped a can of trash into the crusher. Javy tried not to pay too much attention to what all went past. His first couple of weeks on the job, he noticed with fascination what people threw away, but now the stuff grossed him out. He supposed he would eventually become oblivious to it, but then maybe it would be time to start looking for another job.

" 'So I told her,' " Javy said, in the voice of the character in the scene, " 'if you think I'm laying out sixty bucks for a goddamn toaster oven, you got another thing coming.' "

The onshore breeze came up. It blew away the diesel fumes and brought a marshy, low-tide smell from the sea. Soon it would disperse the mist. Javy liked working the early shift; even on foggy days he liked dawn. A few minutes ago, before sunrise, he and Ben had seen a shooting star, surprisingly distinct in the fog.

"So what'd she say?" Ben asked, as if Javy were telling him about a real argument with a real person. Ben was a great audience. The only trouble was, he never bought books. He watched TV. Once in a while he went to a movie. Javy wondered if he ought to try writing the novel as a movie script instead—it would never make it as a TV movie; it was too rough and raw for TV—and take it down to L.A.

The onshore breeze freshened, then stiffened.

Suddenly the loose trash scuttled past Javy's feet like fleeing crabs and the wind blew trash out of the cans, knocking the cans over, swirling up whirlwinds of dust and leaves, whipping past so hard that even Ben had to grab the side of the truck to keep from being pushed over too. Javy stumbled and Ben grabbed him.

The wind stopped as abruptly as it had started. It did not die down or fade away; it simply ceased.

"What the hell was that?" Javy said.

He winced at a sharp pain in his ears. The pain became a high-pitched shriek, a zoned-out whine. Light fell out of the gray dawn. He looked toward it—

—and saw, amid the fog, on a terraced bank above him, a ramp descending, from nothingness, a light shining, from nothingness, and people appearing, from nothingness. He stared, speechless.

Ben grabbed him by the arm and pulled him toward the front of the truck.

"Let's get outta here!"

Too stunned to resist, Javy stumbled up into the driver's seat. Ben shoved him over, flung himself inside, grabbed the wheel, and snatched at the gearshift. He jammed his foot on the gas pedal and released the emergency brake with a jolt as the truck lurched forward.

"Wait!" Javy shouted. He lunged for the door on his side. Ben grabbed him by the shirt collar and dragged him back. Javy struggled with him, but Ben was about twice his size. "Did you see that?"

"No!" Ben shouted. "And neither did you, so shut up!"

For a minute Javy considered jumping out of the truck, but Ben had it going nearly fifty. Javy tried to see behind them in the side mirror, but the light and the ramp had vanished, and he could make out only shadows.

Jim led the way out of the *Bounty* and signaled for the ramp to withdraw. It disappeared into the cloaking field. The hatch closed, cutting off the interior light.

"Do you hear something?" Sulu said.

A low rumble changed pitch, fading.

"It's just traffic," Jim said. "Ground cars, with internal combustion engines. Shouldn't be too many around this early, but later the streets fill up with them."

The oily smoke of the ground cars' exhaust hung close. Trash littered the path and the meadow. Someone had turned over a row of garbage cans and spread their contents around the park. Jim worried about how he and his people would be able to get along within a culture that took so little care of its world, the world that would be theirs. In Jim's time, Earth still bore scars from wounds inflicted during the twentieth century.

Under his breath, McCoy grumbled about the smell. Spock gazed about with detached interest, his only visible reaction to the fumes a slight distension of the nostrils.

"We'll stick together till we get oriented," Jim said. "Uhura, what's the bearing to the whales?"

Uhura consulted her tricorder and gave him the distance and bearing. Before they departed, Jim fixed the surroundings in his mind. He could find the *Bounty* by tricorder, but he could also imagine needing to get back inside the ship without pausing for an instrument reading.

They set off across the meadow in the direction Uhura indicated.

"Everybody remember where we parked," Jim said.

Six

Jim and his shipmates left the park and entered the city at dawn. The sun burnished adobe houses with gold and burned away the fog. Long, fuzzy shadows shortened and sharpened.

Jim had not walked through his adopted home town in a long while. Climbing the steep hills, he began to wish he had come on the voyage in a good pair of walking shoes instead of dress boots.

Ground cars and pedestrians crowded the streets and sidewalks. Jim's tension eased when no one gave him and his group more than a second glance. Even Spock received little notice. Jim could not help but wonder why no one bothered about them, especially when they reached an area in which everyone wore similar clothes—dark jackets, matching trousers or shirts, lighter shirts, a strip of material tied around the neck—and carried similar dark leather cases. But here Jim's group did not even get first glances—

A man suddenly stopped and glared.

"What's *your* problem?"

"Nothing," Jim said, suppressing an irrational urge to tell him. "I don't have a problem."

"You will if you don't watch who you stare at." He shoved past Jim, then looked back. "And how you stare at them!" He turned, nearly ran into Spock, snarled as he circled him, and strode angrily away.

Jim *had* been staring at the people he passed, but he did not understand why one individual had reacted so strongly. He kept going, and he still watched people, but he watched more surreptitiously. He wondered why everyone dressed more or less alike, though not alike enough to be described as "in uniform," at least as he understood the term.

He stopped at an intersection with the other pedestrians. They waited, gazing at lines of ground cars that moved at a crawl in one direction and stood dead still on the cross-street.

A group of glass-screened boxes clustered together, each chained to a steel post.

Good, he thought. *News machines. They might tell me what I need to know. If I can key on whales . . .*

He glanced quickly over the headlines: "I was abducted by aliens from space!"

Jim frowned. Had he stumbled into a first encounter of human beings with another sentient species? If so, he would have to keep his people and his ship well out of the way. But he distinctly remembered—he thought he remembered—that the first contact happened in the twenty-first century. It happened when humans left their solar system, not when another species visited Earth. And he certainly did not recall anything about abductions of humans by extraterrestrials. He would have to ask Spock if he knew for certain, but not here on a crowded street corner where their conversation could be overheard.

Other headlines: "Talk Service Exposé." "Congloms Glom VidBiz." "Dow Jones Bull Turns Bear." The first two he found completely incomprehensible. He assumed the third to be a report on genetic engineering, though he did not quite understand why Jones would want to change a bull into a bear.

"Nuclear Arms Talks Stalled." That one he understood.

"It's a miracle these people ever got out of the twentieth century," McCoy said.

Jim waited for the headline to dissolve into a news story, but nothing happened. He wondered if the news machine was broken. Probably street machines were not as reliable now as they were in his own time. He looked for a way to key it to the subject he needed, but saw no controls. Perhaps it was more sophisticated than it looked and could be operated by voice.

"Excuse me." A man in quasiuniform stepped around Jim, bent over the news machine, inserted metallic disks into it, and opened it. Jim thought he was probably going to repair the machine so its screen would display more than headlines. Instead, the man took a folded bunch of paper from a stack of similar bunches of folded paper inside the machine. It was not an electronic news machine at all, but a dispenser of printed stories. Newspapers? That was it. The antique novels he had read sometimes mentioned newspapers, but never newspaper machines. They described young newspaper carriers running down the street crying "Extra!" Jim wondered how anyone kept up with the news here. These headlines must be hours old.

The man folded his paper under his arm and let the machine's spring door slam. The disks he had fed into it rattled in their container.

"Damn," Jim said softly. "They're still using money. We're going to need some."

"Money?" Chekov said. "We should have landed in Russia. There, we would not want money."

A couple of the twentieth-century people standing around them reacted to Chekov's comment with irritation. Jim heard somebody mutter, "Pinko commie exchange student." He recalled that the stalled nuclear arms talks referred to in the newspaper were arms talks between North Americans and Russians.

"In Russia," Chekov said, "to each according to their need, from each according to their ability." He smiled at a glowering citizen of twentieth-century North America.

The traffic pattern changed. The crowd at the corner flooded into the intersection, dashing around and between ground cars and sweeping away the belligerent citizen. The cars on the cross-street lurched forward, honking and screeching and outmaneuvering each other.

"Mister Chekov," Jim said, *sotto voce,* "I think that keeping quiet about the glories of Russia would be the better part of valor. At least while we're walking around on the streets of North America."

"Very well, Admiral," Chekov said, plainly mystified.

On the other hand, Jim thought, *it would be awfully convenient if we could receive according to our need just long enough to do what we need to do. Maybe we could have vanished before anybody asked us what our abilities might allow us to contribute.*

At any rate, they needed some money, physical money, and they needed it soon. Jim's conspicuous group would not get far with a zeroed-out credit balance.

He tried to remember more history. He thought that the age of electronic credit either had not yet begun or had not yet taken hold. Staring glumly at a sign across the street, "Antiques: We Buy and Sell," he recalled that the economy of twentieth-century Earth was still based on buying and selling.

He had some pieces in his collection back home that even here, a couple of hundred years in the past, might be worth something. But if he sold anything he had brought with him from his own time, he would introduce anachronisms into history. This he must not do. Besides, he could hardly hope to pass off a tricorder or one of McCoy's medical instruments as an antique.

Then he remembered something.

"You people wait here," he said. "And spread out. We look like a cadet review. Spock—"

The others moved apart, looking almost as self-conscious as when they clustered together. Jim started across the street without thinking. Spock followed.

A high shriek, an oily burned smell—a ground car's wheels spread black streaks on the gray street and the nose of the car stopped a handsbreadth from Jim's leg.

"Watch where you're going, you dumb ass!" the driver shouted.

"And—and a *double* dumb ass on you!" Jim yelled, startled into a reaction and still trying to fit in. Flustered, he hurried across the street. The driver blew a deafening blast of the ground car's horn. The car accelerated, leaving a second set of black streaks on the pavement.

On the far curb, Spock gave him an odd look, but said nothing. Jim's pulse raced. It would be ridiculous to travel years and light-years through space-time in order to meet his end under a primitive vehicle in the street of the city where he lived.

He would have to be more careful. All his people would, especially Spock. If the Vulcan had an encounter with contemporary medical authorities, no matter how rudimentary their techniques, his headband would not conceal his extraterrestrial characteristics.

Back on the curb, the shipmates breathed a collective sigh of relief that Kirk and Spock had made it past the traffic.

How disorienting it is, Sulu thought, *to be in a place that looks so familiar yet feels so alien.*

"Ah! Hikaru oji san desu ka?"

Sulu started. He turned to see who had called him by his given name, and called him "uncle" as well. A young boy ran up to him, and addressed him in Japanese.

"Konna tokoro ni nani o shiteru'n desu ka?" The voice spoke informally, as if to a close relative, asking what he was doing here.

"Warui ga, bōya wa hitochigai nasaremashita," Sulu said. To tell the little boy that he had mistaken him for someone else, Sulu had to reach into his memory for his disused Japanese, learned in the classroom and from reading novels not three hundred but a thousand years old.

"Honto desu ne!" the little boy said. *"Anata no nihongo ga okashii'n desu."*

Sulu smiled. *I'm sure he's right, and my Japanese is strange,* he thought. *I probably sound like a character from* The Tale of Genji.

Embarrassed, the little boy started to back away.

"Bōya, machina," Sulu said gently. At his request, the boy stopped. *"Onamae wa nan da?"*

"Sulu Akira desu." The little boy told Sulu his name.

Sulu sat on his heels, and looked at him. The child, Akira Sulu, already possessed the intense gaze and the humor one could see in pictures of him as an adult and as an elderly man.

"Ah sō ka," Sulu said. *"Tashika ni bōya wa shogaianraku ni kurasu."*

The boy blinked, startled to be told by a stranger who looked like his uncle but clearly was not, that he would have a long and happy life.

"Ogisama arigato gozaimasu," he said, thanking Sulu politely.

Sulu stood up again. The little boy ran away down the street.

"What was that all about?" McCoy said. "Who was that?"

"That, Doctor," Sulu said, still watching the little boy, "was my great-great-great grandfather."

McCoy, too, gazed after the child.

On the other side of the street, Jim opened the door of the antique shop and entered, leaving the noisy traffic behind. His vision accustomed itself to the dimmer light of the interior. He stared around, astounded by the items in the shop. Antiques of this quality were nearly impossible to find, at any price, in his time. The years had been too hard on them.

"Can I help you, gentlemen?"

The proprietor, a man of about forty, wore his graying hair long and tied at the back of his neck. Jim believed the period of his costume to be somewhat earlier than the present: antique, perhaps, to fit in with his shop. The antique dealer wore gold spectacles with small round lenses, wide-bottomed blue trousers, patchy and pale with age, leather sandals, and a vest that looked to Jim like museum-quality patchwork.

"What can you tell me about these?" Jim said. He drew his own spectacles from his pocket. They resembled those of the proprietor, but his had rectangular lenses. Light flowed and flared along the cracks in the glass.

The dealer took them and turned them over reverently. He whistled softly. "These are beautiful."

"Antique?"

"Yes—they're eighteenth-century American. They're quite valuable."

"How much will you give me for them?"

"Are you sure you want to part with them?"

"I'm sure." In fact he did not want to part with them at all, but he had no choice, no room for sentiment.

The antique dealer looked at them more carefully, unfolding them and checking the frame. He crossed the shop to get his magnifying glass from the counter, then squinted at the fine engraving on the inner surface of the earpiece.

Spock bent toward Kirk. "Were those not a birthday present from Doctor McCoy?"

"And they will be again, Spock," Kirk said. "That's the beauty of it." He joined the owner on the other side of the shop. "How much?"

"They'd be worth more if the lenses were intact," the antique dealer said. "But I might be able to restore them. It would take some research . . ." He glanced at the glasses again. Jim could tell he wanted them. "I'll give you two hundred bucks, take it or leave it."

"Is that a lot?" Jim asked.

He looked at Jim askance. "I think it's a fair price," he said defensively. "But if you don't like it—" He offered Jim the glasses back.

"My companion did not mean to impugn your fairness," Spock said. "He has been . . . out of the area . . . for some time, and I am only visiting. I am not familiar with prices, or with your current word usage. What is a buck?"

"A buck is a dollar. You know what a dollar is?"

Neither Spock nor Kirk replied.

"The main unit of currency of the good old U.S. of A.? You can buy most of a gallon of gas with it, this week anyway, or most of a loaf of decent bread, or a beer if you choose your bar right. Either you guys have been gone forever, or . . . did we ever meet in the sixties?"

"I think not," Spock said.

They were getting out of their depth. "Two hundred bucks would be fine," Kirk said quickly.

"You aren't interested in selling your belt buckle, are you? Does it have any age on it, or is it contemporary? I've never seen anything quite like it, but it looks a little bit deco."

Jim felt tempted, but he had already pushed his luck by selling his spectacles. McCoy had had the lenses ground to Jim's prescription in their own time. Jim had no idea what an analysis of the glass would show, but he doubted that the results would resemble something from the eighteenth century any more than his belt buckle would look like an alloy from old date nineteen-twenty.

"No," he said. "It . . . doesn't have any age on it. I don't think it would be worth much."

"Okay. Let me draw you a check for these."

Jim followed him to the back of the shop. The antique dealer sat at a beautiful mahogany roll-top, opened a black lacquer lap desk, took out a spiral-bound book, and unscrewed the top of a fountain pen.

"Who should I make this out to?"

"I beg your pardon?"

"What's your name, man?" The owner frowned. "I have to know your name so I can write you a check so you can get your money."

"Can't I just have the money?" Jim said.

The owner turned in his chair and hooked one arm over the back rest. He gestured toward the spectacles, glittering gold on his desk. "Look, man, do you have any paperwork on these?" His voice held a hint of suspicion.

"Paperwork?" Jim said, confused.

"You know, like a sales receipt? Any proof of ownership? I've never had any trouble with stolen stuff, and I'm damned if I want to start now."

"They aren't stolen!" Jim said. Spock's story was wearing rather thin. "I've . . . had them for a long time. But I don't have any paperwork."

"Do you have some I.D.?"

At least he knew what I.D. was, unless the usage had changed between now and then. He shook his head. "I . . . er . . . lost it."

"What about your friend?"

With perfect serenity, Spock said, "I have lost mine as well. Our transportation lost our luggage, thus we find ourselves in our present difficulty."

The dealer's attitude changed abruptly. "Jeez, why didn't you say so in the first place? What a bummer. Did you come all the way from Japan? I always wanted to go there, but I never made it. I spent a lot of time in Asia. Nepal, Tibet, and, well, Nam, but I hardly ever tell anybody that anymore, they think you're going to wig out in front of them, you know?" He cut off his words. "Sorry," he said shortly. He closed his fountain pen and put the checkbook back into the lap desk. He gazed at Jim closely. "You know what?"

"What?" Jim said, not sure he really wanted to know.

"Those glasses better not be stolen, man, because I don't want any trouble with the cops. Or the narcs. Or the feds. The feds are the worst, man, I don't want anything more to do with the feds, ever again. So if you're screwing me around, and you're really a couple high-class cokeheads ripping off your rich friends for your next score, it'll go on your karma, you got that?"

"I got that," Jim said. He got the message, even if the details eluded him. "The spectacles are not stolen." He hoped he was telling the truth. It occurred to him that it was perfectly possible that sometime in their long history his spectacles had been stolen.

"Okay." The antique dealer rose and strode to his cash register. It flung itself open with ringing bells and the crash of its drawer. "Here's your money, no questions asked." He handed Jim a wad of green and gray printed rectangles of paper. "Small bills." He suddenly grinned. "I guess I've got a little anarchy left in me yet."

"I guess so," Jim said. He took the money. "Thank you."

As he stepped out into the sunshine, Jim drew a long breath and let it out slowly.

"Thank you, Mister Spock," he said. "I'm not sure we got away clean, but at least we got away."

"I merely spoke the truth, Admiral," Spock said. "Our transportation did destroy my belongings. The *Enterprise* held virtually everything I possessed."

"Yes . . ." Jim did not want to think about the *Enterprise*. "Spock, I'm not in command of anything right now. You've got to get used to calling me Jim, at least while we're here. Calling me Admiral might draw attention."

"Very well," Spock said. "I will try to form a new habit."

They rejoined the rest of their group, being more careful about crossing the street.

"We were about to send out the cavalry," McCoy said.

"The cavalry, even in its mechanized form, ended some decades ago, Doctor McCoy," Spock said.

"No!" McCoy exclaimed. "Really? I'm devastated!"

Jim fended off another quarrel by showing everyone the money. He explained what he knew of its value. He divided it as evenly as the denomination of the bills allowed among the three teams. He gave seventy bucks—dollars?—to Uhura, seventy to Sulu, and kept sixty for himself and Spock. Perhaps he should have kept strictly to rank order and given the tank team money to McCoy or to Scott, but in all the years Jim had known Scott, the engineer had never had an iota of sense about money. As for McCoy . . . Jim did not know what was going on with McCoy. He almost wished he had kept him on the whale team, where he could keep an eye on him. But then he would have to act as buffer between McCoy and Spock, and he did not know how long his temper would hold if he had to do that.

"That's all there is," he said, "so nobody splurge. Are we set?"

Like him, they put a good face on it. He worried more about sending his people into the past of their own world than he ever had about sending them to the surface of a completely alien planet.

He and Spock headed north. The crush in traffic eased. Ground cars still filled the streets, but the masses of people in quasiuniform gave way to a more casual crowd.

"Well, Spock," Jim said, "thanks to your restored memory and a little bit of luck, we are now in the streets of San Francisco looking for a pair of humpback whales."

Spock did not reply. He certainly did not laugh.

"How do you propose to solve this minor problem?" Jim said.

"Simple logic will suffice," Spock said. "We need a map. That one should do."

Showing not the least surprise at discovering one immediately, he led Jim to an enclosure. It sheltered a bench on which a number of people sat. Near a list of street names, some of them still familiar, and numbers, none of which meant anything to Jim, a diagrammatic map had been painted.

"I will simply superimpose the coordinates on this map and find our destination."

Spock glanced at the map, as if an instant of casual attention would solve the problem. Then he looked more closely. The streets and boundaries had been drawn in a formalized way that had little connection with the true geography of the region. The thick colored lines painted over it helped not at all.

As Spock puzzled over the map, a larger than average ground car pulled up. It belched oily smoke, further polluting air already saturated with suspended fumes and particulates. The doors of the vehicle folded open and the people on the bench lined up to enter it. Jim realized this must be contemporary public transportation.

Then he read the sign on the vehicle's side: "See George and Gracie, the only two humpback whales in captivity. At the Cetacean Institute, Sausalito."

"Mister Spock," he said.

"One moment, Admiral. I believe that in time I can discover a solution—"

"Mister Spock. I think we'll find what we're looking for at the Cetacean Institute. In Sausalito. Two humpbacks called George and Gracie."

Spock turned to him, more puzzled than before. "How do you know this?"

"Simple logic," Jim said.

The driver leaned toward them. "You guys getting on the bus or not?"

"Come on, Spock."

Jim led the way through the front doors of the bus.

A moment later, fuming, he descended from the rear exit.

"What does it mean," Spock said, perplexed, " 'exact change'?"

Sulu followed Scott and Doctor McCoy down the street. Scott forged ahead as if he knew where he was going, but if he did he had not let Sulu or McCoy in on the secret.

"Would you mind telling me," McCoy said, "how we plan to convert the cargo hold into a tank?"

"Ordinarily," Scott said, " 'twould be done wi' transparent aluminum."

"You're a few years early for that," Sulu said.

"Aye, lad, I know it. 'Tis up to us to find a twentieth-century equivalent."

Sulu wished that Scott would stop calling him lad. They walked along in silence for another fifty meters. Halfway down the next block, a billboard loomed over the street: "Can't find it? Try the yellow pages!"

Sulu pointed to it. "What about that?"

Scott squinted to read it.

"Does look promising. But can ye tell me," he said, "what's a yellow pages?"

"Beats me," Sulu said. "We'll have to ask somebody." Preferring a straightforward approach, he headed toward the nearest pedestrian.

McCoy grabbed his arm. "Wait a minute," the doctor said. "That billboard—you're obviously supposed to know already what yellow pages are. Or is. For all we know, maybe we're supposed to know what 'it' is, too. If we go around asking questions blind, somebody's bound to get suspicious."

" 'Tis true," Scott said.

"So maybe they'll think we're a little strange," Sulu said. "Maybe they'll think we're from out of town. But I don't think we have to worry about anybody's suspecting that we're space travelers from the future!"

"Out of town . . ." McCoy said. "Sulu, that's a good idea." He regarded Sulu, then Scott, speculatively. "Which one of us is most likely to be able to pass for somebody from out of town?"

All their clothes were just different enough to stand out, but not different enough to attract inordinate amounts of attention; none was physically remarkable in comparison to the general population of San Francisco.

"Mister Scott," McCoy said. "I think you're elected. Your accent—"

"Accent!" Scott exclaimed. "Ye canna be sayin' that I speak wi' an accent!"

"But . . ." McCoy let his protest trail off. "Everybody here does, so in relation you'll sound like you're from out of town. It's that, or I'll have to do my Centaurian imitation—"

"Never mind!" Scott said. "If I'm elected, I'm elected." He straightened his uniform jacket, glanced around, and left their group to speak to the next pedestrian.

"Begging your pardon, sir," he said. "But I'm from out of town, and I was wondering—"

The pedestrian walked past without acknowledging Scott's presence. Scott watched him go, frowning. He rejoined Sulu and McCoy.

"What d'ye make of that?"

McCoy shrugged. "I can't imagine."

"Try again," Sulu said.

Again Scott straightened his coat; again he approached a pedestrian.

"If I might have a moment of your time, sir—"

"Get out of my face!"

Scott backed off, startled. The pedestrian stormed away without a backward glance, muttering something about panhandlers, tracts, and street crazies.

"This isna working," Scott said to Sulu and McCoy. "Doctor, maybe ye'd better attempt the Centaurian imitation after all."

"Come on, Scotty, once more," McCoy said. "Third try's the charm."

Scott approached a third pedestrian. As he neared her, she dropped something. Scott picked it up.

"Excuse me, ma'am, ye dropped this."

She turned back. "Are you speaking to me?"

"Aye, ma'am, that I am, ye dropped this." He offered her the folded leather parcel.

"That's very kind of you," she said, "but I've never seen that wallet before. Maybe we'd better see if there's any identification inside." She took the wallet, opened it, and looked through it.

"Aye, ma'am, I'm sure ye'd know what's best to do wi' it, but I'm from out of town, and I was wondering—"

"Oh, my goodness," she said. "There isn't any identification, but look at this." She displayed a wad of bills. "There must be a thousand dollars in here!"

Scott had not yet got used to twentieth-century money. It all looked the same to him, so all he could tell was that there was a good bit more of it in the wallet than Admiral Kirk had given Sulu. He shrugged.

"I'm sure ye'd know better than me," Scott said. "In the meantime, could ye tell me what the term 'yellow pages' means?"

"Look, if we turn this in to the police, they'll just disappear it even if somebody claims it. Why don't we split it? We'll both put up some of our own money to show our goodwill, and—" She stopped. "What did you say?"

"I asked ye if ye knew what 'yellow pages' means."

"You're not from around here, are you?"

"I told ye that, too," Scott said, wishing he could figure out why it was so difficult to get a simple answer to what he hoped was a simple question.

"Where are you from?"

"Why, Scotland."

"Don't they have phone books in Scotland?"

"What's a phone book?"

"A directory of phone numbers. The yellow pages are the commercial part. You don't have those in Scotland?"

"Nay," he said. Her expression indicated the necessity of some further explanation. " 'Tis all computerized, ye see."

"Oh." She shook her head, bemused. "I suppose your money is computerized, too, and you don't have any cash on you. I bet you don't have any cash money in this country at all."

"Aye," he said, then suddenly wondered if he had said too much. "Why d'ye ask?"

She sighed. "Never mind, it isn't important. If you need some yellow pages, all you have to do is find a phone—you do have phones in Scotland, don't you?"

"Aye," he said, "I mean, well, in a manner o' speaking."

"Phone." She turned him around and led him to a tall, narrow, glass-sided box. He stood before it, waiting for the door to open. She reached out and pulled the handle, folding the door.

'Tis mechanical, Scott thought, *startled by its primitiveness.*

"Door," she said. She hoisted a heavy, black-covered book that hung by hinges. She put it on a shelf, opened it, backed out of the booth, and pointed again. "Yellow pages."

"Thank ye kindly, ma'am," Scott said. "Ye've been of great help."

"Just call me a good Samaritan," she said. "You have a nice day, now." She started away.

"Ma'am?"

"What is it?"

"That wallet—ye seemed to think 'twould cause ye difficulty. Would ye want me to turn it in for ye? I could try to find the time."

She cocked her head. "No," she said. "No, don't worry about it. I know what to do with it."

"Thank ye again."

She raised her hand in acknowledgment and farewell, already striding down the street.

Scott went into the phone booth and paged through the phone book. After a moment, McCoy and Sulu joined him.

"What was all that about?" McCoy said.

"All what, Doctor?"

"What took you so long?" the doctor snapped. "I thought you were going to take her out on a date."

"I wouldna jeopardize our mission wi' such a digression," Scott said, affronted. "Nay, she found a wallet—I mean, I found a wallet—" As he began to get his bearings in the yellow pages—he found it easier if he thought of it as a printed technical manual—he repeated the conversation to McCoy and Sulu. When he finished, all three agreed that the encounter was incomprehensible.

"Hah!" Scott exclaimed, pointing to a section of a yellow page. "Acrylic sheeting! 'Tis bound to be just what we need. Burlingame Industrial Park. Off wi' us, then."

A few blocks and a few phone booths away, Chekov found what he was looking for. He clapped the reinforced cover of the phone book shut and rejoined Uhura on the sidewalk.

"Find it?" she asked.

"Yes. Under U.S. Government. Now we need directions." He stopped the first passerby he saw. "Excuse me, sir. Can you direct me to Navy base in Alameda?"

The man looked at Chekov, looked at Uhura, and frowned. "The Navy base?"

"Yes," Chekov said. "Where they keep nuclear vessels?"

"Sure," the man said slowly. "Alameda. That's up north. Take BART—there's the station over there—toward Berkeley and all the way to the end of the line. Then catch a bus to Sacramento. You can't miss it."

"Spasiba," Chekov said. "Thank you."

Harry watched the Russian biker in the leather suit and the black woman in the paramilitary uniform head toward the BART station. He scowled after them. Then he smiled with one corner of his mouth. He entered the same phone booth they had left, picked up the receiver, wiped the mouthpiece with his pocket handkerchief, and dialed a number from memory.

It took quick thinking to divert a couple of trained spies like that. He had never expected anything like this to happen to him, right out on the street. He never expected to have this kind of chance.

"FBI."

"This is Gamma," Harry said. He recognized the agent's voice. He had talked to him before. He did not know his name, so he called him Bond. Bond never sounded very sympathetic when Harry called, but he always listened and he always claimed to have taken down the information. Harry suspected Bond never did anything with it, though, because the TV and the newspapers never announced the apprehension of any of the spies Harry detected. Someday Gamma would show Bond what he was worth to the government. Maybe this was the time.

Harry assumed the brief pause on the FBI's end of the line was for Bond to turn on a tape recorder.

"What do you want now?"

"I just talked to two spies."

"Spies. Right."

Harry explained what had happened. "What else could they be but commie spies? They asked for directions to Alameda but I sent them to Sacramento instead. You ought to be able to catch them up at the bus station at the end of the BART line."

"Okay. Thanks much."

"You aren't going to do anything, are you?" Harry said angrily.

"I can't release information about investigations over the phone," Bond said. "You know that."

"But—he was a Russian, I tell you. And that woman with him, I bet she was from—from South Africa. Aren't you guys always saying the Russkies are trying to take over Africa?"

Bond did not reply for so long that Harry wondered if he had to change the tape in the recorder.

"A black South African spy," Bond said.

About time I got through to him, Harry thought. "Yeah. Had to've been."

"Right. Uh, thanks very much." The line went dead.

Harry replaced the receiver. Finally he had Bond listening to him. The FBI man must have hung up fast so he could get a squad of agents out after the saboteurs.

The spies had spent a lot of time in and around this phone booth. Maybe another spy had left something for them to pick up. Or maybe *they* had left something to be collected! That would be something to show to Bond, all right. He searched on top of the phone, around the shelves, above the door, even inside the coin return. City grime covered everything with a thin, dusty film. It made him want to wash his hands. He found a quarter, but nothing in the way of secret documents. Maybe he was looking for a microdot. The trouble was that he had no idea what a microdot looked like. He inspected the quarter carefully but found nothing out of the ordinary.

Then he recalled another sneaky thing the government had found out the Russians did. They covered doorknobs and telephones and money and whatever they could get their hands on with poison dust that glowed, or emitted radiation, or something.

He dropped the quarter, kicked it into the corner of the phone booth, and bolted outside.

Suddenly fearful of being spied on himself, Harry glanced suspiciously around. They left the quarter as bait, and marked it, so the spies must have fingered him as an enemy. He rubbed his contaminated hands down the sides of his trousers. He would have to find a place to wash. But he was too smart to let them trick him into leading them right to his home. He would follow the first pair of spies instead. That would fool the ones following him, all right, if he led them to their cohorts and let them run into each other. Maybe Bond and his group could scoop them all up at once.

He headed for the BART station.

Sliding smoothly underground in the Bay Area Rapid Transit train, Uhura read the advertisements on the walls of the car. She hoped they would tell her something about the culture she was trying to hide inside, but they were all written in a sort of advertising shorthand, almost a code, in which a few words meant a great deal to a member of the community, but very little to a stranger. She turned her attention to the schematic map of the transit routes.

"Pavel," she said. "That fellow sent us off in the wrong direction."

"What? How is this possible?" He jumped up and looked at the map.

Uhura traced the route the man on the street had indicated. "I don't know where Sacramento is," she said, "but if we go through Berkeley and then turn east, in the first place we'll be headed away from the sea, not toward it. At least I don't remember that there's been a sea in that direction for a lot longer in the past than we've come. In the second place, Berkeley is north of us, and we want to go to Alameda, which is south." She touched the city on the map.

"You're right," Pavel said.

"We'll have to get off on the other side of the bay and transfer," she said. "I wonder how much it will cost? This is getting expensive."

"I wonder why he told us wrong thing," Pavel said.

Uhura shook her head. "I don't know. Maybe he's from out of town, too, and just didn't want to seem ignorant."

"That must be explanation."

At the first station on the other side of the bay, they got off, waited, and boarded a train going south. Uhura sat down gratefully, glad to be headed in the right direction without an unnecessary digression. She looked out the window. Another train, heading north, stopped beside them.

"Pavel—look!"

The man who had sent them in the wrong direction sat in the northbound car. Someone sat down next to him. He shifted closer to the window and looked away. His gaze locked with Uhura's. As her train pulled out going south, and his train pulled out going north, he jumped up and stared after her with an expression of shock and anger.

Seven

Changing paper money into a metallic form suitable for use on the bus took more time and more powers of persuasion than obtaining the paper money in the first place. Admiral Kirk walked angrily out of the first two establishments in which they sought help. The first proprietor pointed to a hand-lettered sign stuck to his counter with adhesive strips of transparent plastic: "No change." The second proprietor snarled, "What am I, a bank?" He did not react sympathetically when Spock tried to explain about their lost luggage. He muttered something about foreigners and invited Spock and Kirk to depart.

"My disguise appears to be successful," Spock said when they were once more out on the street.

"Too damned successful," Kirk said.

"Admiral," Spock said, "my understanding is that the amounts of money we possess are not too small to permit us onto the bus, but too large."

"Very astute, Mister Spock."

"In that case, we must purchase something that costs less than the difference between one piece of paper money and the amount of metallic money we must give to the bus."

"Astute again."

"It is simple logic."

"So simple I even figured that one out for myself. I've been trying to avoid buying something nonessential. But I don't see any alternative." Scowling, he strode into a third shop. Spock followed. Kirk plucked a small foil-wrapped disk from a bowl on the counter. "I'll have one of these," he said, and handed the clerk a bill.

She pressed keys on a machine that emitted buzzes and a small slip of paper. She handed Kirk a handful of change and a handful of bills. She put the disk into a plastic bag, folded the slip of paper over the bag's top, and fastened it all securely with a small device that inserted a small piece of wire. This was a ceremonial ritual with which Spock was not familiar. The clerk handed Kirk the bag. "Anything else for you today?"

"Yes, thank you," Kirk said. "I'd like some more of these." He showed her the metallic money and offered her another bill.

"Look, mister, I'm sorry. The boss really gets on my case if I give people bus change—that is what you need, isn't it?—and run out of quarters halfway through the afternoon. If it was up to me—"

"Never mind," Kirk said through clenched teeth. "I'll have *two* of these." He picked up another disk, went through the process all over again, and stalked out of the store. "Here, Spock," he said when they were once more on the street. "Have a mint."

Spock disassembled the package, unwrapped the foil, and sniffed the wafer inside. Kirk ripped open the bag he carried and ate his wafer quickly; Spock put his wafer in his mouth and allowed it to melt as he analyzed the outer and inner tastes.

A bus stopped; they entered; they paid. Once they had prepared themselves, the task became simple.

As is true of so many other endeavors, Spock thought.

They sat in the only remaining seat. A young person sat in the seat in front of them, feet stretched across the second seat, attention centered on a large, rectangular, noise-producing machine.

"Admiral," Spock said, "I believe this confection you have given me contains sucrose."

"What?" Kirk said.

Spock wondered why he spoke so loudly. "Sucrose," he said again, showing Kirk the foil wrapper.

"I can't hear you!" Kirk shouted, and Spock realized the admiral was having trouble sorting voices from the sounds produced by the noise-making machine. The admiral leaned toward the next seat. "Excuse me," he said. He received no response. "Excuse me! Can you please stop that sound?"

The young person glanced up, blinked, raised one fisted hand with the middle finger extended, then pushed the machine aside and stood.

"Want to try to make me?" The young person leaned over the back of his seat toward Admiral Kirk.

"That could be arranged," the admiral said.

The young human punched him. But the admiral blocked the blow. The young man's fist smacked against Kirk's palm.

Before the altercation could escalate, Spock placed his fingers at the junction of the neck and shoulder of the young person. He applied slight pressure. The young person sagged, unconscious. Spock settled him securely in the corner of the seat, inspected the controls of the noise-box, and pressed the control marked "on/off." The noise ceased.

Suddenly the other riders on the bus began to applaud. Spock realized, to his surprise, that they were applauding him.

"Domo arigato gozaimashita!" someone shouted at him. Spock had no idea what that meant. Feeling conspicuous, he sat down again. Admiral Kirk settled beside him. To Spock's relief, the applause subsided and the attention of the other riders returned to their own concerns. He could only assume that the audience had enjoyed the minor spectacle.

"As you observed," Spock said, "a primitive culture."

"Yes," Kirk said rather too loudly in the absence of the noise. He lowered his voice abruptly. "Yes."

"Admiral, may I ask you a question?"

"Spock, dammit, don't call me Admiral!" Kirk whispered. "Can't you remember? You used to call me Jim."

Having been told the same thing by several people whose word he trusted, Spock believed this to be true; but another truth was that he did not actually remember it. He said nothing. He felt rather strange. He tried to shake off the effects of the sucrose and the other active chemicals in the mint.

"What's your question?" Kirk said.

"Your use of language has altered since our arrival. It is currently laced with—shall I say—more colorful images: 'double dumb ass on you,' and so forth."

"You mean profanity. That's simply the way they talk here." He shrugged. "Nobody pays any attention to you if you don't swear every other word. You'll find it in all the literature of the period."

"For example?"

"Oh . . ." Kirk considered. "The complete works of Jacqueline Susann, the novels of Harold Robbins . . ."

"Ah," Spock said. He recognized the names from a list he had scanned: the most successful authors of this time. "The giants."

The bus roared onto the Golden Gate Bridge. Kirk and Spock let their discussion of literature drop, for the Pacific stretched away to one side and the bay and the golden California hills stretched in the other, and the cables of the bridge soared above it all.

Following other visitors to the Cetacean Institute, Jim stepped down from the bus, Spock close behind. The wide, white, multileveled building stretched along the shore before them. The sun warmed the pavement and the salt air sparkled. Jim laid out a few more of the precious dollars for admission. He passed through the doors, entering a huge, cool, high-ceilinged display hall. Life-sized replicas of whales hung overhead, swimming and gliding through the air above a group of visitors.

"Good morning." A young woman faced the group. "I'm your guide today," she said. "I'm Doctor Gillian Taylor. You can call me Gillian. I'm assistant director of the Cetacean Institute. Please follow me, and just give a yell if you can't hear. Okay?"

She was twenty-five or thirty, and she had a lot of presence for someone so young. She had a good smile, too. But Jim got the impression that escorting tourists did not completely occupy her attention. He moved closer. Spock lagged at the back, but Jim supposed the Vulcan could not get himself in too much trouble. He had agreed, for the moment, to let Jim ask the questions. They both assumed Jim had a better chance of fitting in with this culture. Jim hoped they both were right.

"The Cetacean Institute is devoted exclusively to whales," Gillian Taylor said. "We're trying to collect all the research that exists on cetaceans. Even if we succeed, our information will be minuscule compared to what we still have to learn—and what we think we know that's wrong. The first common misconception is that whales are fish."

She passed a striking series of underwater photographs of whales. Jim wanted to inspect them more closely, but he also wanted to listen to Gillian Taylor. Gillian Taylor won out.

"Whales aren't fish," she said. "They're mammals, like us. They're warmblooded. They breathe air. They produce milk to nurse their young. And they're very old mammals: eleven million years, give or take."

A little boy waved his hand to attract her attention. "Do whales really eat people, like in *Moby Dick?*"

"Many whales, baleen whales, like George and Gracie, don't even have teeth," Gillian Taylor said. "They strain plankton and shrimp out of vast amounts of sea water, and that's the limit of their hostility. Moby Dick was a sperm whale. He did have teeth, to hunt giant squid thousands of feet beneath the surface of the sea. But there are very few documented cases of attacks on people by whales. Unfortunately, their principal enemy is far more aggressive."

"You mean human beings," Jim said.

She glanced at him and nodded. "To put it bluntly. Since the dawn of time, people have 'harvested' whales." She accentuated the word *harvested* with considerable sarcasm. "We used the bodies of these creatures for a variety of purposes—most recently for dog food and cosmetics."

Jim noticed that she used few cosmetics herself; the blue of her eyes was natural, unaccented, and intense.

"Every single product whales are used for can be duplicated, naturally or synthetically, and usually more economically than by hunting whales. A hundred years ago, using hand-thrown harpoons, people did plenty of damage. But that was nothing compared to what we've achieved in this century."

She led the group to a large video screen and touched a button. Images appeared, grainy and ill defined by Jim's standards, but affecting nonetheless. The films in the *Bounty*'s computer had been grotesque. These, of a modern whale-processing operation, were gruesome. A helicopter spotted a pod of whales. Following directions from the air, a powered boat singled out the largest whale and pursued it. A cannon blasted a harpoon into the whale's side. The harpoon itself exploded. In a moment, an immense and powerful entity changed to a bleeding, dying hulk. The hunt had been replaced by assembly-line killing and butchery.

The harpoon boat left the whale floating and set out after another victim. The dying whale moved its flukes convulsively, erratically, as if somehow the creature could free itself, escape, and live. But it was not to be. The factory ship engulfed the whale and dismembered it into oil and bones, flesh and entrails.

"This is humanity's legacy," Gillian Taylor said. "Whales have been hunted to the edge of extinction. The largest creature ever to inhabit the earth, the blue whale, is virtually gone. Even if hunting stopped right now, today, we've got no assurance that the population would be able to recover."

Gillian's bitterness cut Jim deeply. Her intensity drew him into bearing some of the responsibility for what had happened in their past, for what was happening in her present, and for what would occur in Jim's present, in the future.

"Despite all attempts to ban whaling, countries and pirates continue to engage in the slaughter of these inoffensive creatures. In the case of the humpback, the species once numbered in the hundreds of thousands. Today, less than seven thousand individuals still live, and the whalers take smaller and smaller victims because the whales no longer have time to reach their full growth. And since it's hard to tell whether a whale is male or female, whalers even take females carrying unborn calves."

"To drive another species to extinction is not logical."

Gillian glared at the back of the crowd, at Spock.

"Whoever said the human race was logical?" Anger tinged her voice, but she repressed it. "If you'll all follow me, I'll introduce you to the Institute's pride and joy."

Gillian led the group out into the sunlight. A wide deck surrounded an enormous tank.

"This is the largest sea water tank in the world," Gillian said. "It contains the only two humpback whales in captivity."

Jim scanned the surface of the water, squinting against the dazzle on the wavelets.

"Our pair wandered into San Francisco Bay as calves. Whales, especially humpbacks, seem to have a well-developed sense of humor. So we call our whales George and Gracie."

On the other side of the tank, the arched black back of a whale broke the surface. The whale's small dorsal fin cut through the water. The whale gathered itself, hesitated, flipped its flukes into the air, and smoothly disappeared.

"They're mature now," Gillian said. "They weigh about forty-five thousand pounds each. Gracie is forty-two feet long and George is thirty-nine. They're mature, but they aren't full-grown. Humpbacks used to average about sixty feet—when full-grown humpbacks still existed. It's a measure of our ignorance of the species that we don't even know how long it will take these individuals to reach their full size."

Jim heard a loud splash. Some members of the audience gasped, but Jim's attention had been on Gillian Taylor, and he had not seen the whale leap. A wave splashed at the edge of the deck.

"That was Gracie leaping out of the water," Gillian said. "What she did is called breaching. They do it a lot, and we don't know why. Maybe it's a signal.

Maybe it's courtship. Or maybe it's because they're playing. Their scientific name is *Megaptera novaeangliae;* we call them humpbacks because of their dorsal fin. But the Russians have the perfect name. They call them *'vessyl kit,'* merry whale."

Jim faded to the back of the group to rejoin Spock.

"It's perfect, Spock!" he whispered. "A male, a female, together in a contained space! We can beam them up together and consider ourselves damned lucky!"

Spock raised an eyebrow.

The whales swam to the edge of the tank nearest Gillian, rose, and spouted the mist of their breath. Gillian knelt on the deck, reached into the water, and stroked one of the whales.

"Aren't they beautiful?" Gillian said. "And they're extremely intelligent. Why shouldn't they be? They're swimming around with the largest brains on Earth."

Jim moved to the front of the group again. All he could make out of the whales was two huge dark shapes beneath the bright water.

"How do you know one's male and one's female?" Jim asked. They looked the same to him. Gillian Taylor glanced at him. She blushed.

"Observational evidence," she said, and quickly continued her lecture. "Despite all the things they're teaching us, we have to return George and Gracie to the open sea."

"Why's that?" Jim asked, startled.

"For one thing, we don't have the money to feed them a couple of tons of shrimp a day, and it takes the whole morning to open all those little cans."

Everybody laughed except Jim, who had no idea what was so funny.

"How soon?" he asked. *A month,* he thought. *Even a week. By then we'll be gone, and you won't have to worry about feeding them anymore. I'll take them to a good home, Doctor Gillian Taylor, I promise you that.*

"Soon," Gillian said. "As you can see, they're very friendly. Wild humpbacks would never come this close to a person. Whales are meant to be free. But I've . . . grown quite attached to George and Gracie." She strode across the deck. "This way." Her voice sounded muffled.

She led the group down a set of spiral stairs, through an arched doorway, and into a blue-lit chamber with one curving wall of glass. At first Jim could see only the water beyond. The glass wall, a section of a sphere, arched overhead. Some meters above, the surface rippled smoothly.

Suddenly a great *slap!* thundered through the chamber. An enormous shape, obscured by bubbles, plunged through the surface toward them.

Gillian laughed. The bubbles rose in a swirling curtain, revealing the colossal shape of a humpback whale.

"This is a much better way to see George and Gracie," Gillian said. "Underwater."

None of the pictures, none of the films, even hinted at the sheer size and grace of the creature. It used its long white pectoral fins like wings, soaring, gliding, banking, turning. It rose surfaceward and with a powerful stroke of its tail it sailed through the surface and out of sight. Its entire majestic body left the water. A moment later, ten meters farther on, it plunged into the water upside-down, flipped around, and undulated toward the viewing bubble. At the limits of vision through the tank's water, a second whale breached, then swam, trailing bubbles, to join its partner at the glass. They glided back and forth across the curve of the window. For a moment Jim felt as if he were enclosed and the whales were free.

Jim had expected the tremendous creatures to be clumsy and lumpish, but underwater their supple bodies moved easily, balancing on their flippers, muscles rippling. They looked as if they were flying, as if they were weightless. Speakers on the walls emitted an occasional whistle, or a groan, and the smooth, silky sound of the whales' motion.

George and Gracie undulated past and away, now parting, now coming together to stroke each other with their long flippers.

Spock kept himself at the back of the crowd, but he too watched the humpback whales cavort and play. Their grace and elegance and power transfixed him. Vulcan possessed no creatures the size of whales. Though Spock knew he had observed enormous creatures in his earlier life, he could remember only pictures, recordings, descriptions.

Spock wondered if it was proper Vulcan behavior to be amazed by two creatures playing. He decided he did not care, for the moment, about proper Vulcan behavior. He merely wanted to watch the whales. Nevertheless, the object of the *Bounty*'s mission remained in his mind. Only now did he fully realize the magnitude of the task. If the two whales found themselves beamed into the storage tank without any knowledge or understanding of why they were being transported or where they were being taken, they might panic. Perhaps twenty-third-century materials could withstand the force of the powerful body of a terrified whale. But Spock had no doubt that the structural integrity of a tank jury-rigged from contemporary materials would be severely compromised by such stress.

Spock felt quite strange. He wondered if he was being affected by human emotions. T'Lar and the other Vulcan adepts had warned him against them. Yet his mother, also an adept, had urged him to experience them rather than shutting them out. Spock wondered if now might be the time to take her advice.

"Humpback whales are unique in a number of ways," Doctor Taylor said. "One is their song." She touched a control on a wall panel.

A rising cry soared from the speakers, surrounding the audience.

"This is whale song that you're hearing," Doctor Taylor said. "It isn't the right season to hear it live; this is a tape. We know far too little about the song. We can't translate it. We believe it's only sung by male humpbacks. George will sing anywhere from six to thirty minutes, then start the song over again. Over time, the song evolves. In the ocean, before the era of engine-powered seagoing vessels, the song could be heard for thousands of miles. It's possible—though it's impossible to know for sure, because human beings make so much noise—that a single song could travel all the way around the world. But the song can still travel long distances, and other whales will pick it up and pass it on."

Gracie glided past the viewing window again. As her eye passed Spock, he had the sensation of being watched. He wondered if she sensed the presence of him and Admiral Kirk; he wondered if the whales had some intimation of the intentions of the visitors from the future.

Will they believe they are being stolen? Spock wondered. *No, not stolen. Stolen implies that someone owns them, and this is not the case. I doubt that Doctor Taylor believes she owns them. Perhaps some governmental body claims possession, but that could have no effect on what the whales perceive. The whales may believe they are being kidnapped or abducted. Suppose they do not wish to leave this time and place? In that case, do we have the right to take them against their will? If, in fact, we do take them against their will, would our actions not defeat our own purpose? If two beings who have been wronged answer the probe, it may respond with more and wider aggression.*

Spock could imagine only one solution to the dilemma: communication. And since Doctor Taylor admitted that human beings could neither communicate with the whales nor translate their songs, Spock saw only a single way of achieving the solution.

He moved to the exit, turned, and swiftly climbed the spiral staircase to the surface level of the whale tank. One of the creatures slid past at his feet, curving its back so its dorsal fin cut the water. It dove again, and he could see only its shadowy form, its white pectoral fins, beneath the ripples. At the far end of the tank, the second whale surfaced and spouted with a blast of vapor and spume. Despite the impressive size of the tank, it was little more than a pond to a creature who could dive one hundred fathoms, and whose species regularly migrated a quarter of the circumference of Earth.

The hot sunlight poured down on Spock. He gazed across the surface of the pool, dropped his robe, and dove.

The cold salt water closed in around him and whale sounds—not a song, but curious creaks and squeaks and moans—engulfed him. The vibrations traveled through the water and through his body; he could both feel and hear them. The whales turned toward him, curious about the intruder, and the inquiring sounds became more intense, more penetrating. One whale swam beneath him and breathed out bubbles that rose around him and tickled his skin. She turned and ascended and hovered at Spock's level. Her great eye peered directly into his face. The warmth of her body radiated through the frigid water.

He reached toward her, slowly enough that she could glide out of his reach if she chose. She hung motionless.

Spock touched the great creature, steeling his psyche for mind-melding's assault.

Instead, a gentle touch soothed and questioned him. The peace of the whale's thoughts surrounded him, incredibly powerful, yet as delicate as a windrider.

The touch questioned, and Spock answered.

Inside the observation chamber, Jim Kirk listened to Gillian Taylor talk about the whales. He was both fascinated by the information and impatient for the lecture to end so he could speak to her alone.

One of the whales glided past the observation window, drawing Spock along with it. Jim smothered a gasp of astonishment.

Damn! he thought. *Of all the harebrained things to do, in front of fifty people! Maybe Bones is right—*

A murmur of surprise rippled over the crowd as one person brought the odd sight to the notice of the next.

And if Spock's headband slips off, Jim thought, *we're going to have a lot more to explain than why my crazy companion wants to take a dive in a whale tank.*

At least Gillian Taylor had not noticed. Perhaps no one would say anything directly . . .

"The song of the humpback whale changes every year. But we still don't know what purpose it serves. Is it navigational? Part of the mating ritual? Or pure communication, beyond our comprehension?"

"Maybe the whale is singing to the man," said one of the spectators. Jim flinched.

Gillian turned. "What the hell—!" She stared at Spock, disbelieving, then spun and sprinted for the stairs. "Excuse me! Wait right here!"

Ignoring her order, Jim rushed after her. At the top of the spiral he burst out into the bright sunlight, blinking.

Spock raised himself from the tank with one smooth push. Water splashed and dripped around his feet. He straightened his headband and shrugged into his robe.

"Who the hell are you?" Gillian shouted. "What were you doing in there?"

Spock glanced toward Jim.

I can't take the chance of us both getting arrested, Jim thought.

"You heard the lady!" Jim said.

"Answer me!" Gillian said. "What the hell do you think you were doing in there?"

"I was attempting the hell to communicate," Spock replied.

"Communicate? Communicate what?" She looked him up and down. "What do you think you are, some kind of Zen ethologist? Why does every bozo who comes down the damned pike think they have a direct line to whale-speak?"

"I have no interest in damned pikes," Spock said. "Only in whales."

"I've been studying whales for ten years and *I* can't communicate with them! What makes you think you can come along and—never mind! You have no right to be here!"

In silence, Spock glanced at Jim. Jim tried once more to hint that they should pretend not to be acquainted.

"Come on, fella!" he snapped. "Speak up!" He realized too late that Spock would take him literally.

"Admiral, if we were to assume these whales are ours to do with as we please, we would be as guilty as those who caused their extinction."

"Extinction . . . ?" Gillian said. She glanced from Jim to Spock and back. "O-*kay*," she said. "I don't know what this is about, but I want you guys out of here, right now. Or I call the cops."

"That isn't necessary," Jim said quickly. "I assure you. I think we can help—"

"The hell you can, buster! Your friend was messing up my tank and messing up my whales—"

"They like you very much," Spock said. "But they are not the hell your whales."

"I suppose they told you that!"

"The hell they did," Spock said.

"Oh, *right*," she said, completely out of patience.

In short order Jim and Spock found themselves escorted with politeness, firmness, and finality from the Cetacean Institute by an elderly unarmed security guard. They could have resisted him easily, but Jim did not even try to talk his way into staying. He thought he could do it, but he also thought that if he did he would attract more attention and cause himself more trouble than if he left quietly.

He trudged down the road, a few paces ahead of Spock. They had found out most of what they needed to know.

But damn! Jim thought. *I'll just* bet *I could have found out when they're planning to release the whales if I'd had a few more minutes . . .*

Spock lengthened his stride and caught up to him.

"I didn't know you could swim, Spock," Jim said with some asperity.

"I find it quite refreshing, though I wonder if it is proper Vulcan behavior," Spock said, oblivious to Jim's irritation. "It is not an ability that is common, or even useful, on my homeworld. Admiral, I do not understand why Doctor Taylor believed I wanted the hell to swim with damned pikes."

"What possessed you to swim with damned whales?" Jim exclaimed.

Spock considered. "It seemed like the logical thing to do at the time."

"In front of fifty people? Where's your judgment, Spock?"

Spock hesitated. "It is perhaps not at its peak at the moment, Admiral. Sucrose has been known the hell to have this effect on Vulcans. I do not usually indulge."

"Indulge? Spock, do you mean to tell me you're *drunk?*"

"In a manner of speaking, Admiral." He sounded embarrassed.

"Where did you get it? Why did you eat it?"

"You gave it to me. I did not realize that the wafer's main constituent was sucrose until I had damned already ingested it."

Jim abandoned that line of conversation. "Listen, Spock," he said.

"Yes?"

"About those colorful idioms we discussed. I don't think you should try to use them."

"Why not?" Spock said.

"For one thing, you haven't quite got the hang of it."

"I see," Spock said stiffly.

"Another thing," Jim said. "It isn't always necessary to tell the truth."

"I cannot tell a lie."

"You don't have to lie. You could keep your mouth shut."

"You yourself instructed me to speak up."

"Never mind that! You could understate. Or you could exaggerate."

"Exaggerate," Spock said in a thoughtful tone.

"You've done it before," Jim said. "Can't you remember?"

"The hell I can't," Spock said.

Jim sighed. "All right, never mind that, either. You mind-melded with the whale, obviously. What else did you learn?"

"They are very unhappy about the way their species has been treated by humanity."

"They have a right to be," Jim said. "Is there any chance they'll help us?"

"I believe I was successful," Spock said, "in communicating our intentions."

With that, Spock fell silent.

"I see," Jim said.

Eight

Gillian tried not to be too obvious about hurrying the audience along, but as soon as the last of them finally disappeared through the museum doors, she ran through the lobby, up the spiral staircase, and out onto the deck around the whale tank. George and Gracie sounded and swam toward her, their pectoral fins ghostly white brush strokes beneath the surface. Gillian kicked off her shoes and sat down with her feet in the water. Gracie made a leisurely turn, rolled sideways, and stroked the bottom of Gillian's foot with her long fin. Her movement set up a wave that sloshed against the side of the tank and splashed over the other side.

Both whales rose and blew, showering Gillian with the fine mist of their breath. Gracie lifted her great head, breaking the surface with her knobby rostrum, her forehead and upper jaw. Unlike wild humpbacks, Gracie and George would come close enough to be touched. Gillian stroked Gracie's warm black skin. Underwater, the whale's eye blinked. She blew again, rolled, raised her flukes, and lobbed them into the water. Gillian was used to being splashed.

Both whales seemed upset to Gillian, not agitated but anxious. She had never seen them act like this before. Of course, this was the first time a stranger had ever actually dived in with them, which was probably lucky. Heaven knows enough nuts picked whales to fixate on.

Maybe, Gillian thought, *I ought to be surprised nobody ever got in the tank before now. But I should have realized something odd was going on with those two guys, the way they were dressed, and the one so quiet, the other so intense and with so many questions.*

"It's all right," she said. "Yes, I know." George nuzzled her leg with one of the sensory bristles on his chin. "It's okay. They didn't mean any harm."

At the sound of footsteps she turned quickly, wondering if the two strangers had returned.

Instead, the director of the Cetacean Institute looked down at her and grinned sympathetically.

"Heard there was some excitement." Bob Briggs kicked off his shoes and rolled up his slacks too. He sat beside her and eased his feet into the cold water.

"Just a couple of kooks," Gillian said. *But if they were only harmless kooks,* she thought, *why were they so interested in when we're letting the whales free?*

Gillian wished Bob would leave her alone with George and Gracie. With some effort, she could get along all right with her boss. He was not deliberately malicious, but his offhand condescension annoyed the hell out of her.

"How're you doing?"

"Fine," she said. "Just fine."

"Don't tell me fish stories, kiddo. I've known you too long."

"It's tearing me apart!" she snapped.

Damn! she thought. *Suckered in again.*

"Want to talk about it? It'll help to get your problems out in the open."

"You've been in California too long," she said.

She stared at the water and at the two whales drifting just under the surface at her feet. Every few minutes one would rise above the glimmer of water, exhale noisily, inhale softly, and sink again.

"I know how you feel," Bob said. "I feel the same. But we're between a rock and a hard place, Gill. We can't keep them without risking their lives and we can't let them go without taking the same chance."

"Yeah," she said. "Why are you lecturing me about this? It was my idea to free them in the first place! I had to fight—"

"I'm lecturing you," he said, "to help you get over your second thoughts."

"I'm not having any second thoughts!" she snapped. She immediately regretted her outburst. "I want them to be free. I want them to be safe, too, but there isn't any place in the world where that can happen. And . . . I'll miss them."

"Gill, they aren't human beings! You keep looking for evidence that they're as smart as we are. I'd be *delighted* if they were as smart as we are. But there isn't any proof—"

"I don't know about you, but my compassion for someone isn't limited to my estimate of their intelligence!" She glared at him angrily. "Maybe they didn't paint the *Mona Lisa* or invent the dirt bike. But they didn't ravish the world, either. And they've never driven another species to extinction!" Water splashed as she rose. Gracie and George moved away from the noise and swam to the center of the tank. "Sorry if I spoke out of turn," Gillian said bitterly.

"Not at all," Bob said. He never lost his temper. That was one of the reasons he was director, and one of the ways he made Gillian so mad. "You always give me things to think about. Gillian, why don't you go home early? You sound pretty wrecked."

"Thanks for the compliment," she said.

"Come on. You know what I mean. Really. Why don't you go home? Stare at the ceiling for a while."

"Yeah," Gillian said. "Why don't I?" She picked up her shoes and walked away.

Gillian flung her shoes into the back of her Land Rover, cranked the ignition, shoved a Waylon Jennings tape into the tape deck, and drove out of the parking lot faster than she should have. The speed helped, though she could not run from the dilemma of the whales. She did not want to run from it. She only wanted to let it blow away with the wind for a little while.

The incident with the two strangers refused to blow away with the wind. Why had the one in the tank referred to George and Gracie as extinct? Endangered, sure. Maybe he was just sloppy with his word choice.

But he sounded like he knew what he was talking about, Gillian thought. *Just what the hell does he know that I don't?*

Waylon was singing "Lonesome, On'ry and Mean." Gillian turned the volume up too loud and put her attention to driving, to the speed and the road and the blast of hot autumn air.

Back at the Institute, Bob Briggs watched the two whales surface and blow at the far end of the tank. With everyone but Gillian, George and Gracie acted like wild whales, coming close enough to watch but not to touch.

The track of Gillian's small wet footprints had begun to dry. He was worried about her. When she left the whales, she always looked as if she feared she would never see them again. And this time . . .

He shrugged off his doubts. He knew he had made the right decision. Gillian would be grateful to him later.

His assistant came out of the museum, blinking in the sunshine, and joined him on the deck.

"All squared away?"

"Looks like it," Bob said.

"She's gonna go berserk."

"It's for her own good," Bob said. "It's the only way. She'll call me names for a while, but then she'll calm down. She'll understand."

"Alameda Naval Base!" Pavel Chekov exclaimed. "Finally!"

"No thanks to our helpful friend," Uhura said. She glanced around.

"What is wrong?"

"Nothing. I just keep expecting to see him again. Lurking. Hiding behind a bush or a shrub."

"I am sure he just made mistake," Pavel said.

"Maybe."

"It was coincidence to see him on train. He realized he gave us incorrect directions. He was embarrassed. He has no earthly reason to feel suspicion."

"No earthly reason?" Uhura said. Pavel grinned.

The trees parted before them. Sunlight glittered off the water of the harbor. Uhura saw the ship. *Enterprise,* CVN 65.

She stopped. She shivered suddenly; the last time she had seen the huge craft, it was in a photo displayed on board the *Starship Enterprise.*

Through generations of ships, from space shuttle to system explorer to early star voyager, the name descended to the starship on which Uhura had spent most of her adult life. In this time and this place, the name belonged to an aircraft carrier. She moved toward it, awed by its size, fascinated by the destructive power it represented. In Uhura's time, structures much larger than this were commonplace, but they were built in space, without the restrictions of gravity and air and water pressure. This century's *Enterprise* existed in spite of those factors. The hull swept upward, then flared out to accommodate the landing deck. Uhura and Pavel entered the shadow of its curving side.

Pavel gestured toward the name. Uhura nodded. Pavel opened his communicator; Uhura set to work with her tricorder.

Pavel transmitted the communicator code. "Team leader, this is team two. Come in please . . ."

Uhura studied the readings. "I have the coordinates of the reactor. Or, anyway, coordinates that will have to do."

Pavel gazed at the carrier. "This gives me great sense of history."

"It gives me a great sense of danger." The emissions from the reactor added distortion to Uhura's information, making it impossible to get a precise idea of the layout of the ship. "We have to beam in *next* to the reactor room, not *in* it."

"Team leader," Pavel repeated, "this is team two. Come in please . . ."

On the other side of the bay, Jim trudged down the road leading from the Cetacean Institute. Several buses had passed them by, despite Jim's waving whenever he saw one coming. Public transportation must stop only at spots marked by shelters like the one in the city, but he had not yet found one on this road. He still wished he had brought a pair of walking shoes. Spock, of course, made no complaint; he simply strode along nearby as if they were on a field trip. Every so often he stopped to inspect some dusty plant by the side of the road. More often than not he would nod and murmur, "Fascinating. An extinct species."

"Spock, dammit!" Jim said. "If you keep referring to plants and animals in this world as extinct, somebody is going to start wondering about you."

"I think it unlikely that anyone will reach the proper conclusion about my origin," Spock said.

"You're probably right. But they might reach an improper conclusion about your sanity, and that could cause us trouble."

"Very well," Spock said. "I shall endeavor to contain my enthusiasm. But are you aware, Admiral, that during this period of humanity's history, your species managed to eradicate at least one other species of plant or animal life each day? That frequency increased considerably before it decreased."

"Fascinating," Jim said grimly. "It's your species, too. In case you've forgotten."

"I have not forgotten," Spock said. "But it is a fact on which I prefer not to dwell."

"You ignore everything about Earth and about humans that you possibly can, yet it was you who recognized the humpback's song! Why *you*, Spock?"

"I believe . . ." Spock hesitated. "I remember . . . I have told you that I taught myself to swim, many years ago on Earth. Once, I swam too far. The current caught me. Its force overcame me. When I had nearly lost myself, I felt a creature nearby. I expected a shark to tear my flesh, to kill me. But when the creature touched me, I felt the warmth of a mammal, and I discerned a young and bright intelligence. A dolphin swam beneath me. She supported me and helped me toward shore. One reads of such behavior in mythology, but I had never given the tales credence. We . . . communicated." Spock reached down and touched a dusty, nondescript plant by the side of the road. "This species, too, is extinct in our time. Like the great whales. But the smaller cetaceans, the dolphins, survive. They preserve the memories of their vanished cousins. They remember—they tell stories, in pictures created of sound—the songs of the humpback. They hold themselves aloof from humans, and who can blame them? But I am not a human being. Not entirely. The dolphin sang to me."

In his imagination, Jim could see the endless ocean and feel the depths of its cold; he could feel the supple warmth of the dolphin and hear its echo of the humpback's call.

"I see, Spock," he said softly. "I understand."

Jim's communicator beeped the signal code. He started, pulled it out, and opened it.

"This is team two. Come in please."

"Team two, Kirk here."

"Admiral," Chekov said, "we have found nuclear vessel."

"Well done, team two."

"And, Admiral, this ship is aircraft carrier . . . *Enterprise.*"

Jim felt a pang of regret for his own ship. He kept his voice carefully controlled. "Understood. What is your plan?"

"We will beam in tonight, collect photons, and beam out. No one will ever know we were there."

"Understood and approved," Jim said. "Keep me informed. Kirk out."

He started to call in to Scott, but heard a vehicle speeding down the road behind him. He quickly put away his communicator.

The ground car screeched to a halt behind them, passed them slowly, and stopped again.

Jim kept walking at a steady pace.

"It's her," he said sidelong to Spock. "Taylor, from the Institute. Spock, if we play our cards right, we may learn when those whales are really leaving."

Spock glanced at him. Jim knew he had one eyebrow quirked, even though the headband obscured it.

"How," the Vulcan said, "will playing cards help?"

Using the rearview mirror, Gillian watched the two men approach. She put the Rover in first gear and started to let out the clutch, then changed her mind and jammed the gearshift to reverse. She backed up the Rover and stopped.

"Well," she said. "If it isn't Robin Hood and Friar Tuck."

"I'm afraid you have us confused with someone else," the one in the maroon jacket said. "My name is Kirk, and his is Spock."

She let the Rover ease forward to keep up with him. "Where're you fellas heading?"

"Back to San Francisco," Kirk said.

"That's a long way to come, just to jump in and swim with the kiddies."

"There's no point in my trying to explain what I was doing. You wouldn't believe me anyway."

"I'll buy that," Gillian said. She nodded toward Spock. "And what about what he was trying to do?"

"He's harmless!" Kirk said. "He had a good reason—" He cut himself off. "Look, back in the sixties he was in Berkeley. The free speech movement, and all that. I think . . . well, he did too much LDS."

"LDS? Are you dyslexic, on top of everything else?" She sighed. A burnt-out druggie and his keeper. She felt sorry for them, now that she was sure they posed no danger to the humpbacks. "Let me give you a lift," she said. She smiled ruefully. "I have a notorious weakness for hard-luck cases. That's why I work with whales."

"We don't want to be any trouble," Kirk said.

"You've already been that. Get in."

Spock got in first, then Kirk slid in and slammed the door. Spock sat stiff and straight and silent. When Gillian reached for the gearshift, her hand brushed past his wrist. His body radiated heat, as if he had a high fever. But he did not look flushed. He drew away and slid his hands into the sleeves of his long white robe.

"Thanks for the ride," Kirk said.

"Don't mention it," Gillian said. "And don't try anything, either. I've got a tire iron right where I can get at it."

"I appreciate it, but I don't need help with a—tire iron?"

"You will, if—oh, never mind."

"What's that noise?"

"What noise?" She listened for a problem with the engine.

"That—" Kirk hummed a few notes off-key with the gravelly voice on the tape.

"That's not noise, that's Waylon Jennings!" She turned it down a little. "Don't you like country-western?" She was used to that reaction from her colleagues. "There's some rock in the box on the floor. Not much sixties, I'm afraid. Some Doors, though."

Kirk moved the tape box and looked around. "I don't see a door down here—oh." He opened the glove compartment. Road maps folded inside out and emergency supplies spilled into his lap. Gillian lunged over and grabbed a handful of stuff and pushed it into the glove compartment.

"What is all this?"

"Just junk, shove it all back. I didn't say 'door,' I said 'Doors.' How could you get through the sixties in Berkeley without knowing about the Doors?"

"I didn't say I was at Berkeley, I said Spock was at Berkeley."

"Yeah, but, still—"

"The Doors were a musical group, Admiral," Spock said. "Mid-nineteen-sixties to—"

"Yes, Spock, I get the idea, thank you."

"Want to hear something really different?" Gillian asked. "I've got some Kvern. And 'Always Coming Home' is in there someplace."

"I'm not much on music," Kirk said. "That's more Mister Spock's department. Can you turn it off? Then we could talk."

"Oh. Well. All right." She turned off the tape and waited for Kirk to start talking. She drove along for a time during which neither man spoke.

"So," she said to Spock, determined to get some kind of straight information out of at least one of them, "you were at Berkeley."

"I was not," Spock said.

"Memory problems, too," Kirk said.

"Uh-huh," she said skeptically. "What about you? Where are you from?"

"I'm from Iowa."

"A landlubber," Gillian said.

"Not exactly."

"Come on," Gillian said. "What the hell were you boys really doing back there? Men's club initiation? Swimming with whales on a dare? If that's all, I'm going to be real disappointed. I hate the macho type."

"Can I ask *you* something?" Kirk said suddenly.

She shrugged. "Go ahead."

"What's going to happen when you release the whales?"

Gillian clenched her hands on the wheel. "They're going to have to take their chances."

"What does that mean, exactly?" Kirk said. " 'Take their chances'?"

"It means that they'll be at risk from whale hunters. Same as the rest of the humpbacks."

"We are aware of whale hunters," Spock said. "What I do not understand is the meaning of 'endangered species,' or the meaning of 'protected,' if hunting is still permitted."

"The words mean just what they say," Gillian said. "To people who agree with them. The trouble is, there isn't any way to stop the people who *don't* agree with them. A bunch of countries still allow whale hunting, and our government always seems to find it expedient not to object." She frowned at Spock. "What did you mean when you said all that stuff back at the Institute about extinction?"

"I meant—"

Kirk interrupted. "He meant what you were saying on the tour. That if things keep on the way they're going, humpbacks will disappear forever."

"That's not what he said, farm boy. He said, 'Admiral, if we were to assume these whales are ours to do with as we please, we would be as guilty as those who *caused*'—past tense—'their extinction.' " She waited. Kirk did not reply. "That *is* what he said."

Spock turned to Kirk. "Are you sure," he said, "that it is not time for a colorful idiom?"

Gillian ignored Spock. "You're not one of those guys from the military, are you?" she said to Kirk. "Trying to teach whales to retrieve torpedoes or some dipshit stuff like that?"

"No, ma'am," Kirk said sincerely. "No dipshit."

"That's something, anyway," she said. "Or I'd've let you off right here."

"Gracie is pregnant," Spock said.

Gillian slammed on the brake and the clutch. Spock moved quickly, bracing one hand on the dashboard even before the tires squealed on the pavement. But the sudden stop flung Kirk forward.

"All right," Gillian shouted. "Who are you? Don't jerk me around anymore! I want to know how you know that!"

Kirk pushed himself back. He looked shaken. "We can't tell you," he said. "You'd better—"

"Please. Just let me finish. I can tell you that we're not in the military and that we intend no harm to the whales." He leaned forward, one hand reaching out, open.

"Then—"

"In fact," Kirk said, "we may be able to help—in ways that you can't possibly imagine."

"Or believe, I'll bet," Gillian said.

"Very likely. You're not exactly catching us at our best."

"That much is certain," Spock said.

"That I *will* believe." Gillian drove on in silence for a mile or so.

"You know," Kirk said, his cheer sounding a little forced, "I've got a hunch we'd all be a lot happier talking over dinner. What do you say?"

Gillian wondered what she had let herself in for. If they were a danger to the whales, she ought to dump them out on the highway right now—except then she would not be able to keep an eye on them.

"You guys like Italian food?" she said.

They looked at each other as if they had no idea what she was talking about.

"No," said Spock.

"Yes," said Kirk.

Gillian sighed.

In the factory reception room, Montgomery Scott paced back and forth with unfeigned agitation. He pretended to be angry, but in truth he had a serious case of nerves.

He glanced at the door leading to the inner office. McCoy had been in there for a very long time.

In the manager's office, Doctor Nichols peered at the screen of his small computer. He was middle-aged and balding, wearing glasses and a rumpled cardigan sweater. He used a fist-sized mechanical box with a button on top to flip through the plant schedule. Each click of the button put a new page on the screen. When he moved the box across the desktop, a pointer on the computer screen moved on an identical path. Nichols frowned with perplexity.

"I don't understand why there's nothing down here about your visit," he said. "Usually the PR people are all too efficient."

"But Professor Scott's come all the way from Edinburgh to study your manufacturing methods. Obviously there's been a mix-up, but the university said the invitation was all arranged. I should have checked—you know academics."

"I do know academics," Nichols said. "Used to be one myself, as a matter of fact."

"Er . . ." Gliding over his *faux pas,* McCoy tried creative hysteria. "Professor Scott is a man of very strong temperament," he said. "I don't know if the university got its signals crossed, or he got the date wrong. All I know is that I'm responsible for bringing him here. If he came all this way and goes all the way back for nothing, I get to be responsible for that, too. Doctor Nichols, he'll make my life a living hell."

"We can't have that," Nichols said with a smile. "I think the office will survive without me for an hour or so. Wouldn't do to have a visiting dignitary go back to Edinburgh with unpleasant memories of American hospitality, would it?" He rose and headed for the outer office. McCoy followed.

"Professor Scott," Nichols said, extending his hand. "I'm Doctor Nichols, the plant manager."

Scott stopped pacing and drew himself up, hands on his hips.

"I'm terribly sorry about the mix-up," Nichols said, overlooking Scott's snub. "Would you believe no one told me about your visit?"

Scott glared balefully at McCoy.

"I've tried to clear things up, Professor Scott," McCoy said quickly. "They didn't have any idea you were coming—"

"Dinna ha' any idea!" Scott exclaimed. He used an impenetrable Scots burr. "D'ye mean t' say I ha' come millions o' miles—"

Doctor Nichols smiled patiently. "Millions?"

"Now, professor, it's only thousands," McCoy said in a soothing tone. "It's understandable that you're upset, but let's not exaggerate."

"—thousands o' miles, to go on a tour o' inspection to which I was *invited*—and then ye mean to tell me ye never invited me i' the first place? I demand—"

"Professor Scott, if you'll just—"

"I demand to see the owners! I demand—"

"Professor, take it easy!" McCoy said. "Doctor Nichols is going to show us around himself."

Scott stopped in the middle of a demand. "He is?"

"With pleasure," Doctor Nichols said.

"That's verra different," Scott said.

"If you'll follow me, Professor," Nichols said.

"Aye," Scott said. "That I will. And—'twould be all right if my assistant tags along as well?"

"Of course."

Doctor Nichols led them from the receptionist's office. Following him, Scott passed McCoy.

"Don't bury yourself in the part," McCoy muttered.

Sulu approached the plastics company's big Huey, entranced. He had seen still photos and battered old film of this helicopter, but none had survived, even in museums, to his time. The Huey was as extinct as the humpback whale. He stroked one hand along its flank.

He climbed up and looked into the cockpit—incredible. Hardly any electronics at all, all the gauges and controls mechanical or hydraulic. Flying it would be like going back to horse-and-buggy days. And he had never driven a horse and buggy.

The craft's engine cowling closed with a loud clang. Sulu heard footsteps.

"Can I help you?"

Sulu turned. "Hi." He gestured toward the helicopter. "Huey 205, isn't it?"

"Right on." The young pilot wiped his hands on a greasy rag. "You fly?"

"Here and there," Sulu said. He patted the helicopter's side. "I flew something similar to this in my Academy days."

"Then this is old stuff to you."

"Old, maybe. But interesting." He jumped to the ground and offered his hand. "I'm Sulu—with the international engineering conference tour?"

The pilot shook his hand. "I didn't know about a tour. They just tell me fly here, fly there, don't drop the merchandise. International, huh? Where you from? Japan?"

"Philippines," Sulu said, just to be safe. He had Japanese in his ancestry, but more of his family came from the Philippines, and he knew far more of its history.

"Hey. You folks really did it. Repossessed your country. What about all the loot, though? Think that will ever make it home again?"

"Oh, I think so, eventually," Sulu said, trying not to sound too certain. He drew the conversation back to the Huey. "I was hoping I'd find a pilot when I saw this helicopter. Mind if I ask a few questions?"

"Fire away."

They chatted about the copter for a while. The pilot glanced at his watch. "I've got to make a delivery," he said. "Want to come along?"

"I'd like nothing better."

The chopper lifted off in an incredible clatter of noise. Sulu watched the pilot work, itching to take over. The young man glanced at him. "If anybody asks," he said, "you never flew this thing."

"If anybody asks," Sulu said, "I've never even been *in* this thing."

The young pilot grinned and turned over the controls.

All day Javy tried to talk about what he and Ben had seen in Golden Gate Park, and all day Ben tried to act as if they had seen nothing. He froze up every time Javy mentioned the shooting star or the wind or the lights or the ramp.

When they got off that afternoon, Javy still felt hyper. He had been awake since three and working since four. He usually went home, dove into the shower, slept for a couple of hours, got up, and stared at half-finished pages in his typewriter for a while. Today, all that changed.

He got into his battered gold Mustang and turned on the radio, but it only worked on alternate Fridays and leap days that fell on Wednesday. He tried to pick out news reports through the static and jumps of a traveling short circuit, but heard nothing about the lights.

He needed a shower. This would look different after he got some sleep. Ben was probably right all along.

But instead of going home, he drove down Van Ness, then turned onto Fell, back to the park. He pulled his car up beside the garbage cans, which he had not finished emptying. He tried to smile at the thought of trying to explain why to their supervisor.

The truck had left a patch of rubber on the street where Ben floored it. It was not easy to lay rubber with a garbage truck.

Javy stayed in his car and looked toward the place where he thought he had seen . . . what? In the mist and the dark, perhaps he had not seen anything. Some people out for a stroll, their flashlights glinting off the fog? In daylight, he could not even be sure where he thought he saw what he thought he saw. Whatever it was, nothing remained of it. He decided to watch for a while anyway, just for interest's sake. He settled back in the driver's seat.

Within a few minutes, he had fallen fast asleep.

Scott followed Doctor Nichols through the plant, wondering how on earth the people in this time had ever managed to achieve anything, much less the beginnings of space exploration. With their incredibly primitive methods, he could just see his way to doing what he needed to do with their materials. He wanted to get away to someplace quiet and think for a bit. Twentieth-century factories were unbelievably noisy.

As the tour progressed, Doctor McCoy drew Doctor Nichols out. The engineer's sharp and ambitious intelligence chafed within the bureaucracy of management.

"I've put in for a transfer back to research," Nichols said. "Upper management never understands when you want to go back to what you're best at doing."

"Aye," Scott said, recalling all the times Starfleet had tried to promote him out of engineering. " 'Tis true."

"Especially if you're working for a plastics company and your first love is metallurgy. I've got some ideas about metallic crystalline structure—" He stopped. "But of course you're interested in acrylic production, Professor Scott."

"Professor Scott—'tis too formal. Call me Montgomery, if ye would."

"Certainly," Nichols said. "If you'll return the courtesy. My name's Mark."

"Verra well, Mark. Not Marcus? Ye are Marcus Nichols?" He grabbed Nichols's hand and pumped it. "I'm verra glad to meet ye! The work ye've done, the inventions—"

Behind Nichols, McCoy waved his hands in warning. Scott realized what he had said. He stopped abruptly.

"My inventions?" Nichols said, startled. "Professor Scott, I only hold two patents, and if you've heard of either in Edinburgh, I'm surprised, to say the least."

"But—er—well—"

"You must have him confused with another Marcus Nichols," McCoy said quickly. "That's the only logical—" He stopped as abruptly as Scott.

"But—I mean, aye, that must be it." Scott subsided, face flaming with embarrassment.

"I see," Nichols said.

Nichols led Scott and McCoy into a glass-walled observation cubicle. Its door swung shut, cutting the sound to nearly nothing.

"So much for the tour of our humble plant." Nichols leaned one hip on the back of a leather-covered couch and gave Scott a long, searching appraisal. "I must say, Professor, your memory for names may not be terrific, but your knowledge of engineering is most impressive."

"Why, back home," McCoy said, "we call him the miracle worker."

"Indeed . . ." Nichols gestured toward the bar at the back of the cubicle. "May I offer you gentlemen anything?"

McCoy and Scott exchanged a glance.

"Doctor Nichols," Scott said tentatively, "I might have something to offer *you*."

Nichols raised an eyebrow at this turn of the conversation. "Yes?"

"I notice ye are still working with polymers," Scott said.

"Still?" Nichols frowned, mystified. "This is a plastics company. What else would I be working with?"

"Ah, what else indeed? Let me put it another way. How thick would ye need to make a sheet of your acrylic"—Scott hesitated a moment, converting meters to feet, wishing the twentieth century had finished getting around to the change—"sixty feet by ten feet, if ye wished it to withstand the pressure o' 18,000 cubic feet o' water?"

"That's easy," Nichols said. "Six inches. We carry stuff that big in stock."

"Aye," Scott said. "I noticed. Now suppose—just suppose—I could show ye a way to manufacture a wall that would do the same job but was only an inch thick. Would that be worth something to ye?"

"Are you joking?" Nichols folded his arms. His body language revealed skepticism, suspicion—and interest.

"He never jokes," McCoy said. "Perhaps the professor could use your computer?"

"Please," Nichols said, gesturing toward it.

Scott sat before the machine. "Computer."

The computer did not reply. McCoy grabbed the control box he had seen Nichols using earlier and shoved it into Scott's hand. Scott thanked him with a nod and spoke into it.

"Computer."

No reply.

"Just use the keyboard," Nichols said, "if you prefer it to the mouse."

"The keyboard," Scott said. " 'Tis quaint."

He laced his fingers together and cracked his knuckles. Fast and two-fingered, he started to type.

Information filled the screen. Scott condensed each formula into a few words as he worked. After half an hour, he pressed a final key.

"And if ye treat it by this method, ye change the crystalline structure so 'twill transmit light in the visible range."

A three-dimensional crystalline structure formed on the computer screen. Scott sat back, satisfied.

"Transparent aluminum?" Nichols said with disbelief.

"That's the ticket, laddie."

"But it would take years just to figure out the dynamics of this matrix!"

"And when you do," McCoy said, "you'll be rich beyond the dreams of avarice."

Nichols's attention remained centered on the screen, which fascinated him far more than dreams of avarice.

"So," Scott said, "is it worth something? Or shall I just punch 'clear'?" He extended one finger toward the keyboard.

"No!" Nichols exclaimed. "No." He stared at the screen, frowning, uncomfortable. "What did you have in mind?"

"A moment alone, please," McCoy said.

Scott started to object.

"Please," McCoy said again.

Unwillingly, Nichols left them alone.

"Scotty," McCoy said, "if we give him the formula, we'll be altering the future!"

"How d'ye know he didn't invent the process?" Scott said.

"But—"

"Doctor McCoy, do ye no' understand? He *did* invent it! Have ye ne'er heard his name?"

"I'm a doctor, not a historian," McCoy growled. He had gone into this masquerade willingly, but now he found himself possessed with the need to make as few changes in the past as he could. The intensity of Jim Kirk's argument for their actions warred with another, alien impulse.

" 'Tisna necessary to be a historian to know o' Marcus Nichols! Why, 'twould be as if I never heard o' . . . er . . ."

"Pasteur?"

"Who?"

"Yalow? Arneghe?"

"Nay, well, ne'er mind, the point is, Nichols *did* invent transparent aluminum! And that was only the beginnin' o' his achievements. 'Tis all right that we gi' the formula to him—perhaps 'tis essential!"

McCoy looked at him with his head cocked in a familiar and yet very un-McCoyish way.

"Then, Scotty, does that mean we succeed? We get the whales and get back to our own time and—"

"Nay, Doctor. It means we gi' him the formula—or he recalls enough o' what I've already shown him to reproduce the effect. What happens back in our time . . . 'tis up to us."

McCoy nodded. He squared his shoulders and opened the door, beckoning Nichols into the transparent cubicle again. The scientist had been standing with his back to the windows, nervously giving his uninvited guests their privacy.

"Now, Doctor Nichols—Mark—" Scott said.

"Just a moment." He paused and took a deep breath. "You know what it is you're offering me."

"Aye," Scott said. "That I do."

"Why?"

"Why? Why what?"

"Why are you offering it to me?"

"Because we need something ye have."

"Such as what? My first-born child? My soul?"

Scott chuckled. "Nay. Acrylic sheets, large ones. Acrylic epoxy. The loan o' transportation."

"What you're asking for is worth a couple of thousand dollars at most. What you're offering in return is worth—if it's true—a whole lot more. As well as recognition, respect . . ."

"But, you see, Mark," McCoy said, "we don't have a couple of thousand dollars. And we need the acrylic sheets. Desperately."

"Does the phrase 'too good to be true' mean anything to you?"

McCoy clapped his hand over his eyes. "What a time to run into an honest man!"

Nichols glanced at the tantalizing computer screen. "What you've shown me looks real," he said. "It's just a beginning, but it feels right. It feels like an answer—and I've been trying just to ask the question for the last two years. On the other hand, scientists smarter than me have been taken in by perpetual motion machines and heaven knows what—all kinds of absurd devices. How do I know—"

"Ye think we're tryin' to trick ye!" Scott exclaimed, astonished.

"The possibility did occur to me," Nichols said mildly. "You could be snowing me with fake formulae. You could be trying to plant some other company's research on me in order to embarrass my company with a charge of industrial espionage."

"I hadna thought o' that," Scott said, downcast.

Nichols glanced at McCoy with a wry grin. "Academics," he said.

"What can we do to persuade you we're legitimate?" McCoy said.

"Are you?"

"Er . . . in a way. In that we're not trying to cheat you or defraud you. Or embarrass your company."

"But if this is real, you could sell it—"

"Do ye no' understand?" Scott cried. "We have no time!"

Nichols hitched one hip on his desk, deliberately turning his back to the information on the computer screen.

"Ordinarily, if you wanted to sell something like this—no, let me finish—you'd take it to a company and license it in return for a royalty."

"But 'tisna royalties we need. 'Tis—"

"Mark," McCoy said, "we don't have time for this. We're going to make this trade with someone. It ought to be you. Don't ask me to explain why. If it is you, I think we can be sure it will be well used. If it'll make you feel better to assign the royalties to your favorite charity, or your Aunt Matilda, go ahead. But we're pretty desperate. If we have to go elsewhere, to find someone with fewer scruples, we will."

Nichols drew one knee up, folded his hands around it, and gazed at them both. Then he turned to the computer, carefully saved Scott's work, and moused a purchase order up on the screen. Beneath "Bill to" he typed "Marcus Nichols."

"Tell me what you need," he said.

Nine

Gillian's Land Rover wound through Golden Gate Park along Kennedy Drive.

"Are you sure you won't come with us, Mister Spock?" Gillian said. "We don't have to have Italian food. I'll take us to a place where you can get a hamburger if you want."

"What is a hamburger?" Spock said.

"A hamburger? It's, you know, ground-up beef. On a bun. With a little lettuce, maybe some tomatoes."

"Beef," Spock said. "This is meat?"

"Yes."

"Sounds pretty good, Spock," Kirk said.

Spock looked green. *Uh-oh,* Gillian thought, *a vegetarian.* She had never seen anyone actually turn green before. Maybe it was a trick of the light on his sallow complexion. But he sure looked green.

"I shall prefer not to accompany you," Spock said.

"Okay."

Spock looked at Kirk. "I thought that among my acquaintances only Saavik eats raw meat," he said. "But, of course, she was raised a Romulan."

"It isn't raw!" Gillian exclaimed. "They cook it! Raw hamburger, bleah."

"I don't think we should discuss Saavik, Mister Spock," Kirk said. "And I hate to disillusion you, but I enjoy a bit of steak tartare on occasion myself."

Mister Spock looked at Kirk askance. Gillian wondered why he reacted like that to the idea of raw meat, considering what sushi is made out of. She considered offering to change their plans and go to a Japanese restaurant instead. Then she wondered what country or city people called Romulans lived in. Maybe Mister Spock's friend Saavik came from a country where the people called themselves something that had nothing to do with the country's name, like Belgium and Walloons. Or maybe Mister Spock did not speak English as well as he seemed to, and he really meant his friend who liked raw meat was Roman. But who ever heard of steak tartare Romano, and what kind of a Japanese name was Spock anyhow?

But if he is *Japanese, or from anyplace in Asia,* Gillian thought, *suddenly suspicious—*

"How do I know you two aren't procurers for the Asian black market in whale meat?" she said angrily.

"What black market?" Kirk said.

"Human beings *consume* whale meat? The flesh of another sentient creature?" Mister Spock sounded appalled. His reaction surprised Gillian. Up until now he had seemed rather cold and unemotional.

"You two pretend to know so much about whales—then you pretend not to know anything—"

"I did not pretend to know that human beings *ate* whales," Spock said.

"Gillian," Kirk said, "if we were black market procurers, wouldn't it be awfully inefficient to come to California to steal two whales, when we could go out in the ocean and hunt them?"

"How should I know? Maybe your boat sank." She jerked her head toward Spock, "Maybe he wants to take Gracie and George away and pen them up like cattle and start a whale-breeding program back in Japan or someplace—"

"I do not intend to take George and Gracie to Japan," Spock said. "I am not from Japan. I have never been to Japan."

"Oh, yeah? Why are you walking around in that Samurai outfit, then? If you're not from Japan, where are you from?"

"I am from—"

"Tibet," Kirk said. "He's from Tibet."

"What?"

"He's from Tibet," Kirk said again. "It's landlocked. It's thousands of meters above sea level. What could he do with a pair of whales back in Tibet?"

"Christ on a crutch," Gillian said.

The Land Rover approached a meadow.

"This will be fine," Kirk said.

Gillian pulled into a parking lot. She did not spend much time in San Francisco proper; she did not like cities. She wondered if it was safe to be in this park at night. Probably not. Though dusk had barely begun to fall, only one other vehicle remained in the lot: a beat-up old muscle car with a young man sleeping in the driver's seat. Gillian felt sorry for him. He probably had nowhere else to stay.

Kirk opened the door and let his strange friend get out.

"Are you sure you won't change your mind?" Gillian said.

Spock cocked his head, puzzled. "Is something wrong with the one I have?"

His tone was so serious that Gillian could not decide whether to laugh or answer in the affirmative.

"Just a little joke," Kirk said quickly. He waved to Mister Spock. "See you later, old friend."

Gillian left the Land Rover in neutral. "Mister Spock, how did you know Gracie's pregnant? Who told you? It's supposed to be a secret."

"It is no secret to Gracie," Mister Spock said. "I will be right here," he said to Kirk, and strolled across the meadow toward a terraced bank planted with bright rhododendrons.

"He's just going to hang around in the bushes while we eat?" Gillian said to Kirk.

"It's his way." Kirk shrugged and smiled.

Gillian put the Land Rover into gear and drove away.

Javy woke with a start.

"Hey, bud, you can't sleep here. Come on, wake up!" The cop rapped sharply on the Mustang's roof.

"Uh, good evening, Officer."

"I know things get tough sometimes," the cop said. "But you're not allowed to sleep here. I can give you the address of a couple of shelters. It's getting late to get into either one of them, but maybe—"

"I don't need a shelter!" Javy said. "You don't understand, Officer. I'm . . ." He got out of his car, pulled out his wallet, flipped it open to flash his city I.D., and flipped it shut again. "We've had trouble with vandalism. I'm supposed to be keeping an eye out." He grinned sheepishly. "I'm kind of new. I thought it'd be easy to keep awake on stakeout, you know, like on TV? But it's boring."

"No kidding," the cop said.

A sparkle of light against the darkness caught Javy's attention.

"Jeez, did you see that?"

He bolted past the cop and sprinted a few steps into the meadow. He stopped. The light and the man-shaped figure both had vanished.

"See what? There's nobody out there, bud. Let me see that I.D. again."

Still staring toward the vanished light, Javy pulled out his wallet. Once the cop had more than a glance at it, he realized what department Javy was really in.

"What do you think you are, detective trash class? Look, I don't know what you're trying to pull, trying to sleep on taxpayers' money, or what—"

"I start work at four a.m.!" Javy said angrily, defensively. He gestured toward his Mustang. "That look like a garbage truck to you?"

"Looks like it belongs *in* a garbage truck," the cop said. "But I'm tired and the shift's almost over and I can't think of any reason to take you in, acting stupid not being against the law. But if you make me—"

"Never mind!" Javy said, annoyed at the cop for insulting him and his car as well, but mostly annoyed with himself for falling asleep and blowing his chance. "I'll leave."

Gillian took Kirk to her favorite pizza place. She wondered if she would have had the nerve to come here if Mister Spock had accompanied them. He was so strange—there was no telling how he would act in a restaurant. Come to think of it, she was not entirely sure how Kirk would act.

"Listen," she said to Kirk. "I like this restaurant, and I want to be able to come back, so you behave yourself. Got it?"

"Got it," he said.

Nevertheless she was relieved when a waiter she did not know took them to their table. She glanced over the menu, though she almost always had the same thing.

"Do you trust me?" she asked Kirk.

"Implicitly," he said without hesitation.

"Good. A large mushroom and pepperoni with extra onions," she said to the waiter. "And a Michelob."

He took it down and turned to Kirk. "And you, sir?"

Kirk frowned over the menu. Gillian had the distinct impression that he had never heard of pizza before. Where was this guy from, anyway? Mars?

"Make it two," Kirk said.

"Big appetite," the waiter said.

"He means two beers," Gillian said.

The waiter nodded, took the menus, and left. Gillian toyed with her water glass, making patterns of damp circles with its base and drawing clear streaks in the condensation on its sides. She glanced at Kirk just as Kirk looked at her, and they saw that they were both doing the same thing.

"So," Kirk said. "How did a nice girl like you get to be a cetacean biologist?"

The slightly condescending comment jolted her. She hoped Kirk meant the lines as a joke. She shrugged unhappily. "Just lucky, I guess."

"You're upset about losing the whales," he said.

"You're very perceptive." She tried to keep the sarcasm down. Just what she needed, Bob Briggs all over again, telling her she shouldn't think about them as if they were human, or even as if they were intelligent. They were animals. Just animals.

And if the whale hunters got to them, they would be dead animals, carcasses, raw meat . . .

"How will you move them, exactly?"

"Haven't you done your homework? It's been in all the papers. There's a 747 fitted out to carry them. We'll fly them to Alaska and release them there."

"And that's the last you'll see of them?"

"See, yes," Gillian said. "But we'll tag them with radio transmitters so we can keep track of them."

The ice in Kirk's water glass rattled.

His hand's trembling! Gillian thought. *What's he so damned nervous about?*

He drew back before he exploded the glass in his grip. "I could take those whales where they wouldn't be hunted."

Gillian started to laugh. "You? Kirk, you can't even get from Sausalito to San Francisco without a lift."

The waiter reappeared. He put plates and glasses and two bottles of beer in front of them.

"Thanks," Gillian said. She picked up the bottle, raised it in a quick salute, and took a deep swig. "Cheers."

"If you have such a low opinion of me," Kirk said grimly, "how come we're having dinner?"

"I told you," Gillian said, "I'm a sucker for hard-luck cases. Besides, I want to know why you travel around with that ditzy guy who knows that Gracie is pregnant . . . and calls you Admiral."

Kirk remained silent, but Gillian was aware of his gaze. She took another swig of her beer and set the bottle down hard.

"Where could you take them?" she said.

"Hmm?"

"My whales! What are you trying to do? Buy them for some marine sideshow where you'd make them jump through hoops—"

"Not at all," he said. "That wouldn't make sense, would it? If I were going to do that, I might as well leave them at the Cetacean Institute."

"The Cetacean Institute isn't a sideshow!"

"Of course not," he said quickly. "That isn't what I meant."

"Then where could you take them where they'd be safe?"

"It isn't so much a matter of a place," Kirk said, "as of a time."

Gillian shook her head. "Sorry. The time would have to be right now."

"What do you mean, *now?*"

Gillian poured beer into her glass. "Gracie's a very young whale. This is her first calf. Whales probably learn about raising baby whales from other whales, like primates learn from primates. If she has her calf here, she won't know what to do. She won't know how to take care of it. But if we let her loose in Alaska, she'll have time to be with other whales. She'll have time to learn parenting. I think. I hope. No humpback born in captivity has ever survived. Did you know that?" She sighed. "The problem is, they won't be a whole lot safer at sea. Because of people who shoot them because they think they eat big fish. Because of the degradation of their environment. Because of the hunting." Her voice grew shaky. "So that, as they say, is that." She cut off her words and dashed the tears from her eyes with her sleeve. "Damn."

Gillian heard a faint beep. "What's that?"

"What's what?" Jim said.

The beep repeated.

"A pocket pager? What are you, a doctor?"

At the third beep, Kirk pulled the pager out and flipped it open angrily.

"What is it?" he snapped. "I thought I told you never to call me—"

"Sorry, Admiral," the beeper said. "I just thought ye'd like to know, we're beaming them in now."

"Oh," Kirk said. "I see." He half-turned from Gillian and spoke in a whisper. Gillian could still hear him. "Scotty, tell them, phasers on stun. And good luck. Kirk out." He closed the beeper and put it away.

Gillian stared at him.

"My concierge," Kirk said. "I just can't get it programmed not to call me at the most inconvenient times." He stopped, smiling apologetically.

"I've had it with that disingenuous grin, Kirk," Gillian said. "You *program* your concierge? I'll bet he loves that. And if this is the most inconvenient time anybody ever called you, I don't know whether to envy you or feel sorry for you. Now. You want to try it from the top?"

"Tell me when the whales are going to be released."

"Why's it so important to you? Who *are* you?" she said. "Jeez, I don't even know the rest of your name!"

"It's James," he said. "Who do you think I am?"

She tried to take another swig from her beer bottle, but she had emptied it into her glass. She picked up the glass, drank, and put it down.

"Don't tell me," she said sarcastically. "You're from outer space."

Kirk blew out his breath. "No," he said. "I really am from Iowa. I just work in outer space."

Gillian rolled her eyes toward the ceiling in supplication. "Well, I was close. I *knew* outer space was going to come into it sooner or later."

"All right," he said. "The truth?"

"All right, Kirk James," she said, "I'm all ears."

"That's what you think," he said with a quick grin that she ignored. "Okay. The truth. I'm from what, on your calendar, would be the late twenty-third century. I've been sent back in time to bring two humpback whales with me in an attempt to repopulate the species."

Gillian began to wish she were drinking something stronger than beer. "Hey, why didn't you *say* so?" she said, going along with him. "Why all the coy disguises?"

"Do you want the details?"

"Are you kidding? I wouldn't miss this for all the tea in China."

"Then tell me when the whales are leaving," Jim said.

"Jesus, you are persistent," Gillian said. She looked down into her beer. "Okay. Your friend is right. Like he said, Gracie is pregnant. Maybe it would be better for her to stay at the Institute till the end of the year. Then we could let her loose in Baja California just before she's ready to calve. But if the news gets out before we release her, we'll be under tremendous pressure to keep her. And maybe we should. But I told you the reasons for freeing her. We're going to let her go. At noon tomorrow."

Kirk looked stunned.

"Noon?" he said. "Tomorrow?"

"Yeah. Why's it so important to you?"

The waiter appeared and placed a large round platter on the table between Jim and Gillian.

"Who gets the bad news?" he said, offering the check to the air between them. Kirk looked up at him blankly.

Gillian took the bill. She had expected to go Dutch, but Kirk could at least offer to pay his share. "Don't tell me," she said. "They don't have money in the twenty-third century."

"Well, we *don't*," he said. He pushed himself to his feet. "Come on. I don't have much time."

He strode out, nearly running into a young man at the door.

Perplexed, Gillian watched Kirk leave. The waiter was staring after him too. Gillian wondered how much of their conversation he had heard. The waiter glanced at her with a confused frown. He could not be more confused than she was, and she had heard the whole thing.

"Uh, can we have this to go?" She gestured to the pizza.

Shaking his head, he went away to get a box, and Gillian wondered if she would ever be able to come back to the restaurant after all.

Uhura re-formed within the cool tingle of the transporter beam. She let out her breath with relief. The beam had placed her in an access corridor that led to the nuclear reactor. The reactor and all its shielding skewed the tricorder readings sufficiently that she had not been absolutely certain where she would appear. She pulled out her communicator and opened it. "I'm in," she whispered. "Send Pavel and the collector."

A moment later Chekov appeared beside her, carrying the photon collector. He started to speak. She gestured for silence. Her tricorder suggested the presence of one human being and a dog on the other side of the door to the access corridor, and many other people in the close to intermediate range. Many were pacing in back-and-forth patterns that suggested guard duty.

406 Vonda N. McIntyre

The dog's sharp single bark startled her. The door transmitted the sound clearly.

"Oh, come on, Narc, there's nothing in there." On the other side of the door, the guard chuckled. "If anybody *did* stow dope in the reactor room, they deserve whatever they get back out." His voice faded as he continued his patrol along the outer corridor. "That's a good one. Radioactive coke. New street sensation. Snort it and your nose glows. Come *on,* Narc."

Uhura could even hear the tapping of toenails on the deck as the dog trotted away. She wondered what in the world the security officer had been talking to his dog about.

"Let's go," she whispered.

As she and Pavel headed deeper into the reactor area, the tricorder's readings grew more erratic. The only steady information it could give her concerned radiation. The shielding was less efficient than she would have liked. She and Pavel should not have to remain within the reactor's influence long enough to be in danger. But fission reactors had caused Earth so many problems, some of which persisted even till her time, that she could not be comfortable around one.

A flashing reddish light reflected rhythmically through the corridor. Uhura rounded a bend. Above the reactor room door, a red warning light blinked on and off, on and off.

A large bright sign reading "DANGER" did not increase Uhura's confidence one bit.

Seeking the highest radiation flux with her tricorder, she found the spot and pointed it out to Pavel. He attached the collector to the wall. The field it created would increase the tunneling coefficient of the reactor shielding, causing the radiation to leak out at an abnormally high rate. It was a sort of vacuum cleaner for high-energy photons, and it could vacuum them up through a wall.

Pavel turned the collector on. It settled; it hummed.

"How long?" Uhura whispered.

Pavel studied the collector's readout. "Depends on amount of shielding, depends on molecular structure of reactor wall."

Uhura hoped the patrol would not come into the reactor looking for coke, whatever that was, radioactive or not.

Gillian parked the Land Rover on a bluff above the sea. The tide was out. The rocky beach gleamed in starlight.

Gillian ate pizza and listened to Kirk James's wild story. He had invented all sorts of details that sounded great. If they had been in a novel, she would have suspended her disbelief willingly.

The only trouble is, she thought, this is reality. He hasn't offered me anything to check the details against. And with this baloney about not leaving anachronistic traces in the past, he has a perfect excuse.

"So, you see," Kirk said at the end of his tale, "Spock doesn't want to take your whales home with him. I want to take your whales home with me."

Gillian handed Kirk a slice of pizza. The corner drooped over his fingers.

He bit a chunk from the outer edge. Cheese strings stretched from his mouth to the piece of pizza.

He's never eaten pizza before, that's for sure, Gillian thought. Whoever heard of somebody who doesn't know you eat the point first? Maybe he really is from Iowa. Via Mars.

"Are you familiar with Occam's Razor?" she said.

"Yes," Kirk said. "It's just as true in the twenty-third century as it is now. If two explanations are possible, the simpler is likely to be true."

"Right. Do you know what that means in your case?"

His shoulders slumped. He put down the half-eaten piece of pizza and scrubbed at the cheese on his fingers with a shredding paper napkin.

"I'm afraid so." He raised his head.

Gillian liked his eyes, and his intensity attracted her. The trouble was, he kept offering evidence that it was the intensity of madness.

"Let me tell you a little more," he said.

One of her professors in graduate school preferred another theory over Occam's Razor for sorting out competing hypotheses. "Gillie," she always said, "if you've got two possibilities, go with the beautiful one, the aesthetically pleasing one." The possibility Kirk wanted her to believe was certainly the aesthetically pleasing one. His stories were almost as good as the stories her grandfather used to tell her when she was little, before.

"Do they have Alzheimer's disease in the twenty-third century?" she asked.

"What's Alzheimer's disease?" Kirk said.

"Never mind." She started the Land Rover and headed back into Golden Gate Park. She wished she could believe in his universe. It sounded like a great place to live.

"Tell me about marine biology in the twenty-third century," she said.

"I can't," he said. "I don't know anything about it."

"Why? Because you spend all your time in space?"

"No. Because when I spend time on boats, it's for recreation."

Gillian chuckled. "You're good. You're really good. Smart, too. Most people, when they try to take somebody in, they try to snow you too far and they catch themselves up. If they thought it'd help, they'd claim to *be* a marine biologist."

"I don't even *know* any marine biologists. My mother's a xenobiologist, and so was my brother."

"Was?"

"He . . . died," Kirk said.

"Then there's no immortality in your universe, either."

"No," he said, smiling sadly. "Not for human beings, anyway."

"Let me tell you some more about whales," Gillian said.

"I'd like to hear anything you've got to tell me," he said. "But if you won't help me, then I'm a little pressed for time."

"People have had killer whales in captivity for a couple of decades," she said. "Do you have killer whales in your world? Orcas?"

"No," he said. "I'm sorry, no. All the larger species are extinct."

"Orcas are predators. They swim fifty miles a day, easy. They have an incredible repertoire of sounds they can make. They talk to each other. A lot. That's what it sounds like they're doing, anyway. But when you put them in a tank, they change. They haven't got anywhere to go. They're kept in a deprived environment. After a couple of years, their range of sounds shrinks. Then they become aphasic—they stop talking at all. They get apathetic. And then . . . they die."

Gillian turned in at the parking lot.

"Gillian, that's a shame. But I don't understand—"

She turned off the engine and stared out into the darkness and the silence.

"George didn't sing this spring."

Kirk reached out, touched her shoulder, and gripped it gently.

"Kirk, humpback whales are meant to be wild. They migrate thousands of miles every year. They're part of an incredibly rich, incredibly complex ecosystem. They have the whole ocean, and a thousand other species to interact with. I was up in Alaska last summer, on a research trip observing humpbacks. We were watching a pod, and a sea lion swam right in beside one of them and dived and flipped and wiggled his flippers. The whale rolled over and waved her pectoral fin in the air, and she dove and surfaced and slapped her flukes on the water— she was playing, Kirk. We had a tape deck on the boat, we were listening to some music. When we put on Emmylou Harris, one of the whales swam within twenty feet of the boat—wild humpbacks just don't come that close—and dove underneath us and came up on the other side and put her head out of water, to listen. I swear, she liked it." She shivered, remembering her own wonder and joy and apprehension when the whale glided beneath her, a darkness against darkness, the long white pectoral fins gleaming on either side, their reach nearly spanning the boat's length. "I'm afraid for George and Gracie, Kirk. I'm afraid the same thing will happen to them that happens to orcas. George didn't sing. Maybe soon they'll both stop playing. And then . . ." Her voice was shaking. She fell silent and looked away.

"We'd take good care of them. They'll be safe."

"I want them safe! But I can keep them safe at the Institute. Till they die. It's freedom that they need most. I like you, Kirk, God knows why. And I'd like to believe you. But, you see, if you're going to keep them safe—imprisoned—it doesn't matter whether they're here at the Institute or with you . . . wherever. Whenever."

"Gillian, if their well-being depends on freedom, I swear to you they'll be free. *And* safe. There are no whale hunters in my time, and the ocean isn't polluted. There aren't any great whales anymore, no orcas, but there are still sea lions to play with. I'll even play country-western music to them, if you think it would make them happy."

"Don't make fun of me."

"I'm not. Believe me, I'm not."

He tempted her. Oh, he tempted her. "If you could prove what you've told me—"

"That's impossible."

"I was afraid of that." She reached over him and opened the door. "Admiral," she said, "this has been the strangest dinner of my life. And the biggest cockamamie fish story I ever heard."

"You did ask," he replied. "Now, will you tell me something?"

She waited.

"George and Gracie's transmitters," Kirk said. "What frequencies are you using?"

She sighed. He never gave up. "Sorry," she said. "That's—classified."

"That's a strange thing to hear from somebody who accused me of being in military intelligence."

"I still don't have a clue who you are!" she said angrily. "You wouldn't want to show me around your spaceship, would you?"

"It wouldn't be my first choice, no."

"So. There we are."

"Let me tell you something," Kirk said, his voice suddenly hard. "I'm here to bring two humpback whales into the twenty-third century. If I have to, I'll go to the open sea to get them. But I'd just as soon take yours. It'd be better for me, better for you . . . and better for them."

"I bet you're a damn good poker player," Gillian said.

"Think about it," Kirk said. "But don't take too long, because we're out of time when they take your whales away. If you change your mind, this is where I'll be."

"Here? In the park?"

"Right."

He kissed her, a quick, light touch of his lips to hers.

"I don't know what else to say to convince you."

"Say good-night, Kirk."

"Good-night." He left the Land Rover and strode through the harsh circle of illumination cast by the street lamp.

Gillian hesitated. She wanted to believe him; she almost wanted to join in his attractive craziness and turn it into a *folie à deux*. Instead, she sensibly shoved the Land Rover into gear and stepped on the gas.

A strange shimmery light reflected from her rearview mirror. She braked and glanced out the back window, wondering what she had seen.

The street lamp must have flickered, for it cast the only illumination over the meadow. Whatever had caused the shimmery effect had disappeared.

And so had Kirk. The meadow was empty.

Ten

Spock watched Admiral Kirk re-form on the transporter platform.

"Did you accomplish your aims in your discussion with Doctor Taylor, Admiral?"

"In a manner of speaking," Admiral Kirk said. "I told her the truth, but she doesn't believe me. Maybe you should try to talk to her. Without your disguise."

"Do you think that wise, Admiral?"

"It wouldn't make any difference. She'd just explain you away with plastic surgery," he said with an ironic smile. "I wish she'd stop explaining me away. As it is, when we beam the whales on board, all Gillian will ever be sure of is that they've disappeared. She won't know if they lost their transmitters, or if they died, or if the whalers killed them." He blew out his breath in frustration. "What's our status?"

"The tank will be finished by morning."

"That's cutting it closer than you know. What about team two?"

"We have received no word since their beam-in. We can only wait for their call."

"Damn!" Kirk said. "Dammit!"

Spock wondered why Kirk employed two similar words of profanity, rather than repeating the same one twice or using two entirely different ones. No doubt the admiral had been correct in his statement that Spock did not yet know how to hang that part of the language.

"We've been so lucky!" Kirk said. "We have the two perfect whales in our hands, but if we don't move quickly, we'll lose them."

"Admiral," Spock said, "Doctor Taylor's whales understand our plans. I made certain promises to them, and they agreed to help us. But if we cannot locate them, my calculations reveal that neither the tank nor the *Bounty* can withstand the power of a frightened wild whale. In that event, the probability is that our mission will fail."

"Our *mission!*" Admiral Kirk shouted. He swung toward Spock, his shoulders hunched and his fists clenched.

Spock drew back, startled.

"Our *mission!* Goddamn it, Spock, you're talking about the end of life on Earth! That includes your father's life! You're half human—haven't you got any goddamn feelings about *that?*" He glared at Spock, then turned, infuriated, and strode down the corridor.

Spock lunged one step after him. "Jim—!" He halted abruptly. The admiral vanished around a corner. He had not heard Spock's protest, and for that Spock felt grateful. He did not understand why he had made it. Spock did not understand the terribly un-Vulcan impulse within him that had led him to make it. He should have repressed it almost before he became aware of it. That was the Vulcan way. James Kirk's anger should have no effect on Spock of Vulcan, for anger was illogical. More than that, it was useless. It led to confusion and misunderstanding and inefficiency.

He knew all that as well as he knew anything. Why, then, did he himself feel anger toward the admiral? How could James Kirk's reaction cause a Vulcan so much pain?

He sought some explanation for Kirk's fury. Worrying about what would happen to Earth if the *Bounty* did not return could have no effect on the fate of the planet; nor could worrying about Sarek's fate save the elder Vulcan. What did Kirk expect him to do? Even if he did feel concern and anguish, what possible benefit could be extracted from revealing the emotions to his superior officer, and humiliating himself with his lack of control?

Spock drew a deep breath, trying to calm himself, wrestling with his confusion and the emotions he could not continue to deny. He wanted to return to his quarters; he wanted to meditate and concentrate until he drew himself completely back into control. But he could not. Too much work remained to be done.

Trying to pretend nothing had happened, or at least that Kirk's outburst had not affected him, Spock squared his shoulders, slipped his hands inside the wide sleeves of his robe, and followed the admiral toward the engine room.

Uhura kept her eye on the tricorder readings as Pavel took a readout on the collector's charge for the tenth time in as many minutes. The process was taking far longer than Mister Scott had estimated. Uhura and Pavel had been at the reactor for nearly an hour. If their luck held for another ten minutes . . .

In the radar room of the aircraft carrier *Enterprise,* the radar operator started a routine equipment test. The image on the screen broke up. Frowning, he fiddled with the controls. He managed to get a clear screen for a moment, then lost it.

"What the hell—? Say, Commander?"

The duty officer joined him. When he saw the screen, he, too, frowned. "I thought you were just running a test program."

"Aye, sir. But we're getting a power drain through the module. It's coming from somewhere in the ship."

The operator kept trying to track down the problem. The duty officer hung over his shoulder until the phone rang and he had to go answer it.

"CIC, Rogerson. . . . Yes, Chief, we're tracking it here, too. What do you make of it?" When he spoke again, his voice was tight. "You sure? Check the videoscan. I need a confirm." He put his hand over the mouthpiece. "He thinks there's an intruder in one of the MMRs."

In the reactor access room, the collector's hum rose in pitch and suddenly ceased.

"Hah!" Pavel said. "Finished." He detached the machine from the wall.

Uhura opened her communicator. "Scotty, we're ready to beam out." Static replied to her message. "Scotty? Uhura here, come in please." She waited. "Come in please. Scotty, do you read?"

"Aye, lass." Static blurred the response. "I hear ye. My transporter power's down to minimum. I must bring ye in one at a time. I'll take you first. Stand by."

Pavel shoved the collector into Uhura's hands.

The beam surrounded her. Its frequency sounded wrong. The usual cool tingle felt like thousands of pinpricks. Finally she vanished.

Pavel waited patiently for the *Bounty*'s transporter to recharge and sweep him from this place. Silence, after the constant high-pitched hum of the energy collector, made him nervous. The reactor's flashing red light gave him a headache.

He started at the sudden shrill of a Klaxon alarm. People shouted between its bleats. Pavel snapped open his communicator.

"Mister Scott," he said, "how soon will transporter be ready? Mister Scott? Hello?"

"Chekov, can ye hear me?" Scott's voice was all but unintelligible through the static.

"Mister Scott, now would be good time—"

The hatch clanged open. A large man leaped into the doorway, an equally large weapon held at the ready and pointing at Pavel. He entered the access chamber. Other large men, all in camouflage uniforms, came in after him.

"Freeze!" the leader shouted.

Pavel looked at him curiously. "Precisely what does this mean," he said, "freeze?"

Pavel tried to pretend he did not care about his communicator, while at the same time he tried to stay within reach of it and hoped desperately that they would not take it away to disassemble it. If he could get ten seconds with the communicator in his hands, he might still escape. But if his captors opened it improperly, it would self-destruct.

Unfortunately, the guards did not look like the type to give him the chance to grab his equipment.

He felt foolish. Not only did they have his communicator, but they had his phaser. They even had his identification, because he had neglected to leave it safely on board the *Bounty*. To make matters worse, he had worn his phaser underneath his jacket, out of reach while the guards covered him with weapons—primitive weapons, perhaps, but powerful at close range. Now he was trapped.

A uniformed interrogator asked him again who he was and who he worked for.

"I am Pavel Chekov," he said. "The rest I cannot tell you."

The interrogator swore softly under his breath. A dark-haired man in civilian dress entered the room. He wore dark spectacles that hid his eyes. The interrogator joined him.

"If the FBI knew this was going to happen," he said angrily, "why didn't you warn us?"

"We didn't know! It's a coincidence! The report came from a nut. He spies on his neighbors and anybody else he can think of and then calls my office and tries to tell me about them. It's embarrassing."

"But he knew—"

"It's a coincidence!" the FBI agent said again. "Watch." Looking disgusted, he approached Pavel. "We caught your friend," he said.

Pavel started. "But—that is impossible!"

The FBI agent turned pale under his tan. "Your black South African friend."

"She is not from south of Africa," Pavel said. "Bantu Nation is—" He stopped. "You did not catch her. You are fooling me."

"Then you weren't alone." The FBI agent looked stunned.

"Yes I was," Pavel said.

The agent left him alone with the guards.

Humiliated by having given his captors evidence of Uhura's existence, Pavel wished the interrogators would chop off his head, or shoot him, or whatever they did to prisoners in the twentieth century.

Would serve me right for stupidity, he thought. *If twentieth-century people shoot me, then Admiral Kirk will not have to be concerned with me. He can rescue whales, take* Bounty *back home, and stop probe.*

He imagined Starfleet's memorial service for Pavel Chekov, fallen hero who had helped save Earth. Admiral Kirk delivered his eulogy. He took some comfort from his fantasy.

His communicator beeped. He snatched at it. One of the guards grabbed him and pushed him back. The interrogator and the FBI agent hurried across the room.

"Let's get rid of that thing," the interrogator said. "It might be a bomb."

"It's not a bomb," said the FBI agent, the man who had fooled him.

"How do you know?"

He shrugged. "It just isn't. It doesn't *look* like a bomb. You develop a feel for these things."

"Uh-huh. Like you develop a feel for loony informants who invent Russian agents and black South African spies."

The agent blushed. "Look, if it were a bomb, our terrorist here would either be sweating, or he'd be threatening us with it."

Pavel wished he had thought of that, but it was too late now.

"Maybe."

"Shall I prove it?" He reached for the communicator.

"No. Leave it alone. I've got somebody from demolition and somebody from electronics coming down to check it out."

"Suit yourself."

Pavel knew that somehow he had to get himself and his equipment out of there before anybody had a chance to inspect it and destroy it. Even his I.D. was causing a good bit of comment.

"Can I see that again?" The FBI agent picked up Chekov's I.D., inspected it, and glanced up again.

"Starfleet?" he said. "United Federation of Planets?"

"I am Lieutenant Commander Pavel Andrei'ich Chekov, Starfleet, United Federation of Planets," Pavel said.

"Yes," the dark-haired agent said sarcastically. "And my name is Bond. All right, Commander, you want to tell us anything?"

"Like what?" Pavel said.

"Like who you really are and what you're doing here and what this stuff is." He gestured to the phaser and the communicator, lying useless on the table just out of Chekov's reach.

"My name is Pavel Andrei'ich Chekov," he said again. "I am lieutenant commander in Starfleet, United Federation of Planets. Service number 656-5827B."

The interrogator sighed. "Let's take it from the top."

"The top of what?" Pavel asked curiously.

"Name?"

"My name?"

"No," the interrogator said. The sarcasm had returned to his tone. "*My* name."

"Your name is Bond," Pavel said.

"My name is *not* Bond!"

"Then I do not know your name," Pavel said, confused.

"You play games with me, and you're through!"

"I am?" Pavel said, surprised. "May I go now?"

With a scowl of exasperation, the agent who had claimed to be named Bond, then denied it, turned his back on Pavel and joined the interrogator.

"What do you think?"

Pavel edged toward the table on which his phaser lay.

The interrogator glared poisonously at Pavel, who pretended he had never moved.

"I think he's a Russian."

"No *kidding*. He's a Russian, all right, but I think he's . . . developmentally disabled."

"We'd better call Washington."

"Washington?" the agent said. "I don't think there's any need to call Washington. I don't know how this guy got onto your boat—"

"Ship. It's a ship. And there's nothing wrong with the security on the *Enterprise*."

"—but he's no more a spy than—"

The guards were distracted by the argument. Pavel lunged and grabbed his phaser.

"Don't move!" he shouted.

Everyone turned toward him, startled.

"Freeze!" Pavel said, hoping they would respond better to their own language.

Bond took one step forward. "Okay," he said. "Make nice and give us the raygun."

"I warn you," Pavel said. "If you don't lie on floor, I will have to stun you."

"Go ahead." The agent sounded tired. "Stun me."

"I'm very sorry, but—" He fired the phaser.

The phaser gurgled and died.

"It must be radiation . . ." Pavel murmured.

Before they could draw their primitive weapons, he grabbed his communicator and I.D., bolted for the door, flung it open, and fled.

"Sound the alarm," the agent yelled. "But don't hurt the crazy bastard."

Pavel ran. A patrol clattered after him. He dodged around a corner and kept running. Voices and footsteps closed in on him. He flung open a hatch and dogged it shut. Another hatch opened into darkness below; a ladder led upward. He swarmed up the ladder. If he could just elude them long enough to communicate with Mister Scott, if he could just stand still long enough for the transporter to lock onto him—

Booted feet clanged on the metal rungs below and behind him. He ran again. He burst out onto the hangar deck. Ranks of sleek jets filled the cavernous space. Even if he could steal a plane, he had no experience with antique aircraft. On the other side of the deck, misty moonlight stretched in a long rectangle. He fled toward it, ducking beneath backswept wings, around awkward landing wheels.

He plunged into the open air and down the gangway. Footsteps clattered behind him; footsteps clattered ahead. He stopped short. A second patrol ran toward him from shore. He was trapped.

A streak of dark water stretched between the dock and the ship. If he could dive in and swim under the pier—

He grabbed the rail. He started to vault, then tried to stop short when he saw what lay below. His boot caught on the decking. He stumbled, bounced into the rail, tumbled over it, flung out his hands to catch himself. The phaser and communicator arced out and splashed into the sea. The wind caught his I.D. and fluttered and spun it away. His fingertips slipped on the wire cable. He cried out.

He fell.

The FBI agent shouldered his way through the shore patrol. They all stood at the edge of the gangway, looking downward, stunned.

"Oh, damn! Get an ambulance!"

The crazy Russian lay sprawled on a barge moored below the gangway. Blood pooled on the deck around his head.

He did not move.

Frightened and frustrated, Uhura hovered at Scott's elbow while he worked frantically over the transporter console.

"His communicator's gone dead," Scott said. "I canna locate him."

"You've got to find him," Uhura said.

"I know that, lass."

Minutes passed without any trace of Chekov.

"I'm going up to the bridge," Uhura said. "I'll try to—"

Admiral Kirk strode into the transporter room. "What's holding things up?" He spoke in this clipped, impatient tone only under conditions of the greatest stress.

"I ha' . . . lost Commander Chekov," Scott said.

"You've *lost* him!"

"You've got to send me back!" Uhura said. "I'll find him, and—"

"Absolutely not!" Admiral Kirk said.

"But, sir—"

"It's out of the question. If he's been taken prisoner, you'd be walking straight into the same trap. And if he's all right, he'll contact us or he'll make his way back on his own."

"I'm responsible—"

"We're all responsible, Uhura! But he voted to take the risk with the rest of us. I need you here, Commander." He inspected the photon collector. "This is it?"

"Aye, sir," Scott said, still fiddling with the transporter controls.

"Then get it in place! Uhura, Scotty, I understand your concern for Chekov. But I've got to have full power in the ship, and I've got to have it soon!" He rose and put one hand on Scott's shoulder. "Scotty, I'll stay here and keep trying to reach Pavel. Go on now."

"Aye, sir." Scott picked up the photon collector. Shoulders slumped, despondent, he left the transporter room.

"Uhura," the admiral said, "you listen in on official communications. If he *was* captured, you may be able to find him that way. But I'll bet he turns up knocking on the hatch within the hour."

"I hope so, sir." Uhura hurried to the control chamber.

She set the computer to monitoring the cacophony of this world's radio transmissions. It would signal when it detected key words. She scanned the frequencies by ear, listening for a few seconds at each channel. Uhura missed the computer on the *Enterprise*. She could have asked it to relay anything unusual to her; she could have explained to it what she meant by unusual. But the computer on the *Bounty* considered everything about the Federation of Planets to be unusual. The centuries-long time jump added to the problem.

Time passed.

"Any luck?"

Uhura started. Admiral Kirk stood beside her.

"Nothing," she said. "I should never have left him."

"Uhura, you did what was necessary. You got the collector back. It wouldn't do any of us any good if you were both lost." He tried to smile. "Keep trying. You'll find him."

The admiral sank into the command chair.

At the power chamber, Scott made a minuscule adjustment of the photon collector as it transferred energy to the dilithium crystals. With Spock's help, Scott had managed to improve the cross-channeling rate. He hoped it was enough. Scott glanced through the observation window. He shook his head. He still could see no difference in the crystals, though both his instruments and Mister Spock claimed they had begun to recrystallize. That was, by a long way, the least that he had hoped for.

The intercom came on. "Mister Scott," Admiral Kirk said, "you promised me an estimate on the dilithium crystals."

Scott rose wearily to reply. "It's going slow, sir, verra slow. It'll be well into tomorrow."

"Not good enough, Scotty! You've got to do better!"

Now I'm expected to speed up quantum reactions, Scott thought. *Perhaps I'll be wanted next to alter the value of Planck's constant. Or the speed of light itself.*

"I'll try, sir. Scott out." He squatted down beside Spock again. "Well now, he's got himself in a bit of a snit, don't he."

"He is a man of deep feelings," Spock said thoughtfully.

"So what else is new?" Grimly, Scott buried himself in the cross-channeling connector.

In the control room, Jim Kirk rubbed his face with both hands. Behind him, the voices Uhura monitored buzzed and jumped. For the first time since leaving Vulcan, Jim had nothing to do. Nothing to do but wait.

And that was the hardest thing of all.

Eleven

Long past midnight, Gillian Taylor drove back toward Sausalito. She had a Springsteen tape playing on the tape deck, too loud as usual. More than twelve hours ago, she had left the Institute early to go home and stare at the ceiling. So much for that.

She would rather be with the whales. She envied the people fifteen or twenty years ago who had lived with dolphins in half-flooded houses in order to do research on human-cetacean communication. But no funding existed anymore for that sort of esoteric, Aquarian-age work. Sometimes Gillian felt like she had been born fifteen years too late.

Or maybe, she thought, *three hundred years too early.*

Then she laughed at herself for taking Kirk's story seriously, even for a second.

She stopped at an intersection. The red light reflected into the Rover. Springsteen was singing "Dancing in the Dark." Gillian turned it up even louder and glanced at her own reflection in the rearview mirror as he got to the line about wanting to change his clothes, his hair, his face.

Yeah, she thought. *Sing it to me, Bruce.*

She wished she could change herself so she could stay with the whales. She allowed herself a wild fantasy of diving into the cold Alaska water with George and Gracie, to help them adapt to their new life, never to be seen again.

No kidding, Gillian, she thought. *Never to be seen again, indeed; you'd die of hypothermia in half an hour. Besides, you know less about whale society than Gracie and George do, even if they did get separated from it as calves. You know as much about them as anybody in the world. But it isn't enough.*

And if Mister Spock knew what he was talking about—which she tried to convince herself she did not believe for a minute—and humpbacks were soon to become extinct, human beings would never know much about the whales.

Her vision blurred. She angrily swiped her forearm across her eyes. The smear of tears glistened beneath the fine, sun-bleached hairs on her arm, changing from red to green with the traffic light. She put the Rover in gear and drove on.

If I could go with them, she thought. *Or if I could protect them. If I could tell them, before they leave, to turn and swim away every time they hear the engine of a boat, or the propeller of a plane, or even a human voice.*

That was what frightened her most. The two humpbacks had known only friendship from human beings. Unlike wild humpbacks, they might swim right up to a boat. They had no way of distinguishing between relatively benign whale-watchers and the cannon-armed harpoon ships of black market whale hunters.

And yet she felt glad that Gracie and George would experience freedom. She tried to reassure herself about their safety. Public opinion and consumer boycotts and just plain economics continued to push toward the end of all whaling. If Gracie and George could survive for a couple of years, they might be safe for the rest of their lives.

She slowed as she approached the turnoff to her house. She ought to go home. She would need to be rested in the morning if she wanted to withstand the stress of moving the whales, and dealing with the reporters that Briggs planned to let in on the story, and most of all saying good-bye.

Instead, she stayed on the main road that led to the Institute.

What the hell, Gillian thought. *So I'll be tired tomorrow. I don't care what Bob Briggs thinks about my feelings for the whales. I'm going to sit on the deck by the tank and wait for sunrise. I'll talk to George and Gracie. And watch them and listen to them. I'll get the boom-box out of my office and let Willie Nelson sing "Blue Skies" to them. It will be the last time, but that's all right. Because whatever happens, they'll be free. And maybe George will sing again.*

Gillian parked the Rover, entered the dark museum, and clattered up the spiral staircase to the deck around the tank. She peered into the darkness. The whales ought to be dozing. Every few minutes they would surface, blow gently, and breathe. But she could not find them.

Maybe they caught a case of nerves from me and everybody else. Maybe they don't feel like sleeping any more than I do.

"Hey, you guys!"

She did not hear the blow and huff of their breathing.

Frightened, Gillian clattered down the spiral stairs to the viewing window. Surely nothing could have happened to them. Not now. Not with their freedom in sight. She pressed her hands against the cold glass, shading her eyes to peer into the tank, afraid she might see one whale dead or injured on the floor of the tank, the other nuzzling the body in grief and confusion and trying to help.

She heard footsteps. She turned.

Bob Briggs stood in the entrance to the viewing area.

"They left last night," he said softly.

Gillian stared at him with complete incomprehension.

"We didn't want a mob scene with the press," he said. "It wouldn't have been good for them. Besides, I thought it would be easier on you this way."

"Easier on me!" She took one step toward him. "You sent them away? Without even letting me say good-bye?" Rage and grief and loss concentrated inside her.

The rage burst out and Gillian slapped Briggs as hard as she could. He staggered back.

"You son of a bitch!" she cried. She did not even wait to see if she had hurt him. "You stupid, condescending son of a bitch!" She fled.

In her car, she leaned her forehead against the steering wheel, sobbing uncontrollably. Her palm hurt. She had never punched anybody, but she wished she had struck Bob Briggs with her fist instead of her open hand.

George and Gracie were free. That was what she wanted. But she wanted them safe, too.

She raised her head. She reached the decision she had been approaching, roundabout and slowly, all night long, and she hoped she had not waited too long to make it. She started the Land Rover, threw it into gear, floored it, and peeled out of the parking lot.

Sulu hoisted the battered helicopter into the air. It flew as if it were a bumblebee and believed the old theory that bumblebees should not be able to fly. It reached the end of the harness around the acrylic sheeting.

The cable snapped tight, pitching the Huey forward with a jolt and a shudder. Adrenaline rushing, Sulu fought to keep the copter in the air. Gradually, it steadied.

Sulu edged the power up and took the copter higher. The acrylic sheeting rose. A breeze, imperceptible on the ground, caught the flat of it and started it swinging. The oscillation transferred to the Huey. Loaded, the copter was far more difficult to fly.

"How the hell did they ever keep these things in the air?" he muttered. He gave it a bit of forward momentum, which helped damp the swing. The sheeting turned edge on to the copter's direction. More steadily now, the Huey clattered and chopped toward Golden Gate Park.

The Land Rover screeched to a stop in the parking lot by the meadow. Gillian leaped out, dodged a clump of garbage cans, and ran across the grass. Mist swirled around her, glowing silver in the dawn.

She stopped in the last place she had seen Kirk.

"Kirk!" She could hardly hear her own voice over the clattery racket of an approaching helicopter. "Kirk!" she cried in fury. "Damn you! If you're a fake— if you lied to me—!"

Gillian turned in a complete circle, searching. But Kirk did not answer. There was nothing there, no Kirk, no strange friend, no invisible spaceship. Tears of anger burned her eyes. She did not even care that Kirk had made a fool of her. He had offered her safety for the humpbacks. She had wanted to believe him, she had made herself believe him, and he had lied.

A downward blast of wind turned the tear tracks cold and whipped her hair around her face. The helicopter, closer now, hovered over a landscaped terrace. A huge pane of glass hung from its cargo harness. The copter lowered the glass slowly toward the blossoming rhododendrons. Beneath it, a man gestured instructions.

Gillian gasped.

The man hung unsupported in the air. But from the waist down, he did not even exist. It was as if he were standing within a structure that could not be seen and that could conceal him as well. An invisible structure . . .

"Kirk!" Gillian cried. "Kirk, listen to me!"

She ran up the bank to the terrace, crashing through the shiny dark green leaves and fluorescent pink and scarlet flowers of the rhododendrons. They flicked back at her, showering her with dew.

Excited and amazed, she clambered headlong over the edge of the terrace. She ran smack into something. She fell, stunned, a metallic *clang* reverberating around her. Still dizzy, she reached out and encountered a strut, cold, hard, solid . . . and invisible. In wonder and joy, she clenched her hands around it and pulled herself to her feet.

The half-visible man above her guided the acrylic sheet, letting it descend into invisibility. He waved off the helicopter. It rose, spun, and clattered away. The prop wash and the noise decreased precipitously.

"Where's Kirk?" Gillian shouted. "Kirk!" she shouted. "God, Kirk, I need you!"

The partly invisible man stared down at her, blinked, bent down, and vanished.

Gillian held the strut more tightly. *Kirk won't disappear on me now,* she thought. *I won't let him!*

She waited a moment for the invisible man to become half-visible again, but he remained hidden and she saw no sign of Kirk. She reached up, feeling for handholds, wondering if she could climb the invisible framework supporting the invisible ship.

Fluid, insubstantial, the strut dissolved from beneath her hands. Her vision blurred and a tingly, excited feeling swept over her.

The park faded away, to be replaced by a bright chamber lit by fixtures of odd, angular construction. The proportions of the room seemed strange to her, and the quality of the light, and the colors.

Not strange, Gillian thought. *Alien.* Alien.

She was standing on a small platform. The glow and hum of a beam of energy faded. In front of her, Kirk James reached up to the controls of a console built to be operated by someone much larger.

"Hello, Alice," Kirk said. "Welcome to Wonderland."

She pushed her tangled hair from her face.

"It is true," she whispered. "It's all true. Everything you said . . ."

"Yes. And I'm glad you're here. Though I'll admit, you picked a hell of a time to drop in." He took her by the elbow. "Steady now. We need your help."

"Have I flipped out?" Gillian asked. She stepped down from the platform, staring around her in amazement. A script she had never seen labeled the controls of the console, but bits of plastic hand-lettered in English were stuck beside some of them. "Is any of this real?"

"It's all real," Kirk said. He guided her around, led her through a corridor, and took her to an echoing enclosed space. Sunlight slanted through the hatch above. The half-invisible man, whole now, secured the large sheet of transparent plastic.

"This is my engineer, Mister Scott," Kirk said.

Scott straightened up and stretched his back. "Aye, how d'ye do." He spoke with a strong Scots burr. " 'Tis finished, Admiral. An hour or so for the epoxy to cure, and it'll hold slime devils, ne'er mind Doctor Taylor's critters."

"It's a tank for the whales," Kirk said to Gillian. "Good work, Scotty."

"But, Kirk—" Gillian said.

"We'll bring them up just like we brought you. It's called a transporter beam—"

"Kirk, listen to me! They're gone!"

He stared at her. "Gone?" he said.

"Briggs—my boss—sent them away last night. Without telling me. To 'protect' me, damn him! They're in Alaska by now."

"Damn." Kirk pressed his closed fist very firmly and very quietly against the transparent surface of the plastic.

"But they're tagged!" Gillian said. "I told you that. Can't we go find them?"

"At the moment," Kirk said, "we can't go anywhere."

Gillian scowled at him. "What kind of spaceship is this, anyway?"

"A spaceship with a missing man," Kirk said.

Mister Spock entered the cargo bay. He still wore his white kimono, but he had taken off his headband. Gillian saw his ears and his eyebrows for the first time.

"Admiral, full power is restored."

"Thank you, Spock," Kirk said. "Gillian, you know Mister Spock."

Gillian stared at him agape.

"Hello, Doctor Taylor," Mister Spock said with perfect calm. "Welcome aboard."

A woman's voice, tense with strain, came over the intercom. "Admiral—are you there?"

Kirk answered. "Yes, Uhura. What's wrong?"

"I've found Chekov, sir. He's been injured. He's going into emergency surgery right now."

"Uhura, *where?*"

"Mercy Hospital."

"That's in the Mission District," Gillian said.

"Admiral, his condition's critical. They said . . . he isn't expected to survive."

Gillian reached out to Kirk, in sympathy with his distress. Spock, on the other hand, listened impassively to the report. Kirk squeezed Gillian's hand gratefully. Another man hurried into the cargo bay.

"You've got to let me go after him!" he exclaimed without preliminaries, without even noticing Gillian. "Don't leave him in the hands of twentieth-century medicine."

"And this, Gillian, is Doctor McCoy," Kirk said. "Bones—" He stopped and turned to Mister Spock instead. "What do you think, Spock?"

He raised one eyebrow. Now Gillian understood why she had never met anyone like him. She had a sudden, irrational urge to laugh. She was standing face to face with a being from another planet. An alien.

Probably, she thought, *an illegal alien.*

"Spock?" Kirk said again.

"As the admiral requested," Spock said, "I am thinking." He continued to think. His face showed no expression. "Commander Chekov is a perfectly normal human being of Earth stock. Only the most detailed autopsy imaginable might hint that he is not from this time. His death here would have only the slightest possible chance of affecting the present or the future."

"You think we should find the whales, return home . . . and leave Pavel to die."

"Now just a minute!" Doctor McCoy exclaimed.

"No, Admiral," Spock said. "I suggest that Doctor McCoy is correct. We must help Commander Chekov."

422 Vonda N. McIntyre

"Is that the logical thing to do, Spock?"

"No, Admiral," Spock said. "But I believe you would call it the human thing to do."

For a moment it seemed to Gillian that a gentler expression might soften his severe and ascetic face. This was practically the first thing Gillian had heard Mister Spock say that did not surprise her, yet Kirk looked surprised by his friend's comment. He hesitated. Spock gazed at him, cool, collected.

"Right," Kirk said abruptly. He turned to Gillian. "Will you help us?"

"Sure," she said. "But how?"

"For one thing," Doctor McCoy said, "we'll need to look like physicians."

This time Gillian paid attention to the transporter beam. The sensation of being lifted, stirred around, and placed somewhere else entirely filled her with astonishment and joy.

Maybe it's just an adrenaline reaction, she thought, *but early trials suggest it as a sure cure for depression.*

When she had completely solidified, darkness surrounded her. She felt her way to the wall, the door, the light switch. She flipped it.

Bingo! she thought. *She had asked Mister Scott to try to place them within a small, deserted cubicle. He had done her proud: not only had they come down in a closet, they had come down in a storage closet of linens, lab coats, and scrub suits.*

"Damned Klingon transporter's even worse than ours," Doctor McCoy muttered.

"What does he mean?" Gillian said. She flipped through a stack of scrubs. Did these things have sizes, or were they one size fits all? Stolen hospital scrubs had enjoyed a minor fashion popularity when she was in graduate school, but she had never had much interest in them. Nor had she ever had a medical student boyfriend to steal one for her. All she knew was that you could wear them inside out or outside in.

"Oh—Doctor McCoy doesn't like transporter beams."

"You don't? God, I think they're great. But I meant why isn't it *your* transporter beam?"

"Our ship—and our transporter—are from the Klingon empire," Kirk said. "Not our . . . regular brand, you might say."

"How come you're flying a foreign ship?" Gillian dug through the stack of scrubs. They only came in three sizes, so she did not have to worry much about the fit.

"It's a long story. The short version is, it was the only one available, so we stole it."

"We don't even have time for short versions of stories!" Doctor McCoy snapped. "Let's find Chekov and get out of here." He reached for the doorknob.

"Wait," Gillian said. She handed McCoy the blue scrub suit. "Thought you wanted to look like a doctor."

"I thought *you* said I would, with my bag," he said grumpily. He hefted his medical kit, a leather satchel hardly different externally from the sort of bag doctors carried in the twentieth century.

"You do. But you won't get into surgery in regular clothes." She slipped the scrub on over her head. "Doctor Gillian Taylor, Ph.D., very recent M.D.," she said.

Suddenly the doorknob turned. Instantly Gillian grabbed both Kirk and McCoy. She drew them toward her, one hand at the back of each man's neck. She kissed Kirk full on the lips. He put his arms around her. Startled, McCoy at first pulled back, then hid his face against her neck.

The door swung open. Gillian pretended to be fully involved. She did not have to pretend too hard. Kirk smelled good. His breath tickled her cheek.

"*Pre*verts," a voice said cheerfully, *tsked* twice, and chuckled. The door closed again.

Gillian let Kirk and McCoy go.

"Um," she said. "Sorry."

McCoy cleared his throat.

"No apologies necessary," Kirk said, flustered.

A moment later, all attired in surgeons' garb, they opened the door cautiously and peered out into the corridor.

"All clear," Kirk said.

On the way out of the storage closet, Gillian snagged a handful of surgical masks in sterile paper packages.

"We'll check this way, Bones," Kirk said. "You try down there."

McCoy strode down the hallway, doing his best to pretend he knew exactly where he was going and what he was doing. He nodded to the people he passed as if he knew them. They all nodded back as if they knew him.

A frail and elderly patient lay on a gurney just outside a room full of esoteric equipment that looked, to McCoy, like medieval instruments of torture. McCoy stopped beside the gurney, hoping to get his bearings.

"Doctor . . ." the frail patient said. She had poor color and her hands trembled. A large black bruise had spread around a vein cut-down on the back of her left hand.

"What's the matter with you?" McCoy asked.

"Kidney," she said. She stared with resignation into the room beyond. "Dialysis . . ."

"*Dialysis?* What is this," McCoy said without thinking, "the dark ages?" He shook his head. To hell with not leaving traces of anachronistic technology. He took a lozenge from his bag and slipped it into the patient's mouth. "Here. Swallow one of these." He strolled away. "And call me if you have any problems," he said over his shoulder.

McCoy looked for a comm terminal—surely the twentieth century must have comm terminals?—to query about the location of surgery. Instead he saw Jim gesturing to him from down the hall. McCoy hurried to join him and Gillian.

"They're holding Chekov in a security corridor one flight up," Jim said. "His condition's still critical. Skull fracture—they're about to operate."

"Good Lord. Why don't they just bore a hole in his head and let the evil spirits out?" A gurney stood empty nearby. McCoy grabbed it. "Come on."

He pushed the gurney into a vacant room and threw back the sheet.

"Give us a couple of those masks," he said to Gillian, "and jump up here."

She handed him the masks, "Wait a minute," she said. "How come I have to be the patient and you guys get to be the doctors?"

"What?" McCoy said, baffled.

"Good lord, Gillian, what difference does it make?" Jim said.

Gillian saw that he honestly did not understand why his suggestion might irritate her, and that gave her a view of his future that attracted her far more than all his descriptions of wonders and marvels. She jumped onto the gurney and covered herself with the sheet.

A moment later, McCoy and Kirk rolled the gurney onto the elevator. Gillian lay still. The two people already on the elevator, paying them not the least bit of attention, continued their discussion of a patient's course of chemotherapy and the attending side effects.

Twentieth-century technology was so close to the breakthroughs that would spare people this sort of torture, and yet this world continued to expend its resources on weapons. "Unbelievable," McCoy muttered.

Both the other elevator passengers turned toward him. "Do you have a different view, Doctor?" one asked.

The elevator doors opened. McCoy scowled. "Sounds like the goddamn Spanish Inquisition," he said. He plunged out of the elevator, leaving startled silence behind him. He had to get Pavel Chekov out of here before these people did too much damage for even the twenty-third century to repair.

Jim followed, pushing the gurney.

Two police officers guarded the operating wing's double doors.

"Out of the way," McCoy said in a peremptory tone.

Neither officer moved. McCoy saw Gillian's eyelids flicker. Suddenly she began to moan.

"Sorry, Doctor—" the police officer said.

Gillian moaned again.

"—we have strict orders—" The officer had to raise his voice to be heard above Gillian's groaning. He glanced down at her, distressed.

"Dammit!" McCoy said. "This patient has immediate postprandial upper abdominal distension! Do you want an acute case on your hands?"

The two officers looked at each other uncertainly.

Gillian wailed loudly.

"Orderly!" McCoy nodded curtly to Jim, who pushed the gurney between the two officers.

The doors opened. Safe on the other side, Jim blew out his breath with relief.

"What did you say she was getting?" he asked McCoy.

"Cramps," McCoy said.

Gillian sat up and threw off the sheet. "I beg your pardon!"

Jim tossed her a surgical mask. He pulled his own mask over his face and led his intrepid group into the operating room. Chekov lay unconscious on the operating table.

A young doctor looked up from examining him. He frowned. "Who are you? Doctor Adams is supposed to assist me."

"We're just—observing," McCoy said.

"Nobody said anything to me about observers."

Ignoring him, McCoy went to Chekov's side, took out his tricorder, and passed it over Chekov's still, pale form.

"What the hell do you think you're doing?" the young doctor said.

"Reading the patient's vital signs."

"It's an experimental device, Doctor," Jim said quickly.

"Experimental! You're not doing any experiments on my patients—even one who's in custody!"

"Tearing of the middle meningeal artery," McCoy muttered.

"What's your degree in?" the other doctor said angrily. "Dentistry?"

"How do *you* explain slowing pulse, low respiratory rate, and coma?"

"Funduscopic examination—"

"Funduscopic examination is unrevealing in these cases!"

The young doctor gave McCoy a condescending smile. "A simple evacuation of the expanding epidural hematoma will relieve the pressure."

"My God, man!" McCoy exclaimed. "Drilling holes in his head is not the answer. The artery must be repaired, without delay, or he'll die! So put away your butcher knives and let me save the patient!"

Their antagonist glowered. "I don't know who the hell you are, but I'm going to have you removed."

He headed for the door. Jim blocked his path.

"Doctors, doctors, this is highly unprofessional—"

The doctor snarled and tried to get around him.

Jim grabbed him at the juncture of neck and shoulder, and caught him as he collapsed.

"Kirk!" Gillian said.

"That never worked before," Jim said, astonished. "And it probably never will again. Give me a hand, will you?"

Gillian helped him carry the unconscious doctor to the adjoining room. Jim closed the door and slagged the lock with his phaser. He and Gillian rejoined McCoy. McCoy had already induced tissue regeneration. He passed his tricorder over Chekov again.

"Chemotherapy!" McCoy growled. "Funduscopic examination! Medievalism!" He closed the vial of regenerator and shoved it back into his bag. Chekov took a deep, strong breath. He breathed out, moaning softly.

"Wake up, man, wake up!"

"Come on, Pavel," Jim said.

Chekov's eyelids flickered and his hands twitched.

"He's coming around, Jim," McCoy said.

"Pavel, can you hear me? Chekov! Give me your name and rank!"

"Chekov, Pavel A.," he murmured. "Rank . . ." He smiled in his dreams. "Admiral . . ."

Jim grinned.

"Don't you guys have any enlisted types?" Gillian said.

Chekov opened his eyes, sat up with Jim's help, and looked around.

"Doctor McCoy . . . ? *Zdrastvuyte!*"

"And hello to you, too, Chekov," McCoy said.

Jim drew out his communicator. He was about to call Scott and have them beamed out when McCoy elbowed him and gestured toward the slagged door. The groggy doctor appeared at the window.

"Let me out of here!" he yelled.

He could not have seen too much of McCoy's operation, and even if he had it would not have been obvious what he was doing; but beaming out in plain sight would be too much.

"Let's go." Jim helped Chekov onto the gurney, threw a surgical drape over him, and pushed the gurney through the double doors and past the two policemen.

"How's the patient?" one of them asked.

"He's going to make it!" Jim exclaimed, hurrying on without pause. Gillian and McCoy followed. As he rounded the corner, Jim began to think they would get away clean.

"He?" one of the officers said. "They went in with a she!"

"One little mistake!" Jim said with disgust. He started running, pushing the gurney before him.

A moment later the loudspeakers blared with alarms. Jim cursed. At an intersection he turned one way, saw dark uniforms through the windows of a set of doors, slid to a halt, spun the gurney around, and headed in the other direction. Gillian and McCoy dodged and followed him as he pelted down the opposite corridor. At the next set of doors he dragged the gurney to a more normal pace and pushed it through. Gillian and McCoy followed sedately.

Before them, an elderly woman sat smiling in a wheelchair. Two doctors conferred intently just behind her. As Jim passed, one said to the other, "So? How do you explain it?"

"According to the CAT scan," the other replied, "she's growing a new kidney!"

Jim glanced back. The elderly woman saw McCoy, reached out, grasped his hand, and held it.

"Doctor, thank you."

"You're welcome, ma'am."

The doors burst open behind them. Hospital security and police officers crowded the corridor. Jim plunged into a run.

"Freeze! Stop, or I'll—" The voice cut itself off. Jim trusted that nobody would be stupid enough to shoot in a hallway full of people. But then they passed into a deserted corridor. The pursuers began to close on them. Jim kept going. Gillian and McCoy ran alongside. Still confused and a little groggy, Chekov raised his head. McCoy reached out and pushed him back down. They were only twenty meters from the elevator. Its doors opened as if Jim had called to them.

Suddenly a guard stepped out of a cross-corridor and barred their way. Jim did not even pause. Pushing the gurney like a battering ram before him he flung himself at the guard. The guard backed up fast and stumbled. Jim plunged into the elevator. Gillian and McCoy piled in after him. He slammed his hand on the "up" button and sagged back against the wall, gasping for breath. The doors closed.

The elevator rose.

"If we keep going up, they'll catch us!" Gillian said.

"Calm yourself, Doctor Taylor," Kirk said. He pulled out his communicator and opened it. "Scotty, get us out of here!"

In the corridor outside, the guard hoisted himself off the floor and grabbed at the edges of the elevator doors just as they closed. He heard the elevator cage moving away. Cursing, he kicked the doors. The indicator light flicked to the next floor. Most of hospital security and a dozen uniformed police officers clattered down the corridor.

"Come on! They're in the elevator!" He headed for the stairs and mounted them three at a time. The others followed, a few stopping at each floor to keep the fugitives from escaping. Walkie-talkies began to buzz and rasp: "They didn't get out. The elevator's still going up."

At the top floor, he raced for the elevator. It had not yet reached this floor. It rose without stopping. He drew his gun.

The elevator doors opened.

"All right—" he said. And stopped.

The elevator was empty.

Gillian reappeared on board the *Bounty*. Again the transporter gave her a feeling of exultation. Kirk and McCoy, supporting Chekov, solidified beside her. Another member of the spaceship crew, an Asian man she had not met before, joined McCoy and helped him take Chekov away. Kirk stayed with Gillian. They walked along the oddly proportioned corridor. Before Gillian realized what was happening, the corridor extended into a ramp and Kirk led her onto the terraced bank beneath the ship. The ramp rose and disappeared behind them. Gillian looked back, but nothing remained of the spaceship. It was as if it had never existed.

"Gillian, would the whales be at sea by now?"

"Yes." Gillian turned eagerly toward the spaceship. "If you've got a chart on board, I can show you."

"All I need is the radio frequency to track them."

"What are you talking about? I'm coming with you."

"You can't. Our next stop is the twenty-third century."

"What do I care? I've got nobody but those whales!"

"Maybe the whales here in the twentieth century need you, too. You can work for their preservation. Maybe they don't have to become extinct."

"And what happens then? Does that mean you won't have to come back, and I never will have met you?" She stopped, tangled in the time paradoxes. "Kirk, don't you understand? There are hundreds—thousands—of people working for the preservation of whales! If Mister Spock is right, nothing they do makes any difference. I can't do anything more. What do you think I'd say? How about, 'I met a man in an invisible alien spaceship from the twenty-third century, and his greenish friend with the pointy ears told me whales were about to become extinct.' Do you think anybody would listen to me? They'd throw me in the loony bin and throw the key into San Francisco Bay!"

"Gillian, I'm sorry. I don't have time to argue. I don't even have time to tell you how much you've meant to us. To me. Please. *The frequency*."

"All right. The frequency is 401 megahertz."

"Thank you." He hesitated. "For everything." He pulled out his communicator and flipped it open. "Beam me up, Scotty."

The familiar sound whined. A faint glittery haze gathered around Kirk's body. He started to disappear.

Twelve

Not knowing what would happen, not caring, Gillian flung herself into the beam and grabbed Kirk around the waist. She felt him dissolving in her hands.

She felt herself dissolving.

They reappeared in the transporter room.

"Surprise!" Gillian said.

Kirk glared at her. "Do you know how dangerous—no, how could you? You could have killed both of us. Never mind. Come on, you'll just have to leave again."

"*Hai!*" She jumped into a karate crouch, both hands raised. "You'll have to fight me to get me out of here."

He put his hands on his hips and appraised her stance. "You don't know the first thing about karate, do you?"

"Maybe not," she said, without backing down. "But you don't know the first thing about whales. I won't let you take George and Gracie and not take me!"

"Gillian, we could all die trying to get home! The whales, my officers, me . . . you."

He made her pause, but he did not change her mind. "So much for your promise to keep my whales safe," she said. "I'm staying."

He sighed, raised his hands above his shoulders, and let them fall to his sides.

"Suit yourself." He strode away.

She followed him through the amazing ship of odd color combinations, odd intersections, odd angles. Finally he reached a room full of controls and computer screens and instruments, all with the same unfamiliar proportions and unusual colors as the transporter room. Here, too, the controls had been relabeled.

Mister Spock stood nearby.

"Mister Spock," Kirk said, "where the hell is the power you promised me?"

"Admiral," Mister Spock said, "you must wait one damn minute."

A black woman glanced up from her console, saw Gillian, and smiled at her. The Asian man who had helped Chekov entered and took his place at another control console. Gillian stared around in wonder. She was in a spaceship that could travel from star to star, among a group of people who lived and worked together without being concerned about race or gender, among people from Earth and a person from another planet. Gillian broke into a grin. Probably a silly grin, she thought, and she did not care.

"I'm ready, Mister Spock," Mister Scott said over the intercom. "Let's go find George and Gracie."

"Mister Sulu?" Kirk said.

Mister Sulu, the slender, good-looking Asian man, touched the controls. "I'm trying to remember how this works," he said with a smile. "I got used to a Huey."

Gillian felt a hint of vibration beneath her feet. Kirk faced her, frowning.

"That was a lousy trick," he said.

"You need me," Gillian replied.

"Ready, sir," Sulu said.

"Go, Mister Sulu."

The alien ship's vibration increased to a roar. On the viewscreen before Gillian, dust and leaves and fallen blossoms swirled in a cloud.

Javy felt awful. He should have stayed awake all night instead of tossing and turning and finally dropping off and then oversleeping. Ben had been bitching at him all day for being late to work. He did not stop griping till they reached the line of trash cans near the meadow in Golden Gate Park. At the entrance to the parking lot Ben hesitated, cursed, and lurched the truck into the lot. They both got down and started unloading the cans.

Trying to pretend it was still a regular spot, Ben started griping again.

"Jeez, Javy, we've hardly made up any time at all. We're three, four hours behind. We're not gonna get done till I don't know when—"

"I already told you thanks for covering for me," Javy said. "Look, you take off at noon like always, and I'll finish the route myself."

Ben immediately demurred, which was worse than if he had accepted Javy's offer. Javy knew Ben just wanted to be persuaded some more, so he started persuading him. But his gaze kept being drawn to the meadow, to the place where he had seen the man disappear. He replaced the last can.

"Hang on a minute, I'll be right back."

"Javy, dammit—"

Javy found nothing in the meadow, no seared spot on the ground, not even any footprints. Maybe he remembered it wrong. He walked in a spiral around the most likely place.

"Javy, if you don't hurry up—!"

An enormous roar vibrated the ground. A wind from nowhere blew downward. Crumpled paper and leaves and brilliant pink rhododendron blossoms whipped around Javy's feet. He looked up. The roar intensified and a wave of heat blasted past.

A huge birdlike shadow cut off the sunlight, moved slowly over him, accelerated across the meadow, and vanished over the trees.

The shadow had come from the direction of a terraced bank and the wind had ripped blossoms from the bushes planted there. Javy sprinted up the hill, slipping between branches of dense foliage. Ben followed, crashing through the plants and yelling at him.

He reached the terrace, pushing past wilted vegetation. The heat surrounded him with a strange pungent odor. Whatever had been here had vanished into the sky.

"Javy, dammit, I think you've gone straight around the bend—Jeez Louise."

Ben stopped at the edge of the terrace, staring. Javy looked down.

Around his feet lay a circle of scorched ground.

Immersed in time-warp calculations, Spock could spare only a minimum of attention for the operation of the *Bounty* or the sight of the receding Earth. He did note that the ship's controls answered Sulu's demands with a slight hesitation. Far below, a green stripe led from the western edge of the city toward its center: Golden Gate Park, its details obscured by distance. San Francisco reached across the water with its tentacles of bridges.

"Cloaking device is stable," Chekov said. "All systems normal."

"Stabilize energy reserve," Admiral Kirk said. "Report, helm."

"Maintaining impulse climb," Sulu said. "Wing five by zero, helm steady."

"Advise reaching ten thousand. Steer three-one-zero."

"Three-one-zero, aye," Sulu replied.

"Uhura, scan for the whales: 401 megahertz."

"Scanning, sir."

"Ten thousand MSL, Admiral," Mister Sulu said.

"Wings to cruise configuration. Full impulse power."

"Aye, sir. Three-one-zero to the Bering Sea. ETA twelve minutes."

The California coast sped beneath them and vanished behind them and they soared over the open sea.

Admiral Kirk opened an intercom channel. "Scotty, are the whale tanks secure?"

" 'Twould be better to give the epoxy more time to cure, but there's no help for it. Maybe 'twill hold, but I'd give my eyeteeth for a force field. Admiral, I've never beamed up four hundred tons before."

"*Four hundred* tons?" Kirk exclaimed.

"It ain't just the whales, it's the water."

"Oh," Kirk said. "Yes. Of course."

Spock gazed at the unfinished equations, troubled.

"Uhura," Admiral Kirk said, "any contact with the whales yet?"

Spock took note of her negative gesture as he continued to puzzle out the formulae. The doors of the control chamber slid open. Doctor McCoy entered. He stopped beside Spock and observed him for some moments.

"You . . . er . . ." McCoy hesitated, then continued in a diplomatic tone. "You present the appearance of a man with a problem."

"Your perception is correct, Doctor," Spock said. "In order to return us to the exact moment at which we left the twenty-third century, I have used our journey back through time as a referent, calculating the coefficient of elapsed time in relation to the deceleration curve."

"Naturally," McCoy said, with apparent comprehension.

Spock raised one eyebrow. Perhaps the doctor's connection with Vulcan rationality had benefited him after all.

"So . . ." McCoy said, "what is your problem?"

"The ship's mass has not remained constant. This will affect our acceleration."

"You're going to have to take your best shot," McCoy said.

"My best shot?"

"*Guess,* Spock. Your best guess."

Spock experienced distress at the idea. "Guessing is not in my nature," he said.

McCoy suddenly grinned. "Well, nobody's perfect."

The speakers produced a noise unfamiliar to Spock.

"That's it!" Gillian Taylor exclaimed.

The sound was more than familiar to Gillian. It was the transponder pattern assigned to Gracie.

"Affirmative," Uhura said. "Contact with the whales."

"Bearing?" Kirk said.

"Bearing three-twenty-seven, range one thousand kilometers."

"Put them on-screen."

"On-screen!" Gillian said. "How can you do that? It's radio!"

Uhura smiled at her. Gillian blushed. She had a lot to learn. She hoped she had a chance to learn it.

"Image translation on-screen," Uhura said.

A faint image appeared and gradually gained resolution. Gillian gasped. George and Gracie swam in the open sea, breaching and playing. Kirk gave an exclamation of triumph.

"*Vessyl kit,*" Chekov whispered.

Under the surface, they swam as eagles flew. Until now, Gillian had seen them only as falcons in hoods and jesses.

"Admiral," Uhura said, "I have a signal closing on the whales. Bearing three-twenty-eight degrees."

"On-screen," Kirk said.

A blurrier image appeared. Gillian froze in disbelief.

"What kind of a ship is that?" Doctor McCoy asked.

"It's a whaling ship, Doctor," Gillian whispered.

"Estimate range, whaler to whales."

"Range two kilometers, Admiral," Uhura said.

"Oh my God," Gillian said, "we're too late!"

"Mister Sulu! Full-power descent!"

The ship tilted and the acceleration increased for an instant before another force—artificial gravity?—compensated for it. Gillian barely noticed the roller-coaster effect. On the screen, the modern ship roared toward the whales, an explosive-powered harpoon gun looming on its bow. These whalers would hardly ever lose their prey.

George and Gracie had no way of knowing they should turn and flee.

"Dive speed is three hundred kilometers per minute. Five kilometers per second," Mister Sulu said. "Estimate reaching whales in one point two minutes."

Gillian knew the routine on the whaler all too well. She had seen the films a hundred, a thousand times. The blurry image cleared to a crystalline intensity. The crew sighted their quarry and prepared their weapons. The whale boat collected itself and surged forward on powerful engines. Its deep wake cut the ocean. Gillian stared at the image as if she could communicate with the whales by will.

The image changed: wispy clouds parted before the alien ship's bow. The open ocean stretched out before it. Far ahead, George and Gracie played. The whale boat sped closer.

"Range to whales," Sulu said, "thirty seconds."

The image was so clear that Gillian could see the whalers loading the harpoon gun and preparing to fire. George and Gracie noticed the ship. They stopped playing and floated in the sea. Gillian urged them in her mind to take fright and swim away.

With a languid stroke of his flukes, George propelled himself toward the whale boat.

Laughing, the whalers aimed.

"Ten seconds, sir!"

"Hover on my mark, Mister Sulu," Kirk said. "Mister Chekov, stand by decloaking. Scotty, ready for power buildup." He paused. "Mark, Mister Sulu."

The *Bounty* shot ahead of the whales and dropped between them and the whaling vessel. The harpoon gun emitted a cloud of gunpowder smoke. The harpoon moved too fast to see.

The *Bounty* reverberated with a tremendous *clang!* The spent harpoon tumbled away from the viewscreen and splashed into the ocean. Beyond it, the whale hunters stared in confusion and disbelief.

"Scotty," Kirk said. "Disengage cloaking device."

"Aye, sir."

Gillian felt a shimmery shiver around her. The walls of the ship flickered so quickly she was not sure she had really seen any change. A wash of light flashed over the whalers and they reacted in terror as Kirk's invisible spaceship became visible. The gunner jerked back from the harpoon cannon, flinging up his hands to protect his eyes. The ship lost way, pitching the gunnery crew forward against the rail, then sideways as the pilot spun the wheel and slewed the boat around so sharply that he nearly swamped it. The boat yawed, straightened, fled.

Sulu let out a whoop of triumph, and the others all cheered. Gillian tried to join them. She gasped. She had been holding her breath.

"Mister Scott," Kirk said. Everyone in the control room fell silent, but the exultation remained. "It's up to you now. Commence buildup for transporter beam."

"I'll give it me best, sir," Scott said. He tried to conceal the concern in his voice. " 'Twould be a right mess if we came all this way and got this far, only to lose Doctor Taylor's wee beasties in a weak transporter beam."

"The cloaking device has strained the power system," Spock said. "The dilithium recrystallization may have reversed."

"Mister Chekov, put everything you can into the transporter charge."

"Aye, sir."

The lights dimmed and the sounds on the bridge faded.

"Any better, Scotty?"

"A bit, sir. I willna let this alien bucket o' bolts gi' ou' on me now, or I'll see i' in a scrap heap. And never mind that Mister Sulu likes to fly it."

"Mister Scott!" Kirk said.

"Stay wi' me, sir," Scott replied. "I need a steeper power curve."

"How long, Scotty?"

"Ten seconds, Admiral. Five . . ."

In the control room, as Mister Scott's voice counted down the last seconds, Gillian clenched her fists and stared at the viewscreen as if her will could force everything to turn out all right.

"Four . . ."

In the sea below the *Bounty,* George and Gracie ceased their playing. They hovered just beneath the surface, watching, waiting, without fear.

"Three . . ."

Gillian wished she could tell the whales that the transporter beam was fun, that they would like it.

"Two . . ."

Perhaps Mister Spock had told them it was fun. But that did not seem very much in character for Mister Spock.

"One . . ."

The whales flickered and vanished in the glittery beam of the transporter. The surface of the ocean collapsed and a circular wave burst away as sea water rushed in to fill the space where they had been.

"Admiral," Scott whispered, "there be whales here."

The viewscreen shifted to show the two whales safely in their tank, massively beautiful, lying still in the cramped space. No one spoke. The eerie cry of a humpback's song filled the ship, the first song George had sung in more than a year. Gillian blinked hard. She looked at Jim.

Jim felt the tension in him quivering, about to break. He wanted to leap up and shout with glee. But he sat motionless, showing no more emotion than Spock—less, perhaps, for the science officer watched the screen with one eyebrow expressively arched.

We're not home free yet, Jim thought. *Not by a long shot.*

"Well done, Mister Scott," he said. "How soon can we be ready for warp-speed?"

"I'll have to reenergize."

"Don't take too long. We're sitting ducks for their radar systems. Mister Sulu, impulse climb."

"Aye, sir."

The *Bounty*'s nose lifted toward the sky and the ship accelerated to the limit of its structural strength. Friction turned air to an ionized plasma. The bow of the ship glowed with heat.

"Unidentified aircraft," Uhura said. "40,000 MSL, range fifty kilometers, bearing zero-one-zero."

Jim swore softly to himself. It would be a fine mess if they returned home after all this, only to find that their presence here had caused the nuclear war that the twentieth century had avoided.

They blasted into the ionosphere. Uhura's instruments showed the Earth aircraft still following, straining to catch them. The air grew thin enough for transition to warp speed to be only moderately dangerous, rather than suicidal.

"Mister Scott—how soon?"

"Stand by, sir. Miracle worker at work."

"Mister Scott, don't make jokes!" Jim snapped. "We are in danger of—"

"Full power, sir," Scott said, in a slightly chiding tone.

Jim reined in his irritation. "Mister Sulu, if you please."

"Aye, sir."

The *Bounty* vanished into warp space.

Jim rose from his place, still keeping himself in complete control. "Mister Sulu, take the conn. Doctor Taylor, would you like to visit your whales?"

Gillian felt shaky with excitement. She did not understand half of what had just happened, but all she really cared about for the moment was that Gracie and George were safe. And she was with them. She grinned at Kirk. He smiled. He looked exhausted and on the brink of exultation. They started for the doors, but Kirk paused at Mister Spock's station.

"Mister Spock, are you able to adjust for the changed variables in your time reentry program?"

"Mister Scott cannot give me exact mass change figures, Admiral," Spock said. "So I will . . ." He hesitated. Gillian thought he looked a little embarrassed. "I will make a guess."

"You?" Kirk exclaimed. He gave a quick laugh of astonishment. "Spock, that's extraordinary." He clasped Spock's hand, very briefly.

After Admiral Kirk and Doctor Taylor departed, Spock shook his head, thoroughly puzzled. Through their handshake, he had experienced Admiral Kirk's astonishment and joy. He did not believe that he understood either emotion in the abstract, and he certainly did not comprehend why the admiral should react with joy to being told their survival rested on a guess.

"I do not think he understands," Spock said.

McCoy chuckled. "No, Spock, he understands. He means he feels safer about your guesses than about most other people's facts."

Spock considered McCoy's statement for some moments. "You are saying," he said, offering a tentative conclusion for analysis, "that it is a compliment."

"It is," McCoy said. "It is indeed."

Spock squared his shoulders. "I will, of course, try to make the best guess I can."

Gillian walked with Kirk through the neck of the *Bounty* toward the cargo bay.

"Congratulations, Gillian," he said.

"Shouldn't I be saying that to you, Kirk?"

"No," he said thoughtfully. "I think I've got it right. But I've been meaning to tell you, it's my family name that's Kirk. James is my given name. Most of my friends call me Jim."

"Oh." She wondered why he had not said so before. "Gee. I've kind of got used to calling you Kirk."

"You still can, if you want to. I've kind of got used to you calling me Kirk."

Gillian stopped. The music of the humpback echoed through the *Bounty,* surrounding her with an eerie song of cries and clicks, wails and glissandos.

"If you go sailing around humpbacks, you can hear their song through the hull of your boat," Gillian said. "When you're lying at anchor, late at night, you can imagine how it must have sounded to sailors two or three thousand years ago, before anyone knew what the music was. They thought it was a siren song, calling men to their deaths."

"But this siren song may call a whole planet back to life," Jim said.

The cool salt tang of sea water filled the air. Gillian hurried ahead. She strode past Mister Scott, who stared fascinated at the whales. Gillian placed her hands flat against the cold, transparent plastic. George and Gracie, cramped but calm in the huge tank that for them was tiny, shifted to look at Gillian. The song filled the cargo bay.

Jim joined Gillian beside the tank.

"Ironic," he said. "When human beings killed these creatures, they destroyed their own future."

"The beasties seem happy to see ye, Doctor," Scott said to Gillian. "I hope ye like our little aquarium."

"A miracle, Mister Scott."

Scott sighed and headed off to check the power supply. "The miracle is yet to come," he said.

"What does he mean?" Gillian asked.

"He means our chances of getting home aren't very good," Jim said. "You might have lived a longer life if you'd stayed where you belong."

"I belong here," Gillian said.

Kirk's skeptical glance made Gillian fear that he planned to try again to persuade her to remain in her own time, or even to send her back against her will.

"Listen, Kirk," she said, "suppose you pull off this miracle and get them through. Who in the twenty-third century knows anything about humpback whales?"

He looked at the whales in silence. "I concede your point."

The ship trembled around them. Gillian pressed her hand against the tank, trying to give the whales a confidence she did not entirely feel. Gracie and George flexed their massive bodies and blew bright spray into the air, no more afraid of anything in space than they were of anything in the sea.

Kirk touched Gillian's hand in an equally comforting gesture. The irregular vibration continued.

"Ye'd better get forward, Admiral," Scott said. "We're having some power fall-off."

"On my way." Kirk squeezed Gillian's hand, then hurried out.

"Buckle up, lassie," Mister Scott said. "It gets bumpy from here."

As Jim raced through the neck of the *Bounty,* the vibration increased. The Klingon ship had never been intended for such extreme gravitational stresses. A resonant frequency increased the intensity of the shudder and threatened to rip the *Bounty* apart. The control room doors opened. The ship bucked. Jim lunged for his chair, grabbed the back to steady himself, then sidled around to take his place.

On the viewscreen, the sun blazed in silent violence. The screen damped out the brightest central light, but left the corona brilliantly flaming.

Scott announced their increasing velocity. "Warp seven point five . . . seven point nine . . . Mister Sulu, that's all I can gi' ye!"

"Shields at maximum," Chekov said.

Jim made his way to Spock's station. "Can we make breakaway speed?"

"Hardly, Admiral, with such limited power. I cannot even guarantee we will escape the sun's gravity. I will attempt to compensate by altering our trajectory. This will, however, place the ship at considerable risk."

Jim essayed a smile. "A calculated one, I trust, Mister Spock."

"No, Admiral," Spock said without expression.

"Warp eight," Sulu said. "Eight point one . . ." He waited, then glanced at Jim. "Maximum speed, sir."

Spock straightened from his computer. "Admiral, I need thruster control."

"Acceleration thrusters at Spock's command," Jim said without hesitation.

Spock gazed into the sensor. Its light rippled across his face and hands. He could hear the nearly imperceptible wash of the solar wind that penetrated the *Bounty*'s shields; he could feel the beginnings of the increase in temperature. The human beings would soon perceive the heat. If he made an error, they would succumb to it sooner than a Vulcan. If he made an error, he would live only a few more moments than they. The moments would not be pleasant.

The gravitational whirlpool around the sun pummeled the fragile starship. Spock gripped the console tightly to keep himself from shifting.

Spock could smell tension. He raised his head for an instant. Everyone on the bridge watched him intently.

He realized they were frightened. And he understood their fear.

"Steady," he said. He bent over the console again. "Steady."

His decision now meant the lives of all these people, his friends; and the future of all life on Earth.

"Now."

Sulu blasted the thrusters on full.

Spock felt the jolt of additional acceleration. The sun's face touched the edges of the viewscreen, then filled it completely. A sunspot expanded rapidly as the *Bounty* plunged downward.

The viewscreen flickered and died, its receptors burned dead by the radiation of Sol. Spock's eyes adapted to the change in the light level. Around him, the human beings blinked and squinted, trying to see. Gravity and acceleration buffeted the ship, brutally wrenching its structure. The sun's heat and radiation penetrated the *Bounty*'s shields.

Spock recalled an earlier, similar death, heat and radiation blasting around him as he struggled to save the *Enterprise*. That time he had succeeded. This time he feared he must have failed. He glanced for an instant at each of the people in the control room, at each of his friends.

Only Leonard McCoy returned his gaze. The doctor looked at him for a long moment. Sweat glistened on his face. The ship plunged obliquely and McCoy had to snatch at the railing to keep his feet. He straightened again. He was frightened, but he showed no evidence of terror or panic.

To Spock's astonishment, he smiled.

Spock had no idea how to respond.

Abruptly, impossibly, the *Bounty*'s torture ceased. Silence gripped the starship, a silence of such intensity that even a breath would seem an intrusion.

The viewscreen remained dark and Spock's sensor readings hummed in useless monotone.

"Spock . . ." James Kirk's voice broke the hypnotic stasis. "Did braking thrusters fire?"

Spock collected himself quickly. "They did, Admiral."

"Then where the hell are we?"

Spock had no answer.

In the silence, the humpback's song whispered through the ship.

The quiet threat of the probe's wail answered.

Thirteen

The traveler's joy overcame the distress of losing contact with the beings on this little world. The planet lay enshrouded in an impenetrable cloud. Soon the insignificant life that remained would perish from the cold.

Until then, the traveler need only wait.

Turbulence blasted through the silence. The *Bounty* trembled and shook. Only the wail of the probe seemed real and solid.

"Spock! Condition report."

"No data, Admiral. Computers are nonfunctional."

"Mister Sulu, switch to manual control."

"I have no control, sir."

"Picture, Uhura?"

"I can't, sir, there's nothing!"

Jim cursed softly. "Out of control, and blind as a bat!"

"For God's sake, Jim," McCoy said, "where are we?"

In all his years on Vulcan, on earth, and on many worlds in between, Sarek had never observed such weather.

James Kirk is coming to earth, Sarek thought. *All ships have been ordered away. But instead of obeying, he will come. He has been ordered to Earth. But instead of disobeying, he will come.*

James Kirk was incapable of standing by while his homeworld died. But Sarek also knew that there was no logical way to save Earth. The Klingon ship would face the probe and be destroyed. So, too, Kirk and all his companions would die.

"Analysis." Kirk's voice rose and faded in the static and the resonance. A strange cry whistled and moaned in the background. "Probe call . . . Captain Spock's opinion . . . extinct species . . . humpback whale . . . proper response . . ."

Kirk's voice and image both failed, but Sarek had already gleaned Spock's explanation of the probe's intent and desire. A bright stroke of pride touched the elder Vulcan's equanimity.

"Stabilize!" Cartwright exclaimed. "Emergency reserve!"

438 Vonda N. McIntyre

"Do you read me?" Kirk said clearly. His image snapped into focus, then deteriorated. "Starfleet, if you read, we are going to attempt time travel. We are computing our trajectory . . ."

"What in heaven's name?" the fleet commander said.

The power failed utterly.

"Emergency reserve!" Cartwright said again, his voice hoarse.

"There *is* no emergency reserve," the comm officer said.

The groan of tortured glass and metal cut through the scream of the wind and the pounding of rain and waves. Sarek understood what Kirk proposed to do. Somehow, in the madness of its desperation, the plan possessed an element of rationality.

"Good luck, Kirk," Sarek said. "To you, and to all who go with you."

The shoring struts on the window failed. The glass imploded. Sarek heard cries of pain and fear. Cold, sharp shards of glass spattered around him, and freezing needles of sleet and wind impaled him.

Sarek dragged himself up, trying to protect his face from wind and debris. Fleet Commander Cartwright held himself steady against the railing of the observation deck. Sarek detected a strange motion beyond the blasted window and the howling wind. Shielding his eyes as best he could, he peered out.

"Look!" he said.

Cartwright exclaimed in horror.

Sarek and Cartwright watched in disbelief as the Klingon fighter ship streaked across the sky. It plunged downward in an unpowered glide, its engines dead, held aloft only by the structure of its wings.

Kirk's plan failed, Sarek thought.

The Golden Gate Bridge lay directly in the ship's path. Sarek thought, Better to die quickly than to perish in endless cold. But another thought kept coming to his mind, with bitterness: *Kirk, after all your successes, this time you have failed.*

Sarek steeled himself for the explosion and the flames. The Klingon starship reached the bridge—and skimmed beneath it and safely out the other side. Sarek remembered something Amanda once had said. Something about blind luck.

Sulu gritted his teeth and clenched his hands on the *Bounty*'s controls. Suddenly he felt a response. Though he did not know where they were or what lay ahead, atmospheric turbulence buffeted the ship. It was plunging toward a planetary surface at terminal velocity.

"Sir—I've got some back pressure on manual!" Sulu wrestled *Bounty*'s nose up.

"Ground cushion! Keep the nose up if you can!"

The flight characteristics deteriorated as the ship disintegrated beneath the force of friction, vibration, and wind shear. He knew he had lost the ship already. After this voyage, it would never fly. The only question to be answered was whether he could keep the passengers—human, Vulcan, and cetacean—alive when it crashed. The *Bounty* struggled to respond to his commands. When the bow crept up, the aerodynamics changed. Destructive forces increased. The airspeed decreased, but stressed metal shrieked and groaned. Sulu eased some power into the retro-thrusters, but did not dare take too much from the ground cushion. The probe wailed.

The *Bounty* hit with a tremendous, wrenching crash. The impact flung Sulu from the console. He staggered up, aware of his ship dying around him and his shipmates in distress.

Then, to his astonishment, all the sounds of destruction ceased. A few interminable seconds passed as he and the others struggled back into position and clung there.

A second blow struck. The ship screamed in agony. Again, the battering stopped. For another long moment Sulu could not understand how they still survived.

We came in almost flat! he thought. *We came in horizontal, and we came in over the sea! Now we're skipping across the water like a stone—*

He grabbed for the controls, fighting to raise the bow so the ship would skim instead of bounce. The *Bounty* crashed again. The third time, it did not regain the air. It plunged forward and down, pitching Sulu over the control console. He struck the bulkhead and fell back, stunned.

Jim Kirk flinched at the horrible high-frequency squeal of rending metal. He struggled to his feet. A wave of frigid sea water crashed through the broken bulkheads, washed past Jim, and slapped Sulu down. Gasping and coughing, Sulu tried to rise.

Jim grabbed his arm and helped him up. The deck tilted beneath them as the tail section of the *Bounty* began to sink.

"Blow the hatch!" Jim shouted.

Against the sound of the wind and the sea and the dying ship, against the omnipresent crying of the probe, the explosive bolts made a restrained thudding noise. The force flung the hatch open. Rain pounded through it. Waves beat against the *Bounty*. Torrents rushed through its stove-in sides. The water shorted systems, adding a pall of ozone-tinged smoke to the crashing rain and sea.

Jim glanced at Sulu.

"I'm all right now, sir," Sulu said. "Thanks." He looked dazed but coherent.

Jim flung his dripping hair back off his forehead. He and Sulu struggled toward the hatch against the steepening grade of the deck. Uhura and Chekov and McCoy clung to a console near Spock. Somehow, everyone on the bridge had survived. "Get topside!" Jim shouted at Sulu. "Help the others out!" High above, clouds roiled and vibrated with the calling of the probe. Jim boosted Sulu through the hatch and turned to Spock. "Spock, you got us to the right place!" His voice nearly disappeared in the violence of the storm. "Mister Spock, see to the safety of all hands."

"I will, Admiral."

While Spock helped the others out of the dying starship, Jim struggled back to the comm. "Mister Scott, come in. Gillian? Scotty?" He waited, but received no reply. "Damn!"

Jim waded through knee-deep water to the exit. He had to force the doors apart. They crashed open and he ran into the neck of the *Bounty*. The water deepened, slowing his headlong plunge. By the time he reached the cargo bay the water rose to his waist. Leaks sprang through the seals of the cargo bay doors. On the other side, someone fought desperately to get the doors open.

Jim grabbed the emergency release and pulled it. Nothing happened. He pulled again. For an awful moment he thought he would not budge it. If he failed, Gillian and Scotty and the whales would drown without his ever reaching them. Odd to think that two marine creatures could drown, but without air Gracie and George would perish along with the human people, only a little more slowly.

With the whole force of his body, he wrenched the release. The jolt blew it open. The doors parted as smoothly as if the ship were cruising the gentlest region of space. Water gushed through, carrying Gillian and Scotty into the corridor and sweeping Jim off his feet. He splashed up, coughing, and dragged Scott out of the current. Gillian waded against the rush of water, trying to return to the cargo bay. The doors opened to their limits, more than far enough for a person to pass. A human person. Not a whale.

"The whales?" Jim shouted.

The juncture between the *Bounty*'s neck and body ripped apart. Water sprayed in all around. Wind whistled, blowing sea foam through the openings.

"They're alive!" Gillian cried. "But they're trapped!"

"No power to the bay doors," Scott said.

"What about the explosive override?"

" 'Tis underwater! There isna any way to reach it!"

"Go on ahead!" Jim shouted.

"Admiral, you'll be trapped!"

"Kirk, I won't—!"

Jim plunged between the doors and closed and secured them so Gillian could not follow. The doors muffled the sound of wind and rain, giving an eerie illusion of peace. Gillian shouted for him to open the door and Scott pounded on the metal. He ignored their pleas. Though he could hear them, though he was perfectly aware of them, they were a step removed from the reality of what he had to do.

Breathing deeply to build up his reserves of oxygen, Jim waded deeper. Water crept to his thighs, to his waist. The pressure of the sea forced spray through sprung seals above him. Luminous wall panels glowed with the eerie blue of emergency light. In the far end of the cargo bay, the water nearly reached the top of the acrylic tank. Gracie raised her flukes and slapped them down into the tank, splashing water into the flooding compartment. Soon both whales would be able to swim out. But if Jim could not open the bay doors, they would be freed into a larger coffin. He kicked off his boots, took one last deep breath, and dove.

The freezing water clamped around his chest like a jolt of electricity. He clenched his teeth to keep from gasping. He kicked himself forward, groping for the override. It ought to be—he wondered if he had lost his sense of direction in the dimness and the cold, with the screaming gibberish of the probe whipping through him. His breath burned in his lungs.

Outside the cargo bay, Gillian leaned her head against the locked doors and cried.

"Kirk, let me in," she whispered. The wind dragged her hair across her face.

"Come along, lassie," Mister Scott shouted above the pelting of the rain. "If anyone can get your beasties free, the admiral can. Ye canna help him now." He took her arm and guided her around and led her up the steep slope toward the control room. The rain and her tears blinded her.

Fighting the instinct to breathe, Jim kicked through the deep water. He broke the surface and flung up his arm to fend off the ceiling. The sprung seals had allowed most of the air to escape. Only a handsbreadth of airspace remained between the water and the top of the cargo bay. Gasping, treading water, he tilted his head back so his nose and mouth remained in the air. He took a long, deep breath, and dove again.

The series of crashes had buckled panels and knocked the bay into wreckage. He swam through a drowned dark junkyard forest, searching through a directionless melange for a single panel. His heart pounded in counterpoint with the cruel music of the probe.

He took the risk of a pause. He hung suspended in the water and reached with all his senses to get his bearings.

Jim stroked around and swam directly to a tangle of wreckage. He pushed it aside. The panel lay beneath. He dragged it open with his fingernails and yanked the override.

A pressure wave flung him against the bulkhead. The impact drove half the air from his lungs. His ears rang. Unconsciousness drew him. Another, deeper darkness opened beneath him as the cargo bay doors slowly parted.

Every instinct pulled him upward into the airless trap of the water-filled cargo hold. Instead, he dove deeper. He passed from the protection of the *Bounty* into the open sea. Following the outer hull, he kicked and pulled himself along its curve. He broke the surface, gasping. A powerful wave smacked him in the face, blinding him, filling his nose and mouth. Water burned in his throat and his lungs. He coughed and choked and finally drew breath.

Jim struggled to see over the waves and through the pounding sleet, willing the whales to fling themselves upward in a joyous leap of freedom, willing them to swim into the sea and sing their song. But he saw nothing, nothing but the ocean and the slowly sinking ship. Through the ringing in his ears he heard nothing but the storm, and the unremitting, piercing, amelodic probe.

With an intake of breath like a sob, he dove again, following the curve of the *Bounty*'s side. He passed the open cargo bay doors and gazed up into the ship's belly. He used some of his precious breath to power one inarticulate shout.

Slowly, gracefully, with perfect ease and composure, the two humpback whales glided from the ship. Joy and wonder rushed through Jim's spirit. He wished he could swim away with them to explore the mysteries that still remained in the sea.

But suddenly a current slammed the crippled *Bounty* around, catching Jim and pushing him inexorably toward the angle between the cargo bay door and the hull. He swam hard, but could make no headway against the strength of the sea. His air was nearly exhausted. Cold and exertion had drained his strength.

Gracie eased through the water, balancing on her pectoral fins like a massive bird. She slid beneath Jim on the powerful stroke of her tail. Her flukes brushed past him. In desperation he grabbed and held on. The whale drew him easily from the grasp of the current and pulled him free of the ship. She glided upward, then curved her body so she barely broke the rough interface between air and water. She gathered herself, arched her back, and lifted her flukes. The vertical flip pulled Jim to the surface. Gracie sounded and disappeared.

"Kirk!"

Jim turned. A wave slapped the back of his head, but raised him high enough to see the floating control sphere of the *Bounty*. All his shipmates clung to the smooth surface. Gillian reached toward him. He floundered through the chop to the pitching solidity of the sphere. Gillian and Spock helped him clamber up its side.

Unabated, the probe continued its cry.

Jim looked for the whales, but they had vanished.

"Why don't they answer?" he shouted. "Dammit, why don't they sing?"

Gillian touched her fingertips to his. He could not tell if rain or tears streaked her face, or if the tears were of joy or despair.

Shivering violently, he pressed himself against the cold, slick metal. Sleet spat needles against his face and hands. The cargo bay had broken off and vanished, and soon, inevitably, the control sphere would sink. No one could be spared to come and rescue him and his shipmates; perhaps no one was left to do so. If he was to fail anyway, he wished the *Bounty* had perished in the fire of the sun. He preferred a quick and blazing failure to watching his friends die a slow death of cold and exposure.

A whale song whispered to him. A second song answered. Both whales, male and female, began to sing.

The sea transmitted it to the control sphere and the control sphere focused and amplified it. Jim pressed his ear, his hands, his whole body against the hull, taking the music into himself. It soared above the range of his hearing, then fell, groaning to a level that he could not hear, only feel. He looked up at Gillian. He wanted to laugh, to cry. She was doing both.

The probe's call paused. The humpbacks' song expanded into the hesitation, rising above the crashing wind and water.

Basking in the bright, unfiltered radiation of deep space, the traveler paused in the midst of turning the blue world white with snow and ice and sterility. Something was occurring that had never occurred before in the myriad of millennia of the traveler's existence. From a silent planet, a song replied.

The information spiraled inward. Even at the speed of light, seconds passed before the song reached the most central point of the traveler's intelligence. Even in the superconductive state in which that intelligence operated, it required long moments to recover from the shock of a unique event.

Tentatively, with some suspicion, it responded to the song of the beings on the world below.

Why did you remain silent for so long?

They tried to explain, but it reacted in surprise and disbelief.

Where were you? it asked.

We were not here, they replied, *but now we have returned. We cannot explain, traveler, because we do not yet understand all that has happened to us.*

By "us," the traveler understood them to mean themselves as individuals and all their kind for millions of years in the past. By their song it recognized them as youths.

Who are you? it asked. *Where are the others? Where are the elders?*

They are gone, the whales sang, with sadness. *They have passed into the deep, they have vanished upon white shores. We alone survive.*

Your song is simple, the traveler said, chiding. It was not above petulance. *Where are the tales you have invented in all this time, and where are the stories of your families?*

They are lost, replied the whale song. *All lost. We must begin again. We must evolve our civilization again. We have no other answer.*

The traveler hesitated. It wondered if perhaps it should sterilize the planet anyway despite the presence of the untaught singing youths. But if it began a new evolution here, the planet would be silent at least as long as it would take the traveler to circumscribe the galaxy. The traveler would have to endure the pain of the world's silence. Organic evolution required so much time. However, the traveler possessed very little cruelty. It could consider destroying the young singers, but the conception caused great distress. It abandoned the idea.

Very well, it said. *I shall anticipate young stories. Fare thee well.*

The traveler fell silent. The whales bid it farewell.

The traveler collected its energy. It ended its interference with the patterns of the blue-white planet. It ceased to power the violent storms ravaging the surface. It sought its usual course, oriented itself properly, and sailed on a tail of flame into the brilliant blackness of the galaxy.

The whale song, attenuated by distance, faded below the limits of Jim's hearing.

Only wilderness existed in this kind of utter silence. Jim recalled such moments of quiet, when he stood on a hilltop and heard the sunlight fall upon the ground, heard its heat melting the pine pitch from the trees to fill the air with a heavy pungency.

He looked up. The rain stopped. The sea calmed. The control chamber moved as gently as a soap bubble in still air. The clouds roiled, then broke, and a brilliant streak of blue cut through them. Sunlight poured onto the sea. Speechless, Jim clambered to the upper curve of the control sphere. He and his shipmates gazed at the world and at each other, in wonder.

Sarek and Cartwright lost sight of the Klingon fighter when it crashed into the sea. Sarek feared that Spock must be dead, lost. That he did not outwardly show his grief helped in no way to attenuate it. Sleet battered him.

Only when the probe's cry hesitated did he feel, against his will and judgment, a blossom of hope.

When the searing wail ended and did not return, when the sun broke through the clouds, he hurried to the edge of the shattered window and strained to see what lay on the surface of the sea.

"Mister President!" Fleet Commander Cartwright exclaimed. "We have power!"

Reviving electronic machines chattered to each other. New light glowed in

Sarek's peripheral vision. But he could spare none of it his attention. Far distant, metal caught and reflected the new sunlight.

"Look." His voice was quiet.

The council president joined him. "By God!" he exclaimed. "Do we have a working shuttle left?"

Cartwright saw what they had found on the surface of the sea.

"I'll find one," he said. "I'll find one somewhere."

The sky had almost cleared, Jim turned toward the sun, letting its heat steam the cold out of his exhausted body and his bedraggled clothes. He glanced at his shipmates with a smile.

"We look like we've been out here a week," he said.

"I want to grow a beard if I'm going to be a castaway," McCoy said. He perched precariously on the control sphere, his knees drawn up and his forearms resting on them, his hands dangling relaxed. He grinned. "Congratulations, Jim. I think you've saved the Earth."

Jim glanced at Gillian, squeezed her hand, and searched the sea. Gillian nudged him and pointed.

"Not me, Bones," Jim said. "*They* did it."

In the distance, one of the humpbacks leaped. It cleared the water completely. Jim recognized which one it was, but human names meant nothing to the humpbacks anymore. The whale made a leisurely spiral in the air and landed back first and pectoral fins extended with a tremendous splash. Beside the first whale, the second humpback leaped and breached.

Gillian laughed. *"Vessyl kit,"* she said. "Merry whale."

A great double rainbow glowed against the sky. The inner arc began with violet and ended with red; its shadow, as intense as any ordinary rainbow, began with red and ended with violet.

"Oh, jeez," Gillian said, and burst into tears.

Epilogue

Leonard McCoy strode through the gateway, across the manicured lawn, and up the steps of the Vulcan embassy. He pounded on the carved wooden door. When it did not open in a few seconds, he pounded again.

"Let me in!" He was in no mood to be polite. He had been trying to reach Spock for days. "Spock, dammit, if you won't take my calls, I'm staying on your front porch till you talk to me!" He raised his fist to hit the heavy polished wood for a third time.

The door swung open. "Proceed."

Alone except for the disembodied voice, McCoy entered the elegant old mansion. The Vulcans had changed the house very little, or they had furnished it in the style of its world and its time. Oriental carpets covered golden hardwood floors; heavy velvet-covered furniture hunkered in the rooms he passed. The voice directed him down a long hallway to a set of wide glass doors. They swung open as he approached, admitting a hot, dry breeze. He might have expected the house's atrium to contain a gazebo, a topiary, even a maze. Instead it held a sere expanse of swept sand and wind-polished granite blocks, reddened light and thin air, concentrated heat. The microclimate and the illusion of a great scarlet sun banished the morning's fog.

Spock stood in full sunlight in the center of the atrium, robed but bareheaded. McCoy started toward him without waiting for Spock to acknowledge his presence. The sand scraped beneath his boots.

"Spock!"

"Yes, Doctor McCoy," Spock said.

"Why didn't you answer my call?"

"I was helping Doctor Taylor ensure the safety and well-being and the freedom of the whales. Afterward, I found it necessary to meditate. If you had been patient—" He stopped and gazed at McCoy; he smiled very slightly. "But of course you are a doctor, not a patient."

"I—*what?*" He really had heard Spock say what he thought he heard him say.

"It is of no consequence, Doctor McCoy," Spock said. "Did you come to take me to task?"

"No. Why do you think I've come to take you to task? Take you to task for what?"

"For occupying myself elsewhere while you and Admiral Kirk and my other shipmates await the judgment of the tribunal."

"No. I—" McCoy realized he had not even considered berating Spock for his absence. "I understand why you didn't stay. You testified, you did all you could. It wasn't logical . . ." Groaning, he buried his face in his hands. "It's driving me crazy, Spock!" he cried. "To understand you so well. T'Lar said you were whole again. She swore she'd freed us of each other!"

"Doctor McCoy, sit down. Please."

McCoy collapsed on one of the polished granite boulders. Spock sat nearby.

"Is it so terrible," the Vulcan said, "to understand me?"

"I—" McCoy managed to smile. "It isn't something I'm used to." He rubbed his hands down the smooth, stippled sides of the sun-warmed boulder. Between him and the mansion, the deep line of his footprints began to blur and vanish. "No, Spock, the understanding isn't so terrible. It isn't terrible at all—though I'm not sure I believe I'm admitting that. But it shouldn't be happening! I feel like I'm losing myself again. Spock . . . I'm afraid."

Spock leaned toward him, elbows on knees. "Doctor, you are not alone in this experience."

McCoy rubbed his temples. The facilitation sessions horrified him. He had thought he would do anything, even conceal the madness he feared, to avoid enduring another one. Only the sensation of having another entity taking over his mind could be worse.

"It depends on the tribunal's verdict," McCoy said, staring into the sand. "The terms may not permit me the freedom to return to Vulcan. Maybe, if you aren't yet healed, if your sanity requires my presence—"

"But the facilitation sessions are complete. We need not return to Vulcan."

McCoy glanced up.

"Doctor McCoy," Spock said, "T'Lar spoke the truth. To the degree that is possible to achieve, we are free, each of the other. But we have our own true memories. We retain resonances of each other. I understand you better, too. Can you accept what has occurred? If you cannot, you will suffer. But it will be your own suffering, not mine. If you can take yourself beyond your fear, you will take yourself beyond danger as well."

"Is it true?" McCoy whispered.

Spock nodded.

The Vulcan spoke of resonances: the truth of what he said resonated within McCoy.

He rose. "Thank you, Mister Spock. You've eased my mind considerably. I'll leave you to your meditation. I have to return to Starfleet headquarters. To wait with Jim and the others."

"Spock."

Spock rose. "Yes, Father."

McCoy glanced back. Sarek crossed the sand toward them. The desert garden began to obliterate his footprints.

"The tribunal has signaled its intention to deliver a verdict."

"I've got to hurry," McCoy said.

"We will accompany you," Spock said.

In a pleasant room with a wall of windows, Admiral James T. Kirk stared into San Francisco Bay and pretended a calm that he did not feel. The water glittered in the sunlight. Somewhere out there, a hundred fathoms deep, lay the battered remains of the *Bounty*. Somewhere more distant, out in the Pacific, two whales swam free. Jim was imprisoned, bound by his word of honor to stay.

I can't believe this is happening, he thought angrily. *After all we've been through—I can't believe Starfleet still insists on a court-martial.*

Earth was recovering from the effects of the probe. Because of the evacuation of the coasts, few lives had been lost on Earth. Most of the neutralized Starfleet ships had been crippled, not killed; they had sustained few casualties. Jim was glad of that. He had seen too much death, too recently. He touched the narrow black mourning band on his cuff. His grief over David's death returned suddenly, as it often did at unexpected times, and struck him with its full force. If Carol would only speak to him, if they could offer each other both sorrow and comfort . . . but she remained on Delta, refusing his attempts to contact her. Jim looked down, blinking rapidly, forcing his vision to clear.

He tried to take comfort in the resurrection of his friend, in the survival of his homeworld, and in the recovery of an extinct species of sentient being. Spock had made promises to the whales. The work that would carry out those promises had kept Spock and Gillian away from the trial.

Samples of whale cells, preserved in the twentieth century, would add to the species' genetic diversity through cloning. Legends and myths to the contrary, two individuals—even three, when Gracie's calf was born—were not sufficient to reestablish any species. The whales would never again be hunted, and their freedom would never again be curtailed.

Gracie and George, youths trying to rebuild their species' civilization, seemed undaunted by the scope of the task. It would take far longer than rebuilding their minuscule population. But, according to Spock, humpbacks thought in terms of generations and centuries, not in minutes or seasons or years.

Jim smoothed the mourning band and the sleeve of his uniform jacket.

Will I still have the right to wear my uniform or my insignia after the next few hours? he wondered. He could not answer the question. He could not even be certain how he would react when the tribunal delivered its judgment.

He wondered how the others were holding up. His officers, lacking McCoy, had gathered here this morning to wait through another day. No one spoke much. Scott sat nearby, fidgeting, glowering, hating the wait. Every so often Chekov tried to make a joke, and Uhura tried to laugh.

Sulu stood alone, staring out the far window. Perhaps he was gazing at the spot where the *Bounty* had gone down. It might be the last starship he ever flew, if Jim's attempt to shield his shipmates failed. Jim rose and crossed the room to stand with Sulu.

"It was a good little ship," Jim said.

The young commander did not reply. Of all his shipmates, Jim worried most about him. Outrage lit Sulu from within.

"Commander Sulu, whatever happens, you aren't to make any foolish gestures."

"I have no idea what you're talking about, Admiral," Sulu said stonily.

"A protest. An outburst, or resignation. The sacrifice of your career, to make a point. I think you do know what I mean."

Sulu faced him, his dark eyes intense. "And do you also think nobody noticed what you were doing during the testimony? Taking everything as your own responsibility? If you want to convince somebody not to make a sacrifice, you haven't got much moral ground to stand on! I'll tell you what I think. I think this court-martial stinks, and I don't intend to keep my mouth shut on the subject no matter what you order!"

Jim frowned. "Be careful how you speak to me, Commander. It *was* my responsibility—"

"No, Admiral, it wasn't. We all made our own choices. If you try to stand alone, if you deny our accountability for what we did, where does that leave us? As mindless puppets, following blindly without any sense of our own ethics."

"Now wait one minute!" Jim started to protest, then cut himself off. He could see Sulu's point. By trying to draw all the blame to himself, Jim had, in a strange way, behaved thoughtlessly and selfishly. "No. You're right. What we did, none of us could have done alone. Commander Sulu, I won't discount the participation—or the responsibility—of my officers again."

He offered his hand. After a moment, Sulu grasped it hard.

The door opened. Everyone in the room fell silent. The chancellor appeared in the entryway.

"The council has returned," she said.

The shipmates gathered together. Jim led them from the anteroom. McCoy joined them in the corridor, hurrying, out of breath.

As Jim entered the council chamber, whispers brushed his hearing. Spectators filled the observation seats and the spaces around the walls. Gillian Taylor sat with Christine Chapel and Janice Rand, and, to Jim's surprise, with Sarek and Spock. Though grateful for their support, Jim did not acknowledge their presence. Eyes front, he strode to the center of the council chamber. His shipmates lined up beside him. On the floor, the seal of the United Federation of Planets formed an inlaid circle around them.

Behind the wide bench, the members of the council gazed down at Jim and his shipmates. Their expressions revealed no hint of their decision.

A louder murmur, a collective whisper of astonishment, rippled across the audience. Someone walked across the chamber with long, quiet strides.

Spock stopped beside Jim and came to attention like the others. He, too, wore a Starfleet uniform.

"Captain Spock," the council president said, "you do not stand accused."

"I stand with my shipmates," Spock replied. "Their fate shall be mine."

"As you wish." The president touched each of them with his intent gaze. "The charges and specifications are conspiracy; assault on Federation officers; theft of the *Starship Enterprise,* Federation property; sabotage of the *Starship Excelsior,* Federation property; willful destruction of the aforementioned *U.S.S. Enterprise,* Federation property; and, finally, disobeying direct orders of Commander, Starfleet. How do you plead?"

Admiral James Kirk formally repeated his plea. "On behalf of all of us, Mister President, I am authorized to plead guilty."

"So entered. Hear now the sentence of the Federation Council." He glanced down at his papers, cleared his throat, and looked up again. "Mitigating circumstances impel the tribunal to dismiss all charges except one."

The spectators reacted. A glance from the president quieted them.

"I direct the final charge, disobeying the orders of a superior officer, at Admiral Kirk alone." He gazed at Jim, his expression somber. "I am sure the admiral will recognize the necessity of discipline in any chain of command."

"I do, sir," Kirk replied. It was too late to argue about self-reliance and initiative.

"James T. Kirk, it is the verdict of this tribunal that you are guilty of the charge against you."

Jim stared ahead, stony-faced, but inside he flinched.

"Furthermore, it is the judgment of this tribunal that you be reduced in rank. You are relieved of the rank, duties, and privileges of flag officer. The tribunal decrees that Captain James T. Kirk return to the duties for which he has repeatedly demonstrated unswerving ability: the command of a starship."

The reaction of the crowd washed over him. Jim forced himself not to react. But a shout of astonishment and relief, a shout of pure happiness, trembled beside his heart.

"Silence!" the president exclaimed. Slowly, the audience obeyed. "Captain Kirk, your new command awaits you. You and your officers have saved this planet from its own shortsightedness, and we are forever in your debt."

"Bravo!"

Jim recognized Gillian's voice, but a hundred other voices drowned her out. In another moment he was surrounded by well-wishers, acquaintances, strangers, all wanting to congratulate him, to shake his hand. He complied, but he hardly heard or saw them. He was searching for his shipmates. He saw McCoy, reached out, grabbed him, and drew him into a bear hug. McCoy returned it, then grasped Jim by the shoulders and looked him straight in the eye.

"You can always appeal, you know," he said.

Jim stared at him for a moment, speechless, his fear for the doctor renewed. And then he noticed the smile McCoy tried to hide. Jim started to laugh. McCoy gave up trying to keep a straight face. He laughed, too—finally, after too long, back to his old self.

They eased their way between spectators till they reached Chekov and Scott and Uhura, hugging each other and shaking hands. Sulu stood nearby, perhaps more stunned by a positive verdict than by the negative one for which he had prepared himself.

"Congratulations, Admi—I mean, Captain Kirk," he said.

"The congratulations are for all of us, Commander Sulu," Jim said. He wanted to tell him something more, but the onlookers pushed between them.

In San Francisco, in the twentieth century, Javy and Ben climbed down the terraced bank and headed for their dieseling truck. Despite everything, the rest of their day's work remained.

"I'm really sorry, Javy," Ben said. "I should of believed you right off. Maybe if I had we would of seen what made that burn."

"I saw it," Javy said. "I saw its shadow, anyway."

"But, I mean, we would of seen it and we would of been able to show it to other people. To a reporter, maybe, and they'd write us up in a book and maybe we'd get on Johnny Carson." He brightened. "Maybe if we show them the burned place—"

"Maybe if we show them the burned place, they'll arrest us for arson. Or they'll write us up as a couple of nut cases," Javy said. "And maybe they'd be right. We don't have any proof. A burned place and a shadow."

"I'm really sorry," Ben said again, downcast.

"Don't be, Ben, it's okay, honest."

"I'd be mad, if I were you."

"Maybe I ought to be," Javy said. "Except . . ." He hesitated, not sure he wanted to say it out loud before he was certain it was true.

"What?"

What the hell. Telling Ben the story had always worked before. Javy grinned. "I figured out how to end my novel," he said.

The FBI agent put all the reports together and looked at them and wished the lights were brighter so he could put on his sunglasses.

I might as well be named Bond, he thought. Nobody outside a spy novel would believe this stuff. My boss sure won't, and my partner will say I've been talking to Gamma too much.

"*I* don't even believe it," he muttered. "I don't even believe the parts I saw with my own eyes." The radar reports from San Francisco and Nome did nothing to improve his mood.

Maybe the report will get lost when it's filed, he thought. *Stuff sometimes does. Before anybody has a chance to read it. With any luck . . .*

But he trusted Murphy's Law more than he trusted luck. He decided to file the report himself.

He picked it up, took it to the proper place, and filed it.

In the circular file.

Finally the crowd in the Federation Council chamber dispersed. Jim felt wrung out. He glanced around, looking for an escape, and found himself face to face with Gillian Taylor.

"My own exonerated Kirk!" she exclaimed. "I'm so juiced, I can't tell you!" She gave him a quick kiss. "I have to hurry. So long, Kirk. And thanks." She headed for the arched exit.

"Hey!" Jim cried. "Where are you going?"

"You're going to your ship, I'm going to mine. Science vessel, bound for Mer to recruit some divers to help the whales. Why, the next time you see me, I may have learned to breathe underwater!" She grinned, honestly and completely happy for the first time since Jim had met her. "I've got three hundred years of catchup learning to do," she said.

Though glad for her happiness, he could not help feeling disappointment as well.

"You mean this is—good-bye?" he said.

"Why does it have to be good-bye?" she asked, mystified.

"I . . . as they say in your century, I don't even have your phone number. How will I find you?"

"Don't worry," she said. "I'll find you." She raised her hand in farewell. "See you 'round the galaxy!" She strode away.

Just farewell, Jim told himself. *Not good-bye.* He shook his head fondly as she vanished through the wide, arched doorway of the council hall.

In a secluded corner, Spock waited for the last spectators to disperse. He wished to leave, but he did not want to go anywhere on this planet. Spock knew now—he had learned again, or he had remembered; it did not matter which—that he had never felt at home on Earth or on Vulcan, or indeed on any planet. He felt at home in space.

Sarek, tall and dignified, his face expressionless, approached him.

"Father," Spock said.

"I will take passage to Vulcan within the hour," Sarek said. "I wanted to take my leave of you."

"It is kind of you to make this effort."

"It is not an effort. You are my son." He stopped abruptly, controlling his instant's lapse. "Besides," he said, "I wished to tell you that I am most impressed with your performance in this crisis."

"Most kind, Father," Spock said, and again Sarek had no suitable response for the charge of kindness.

"I opposed your enlistment in Starfleet," Sarek said. "It is possible that my judgment was incorrect."

Spock raised his eyebrow. He could not recall his father's ever having confessed to an error before, or, indeed, ever having committed an error.

"Your associates are people of good character," Sarek said.

"They are my friends," Spock said.

"Yes," Sarek said. "Yes, of course." He spoke in a tone of acceptance and the beginnings of understanding. "Spock, do you have any message for your mother?"

Spock considered. "Yes," he said. "Please tell her . . . I feel fine."

Spock took his leave of his bemused father and crossed the council chamber to join James Kirk and his other shipmates.

"Are you coming with us, Mister Spock?" the captain asked.

"Of course, Captain," Spock said. "Did you believe otherwise?"

"I haven't been quite sure what to believe, the last few days."

"Sarek offered you a compliment," Spock said.

"Oh, really? What might that be?"

"He said you were of good character."

Kirk stopped, nonplussed, then recovered himself.

"Sarek is getting effusive in his retirement," Kirk said. "I wonder what I did after all these years to make him come to that conclusion?"

Spock felt astonished that Captain Kirk did not understand. "Captain—Jim—!" he said in protest. Then he noted James Kirk's smile. Solemnly he replied, "I am sure that I do not know."

Jim Kirk began to laugh.

Inside Spacedock, a shuttlecraft dove through the great cavern of a docking bay. The *Enterprise* shipmates searched among ships and tenders and repair scows, curious to discover their destination.

They passed the *Saratoga,* being towed in for inspection. Its captain—

Alexander, isn't it? Jim thought—had saved her officers and crew in stasis before the life-support systems gave out entirely.

"The bureaucratic mentality is the only constant in the universe," McCoy said. "We're gonna get a freighter."

Jim remained silent, but he tightened his hand around the envelope of thick, textured paper that he carried. The envelope held written orders, not a computer memory chip, and by that alone Jim knew that the orders were something very special. But he was forbidden to break the holographic epoxy of the Starfleet seal until he had accepted his new command and taken it beyond the solar system.

He turned the envelope over and over, then pulled his attention back to the conversation.

"—I'm counting on *Excelsior*," Sulu was saying to McCoy.

"Excelsior!" Scott exclaimed. "Why in God's name would you want that bucket of bolts?"

Before Sulu could retort and the two men could embark on one of their interminable arguments about the merits of *Excelsior*, Jim cut in.

"Scotty, don't be judgmental. A ship is a ship." At the same time he had to wonder how Sulu would handle being subordinate to James Kirk on a ship that should have been Sulu's own.

It appeared that they were indeed heading for *Excelsior*. The massive ship filled the wide shuttlecraft windows. Scott watched it apprehensively.

"Whatever you say, sir," he said, resigned. Under his breath he added, "Thy will be done."

To Jim's surprise the shuttlecraft sped past *Excelsior*.

Jim blinked. In the next slip, a *Constellation*-class starship echoed the lines of his own *Enterprise*. And this time the shuttlecraft did not duck around it. On the saucer section of the ship, Jim made out the name and the registration number.

U.S.S. Enterprise. NCC 1701-A.

A suited-up space tech put the finishing touches on the "A," turned, saw the shuttlecraft, waved jauntily, and powered away on travel jets.

Everyone in the shuttlecraft gazed in wonder at the ship. Spock, silent, stood at Jim's right and McCoy, chuckling, at his left. Scotty leaned forward with his nose practically pressed against the port. Sulu and Chekov clapped each other on the shoulder, and Uhura smiled her quiet smile.

"My friends," Jim said softly, "we've come home."

When he took his place on the bridge of the *Enterprise*, Jim Kirk gripped the sealed envelope so tightly he crumpled it. "Clear all moorings. Reverse thrust."

Jim unclenched his hands, still trying to keep them from trembling with excitement. He settled into the difference of the ship, and the sameness.

"Rotate and hold."

Below, Scotty would be mother-henning the engines. Sulu and Chekov held their places at navigation and helm. Uhura conferred with Spacedock control, and Spock bent over his computer console.

The *Enterprise* spun slowly and hovered as Spacedock's doors slid open.

McCoy lounged easily against the arm of the captain's chair.

"Well, Captain?" he said. "Are we just going to sit here?"

Deep space stretched out before them.

"Thrusters ahead one-quarter," Captain Kirk said.

"Course, Captain?" Chekov said.

Beside Jim, McCoy grinned. "Thataway, Mister Chekov," the doctor said.

Spock glanced up from the science station. "That is, I trust, a technical term."

The impulse engines pressed them beyond Spacedock.

Jim wanted to laugh with joy. "Let's see what she's got, Mister Sulu." He rubbed his fingertips across the glimmering Starfleet seal. "Warp speed."

"Aye, sir!"

The *Enterprise* plunged into the radiant spectrum of warp space, heading toward strange new worlds, new life, and new civilizations.